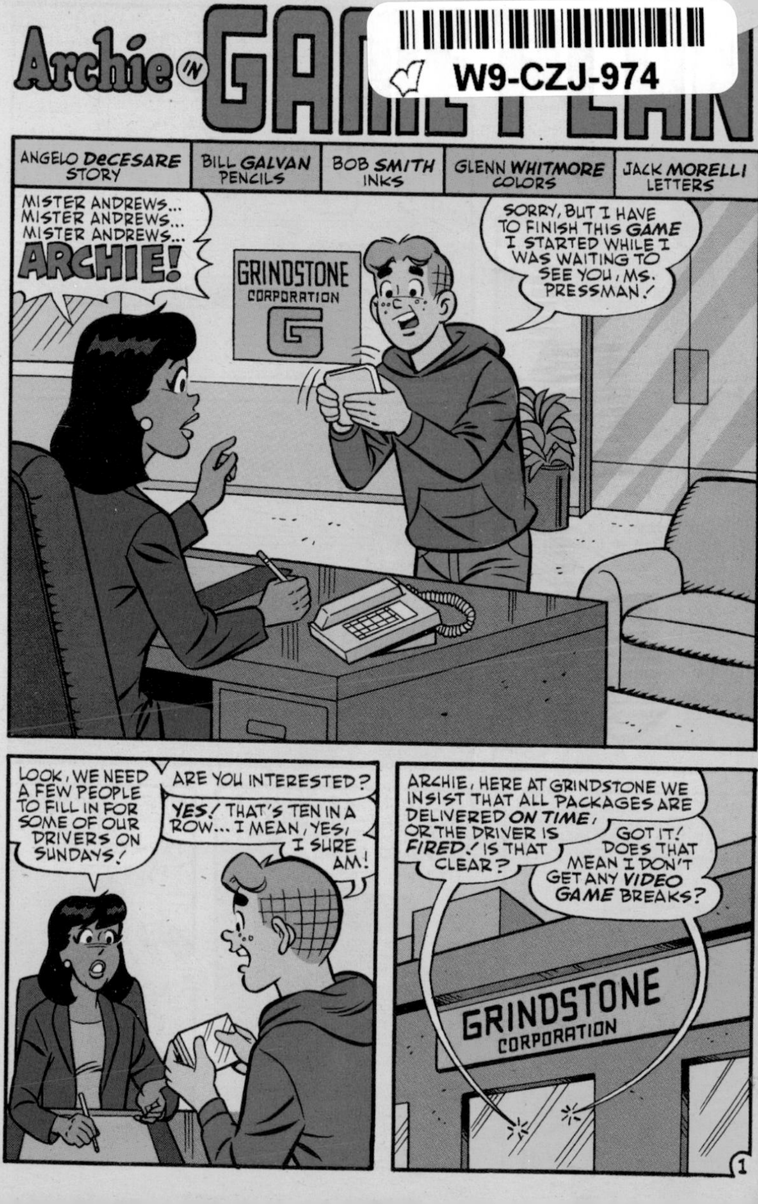
Archie IN
ANGELO DeCESARE STORY
BILL GALVAN PENCILS
BOB SMITH INKS
GLENN WHITMORE COLORS
JACK MORELLI LETTERS
MISTER ANDREWS... MISTER ANDREWS... MISTER ANDREWS... ARCHIE!
GRINDSTONE CORPORATION G
SORRY, BUT I HAVE TO FINISH THIS GAME I STARTED WHILE I WAS WAITING TO SEE YOU, MS. PRESSMAN!
LOOK, WE NEED A FEW PEOPLE TO FILL IN FOR SOME OF OUR DRIVERS ON SUNDAYS!
ARE YOU INTERESTED?
YES! THAT'S TEN IN A ROW... I MEAN, YES, I SURE AM!
ARCHIE, HERE AT GRINDSTONE WE INSIST THAT ALL PACKAGES ARE DELIVERED ON TIME, OR THE DRIVER IS FIRED! IS THAT CLEAR?
GOT IT! DOES THAT MEAN I DON'T GET ANY VIDEO GAME BREAKS?
GRINDSTONE CORPORATION

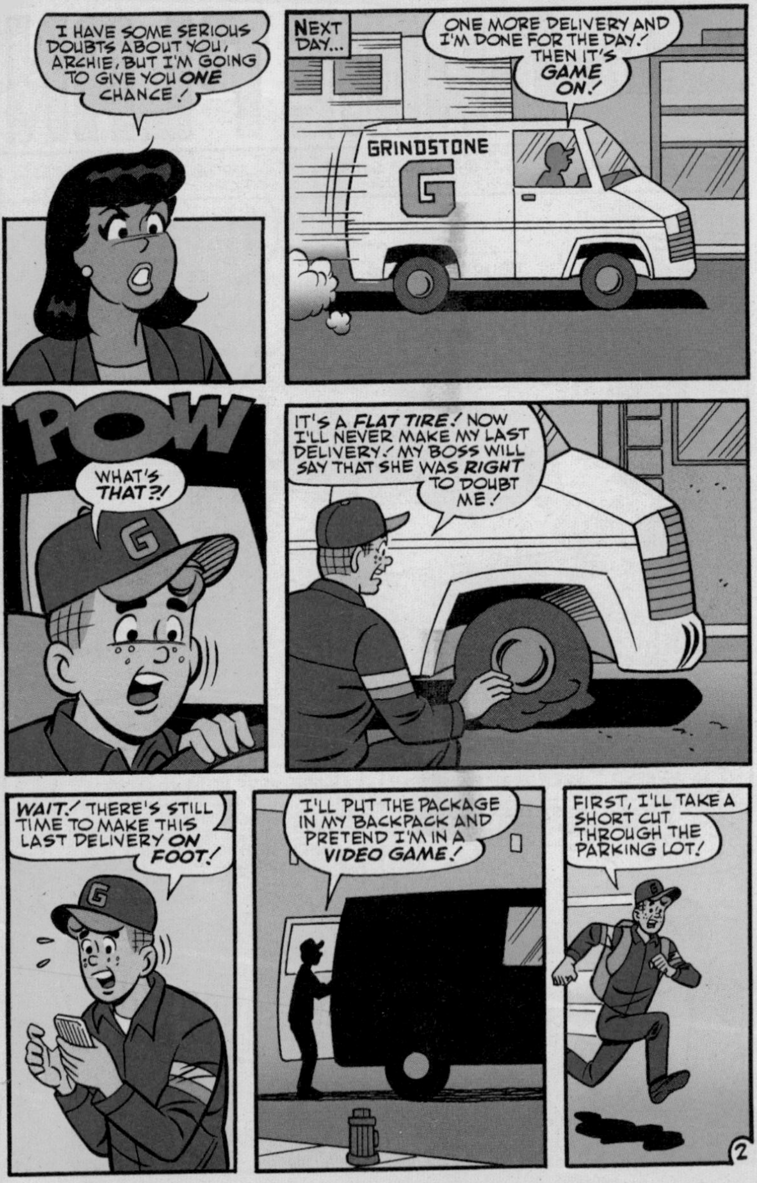
I HAVE SOME SERIOUS DOUBTS ABOUT YOU, ARCHIE, BUT I'M GOING TO GIVE YOU ONE CHANCE!
NEXT DAY...
ONE MORE DELIVERY AND I'M DONE FOR THE DAY! THEN IT'S GAME ON!
GRINDSTONE
G
POW
WHAT'S THAT?!
IT'S A FLAT TIRE! NOW I'LL NEVER MAKE MY LAST DELIVERY! MY BOSS WILL SAY THAT SHE WAS RIGHT TO DOUBT ME!
WAIT! THERE'S STILL TIME TO MAKE THIS LAST DELIVERY ON FOOT!
I'LL PUT THE PACKAGE IN MY BACKPACK AND PRETEND I'M IN A VIDEO GAME!
FIRST, I'LL TAKE A SHORT CUT THROUGH THE PARKING LOT!
2

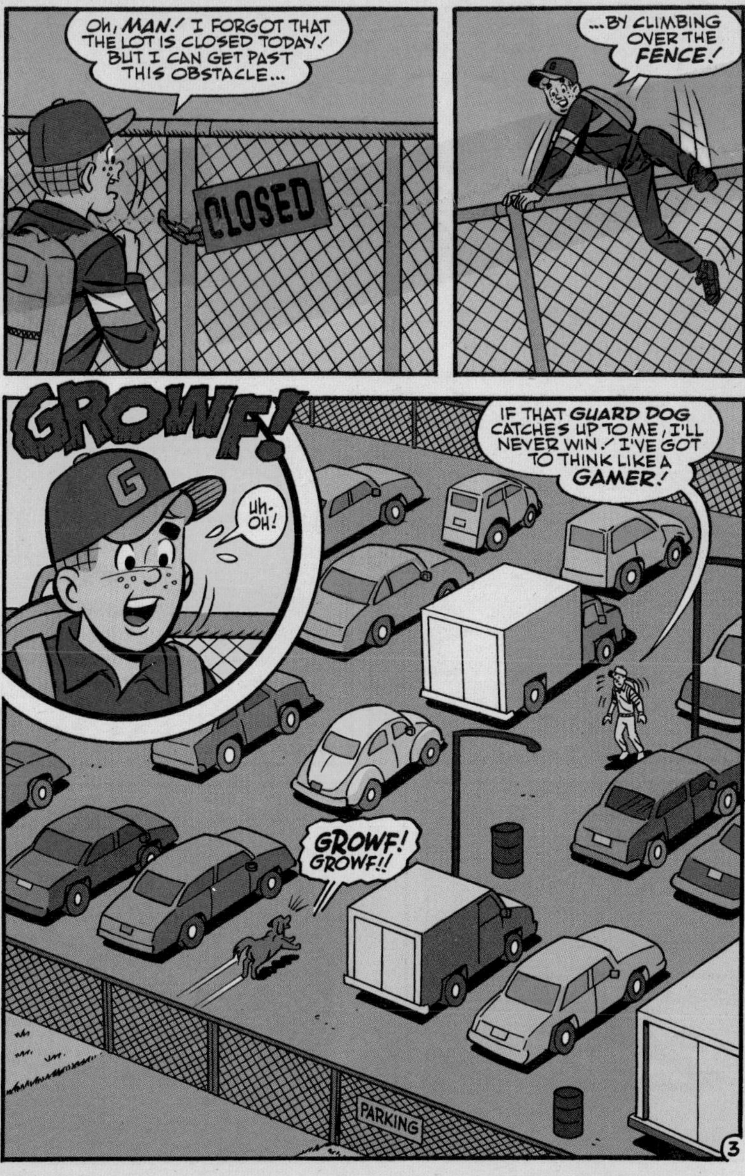
OH, MAN! I FORGOT THAT THE LOT IS CLOSED TODAY! BUT I CAN GET PAST THIS OBSTACLE...
CLOSED
...BY CLIMBING OVER THE FENCE!
GROWF!
UH-OH!
IF THAT GUARD DOG CATCHES UP TO ME, I'LL NEVER WIN! I'VE GOT TO THINK LIKE A GAMER!
GROWF! GROWF!!
PARKING
3

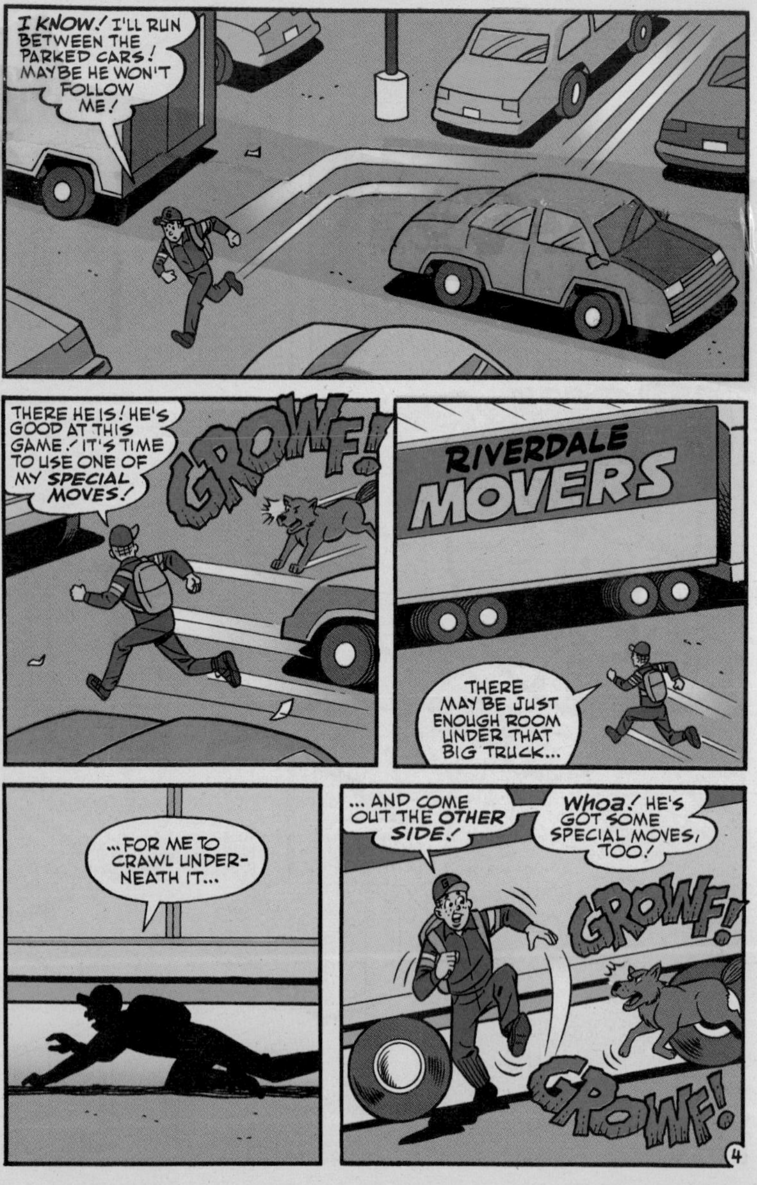
I KNOW! I'LL RUN BETWEEN THE PARKED CARS! MAYBE HE WON'T FOLLOW ME!
THERE HE IS! HE'S GOOD AT THIS GAME! IT'S TIME TO USE ONE OF MY SPECIAL MOVES!
GROWF!
RIVERDALE MOVERS
THERE MAY BE JUST ENOUGH ROOM UNDER THAT BIG TRUCK...
...FOR ME TO CRAWL UNDER-NEATH IT...
... AND COME OUT THE OTHER SIDE!
Whoa! HE'S GOT SOME SPECIAL MOVES, TOO!
GROWF!
GROWF!
4

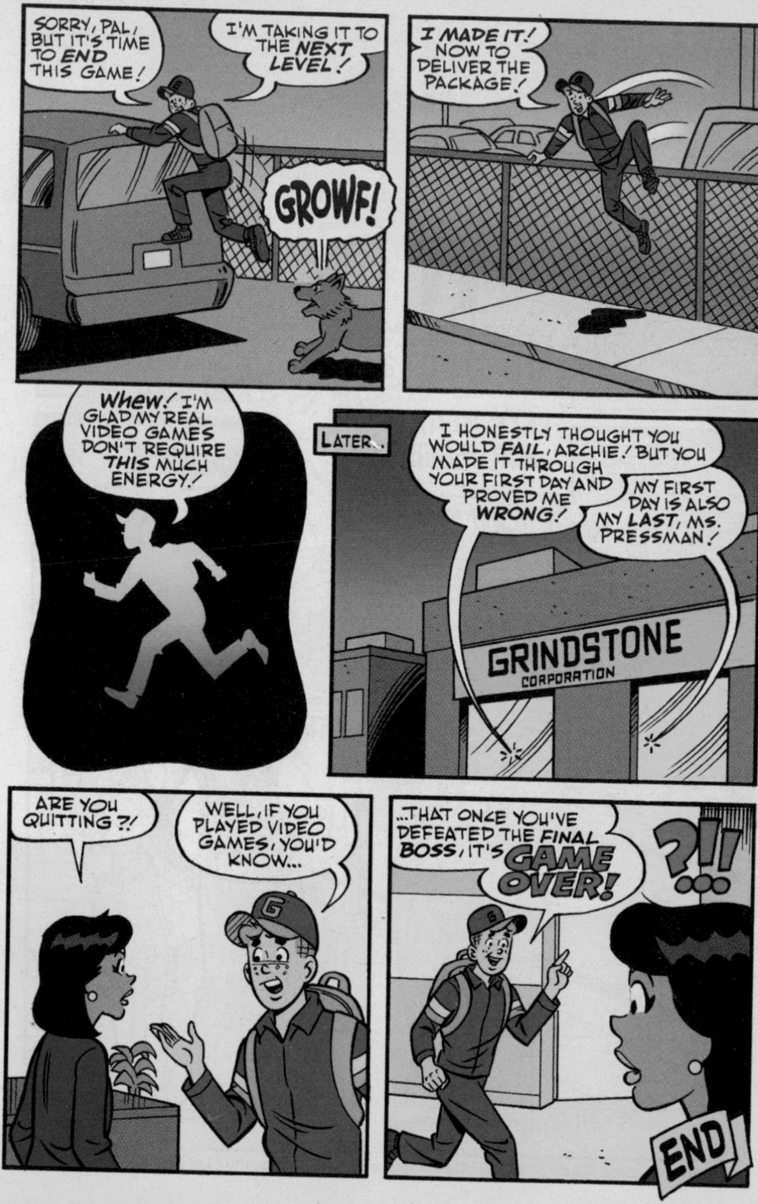
SORRY, PAL, BUT IT'S TIME TO END THIS GAME!
I'M TAKING IT TO THE NEXT LEVEL!
GROWF!
I MADE IT! NOW TO DELIVER THE PACKAGE!
Whew! I'M GLAD MY REAL VIDEO GAMES DON'T REQUIRE THIS MUCH ENERGY!
LATER...
I HONESTLY THOUGHT YOU WOULD FAIL, ARCHIE! BUT YOU MADE IT THROUGH YOUR FIRST DAY AND PROVED ME WRONG!
MY FIRST DAY IS ALSO MY LAST, MS. PRESSMAN!
GRINDSTONE
CORPORATION
ARE YOU QUITTING?!
WELL, IF YOU PLAYED VIDEO GAMES, YOU'D KNOW...
...THAT ONCE YOU'VE DEFEATED THE FINAL BOSS, IT'S GAME OVER!
?!!...
END

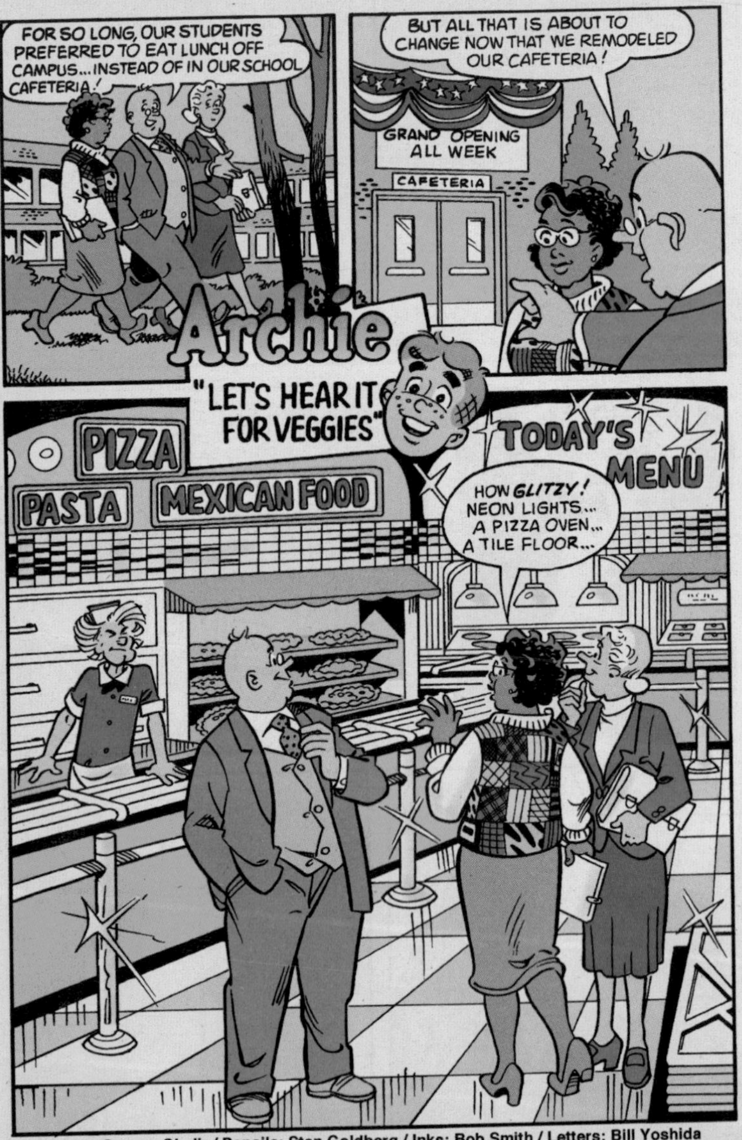
FOR SO LONG, OUR STUDENTS PREFERRED TO EAT LUNCH OFF CAMPUS... INSTEAD OF IN OUR SCHOOL CAFETERIA!
BUT ALL THAT IS ABOUT TO CHANGE NOW THAT WE REMODELED OUR CAFETERIA!
GRAND OPENING ALL WEEK
CAFETERIA
Archie
"LET'S HEAR IT FOR VEGGIES"
PIZZA
PASTA
MEXICAN FOOD
TODAY'S MENU
HOW GLITZY! NEON LIGHTS... A PIZZA OVEN... A TILE FLOOR...

Script: George Gladir / Pencils: Stan Goldberg / Inks: Bob Smith / Letters: Bill Yoshida

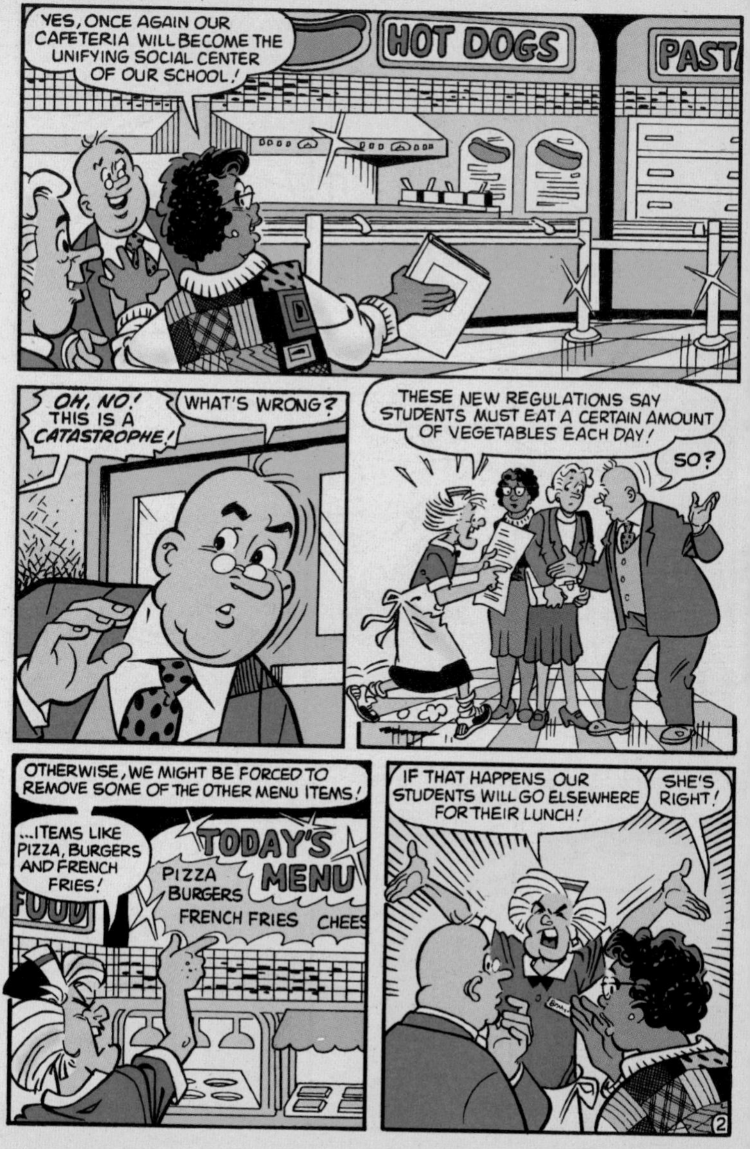
YES, ONCE AGAIN OUR CAFETERIA WILL BECOME THE UNIFYING SOCIAL CENTER OF OUR SCHOOL!
HOT DOGS
OH, NO! THIS IS A CATASTROPHE!
WHAT'S WRONG?
THESE NEW REGULATIONS SAY STUDENTS MUST EAT A CERTAIN AMOUNT OF VEGETABLES EACH DAY!
SO?
OTHERWISE, WE MIGHT BE FORCED TO REMOVE SOME OF THE OTHER MENU ITEMS!
...ITEMS LIKE PIZZA, BURGERS AND FRENCH FRIES!
TODAY'S MENU
PIZZA
BURGERS
FRENCH FRIES
IF THAT HAPPENS OUR STUDENTS WILL GO ELSEWHERE FOR THEIR LUNCH!
SHE'S RIGHT!
2

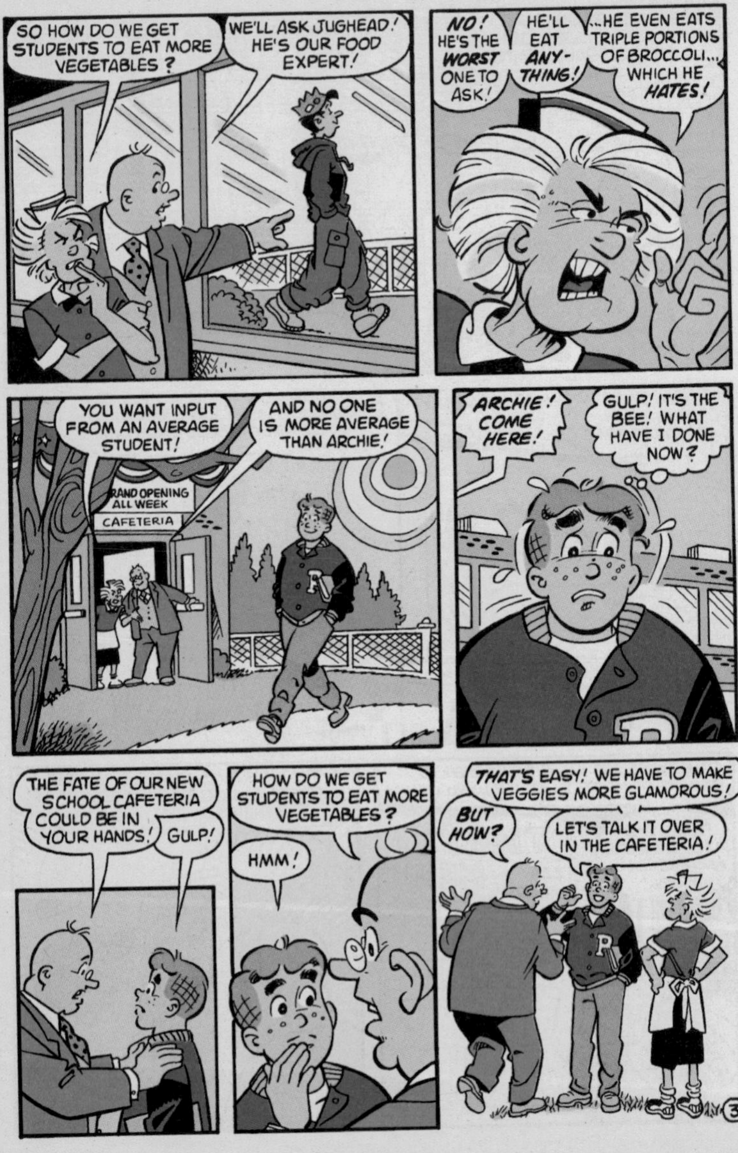
SO HOW DO WE GET STUDENTS TO EAT MORE VEGETABLES?
WE'LL ASK JUGHEAD! HE'S OUR FOOD EXPERT!
NO! HE'S THE WORST ONE TO ASK!
HE'LL EAT ANY-THING!
...HE EVEN EATS TRIPLE PORTIONS OF BROCCOLI... WHICH HE HATES!
YOU WANT INPUT FROM AN AVERAGE STUDENT!
AND NO ONE IS MORE AVERAGE THAN ARCHIE!
RAND OPENING ALL WEEK
CAFETERIA
ARCHIE! COME HERE!
GULP! IT'S THE BEE! WHAT HAVE I DONE NOW?
THE FATE OF OUR NEW SCHOOL CAFETERIA COULD BE IN YOUR HANDS!
GULP!
HOW DO WE GET STUDENTS TO EAT MORE VEGETABLES?
HMM!
THAT'S EASY! WE HAVE TO MAKE VEGGIES MORE GLAMOROUS!
BUT HOW?
LET'S TALK IT OVER IN THE CAFETERIA!
3

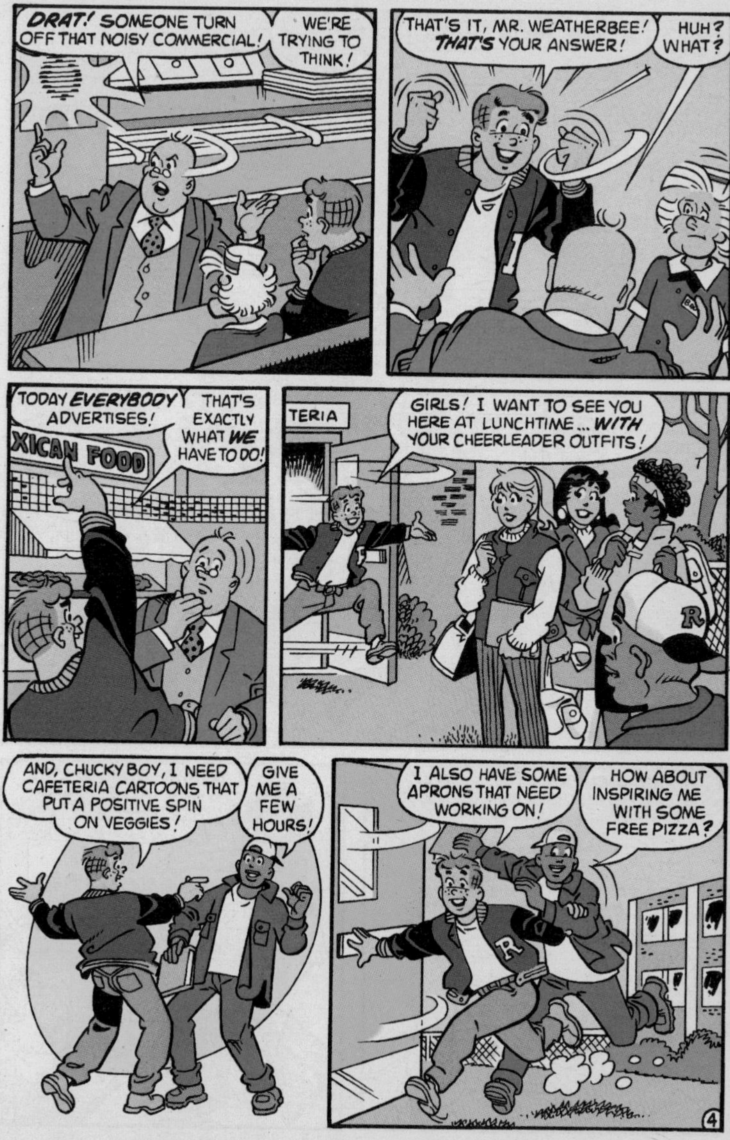
DRAT! SOMEONE TURN OFF THAT NOISY COMMERCIAL!
WE'RE TRYING TO THINK!
THAT'S IT, MR. WEATHERBEE! THAT'S YOUR ANSWER!
HUH? WHAT?
TODAY EVERYBODY ADVERTISES!
THAT'S EXACTLY WHAT WE HAVE TO DO!
XICAN FOOD
TERIA
GIRLS! I WANT TO SEE YOU HERE AT LUNCHTIME... WITH YOUR CHEERLEADER OUTFITS!
AND, CHUCKY BOY, I NEED CAFETERIA CARTOONS THAT PUT A POSITIVE SPIN ON VEGGIES!
GIVE ME A FEW HOURS!
I ALSO HAVE SOME APRONS THAT NEED WORKING ON!
HOW ABOUT INSPIRING ME WITH SOME FREE PIZZA?
4

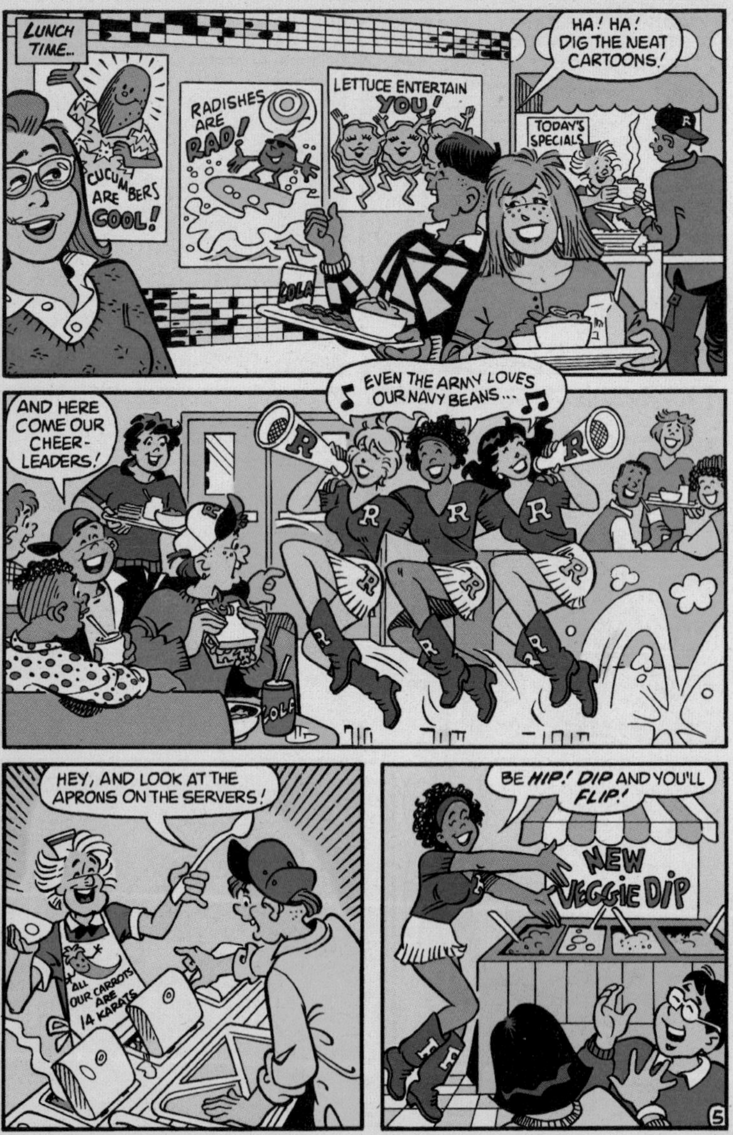
LUNCH TIME...
CUCUMBERS ARE COOL!
RADISHES ARE RAD!
LETTUCE ENTERTAIN YOU!
HA! HA! DIG THE NEAT CARTOONS!
TODAY'S SPECIALS
COLA
AND HERE COME OUR CHEER-LEADERS!
EVEN THE ARMY LOVES OUR NAVY BEANS...
HEY, AND LOOK AT THE APRONS ON THE SERVERS!
ALL OUR CARROTS ARE 14 KARATS
BE HIP! DIP AND YOU'LL FLIP!
NEW VEGGIE DIP
5

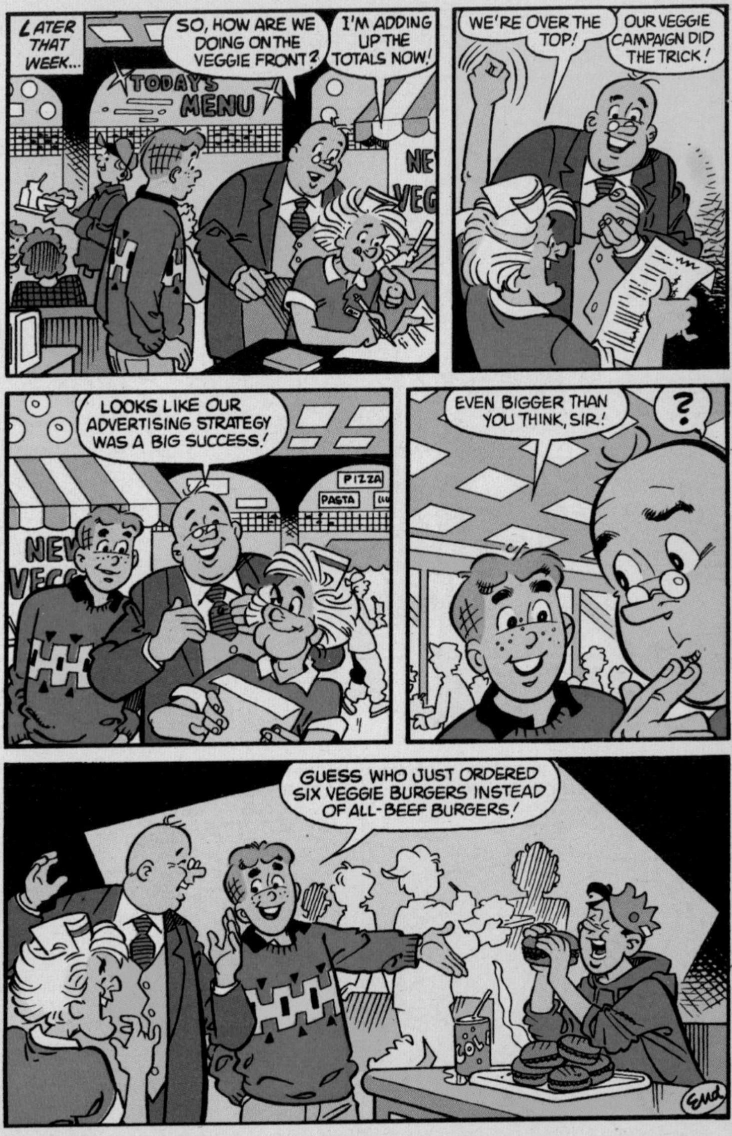
LATER THAT WEEK...
SO, HOW ARE WE DOING ON THE VEGGIE FRONT?
I'M ADDING UP THE TOTALS NOW!
TODAY'S MENU
WE'RE OVER THE TOP!
OUR VEGGIE CAMPAIGN DID THE TRICK!
LOOKS LIKE OUR ADVERTISING STRATEGY WAS A BIG SUCCESS!
PIZZA
PASTA
EVEN BIGGER THAN YOU THINK, SIR!
?
GUESS WHO JUST ORDERED SIX VEGGIE BURGERS INSTEAD OF ALL-BEEF BURGERS!
End

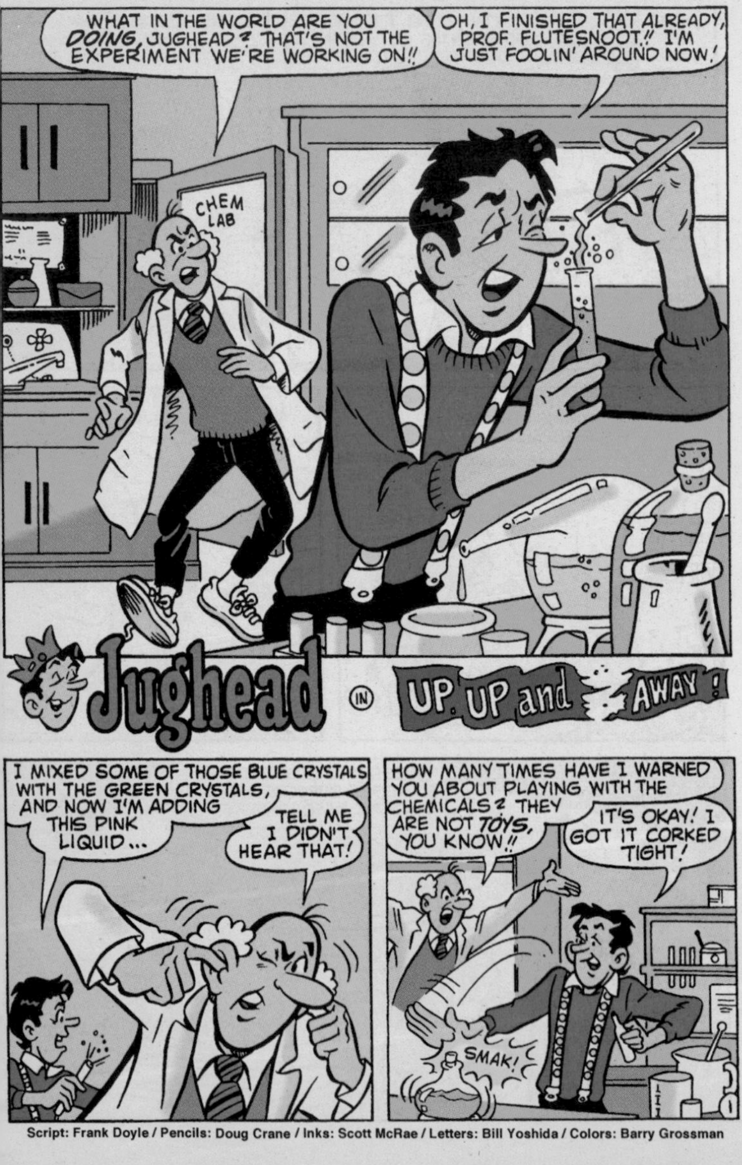
WHAT IN THE WORLD ARE YOU DOING, JUGHEAD? THAT'S NOT THE EXPERIMENT WE'RE WORKING ON!!
OH, I FINISHED THAT ALREADY, PROF. FLUTESNOOT!! I'M JUST FOOLIN' AROUND NOW!
CHEM LAB
Jughead IN UP, UP and AWAY!
I MIXED SOME OF THOSE BLUE CRYSTALS WITH THE GREEN CRYSTALS, AND NOW I'M ADDING THIS PINK LIQUID...
TELL ME I DIDN'T HEAR THAT!
HOW MANY TIMES HAVE I WARNED YOU ABOUT PLAYING WITH THE CHEMICALS? THEY ARE NOT TOYS, YOU KNOW!!
IT'S OKAY! I GOT IT CORKED TIGHT!
SMAK!

Script: Frank Doyle / Pencils: Doug Crane / Inks: Scott McRae / Letters: Bill Yoshida / Colors: Barry Grossman

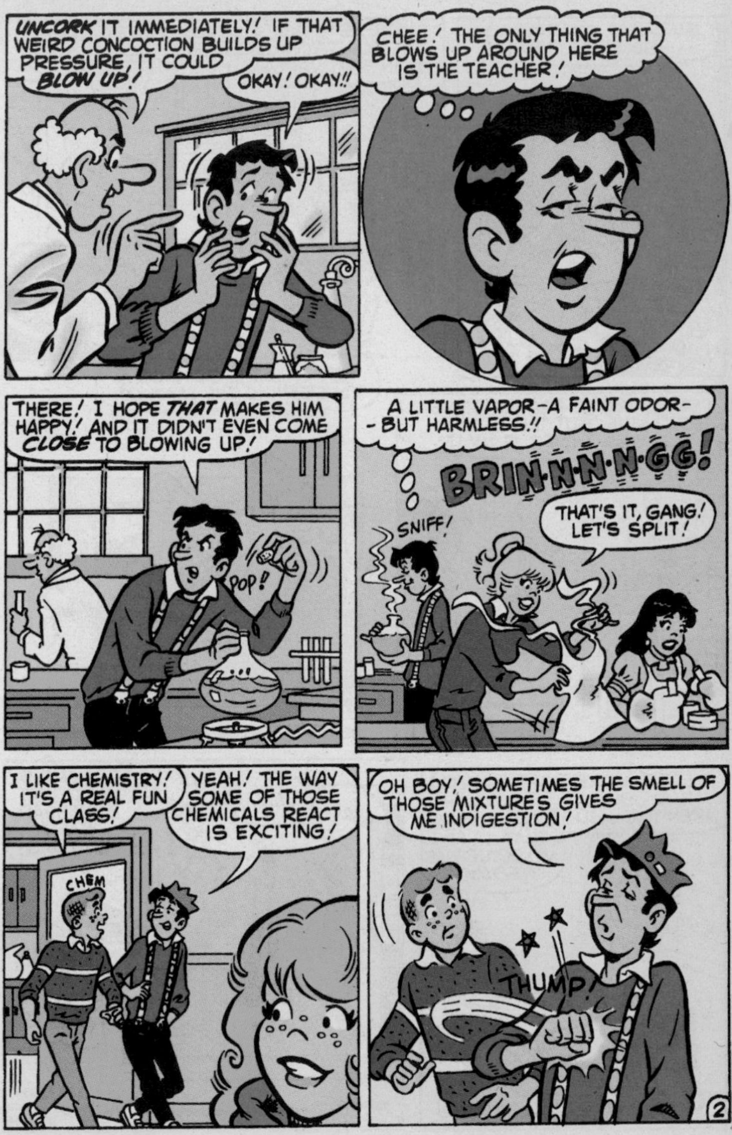
UNCORK IT IMMEDIATELY! IF THAT WEIRD CONCOCTION BUILDS UP PRESSURE, IT COULD BLOW UP!
OKAY! OKAY!!
CHEE! THE ONLY THING THAT BLOWS UP AROUND HERE IS THE TEACHER!
THERE! I HOPE THAT MAKES HIM HAPPY! AND IT DIDN'T EVEN COME CLOSE TO BLOWING UP!
POP!
A LITTLE VAPOR-A FAINT ODOR- -BUT HARMLESS!!
BRIN-N-N-N-GG!
SNIFF!
THAT'S IT, GANG! LET'S SPLIT!
I LIKE CHEMISTRY! IT'S A REAL FUN CLASS!
YEAH! THE WAY SOME OF THOSE CHEMICALS REACT IS EXCITING!
CHEM
OH BOY! SOMETIMES THE SMELL OF THOSE MIXTURES GIVES ME INDIGESTION!
THUMP!
2

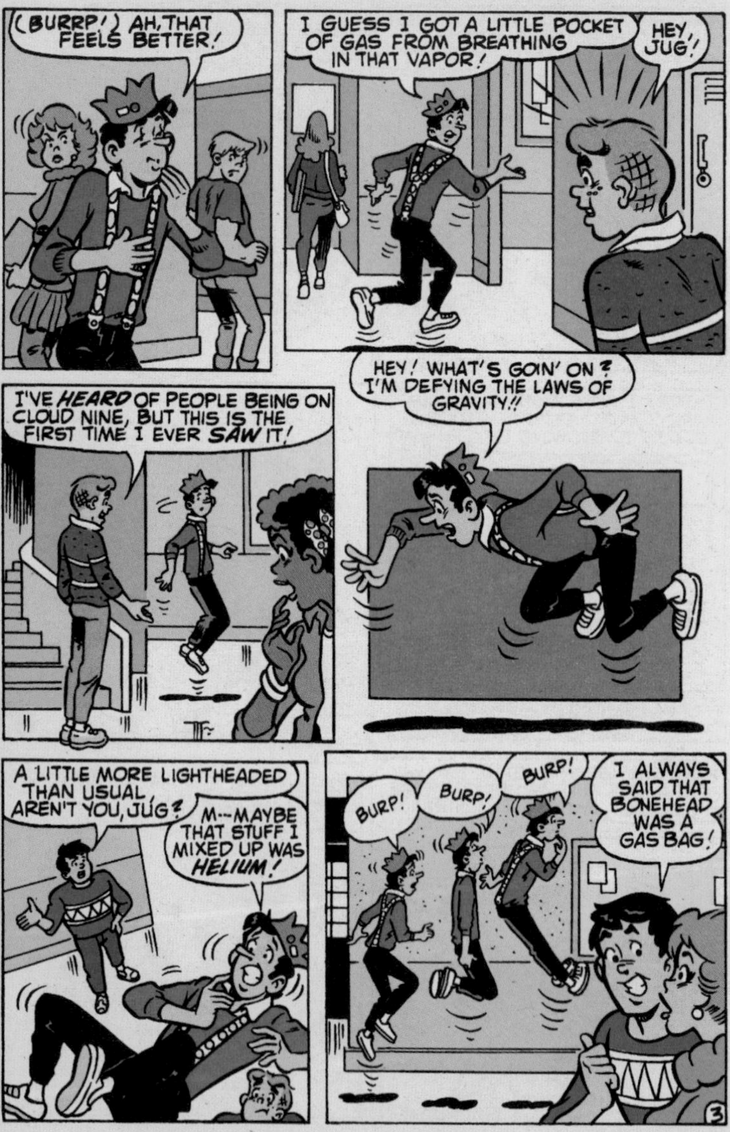

(BURRP!) AH, THAT FEELS BETTER!
I GUESS I GOT A LITTLE POCKET OF GAS FROM BREATHING IN THAT VAPOR!
HEY, JUG!
I'VE HEARD OF PEOPLE BEING ON CLOUD NINE, BUT THIS IS THE FIRST TIME I EVER SAW IT!
HEY! WHAT'S GOIN' ON? I'M DEFYING THE LAWS OF GRAVITY!!
A LITTLE MORE LIGHTHEADED THAN USUAL, AREN'T YOU, JUG?
M--MAYBE THAT STUFF I MIXED UP WAS HELIUM!
BURP!
BURP!
BURP!
I ALWAYS SAID THAT BONEHEAD WAS A GAS BAG!
3

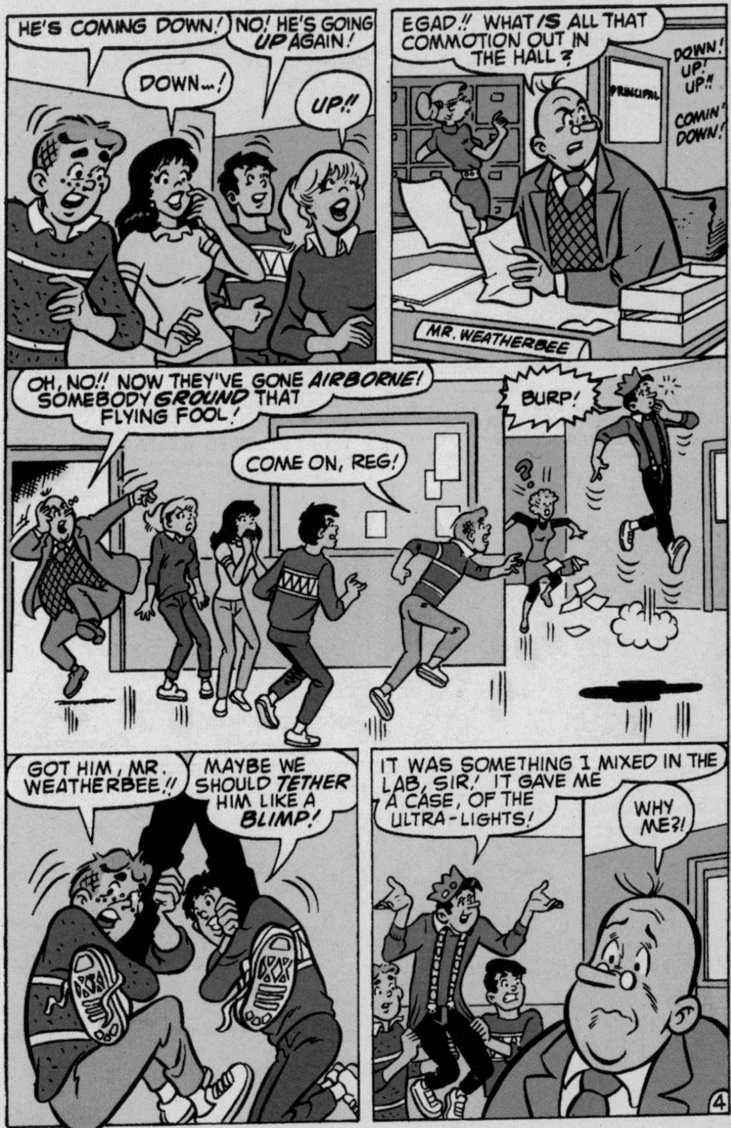
HE'S COMING DOWN!
NO! HE'S GOING UP AGAIN!
DOWN...!
UP!!
EGAD!! WHAT IS ALL THAT COMMOTION OUT IN THE HALL?
DOWN! UP! UP!! COMIN' DOWN!
PRINCIPAL
MR. WEATHERBEE
OH, NO!! NOW THEY'VE GONE AIRBORNE! SOMEBODY GROUND THAT FLYING FOOL!
BURP!
COME ON, REG!
GOT HIM, MR. WEATHERBEE!!
MAYBE WE SHOULD TETHER HIM LIKE A BLIMP!
IT WAS SOMETHING I MIXED IN THE LAB, SIR! IT GAVE ME A CASE, OF THE ULTRA-LIGHTS!
WHY ME?!
4

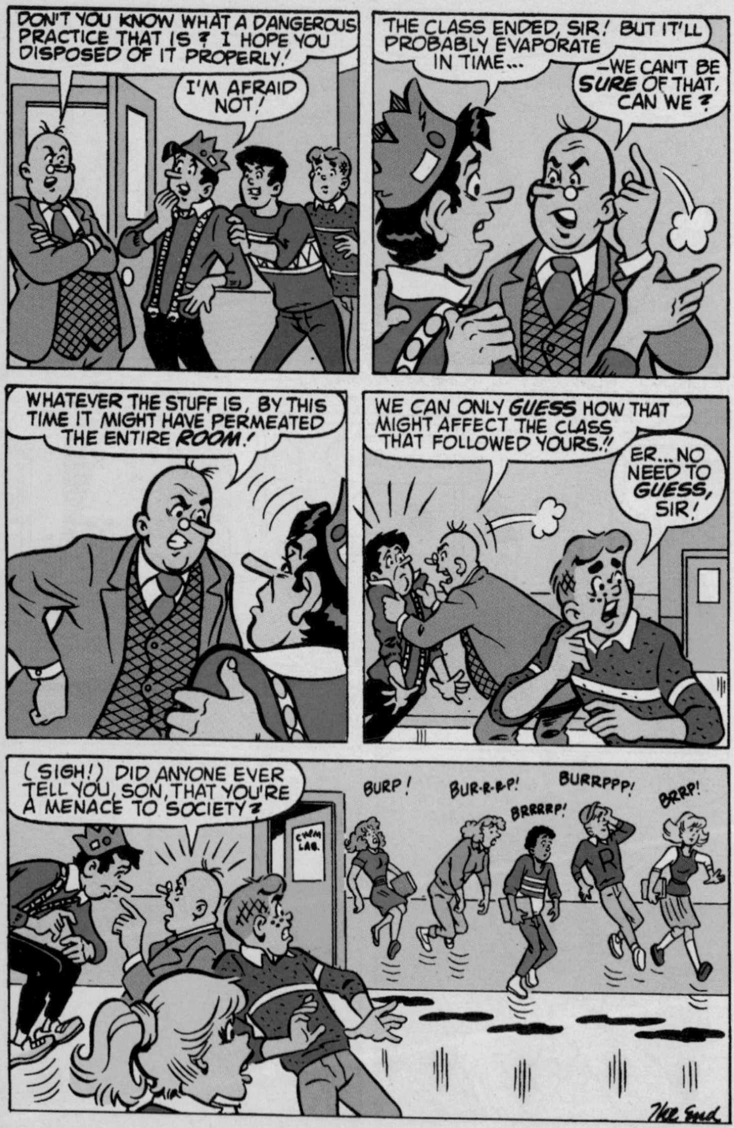
DON'T YOU KNOW WHAT A DANGEROUS PRACTICE THAT IS ? I HOPE YOU DISPOSED OF IT PROPERLY!
I'M AFRAID NOT!
THE CLASS ENDED, SIR! BUT IT'LL PROBABLY EVAPORATE IN TIME...
—WE CAN'T BE SURE OF THAT, CAN WE ?
WHATEVER THE STUFF IS, BY THIS TIME IT MIGHT HAVE PERMEATED THE ENTIRE ROOM!
WE CAN ONLY GUESS HOW THAT MIGHT AFFECT THE CLASS THAT FOLLOWED YOURS!!
ER... NO NEED TO GUESS, SIR!
(SIGH!) DID ANYONE EVER TELL YOU, SON, THAT YOU'RE A MENACE TO SOCIETY ?
CHEM LAB.
BURP!
BUR-R-R-P!
BRRRRP!
BURRPPP!
BRRP!

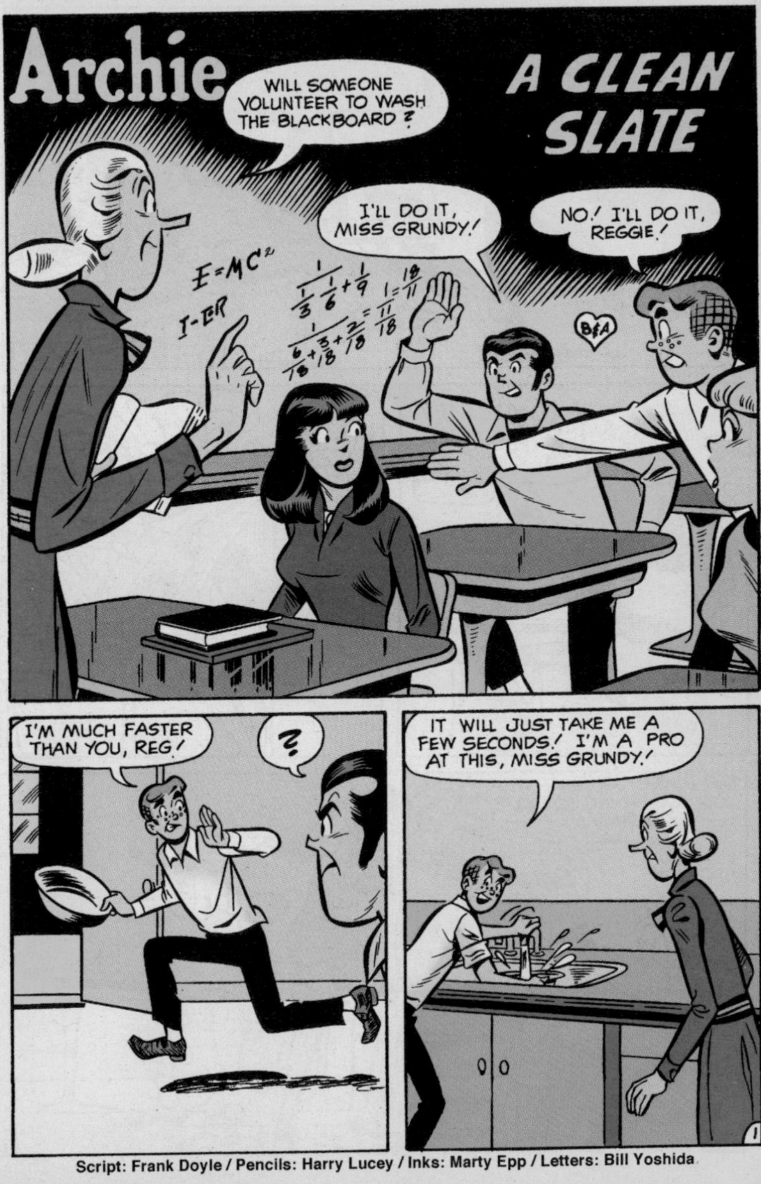
Archie
A CLEAN SLATE
WILL SOMEONE VOLUNTEER TO WASH THE BLACKBOARD ?
I'LL DO IT, MISS GRUNDY!
NO! I'LL DO IT, REGGIE!
B&A
I'M MUCH FASTER THAN YOU, REG!
?
IT WILL JUST TAKE ME A FEW SECONDS! I'M A PRO AT THIS, MISS GRUNDY!
1

Script: Frank Doyle / Pencils: Harry Lucey / Inks: Marty Epp / Letters: Bill Yoshida

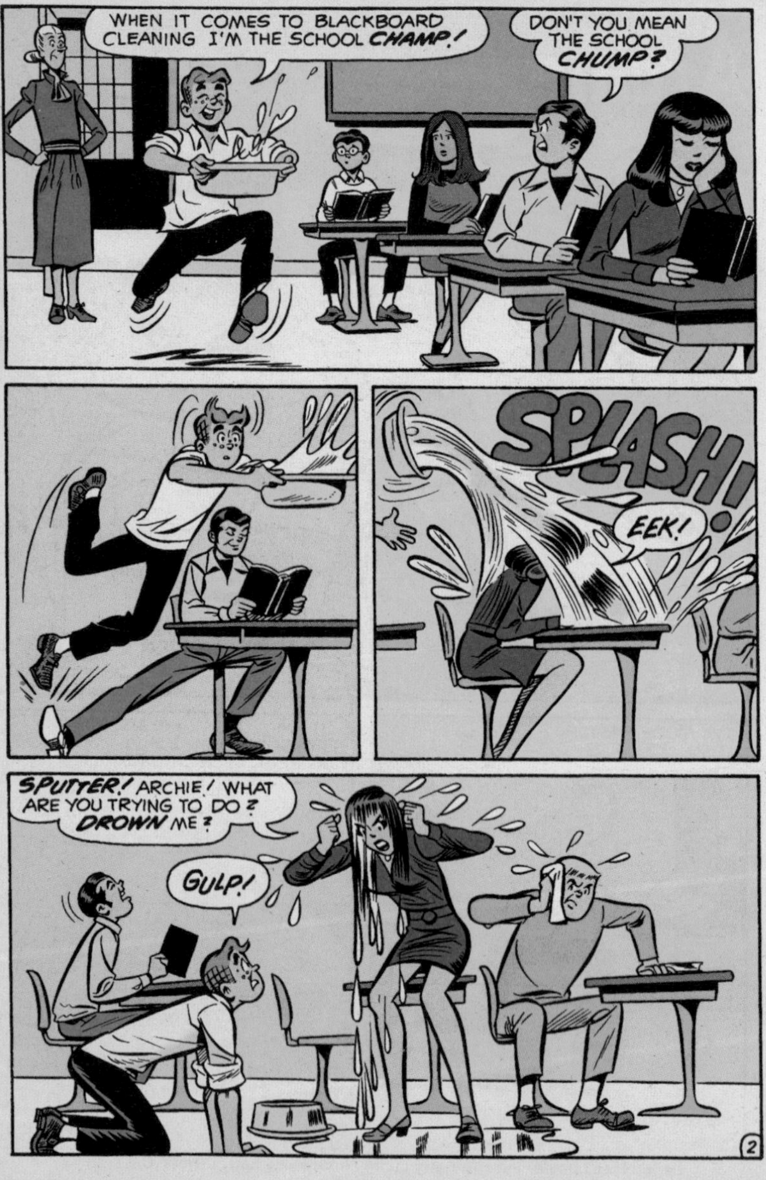

WHEN IT COMES TO BLACKBOARD CLEANING I'M THE SCHOOL CHAMP!
DON'T YOU MEAN THE SCHOOL CHUMP?
SPLASH!
EEK!
SPUTTER! ARCHIE! WHAT ARE YOU TRYING TO DO? DROWN ME?
GULP!

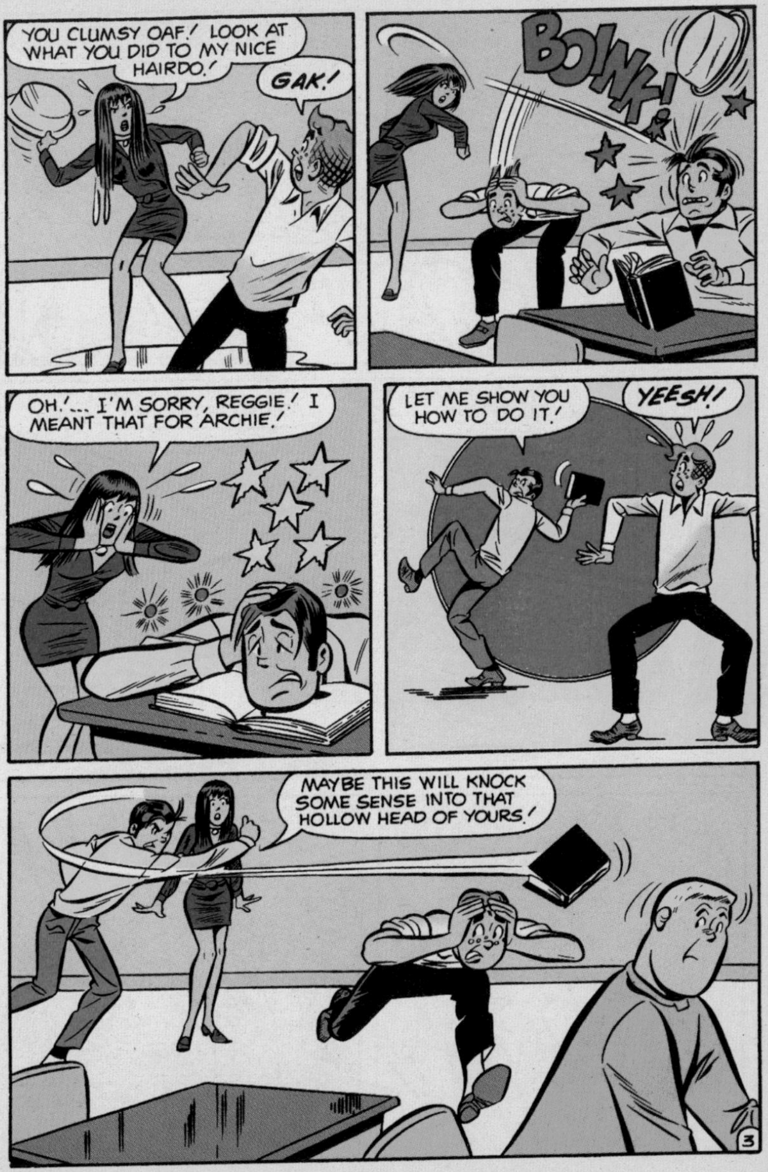
YOU CLUMSY OAF! LOOK AT WHAT YOU DID TO MY NICE HAIRDO!
GAK!
BOINK!
OH!... I'M SORRY, REGGIE! I MEANT THAT FOR ARCHIE!
LET ME SHOW YOU HOW TO DO IT!
YEESH!
MAYBE THIS WILL KNOCK SOME SENSE INTO THAT HOLLOW HEAD OF YOURS!
3

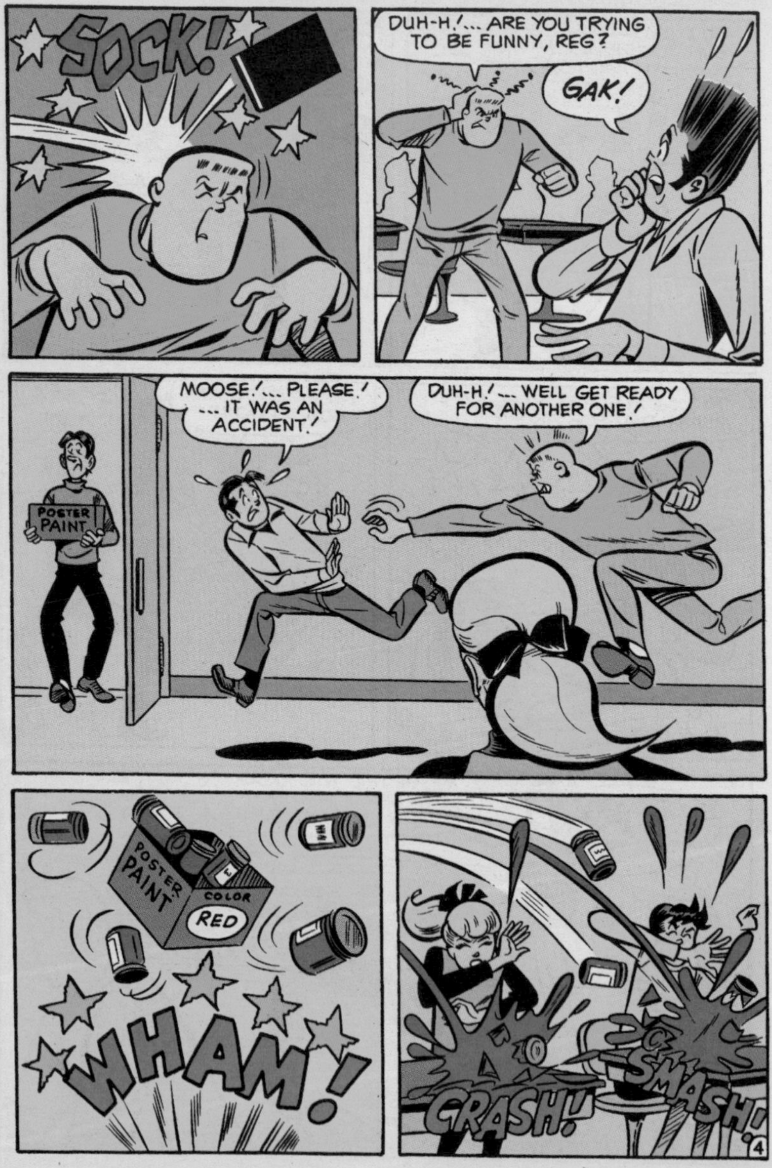
SOCK!
DUH-H.!... ARE YOU TRYING TO BE FUNNY, REG?
GAK!
MOOSE!... PLEASE! ... IT WAS AN ACCIDENT!
DUH-H.!... WELL GET READY FOR ANOTHER ONE!
POSTER PAINT
POSTER PAINT
COLOR
RED
WHAM!
CRASH!
SMASH!
4

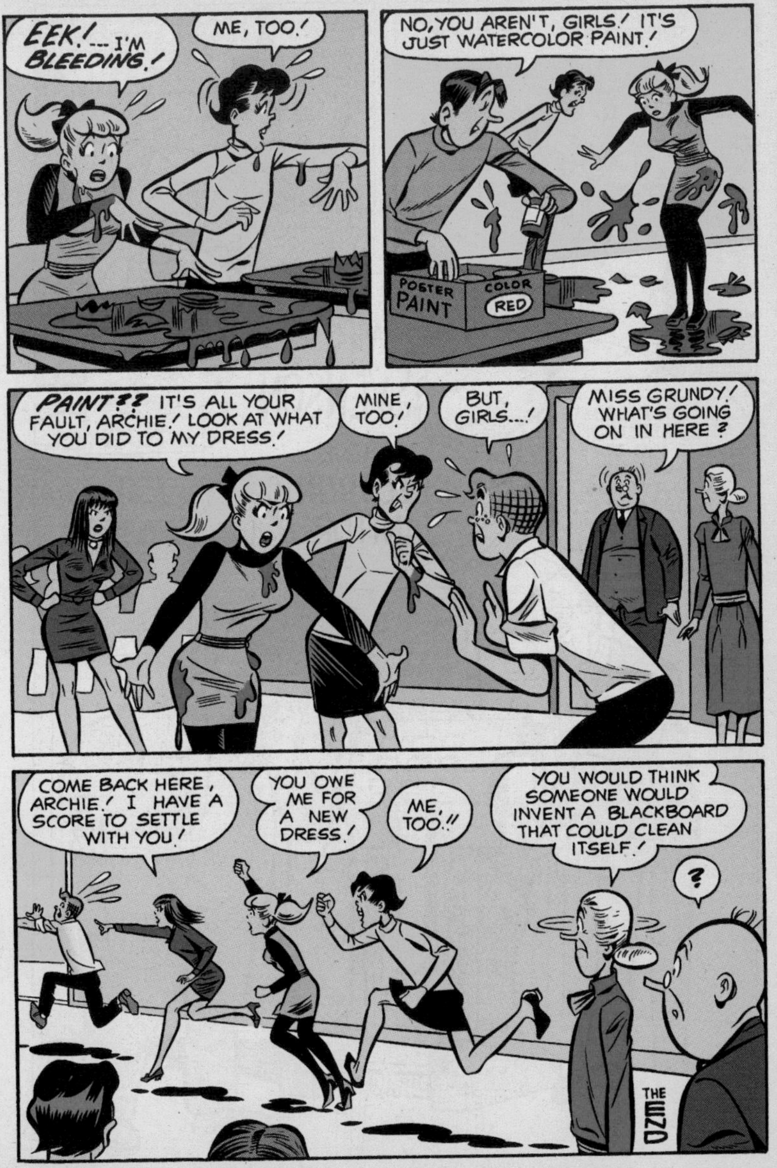
EEK! --- I'M BLEEDING!
ME, TOO!
NO, YOU AREN'T, GIRLS! IT'S JUST WATERCOLOR PAINT!
POSTER PAINT
COLOR RED
PAINT?? IT'S ALL YOUR FAULT, ARCHIE! LOOK AT WHAT YOU DID TO MY DRESS!
MINE, TOO!
BUT, GIRLS...!
MISS GRUNDY! WHAT'S GOING ON IN HERE?
COME BACK HERE, ARCHIE! I HAVE A SCORE TO SETTLE WITH YOU!
YOU OWE ME FOR A NEW DRESS!
ME, TOO!!
YOU WOULD THINK SOMEONE WOULD INVENT A BLACKBOARD THAT COULD CLEAN ITSELF!
?
THE END

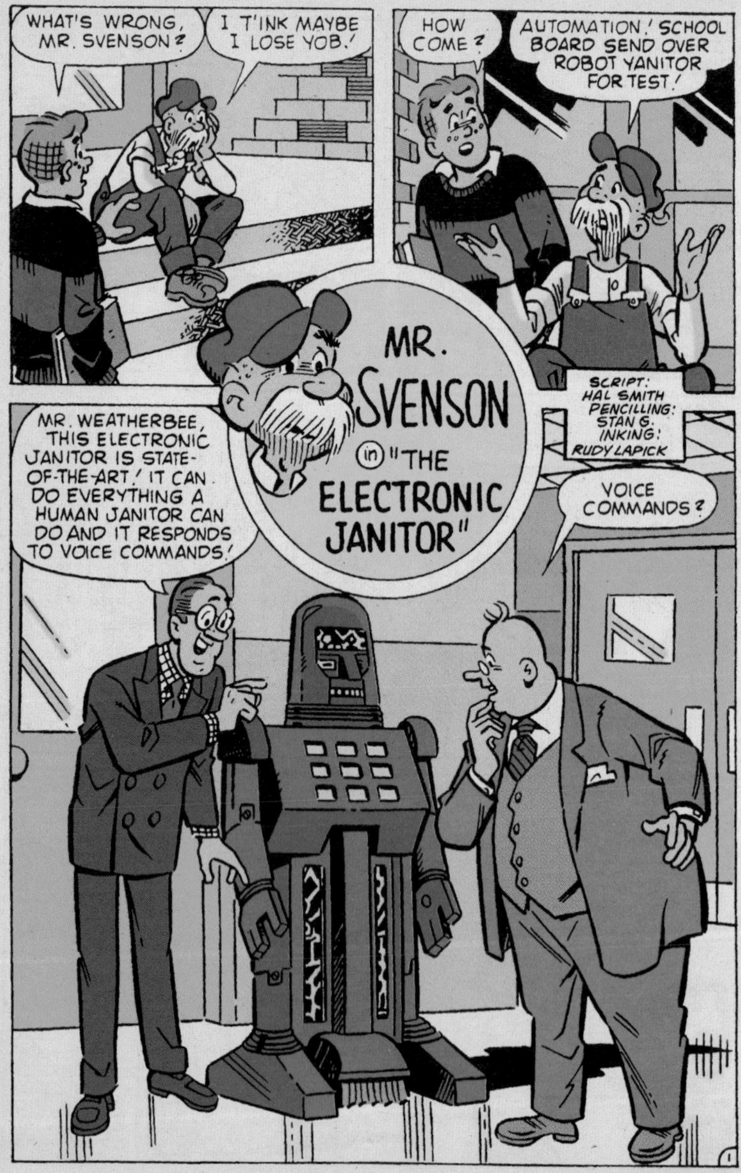
WHAT'S WRONG, MR. SVENSON?
I T'INK MAYBE I LOSE YOB!
HOW COME?
AUTOMATION! SCHOOL BOARD SEND OVER ROBOT YANITOR FOR TEST!
MR. SVENSON in "THE ELECTRONIC JANITOR"
SCRIPT: HAL SMITH
PENCILLING: STAN G.
INKING: RUDY LAPICK
MR. WEATHERBEE, THIS ELECTRONIC JANITOR IS STATE-OF-THE-ART! IT CAN DO EVERYTHING A HUMAN JANITOR CAN DO AND IT RESPONDS TO VOICE COMMANDS!
VOICE COMMANDS?
1

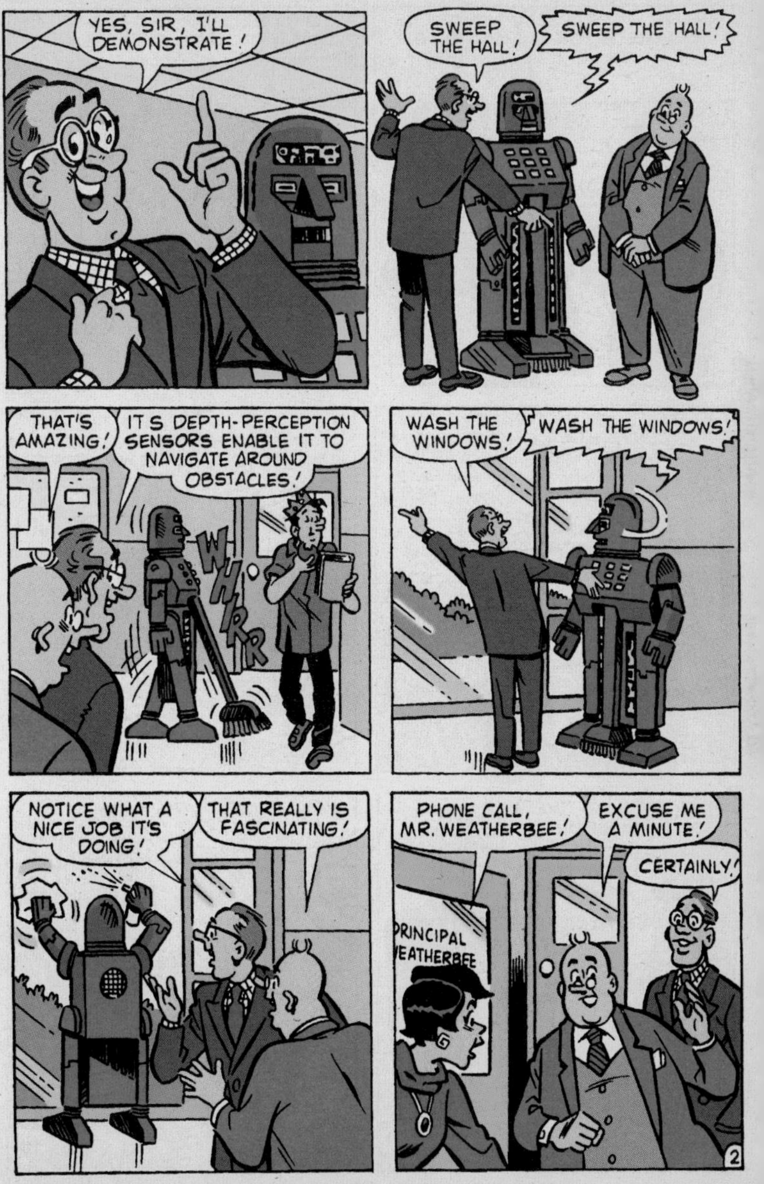
YES, SIR, I'LL DEMONSTRATE!
SWEEP THE HALL!
SWEEP THE HALL!
THAT'S AMAZING!
IT S DEPTH-PERCEPTION SENSORS ENABLE IT TO NAVIGATE AROUND OBSTACLES!
WHIRRR
WASH THE WINDOWS!
WASH THE WINDOWS!
NOTICE WHAT A NICE JOB IT'S DOING!
THAT REALLY IS FASCINATING!
PHONE CALL, MR. WEATHERBEE!
EXCUSE ME A MINUTE!
CERTAINLY!
PRINCIPAL WEATHERBEE
2

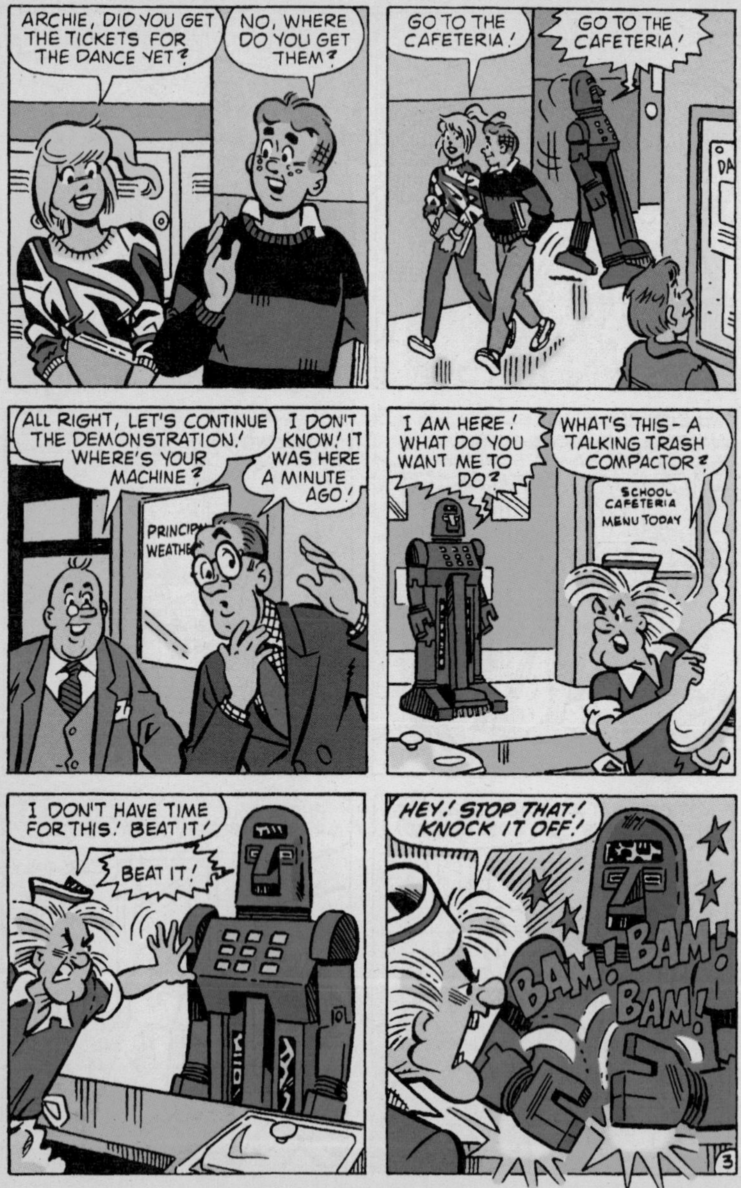
ARCHIE, DID YOU GET THE TICKETS FOR THE DANCE YET?
NO, WHERE DO YOU GET THEM?
GO TO THE CAFETERIA!
GO TO THE CAFETERIA!
ALL RIGHT, LET'S CONTINUE THE DEMONSTRATION! WHERE'S YOUR MACHINE?
I DON'T KNOW! IT WAS HERE A MINUTE AGO!
I AM HERE! WHAT DO YOU WANT ME TO DO?
WHAT'S THIS - A TALKING TRASH COMPACTOR?
SCHOOL CAFETERIA MENU TODAY
I DON'T HAVE TIME FOR THIS! BEAT IT!
BEAT IT!
HEY! STOP THAT! KNOCK IT OFF!
BAM! BAM! BAM!
3

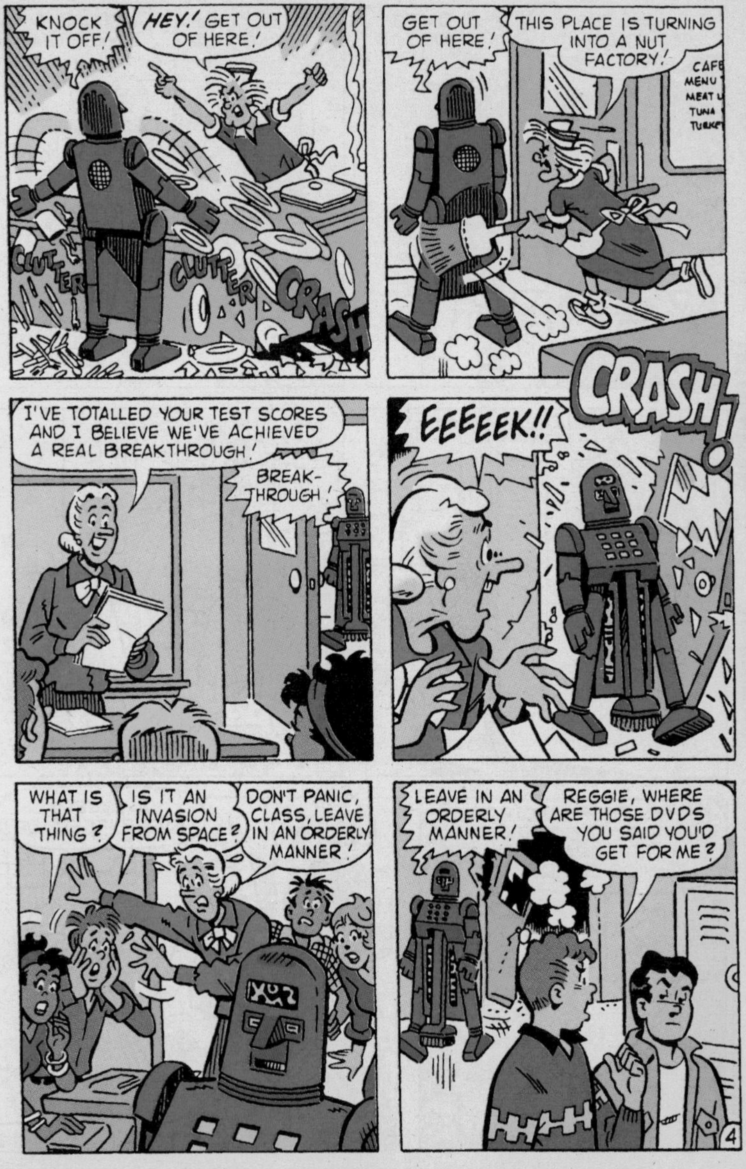

KNOCK IT OFF!
HEY! GET OUT OF HERE!
CLUTTER
CLUTTER
CRASH
GET OUT OF HERE!
THIS PLACE IS TURNING INTO A NUT FACTORY!
CAFE MENU
MEAT
TUNA
TURKEY
I'VE TOTALLED YOUR TEST SCORES AND I BELIEVE WE'VE ACHIEVED A REAL BREAKTHROUGH!
BREAK-THROUGH!
EEEEEK!!
CRASH!
WHAT IS THAT THING?
IS IT AN INVASION FROM SPACE?
DON'T PANIC, CLASS, LEAVE IN AN ORDERLY MANNER!
LEAVE IN AN ORDERLY MANNER!
REGGIE, WHERE ARE THOSE DVDS YOU SAID YOU'D GET FOR ME?

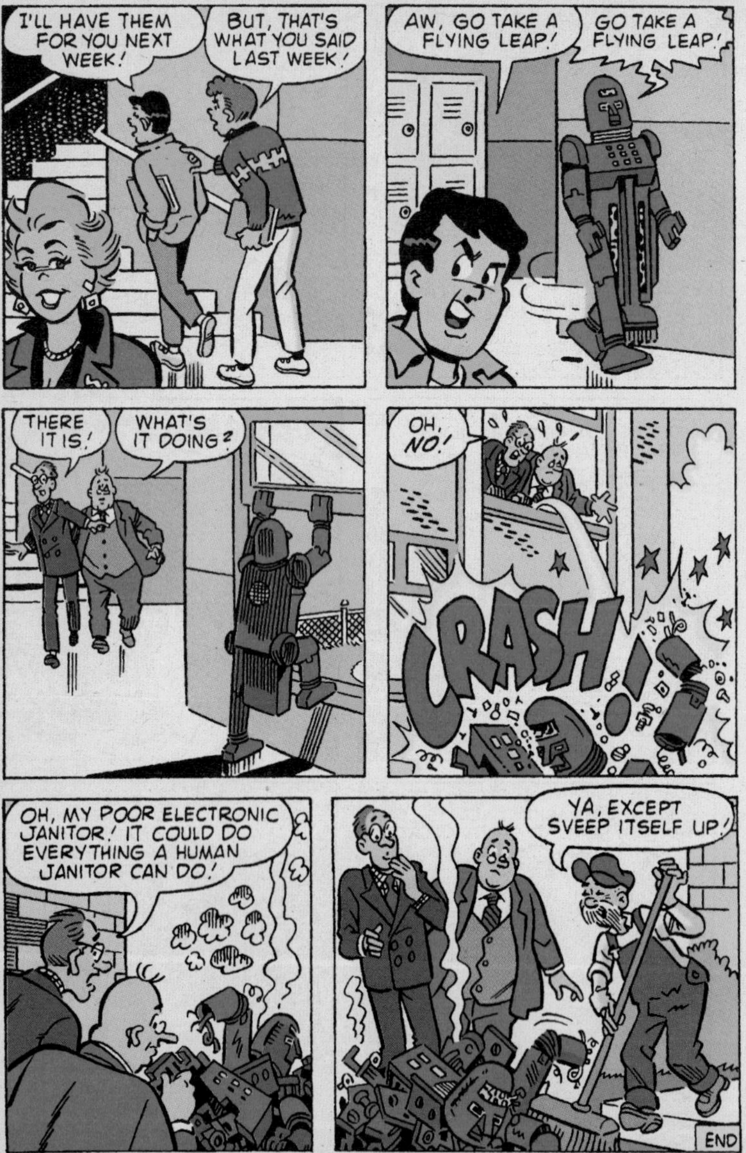

I'LL HAVE THEM FOR YOU NEXT WEEK!
BUT, THAT'S WHAT YOU SAID LAST WEEK!
AW, GO TAKE A FLYING LEAP!
GO TAKE A FLYING LEAP!
THERE IT IS!
WHAT'S IT DOING?
OH, NO!
CRASH!
OH, MY POOR ELECTRONIC JANITOR! IT COULD DO EVERYTHING A HUMAN JANITOR CAN DO!
YA, EXCEPT SVEEP ITSELF UP!
END

Archie in The ULTRA COOL SCHOOL

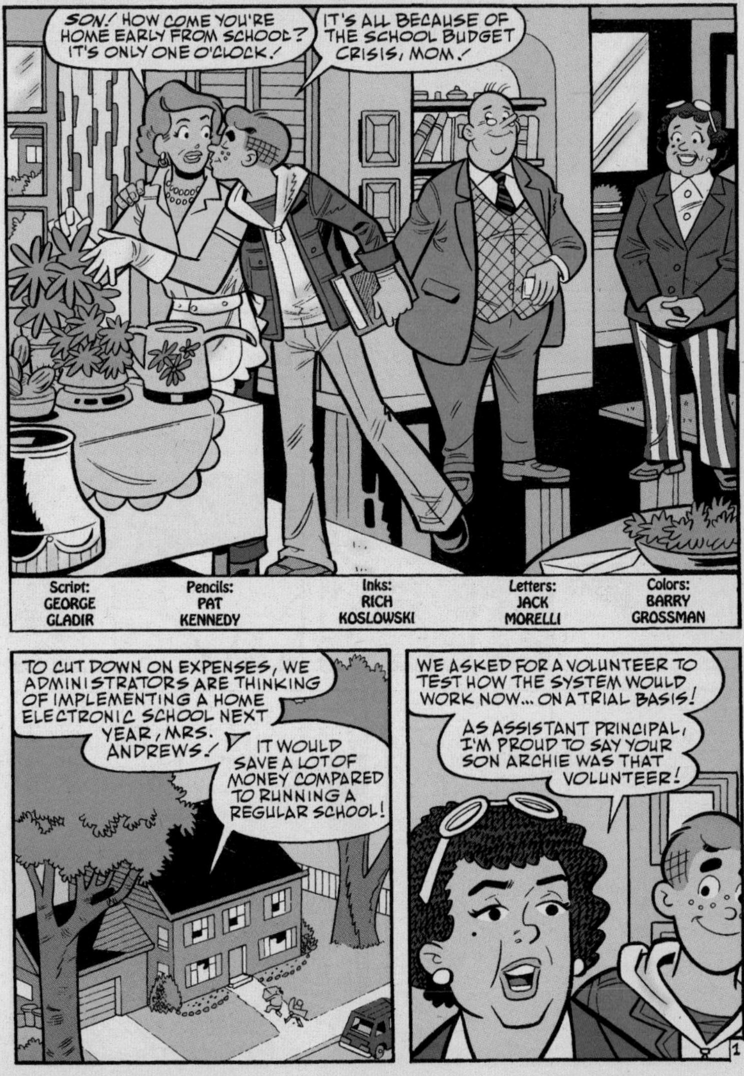

SON! HOW COME YOU'RE HOME EARLY FROM SCHOOL? IT'S ONLY ONE O'CLOCK!
IT'S ALL BECAUSE OF THE SCHOOL BUDGET CRISIS, MOM!
Script: GEORGE GLADIR
Pencils: PAT KENNEDY
Inks: RICH KOSLOWSKI
Letters: JACK MORELLI
Colors: BARRY GROSSMAN
TO CUT DOWN ON EXPENSES, WE ADMINISTRATORS ARE THINKING OF IMPLEMENTING A HOME ELECTRONIC SCHOOL NEXT YEAR, MRS. ANDREWS!
IT WOULD SAVE A LOT OF MONEY COMPARED TO RUNNING A REGULAR SCHOOL!
WE ASKED FOR A VOLUNTEER TO TEST HOW THE SYSTEM WOULD WORK NOW... ON A TRIAL BASIS!
AS ASSISTANT PRINCIPAL, I'M PROUD TO SAY YOUR SON ARCHIE WAS THAT VOLUNTEER!

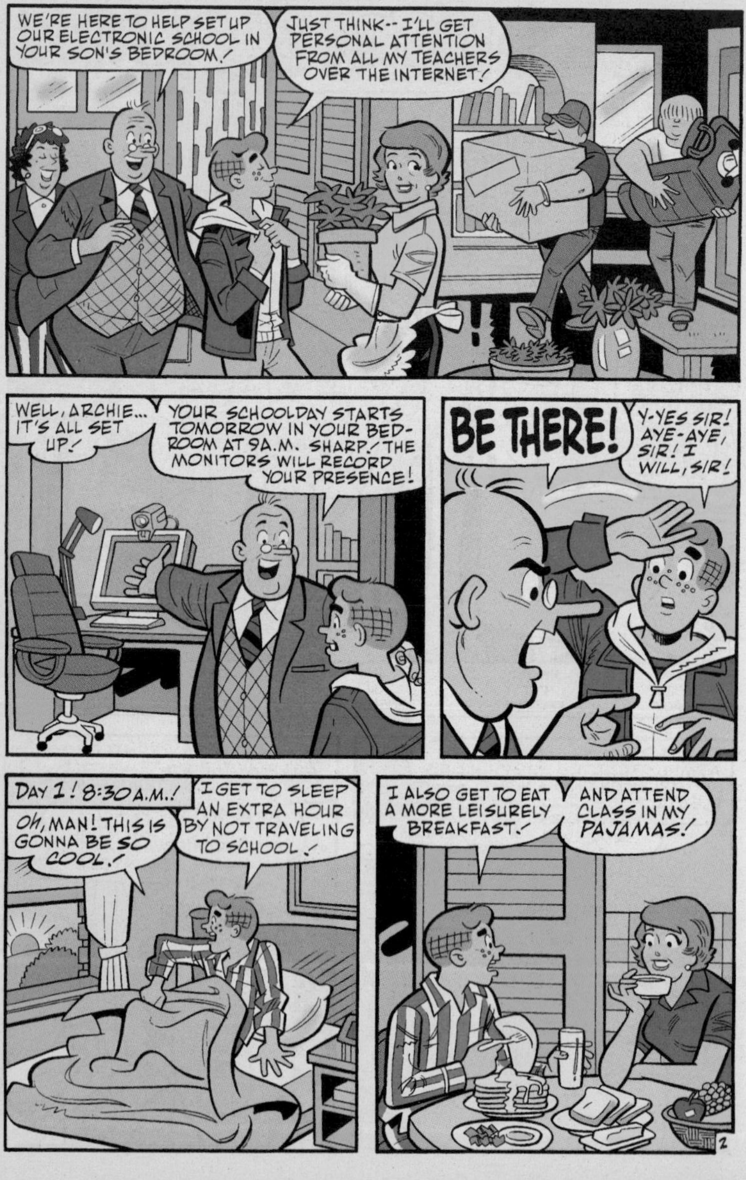
WE'RE HERE TO HELP SET UP OUR ELECTRONIC SCHOOL IN YOUR SON'S BEDROOM!
JUST THINK-- I'LL GET PERSONAL ATTENTION FROM ALL MY TEACHERS OVER THE INTERNET!
WELL, ARCHIE... IT'S ALL SET UP!
YOUR SCHOOLDAY STARTS TOMORROW IN YOUR BEDROOM AT 9A.M. SHARP! THE MONITORS WILL RECORD YOUR PRESENCE!
BE THERE!
Y-YES SIR! AYE-AYE, SIR! I WILL, SIR!
DAY 1! 8:30 A.M.!
Oh, MAN! THIS IS GONNA BE SO COOL!
I GET TO SLEEP AN EXTRA HOUR BY NOT TRAVELING TO SCHOOL!
I ALSO GET TO EAT A MORE LEISURELY BREAKFAST!
AND ATTEND CLASS IN MY PAJAMAS!
2

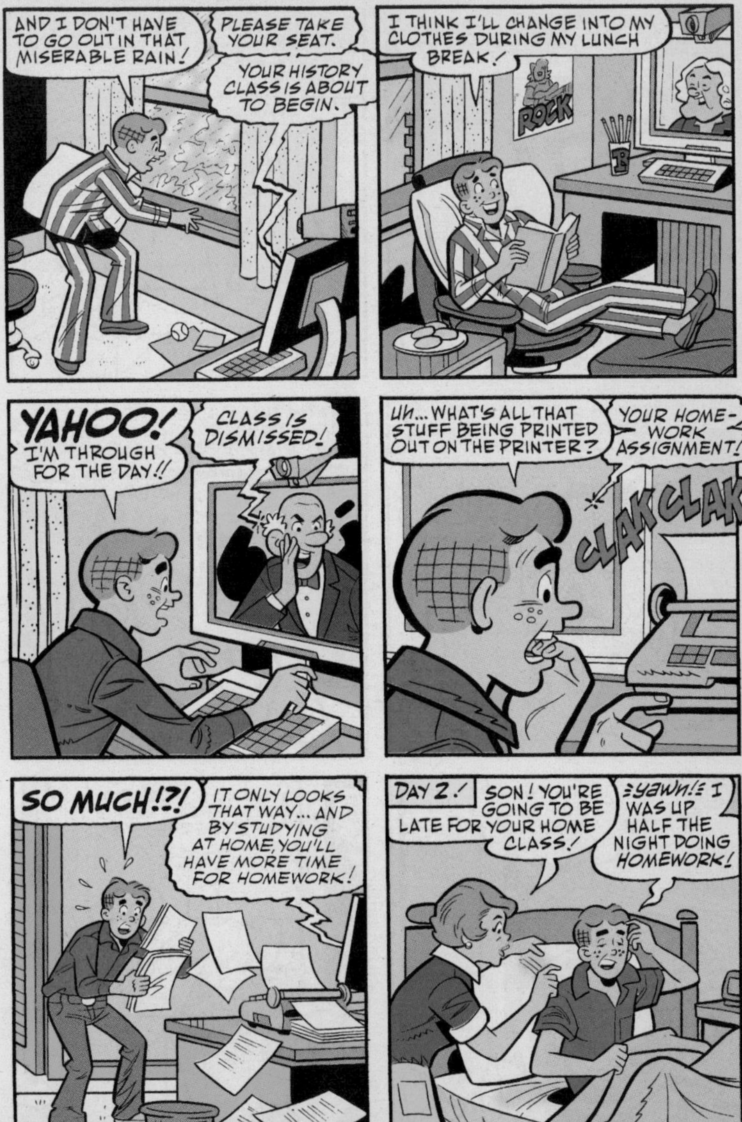
AND I DON'T HAVE TO GO OUT IN THAT MISERABLE RAIN!
PLEASE TAKE YOUR SEAT.
YOUR HISTORY CLASS IS ABOUT TO BEGIN.
I THINK I'LL CHANGE INTO MY CLOTHES DURING MY LUNCH BREAK!
ROCK
YAHOO! I'M THROUGH FOR THE DAY!!
CLASS IS DISMISSED!
UH... WHAT'S ALL THAT STUFF BEING PRINTED OUT ON THE PRINTER?
YOUR HOME-WORK ASSIGNMENT!
CLAK CLAK
SO MUCH!?!
IT ONLY LOOKS THAT WAY... AND BY STUDYING AT HOME, YOU'LL HAVE MORE TIME FOR HOMEWORK!
DAY 2!
SON! YOU'RE GOING TO BE LATE FOR YOUR HOME CLASS!
yawn! I WAS UP HALF THE NIGHT DOING HOMEWORK!

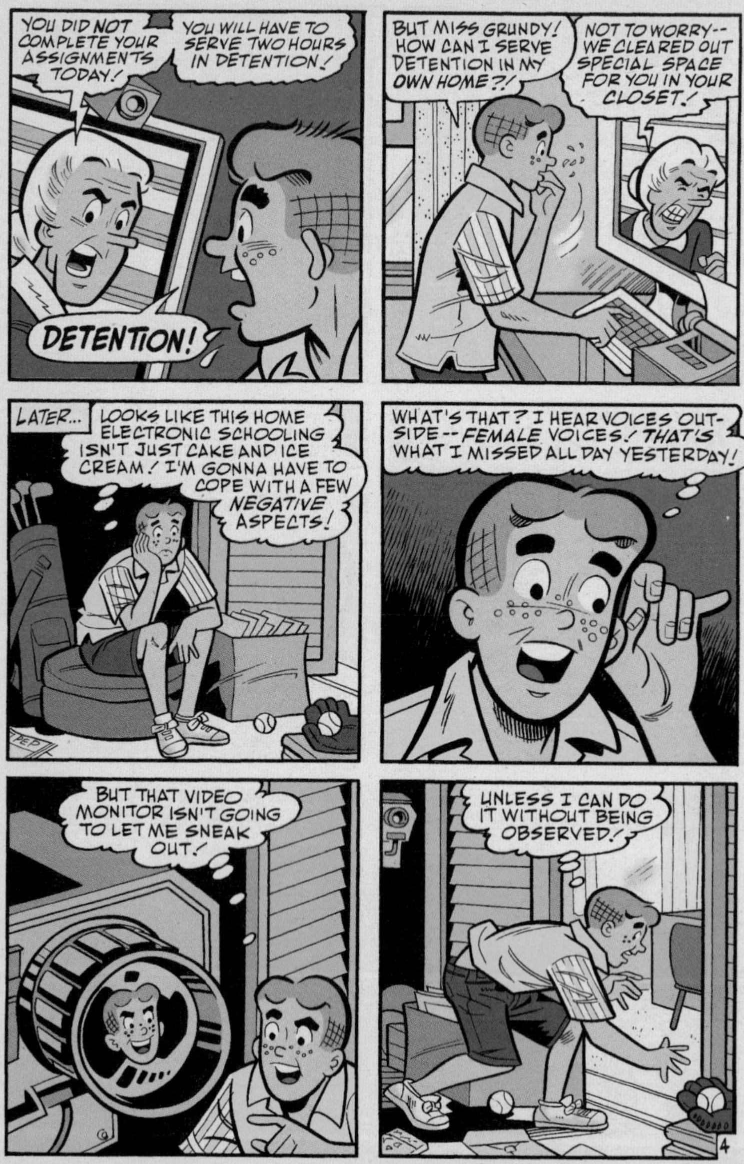
YOU DID NOT COMPLETE YOUR ASSIGNMENTS TODAY!
YOU WILL HAVE TO SERVE TWO HOURS IN DETENTION!
DETENTION!
BUT MISS GRUNDY! HOW CAN I SERVE DETENTION IN MY OWN HOME?!
NOT TO WORRY-- WE CLEARED OUT SPECIAL SPACE FOR YOU IN YOUR CLOSET!
LATER...
LOOKS LIKE THIS HOME ELECTRONIC SCHOOLING ISN'T JUST CAKE AND ICE CREAM! I'M GONNA HAVE TO COPE WITH A FEW NEGATIVE ASPECTS!
PEP
WHAT'S THAT? I HEAR VOICES OUT-SIDE-- FEMALE VOICES! THAT'S WHAT I MISSED ALL DAY YESTERDAY!
BUT THAT VIDEO MONITOR ISN'T GOING TO LET ME SNEAK OUT!
UNLESS I CAN DO IT WITHOUT BEING OBSERVED!

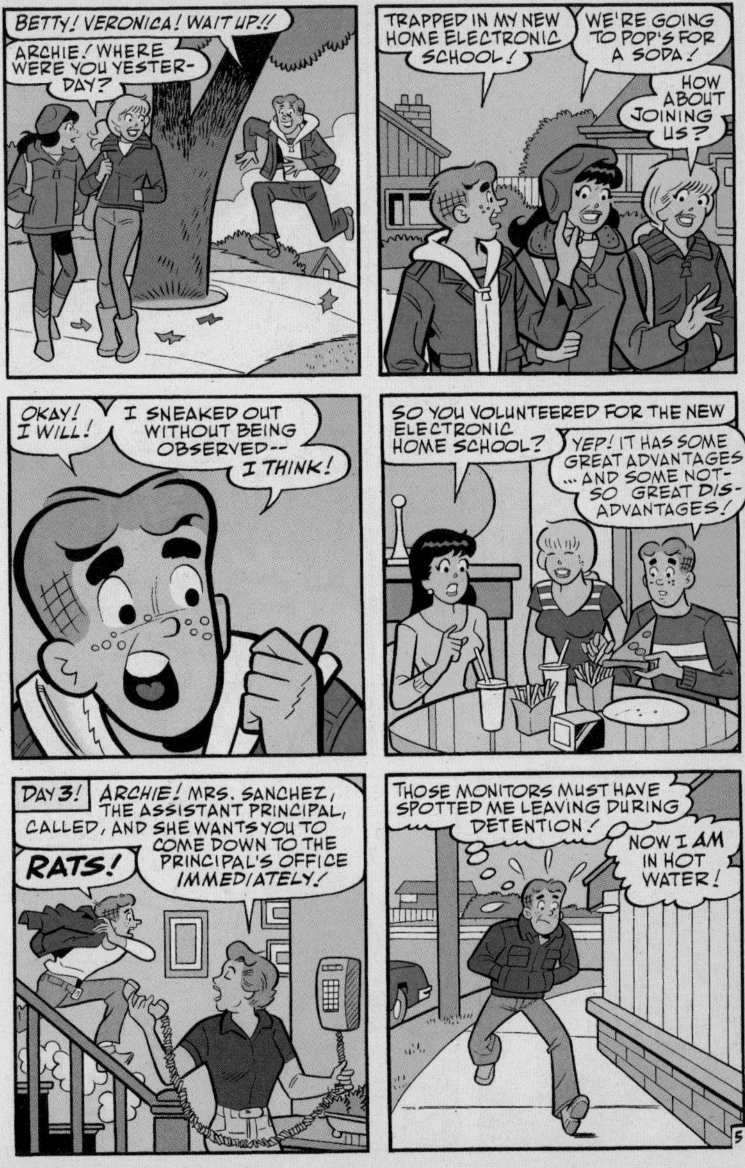
BETTY! VERONICA! WAIT UP!!
ARCHIE! WHERE WERE YOU YESTER-DAY?
TRAPPED IN MY NEW HOME ELECTRONIC SCHOOL!
WE'RE GOING TO POP'S FOR A SODA!
HOW ABOUT JOINING US?
OKAY! I WILL!
I SNEAKED OUT WITHOUT BEING OBSERVED-- I THINK!
SO YOU VOLUNTEERED FOR THE NEW ELECTRONIC HOME SCHOOL?
YEP! IT HAS SOME GREAT ADVANTAGES ...AND SOME NOT-SO GREAT DIS-ADVANTAGES!
DAY 3!
ARCHIE! MRS. SANCHEZ, THE ASSISTANT PRINCIPAL, CALLED, AND SHE WANTS YOU TO COME DOWN TO THE PRINCIPAL'S OFFICE IMMEDIATELY!
RATS!
THOSE MONITORS MUST HAVE SPOTTED ME LEAVING DURING DETENTION!
NOW I AM IN HOT WATER!

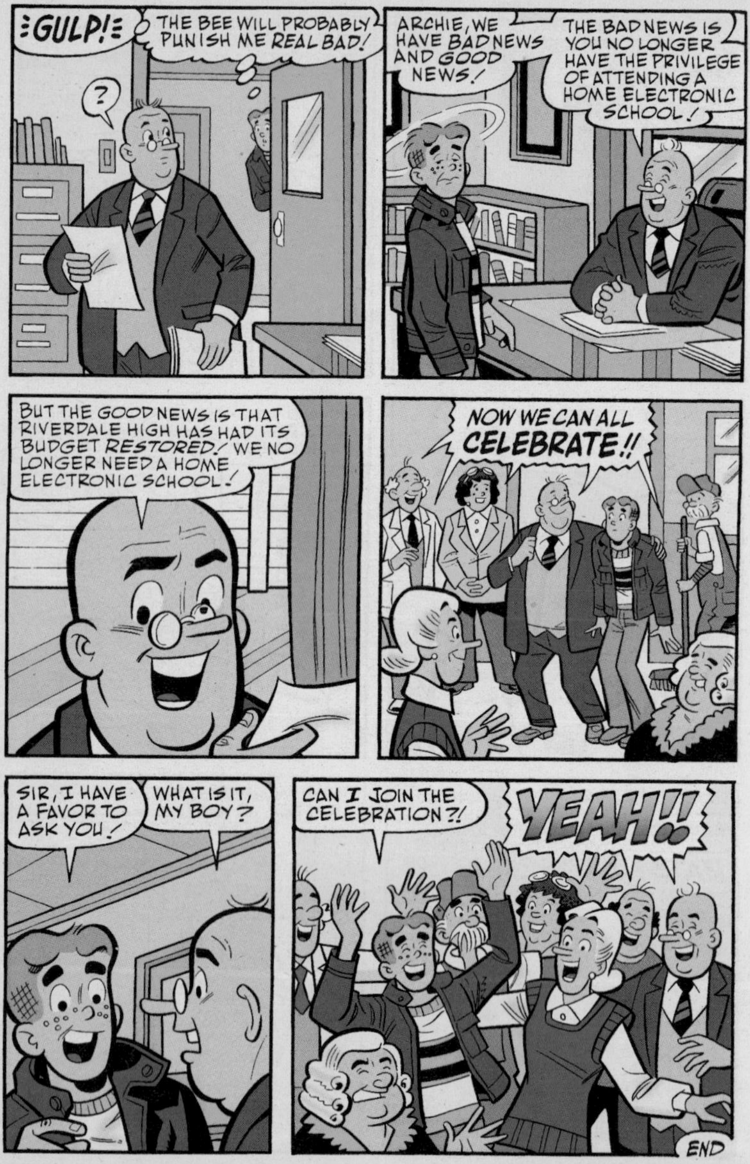
GULP!
THE BEE WILL PROBABLY PUNISH ME REAL BAD!
?
ARCHIE, WE HAVE BAD NEWS AND GOOD NEWS!
THE BAD NEWS IS YOU NO LONGER HAVE THE PRIVILEGE OF ATTENDING A HOME ELECTRONIC SCHOOL!
BUT THE GOOD NEWS IS THAT RIVERDALE HIGH HAS HAD ITS BUDGET RESTORED! WE NO LONGER NEED A HOME ELECTRONIC SCHOOL!
NOW WE CAN ALL CELEBRATE!!
SIR, I HAVE A FAVOR TO ASK YOU!
WHAT IS IT, MY BOY?
CAN I JOIN THE CELEBRATION?!
YEAH!!
END

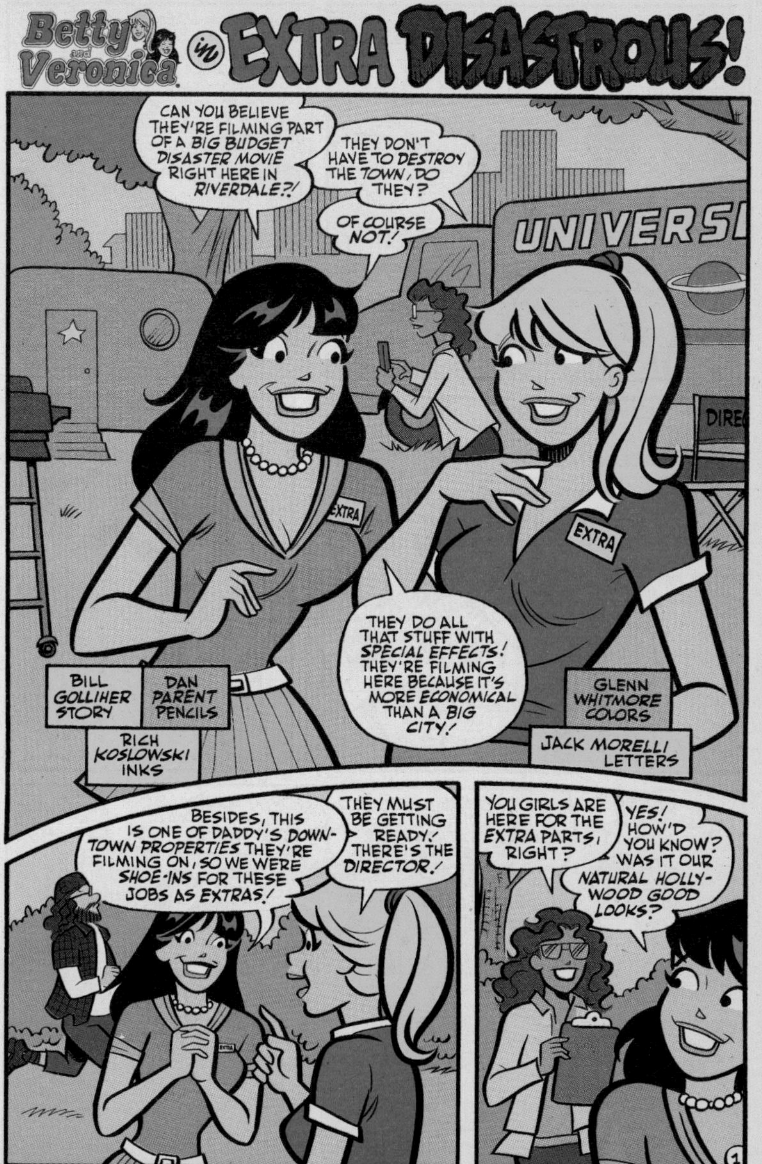
Betty and Veronica in EXTRA DISASTROUS!
CAN YOU BELIEVE THEY'RE FILMING PART OF A BIG BUDGET DISASTER MOVIE RIGHT HERE IN RIVERDALE?!
THEY DON'T HAVE TO DESTROY THE TOWN, DO THEY?
OF COURSE NOT!
UNIVERSI
THEY DO ALL THAT STUFF WITH SPECIAL EFFECTS! THEY'RE FILMING HERE BECAUSE IT'S MORE ECONOMICAL THAN A BIG CITY!
EXTRA
EXTRA
BILL GOLLIHER STORY
DAN PARENT PENCILS
RICH KOSLOWSKI INKS
GLENN WHITMORE COLORS
JACK MORELLI LETTERS
BESIDES, THIS IS ONE OF DADDY'S DOWNTOWN PROPERTIES THEY'RE FILMING ON, SO WE WERE SHOE-INS FOR THESE JOBS AS EXTRAS!
THEY MUST BE GETTING READY! THERE'S THE DIRECTOR!
YOU GIRLS ARE HERE FOR THE EXTRA PARTS, RIGHT?
YES! HOW'D YOU KNOW? WAS IT OUR NATURAL HOLLYWOOD GOOD LOOKS?
1

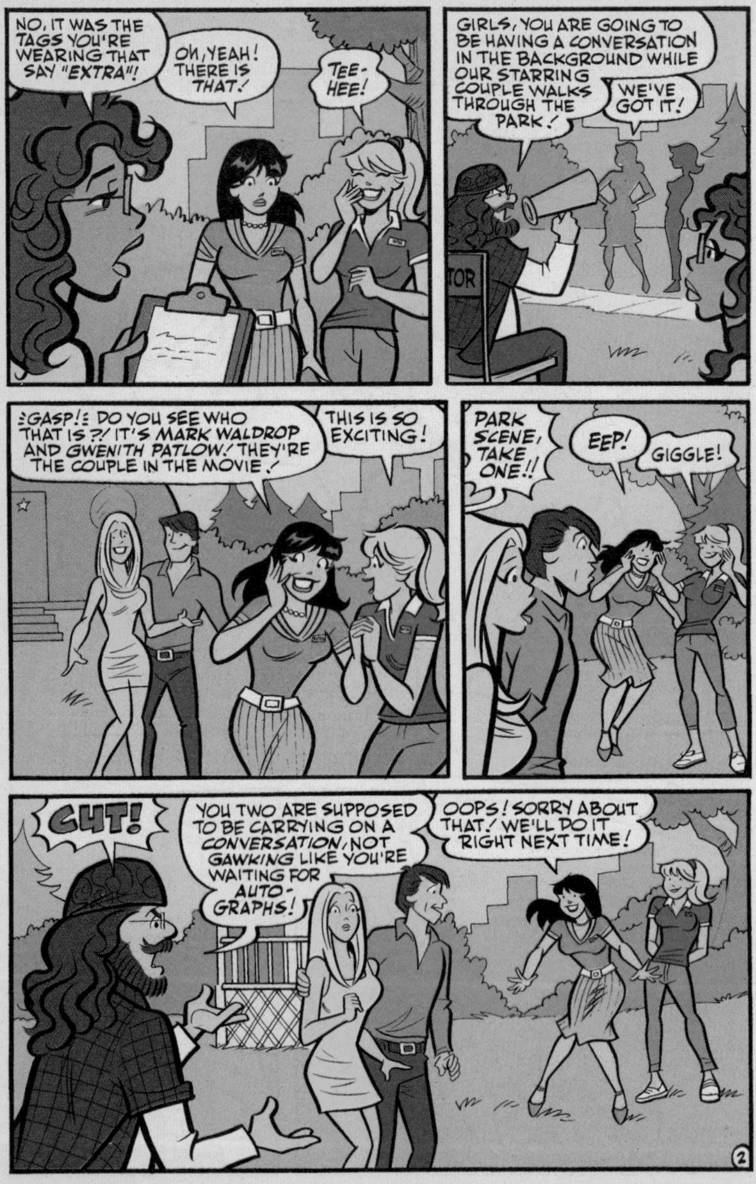

NO, IT WAS THE TAGS YOU'RE WEARING THAT SAY "EXTRA"!
OH, YEAH! THERE IS THAT!
TEE-HEE!
GIRLS, YOU ARE GOING TO BE HAVING A CONVERSATION IN THE BACKGROUND WHILE OUR STARRING COUPLE WALKS THROUGH THE PARK!
WE'VE GOT IT!
TOR
:GASP!: DO YOU SEE WHO THAT IS?! IT'S MARK WALDROP AND GWENITH PATLOW! THEY'RE THE COUPLE IN THE MOVIE!
THIS IS SO EXCITING!
PARK SCENE, TAKE ONE!!
EEP!
GIGGLE!
CUT!
YOU TWO ARE SUPPOSED TO BE CARRYING ON A CONVERSATION, NOT GAWKING LIKE YOU'RE WAITING FOR AUTO-GRAPHS!
OOPS! SORRY ABOUT THAT! WE'LL DO IT RIGHT NEXT TIME!
2

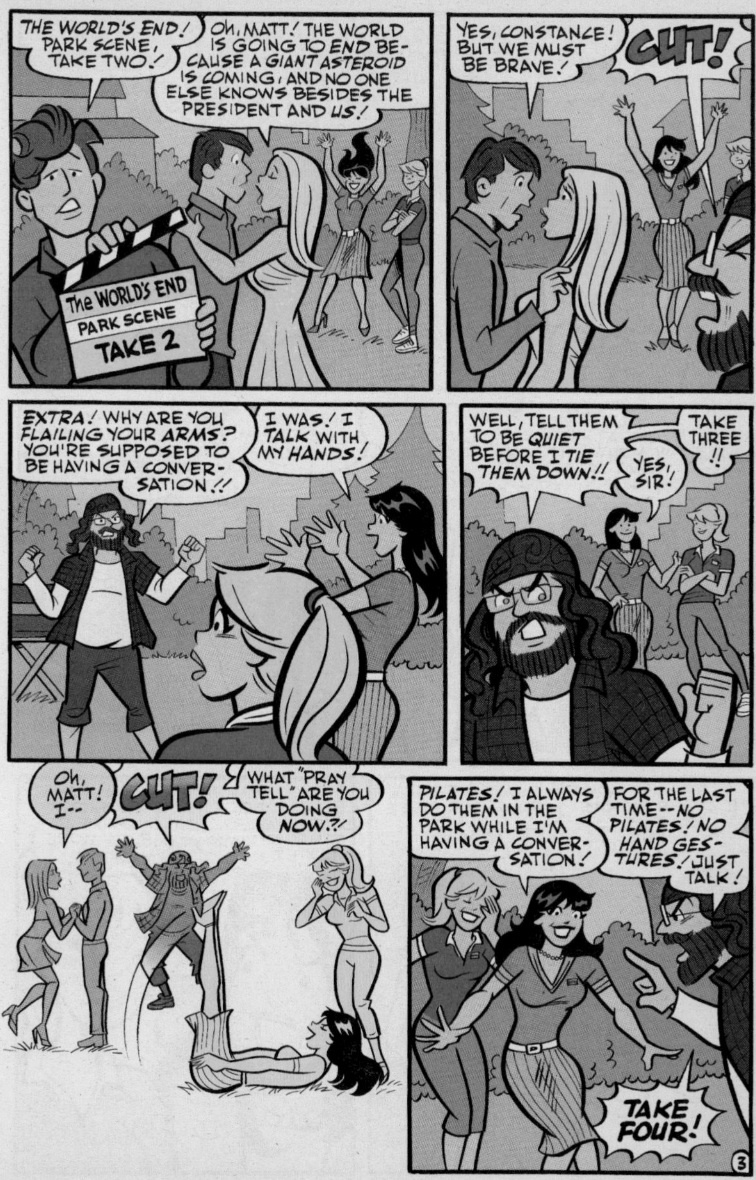

THE WORLD'S END! PARK SCENE, TAKE TWO!
Oh, MATT! THE WORLD IS GOING TO END BECAUSE A GIANT ASTEROID IS COMING, AND NO ONE ELSE KNOWS BESIDES THE PRESIDENT AND US!
The WORLD'S END
PARK SCENE
TAKE 2
YES, CONSTANCE! BUT WE MUST BE BRAVE!
CUT!
EXTRA! WHY ARE YOU FLAILING YOUR ARMS? YOU'RE SUPPOSED TO BE HAVING A CONVERSATION!!
I WAS! I TALK WITH MY HANDS!
WELL, TELL THEM TO BE QUIET BEFORE I TIE THEM DOWN!!
YES, SIR!
TAKE THREE!!
Oh, MATT! I--
CUT!
WHAT "PRAY TELL" ARE YOU DOING NOW?!
PILATES! I ALWAYS DO THEM IN THE PARK WHILE I'M HAVING A CONVERSATION!
FOR THE LAST TIME--NO PILATES! NO HAND GESTURES! JUST TALK!
TAKE FOUR!
3

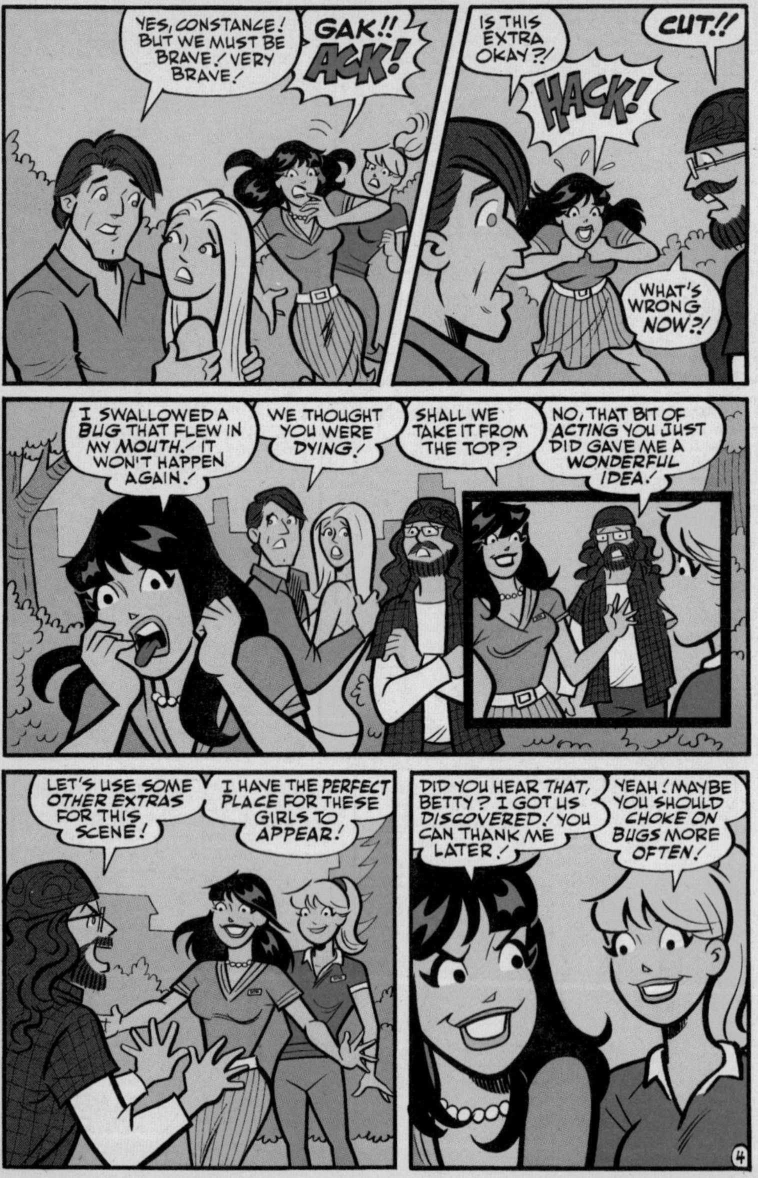

YES, CONSTANCE! BUT WE MUST BE BRAVE! VERY BRAVE!
GAK!! ACK!
IS THIS EXTRA OKAY?!
HACK!
CUT!!
WHAT'S WRONG NOW?!
I SWALLOWED A BUG THAT FLEW IN MY MOUTH! IT WON'T HAPPEN AGAIN!
WE THOUGHT YOU WERE DYING!
SHALL WE TAKE IT FROM THE TOP?
NO, THAT BIT OF ACTING YOU JUST DID GAVE ME A WONDERFUL IDEA!
LET'S USE SOME OTHER EXTRAS FOR THIS SCENE!
I HAVE THE PERFECT PLACE FOR THESE GIRLS TO APPEAR!
DID YOU HEAR THAT, BETTY? I GOT US DISCOVERED! YOU CAN THANK ME LATER!
YEAH! MAYBE YOU SHOULD CHOKE ON BUGS MORE OFTEN!
4

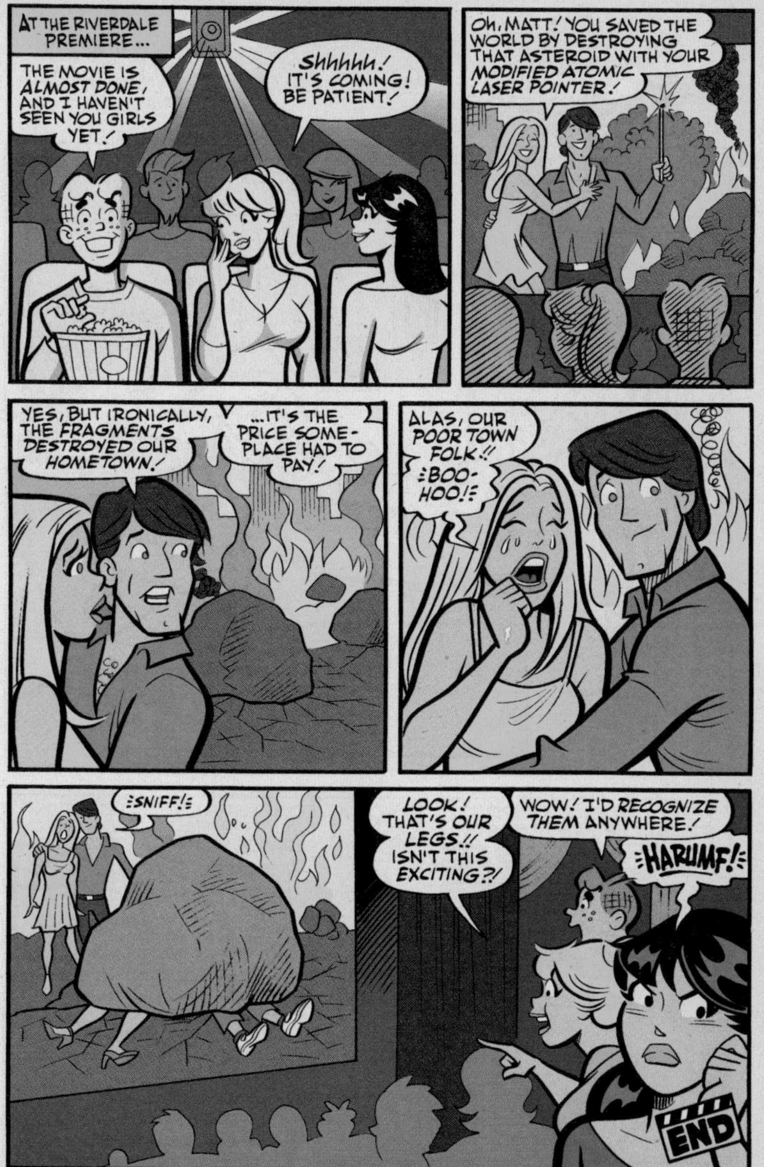
AT THE RIVERDALE PREMIERE...
THE MOVIE IS ALMOST DONE, AND I HAVEN'T SEEN YOU GIRLS YET!
Shhhhh! IT'S COMING! BE PATIENT!
Oh, MATT! YOU SAVED THE WORLD BY DESTROYING THAT ASTEROID WITH YOUR MODIFIED ATOMIC LASER POINTER!
YES, BUT IRONICALLY, THE FRAGMENTS DESTROYED OUR HOMETOWN!
...IT'S THE PRICE SOME-PLACE HAD TO PAY!
ALAS, OUR POOR TOWN FOLK!!
BOO-HOO!!
SNIFF!
LOOK! THAT'S OUR LEGS!! ISN'T THIS EXCITING?!
WOW! I'D RECOGNIZE THEM ANYWHERE!
HARUMF!
END

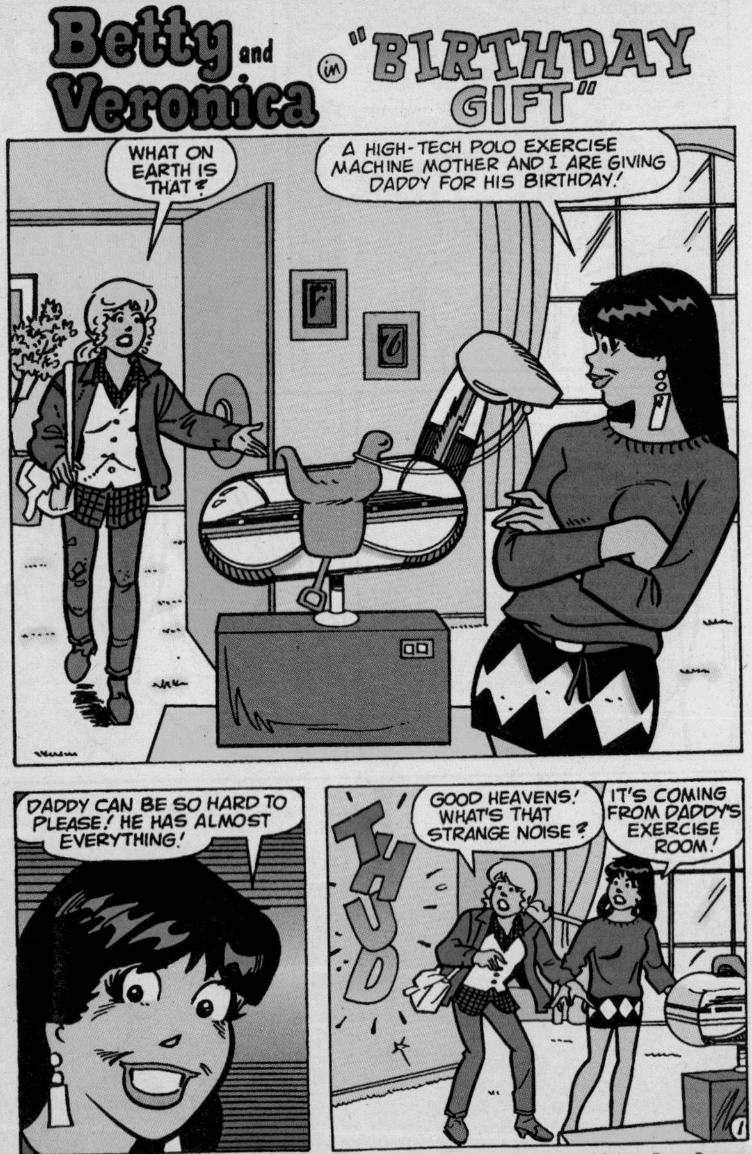
Betty and Veronica in "BIRTHDAY GIFT"
WHAT ON EARTH IS THAT?
A HIGH-TECH POLO EXERCISE MACHINE MOTHER AND I ARE GIVING DADDY FOR HIS BIRTHDAY!
DADDY CAN BE SO HARD TO PLEASE! HE HAS ALMOST EVERYTHING!
THUD
GOOD HEAVENS! WHAT'S THAT STRANGE NOISE?
IT'S COMING FROM DADDY'S EXERCISE ROOM!
1

Script: George Gladir / Pencils: Dan DeCarlo / Inks: Alison Flood / Letters: Bill Yoshida / Colors: Barry Grossman

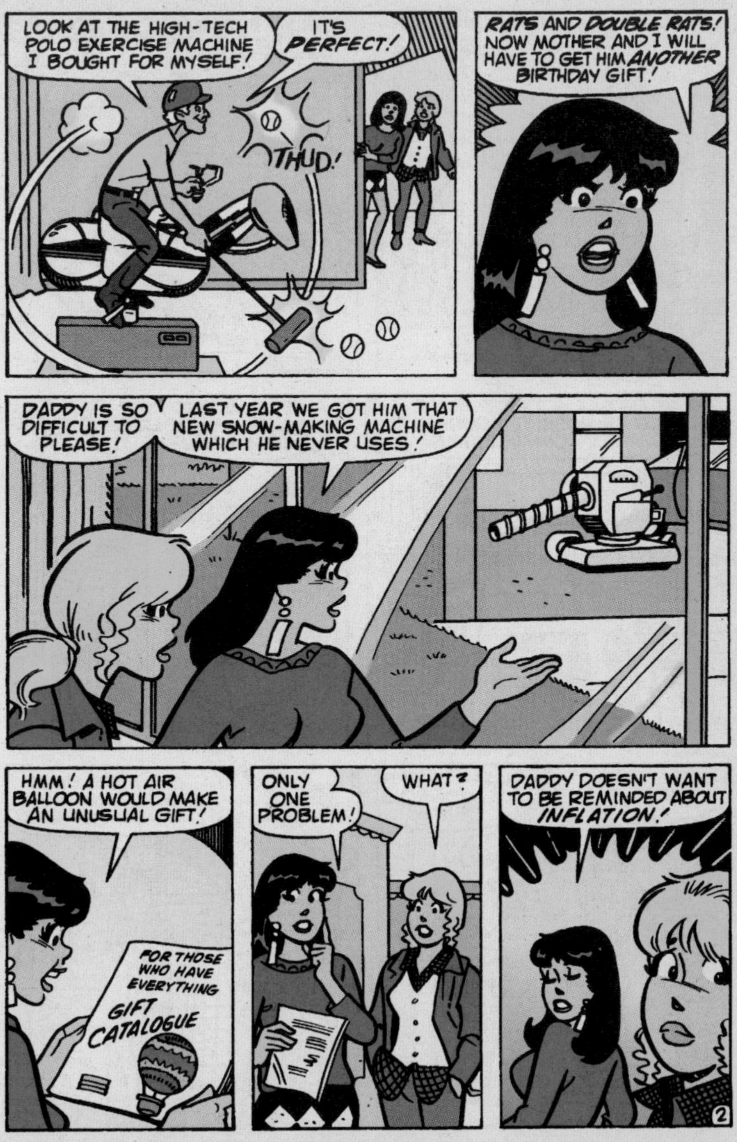
LOOK AT THE HIGH-TECH POLO EXERCISE MACHINE I BOUGHT FOR MYSELF!
IT'S PERFECT!
THUD!
RATS AND DOUBLE RATS! NOW MOTHER AND I WILL HAVE TO GET HIM ANOTHER BIRTHDAY GIFT!
DADDY IS SO DIFFICULT TO PLEASE!
LAST YEAR WE GOT HIM THAT NEW SNOW-MAKING MACHINE WHICH HE NEVER USES!
HMM! A HOT AIR BALLOON WOULD MAKE AN UNUSUAL GIFT!
FOR THOSE WHO HAVE EVERYTHING
GIFT CATALOGUE
ONLY ONE PROBLEM!
WHAT?
DADDY DOESN'T WANT TO BE REMINDED ABOUT INFLATION!
2

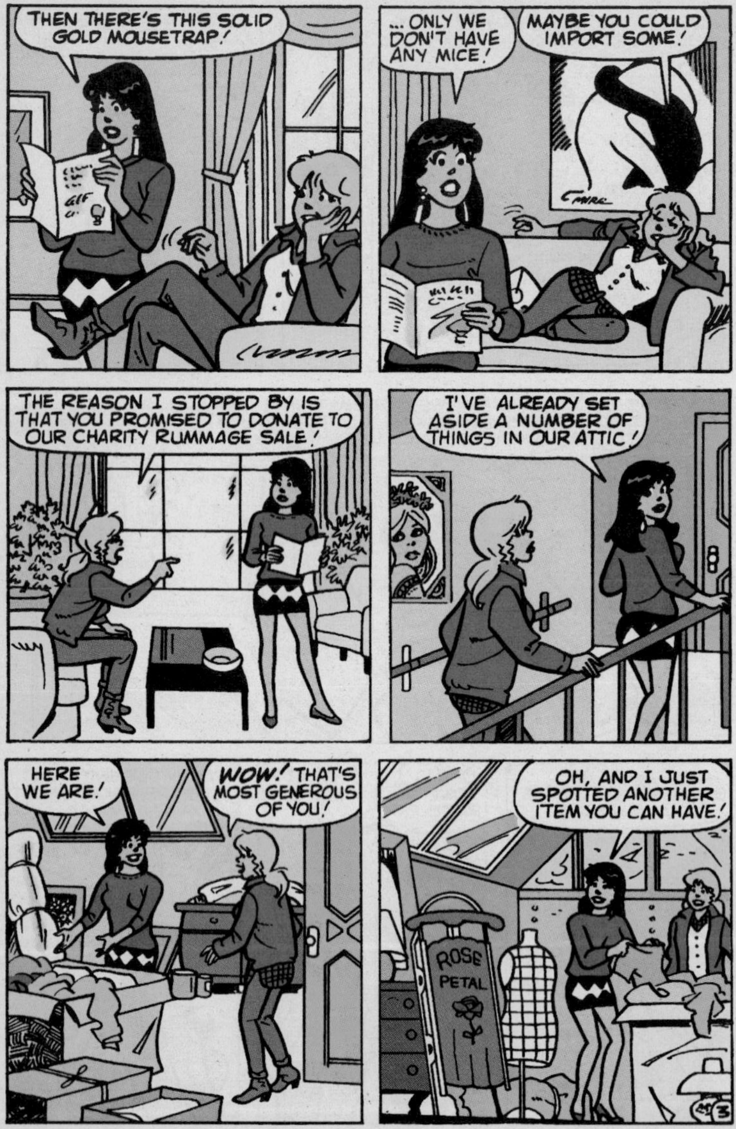
THEN THERE'S THIS SOLID GOLD MOUSETRAP!
... ONLY WE DON'T HAVE ANY MICE!
MAYBE YOU COULD IMPORT SOME!
THE REASON I STOPPED BY IS THAT YOU PROMISED TO DONATE TO OUR CHARITY RUMMAGE SALE!
I'VE ALREADY SET ASIDE A NUMBER OF THINGS IN OUR ATTIC!
HERE WE ARE!
WOW! THAT'S MOST GENEROUS OF YOU!
OH, AND I JUST SPOTTED ANOTHER ITEM YOU CAN HAVE!
ROSE PETAL
3

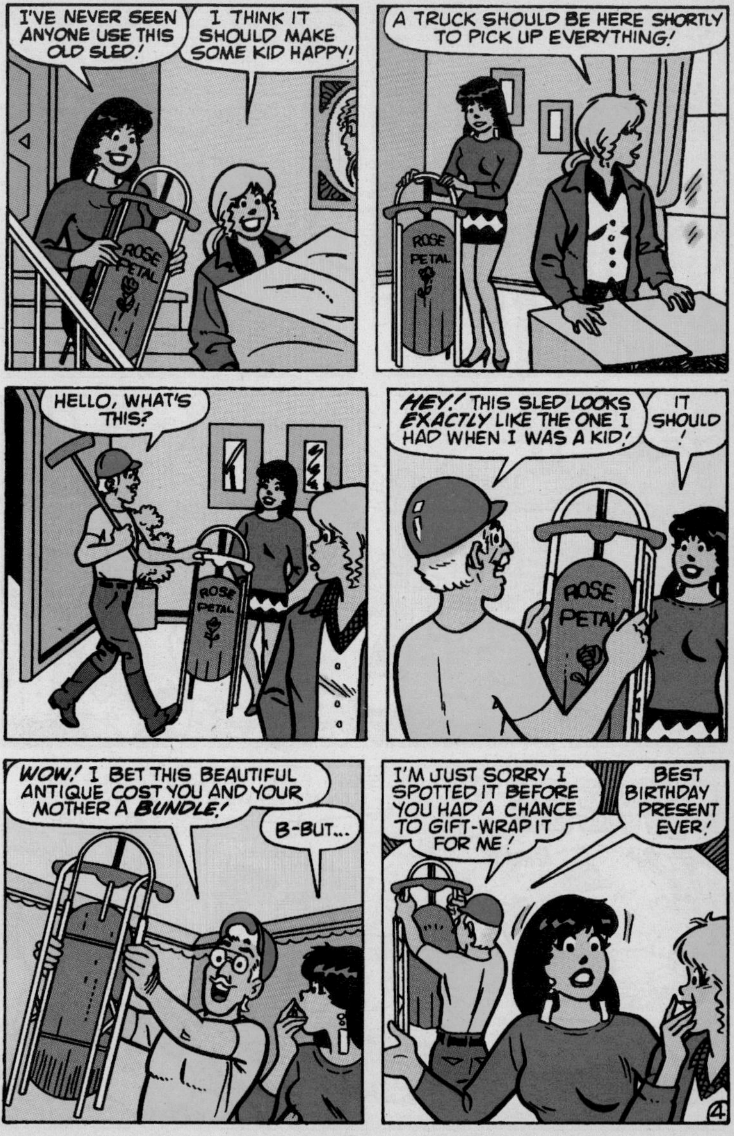
I'VE NEVER SEEN ANYONE USE THIS OLD SLED!
I THINK IT SHOULD MAKE SOME KID HAPPY!
ROSE PETAL
A TRUCK SHOULD BE HERE SHORTLY TO PICK UP EVERYTHING!
ROSE PETAL
HELLO, WHAT'S THIS?
ROSE PETAL
HEY! THIS SLED LOOKS EXACTLY LIKE THE ONE I HAD WHEN I WAS A KID!
IT SHOULD!
ROSE PETAL
WOW! I BET THIS BEAUTIFUL ANTIQUE COST YOU AND YOUR MOTHER A BUNDLE!
B-BUT...
I'M JUST SORRY I SPOTTED IT BEFORE YOU HAD A CHANCE TO GIFT-WRAP IT FOR ME!
BEST BIRTHDAY PRESENT EVER!
4

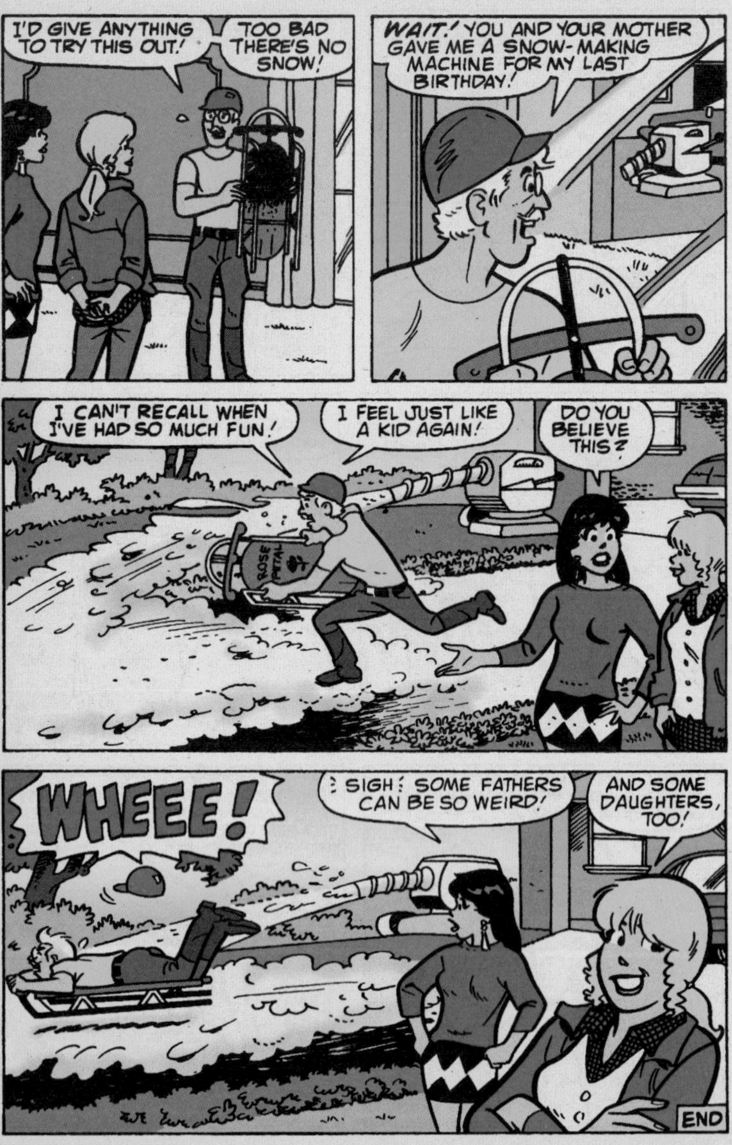
I'D GIVE ANYTHING TO TRY THIS OUT!
TOO BAD THERE'S NO SNOW!
WAIT! YOU AND YOUR MOTHER GAVE ME A SNOW-MAKING MACHINE FOR MY LAST BIRTHDAY!
I CAN'T RECALL WHEN I'VE HAD SO MUCH FUN!
I FEEL JUST LIKE A KID AGAIN!
DO YOU BELIEVE THIS?
ROSE PETAL
WHEEE!
SIGH! SOME FATHERS CAN BE SO WEIRD!
AND SOME DAUGHTERS, TOO!
END

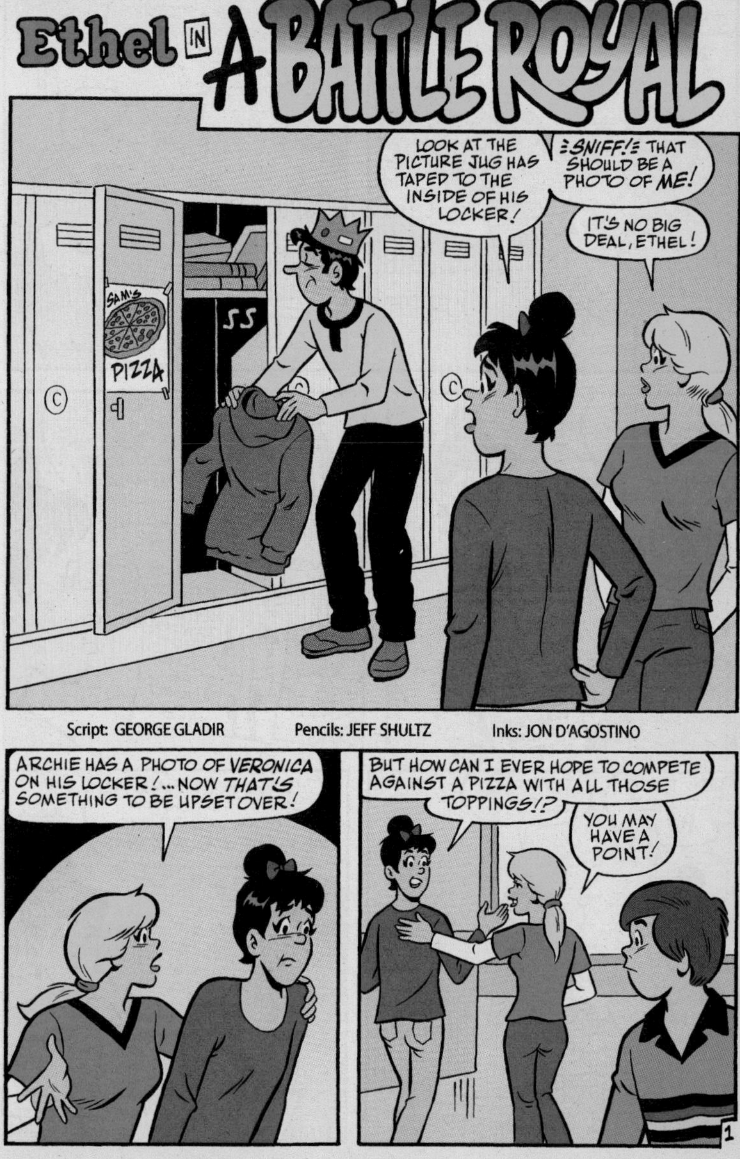
Ethel IN A BATTLE ROYAL
LOOK AT THE PICTURE JUG HAS TAPED TO THE INSIDE OF HIS LOCKER!
SNIFF! THAT SHOULD BE A PHOTO OF ME!
IT'S NO BIG DEAL, ETHEL!
SAM'S PIZZA
ARCHIE HAS A PHOTO OF VERONICA ON HIS LOCKER! ...NOW THAT'S SOMETHING TO BE UPSET OVER!
BUT HOW CAN I EVER HOPE TO COMPETE AGAINST A PIZZA WITH ALL THOSE TOPPINGS!?
YOU MAY HAVE A POINT!
1

Script: GEORGE GLADIR Pencils: JEFF SHULTZ Inks: JON D'AGOSTINO

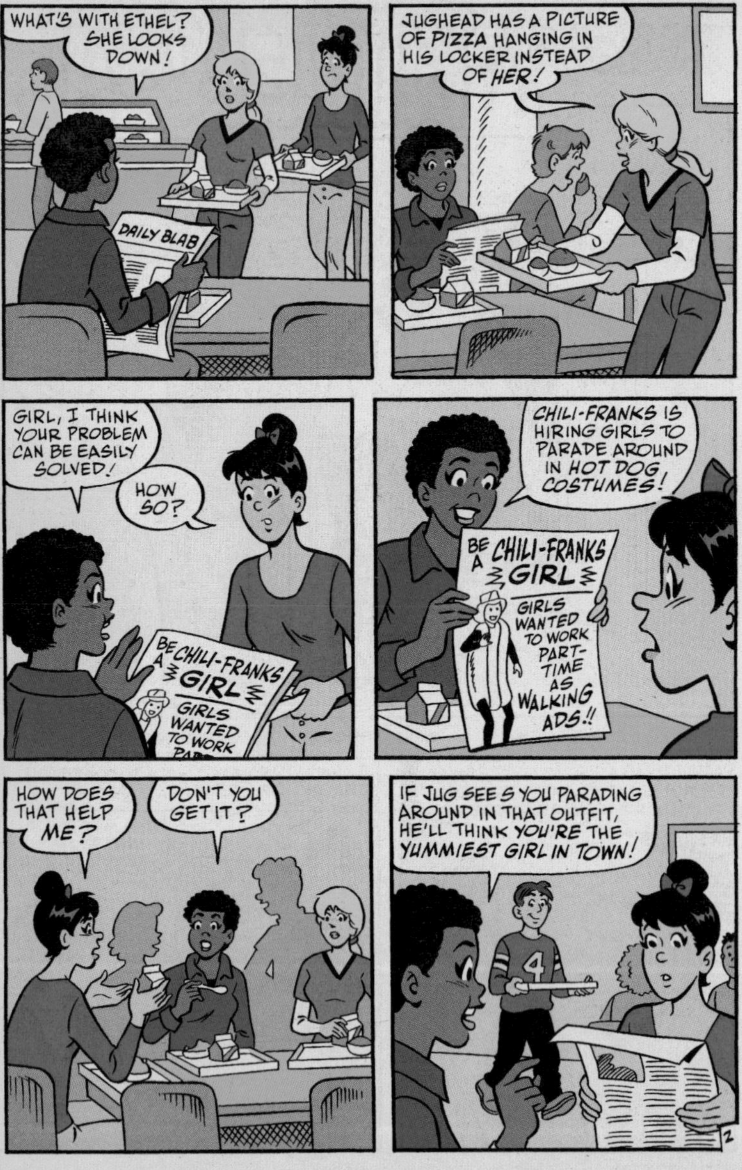
WHAT'S WITH ETHEL? SHE LOOKS DOWN!
DAILY BLAB
JUGHEAD HAS A PICTURE OF PIZZA HANGING IN HIS LOCKER INSTEAD OF HER!
GIRL, I THINK YOUR PROBLEM CAN BE EASILY SOLVED!
HOW SO?
CHILI-FRANKS IS HIRING GIRLS TO PARADE AROUND IN HOT DOG COSTUMES!
BE A CHILI-FRANKS GIRL
GIRLS WANTED TO WORK PART-TIME AS WALKING ADS!!
HOW DOES THAT HELP ME?
DON'T YOU GET IT?
IF JUG SEES YOU PARADING AROUND IN THAT OUTFIT, HE'LL THINK YOU'RE THE YUMMIEST GIRL IN TOWN!
2

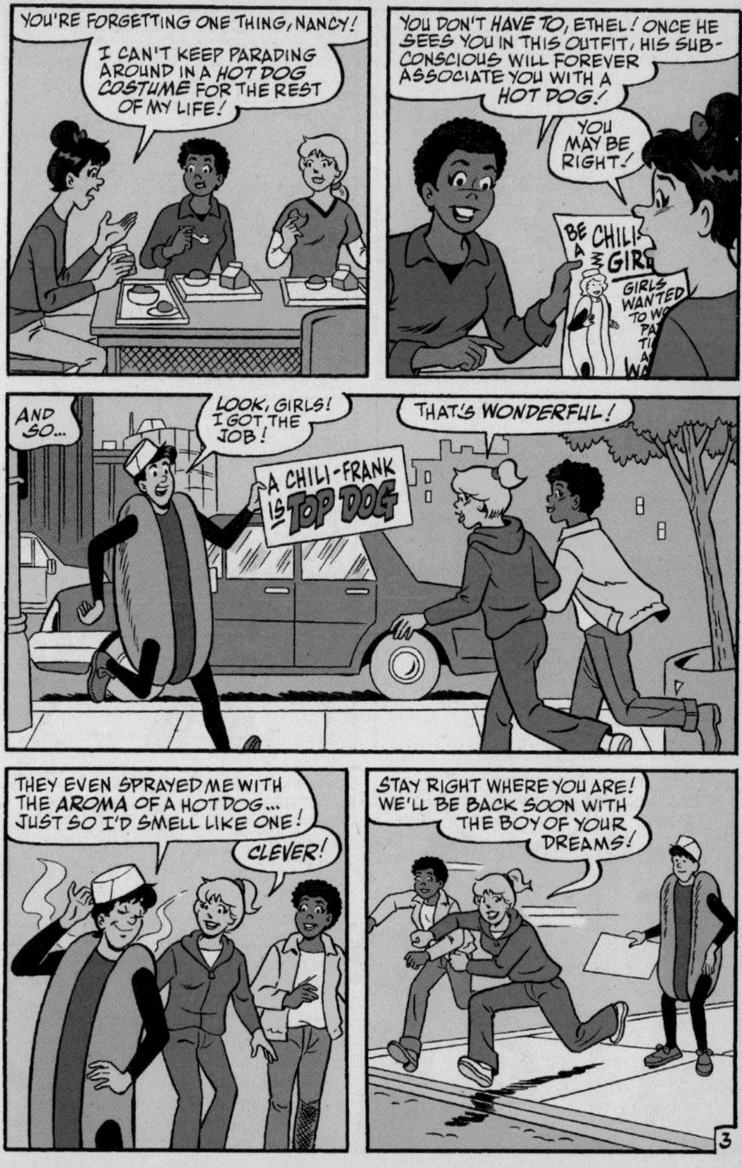
YOU'RE FORGETTING ONE THING, NANCY!
I CAN'T KEEP PARADING AROUND IN A HOT DOG COSTUME FOR THE REST OF MY LIFE!
YOU DON'T HAVE TO, ETHEL! ONCE HE SEES YOU IN THIS OUTFIT, HIS SUB-CONSCIOUS WILL FOREVER ASSOCIATE YOU WITH A HOT DOG!
YOU MAY BE RIGHT!
BE A CHILI
GIRLS WANTED
AND SO...
LOOK, GIRLS! I GOT THE JOB!
A CHILI-FRANK IS TOP DOG
THAT'S WONDERFUL!
THEY EVEN SPRAYED ME WITH THE AROMA OF A HOT DOG... JUST SO I'D SMELL LIKE ONE!
CLEVER!
STAY RIGHT WHERE YOU ARE! WE'LL BE BACK SOON WITH THE BOY OF YOUR DREAMS!
3

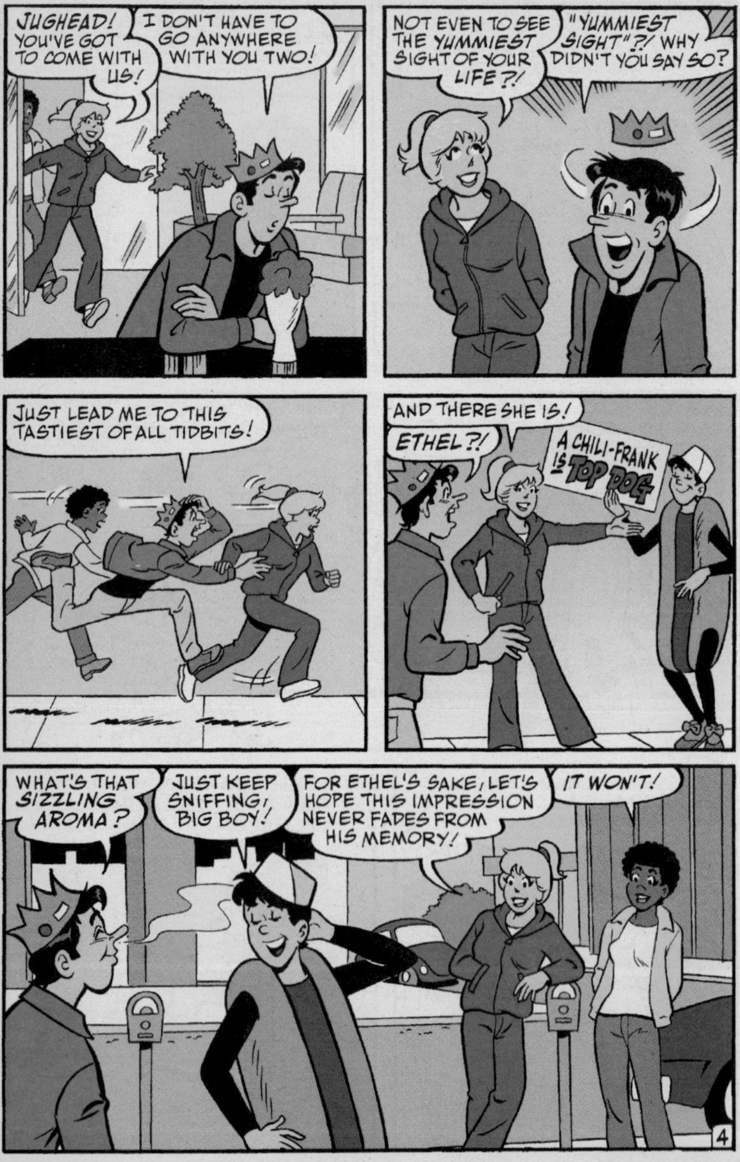
JUGHEAD! YOU'VE GOT TO COME WITH US!
I DON'T HAVE TO GO ANYWHERE WITH YOU TWO!
NOT EVEN TO SEE THE YUMMIEST SIGHT OF YOUR LIFE?!
"YUMMIEST SIGHT"?! WHY DIDN'T YOU SAY SO?
JUST LEAD ME TO THIS TASTIEST OF ALL TIDBITS!
AND THERE SHE IS!
ETHEL?!
A CHILI-FRANK IS TOP DOG
WHAT'S THAT SIZZLING AROMA?
JUST KEEP SNIFFING, BIG BOY!
FOR ETHEL'S SAKE, LET'S HOPE THIS IMPRESSION NEVER FADES FROM HIS MEMORY!
IT WON'T!
4

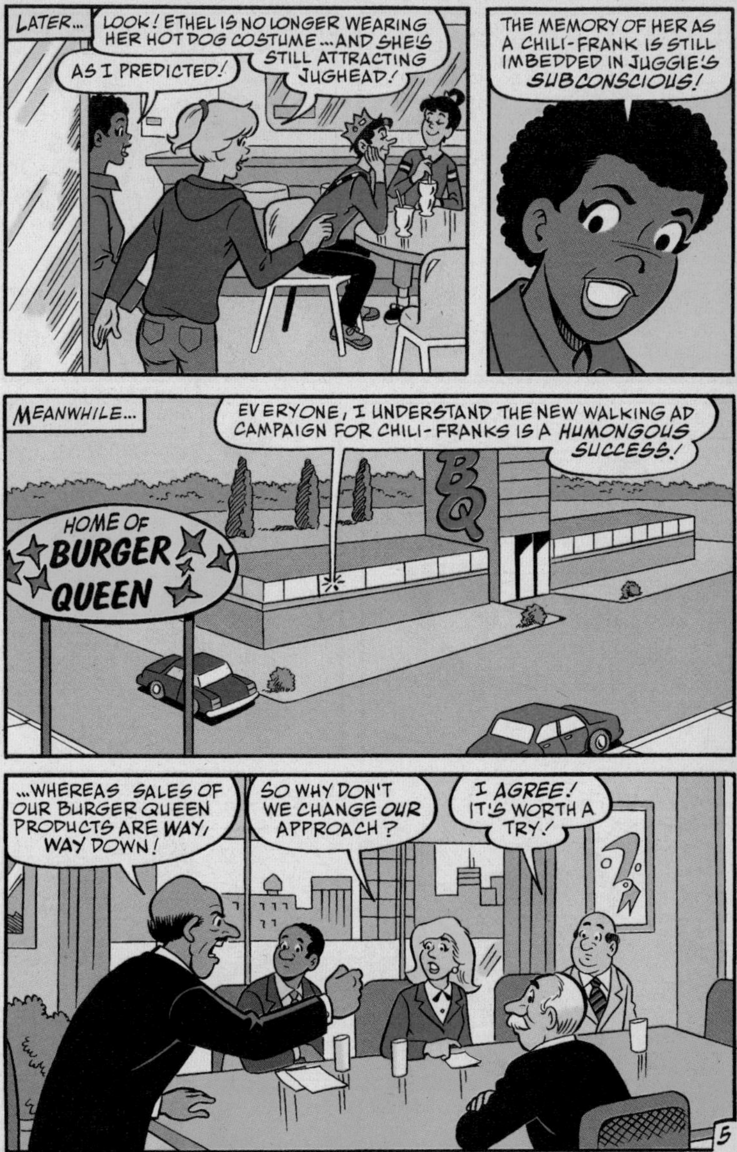

LATER...
LOOK! ETHEL IS NO LONGER WEARING HER HOT DOG COSTUME...AND SHE'S STILL ATTRACTING JUGHEAD!
AS I PREDICTED!
THE MEMORY OF HER AS A CHILI-FRANK IS STILL IMBEDDED IN JUGGIE'S SUBCONSCIOUS!
MEANWHILE...
EVERYONE, I UNDERSTAND THE NEW WALKING AD CAMPAIGN FOR CHILI-FRANKS IS A HUMONGOUS SUCCESS!
HOME OF BURGER QUEEN
BQ
...WHEREAS SALES OF OUR BURGER QUEEN PRODUCTS ARE WAY, WAY DOWN!
SO WHY DON'T WE CHANGE OUR APPROACH?
I AGREE! IT'S WORTH A TRY!
5

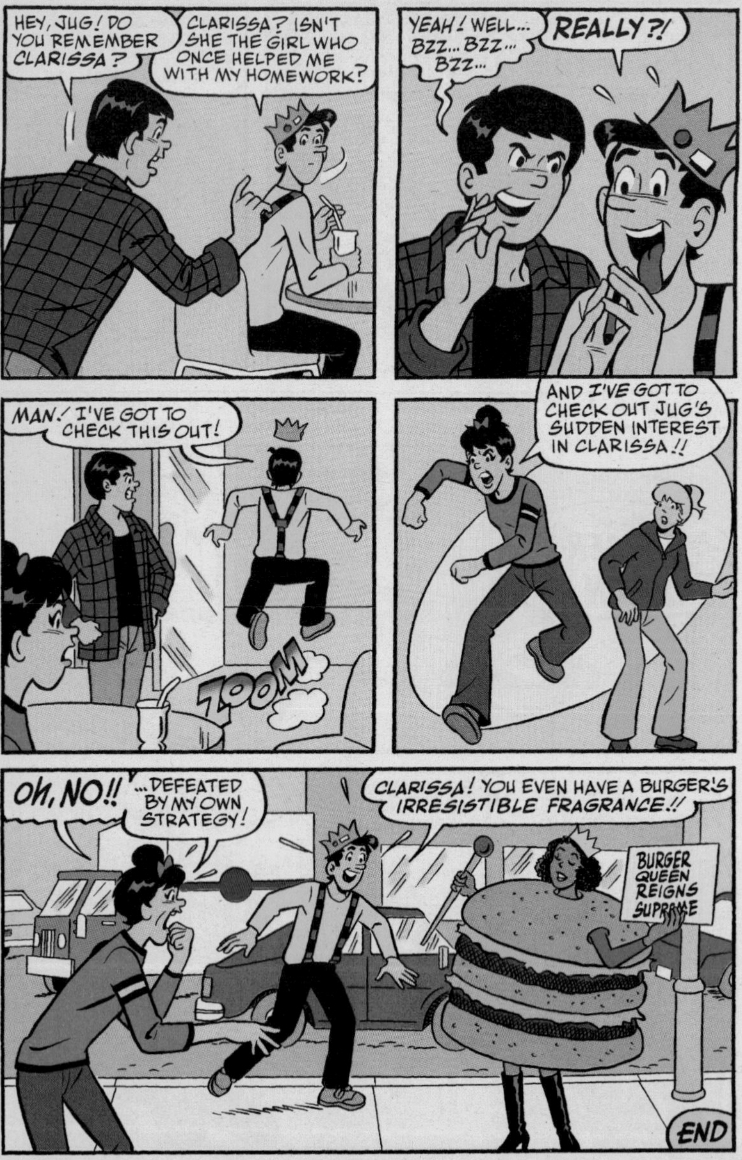
HEY, JUG! DO YOU REMEMBER CLARISSA?
CLARISSA? ISN'T SHE THE GIRL WHO ONCE HELPED ME WITH MY HOMEWORK?
YEAH! WELL... BZZ... BZZ... BZZ...
REALLY?!
MAN! I'VE GOT TO CHECK THIS OUT!
ZOOM
AND I'VE GOT TO CHECK OUT JUG'S SUDDEN INTEREST IN CLARISSA!!
OH, NO!!
...DEFEATED BY MY OWN STRATEGY!
CLARISSA! YOU EVEN HAVE A BURGER'S IRRESISTIBLE FRAGRANCE!!
BURGER QUEEN REIGNS SUPREME
END

Betty and Veronica in "GIRLS JUST WANNA HAVE FUN"

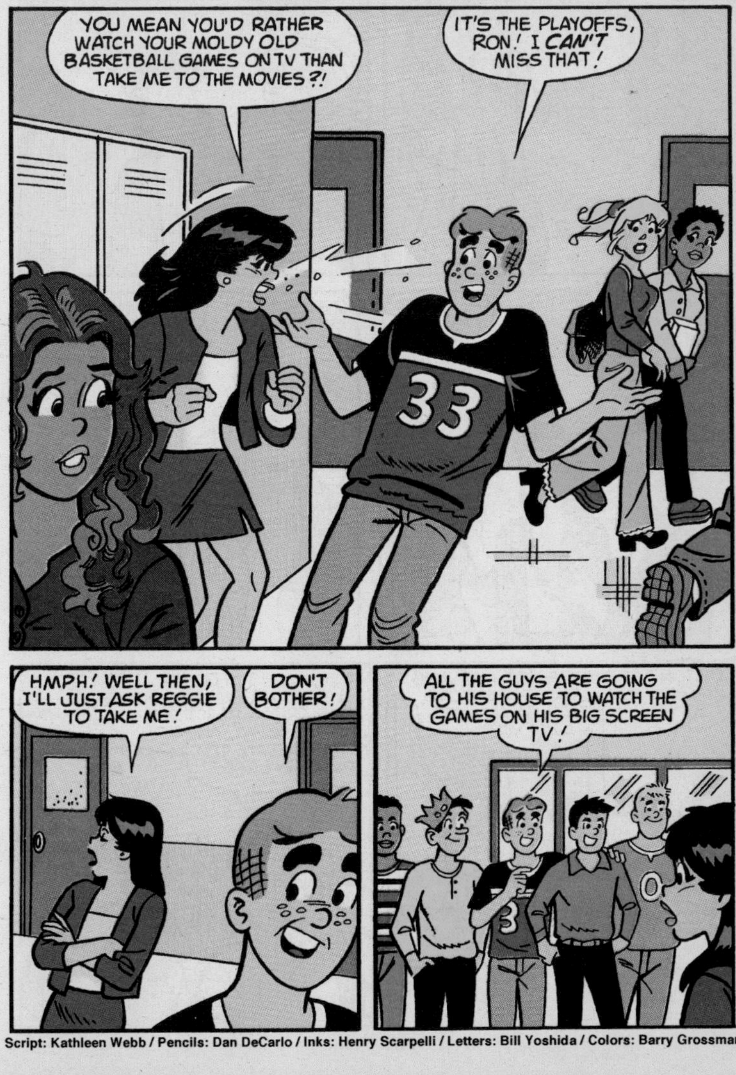
YOU MEAN YOU'D RATHER WATCH YOUR MOLDY OLD BASKETBALL GAMES ON TV THAN TAKE ME TO THE MOVIES?!
IT'S THE PLAYOFFS, RON! I CAN'T MISS THAT!
33
HMPH! WELL THEN, I'LL JUST ASK REGGIE TO TAKE ME!
DON'T BOTHER!
ALL THE GUYS ARE GOING TO HIS HOUSE TO WATCH THE GAMES ON HIS BIG SCREEN TV!

Script: Kathleen Webb / Pencils: Dan DeCarlo / Inks: Henry Scarpelli / Letters: Bill Yoshida / Colors: Barry Grossman

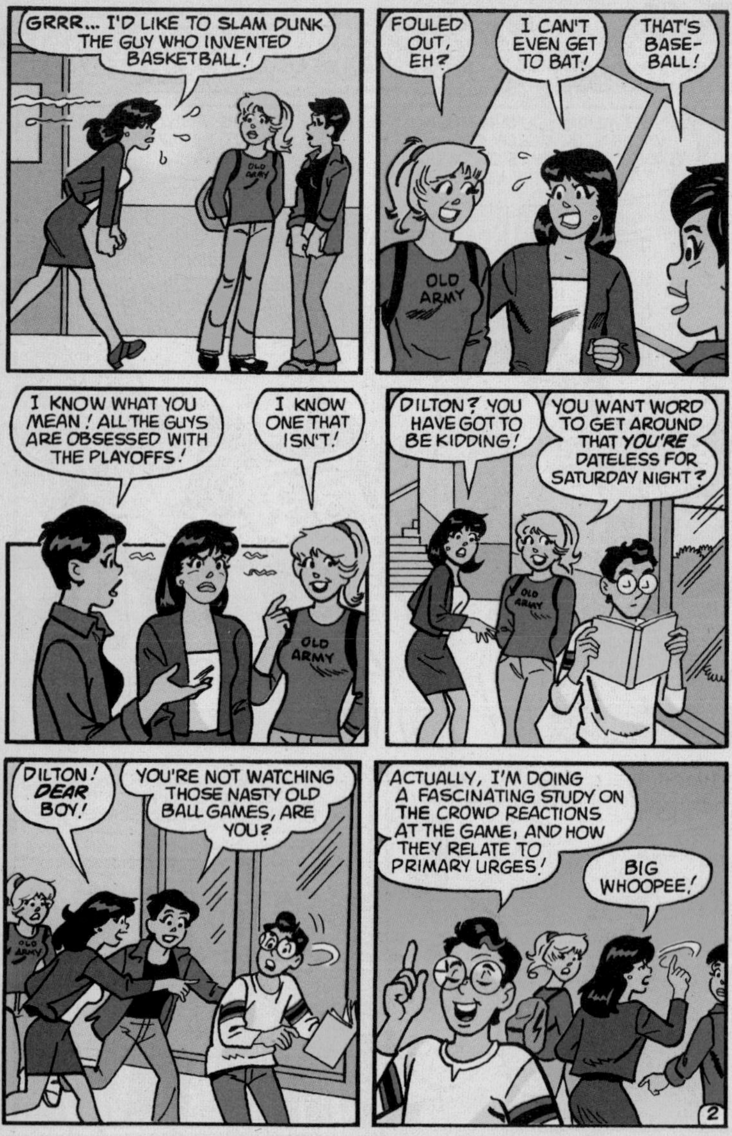
GRRR... I'D LIKE TO SLAM DUNK THE GUY WHO INVENTED BASKETBALL!
FOULED OUT, EH?
I CAN'T EVEN GET TO BAT!
THAT'S BASE-BALL!
I KNOW WHAT YOU MEAN! ALL THE GUYS ARE OBSESSED WITH THE PLAYOFFS!
I KNOW ONE THAT ISN'T!
DILTON? YOU HAVE GOT TO BE KIDDING!
YOU WANT WORD TO GET AROUND THAT YOU'RE DATELESS FOR SATURDAY NIGHT?
DILTON! DEAR BOY!
YOU'RE NOT WATCHING THOSE NASTY OLD BALL GAMES, ARE YOU?
ACTUALLY, I'M DOING A FASCINATING STUDY ON THE CROWD REACTIONS AT THE GAME, AND HOW THEY RELATE TO PRIMARY URGES!
BIG WHOOPEE!
2

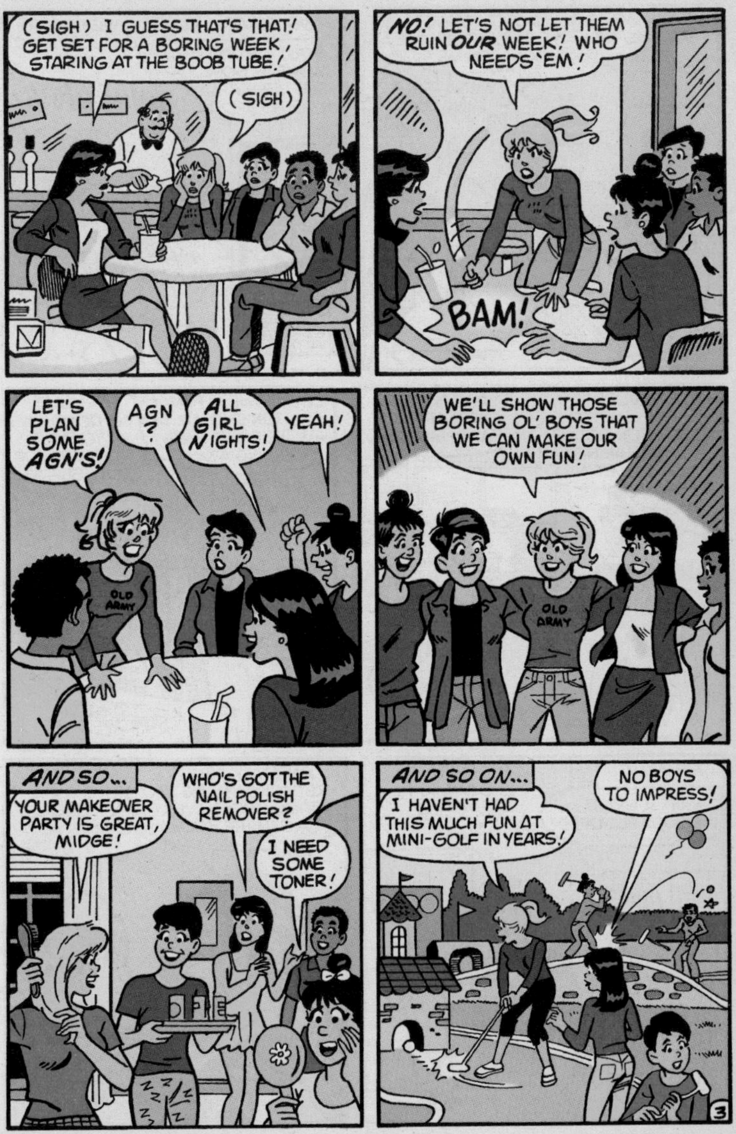
(SIGH) I GUESS THAT'S THAT! GET SET FOR A BORING WEEK, STARING AT THE BOOB TUBE!
(SIGH)
NO! LET'S NOT LET THEM RUIN OUR WEEK! WHO NEEDS 'EM!
BAM!
LET'S PLAN SOME AGN'S!
AGN?
ALL GIRL NIGHTS!
YEAH!
OLD ARMY
WE'LL SHOW THOSE BORING OL' BOYS THAT WE CAN MAKE OUR OWN FUN!
OLD ARMY
AND SO...
YOUR MAKEOVER PARTY IS GREAT, MIDGE!
WHO'S GOT THE NAIL POLISH REMOVER?
I NEED SOME TONER!
AND SO ON...
I HAVEN'T HAD THIS MUCH FUN AT MINI-GOLF IN YEARS!
NO BOYS TO IMPRESS!
3

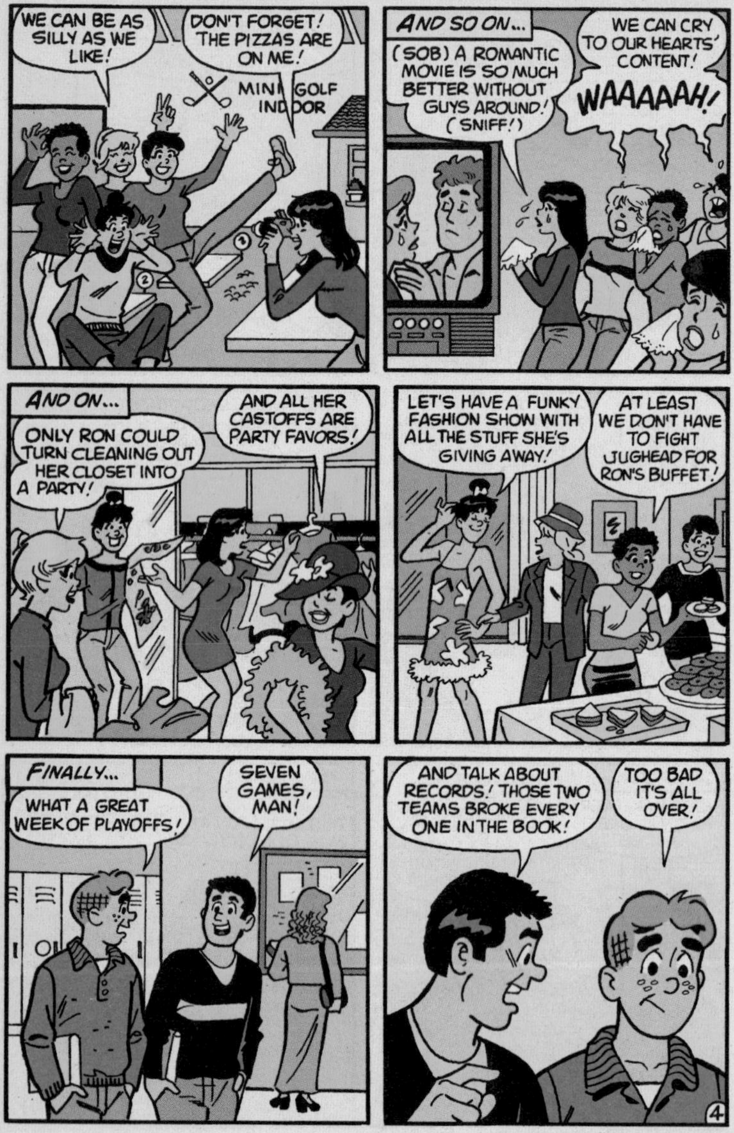
WE CAN BE AS SILLY AS WE LIKE!
DON'T FORGET! THE PIZZAS ARE ON ME!
MINI GOLF INDOOR
AND SO ON...
(SOB) A ROMANTIC MOVIE IS SO MUCH BETTER WITHOUT GUYS AROUND! (SNIFF!)
WE CAN CRY TO OUR HEARTS' CONTENT!
WAAAAAH!
AND ON...
ONLY RON COULD TURN CLEANING OUT HER CLOSET INTO A PARTY!
AND ALL HER CASTOFFS ARE PARTY FAVORS!
LET'S HAVE A FUNKY FASHION SHOW WITH ALL THE STUFF SHE'S GIVING AWAY!
AT LEAST WE DON'T HAVE TO FIGHT JUGHEAD FOR RON'S BUFFET!
FINALLY...
WHAT A GREAT WEEK OF PLAYOFFS!
SEVEN GAMES, MAN!
AND TALK ABOUT RECORDS! THOSE TWO TEAMS BROKE EVERY ONE IN THE BOOK!
TOO BAD IT'S ALL OVER!
4

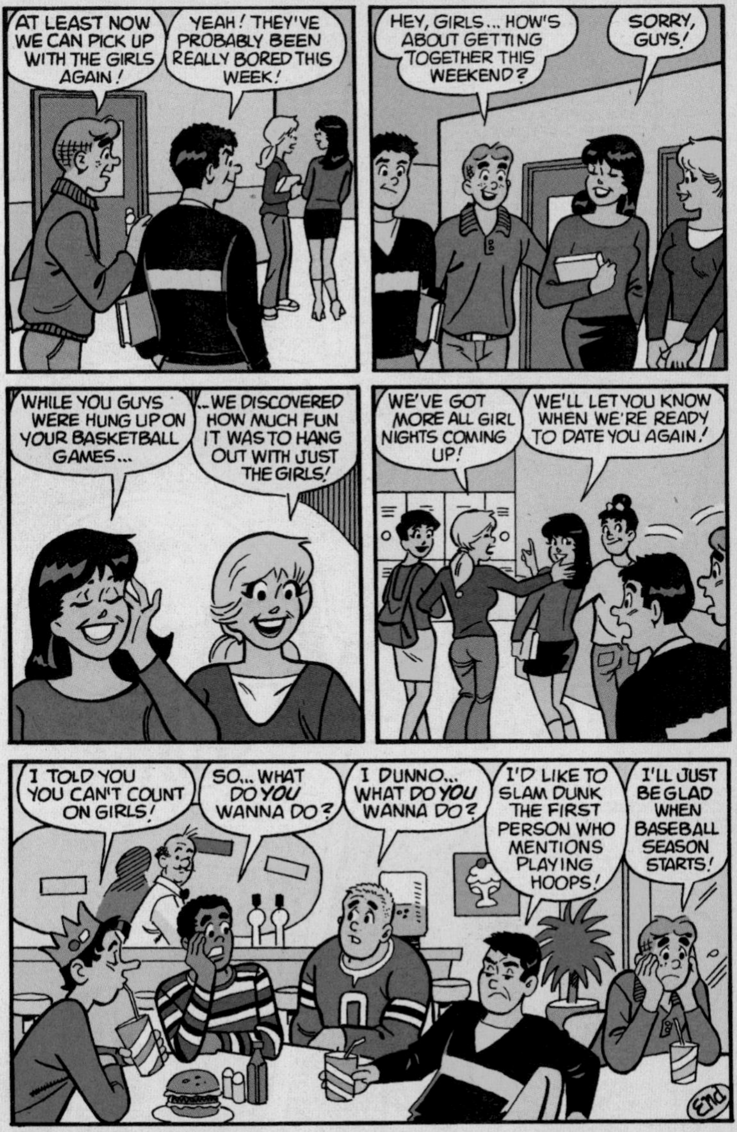
AT LEAST NOW WE CAN PICK UP WITH THE GIRLS AGAIN!
YEAH! THEY'VE PROBABLY BEEN REALLY BORED THIS WEEK!
HEY, GIRLS... HOW'S ABOUT GETTING TOGETHER THIS WEEKEND?
SORRY, GUYS!
WHILE YOU GUYS WERE HUNG UP ON YOUR BASKETBALL GAMES...
...WE DISCOVERED HOW MUCH FUN IT WAS TO HANG OUT WITH JUST THE GIRLS!
WE'VE GOT MORE ALL GIRL NIGHTS COMING UP!
WE'LL LET YOU KNOW WHEN WE'RE READY TO DATE YOU AGAIN!
I TOLD YOU YOU CAN'T COUNT ON GIRLS!
SO... WHAT DO YOU WANNA DO?
I DUNNO... WHAT DO YOU WANNA DO?
I'D LIKE TO SLAM DUNK THE FIRST PERSON WHO MENTIONS PLAYING HOOPS!
I'LL JUST BE GLAD WHEN BASEBALL SEASON STARTS!
End

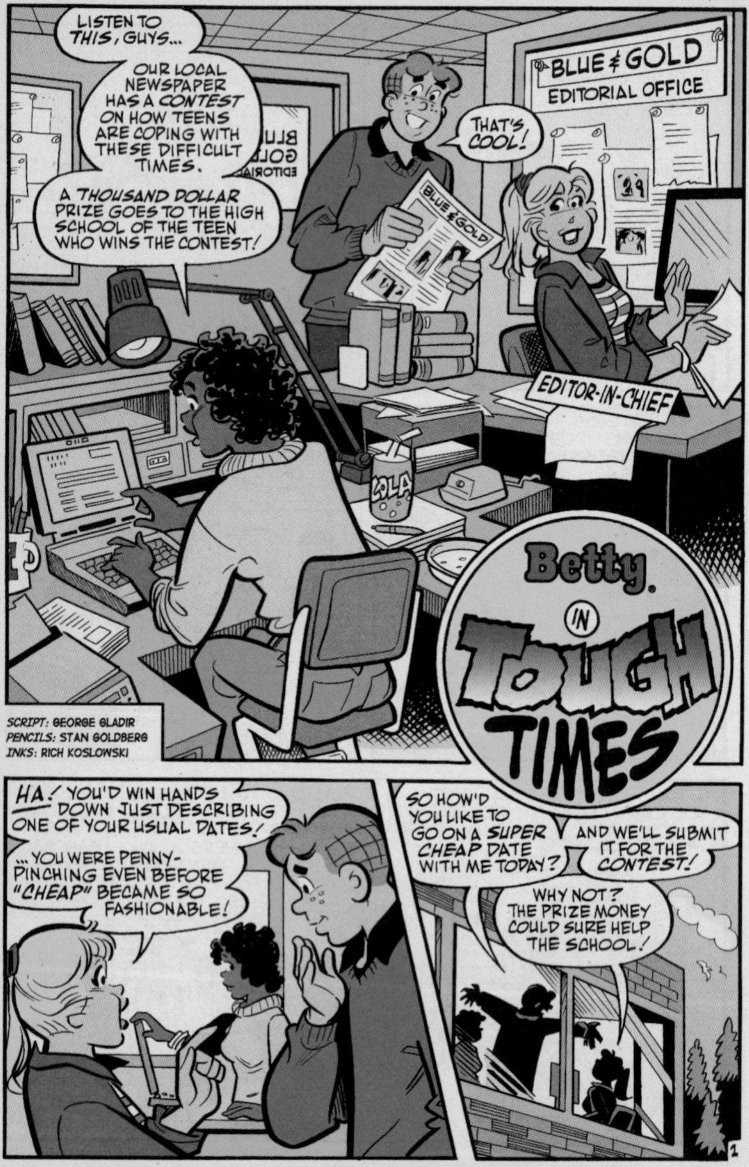
LISTEN TO THIS, GUYS...
OUR LOCAL NEWSPAPER HAS A CONTEST ON HOW TEENS ARE COPING WITH THESE DIFFICULT TIMES.
A THOUSAND DOLLAR PRIZE GOES TO THE HIGH SCHOOL OF THE TEEN WHO WINS THE CONTEST!
THAT'S COOL!
BLUE & GOLD
EDITORIAL OFFICE
BLUE & GOLD
EDITOR-IN-CHIEF
COLA
Betty
IN
TOUGH TIMES
SCRIPT: GEORGE GLADIR
PENCILS: STAN GOLDBERG
INKS: RICH KOSLOWSKI
HA! YOU'D WIN HANDS DOWN JUST DESCRIBING ONE OF YOUR USUAL DATES!
... YOU WERE PENNY-PINCHING EVEN BEFORE "CHEAP" BECAME SO FASHIONABLE!
SO HOW'D YOU LIKE TO GO ON A SUPER CHEAP DATE WITH ME TODAY?
AND WE'LL SUBMIT IT FOR THE CONTEST!
WHY NOT? THE PRIZE MONEY COULD SURE HELP THE SCHOOL!

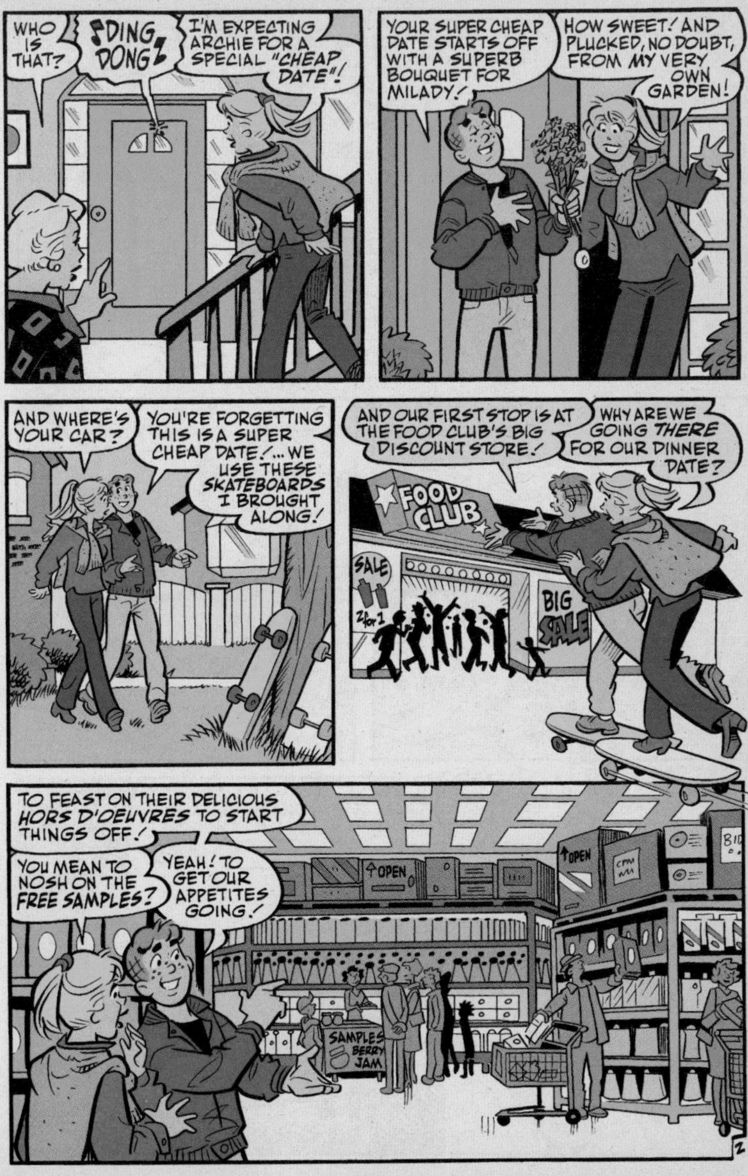
WHO IS THAT?
DING DONG
I'M EXPECTING ARCHIE FOR A SPECIAL "CHEAP DATE"!
YOUR SUPER CHEAP DATE STARTS OFF WITH A SUPERB BOUQUET FOR MILADY!
HOW SWEET! AND PLUCKED, NO DOUBT, FROM MY VERY OWN GARDEN!
AND WHERE'S YOUR CAR?
YOU'RE FORGETTING THIS IS A SUPER CHEAP DATE! ... WE USE THESE SKATEBOARDS I BROUGHT ALONG!
AND OUR FIRST STOP IS AT THE FOOD CLUB'S BIG DISCOUNT STORE!
WHY ARE WE GOING THERE FOR OUR DINNER DATE?
FOOD CLUB
SALE
2 for 1
BIG SALE
TO FEAST ON THEIR DELICIOUS HORS D'OEUVRES TO START THINGS OFF!
YOU MEAN TO NOSH ON THE FREE SAMPLES?
YEAH! TO GET OUR APPETITES GOING!
OPEN
OPEN
SAMPLES BERRY JAM
2

Panel 1: ≡BURP!≡ THIS IS SUPERB!

SHALL WE GO FOR A SECOND ROUND?

NO, I EXPECT SOME VARIETY, EVEN ON THIS "CHEAP DATE"!

Panel 2: IS THIS GOING TO BE OUR NEXT COURSE?

YES! THEY HAVE GREAT ENTREES!

JILL IN THE BOX

Panel 3: ...BUT MORE IMPORTANTLY, THEY HAVE THESE SUPER DISCOUNT COUPONS FOR THEIR MEALS!

TWO FOR THE PRICE OF ONE!

FRIES SHAKE

JILL BUR

JILL BURGER

Panel 4: THAT WAS DEE-LISH! WHAT'S NEXT?

WE GO TO THE MOVIES!

Panel 5: AREN'T WE GOING SOMEWHAT FAR FOR A MOVIE?

I WON FREE TICKETS TO A THEATER IN SMITHTOWN!

Panel 6: YOU WON TWO FREE TICKETS?

IT WAS A CONTEST DRAWING ... I WAS ONE OF A HUNDRED PEOPLE TO WIN!

EXIT

3

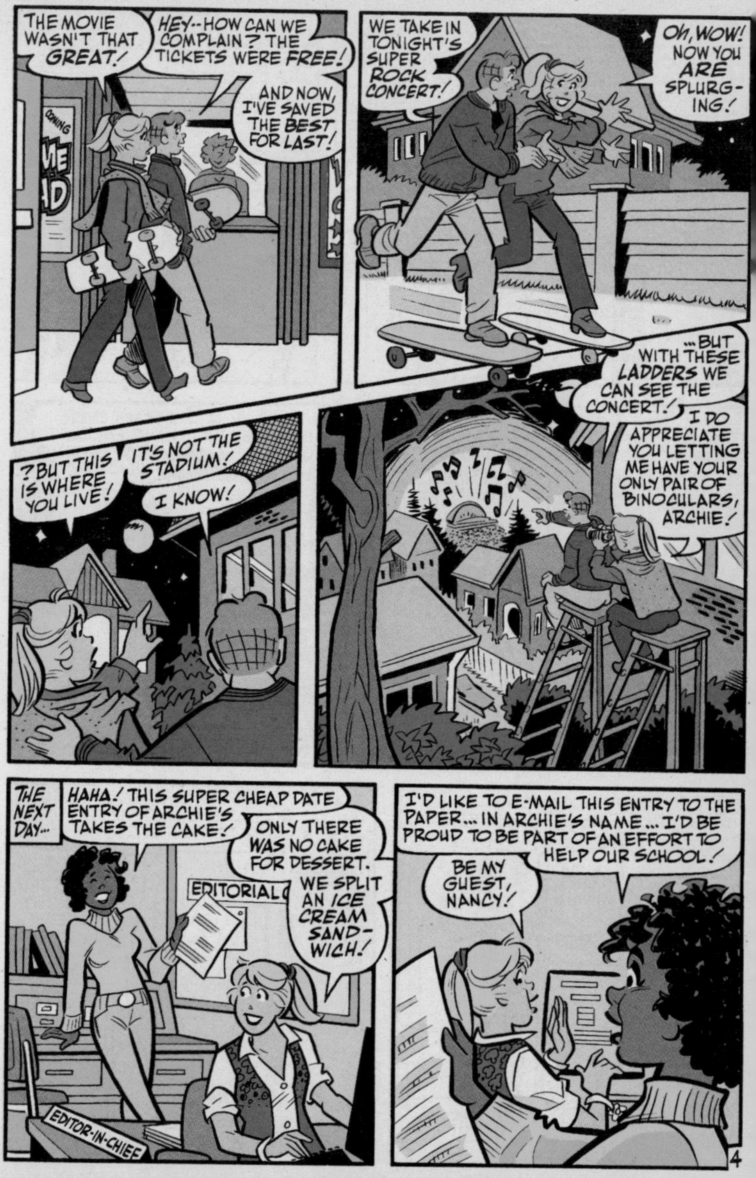
THE MOVIE WASN'T THAT GREAT!
HEY--HOW CAN WE COMPLAIN? THE TICKETS WERE FREE!
AND NOW, I'VE SAVED THE BEST FOR LAST!
WE TAKE IN TONIGHT'S SUPER ROCK CONCERT!
Oh, WOW! NOW YOU ARE SPLURG-ING!
? BUT THIS IS WHERE YOU LIVE!
IT'S NOT THE STADIUM!
I KNOW!
...BUT WITH THESE LADDERS WE CAN SEE THE CONCERT!
I DO APPRECIATE YOU LETTING ME HAVE YOUR ONLY PAIR OF BINOCULARS, ARCHIE!
THE NEXT DAY...
HAHA! THIS SUPER CHEAP DATE ENTRY OF ARCHIE'S TAKES THE CAKE!
ONLY THERE WAS NO CAKE FOR DESSERT.
WE SPLIT AN ICE CREAM SAND-WICH!
EDITORIAL
EDITOR-IN-CHIEF
I'D LIKE TO E-MAIL THIS ENTRY TO THE PAPER... IN ARCHIE'S NAME... I'D BE PROUD TO BE PART OF AN EFFORT TO HELP OUR SCHOOL!
BE MY GUEST, NANCY!

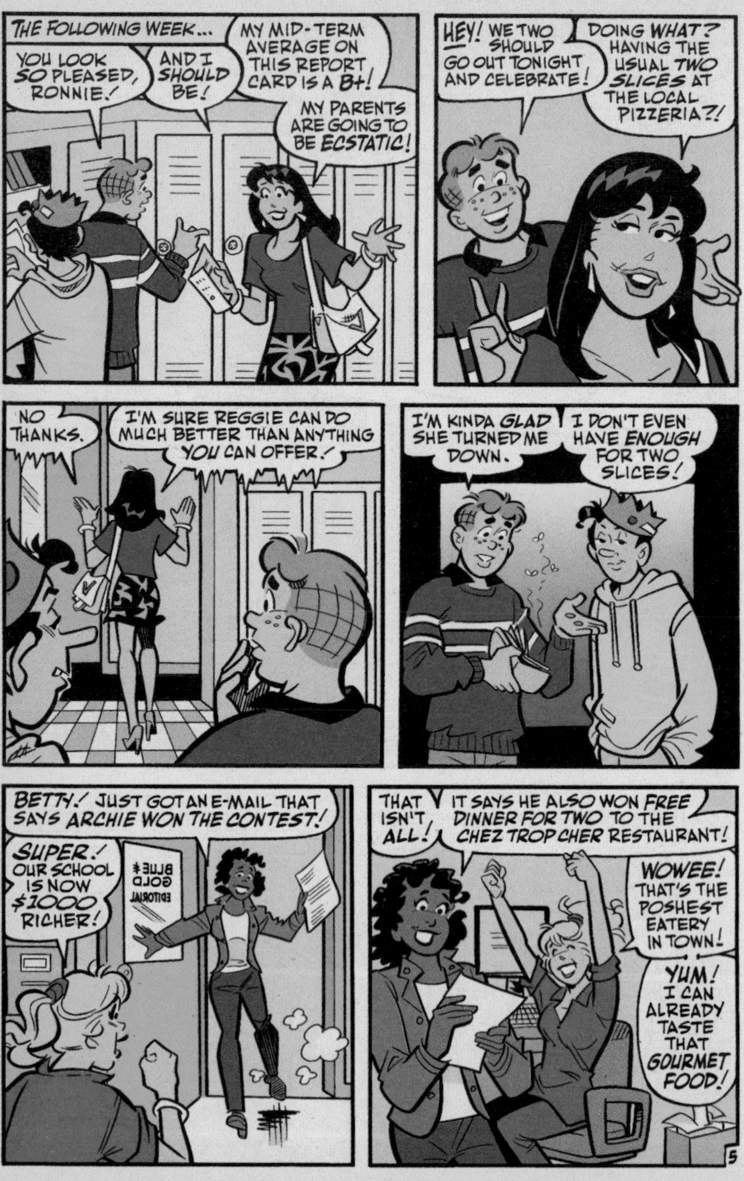
THE FOLLOWING WEEK...
YOU LOOK SO PLEASED, RONNIE!
AND I SHOULD BE!
MY MID-TERM AVERAGE ON THIS REPORT CARD IS A B+!
MY PARENTS ARE GOING TO BE ECSTATIC!
HEY! WE TWO SHOULD GO OUT TONIGHT AND CELEBRATE!
DOING WHAT? HAVING THE USUAL TWO SLICES AT THE LOCAL PIZZERIA?!
NO THANKS.
I'M SURE REGGIE CAN DO MUCH BETTER THAN ANYTHING YOU CAN OFFER!
I'M KINDA GLAD SHE TURNED ME DOWN.
I DON'T EVEN HAVE ENOUGH FOR TWO SLICES!
BETTY! JUST GOT AN E-MAIL THAT SAYS ARCHIE WON THE CONTEST!
SUPER! OUR SCHOOL IS NOW $1000 RICHER!
BLUE & GOLD EDITORIAL
THAT ISN'T ALL!
IT SAYS HE ALSO WON FREE DINNER FOR TWO TO THE CHEZ TROP CHER RESTAURANT!
WOWEE! THAT'S THE POSHEST EATERY IN TOWN!
YUM! I CAN ALREADY TASTE THAT GOURMET FOOD!

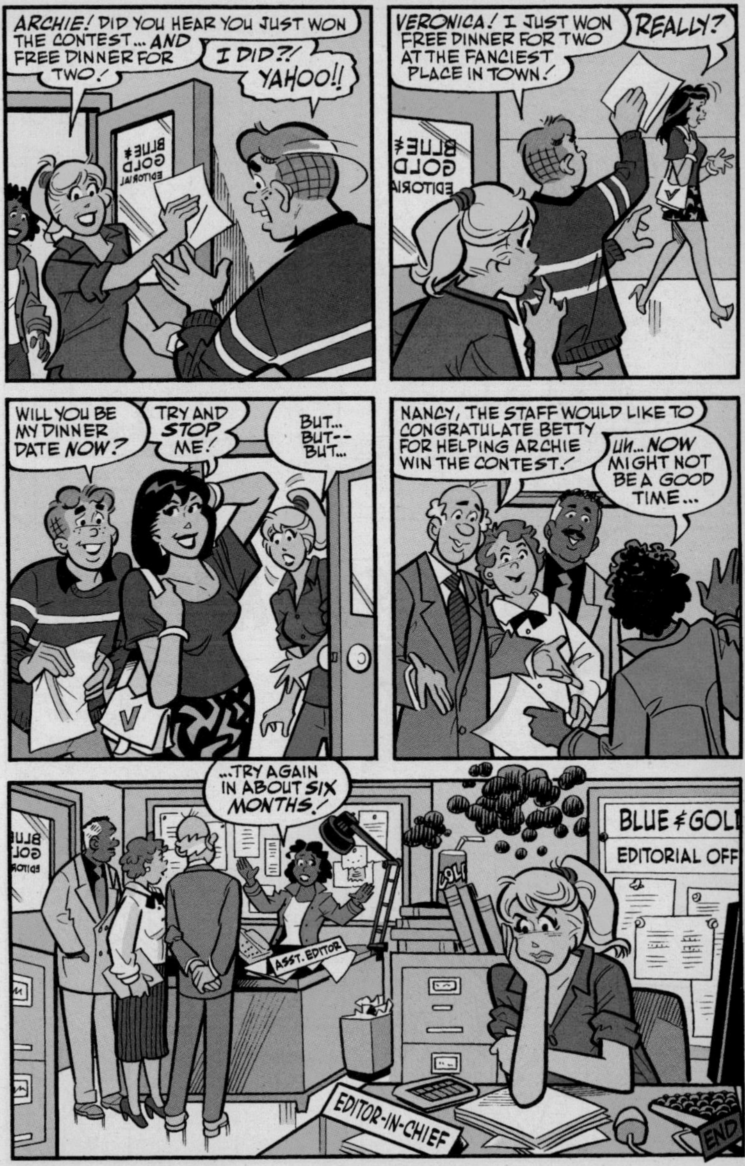
ARCHIE! DID YOU HEAR YOU JUST WON THE CONTEST... AND FREE DINNER FOR TWO!
I DID?!
YAHOO!!
BLUE & GOLD EDITORIAL
VERONICA! I JUST WON FREE DINNER FOR TWO AT THE FANCIEST PLACE IN TOWN!
REALLY?
BLUE & GOLD EDITORIAL
WILL YOU BE MY DINNER DATE NOW?
TRY AND STOP ME!
BUT... BUT-- BUT...
NANCY, THE STAFF WOULD LIKE TO CONGRATULATE BETTY FOR HELPING ARCHIE WIN THE CONTEST!
UH... NOW MIGHT NOT BE A GOOD TIME...
...TRY AGAIN IN ABOUT SIX MONTHS!
BLUE & GOL
EDITORIAL OFF
ASST. EDITOR
EDITOR-IN-CHIEF
END

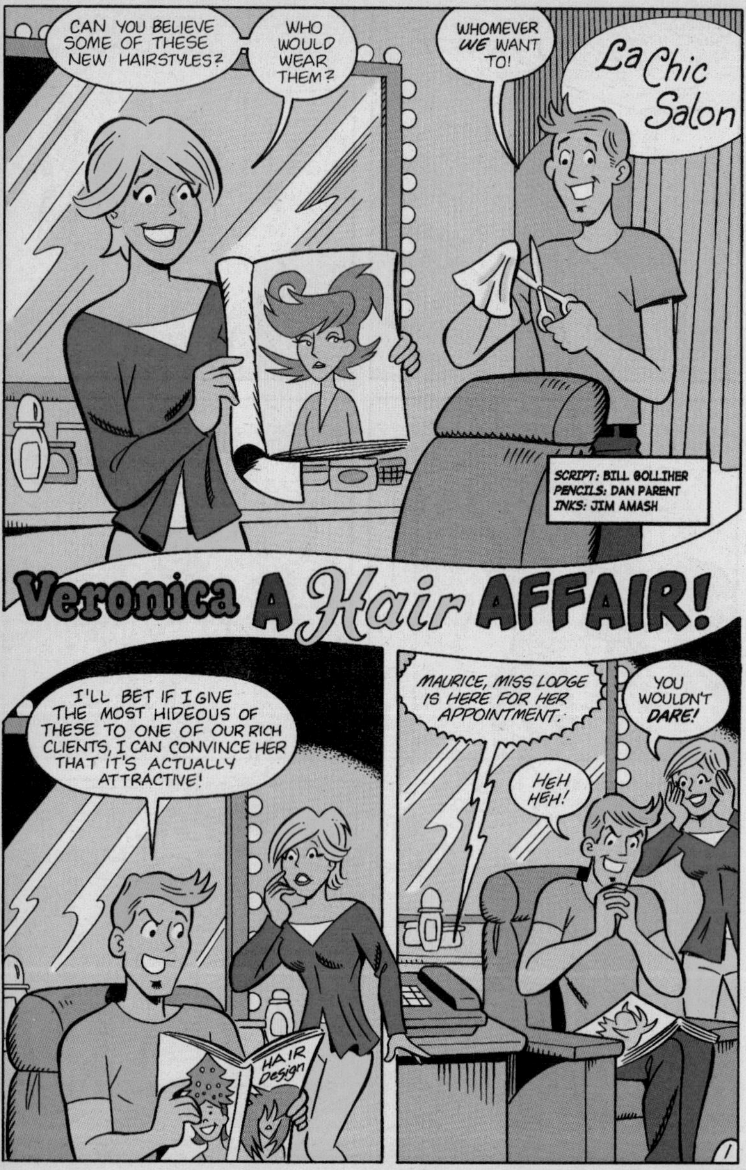
CAN YOU BELIEVE SOME OF THESE NEW HAIRSTYLES?
WHO WOULD WEAR THEM?
WHOMEVER *WE* WANT TO!
La Chic Salon
SCRIPT: BILL GOLLIHER
PENCILS: DAN PARENT
INKS: JIM AMASH
Veronica A Hair AFFAIR!
I'LL BET IF I GIVE THE MOST HIDEOUS OF THESE TO ONE OF OUR RICH CLIENTS, I CAN CONVINCE HER THAT IT'S ACTUALLY ATTRACTIVE!
HAIR Design
MAURICE, MISS LODGE IS HERE FOR HER APPOINTMENT.
YOU WOULDN'T *DARE!*
HEH HEH!
1

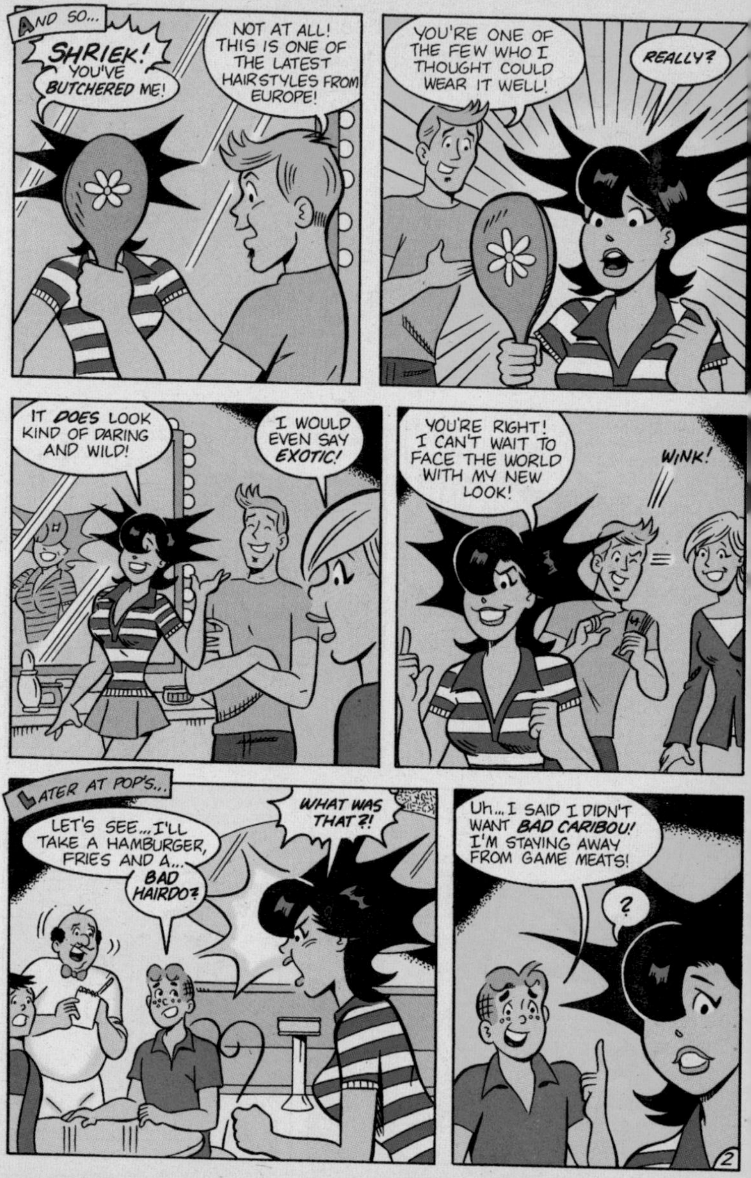
AND SO...
SHRIEK! YOU'VE BUTCHERED ME!
NOT AT ALL! THIS IS ONE OF THE LATEST HAIRSTYLES FROM EUROPE!
YOU'RE ONE OF THE FEW WHO I THOUGHT COULD WEAR IT WELL!
REALLY?
IT DOES LOOK KIND OF DARING AND WILD!
I WOULD EVEN SAY EXOTIC!
YOU'RE RIGHT! I CAN'T WAIT TO FACE THE WORLD WITH MY NEW LOOK!
WINK!
LATER AT POP'S...
LET'S SEE...I'LL TAKE A HAMBURGER, FRIES AND A... BAD HAIRDO?
WHAT WAS THAT?!
Uh...I SAID I DIDN'T WANT BAD CARIBOU! I'M STAYING AWAY FROM GAME MEATS!
?
2

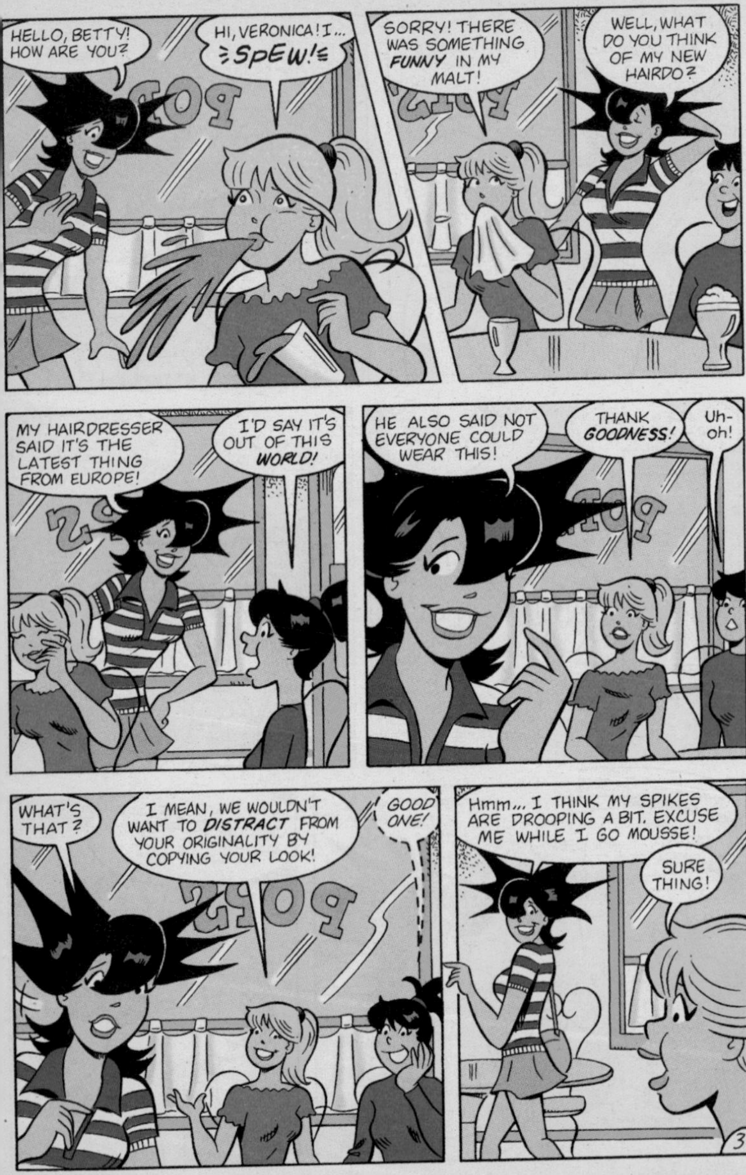
HELLO, BETTY! HOW ARE YOU?
HI, VERONICA! I... SPEW!
SORRY! THERE WAS SOMETHING FUNNY IN MY MALT!
WELL, WHAT DO YOU THINK OF MY NEW HAIRDO?
MY HAIRDRESSER SAID IT'S THE LATEST THING FROM EUROPE!
I'D SAY IT'S OUT OF THIS WORLD!
HE ALSO SAID NOT EVERYONE COULD WEAR THIS!
THANK GOODNESS!
Uh-oh!
WHAT'S THAT?
I MEAN, WE WOULDN'T WANT TO DISTRACT FROM YOUR ORIGINALITY BY COPYING YOUR LOOK!
GOOD ONE!
Hmm... I THINK MY SPIKES ARE DROOPING A BIT. EXCUSE ME WHILE I GO MOUSSE!
SURE THING!
3

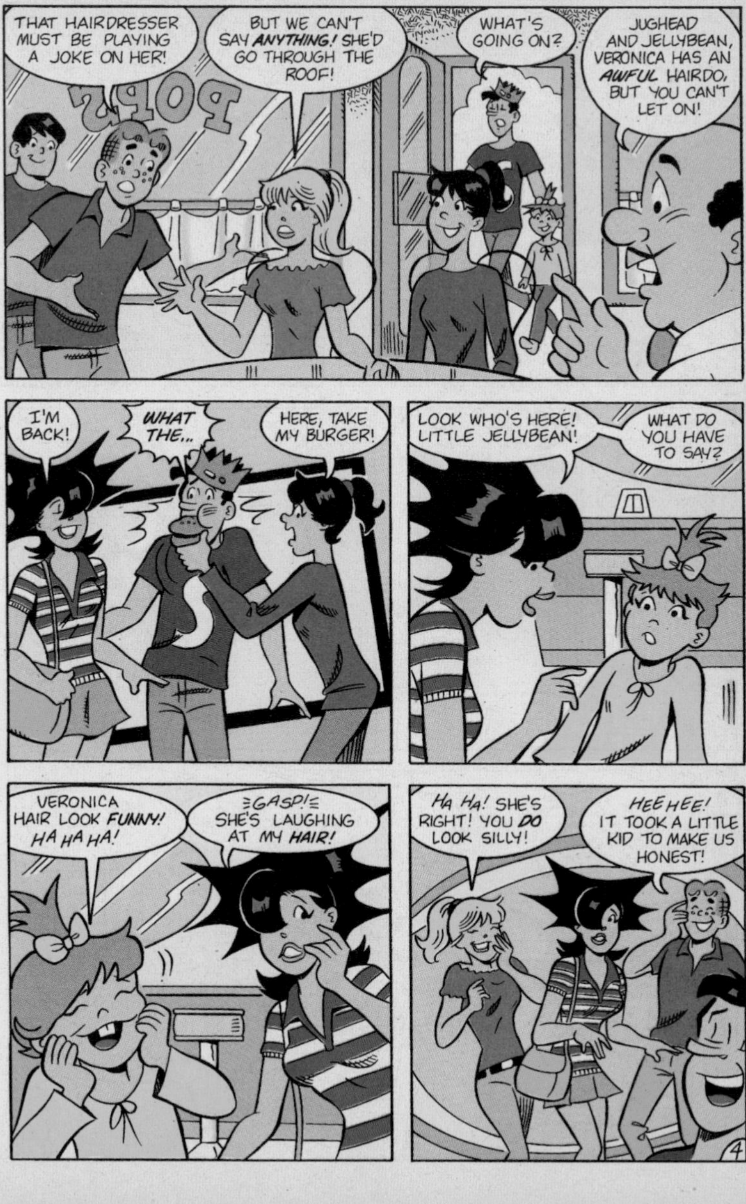
THAT HAIRDRESSER MUST BE PLAYING A JOKE ON HER!
BUT WE CAN'T SAY ANYTHING! SHE'D GO THROUGH THE ROOF!
POPS
WHAT'S GOING ON?
JUGHEAD AND JELLYBEAN, VERONICA HAS AN AWFUL HAIRDO, BUT YOU CAN'T LET ON!
I'M BACK!
WHAT THE...
HERE, TAKE MY BURGER!
LOOK WHO'S HERE! LITTLE JELLYBEAN!
WHAT DO YOU HAVE TO SAY?
VERONICA HAIR LOOK FUNNY! HA HA HA!
GASP! SHE'S LAUGHING AT MY HAIR!
HA HA! SHE'S RIGHT! YOU DO LOOK SILLY!
HEE HEE! IT TOOK A LITTLE KID TO MAKE US HONEST!
4

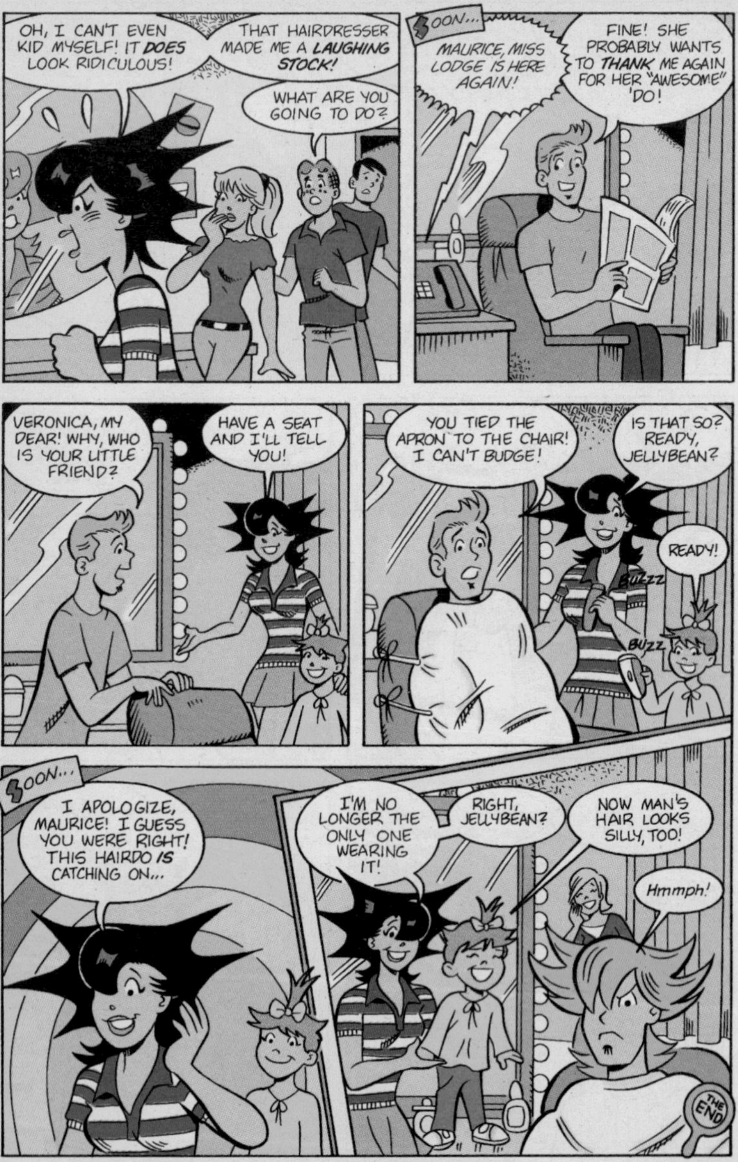
OH, I CAN'T EVEN KID MYSELF! IT DOES LOOK RIDICULOUS!
THAT HAIRDRESSER MADE ME A LAUGHING STOCK!
WHAT ARE YOU GOING TO DO?
SOON...
MAURICE, MISS LODGE IS HERE AGAIN!
FINE! SHE PROBABLY WANTS TO THANK ME AGAIN FOR HER "AWESOME" 'DO!
VERONICA, MY DEAR! WHY, WHO IS YOUR LITTLE FRIEND?
HAVE A SEAT AND I'LL TELL YOU!
YOU TIED THE APRON TO THE CHAIR! I CAN'T BUDGE!
IS THAT SO? READY, JELLYBEAN?
READY!
BUZZZ
BUZZ
SOON...
I APOLOGIZE, MAURICE! I GUESS YOU WERE RIGHT! THIS HAIRDO IS CATCHING ON...
I'M NO LONGER THE ONLY ONE WEARING IT!
RIGHT, JELLYBEAN?
NOW MAN'S HAIR LOOKS SILLY, TOO!
Hmmph!
THE END

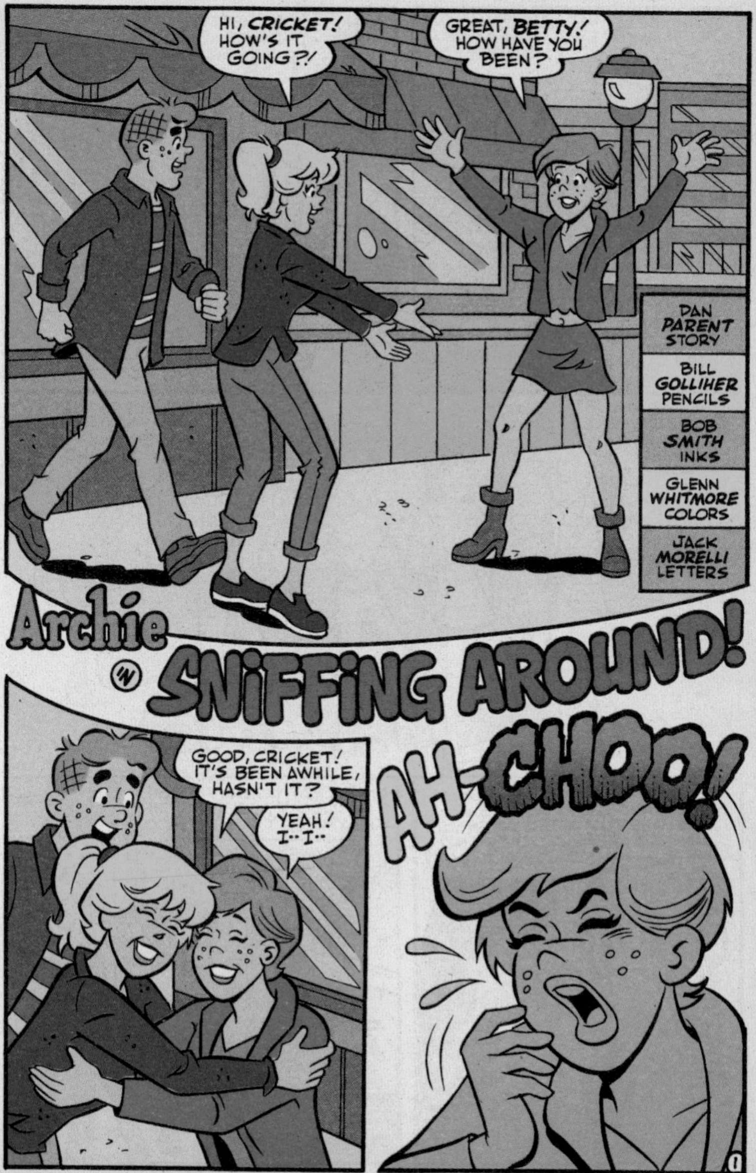
HI, CRICKET! HOW'S IT GOING?!
GREAT, BETTY! HOW HAVE YOU BEEN?
DAN PARENT STORY
BILL GOLLIHER PENCILS
BOB SMITH INKS
GLENN WHITMORE COLORS
JACK MORELLI LETTERS
Archie IN SNIFFING AROUND!
GOOD, CRICKET! IT'S BEEN AWHILE, HASN'T IT?
YEAH! I-- I--
AH-CHOO!
1

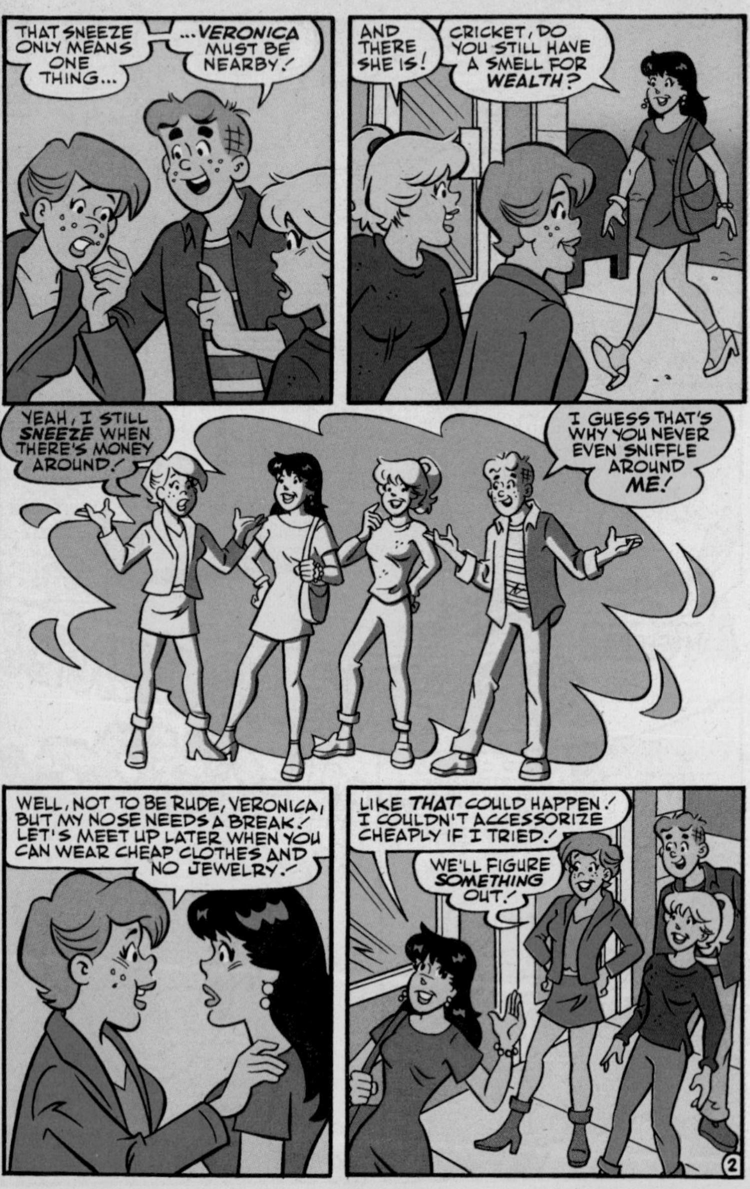
THAT SNEEZE ONLY MEANS ONE THING...
...VERONICA MUST BE NEARBY!
AND THERE SHE IS!
CRICKET, DO YOU STILL HAVE A SMELL FOR WEALTH?
YEAH, I STILL SNEEZE WHEN THERE'S MONEY AROUND!
I GUESS THAT'S WHY YOU NEVER EVEN SNIFFLE AROUND ME!
WELL, NOT TO BE RUDE, VERONICA, BUT MY NOSE NEEDS A BREAK! LET'S MEET UP LATER WHEN YOU CAN WEAR CHEAP CLOTHES AND NO JEWELRY!
LIKE THAT COULD HAPPEN! I COULDN'T ACCESSORIZE CHEAPLY IF I TRIED!
WE'LL FIGURE SOMETHING OUT!
2

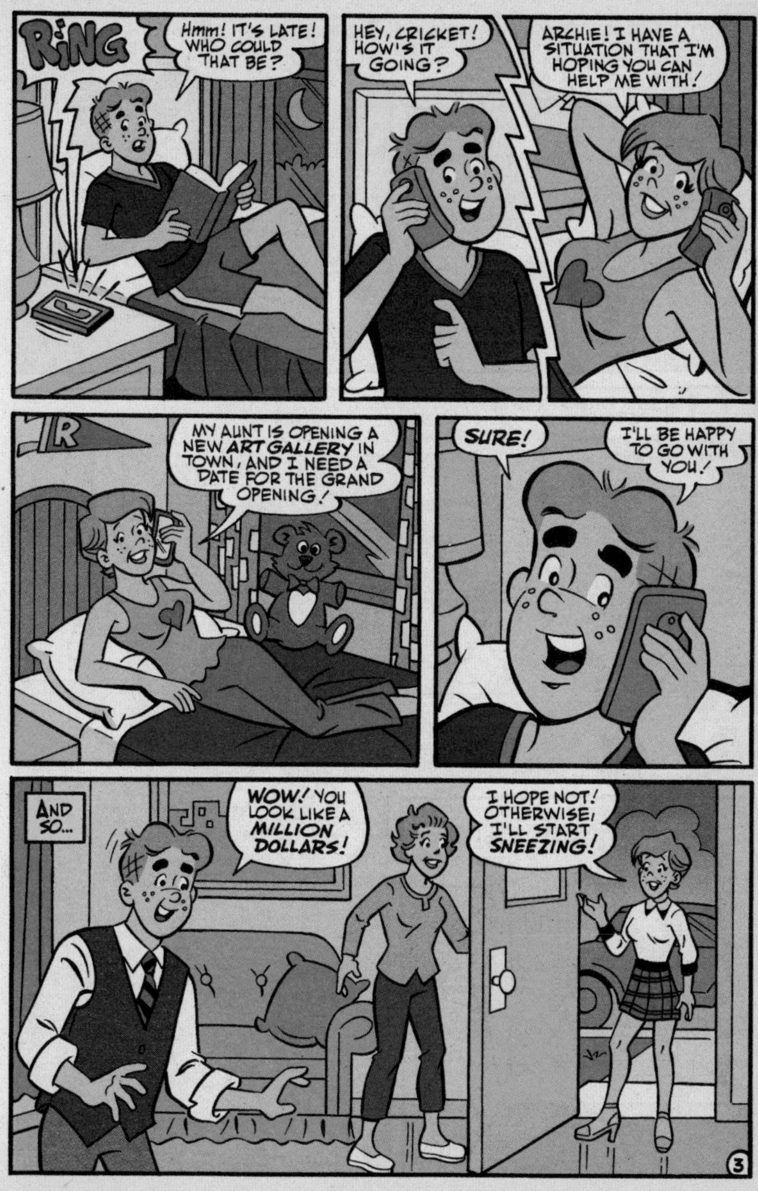
RING
Hmm! IT'S LATE! WHO COULD THAT BE?
HEY, CRICKET! HOW'S IT GOING?
ARCHIE! I HAVE A SITUATION THAT I'M HOPING YOU CAN HELP ME WITH!
MY AUNT IS OPENING A NEW ART GALLERY IN TOWN, AND I NEED A DATE FOR THE GRAND OPENING!
SURE!
I'LL BE HAPPY TO GO WITH YOU!
AND SO...
WOW! YOU LOOK LIKE A MILLION DOLLARS!
I HOPE NOT! OTHERWISE, I'LL START SNEEZING!
3

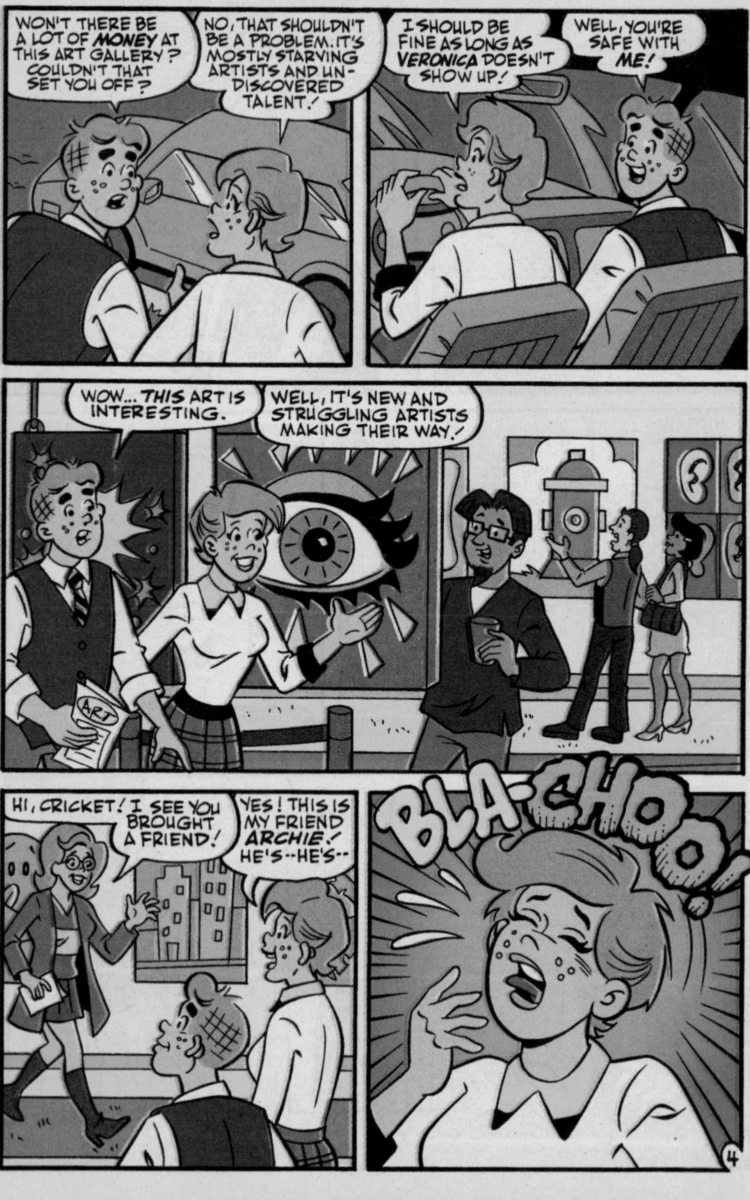
WON'T THERE BE A LOT OF MONEY AT THIS ART GALLERY? COULDN'T THAT SET YOU OFF?
NO, THAT SHOULDN'T BE A PROBLEM. IT'S MOSTLY STARVING ARTISTS AND UN-DISCOVERED TALENT!
I SHOULD BE FINE AS LONG AS VERONICA DOESN'T SHOW UP!
WELL, YOU'RE SAFE WITH ME!
WOW... THIS ART IS INTERESTING.
WELL, IT'S NEW AND STRUGGLING ARTISTS MAKING THEIR WAY!
ART
HI, CRICKET! I SEE YOU BROUGHT A FRIEND!
YES! THIS IS MY FRIEND ARCHIE! HE'S--HE'S--
BLA-CHOO!
4

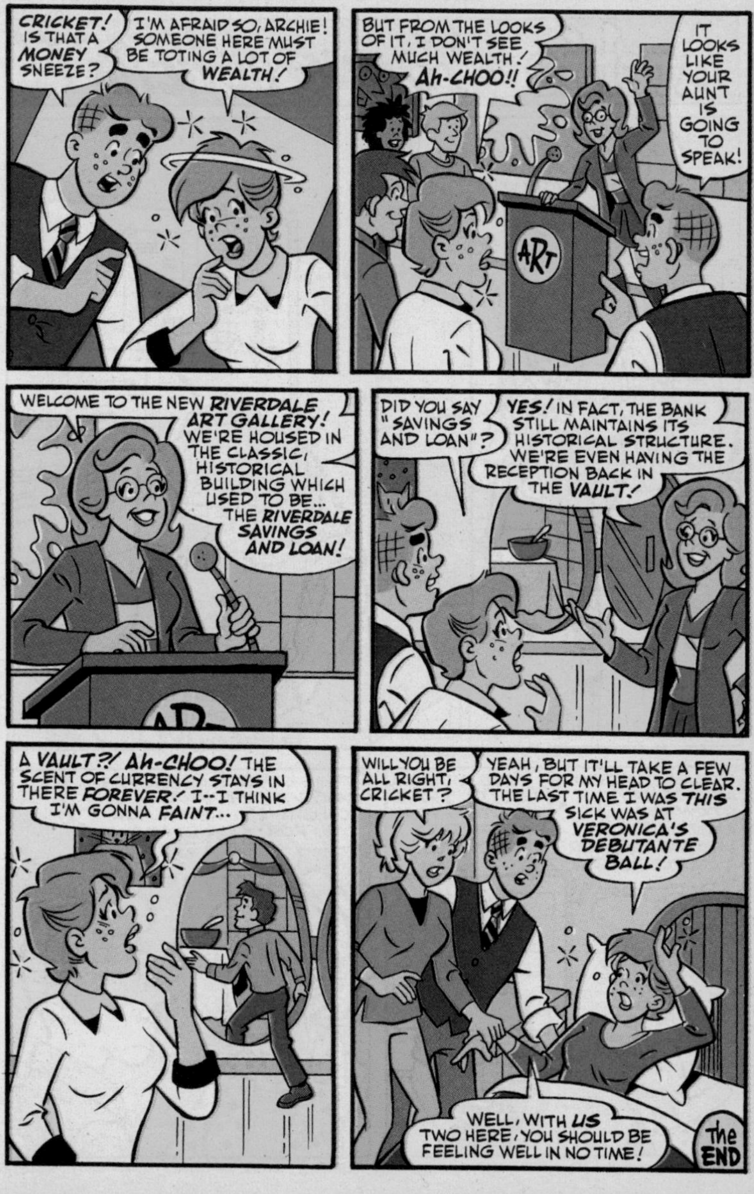
CRICKET! IS THAT A MONEY SNEEZE?
I'M AFRAID SO, ARCHIE! SOMEONE HERE MUST BE TOTING A LOT OF WEALTH!
BUT FROM THE LOOKS OF IT, I DON'T SEE MUCH WEALTH! Ah-CHOO!!
IT LOOKS LIKE YOUR AUNT IS GOING TO SPEAK!
ART
WELCOME TO THE NEW RIVERDALE ART GALLERY! WE'RE HOUSED IN THE CLASSIC, HISTORICAL BUILDING WHICH USED TO BE... THE RIVERDALE SAVINGS AND LOAN!
DID YOU SAY "SAVINGS AND LOAN"?
YES! IN FACT, THE BANK STILL MAINTAINS ITS HISTORICAL STRUCTURE. WE'RE EVEN HAVING THE RECEPTION BACK IN THE VAULT!
A VAULT?! Ah-CHOO! THE SCENT OF CURRENCY STAYS IN THERE FOREVER! I--I THINK I'M GONNA FAINT...
WILL YOU BE ALL RIGHT, CRICKET?
YEAH, BUT IT'LL TAKE A FEW DAYS FOR MY HEAD TO CLEAR. THE LAST TIME I WAS THIS SICK WAS AT VERONICA'S DEBUTANTE BALL!
WELL, WITH US TWO HERE, YOU SHOULD BE FEELING WELL IN NO TIME!
The END

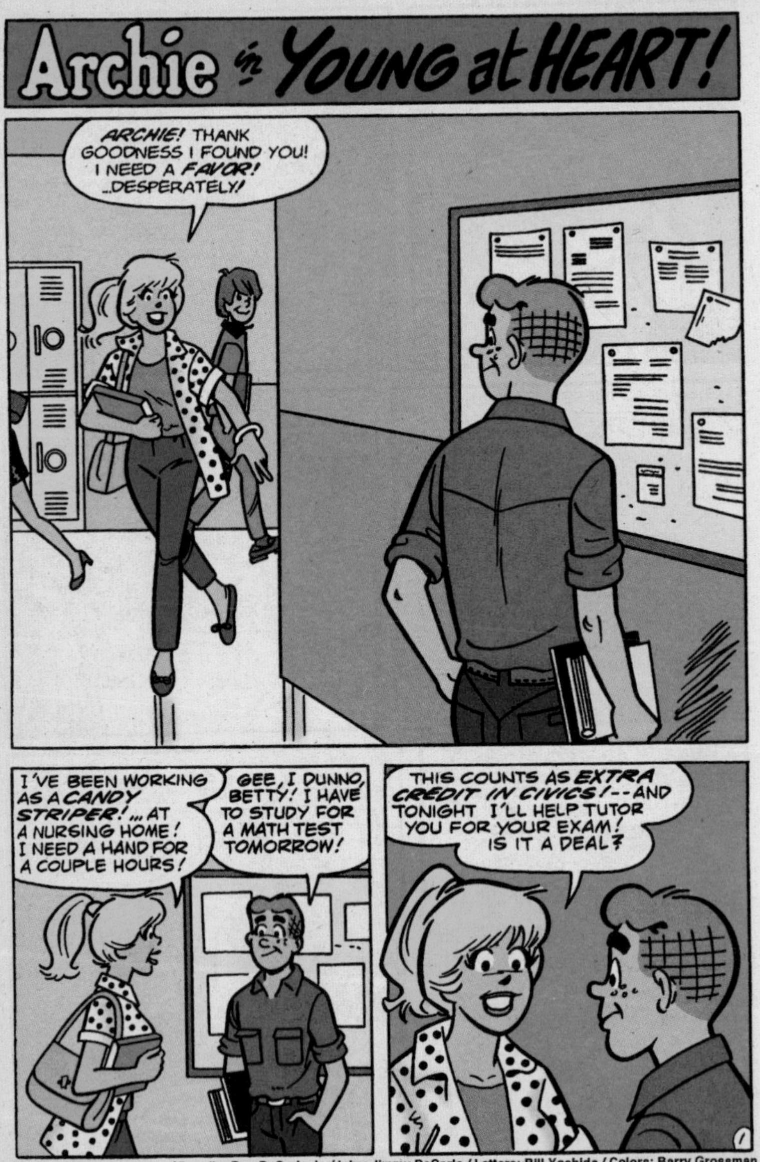
Archie in YOUNG at HEART!
ARCHIE! THANK GOODNESS I FOUND YOU! I NEED A FAVOR! ..DESPERATELY!
I'VE BEEN WORKING AS A CANDY STRIPER! ... AT A NURSING HOME! I NEED A HAND FOR A COUPLE HOURS!
GEE, I DUNNO, BETTY! I HAVE TO STUDY FOR A MATH TEST TOMORROW!
THIS COUNTS AS EXTRA CREDIT IN CIVICS! -- AND TONIGHT I'LL HELP TUTOR YOU FOR YOUR EXAM! IS IT A DEAL?
1

Script: Rich Margopoulos / Pencils: Dan DeCarlo Jr. / Inks: Jimmy DeCarlo / Letters: Bill Yoshida / Colors: Barry Grossman

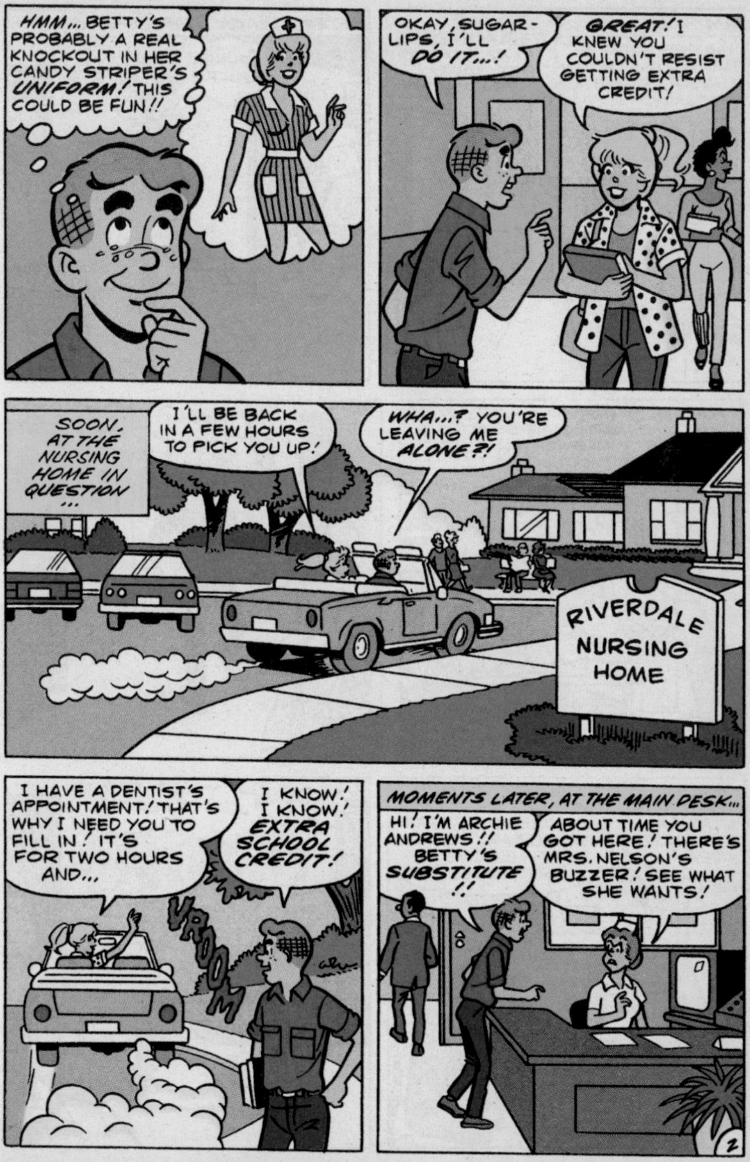
HMM... BETTY'S PROBABLY A REAL KNOCKOUT IN HER CANDY STRIPER'S UNIFORM! THIS COULD BE FUN!!
OKAY, SUGAR-LIPS, I'LL DO IT...!
GREAT! I KNEW YOU COULDN'T RESIST GETTING EXTRA CREDIT!
SOON, AT THE NURSING HOME IN QUESTION ...
I'LL BE BACK IN A FEW HOURS TO PICK YOU UP!
WHA...? YOU'RE LEAVING ME ALONE?!
RIVERDALE NURSING HOME
I HAVE A DENTIST'S APPOINTMENT! THAT'S WHY I NEED YOU TO FILL IN! IT'S FOR TWO HOURS AND...
I KNOW! I KNOW! EXTRA SCHOOL CREDIT!
VROOM
MOMENTS LATER, AT THE MAIN DESK...
HI! I'M ARCHIE ANDREWS!! BETTY'S SUBSTITUTE!!
ABOUT TIME YOU GOT HERE! THERE'S MRS. NELSON'S BUZZER! SEE WHAT SHE WANTS!
2

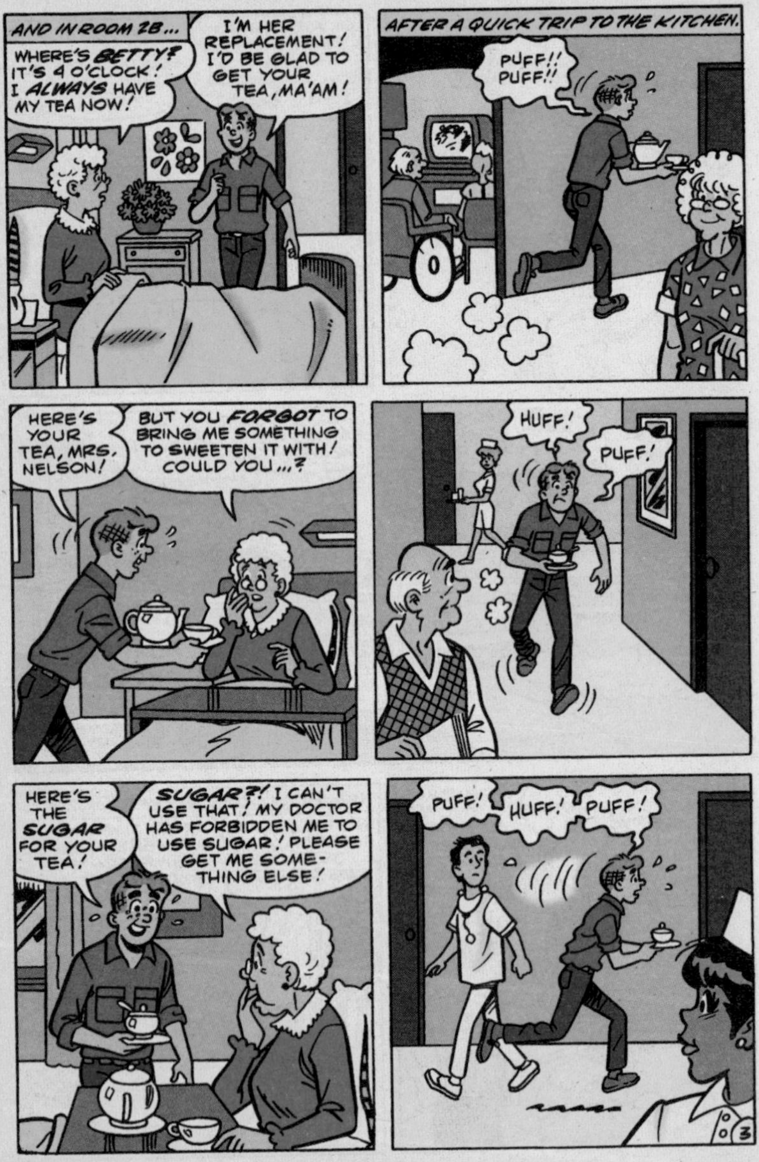
AND IN ROOM 2B...
WHERE'S BETTY? IT'S 4 O'CLOCK! I ALWAYS HAVE MY TEA NOW!
I'M HER REPLACEMENT! I'D BE GLAD TO GET YOUR TEA, MA'AM!
AFTER A QUICK TRIP TO THE KITCHEN.
PUFF!! PUFF!!
HERE'S YOUR TEA, MRS. NELSON!
BUT YOU FORGOT TO BRING ME SOMETHING TO SWEETEN IT WITH! COULD YOU...?
HUFF!
PUFF!
HERE'S THE SUGAR FOR YOUR TEA!
SUGAR?! I CAN'T USE THAT! MY DOCTOR HAS FORBIDDEN ME TO USE SUGAR! PLEASE GET ME SOME-THING ELSE!
PUFF!
HUFF!
PUFF!
3

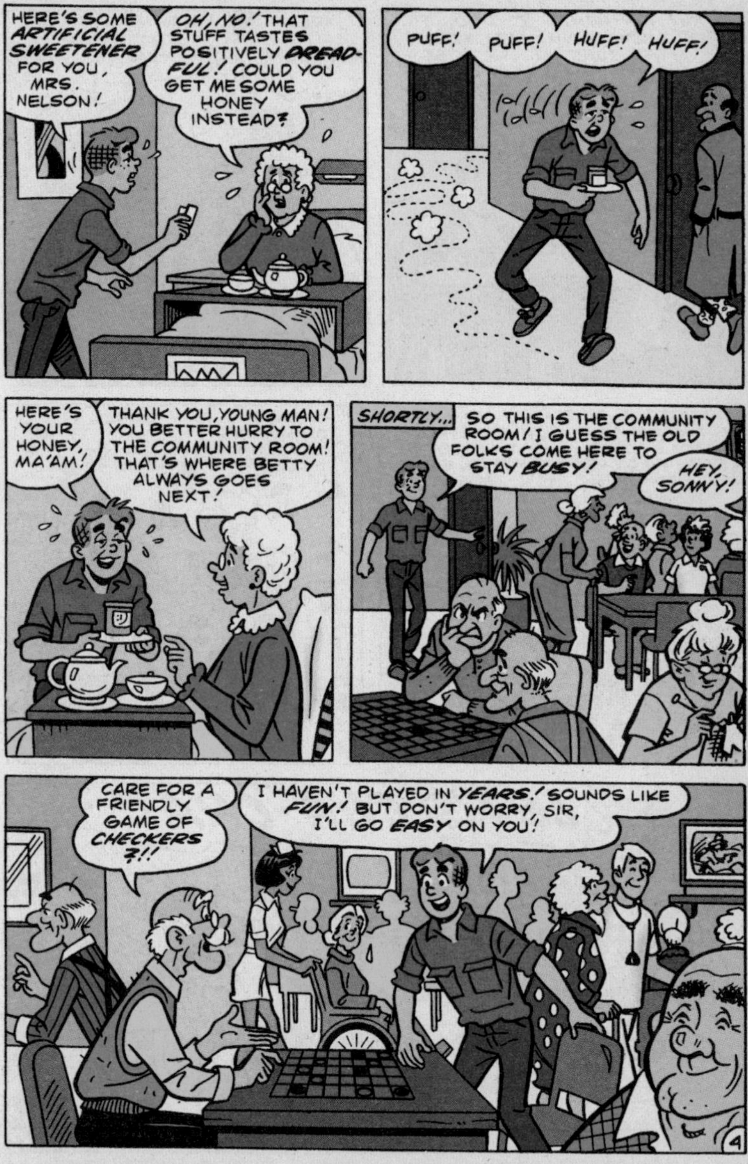

HERE'S SOME ARTIFICIAL SWEETENER FOR YOU, MRS. NELSON!
OH, NO! THAT STUFF TASTES POSITIVELY DREAD-FUL! COULD YOU GET ME SOME HONEY INSTEAD?
PUFF! PUFF! HUFF! HUFF!
HERE'S YOUR HONEY, MA'AM!
THANK YOU, YOUNG MAN! YOU BETTER HURRY TO THE COMMUNITY ROOM! THAT'S WHERE BETTY ALWAYS GOES NEXT!
SHORTLY...
SO THIS IS THE COMMUNITY ROOM! I GUESS THE OLD FOLKS COME HERE TO STAY BUSY!
HEY, SONNY!
CARE FOR A FRIENDLY GAME OF CHECKERS ?!!
I HAVEN'T PLAYED IN YEARS! SOUNDS LIKE FUN! BUT DON'T WORRY, SIR, I'LL GO EASY ON YOU!
4

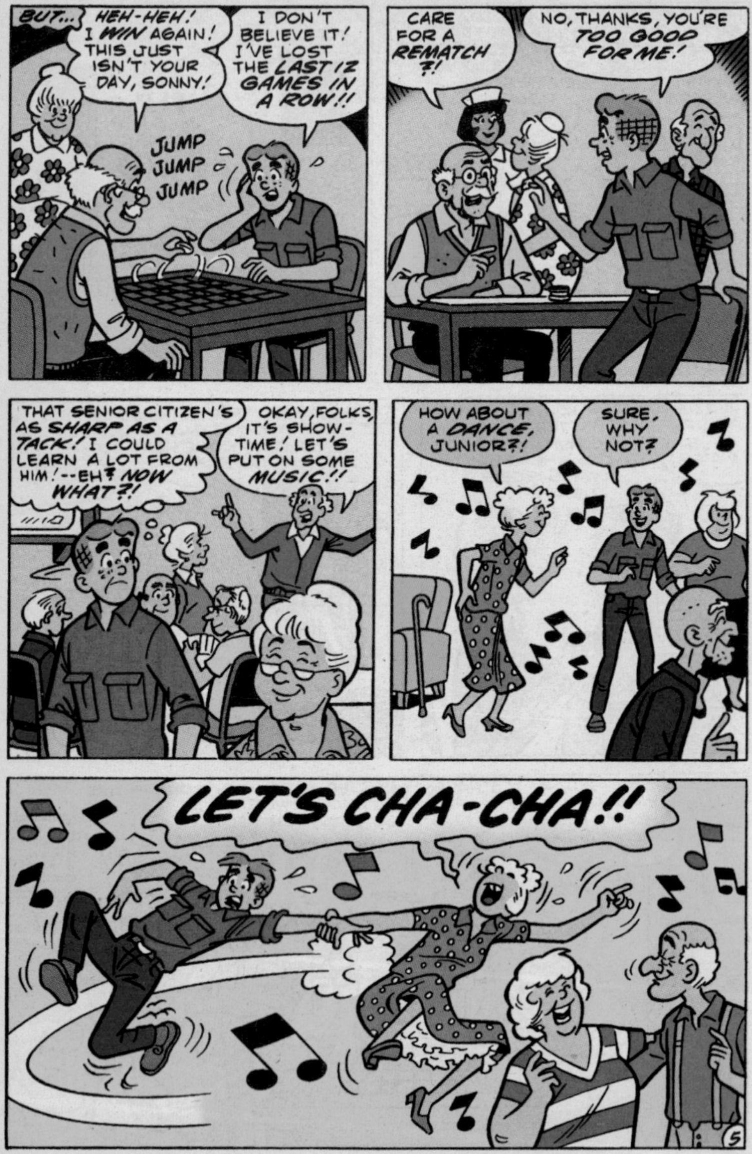
BUT...
HEH-HEH! I WIN AGAIN! THIS JUST ISN'T YOUR DAY, SONNY!
I DON'T BELIEVE IT! I'VE LOST THE LAST 12 GAMES IN A ROW!!
JUMP JUMP JUMP
CARE FOR A REMATCH?!
NO, THANKS, YOU'RE TOO GOOD FOR ME!
THAT SENIOR CITIZEN'S AS SHARP AS A TACK! I COULD LEARN A LOT FROM HIM! --EH? NOW WHAT?!
OKAY, FOLKS, IT'S SHOW-TIME! LET'S PUT ON SOME MUSIC!!
HOW ABOUT A DANCE, JUNIOR?!
SURE, WHY NOT?
LET'S CHA-CHA!!
5

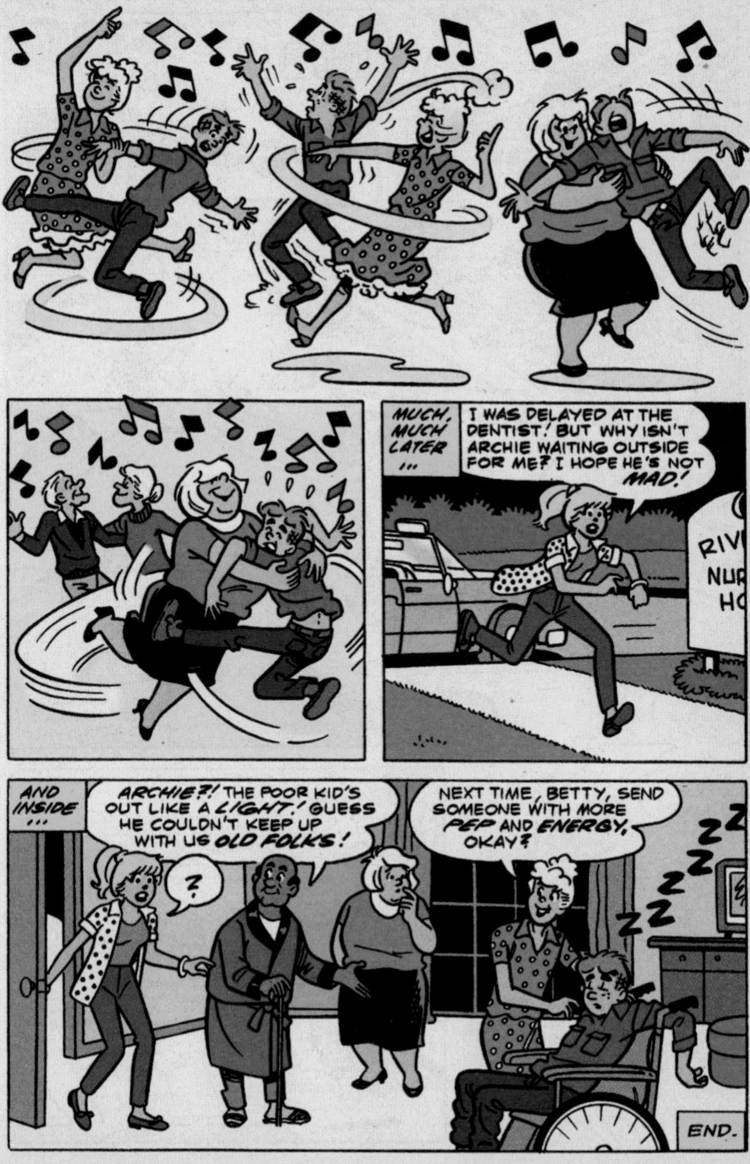
MUCH, MUCH LATER ...
I WAS DELAYED AT THE DENTIST! BUT WHY ISN'T ARCHIE WAITING OUTSIDE FOR ME? I HOPE HE'S NOT MAD!
AND INSIDE ...
ARCHIE?! THE POOR KID'S OUT LIKE A LIGHT! GUESS HE COULDN'T KEEP UP WITH US OLD FOLKS!
?
NEXT TIME, BETTY, SEND SOMEONE WITH MORE PEP AND ENERGY, OKAY?
Z Z Z Z Z Z
END.

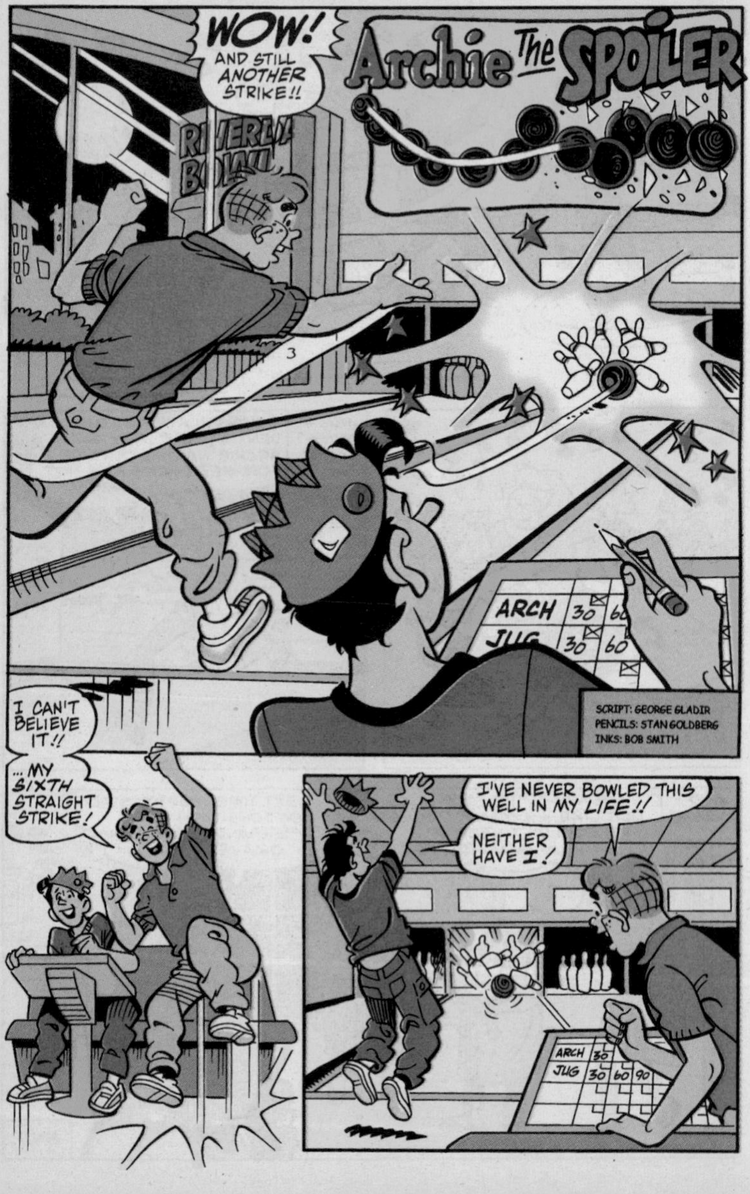

WOW! AND STILL ANOTHER STRIKE!!
Archie The SPOILER
ARCH 30 60
JUG 30 60
SCRIPT: GEORGE GLADIR
PENCILS: STAN GOLDBERG
INKS: BOB SMITH
I CAN'T BELIEVE IT!!
...MY SIXTH STRAIGHT STRIKE!
I'VE NEVER BOWLED THIS WELL IN MY LIFE!!
NEITHER HAVE I!
ARCH 30
JUG 30 60 90

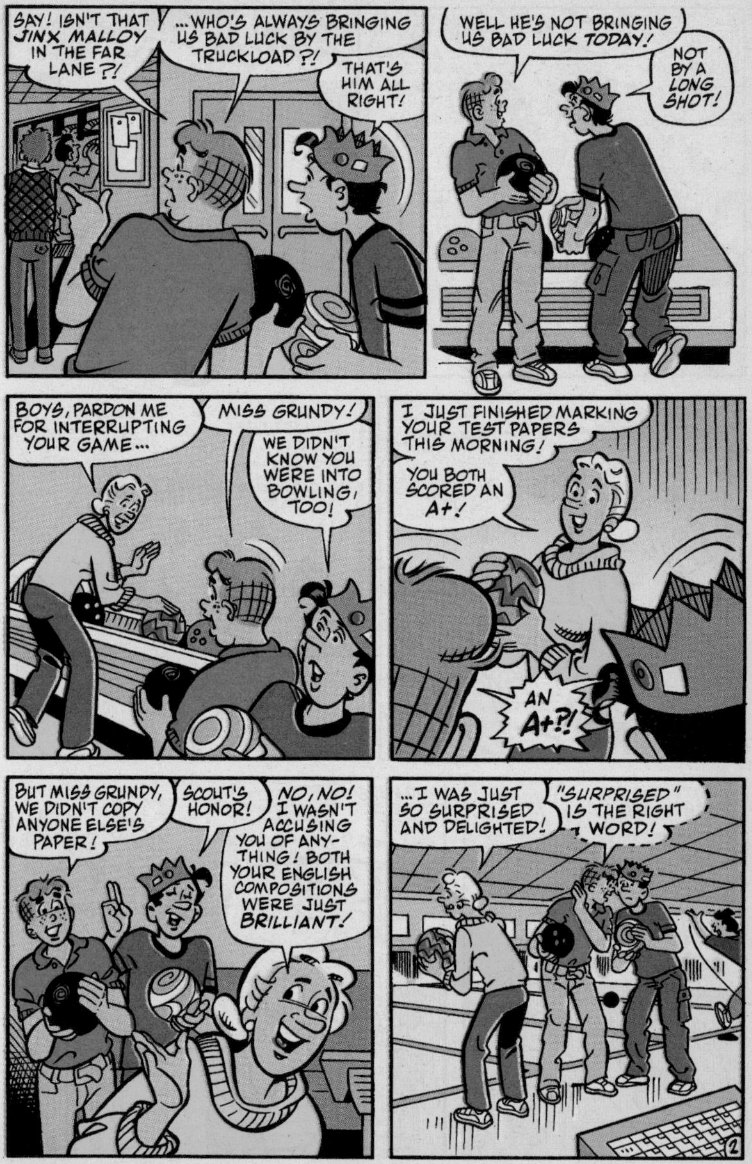
SAY! ISN'T THAT JINX MALLOY IN THE FAR LANE?!
...WHO'S ALWAYS BRINGING US BAD LUCK BY THE TRUCKLOAD?!
THAT'S HIM ALL RIGHT!
WELL HE'S NOT BRINGING US BAD LUCK TODAY!
NOT BY A LONG SHOT!
BOYS, PARDON ME FOR INTERRUPTING YOUR GAME...
MISS GRUNDY!
WE DIDN'T KNOW YOU WERE INTO BOWLING, TOO!
I JUST FINISHED MARKING YOUR TEST PAPERS THIS MORNING!
YOU BOTH SCORED AN A+!
AN A+?!
BUT MISS GRUNDY, WE DIDN'T COPY ANYONE ELSE'S PAPER!
SCOUT'S HONOR!
NO, NO! I WASN'T ACCUSING YOU OF ANYTHING! BOTH YOUR ENGLISH COMPOSITIONS WERE JUST BRILLIANT!
...I WAS JUST SO SURPRISED AND DELIGHTED!
"SURPRISED" IS THE RIGHT WORD!
2

SAY! DO YOU THINK THE JINX IS NOW BRINGING US GOOD LUCK?

COULD BE!

MAYBE HE'S TRYING TO MAKE AMENDS FOR ALL THE BAD LUCK HE THREW OUR WAY IN THE PAST!

yahoo!

MY SEVENTH STRAIGHT STRIKE!

THE BOWLER IN LANE 11 HAS JUST THROWN SEVEN STRAIGHT STRIKES!!

| ARCH | 30 | 60 | 90 | 120 | 150 |
| HUG | 30 | 60 | | | |

...IT'S THE ALLEY'S NEW POLICY TO AWARD FREE SNACKS TO ANYONE ACCOMPLISHING THIS FEAT!!

WOWEE!

AND THIS IS MY SEVENTH STRIKE!!

AND HERE COME OUR FREE SNACKS!!

FOOD COURT

Menu

3

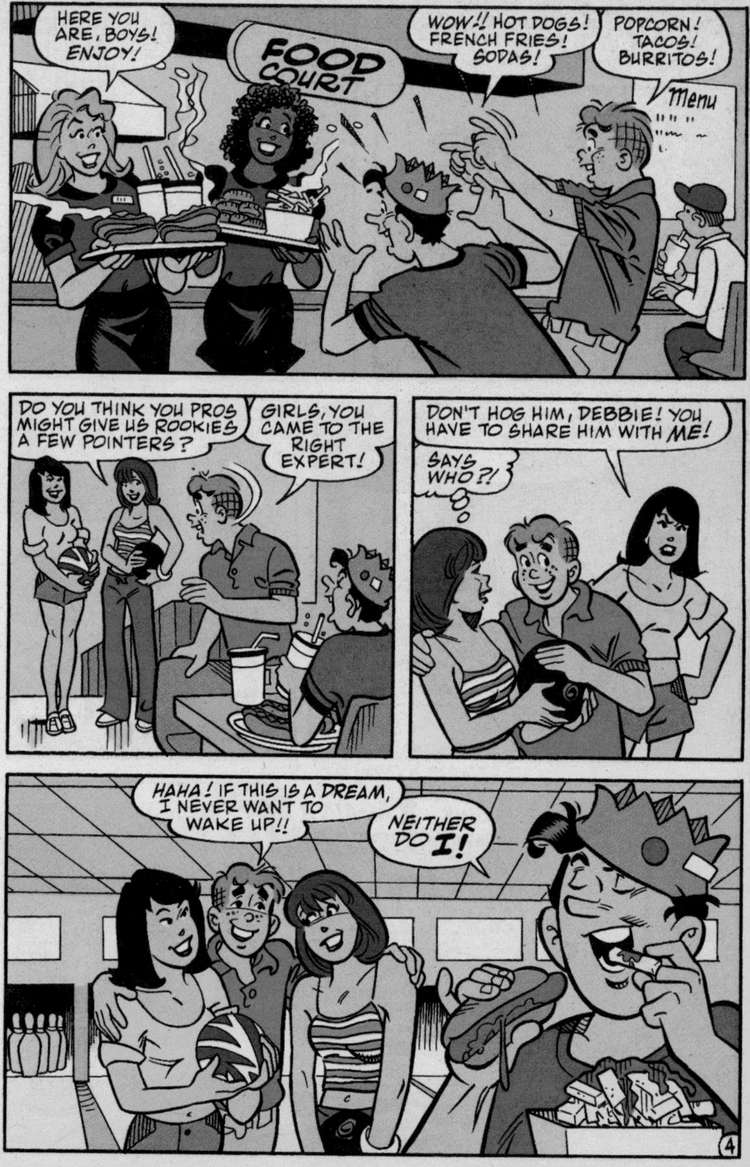
HERE YOU ARE, BOYS! ENJOY!
FOOD COURT
WOW!! HOT DOGS! FRENCH FRIES! SODAS!
POPCORN! TACOS! BURRITOS!
Menu
DO YOU THINK YOU PROS MIGHT GIVE US ROOKIES A FEW POINTERS?
GIRLS, YOU CAME TO THE RIGHT EXPERT!
DON'T HOG HIM, DEBBIE! YOU HAVE TO SHARE HIM WITH ME!
SAYS WHO?!
HAHA! IF THIS IS A DREAM, I NEVER WANT TO WAKE UP!!
NEITHER DO I!
4

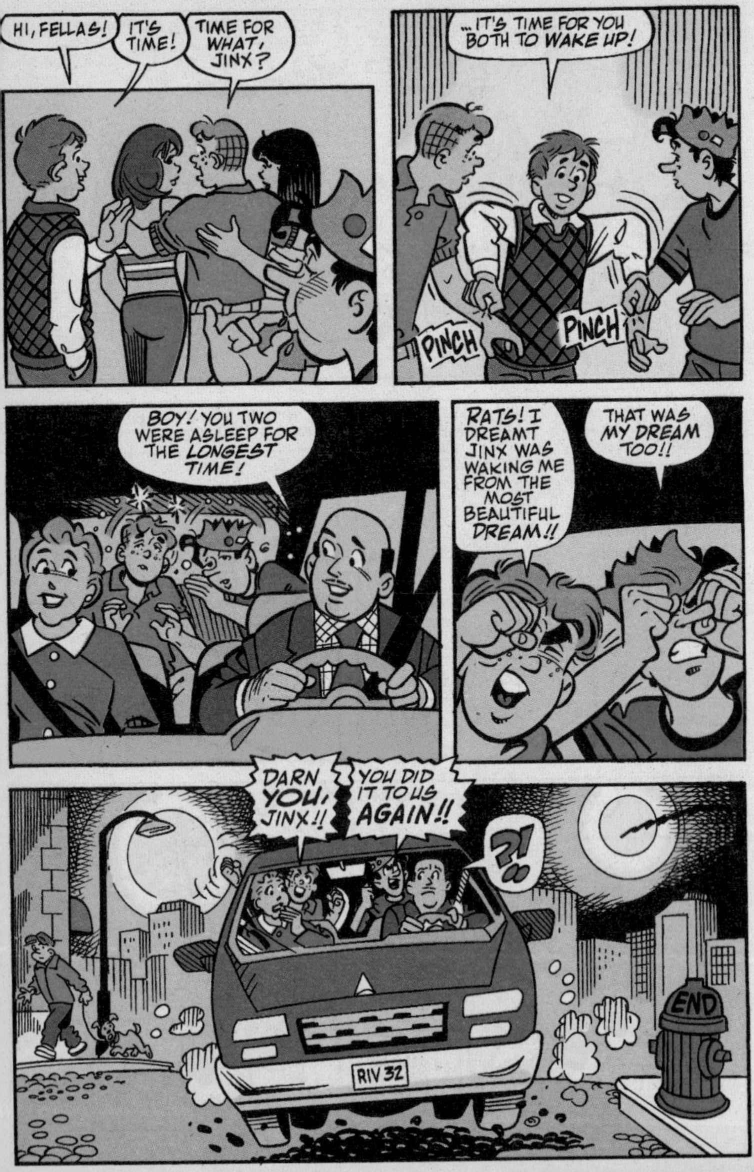
HI, FELLAS!
IT'S TIME!
TIME FOR WHAT, JINX?
...IT'S TIME FOR YOU BOTH TO WAKE UP!
PINCH
PINCH
BOY! YOU TWO WERE ASLEEP FOR THE LONGEST TIME!
RATS! I DREAMT JINX WAS WAKING ME FROM THE MOST BEAUTIFUL DREAM!!
THAT WAS MY DREAM TOO!!
DARN YOU, JINX!!
YOU DID IT TO US AGAIN!!
?!
RIV 32
END

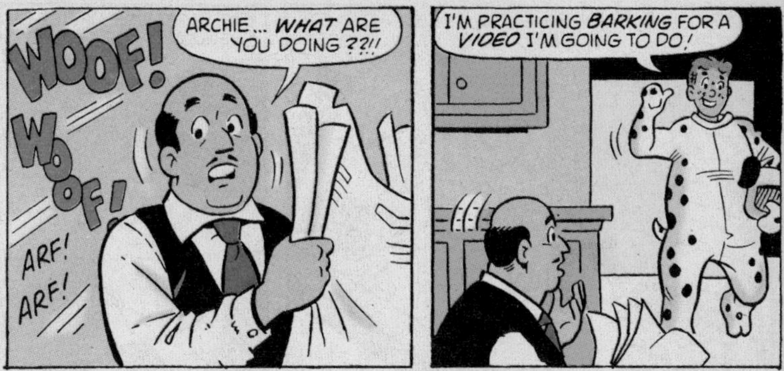
WOOF!
WOOF!
ARF! ARF!
ARCHIE... WHAT ARE YOU DOING ??!!
I'M PRACTICING BARKING FOR A VIDEO I'M GOING TO DO!

Script: George Gladir / Pencils: Tim Kennedy / Inks: Rudy Lapick / Letters: Bill Yoshida

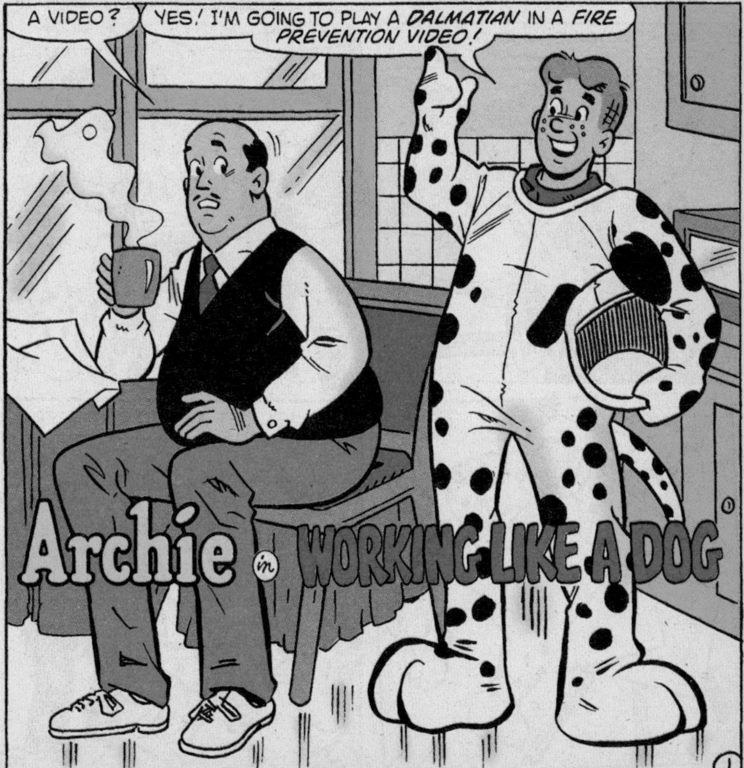
A VIDEO?
YES! I'M GOING TO PLAY A DALMATIAN IN A FIRE PREVENTION VIDEO!
Archie in WORKING LIKE A DOG

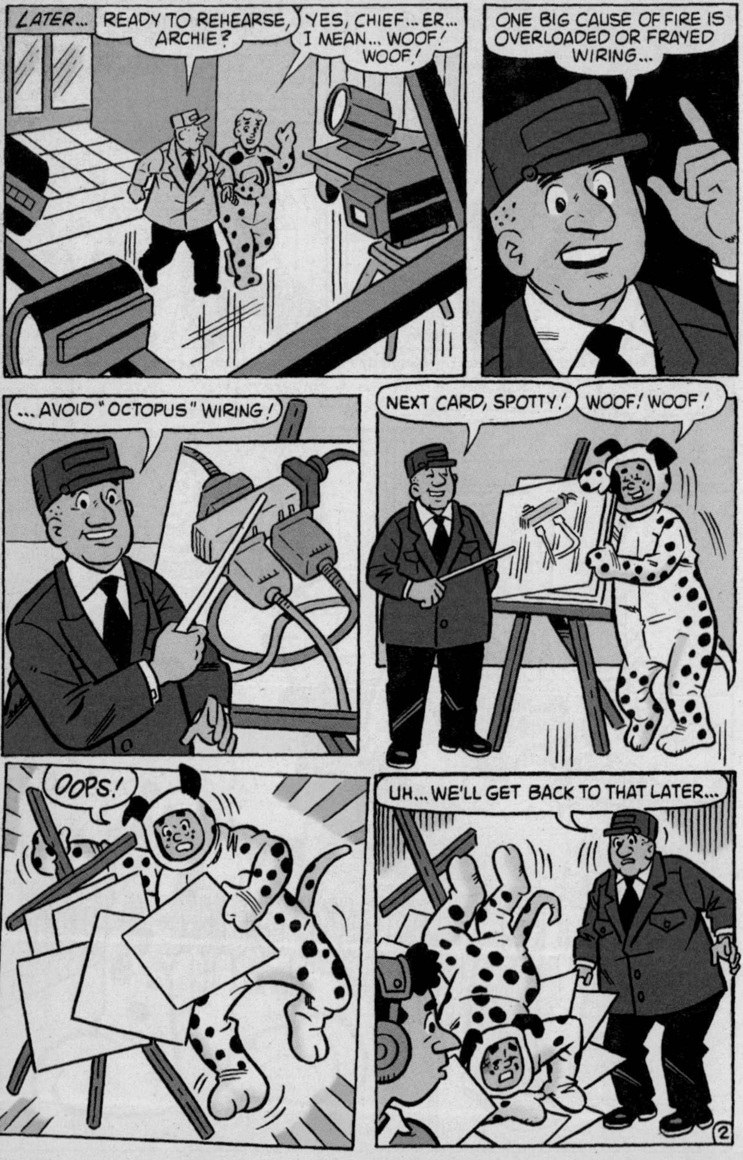

LATER...
READY TO REHEARSE, ARCHIE?
YES, CHIEF... ER... I MEAN... WOOF! WOOF!
ONE BIG CAUSE OF FIRE IS OVERLOADED OR FRAYED WIRING...
... AVOID "OCTOPUS" WIRING!
NEXT CARD, SPOTTY!
WOOF! WOOF!
OOPS!
UH... WE'LL GET BACK TO THAT LATER...
2

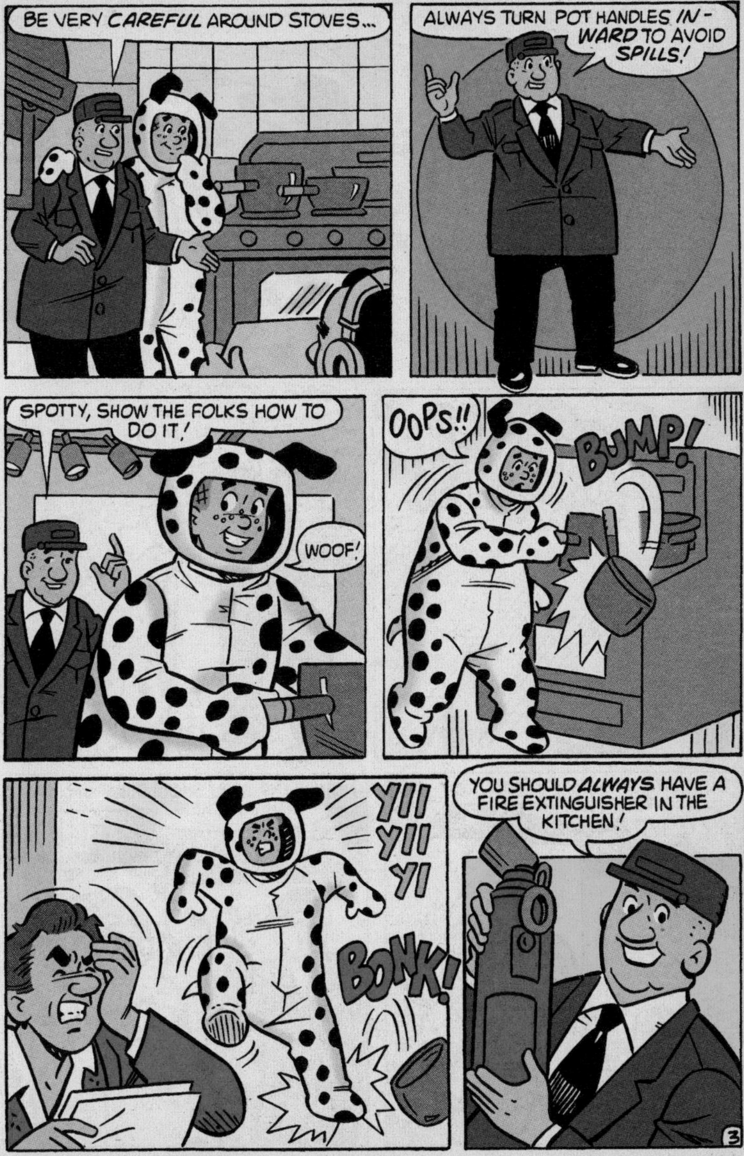
BE VERY CAREFUL AROUND STOVES...
ALWAYS TURN POT HANDLES IN-WARD TO AVOID SPILLS!
SPOTTY, SHOW THE FOLKS HOW TO DO IT!
WOOF!
OOPS!!
BUMP!
YII YII YI
BONK!
YOU SHOULD ALWAYS HAVE A FIRE EXTINGUISHER IN THE KITCHEN!
3

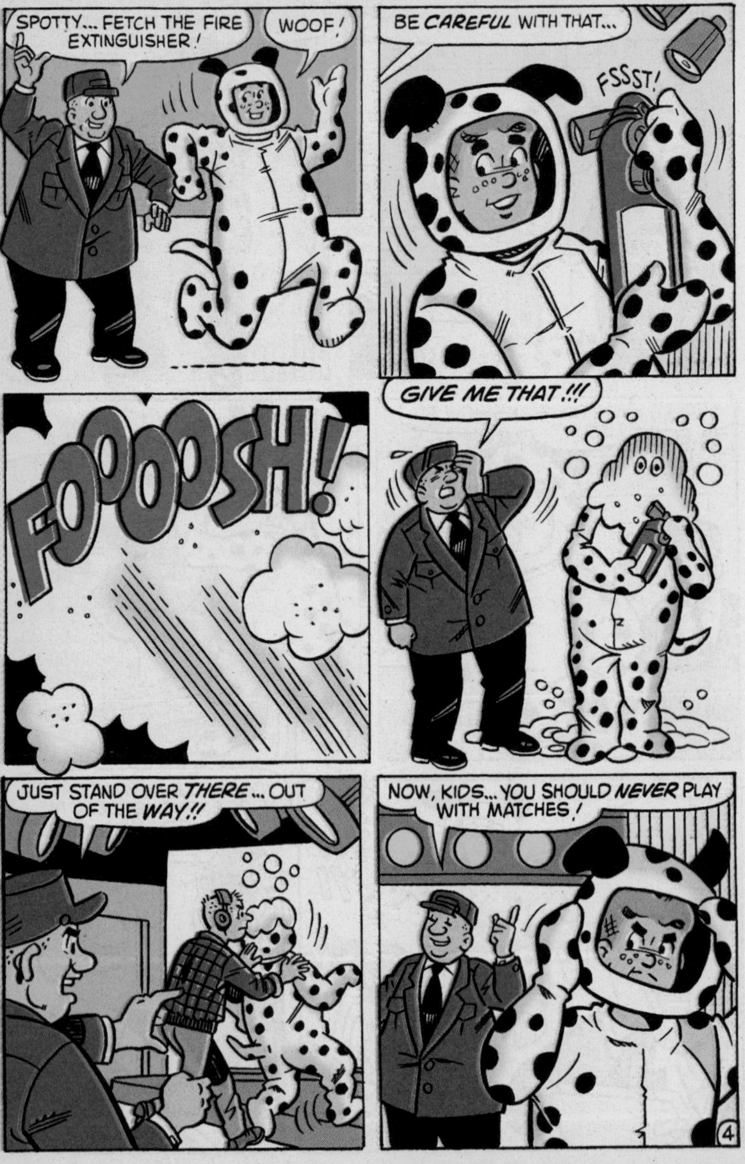

SPOTTY... FETCH THE FIRE EXTINGUISHER!
WOOF!
BE CAREFUL WITH THAT...
FSSST!
FOOOOSH!
GIVE ME THAT!!!
JUST STAND OVER THERE... OUT OF THE WAY!!
NOW, KIDS... YOU SHOULD NEVER PLAY WITH MATCHES!
4

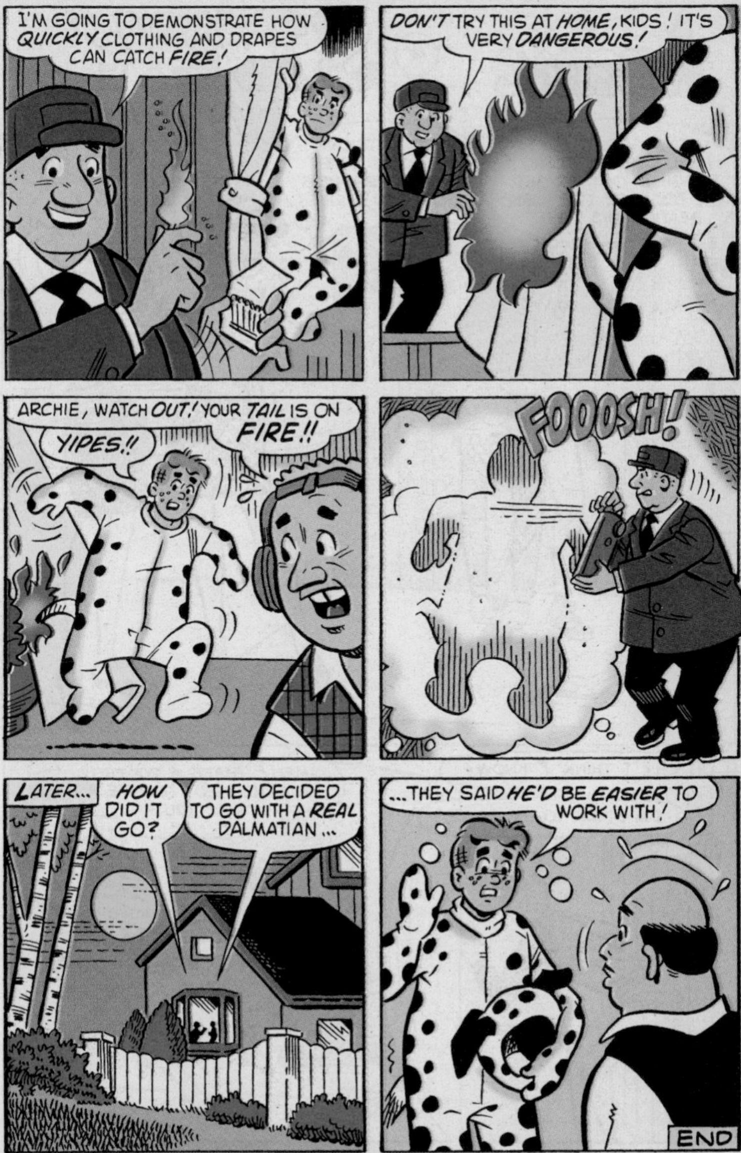
I'M GOING TO DEMONSTRATE HOW QUICKLY CLOTHING AND DRAPES CAN CATCH FIRE!
DON'T TRY THIS AT HOME, KIDS! IT'S VERY DANGEROUS!
ARCHIE, WATCH OUT! YOUR TAIL IS ON FIRE!!
YIPES!!
FOOOSH!
LATER...
HOW DID IT GO?
THEY DECIDED TO GO WITH A REAL DALMATIAN...
...THEY SAID HE'D BE EASIER TO WORK WITH!
END

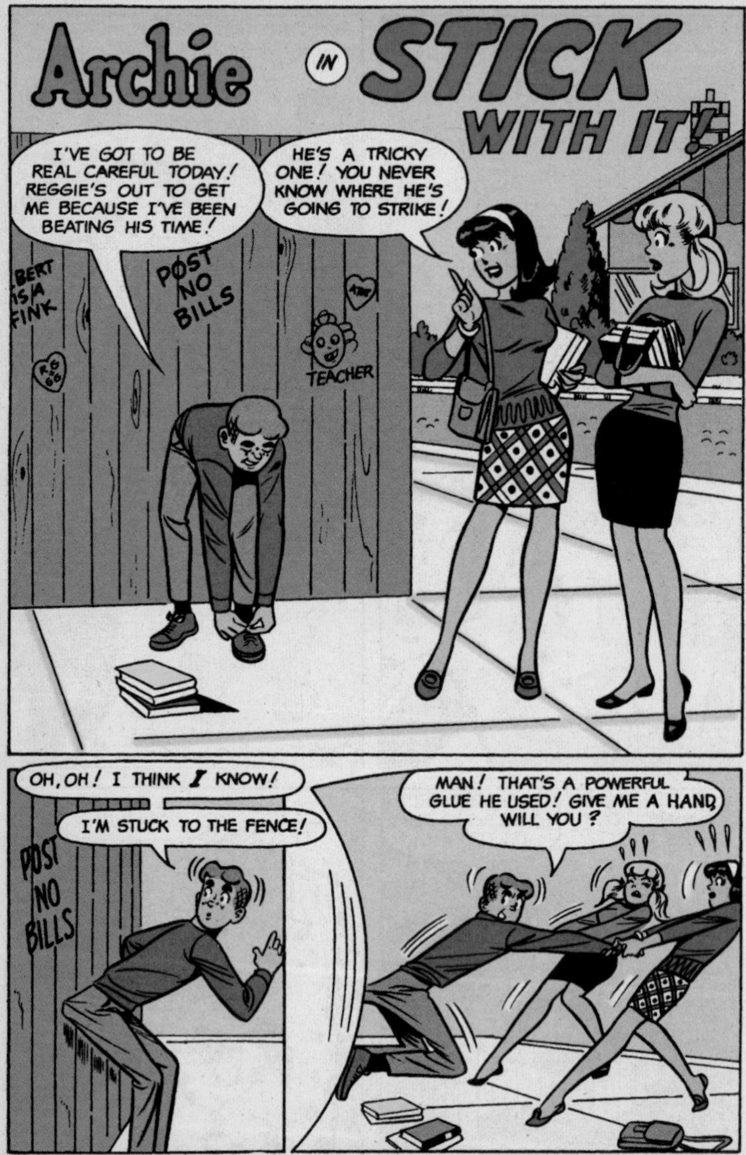
Archie
IN
STICK WITH IT!
I'VE GOT TO BE REAL CAREFUL TODAY! REGGIE'S OUT TO GET ME BECAUSE I'VE BEEN BEATING HIS TIME!
HE'S A TRICKY ONE! YOU NEVER KNOW WHERE HE'S GOING TO STRIKE!
POST NO BILLS
TEACHER
OH, OH! I THINK I KNOW!
I'M STUCK TO THE FENCE!
POST NO BILLS
MAN! THAT'S A POWERFUL GLUE HE USED! GIVE ME A HAND, WILL YOU?

Script: Frank Doyle / Art: Harry Lucey / Letters: Bill Yoshida / Colors: Barry Grossman

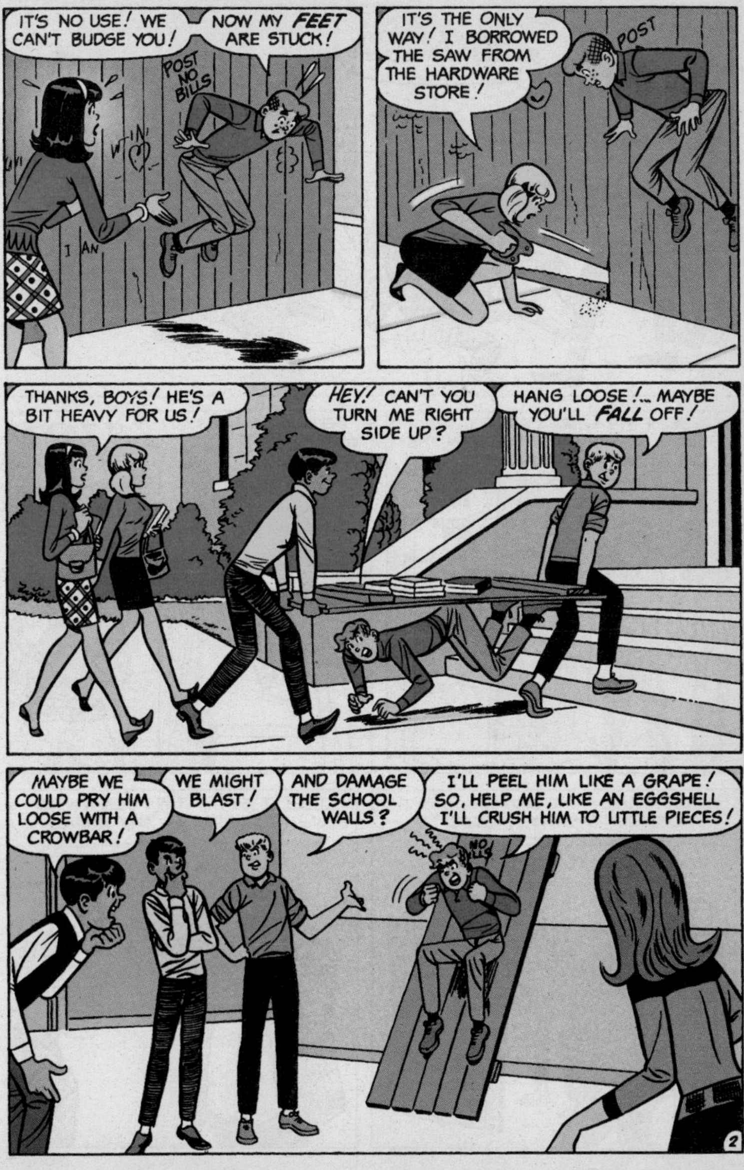
IT'S NO USE! WE CAN'T BUDGE YOU!
NOW MY FEET ARE STUCK!
POST NO BILLS
IT'S THE ONLY WAY! I BORROWED THE SAW FROM THE HARDWARE STORE!
POST
THANKS, BOYS! HE'S A BIT HEAVY FOR US!
HEY! CAN'T YOU TURN ME RIGHT SIDE UP?
HANG LOOSE!... MAYBE YOU'LL FALL OFF!
MAYBE WE COULD PRY HIM LOOSE WITH A CROWBAR!
WE MIGHT BLAST!
AND DAMAGE THE SCHOOL WALLS?
I'LL PEEL HIM LIKE A GRAPE! SO, HELP ME, LIKE AN EGGSHELL I'LL CRUSH HIM TO LITTLE PIECES!
2

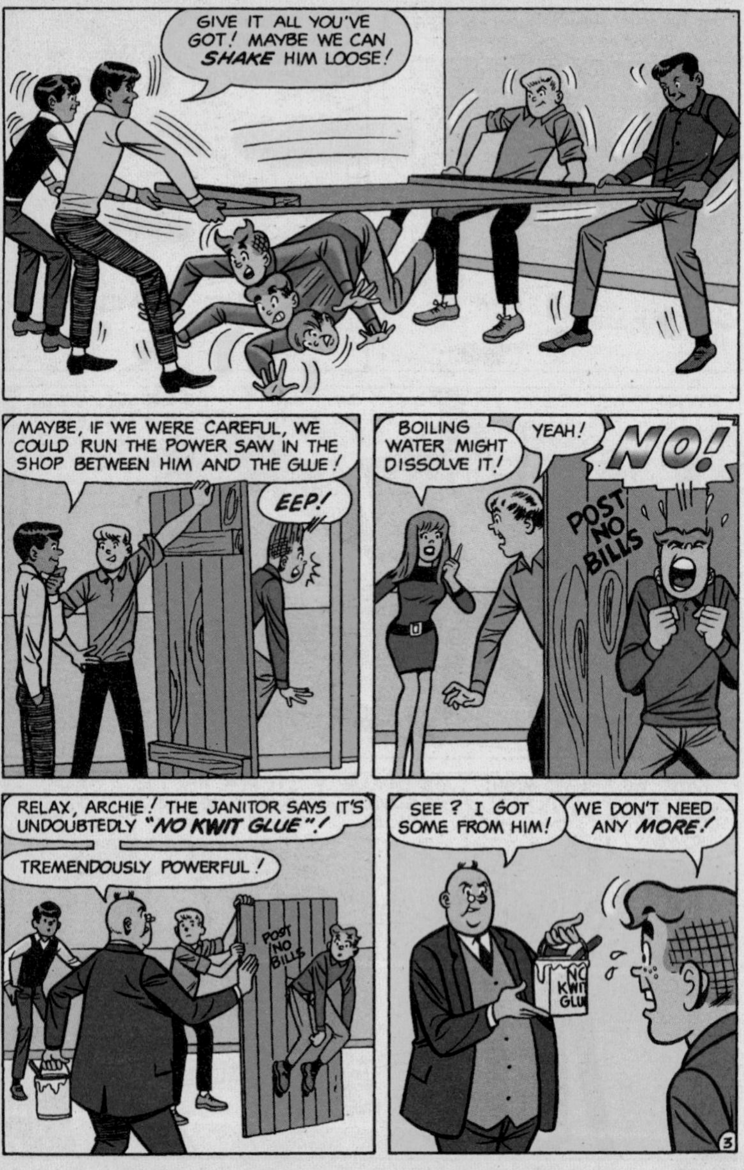

GIVE IT ALL YOU'VE GOT! MAYBE WE CAN *SHAKE* HIM LOOSE!
MAYBE, IF WE WERE CAREFUL, WE COULD RUN THE POWER SAW IN THE SHOP BETWEEN HIM AND THE GLUE!
EEP!
BOILING WATER MIGHT DISSOLVE IT!
YEAH!
NO!
POST NO BILLS
RELAX, ARCHIE! THE JANITOR SAYS IT'S UNDOUBTEDLY *"NO KWIT GLUE"*!
TREMENDOUSLY POWERFUL!
POST NO BILLS
SEE? I GOT SOME FROM HIM!
WE DON'T NEED ANY *MORE*!
NO KWIT GLU
3

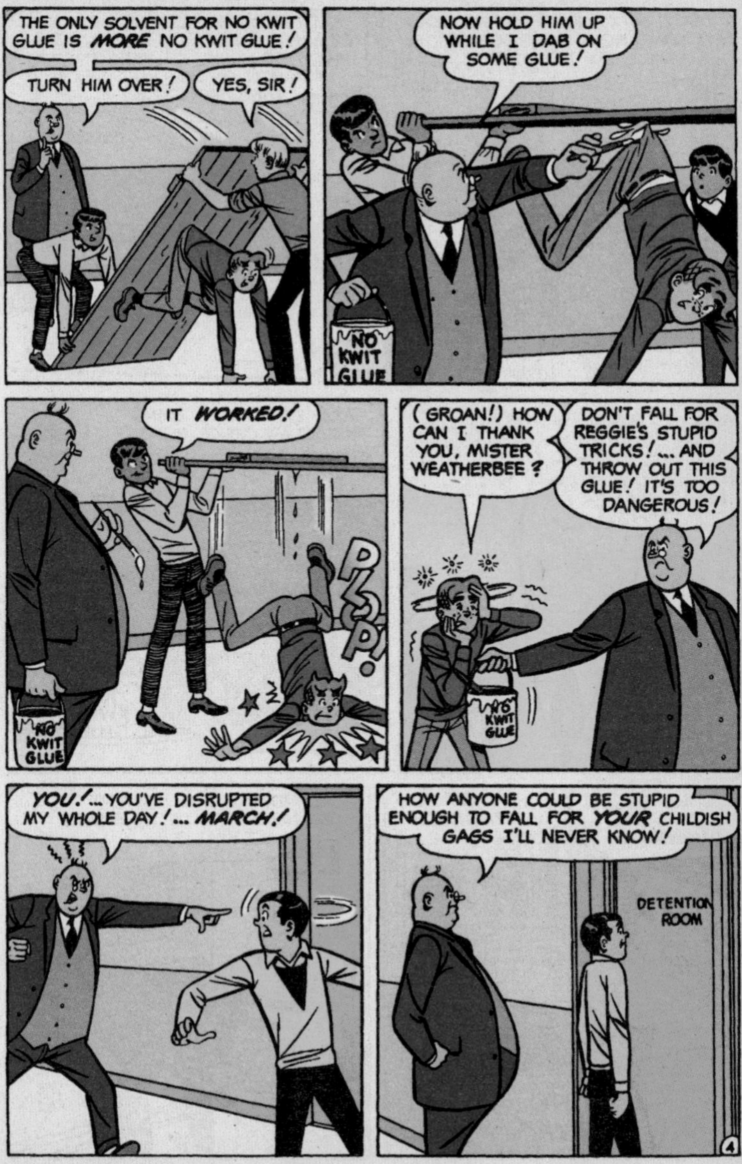
THE ONLY SOLVENT FOR NO KWIT GLUE IS MORE NO KWIT GLUE!
TURN HIM OVER!
YES, SIR!
NOW HOLD HIM UP WHILE I DAB ON SOME GLUE!
NO KWIT GLUE
IT WORKED!
PLOP!
NO KWIT GLUE
(GROAN!) HOW CAN I THANK YOU, MISTER WEATHERBEE?
DON'T FALL FOR REGGIE'S STUPID TRICKS! ... AND THROW OUT THIS GLUE! IT'S TOO DANGEROUS!
NO KWIT GLUE
YOU! ... YOU'VE DISRUPTED MY WHOLE DAY! ... MARCH!
HOW ANYONE COULD BE STUPID ENOUGH TO FALL FOR YOUR CHILDISH GAGS I'LL NEVER KNOW!
DETENTION ROOM
4

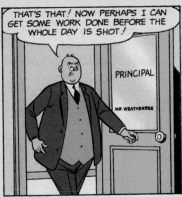

THAT'S THAT! NOW PERHAPS I CAN GET SOME WORK DONE BEFORE THE WHOLE DAY IS SHOT!

PRINCIPAL

MR. WEATHERBEE

YOU'D THINK BY NOW ARCHIE WOULD BE SHARP ENOUGH TO SPOT SOME-THING AS CORNY AS REGGIE'S VARIATION ON THE OLD GLUE ON THE CHAIR TRICK!

GLUE ON THE CHAIR??

ARCHIE!... WAIT!... BRING THAT TO MY OFFICE, PLEASE!

NO KWIT GLUE

I THOUGHT YOU SAID IT WAS DANGEROUS!

IT IS!... BUT SO IS REGGIE!

NO KWIT

... AND THE ONLY SOLVENT FOR NO KWIT GLUE IS MORE NO KWIT GLUE!

THE End

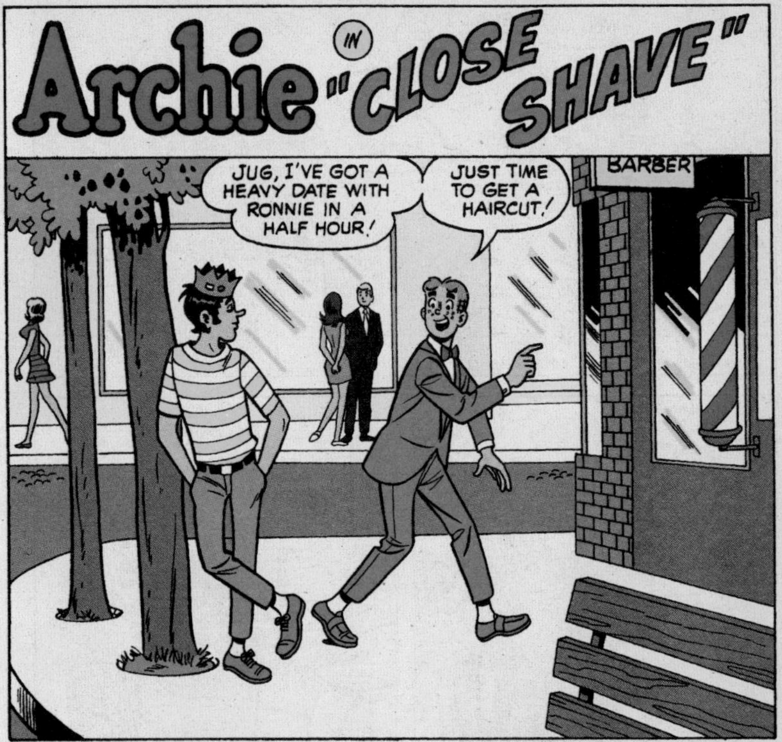
Archie
IN
"CLOSE SHAVE"
JUG, I'VE GOT A HEAVY DATE WITH RONNIE IN A HALF HOUR!
JUST TIME TO GET A HAIRCUT!
BARBER

Script & Pencils: Al Hartley / Inks: Jon D'Agostino / Letters: Bill Yoshida / Colors: Carlos Antunes

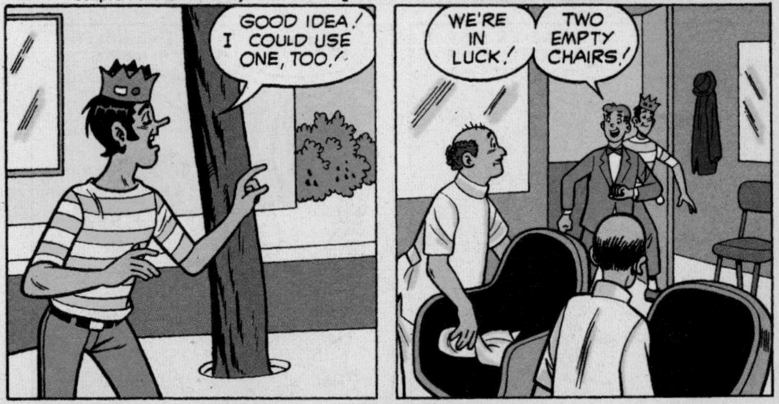
GOOD IDEA! I COULD USE ONE, TOO!
WE'RE IN LUCK!
TWO EMPTY CHAIRS!

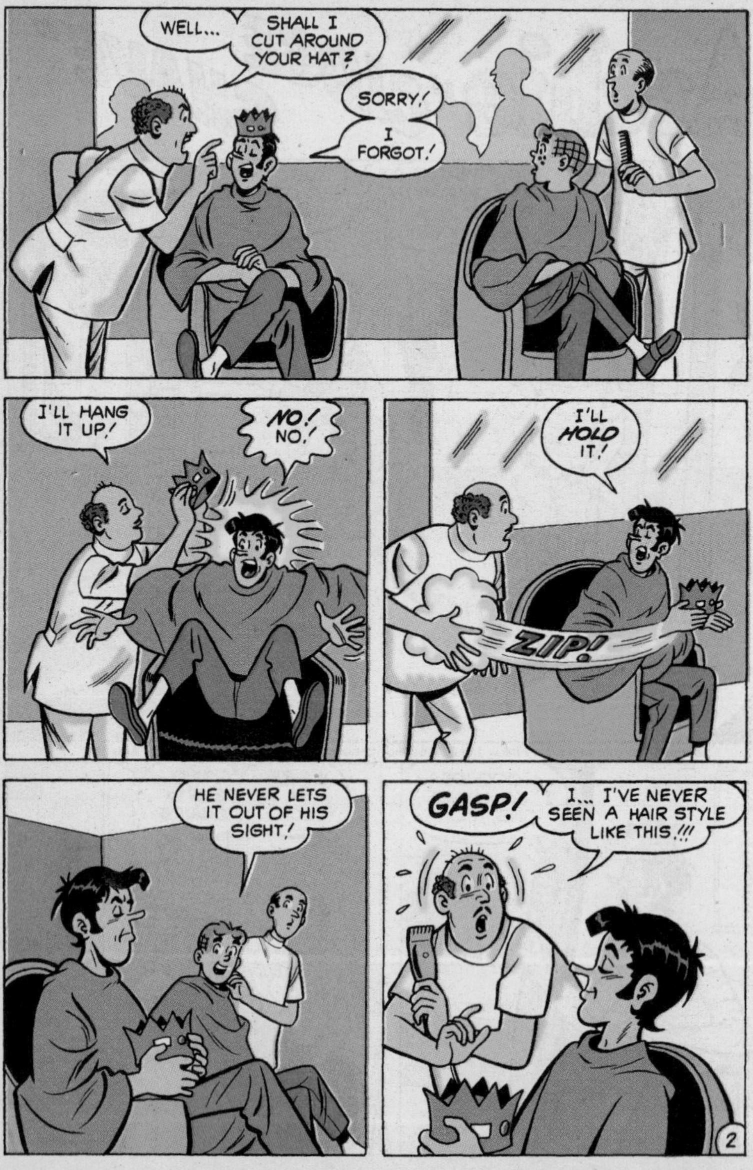
WELL...
SHALL I CUT AROUND YOUR HAT?
SORRY! I FORGOT!
I'LL HANG IT UP!
NO! NO!
I'LL HOLD IT!
ZIP!
HE NEVER LETS IT OUT OF HIS SIGHT!
GASP!
I... I'VE NEVER SEEN A HAIR STYLE LIKE THIS!!!
2

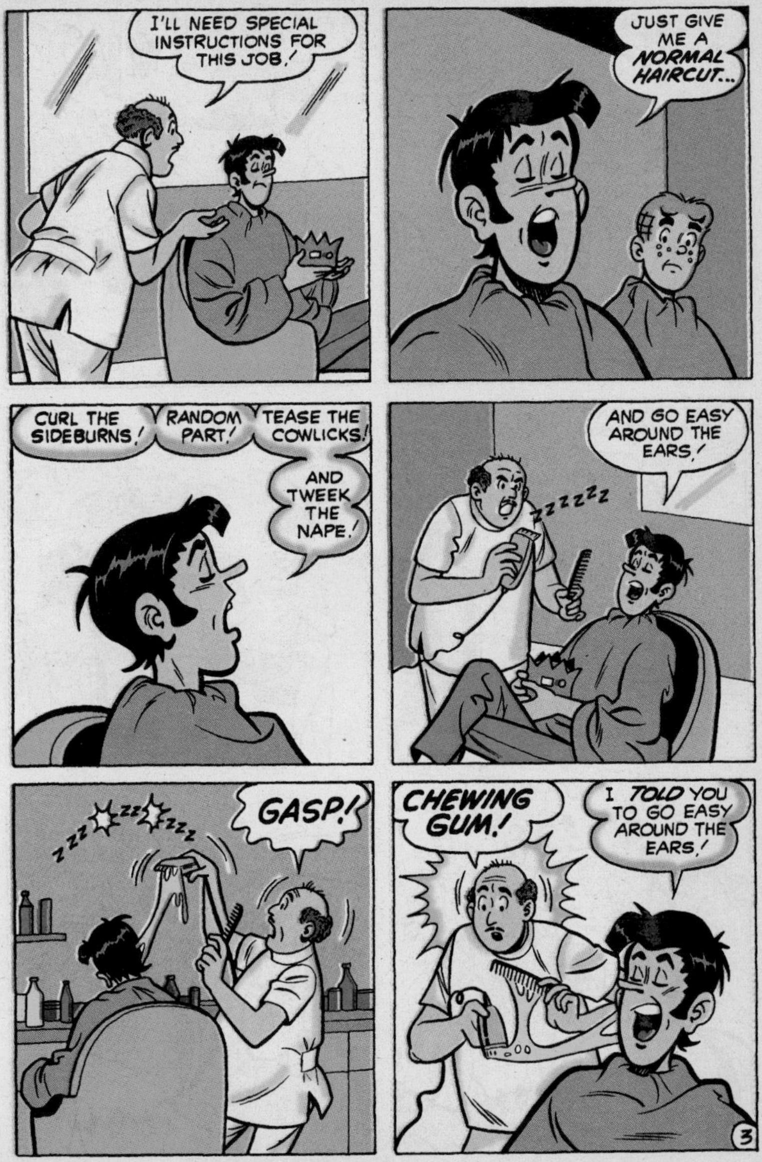
I'LL NEED SPECIAL INSTRUCTIONS FOR THIS JOB!
JUST GIVE ME A *NORMAL HAIRCUT*...
CURL THE SIDEBURNS!
RANDOM PART!
TEASE THE COWLICKS!
AND TWEEK THE NAPE!
AND GO EASY AROUND THE EARS!
ZZZZZZZ
GASP!
CHEWING GUM!
I *TOLD* YOU TO GO EASY AROUND THE EARS!
3

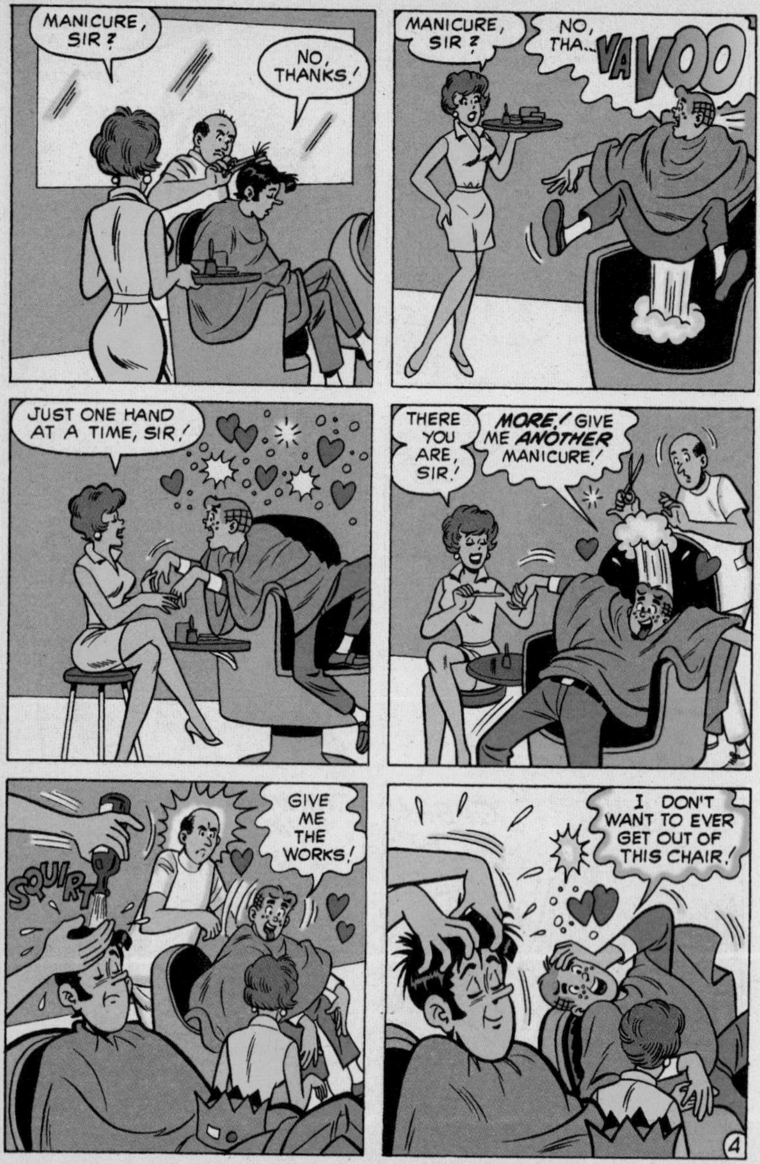
MANICURE, SIR?
NO, THANKS!
MANICURE, SIR?
NO, THA...
VAVOO
JUST ONE HAND AT A TIME, SIR!
THERE YOU ARE, SIR!
MORE! GIVE ME ANOTHER MANICURE!
GIVE ME THE WORKS!
SQUIRT
I DON'T WANT TO EVER GET OUT OF THIS CHAIR!
4

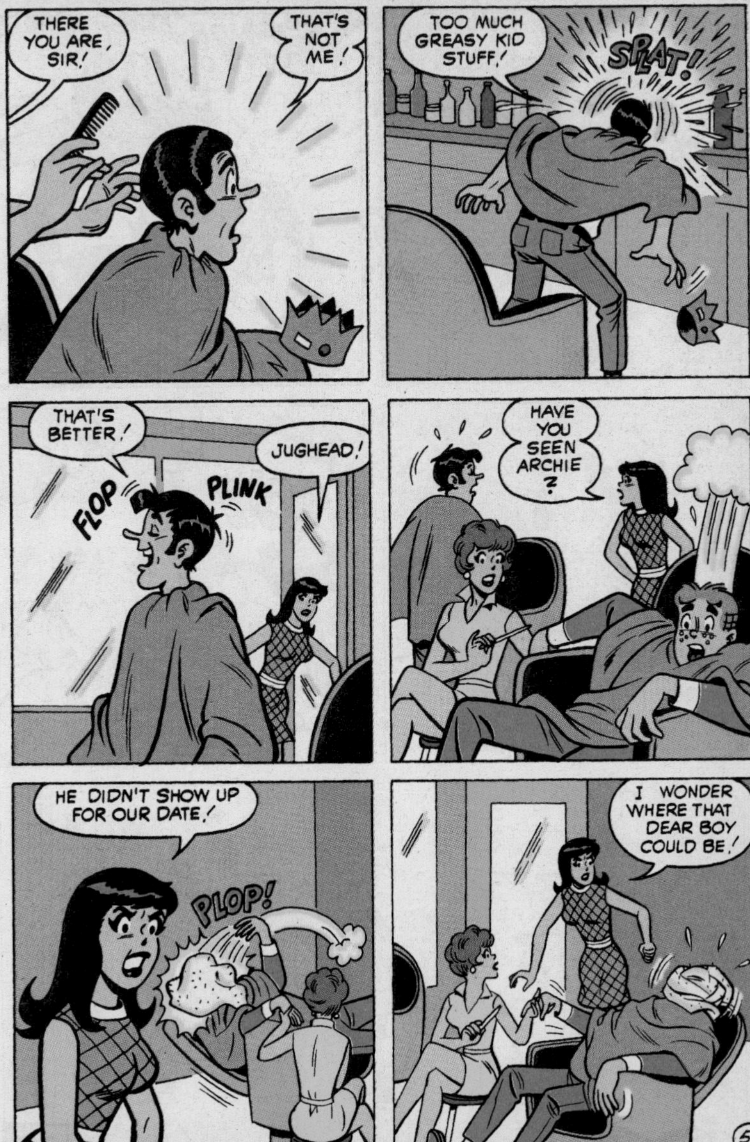
THERE YOU ARE, SIR!
THAT'S NOT ME!
TOO MUCH GREASY KID STUFF!
SPLAT!
THAT'S BETTER!
FLOP
PLINK
JUGHEAD!
HAVE YOU SEEN ARCHIE?
HE DIDN'T SHOW UP FOR OUR DATE!
PLOP!
I WONDER WHERE THAT DEAR BOY COULD BE!
5

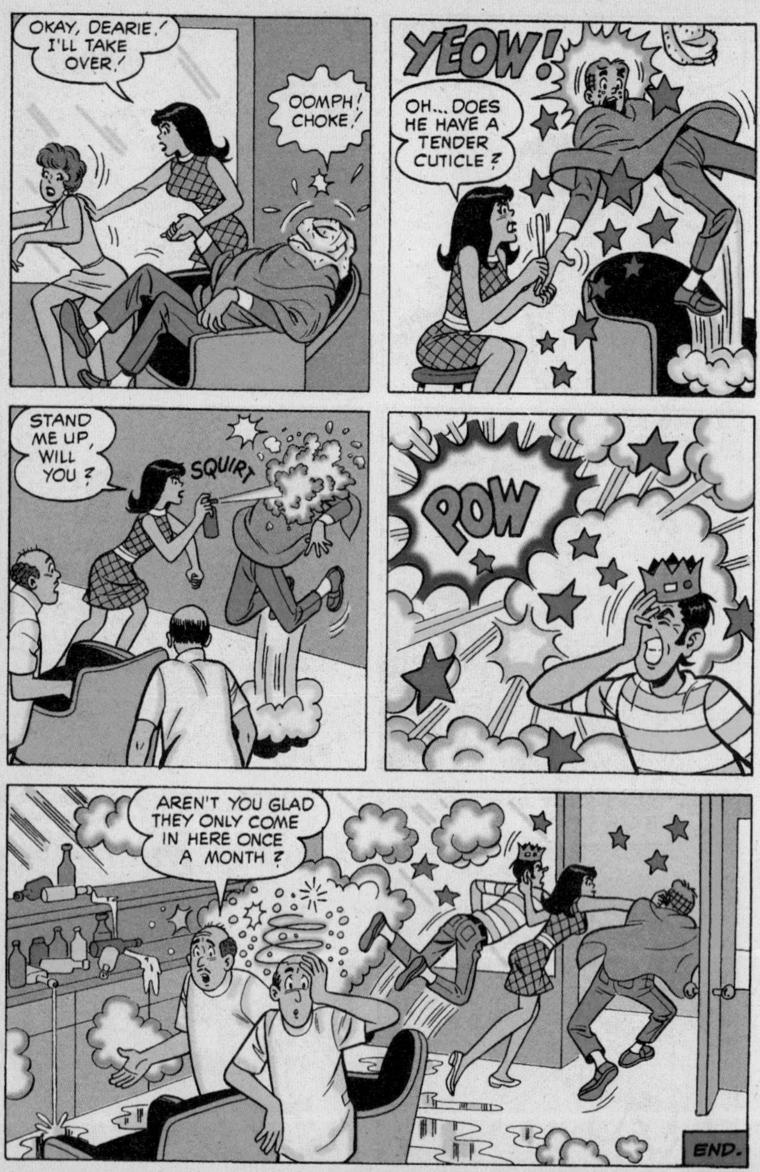

OKAY, DEARIE! I'LL TAKE OVER!
OOMPH! CHOKE!
YEOW!
OH... DOES HE HAVE A TENDER CUTICLE ?
STAND ME UP, WILL YOU ?
SQUIRT
POW
AREN'T YOU GLAD THEY ONLY COME IN HERE ONCE A MONTH ?
END.

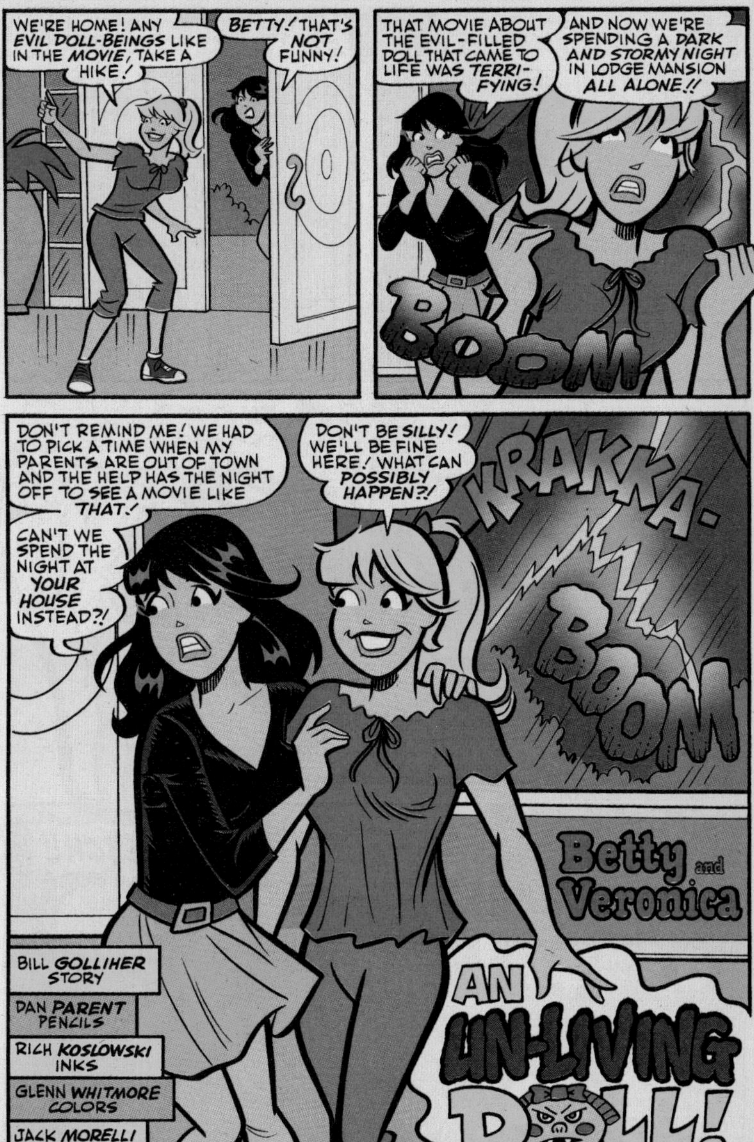
WE'RE HOME! ANY EVIL DOLL-BEINGS LIKE IN THE MOVIE, TAKE A HIKE!
BETTY! THAT'S NOT FUNNY!
THAT MOVIE ABOUT THE EVIL-FILLED DOLL THAT CAME TO LIFE WAS TERRI-FYING!
AND NOW WE'RE SPENDING A DARK AND STORMY NIGHT IN LODGE MANSION ALL ALONE!!
BOOM
DON'T REMIND ME! WE HAD TO PICK A TIME WHEN MY PARENTS ARE OUT OF TOWN AND THE HELP HAS THE NIGHT OFF TO SEE A MOVIE LIKE THAT!
CAN'T WE SPEND THE NIGHT AT YOUR HOUSE INSTEAD?!
DON'T BE SILLY! WE'LL BE FINE HERE! WHAT CAN POSSIBLY HAPPEN?!
KRAKKA-BOOM
Betty and Veronica
AN UN-LIVING DOLL!
BILL GOLLIHER STORY
DAN PARENT PENCILS
RICH KOSLOWSKI INKS
GLENN WHITMORE COLORS
JACK MORELLI LETTERS

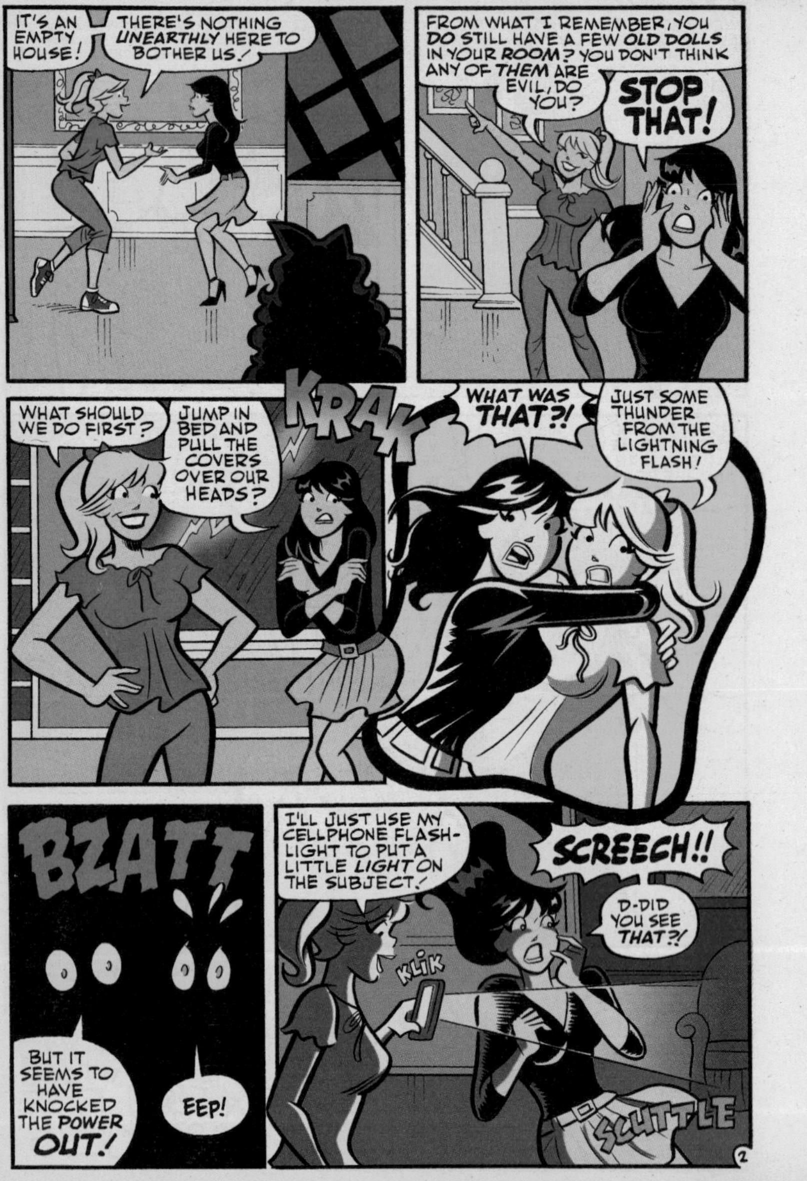
IT'S AN EMPTY HOUSE!
THERE'S NOTHING UNEARTHLY HERE TO BOTHER US.!
FROM WHAT I REMEMBER, YOU DO STILL HAVE A FEW OLD DOLLS IN YOUR ROOM? YOU DON'T THINK ANY OF THEM ARE EVIL, DO YOU?
STOP THAT!
KRAK
WHAT SHOULD WE DO FIRST?
JUMP IN BED AND PULL THE COVERS OVER OUR HEADS?
WHAT WAS THAT?!
JUST SOME THUNDER FROM THE LIGHTNING FLASH!
BZATT
BUT IT SEEMS TO HAVE KNOCKED THE POWER OUT!
EEP!
I'LL JUST USE MY CELLPHONE FLASH-LIGHT TO PUT A LITTLE LIGHT ON THE SUBJECT.!
SCREECH!!
D-DID YOU SEE THAT?!
KLIK
SCUTTLE

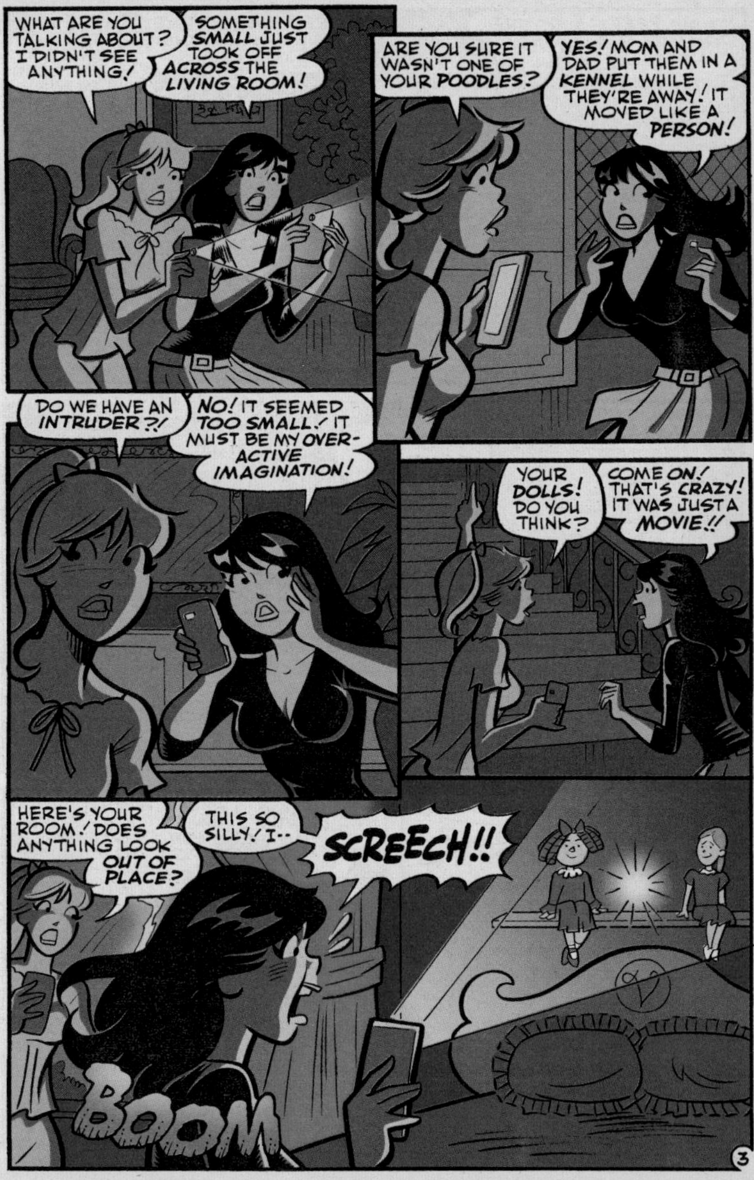

WHAT ARE YOU TALKING ABOUT? I DIDN'T SEE ANYTHING!
SOMETHING SMALL JUST TOOK OFF ACROSS THE LIVING ROOM!
ARE YOU SURE IT WASN'T ONE OF YOUR POODLES?
YES! MOM AND DAD PUT THEM IN A KENNEL WHILE THEY'RE AWAY! IT MOVED LIKE A PERSON!
DO WE HAVE AN INTRUDER?!
NO! IT SEEMED TOO SMALL! IT MUST BE MY OVER-ACTIVE IMAGINATION!
YOUR DOLLS! DO YOU THINK?
COME ON! THAT'S CRAZY! IT WAS JUST A MOVIE!!
HERE'S YOUR ROOM! DOES ANYTHING LOOK OUT OF PLACE?
THIS SO SILLY! I--
SCREECH!!
BOOM

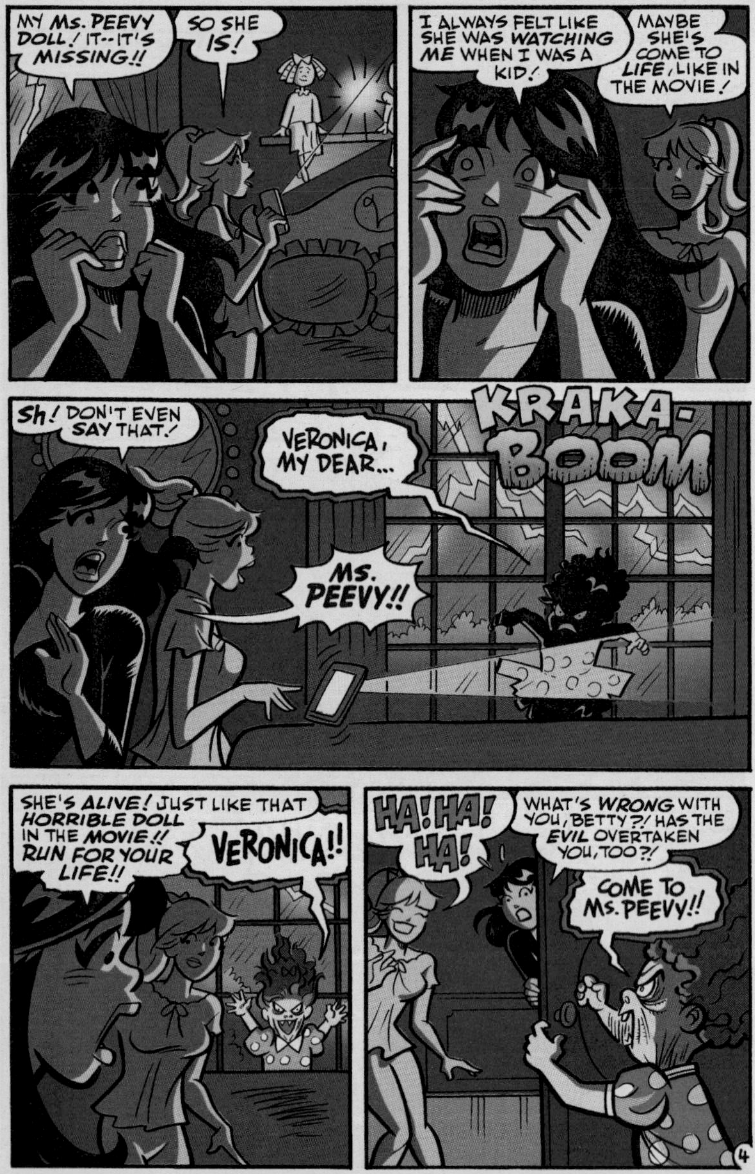
MY MS. PEEVY DOLL! IT--IT'S MISSING!!
SO SHE IS!
I ALWAYS FELT LIKE SHE WAS WATCHING ME WHEN I WAS A KID!
MAYBE SHE'S COME TO LIFE, LIKE IN THE MOVIE!
Sh! DON'T EVEN SAY THAT!
VERONICA, MY DEAR...
KRAKA-BOOM
MS. PEEVY!!
SHE'S ALIVE! JUST LIKE THAT HORRIBLE DOLL IN THE MOVIE!! RUN FOR YOUR LIFE!!
VERONICA!!
HA! HA! HA!
WHAT'S WRONG WITH YOU, BETTY?! HAS THE EVIL OVERTAKEN YOU, TOO?!
COME TO MS. PEEVY!!
4

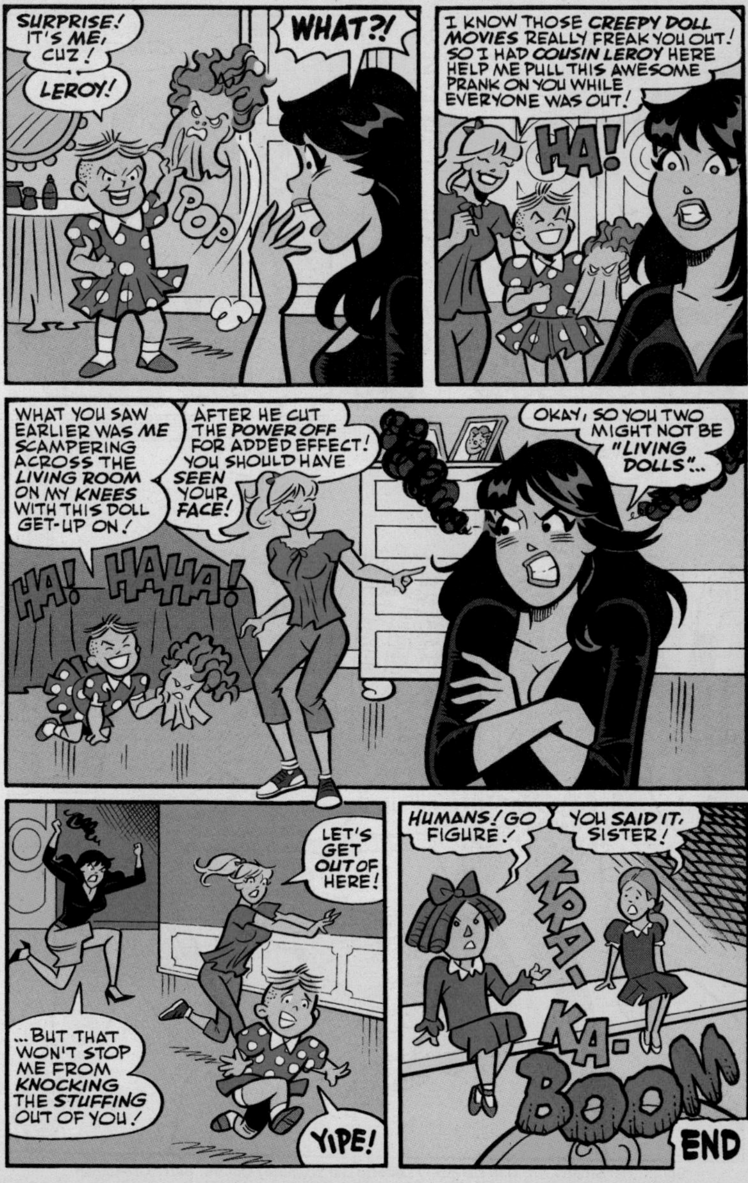

SURPRISE! IT'S ME, CUZ!
LEROY!
WHAT?!
POP
I KNOW THOSE CREEPY DOLL MOVIES REALLY FREAK YOU OUT! SO I HAD COUSIN LEROY HERE HELP ME PULL THIS AWESOME PRANK ON YOU WHILE EVERYONE WAS OUT!
HA!
WHAT YOU SAW EARLIER WAS ME SCAMPERING ACROSS THE LIVING ROOM ON MY KNEES WITH THIS DOLL GET-UP ON!
AFTER HE CUT THE POWER OFF FOR ADDED EFFECT! YOU SHOULD HAVE SEEN YOUR FACE!
OKAY, SO YOU TWO MIGHT NOT BE "LIVING DOLLS"...
HA! HAHA!
LET'S GET OUT OF HERE!
...BUT THAT WON'T STOP ME FROM KNOCKING THE STUFFING OUT OF YOU!
YIPE!
HUMANS! GO FIGURE!
YOU SAID IT, SISTER!
KRA-KA-BOOM
END

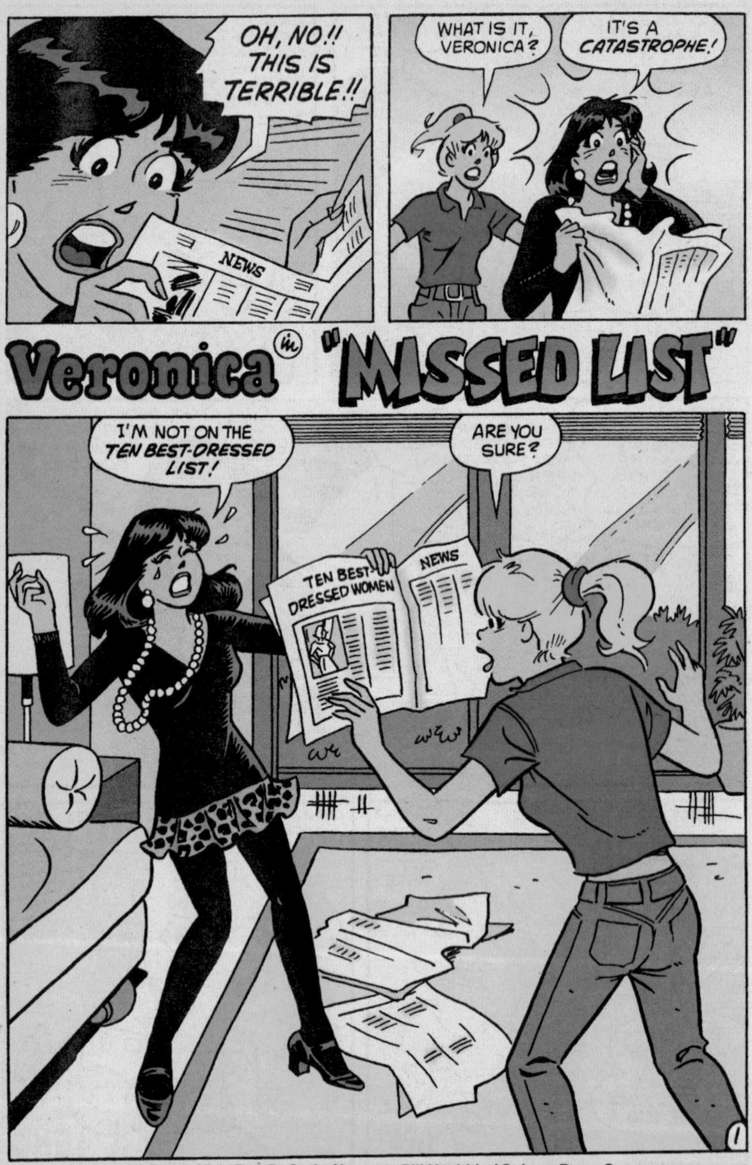
OH, NO!! THIS IS TERRIBLE!!
NEWS
WHAT IS IT, VERONICA?
IT'S A CATASTROPHE!
Veronica in "MISSED LIST"
I'M NOT ON THE TEN BEST-DRESSED LIST!
ARE YOU SURE?
NEWS
TEN BEST-DRESSED WOMEN
1

Script: Hal Smith / Art: Dan DeCarlo / Letters: Bill Yoshida / Colors: Barry Grossman

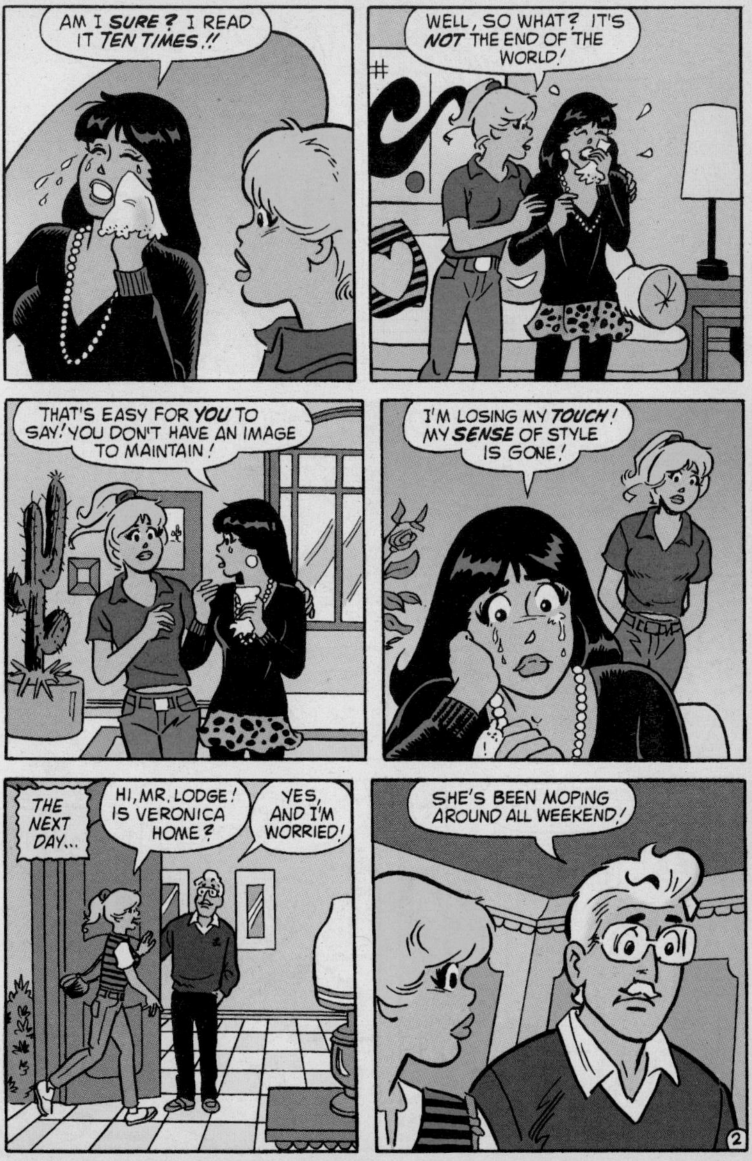

AM I SURE? I READ IT TEN TIMES.!!
WELL, SO WHAT? IT'S NOT THE END OF THE WORLD!
THAT'S EASY FOR YOU TO SAY! YOU DON'T HAVE AN IMAGE TO MAINTAIN!
I'M LOSING MY TOUCH! MY SENSE OF STYLE IS GONE!
THE NEXT DAY...
HI, MR. LODGE! IS VERONICA HOME?
YES, AND I'M WORRIED!
SHE'S BEEN MOPING AROUND ALL WEEKEND!
2

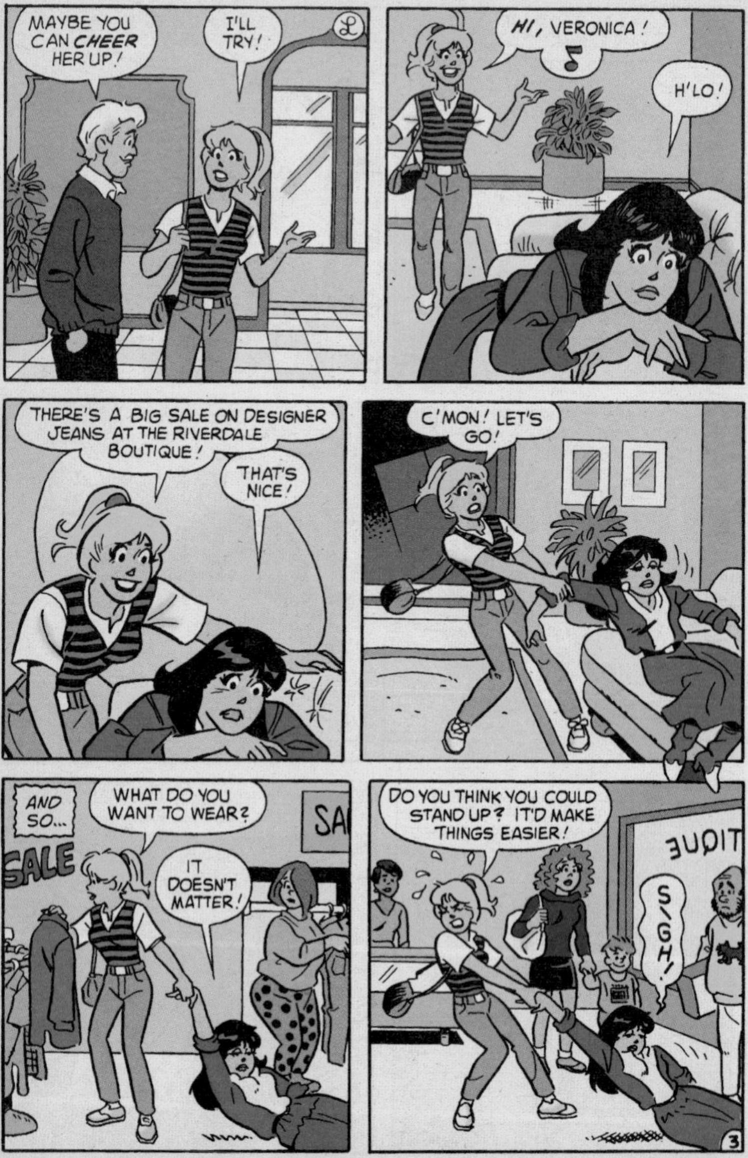

MAYBE YOU CAN CHEER HER UP!
I'LL TRY!
HI, VERONICA!
H'LO!
THERE'S A BIG SALE ON DESIGNER JEANS AT THE RIVERDALE BOUTIQUE!
THAT'S NICE!
C'MON! LET'S GO!
AND SO...
WHAT DO YOU WANT TO WEAR?
SALE
IT DOESN'T MATTER!
DO YOU THINK YOU COULD STAND UP? IT'D MAKE THINGS EASIER!
SIGH!

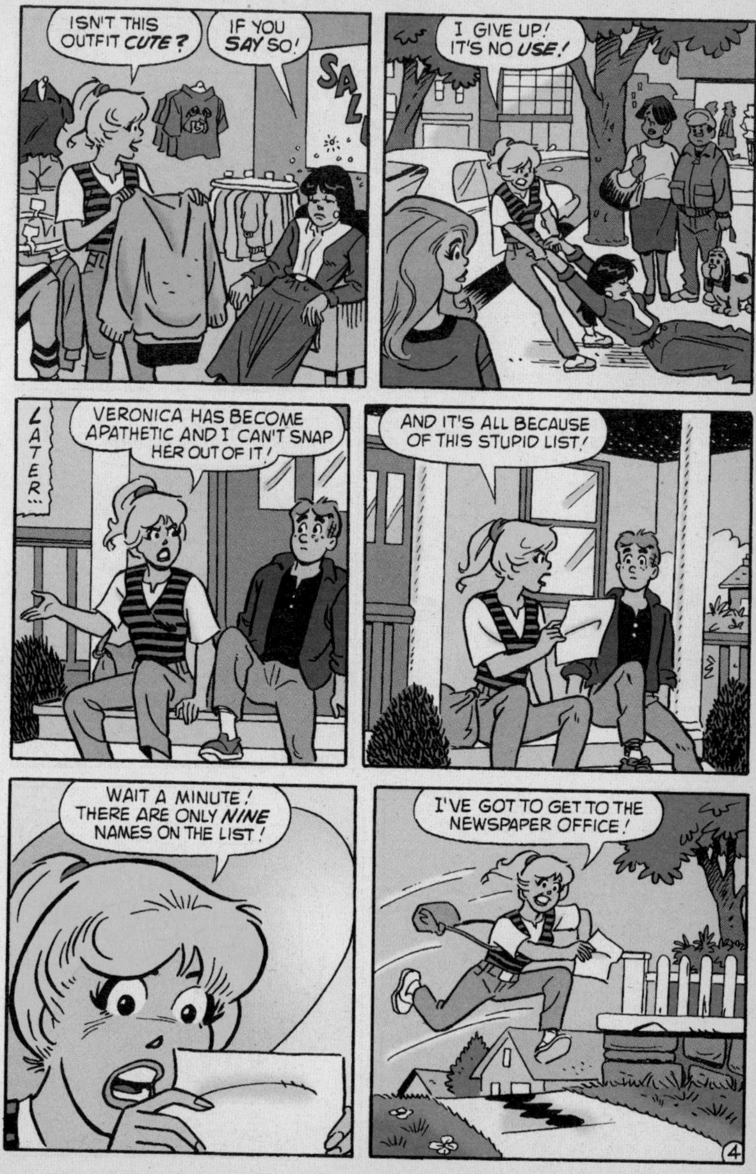

ISN'T THIS OUTFIT CUTE?
IF YOU SAY SO!
SAL
I GIVE UP! IT'S NO USE!
LATER...
VERONICA HAS BECOME APATHETIC AND I CAN'T SNAP HER OUT OF IT!
AND IT'S ALL BECAUSE OF THIS STUPID LIST!
WAIT A MINUTE! THERE ARE ONLY NINE NAMES ON THE LIST!
I'VE GOT TO GET TO THE NEWSPAPER OFFICE!
4

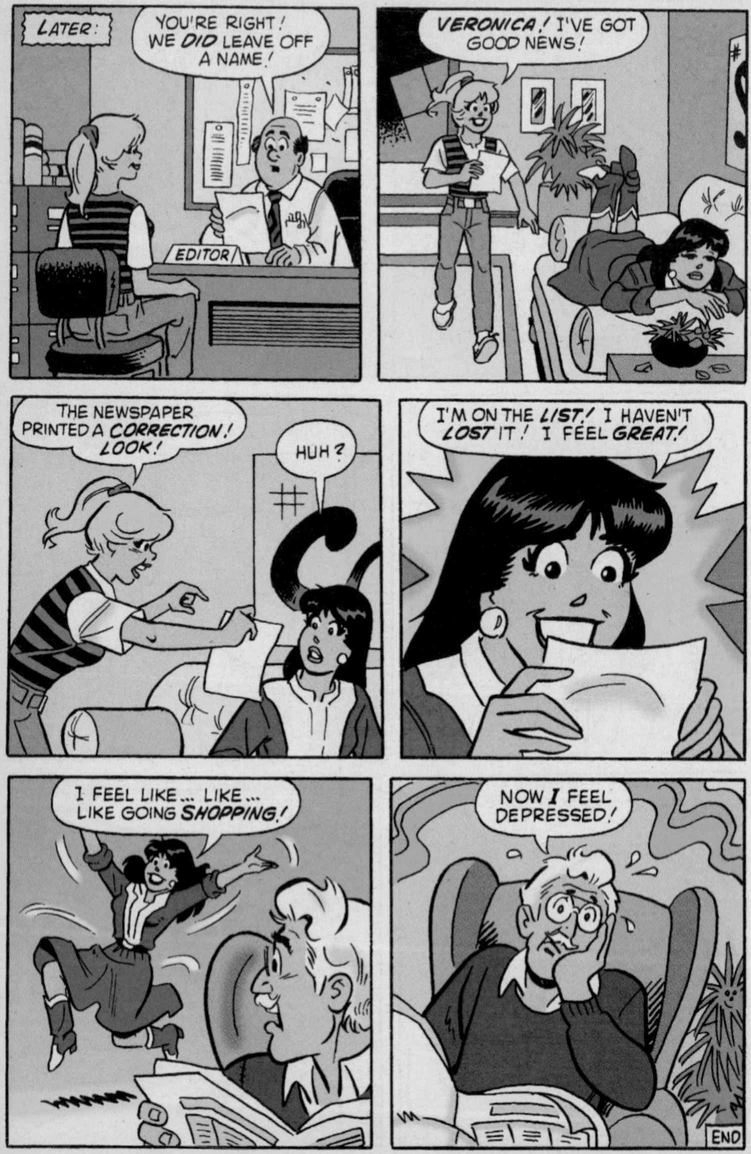
LATER:
YOU'RE RIGHT! WE DID LEAVE OFF A NAME!
EDITOR
VERONICA! I'VE GOT GOOD NEWS!
THE NEWSPAPER PRINTED A CORRECTION! LOOK!
HUH?
I'M ON THE LIST! I HAVEN'T LOST IT! I FEEL GREAT!
I FEEL LIKE... LIKE... LIKE GOING SHOPPING!
NOW I FEEL DEPRESSED!
END

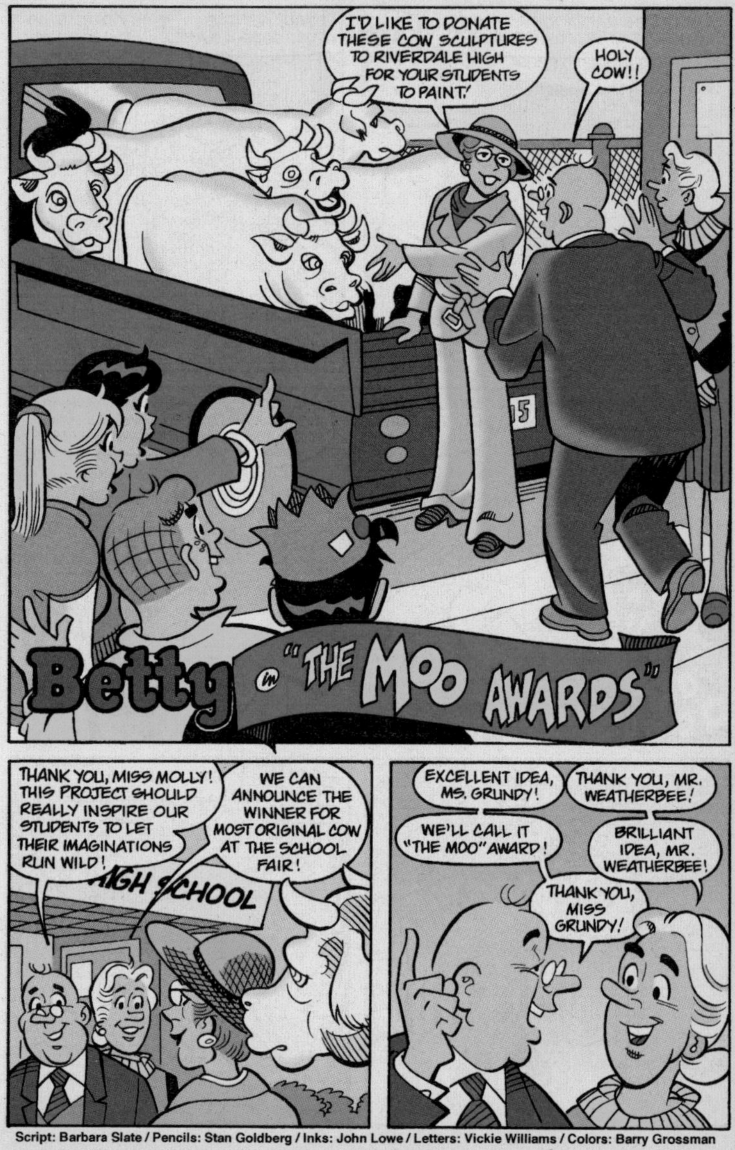
I'D LIKE TO DONATE THESE COW SCULPTURES TO RIVERDALE HIGH FOR YOUR STUDENTS TO PAINT!
HOLY COW!!
Betty in "THE MOO AWARDS"
THANK YOU, MISS MOLLY! THIS PROJECT SHOULD REALLY INSPIRE OUR STUDENTS TO LET THEIR IMAGINATIONS RUN WILD!
WE CAN ANNOUNCE THE WINNER FOR MOST ORIGINAL COW AT THE SCHOOL FAIR!
HIGH SCHOOL
EXCELLENT IDEA, MS. GRUNDY!
THANK YOU, MR. WEATHERBEE!
WE'LL CALL IT "THE MOO" AWARD!
BRILLIANT IDEA, MR. WEATHERBEE!
THANK YOU, MISS GRUNDY!

Script: Barbara Slate / Pencils: Stan Goldberg / Inks: John Lowe / Letters: Vickie Williams / Colors: Barry Grossman

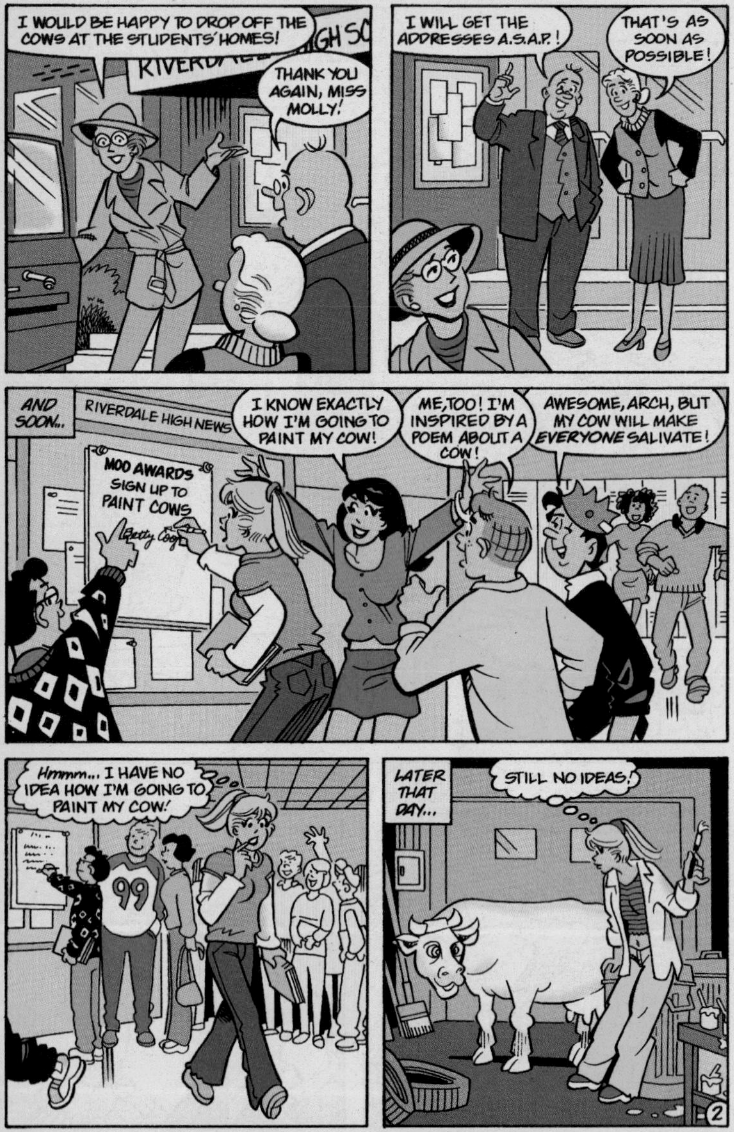
I WOULD BE HAPPY TO DROP OFF THE COWS AT THE STUDENTS' HOMES!
RIVERDALE HIGH SC
THANK YOU AGAIN, MISS MOLLY!
I WILL GET THE ADDRESSES A.S.A.P.!
THAT'S AS SOON AS POSSIBLE!
AND SOON...
RIVERDALE HIGH NEWS
MOO AWARDS SIGN UP TO PAINT COWS
Betty Coop
I KNOW EXACTLY HOW I'M GOING TO PAINT MY COW!
ME, TOO! I'M INSPIRED BY A POEM ABOUT A COW!
AWESOME, ARCH, BUT MY COW WILL MAKE EVERYONE SALIVATE!
Hmmm... I HAVE NO IDEA HOW I'M GOING TO PAINT MY COW!
99
LATER THAT DAY...
STILL NO IDEAS!
2

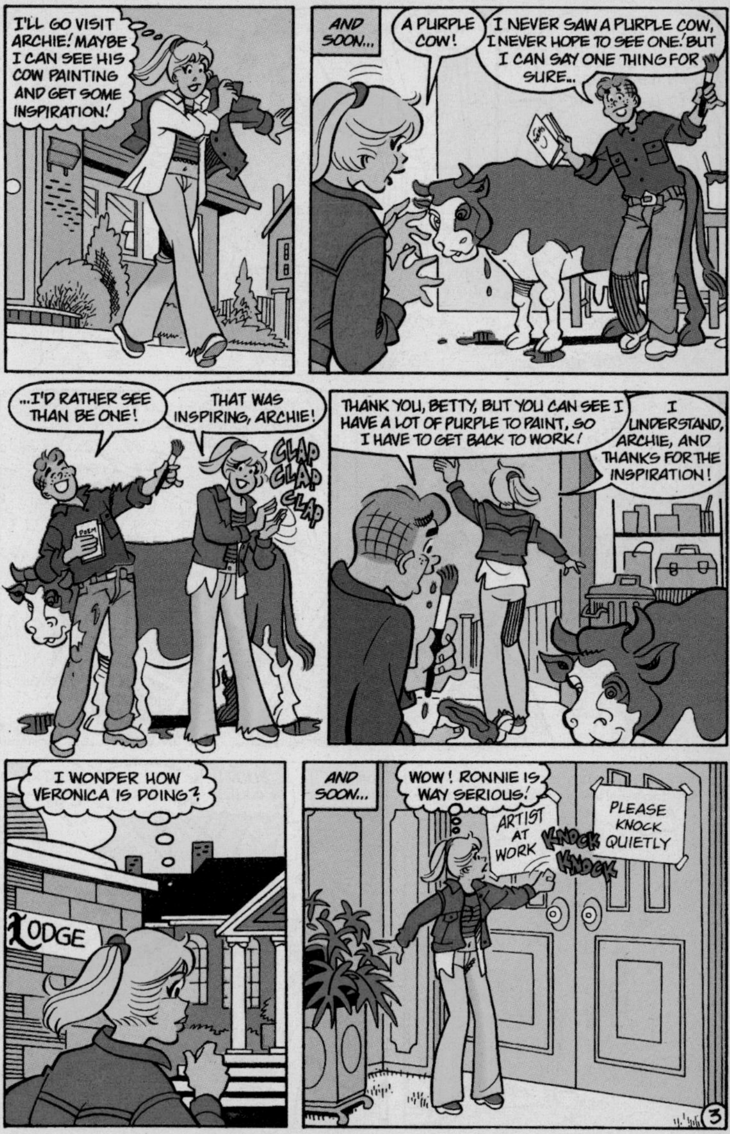
I'LL GO VISIT ARCHIE! MAYBE I CAN SEE HIS COW PAINTING AND GET SOME INSPIRATION!
AND SOON...
A PURPLE COW!
I NEVER SAW A PURPLE COW, I NEVER HOPE TO SEE ONE! BUT I CAN SAY ONE THING FOR SURE...
...I'D RATHER SEE THAN BE ONE!
THAT WAS INSPIRING, ARCHIE!
CLAP CLAP CLAP
POEM
THANK YOU, BETTY, BUT YOU CAN SEE I HAVE A LOT OF PURPLE TO PAINT, SO I HAVE TO GET BACK TO WORK!
I UNDERSTAND, ARCHIE, AND THANKS FOR THE INSPIRATION!
I WONDER HOW VERONICA IS DOING?
LODGE
AND SOON...
WOW! RONNIE IS WAY SERIOUS!
ARTIST AT WORK
PLEASE KNOCK QUIETLY
KNOCK KNOCK

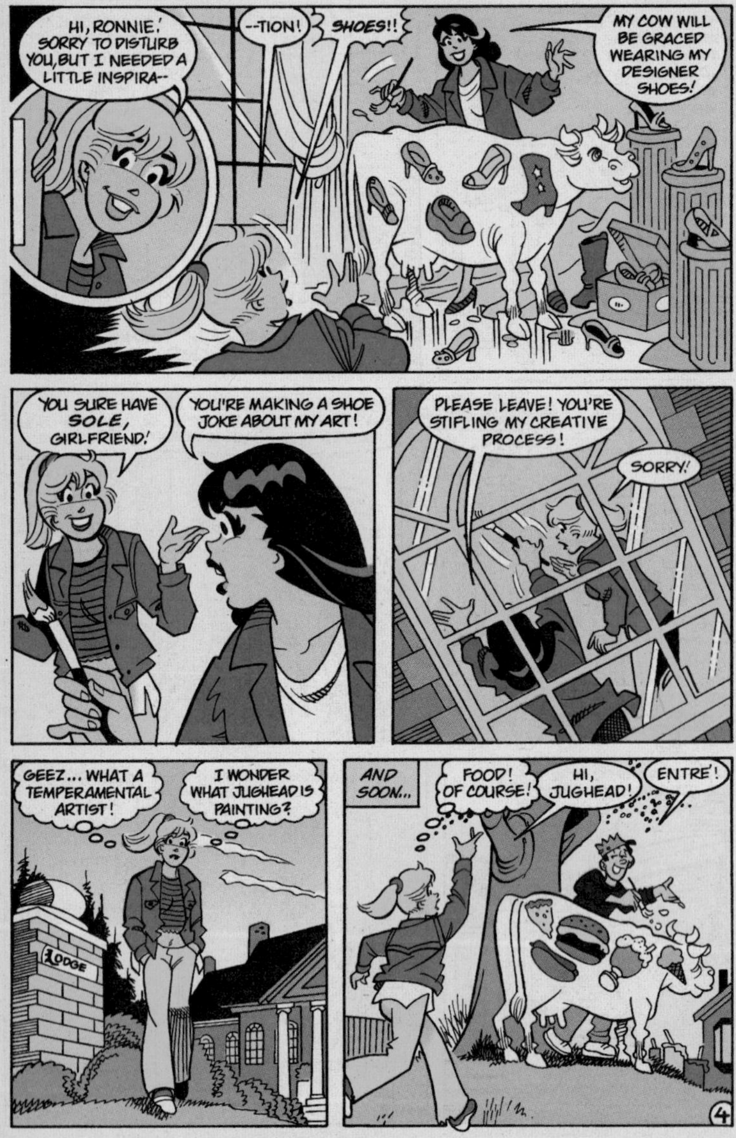
HI, RONNIE! SORRY TO DISTURB YOU, BUT I NEEDED A LITTLE INSPIRA--
--TION!
SHOES!!
MY COW WILL BE GRACED WEARING MY DESIGNER SHOES!
YOU SURE HAVE SOLE, GIRLFRIEND!
YOU'RE MAKING A SHOE JOKE ABOUT MY ART!
PLEASE LEAVE! YOU'RE STIFLING MY CREATIVE PROCESS!
SORRY!
GEEZ... WHAT A TEMPERAMENTAL ARTIST!
I WONDER WHAT JUGHEAD IS PAINTING?
LODGE
AND SOON...
FOOD! OF COURSE!
HI, JUGHEAD!
ENTRE'!
4

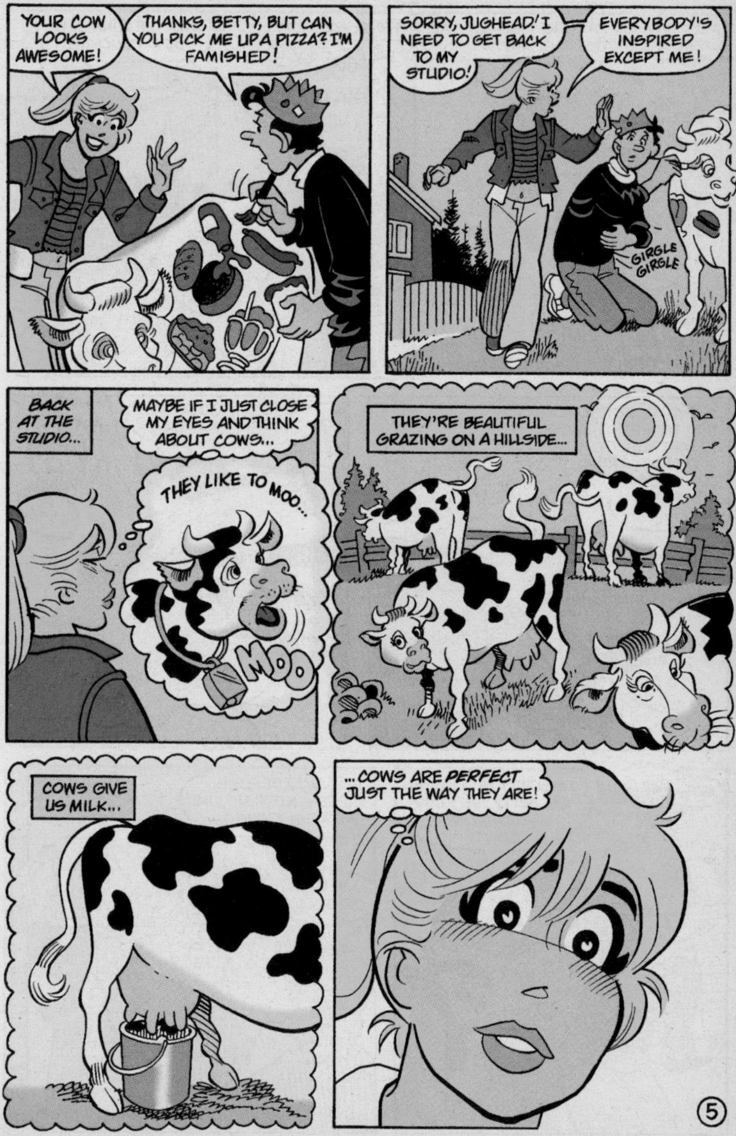
YOUR COW LOOKS AWESOME!
THANKS, BETTY, BUT CAN YOU PICK ME UP A PIZZA? I'M FAMISHED!
SORRY, JUGHEAD! I NEED TO GET BACK TO MY STUDIO!
EVERYBODY'S INSPIRED EXCEPT ME!
GIRGLE GIRGLE
BACK AT THE STUDIO...
MAYBE IF I JUST CLOSE MY EYES AND THINK ABOUT COWS...
THEY LIKE TO MOO...
MOO
THEY'RE BEAUTIFUL GRAZING ON A HILLSIDE...
COWS GIVE US MILK...
...COWS ARE PERFECT JUST THE WAY THEY ARE!
5

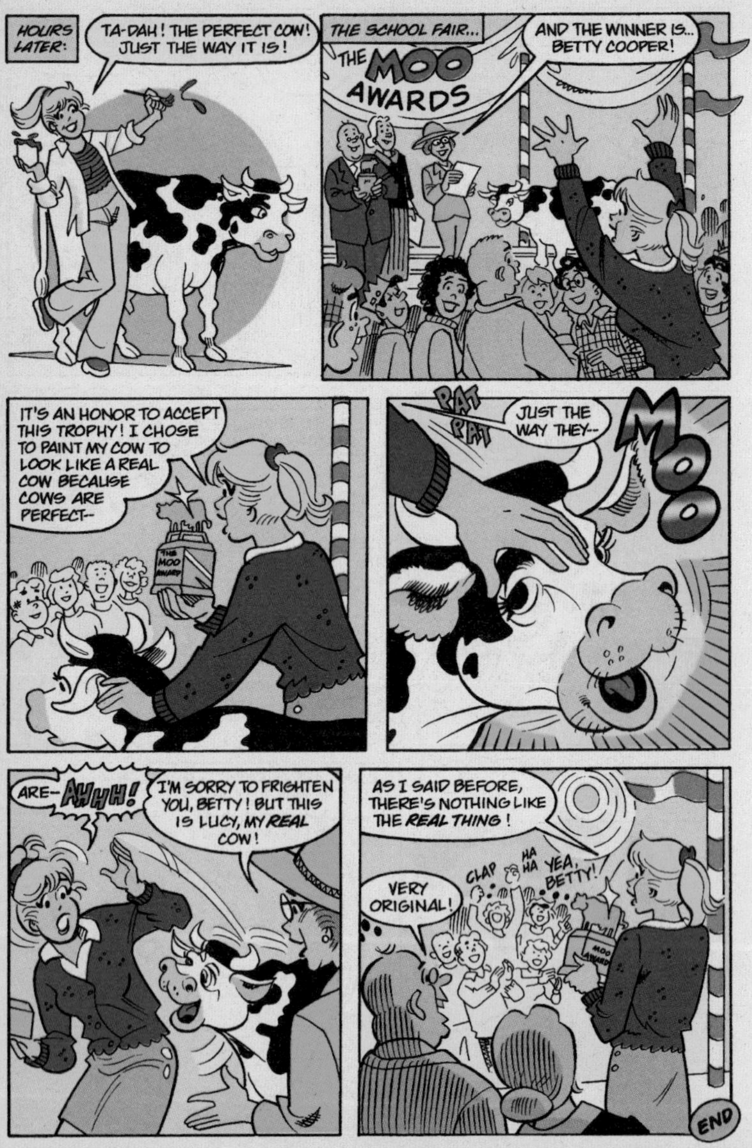
HOURS LATER:
TA-DAH! THE PERFECT COW! JUST THE WAY IT IS!
THE SCHOOL FAIR...
THE MOO AWARDS
AND THE WINNER IS... BETTY COOPER!
IT'S AN HONOR TO ACCEPT THIS TROPHY! I CHOSE TO PAINT MY COW TO LOOK LIKE A REAL COW BECAUSE COWS ARE PERFECT--
THE MOO AWARD
PAT PAT
JUST THE WAY THEY--
MOO
ARE-- AHHH!
I'M SORRY TO FRIGHTEN YOU, BETTY! BUT THIS IS LUCY, MY REAL COW!
AS I SAID BEFORE, THERE'S NOTHING LIKE THE REAL THING!
CLAP
HA HA
YEA, BETTY!
VERY ORIGINAL!
MOO AWARD
END

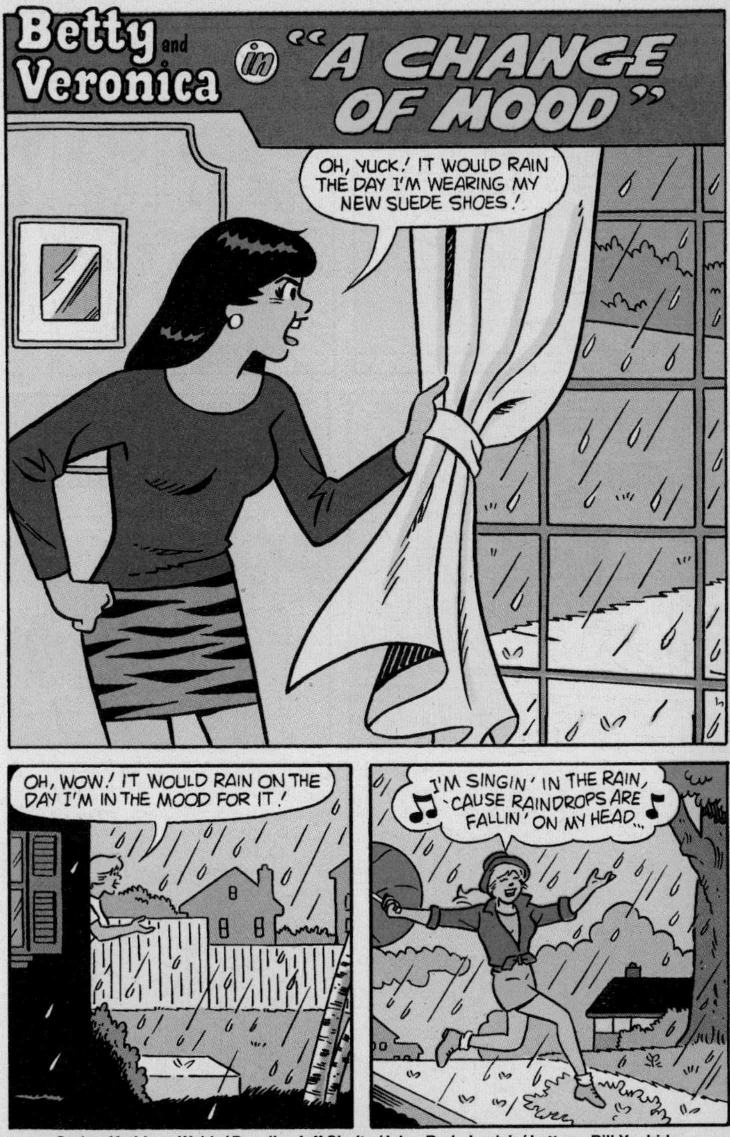
Betty and Veronica in "A CHANGE OF MOOD"
OH, YUCK! IT WOULD RAIN THE DAY I'M WEARING MY NEW SUEDE SHOES!
OH, WOW! IT WOULD RAIN ON THE DAY I'M IN THE MOOD FOR IT!
I'M SINGIN' IN THE RAIN, 'CAUSE RAINDROPS ARE FALLIN' ON MY HEAD...

Script: Kathleen Webb / Pencils: Jeff Shultz / Inks: Rudy Lapick / Letters: Bill Yoshida

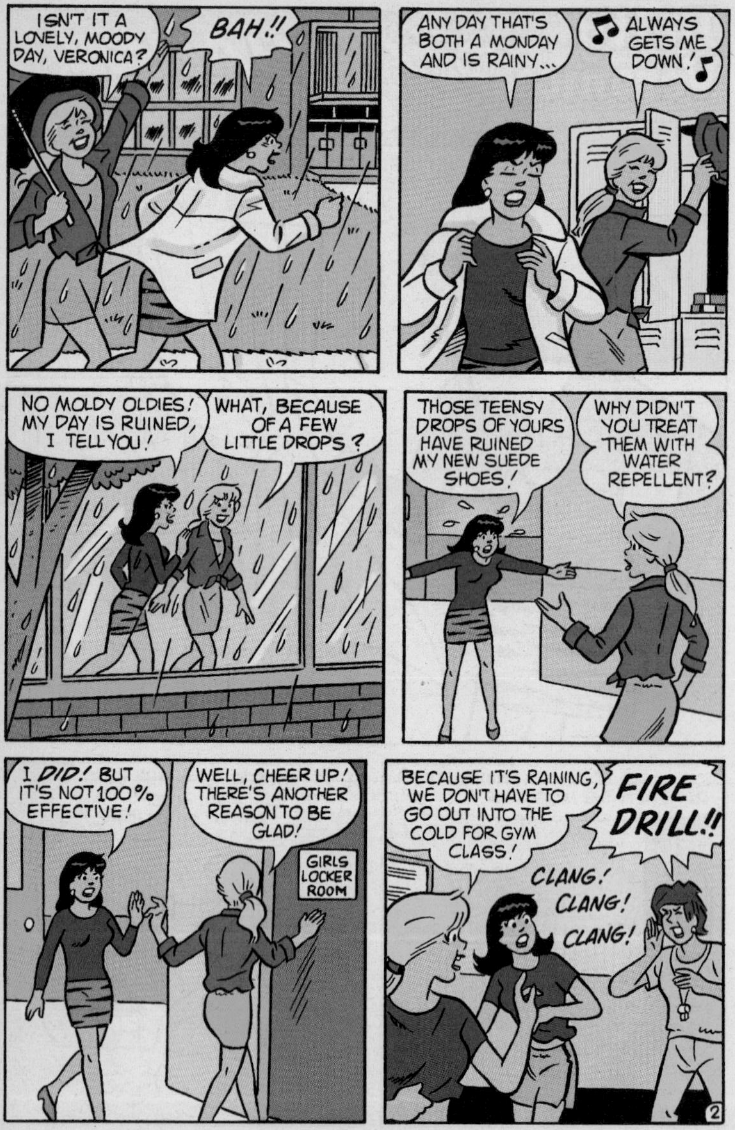
ISN'T IT A LOVELY, MOODY DAY, VERONICA?
BAH!!
ANY DAY THAT'S BOTH A MONDAY AND IS RAINY...
ALWAYS GETS ME DOWN!
NO MOLDY OLDIES! MY DAY IS RUINED, I TELL YOU!
WHAT, BECAUSE OF A FEW LITTLE DROPS?
THOSE TEENSY DROPS OF YOURS HAVE RUINED MY NEW SUEDE SHOES!
WHY DIDN'T YOU TREAT THEM WITH WATER REPELLENT?
I DID! BUT IT'S NOT 100% EFFECTIVE!
WELL, CHEER UP! THERE'S ANOTHER REASON TO BE GLAD!
GIRLS LOCKER ROOM
BECAUSE IT'S RAINING, WE DON'T HAVE TO GO OUT INTO THE COLD FOR GYM CLASS!
FIRE DRILL!!
CLANG! CLANG! CLANG!
2

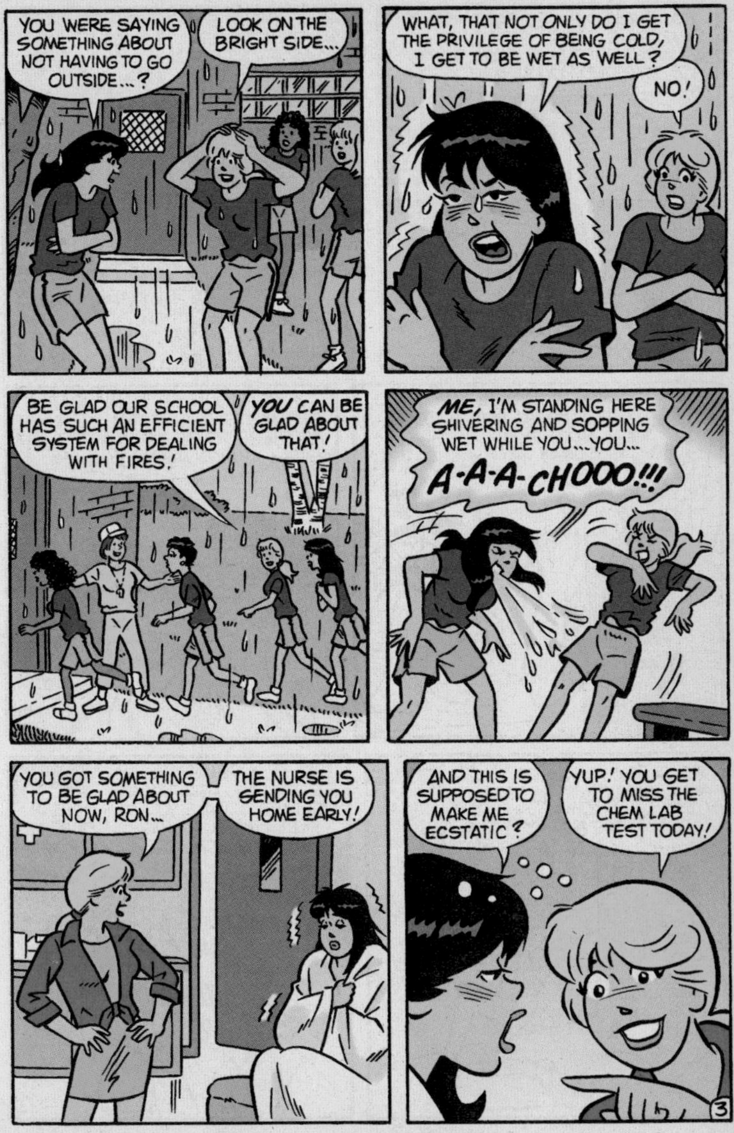

YOU WERE SAYING SOMETHING ABOUT NOT HAVING TO GO OUTSIDE...?
LOOK ON THE BRIGHT SIDE...
WHAT, THAT NOT ONLY DO I GET THE PRIVILEGE OF BEING COLD, I GET TO BE WET AS WELL?
NO!
BE GLAD OUR SCHOOL HAS SUCH AN EFFICIENT SYSTEM FOR DEALING WITH FIRES!
YOU CAN BE GLAD ABOUT THAT!
ME, I'M STANDING HERE SHIVERING AND SOPPING WET WHILE YOU...YOU...
A-A-A-CHOOO!!!
YOU GOT SOMETHING TO BE GLAD ABOUT NOW, RON...
THE NURSE IS SENDING YOU HOME EARLY!
AND THIS IS SUPPOSED TO MAKE ME ECSTATIC?
YUP! YOU GET TO MISS THE CHEM LAB TEST TODAY!
3

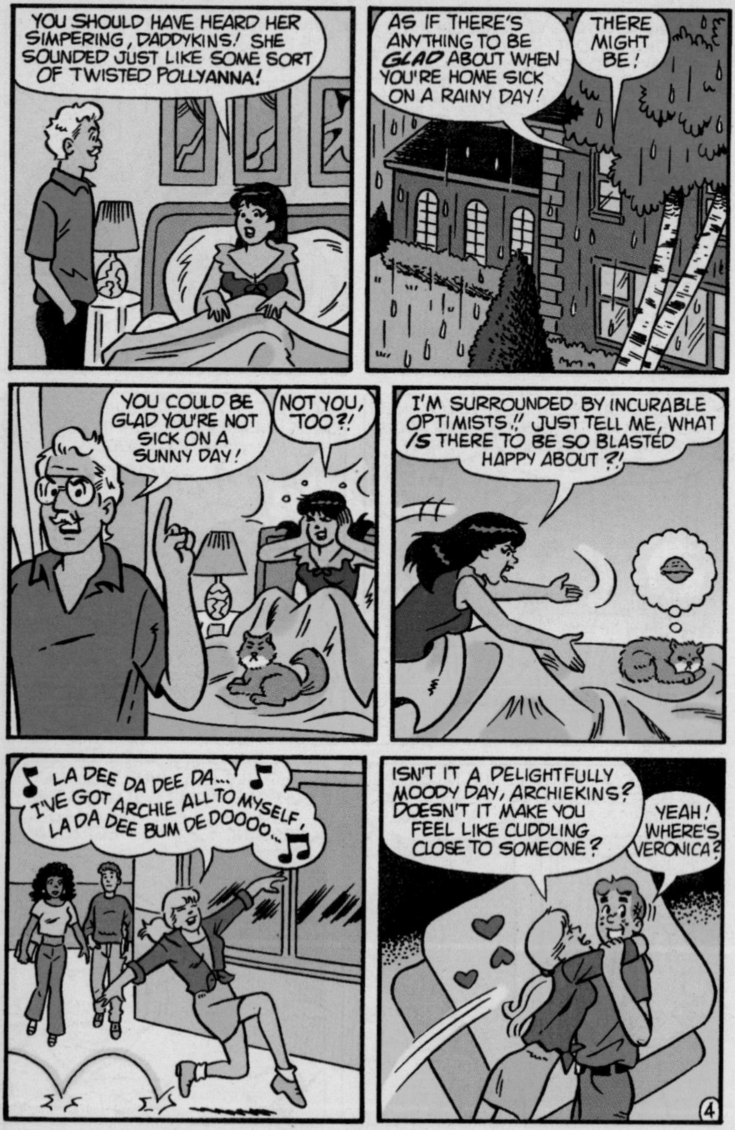
YOU SHOULD HAVE HEARD HER SIMPERING, DADDYKINS! SHE SOUNDED JUST LIKE SOME SORT OF TWISTED POLLYANNA!
AS IF THERE'S ANYTHING TO BE GLAD ABOUT WHEN YOU'RE HOME SICK ON A RAINY DAY!
THERE MIGHT BE!
YOU COULD BE GLAD YOU'RE NOT SICK ON A SUNNY DAY!
NOT YOU, TOO?!
I'M SURROUNDED BY INCURABLE OPTIMISTS!! JUST TELL ME, WHAT IS THERE TO BE SO BLASTED HAPPY ABOUT?!
LA DEE DA DEE DA... I'VE GOT ARCHIE ALL TO MYSELF, LA DA DEE BUM DE DOOOO...
ISN'T IT A DELIGHTFULLY MOODY DAY, ARCHIEKINS? DOESN'T IT MAKE YOU FEEL LIKE CUDDLING CLOSE TO SOMEONE?
YEAH! WHERE'S VERONICA?
4

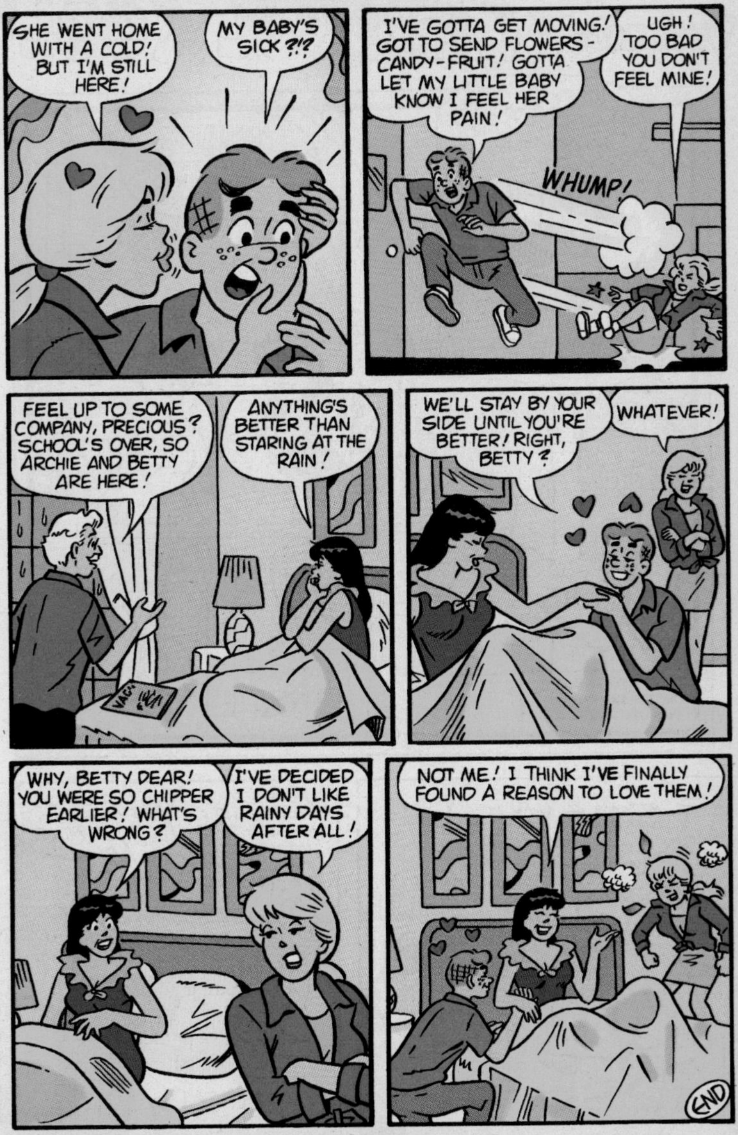
SHE WENT HOME WITH A COLD! BUT I'M STILL HERE!
MY BABY'S SICK?!?
I'VE GOTTA GET MOVING! GOT TO SEND FLOWERS - CANDY - FRUIT! GOTTA LET MY LITTLE BABY KNOW I FEEL HER PAIN!
UGH! TOO BAD YOU DON'T FEEL MINE!
WHUMP!
FEEL UP TO SOME COMPANY, PRECIOUS? SCHOOL'S OVER, SO ARCHIE AND BETTY ARE HERE!
ANYTHING'S BETTER THAN STARING AT THE RAIN!
WE'LL STAY BY YOUR SIDE UNTIL YOU'RE BETTER! RIGHT, BETTY?
WHATEVER!
WHY, BETTY DEAR! YOU WERE SO CHIPPER EARLIER! WHAT'S WRONG?
I'VE DECIDED I DON'T LIKE RAINY DAYS AFTER ALL!
NOT ME! I THINK I'VE FINALLY FOUND A REASON TO LOVE THEM!
END

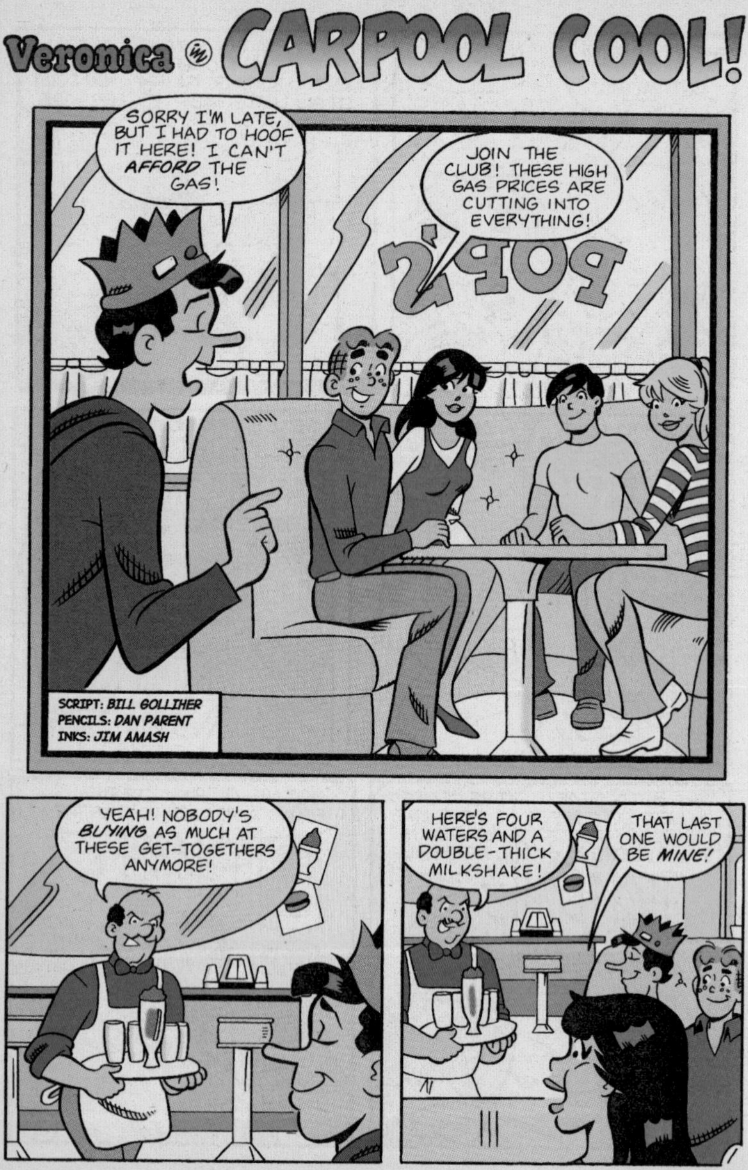
Veronica in CARPOOL COOL!
SORRY I'M LATE, BUT I HAD TO HOOF IT HERE! I CAN'T AFFORD THE GAS!
JOIN THE CLUB! THESE HIGH GAS PRICES ARE CUTTING INTO EVERYTHING!
POP'S
SCRIPT: BILL GOLLIHER
PENCILS: DAN PARENT
INKS: JIM AMASH
YEAH! NOBODY'S BUYING AS MUCH AT THESE GET-TOGETHERS ANYMORE!
HERE'S FOUR WATERS AND A DOUBLE-THICK MILKSHAKE!
THAT LAST ONE WOULD BE MINE!

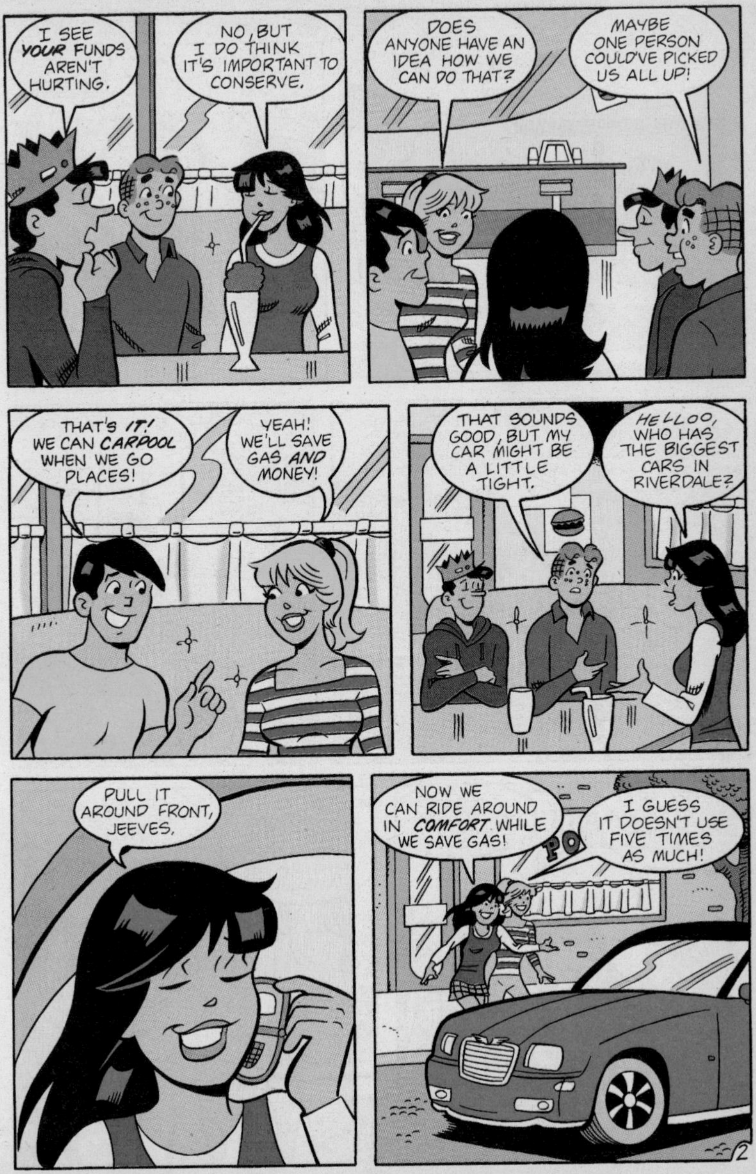
I SEE YOUR FUNDS AREN'T HURTING.
NO, BUT I DO THINK IT'S IMPORTANT TO CONSERVE.
DOES ANYONE HAVE AN IDEA HOW WE CAN DO THAT?
MAYBE ONE PERSON COULD'VE PICKED US ALL UP!
THAT'S IT! WE CAN CARPOOL WHEN WE GO PLACES!
YEAH! WE'LL SAVE GAS AND MONEY!
THAT SOUNDS GOOD, BUT MY CAR MIGHT BE A LITTLE TIGHT.
HELLOO, WHO HAS THE BIGGEST CARS IN RIVERDALE?
PULL IT AROUND FRONT, JEEVES.
NOW WE CAN RIDE AROUND IN COMFORT WHILE WE SAVE GAS!
I GUESS IT DOESN'T USE FIVE TIMES AS MUCH!

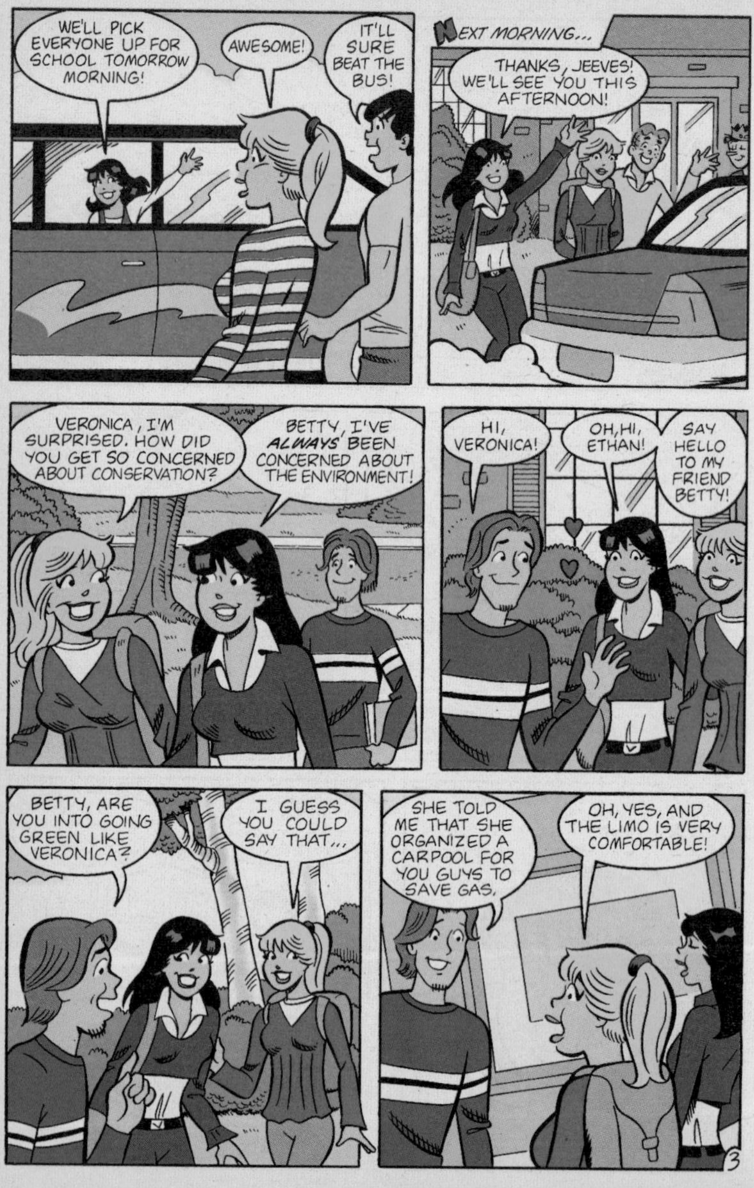

WE'LL PICK EVERYONE UP FOR SCHOOL TOMORROW MORNING!
AWESOME!
IT'LL SURE BEAT THE BUS!
NEXT MORNING...
THANKS, JEEVES! WE'LL SEE YOU THIS AFTERNOON!
VERONICA, I'M SURPRISED. HOW DID YOU GET SO CONCERNED ABOUT CONSERVATION?
BETTY, I'VE ALWAYS BEEN CONCERNED ABOUT THE ENVIRONMENT!
HI, VERONICA!
OH, HI, ETHAN!
SAY HELLO TO MY FRIEND BETTY!
BETTY, ARE YOU INTO GOING GREEN LIKE VERONICA?
I GUESS YOU COULD SAY THAT...
SHE TOLD ME THAT SHE ORGANIZED A CARPOOL FOR YOU GUYS TO SAVE GAS.
OH, YES, AND THE LIMO IS VERY COMFORTABLE!

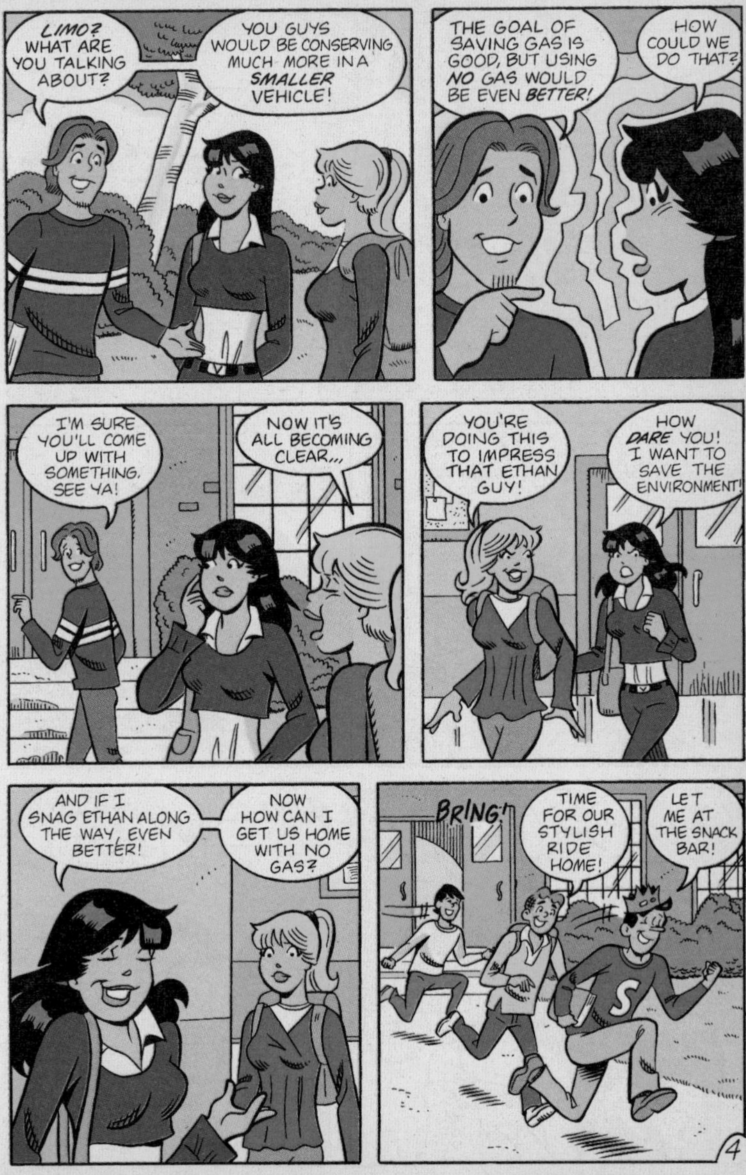
LIMO? WHAT ARE YOU TALKING ABOUT?
YOU GUYS WOULD BE CONSERVING MUCH MORE IN A SMALLER VEHICLE!
THE GOAL OF SAVING GAS IS GOOD, BUT USING NO GAS WOULD BE EVEN BETTER!
HOW COULD WE DO THAT?
I'M SURE YOU'LL COME UP WITH SOMETHING. SEE YA!
NOW IT'S ALL BECOMING CLEAR...
YOU'RE DOING THIS TO IMPRESS THAT ETHAN GUY!
HOW DARE YOU! I WANT TO SAVE THE ENVIRONMENT!
AND IF I SNAG ETHAN ALONG THE WAY, EVEN BETTER!
NOW HOW CAN I GET US HOME WITH NO GAS?
BRING!
TIME FOR OUR STYLISH RIDE HOME!
LET ME AT THE SNACK BAR!
4

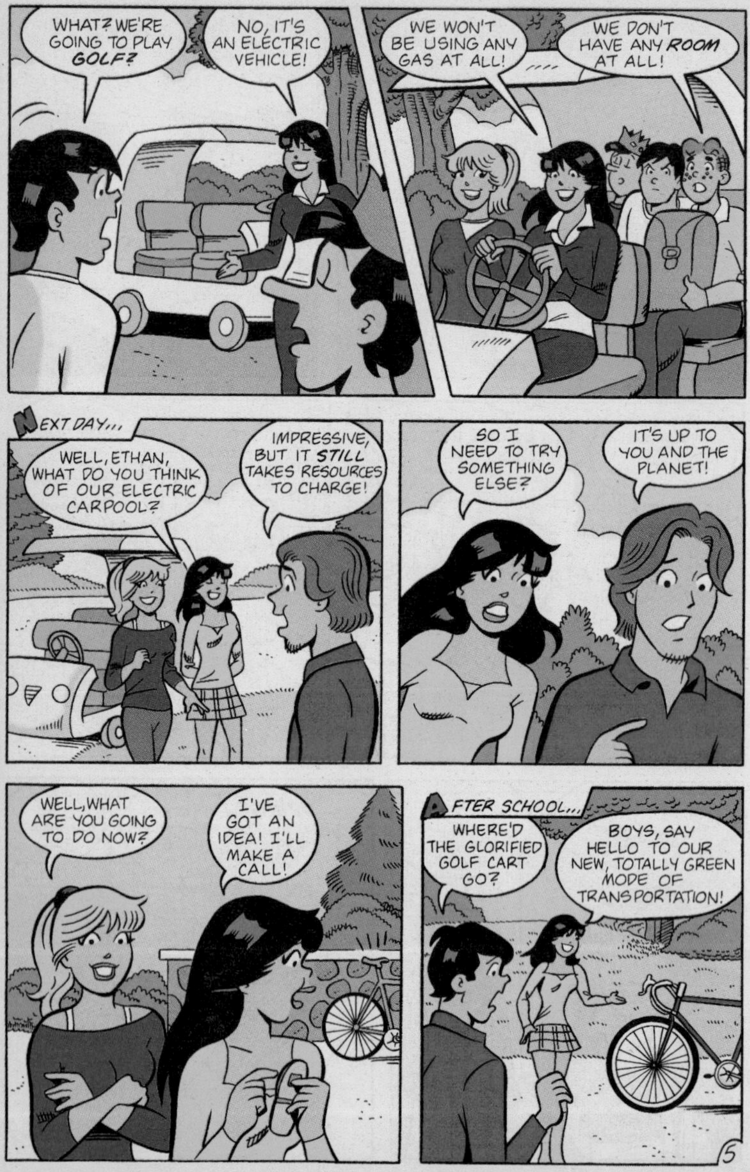

WHAT? WE'RE GOING TO PLAY GOLF?
NO, IT'S AN ELECTRIC VEHICLE!
WE WON'T BE USING ANY GAS AT ALL!
WE DON'T HAVE ANY ROOM AT ALL!
NEXT DAY...
WELL, ETHAN, WHAT DO YOU THINK OF OUR ELECTRIC CARPOOL?
IMPRESSIVE, BUT IT STILL TAKES RESOURCES TO CHARGE!
SO I NEED TO TRY SOMETHING ELSE?
IT'S UP TO YOU AND THE PLANET!
WELL, WHAT ARE YOU GOING TO DO NOW?
I'VE GOT AN IDEA! I'LL MAKE A CALL!
AFTER SCHOOL...
WHERE'D THE GLORIFIED GOLF CART GO?
BOYS, SAY HELLO TO OUR NEW, TOTALLY GREEN MODE OF TRANSPORTATION!

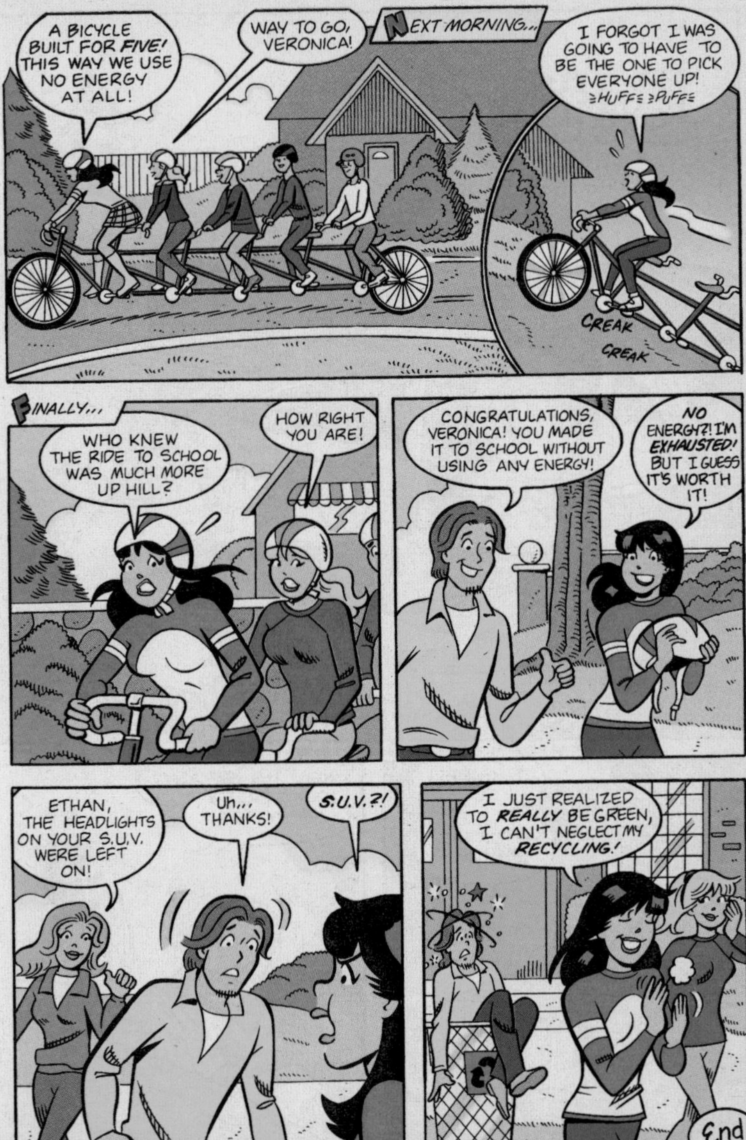
A BICYCLE BUILT FOR FIVE! THIS WAY WE USE NO ENERGY AT ALL!
WAY TO GO, VERONICA!
NEXT MORNING...
I FORGOT I WAS GOING TO HAVE TO BE THE ONE TO PICK EVERYONE UP!
HUFF PUFF
CREAK
CREAK
FINALLY...
WHO KNEW THE RIDE TO SCHOOL WAS MUCH MORE UP HILL?
HOW RIGHT YOU ARE!
CONGRATULATIONS, VERONICA! YOU MADE IT TO SCHOOL WITHOUT USING ANY ENERGY!
NO ENERGY?! I'M EXHAUSTED! BUT I GUESS IT'S WORTH IT!
ETHAN, THE HEADLIGHTS ON YOUR S.U.V. WERE LEFT ON!
Uh... THANKS!
S.U.V.?!
I JUST REALIZED TO REALLY BE GREEN, I CAN'T NEGLECT MY RECYCLING!
End

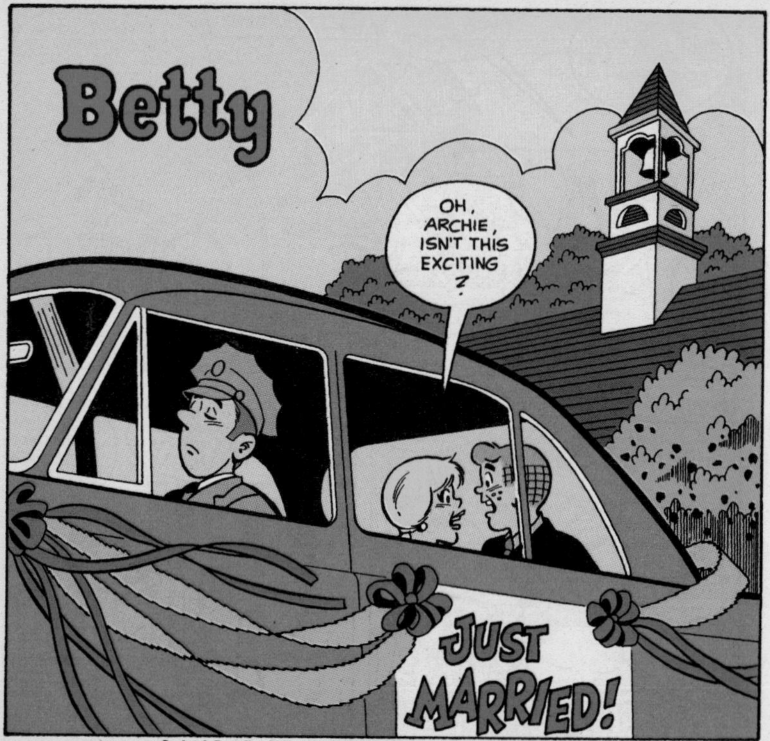
Betty
OH, ARCHIE, ISN'T THIS EXCITING?
JUST MARRIED!

Script & Pencils: Al Hartley / Inks: Jon D'Agostino / Letters: Bill Yoshida

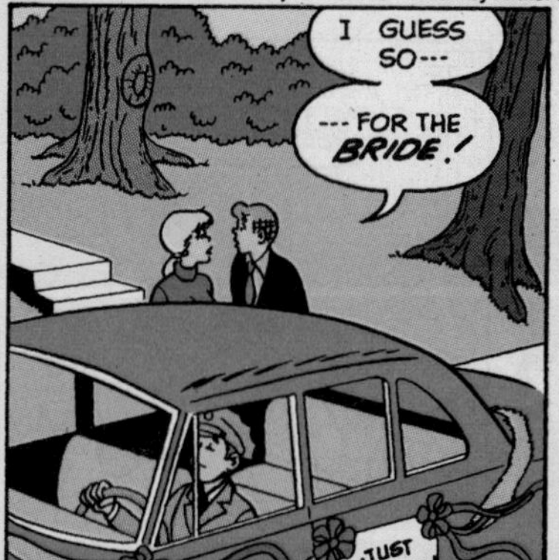
I GUESS SO---
--- FOR THE BRIDE!
JUST MARRIED!

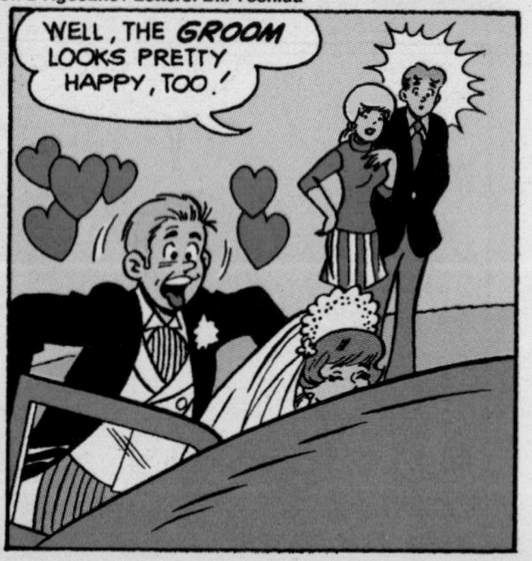
WELL, THE GROOM LOOKS PRETTY HAPPY, TOO!

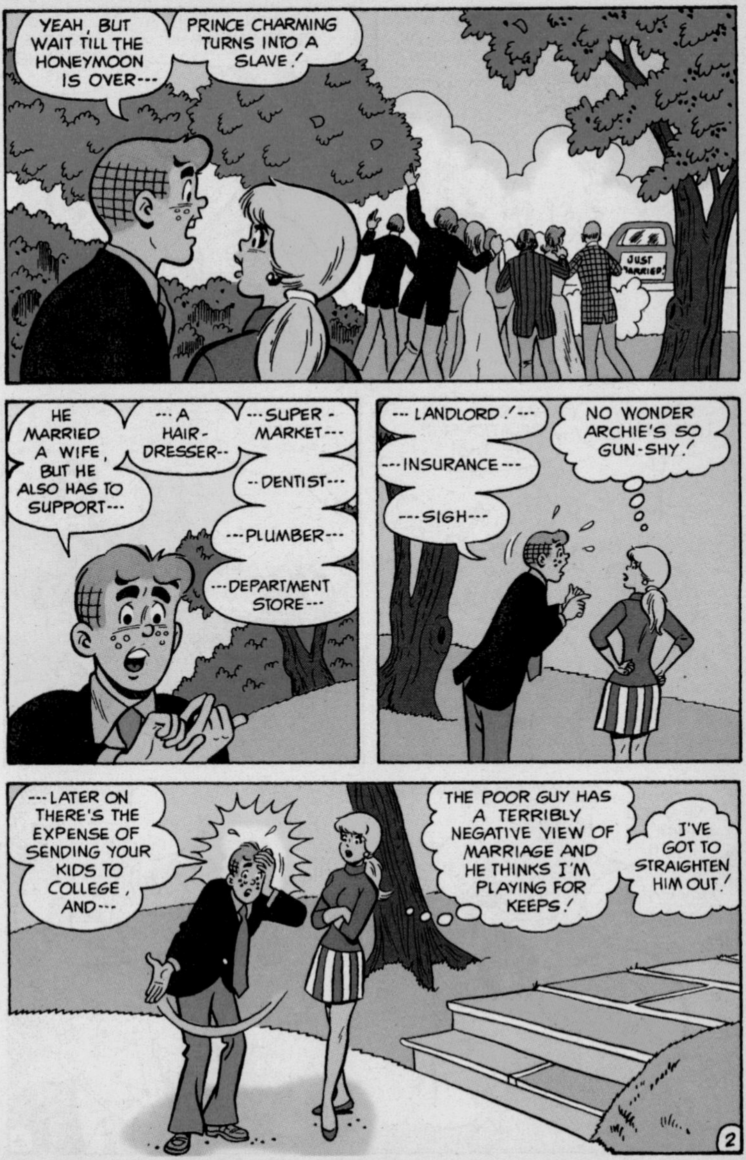
YEAH, BUT WAIT TILL THE HONEYMOON IS OVER---
PRINCE CHARMING TURNS INTO A SLAVE!
JUST MARRIED!
HE MARRIED A WIFE, BUT HE ALSO HAS TO SUPPORT---
--- A HAIR-DRESSER--
---SUPER-MARKET---
--DENTIST---
---PLUMBER---
---DEPARTMENT STORE---
--- LANDLORD!---
---INSURANCE---
---SIGH---
NO WONDER ARCHIE'S SO GUN-SHY!
---LATER ON THERE'S THE EXPENSE OF SENDING YOUR KIDS TO COLLEGE, AND---
THE POOR GUY HAS A TERRIBLY NEGATIVE VIEW OF MARRIAGE AND HE THINKS I'M PLAYING FOR KEEPS!
I'VE GOT TO STRAIGHTEN HIM OUT!
2

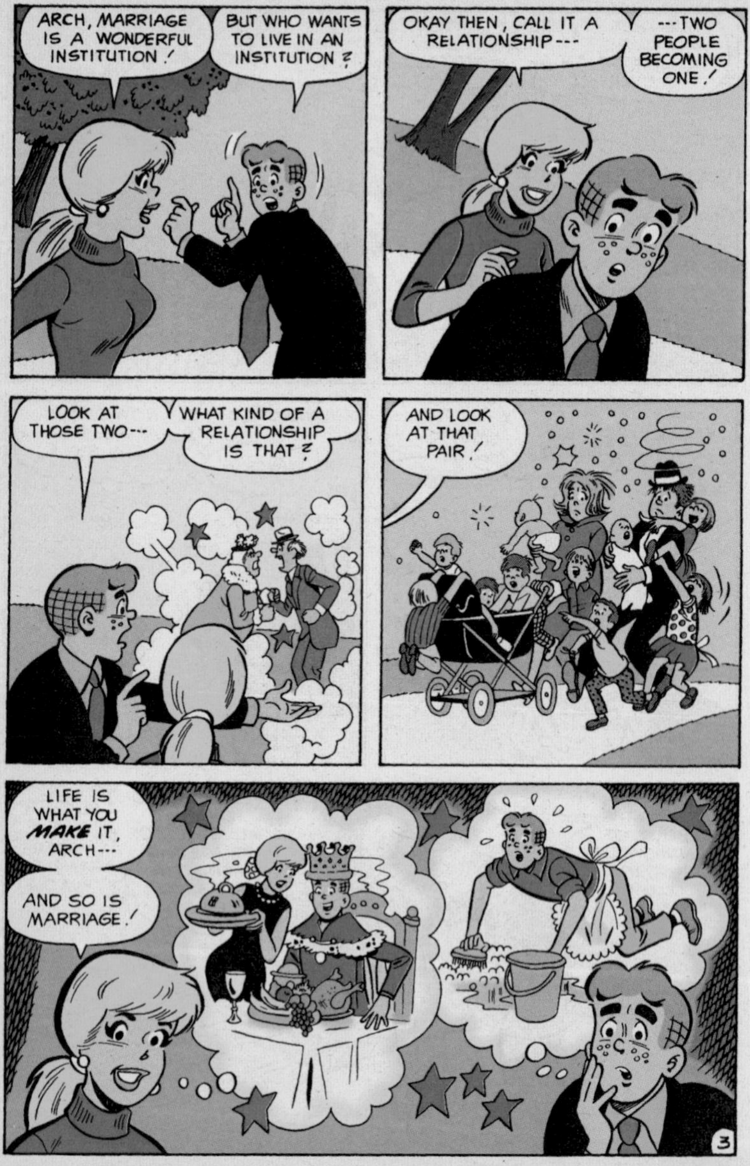

ARCH, MARRIAGE IS A WONDERFUL INSTITUTION!
BUT WHO WANTS TO LIVE IN AN INSTITUTION?
OKAY THEN, CALL IT A RELATIONSHIP---
---TWO PEOPLE BECOMING ONE!
LOOK AT THOSE TWO---
WHAT KIND OF A RELATIONSHIP IS THAT?
AND LOOK AT THAT PAIR!
LIFE IS WHAT YOU *MAKE* IT, ARCH---
AND SO IS MARRIAGE!
3

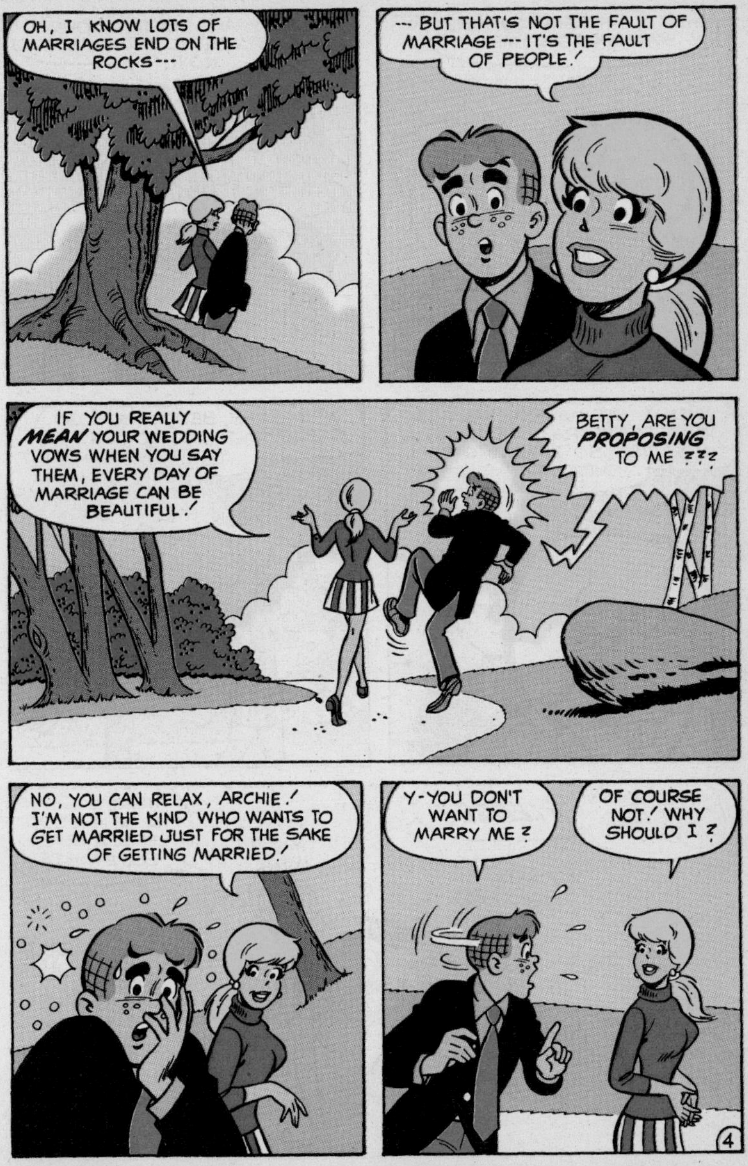
OH, I KNOW LOTS OF MARRIAGES END ON THE ROCKS---
--- BUT THAT'S NOT THE FAULT OF MARRIAGE --- IT'S THE FAULT OF PEOPLE!
IF YOU REALLY MEAN YOUR WEDDING VOWS WHEN YOU SAY THEM, EVERY DAY OF MARRIAGE CAN BE BEAUTIFUL!
BETTY, ARE YOU PROPOSING TO ME ???
NO, YOU CAN RELAX, ARCHIE! I'M NOT THE KIND WHO WANTS TO GET MARRIED JUST FOR THE SAKE OF GETTING MARRIED!
Y-YOU DON'T WANT TO MARRY ME?
OF COURSE NOT! WHY SHOULD I?

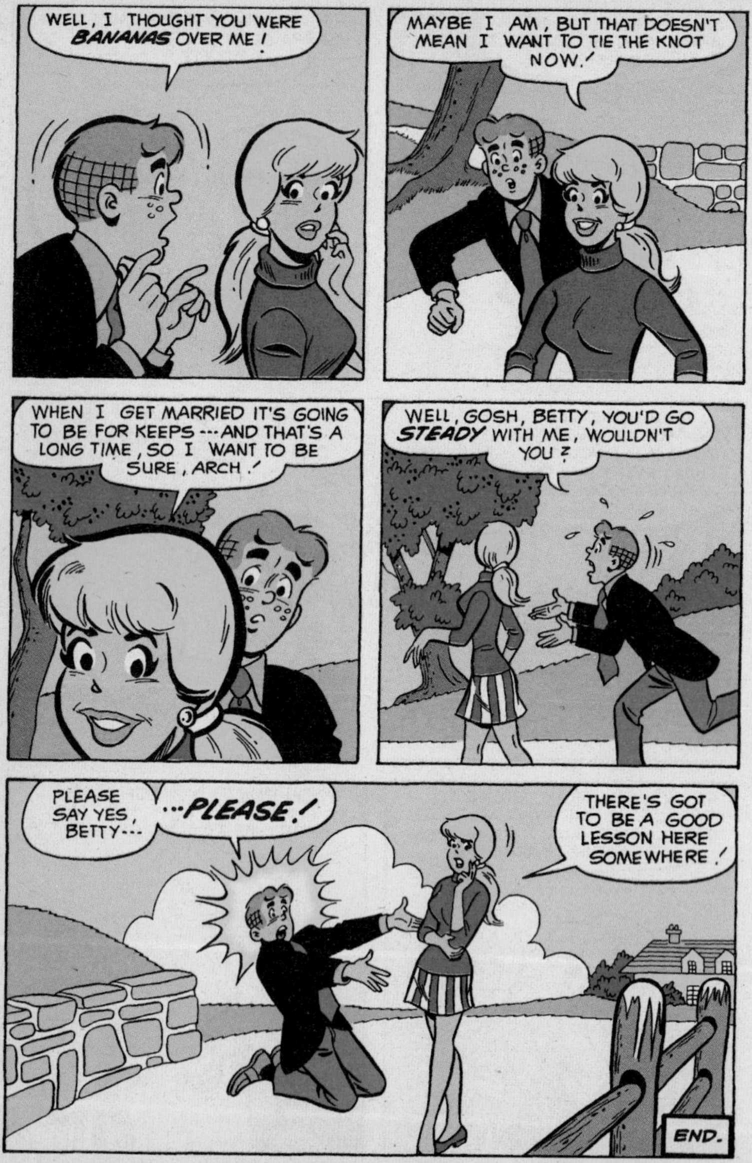

WELL, I THOUGHT YOU WERE BANANAS OVER ME!
MAYBE I AM, BUT THAT DOESN'T MEAN I WANT TO TIE THE KNOT NOW!
WHEN I GET MARRIED IT'S GOING TO BE FOR KEEPS --- AND THAT'S A LONG TIME, SO I WANT TO BE SURE, ARCH!
WELL, GOSH, BETTY, YOU'D GO STEADY WITH ME, WOULDN'T YOU?
PLEASE SAY YES, BETTY---
...PLEASE!
THERE'S GOT TO BE A GOOD LESSON HERE SOMEWHERE!
END.

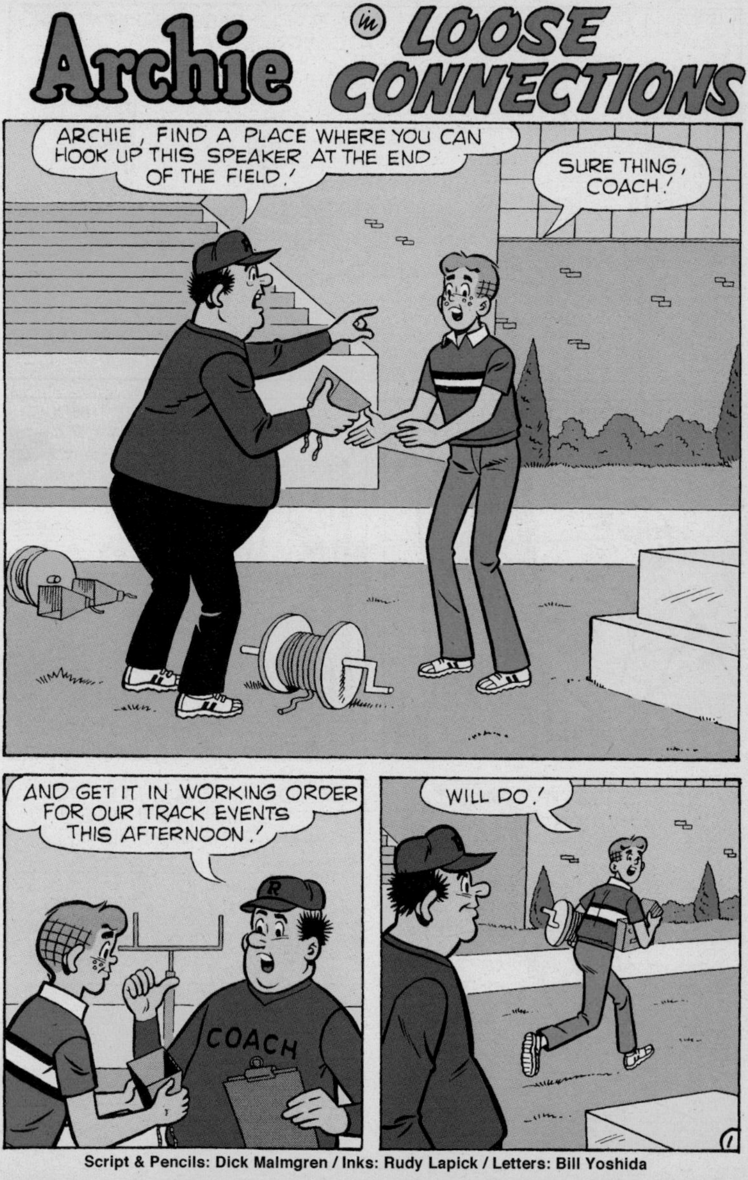
Archie in LOOSE CONNECTIONS
ARCHIE, FIND A PLACE WHERE YOU CAN HOOK UP THIS SPEAKER AT THE END OF THE FIELD!
SURE THING, COACH!
AND GET IT IN WORKING ORDER FOR OUR TRACK EVENTS THIS AFTERNOON!
COACH
WILL DO!
1

Script & Pencils: Dick Malmgren / Inks: Rudy Lapick / Letters: Bill Yoshida

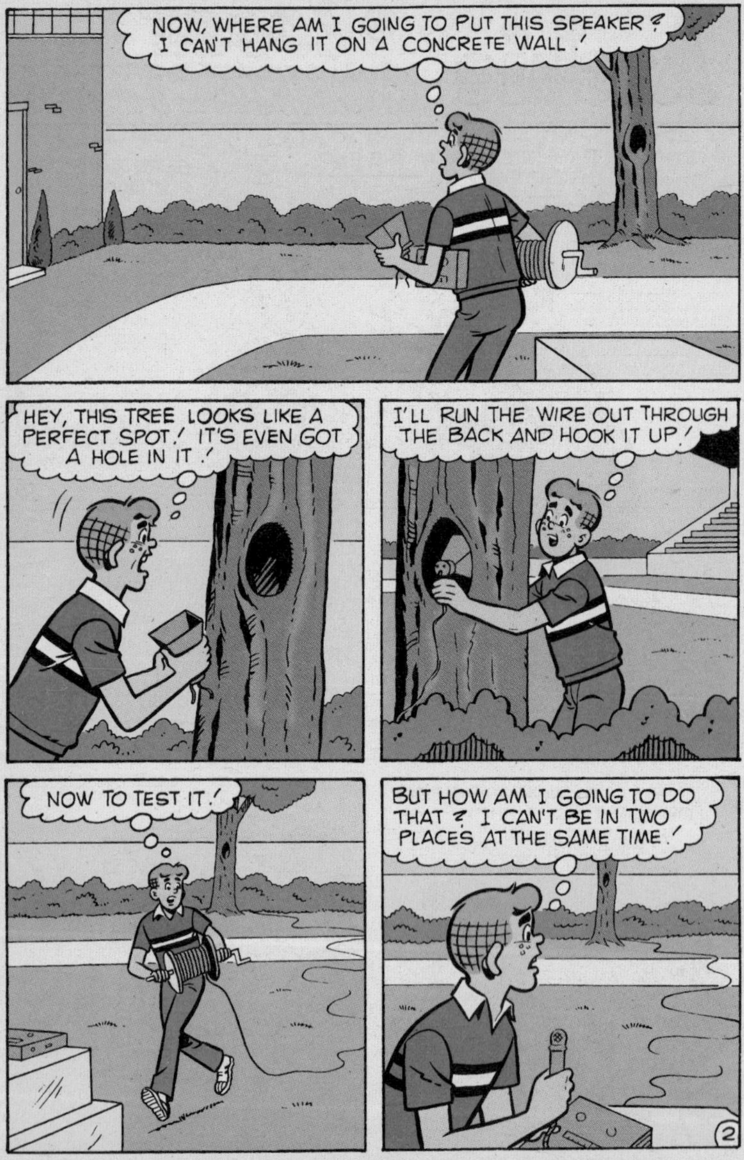
NOW, WHERE AM I GOING TO PUT THIS SPEAKER? I CAN'T HANG IT ON A CONCRETE WALL!
HEY, THIS TREE LOOKS LIKE A PERFECT SPOT! IT'S EVEN GOT A HOLE IN IT!
I'LL RUN THE WIRE OUT THROUGH THE BACK AND HOOK IT UP!
NOW TO TEST IT!
BUT HOW AM I GOING TO DO THAT? I CAN'T BE IN TWO PLACES AT THE SAME TIME!
2

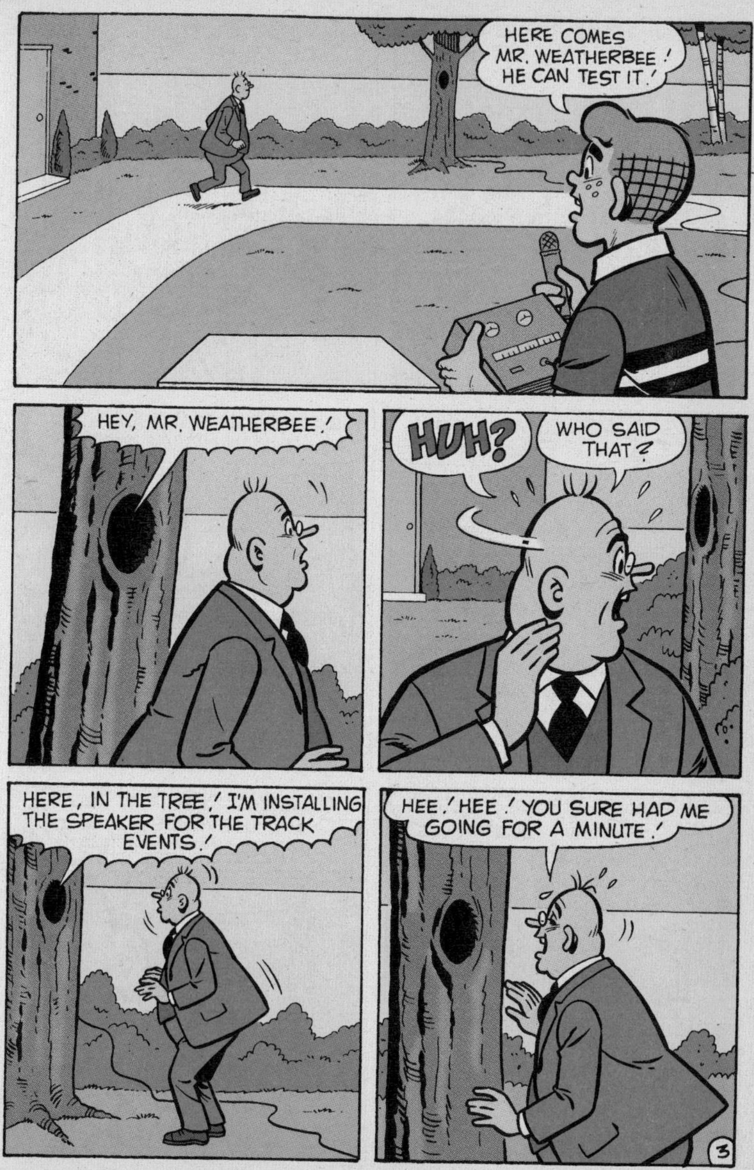
HERE COMES MR. WEATHERBEE! HE CAN TEST IT!
HEY, MR. WEATHERBEE!
HUH?
WHO SAID THAT?
HERE, IN THE TREE! I'M INSTALLING THE SPEAKER FOR THE TRACK EVENTS!
HEE! HEE! YOU SURE HAD ME GOING FOR A MINUTE!
3

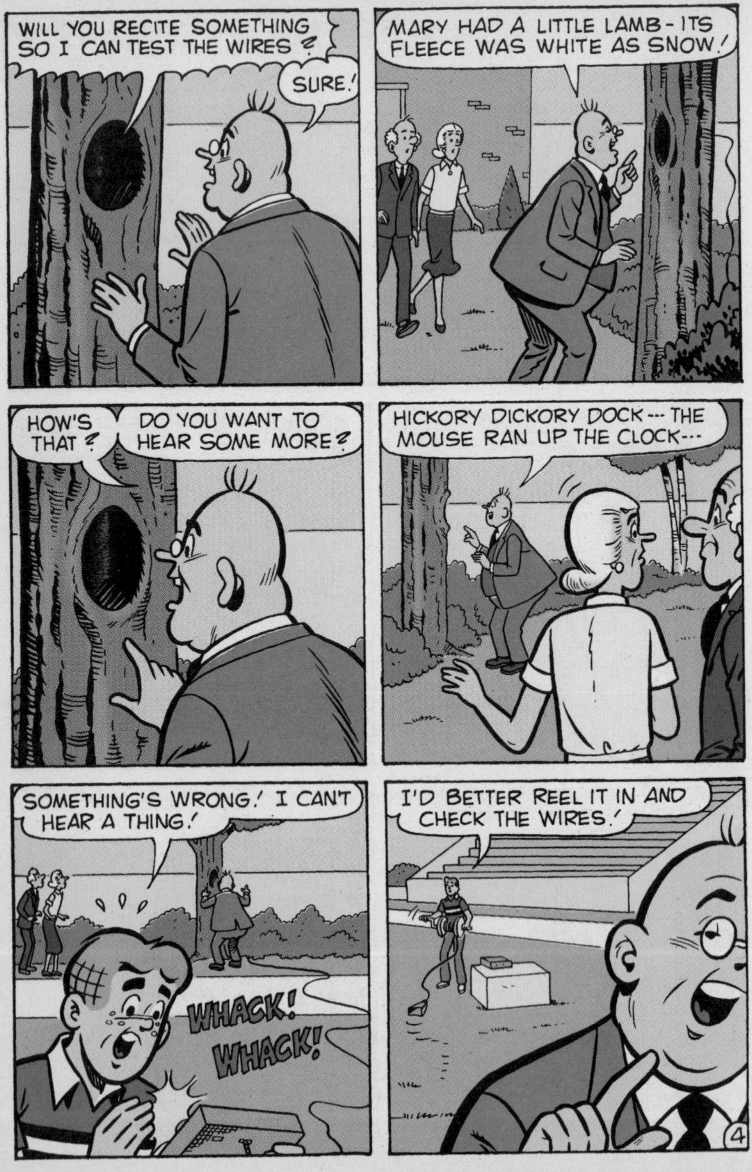
WILL YOU RECITE SOMETHING SO I CAN TEST THE WIRES ?
SURE!
MARY HAD A LITTLE LAMB - ITS FLEECE WAS WHITE AS SNOW!
HOW'S THAT ?
DO YOU WANT TO HEAR SOME MORE ?
HICKORY DICKORY DOCK --- THE MOUSE RAN UP THE CLOCK---
SOMETHING'S WRONG! I CAN'T HEAR A THING!
WHACK!
WHACK!
I'D BETTER REEL IT IN AND CHECK THE WIRES!
4

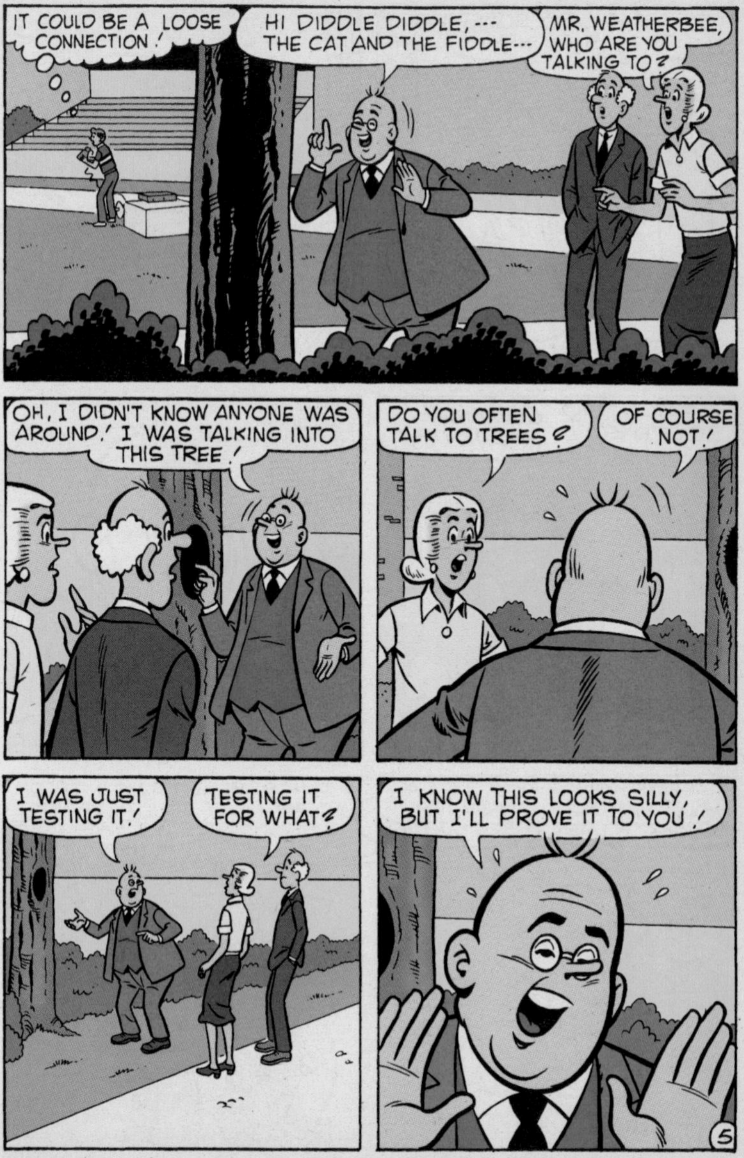
IT COULD BE A LOOSE CONNECTION!
HI DIDDLE DIDDLE, --- THE CAT AND THE FIDDLE---
MR. WEATHERBEE, WHO ARE YOU TALKING TO?
OH, I DIDN'T KNOW ANYONE WAS AROUND! I WAS TALKING INTO THIS TREE!
DO YOU OFTEN TALK TO TREES?
OF COURSE NOT!
I WAS JUST TESTING IT!
TESTING IT FOR WHAT?
I KNOW THIS LOOKS SILLY, BUT I'LL PROVE IT TO YOU!
5

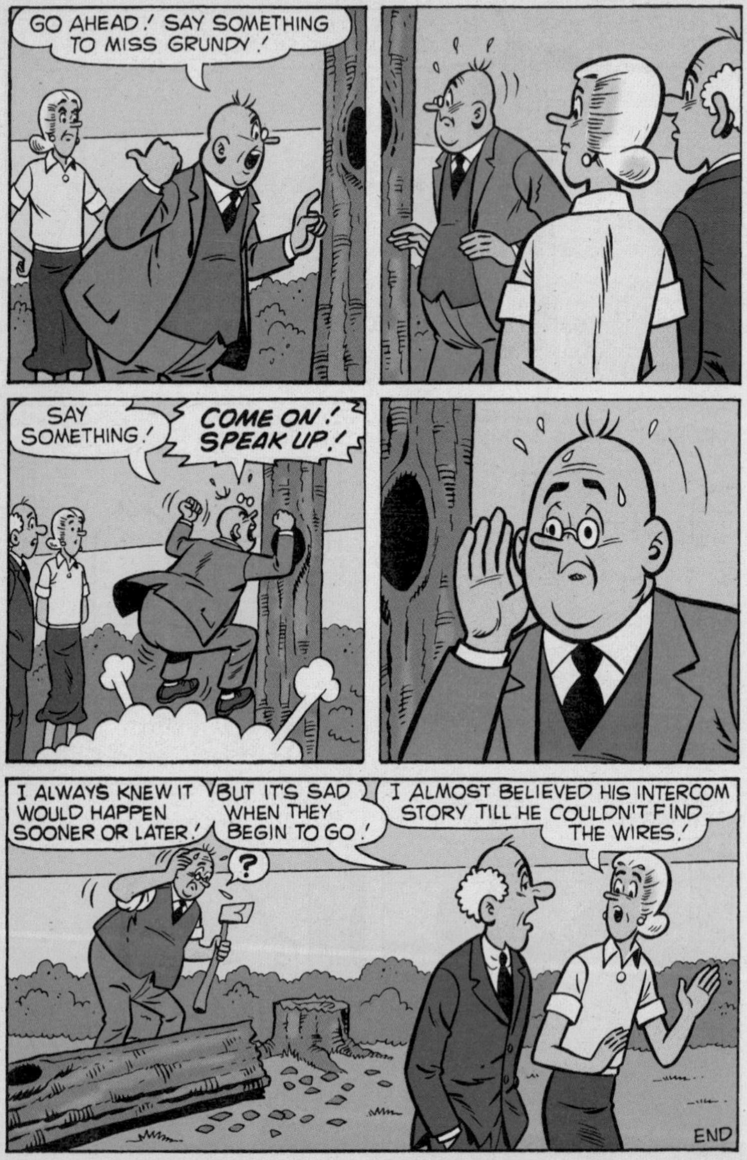

GO AHEAD! SAY SOMETHING TO MISS GRUNDY!
SAY SOMETHING!
COME ON! SPEAK UP!
I ALWAYS KNEW IT WOULD HAPPEN SOONER OR LATER!
BUT IT'S SAD WHEN THEY BEGIN TO GO!
?
I ALMOST BELIEVED HIS INTERCOM STORY TILL HE COULDN'T FIND THE WIRES!
END

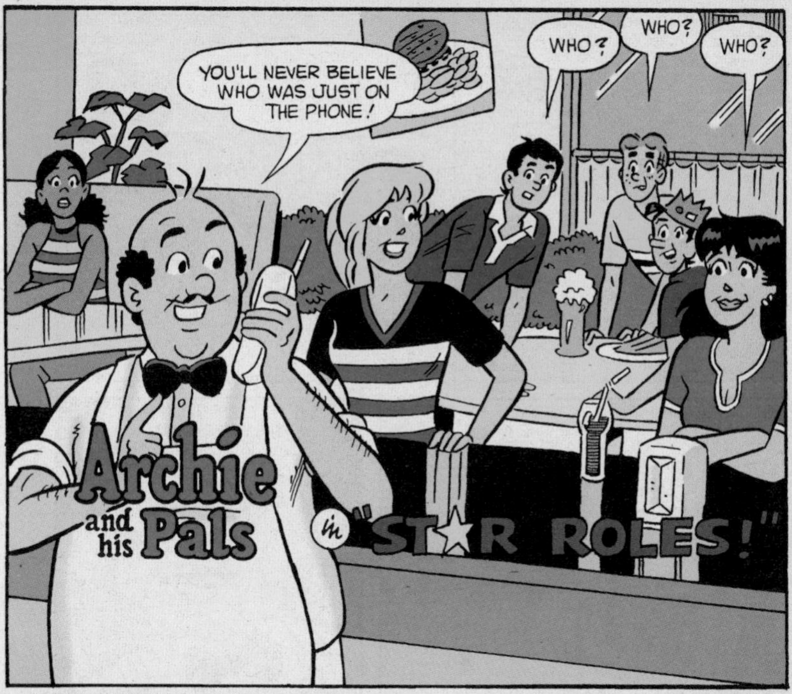
YOU'LL NEVER BELIEVE WHO WAS JUST ON THE PHONE!
WHO?
WHO?
WHO?
Archie and his Pals in "STAR ROLES!"

Script: Mike Pellowski / Pencils: Fernando Ruiz / Inks: Rudy Lapick / Letters: Bill Yoshida / Colors: Barry Grossman

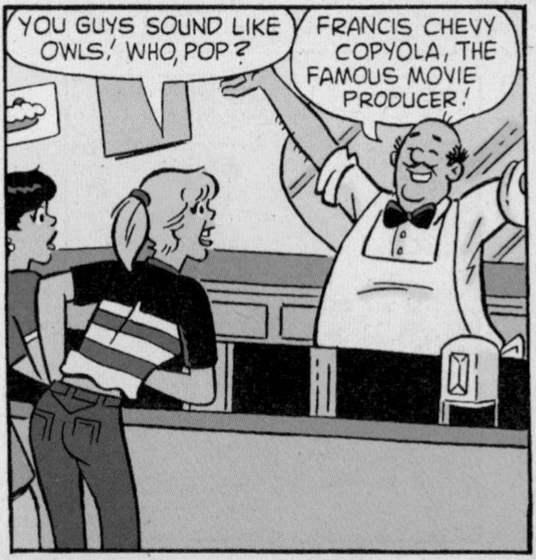
YOU GUYS SOUND LIKE OWLS! WHO, POP?
FRANCIS CHEVY COPYOLA, THE FAMOUS MOVIE PRODUCER!

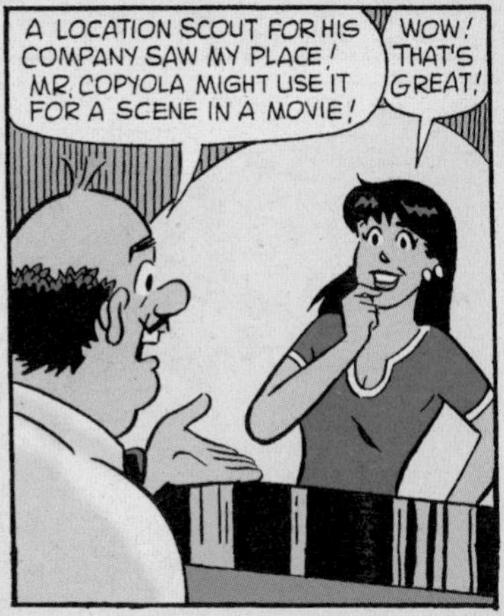
A LOCATION SCOUT FOR HIS COMPANY SAW MY PLACE! MR. COPYOLA MIGHT USE IT FOR A SCENE IN A MOVIE!
WOW! THAT'S GREAT!

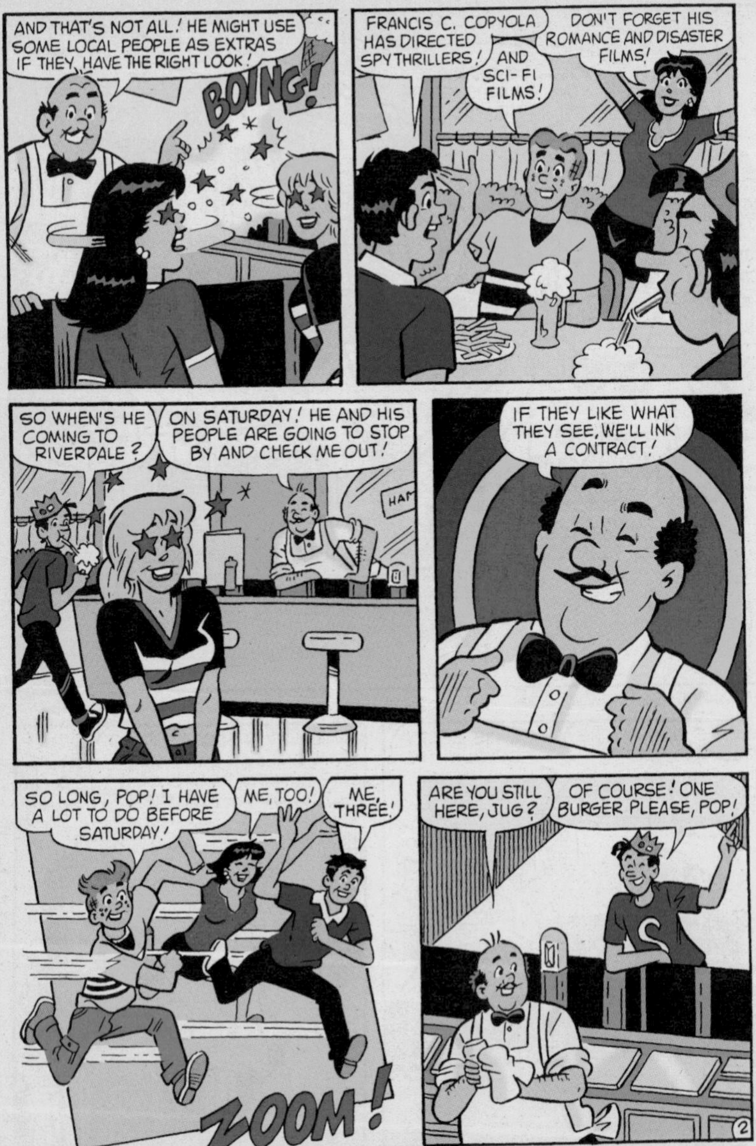
AND THAT'S NOT ALL! HE MIGHT USE SOME LOCAL PEOPLE AS EXTRAS IF THEY HAVE THE RIGHT LOOK!
BOING!
FRANCIS C. COPYOLA HAS DIRECTED SPY THRILLERS!
AND SCI-FI FILMS!
DON'T FORGET HIS ROMANCE AND DISASTER FILMS!
SO WHEN'S HE COMING TO RIVERDALE?
ON SATURDAY! HE AND HIS PEOPLE ARE GOING TO STOP BY AND CHECK ME OUT!
IF THEY LIKE WHAT THEY SEE, WE'LL INK A CONTRACT!
SO LONG, POP! I HAVE A LOT TO DO BEFORE SATURDAY!
ME, TOO!
ME, THREE!
ZOOM!
ARE YOU STILL HERE, JUG?
OF COURSE! ONE BURGER PLEASE, POP!
2

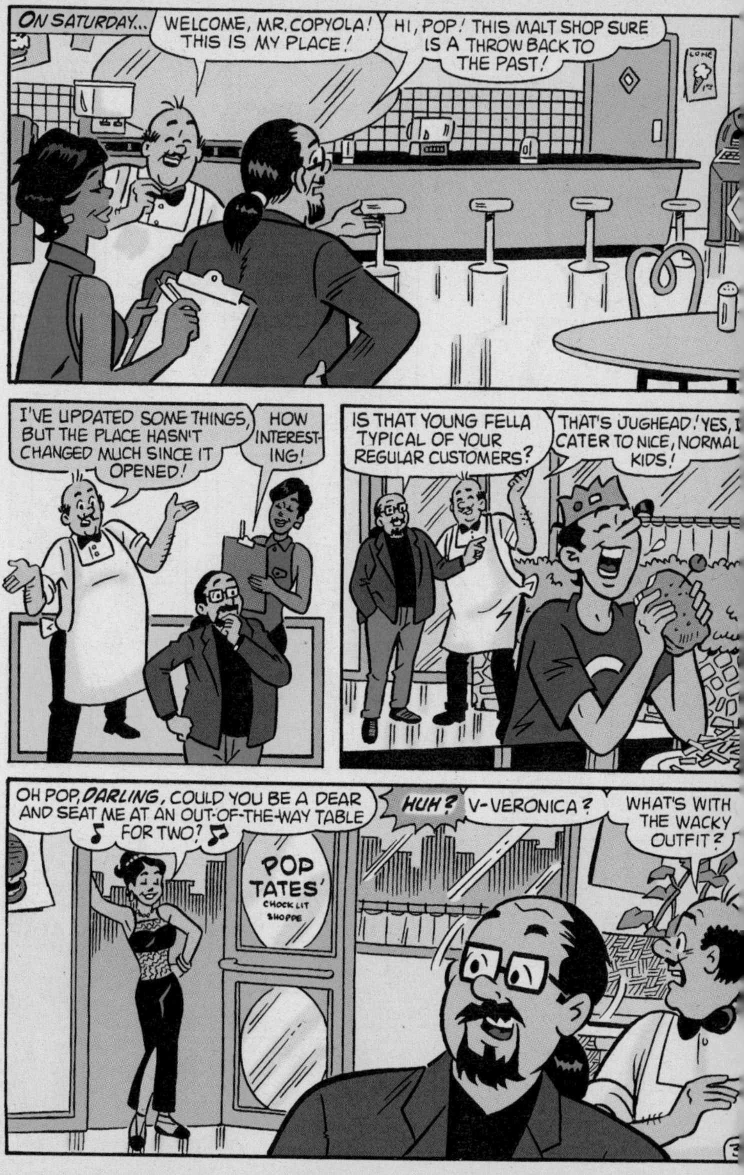

ON SATURDAY...
WELCOME, MR. COPYOLA! THIS IS MY PLACE!
HI, POP! THIS MALT SHOP SURE IS A THROW BACK TO THE PAST!
I'VE UPDATED SOME THINGS, BUT THE PLACE HASN'T CHANGED MUCH SINCE IT OPENED!
HOW INTEREST-ING!
IS THAT YOUNG FELLA TYPICAL OF YOUR REGULAR CUSTOMERS?
THAT'S JUGHEAD! YES, I CATER TO NICE, NORMAL KIDS!
OH POP, DARLING, COULD YOU BE A DEAR AND SEAT ME AT AN OUT-OF-THE-WAY TABLE FOR TWO?
HUH? V-VERONICA?
WHAT'S WITH THE WACKY OUTFIT?
POP TATES' CHOCK LIT SHOPPE

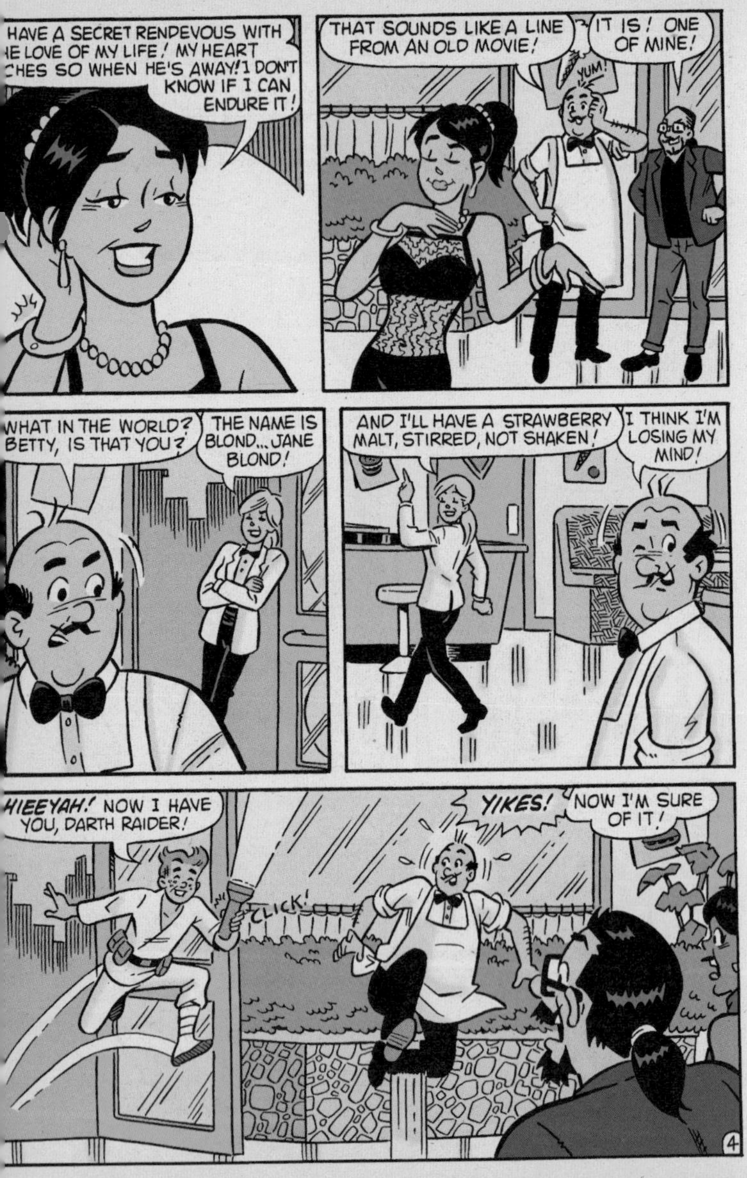
HAVE A SECRET RENDEVOUS WITH
IE LOVE OF MY LIFE! MY HEART
CHES SO WHEN HE'S AWAY! I DON'T KNOW IF I CAN ENDURE IT!
THAT SOUNDS LIKE A LINE FROM AN OLD MOVIE!
IT IS! ONE OF MINE!
YUM!
WHAT IN THE WORLD? BETTY, IS THAT YOU?
THE NAME IS BLOND... JANE BLOND!
AND I'LL HAVE A STRAWBERRY MALT, STIRRED, NOT SHAKEN!
I THINK I'M LOSING MY MIND!
HIEEYAH! NOW I HAVE YOU, DARTH RAIDER!
CLICK!
YIKES!
NOW I'M SURE OF IT!
4

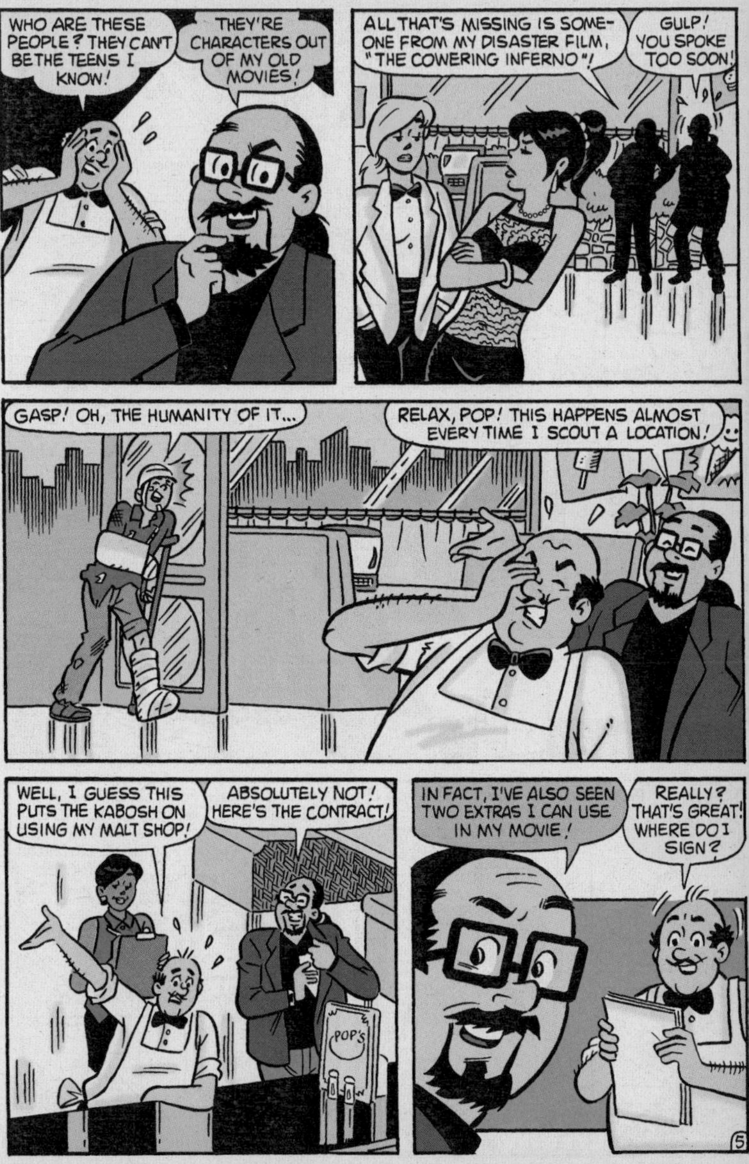
WHO ARE THESE PEOPLE? THEY CAN'T BE THE TEENS I KNOW!
THEY'RE CHARACTERS OUT OF MY OLD MOVIES!
ALL THAT'S MISSING IS SOME-ONE FROM MY DISASTER FILM, "THE COWERING INFERNO"!
GULP! YOU SPOKE TOO SOON!
GASP! OH, THE HUMANITY OF IT...
RELAX, POP! THIS HAPPENS ALMOST EVERY TIME I SCOUT A LOCATION!
WELL, I GUESS THIS PUTS THE KABOSH ON USING MY MALT SHOP!
ABSOLUTELY NOT! HERE'S THE CONTRACT!
POP'S
IN FACT, I'VE ALSO SEEN TWO EXTRAS I CAN USE IN MY MOVIE!
REALLY? THAT'S GREAT! WHERE DO I SIGN?

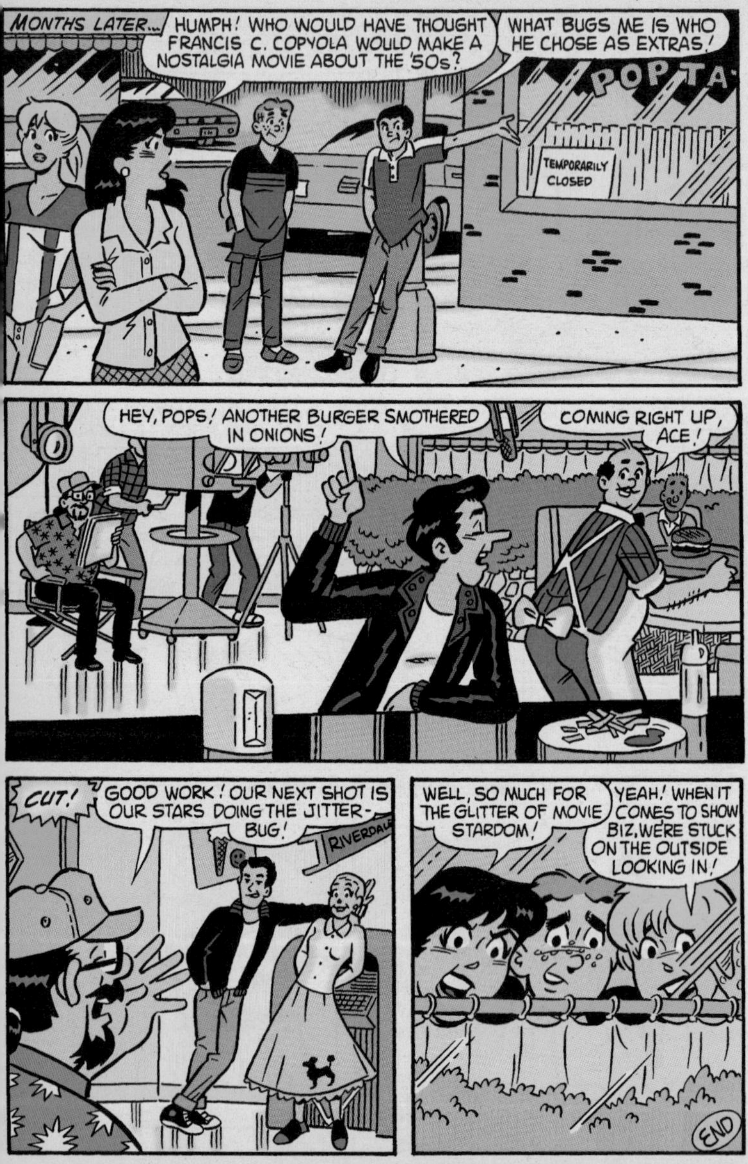
MONTHS LATER...
HUMPH! WHO WOULD HAVE THOUGHT FRANCIS C. COPYOLA WOULD MAKE A NOSTALGIA MOVIE ABOUT THE '50s?
WHAT BUGS ME IS WHO HE CHOSE AS EXTRAS!
POP TA
TEMPORARILY CLOSED
HEY, POPS! ANOTHER BURGER SMOTHERED IN ONIONS!
COMING RIGHT UP, ACE!
CUT!
GOOD WORK! OUR NEXT SHOT IS OUR STARS DOING THE JITTER-BUG!
RIVERDA
WELL, SO MUCH FOR THE GLITTER OF MOVIE STARDOM!
YEAH! WHEN IT COMES TO SHOW BIZ, WE'RE STUCK ON THE OUTSIDE LOOKING IN!
END

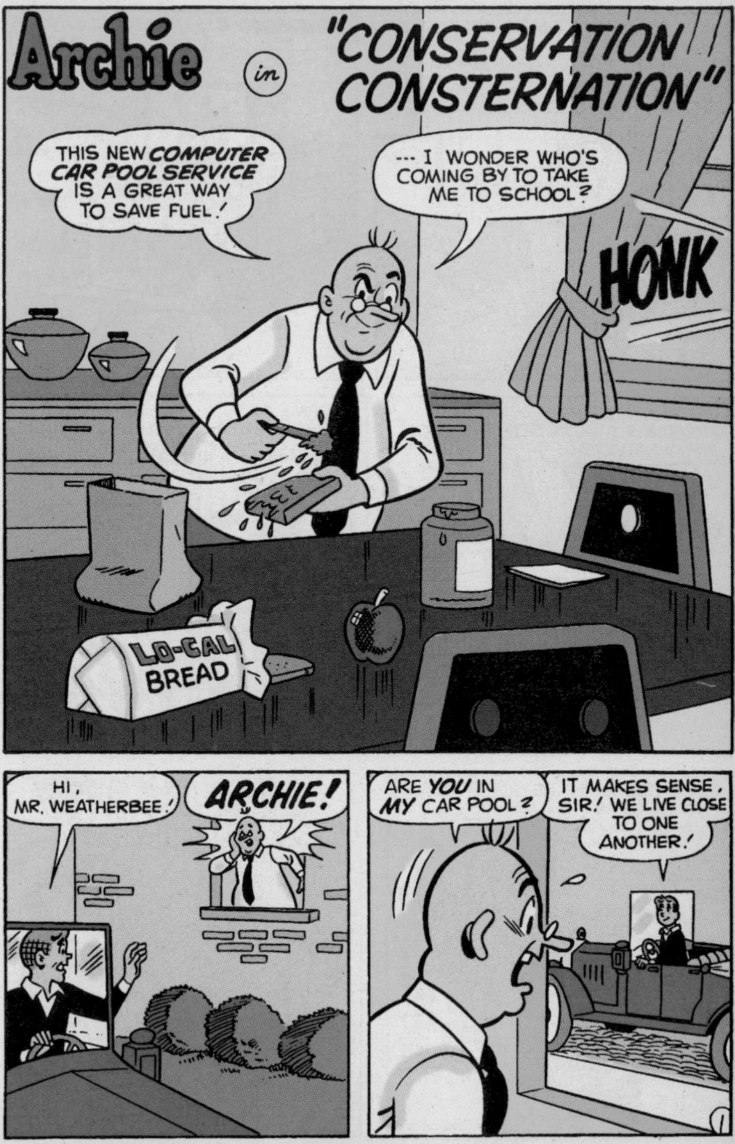
Archie in "CONSERVATION CONSTERNATION"
THIS NEW COMPUTER CAR POOL SERVICE IS A GREAT WAY TO SAVE FUEL!
--- I WONDER WHO'S COMING BY TO TAKE ME TO SCHOOL?
HONK
LO-CAL BREAD
HI, MR. WEATHERBEE!
ARCHIE!
ARE YOU IN MY CAR POOL?
IT MAKES SENSE, SIR! WE LIVE CLOSE TO ONE ANOTHER!

Script & Pencils: Joe Edwards / Inks: Rudy Lapick / Letters: Bill Yoshida

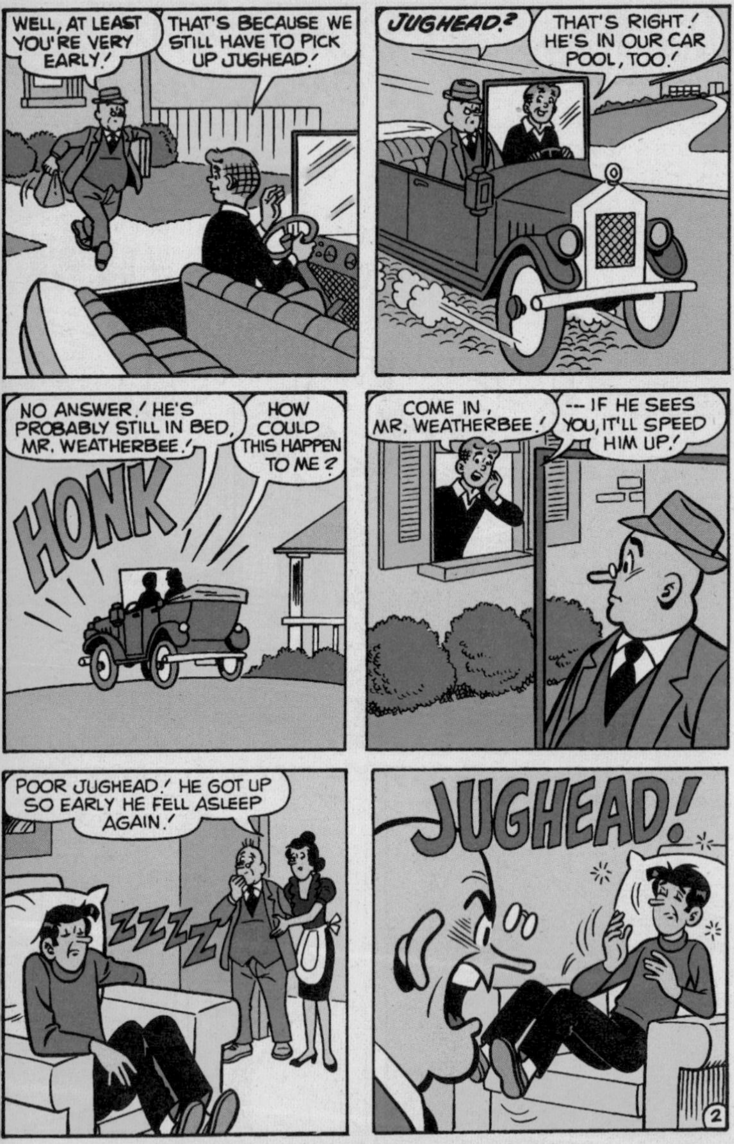
WELL, AT LEAST YOU'RE VERY EARLY!
THAT'S BECAUSE WE STILL HAVE TO PICK UP JUGHEAD!
JUGHEAD?
THAT'S RIGHT! HE'S IN OUR CAR POOL, TOO!
NO ANSWER! HE'S PROBABLY STILL IN BED, MR. WEATHERBEE!
HOW COULD THIS HAPPEN TO ME?
HONK
COME IN, MR. WEATHERBEE!
--- IF HE SEES YOU, IT'LL SPEED HIM UP!
POOR JUGHEAD! HE GOT UP SO EARLY HE FELL ASLEEP AGAIN!
ZZZZ
JUGHEAD!
2

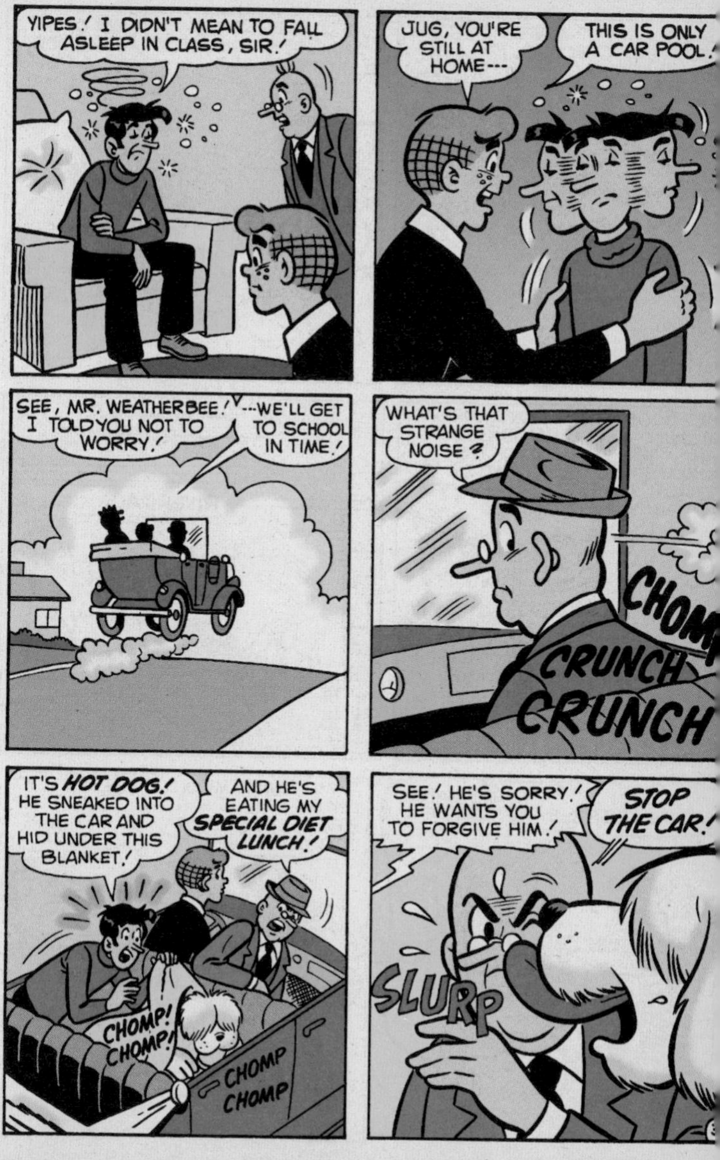

YIPES! I DIDN'T MEAN TO FALL ASLEEP IN CLASS, SIR!
JUG, YOU'RE STILL AT HOME---
THIS IS ONLY A CAR POOL!
SEE, MR. WEATHERBEE! I TOLD YOU NOT TO WORRY!
---WE'LL GET TO SCHOOL IN TIME!
WHAT'S THAT STRANGE NOISE?
CHOMP
CRUNCH
CRUNCH
IT'S HOT DOG! HE SNEAKED INTO THE CAR AND HID UNDER THIS BLANKET!
AND HE'S EATING MY SPECIAL DIET LUNCH!
CHOMP! CHOMP!
CHOMP CHOMP
SEE! HE'S SORRY! HE WANTS YOU TO FORGIVE HIM!
STOP THE CAR!
SLURP

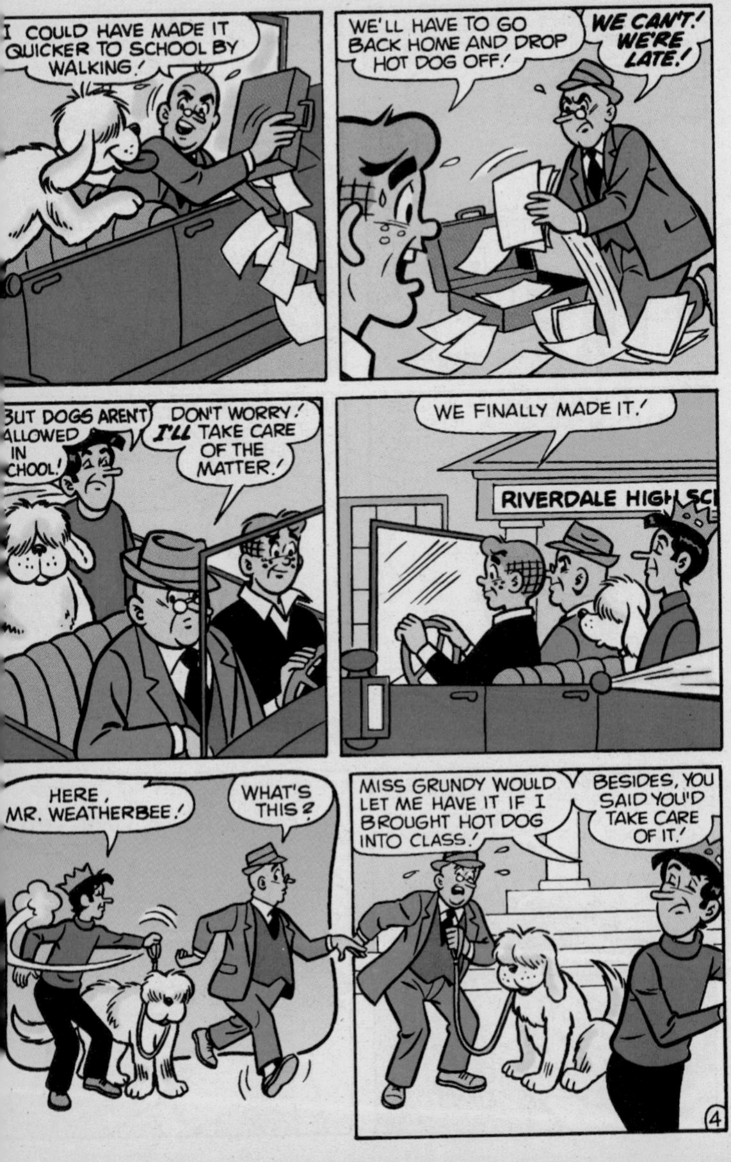
I COULD HAVE MADE IT QUICKER TO SCHOOL BY WALKING!
WE'LL HAVE TO GO BACK HOME AND DROP HOT DOG OFF!
WE CAN'T! WE'RE LATE!
BUT DOGS AREN'T ALLOWED IN SCHOOL!
DON'T WORRY! I'LL TAKE CARE OF THE MATTER!
WE FINALLY MADE IT!
RIVERDALE HIGH SC
HERE, MR. WEATHERBEE!
WHAT'S THIS?
MISS GRUNDY WOULD LET ME HAVE IT IF I BROUGHT HOT DOG INTO CLASS!
BESIDES, YOU SAID YOU'D TAKE CARE OF IT!
4

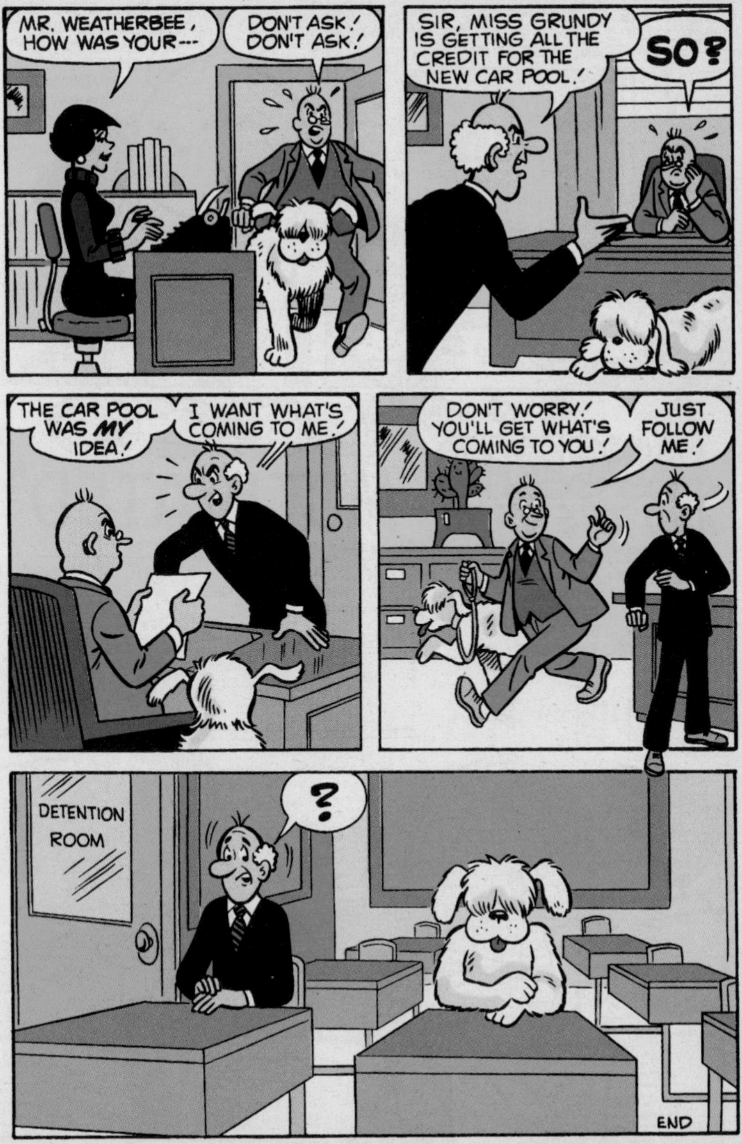
MR. WEATHERBEE, HOW WAS YOUR---
DON'T ASK! DON'T ASK!
SIR, MISS GRUNDY IS GETTING ALL THE CREDIT FOR THE NEW CAR POOL!
SO?
THE CAR POOL WAS *MY* IDEA!
I WANT WHAT'S COMING TO ME!
DON'T WORRY! YOU'LL GET WHAT'S COMING TO YOU!
JUST FOLLOW ME!
DETENTION ROOM
?
END

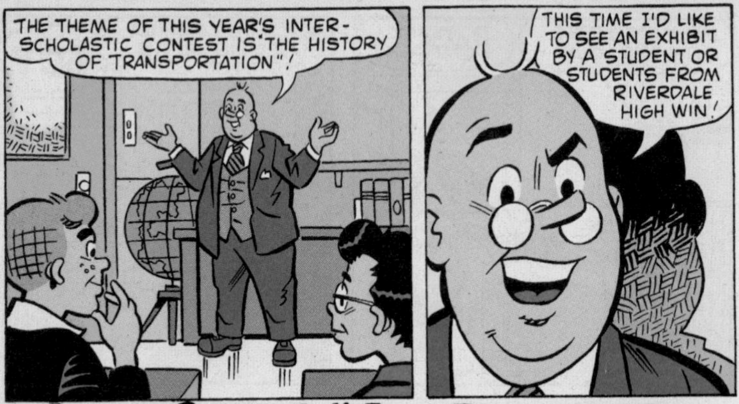
THE THEME OF THIS YEAR'S INTER-SCHOLASTIC CONTEST IS "THE HISTORY OF TRANSPORTATION"!
THIS TIME I'D LIKE TO SEE AN EXHIBIT BY A STUDENT OR STUDENTS FROM RIVERDALE HIGH WIN!

Archie AND THE GANG in "LOCO MOTIVATED"

Script: Hal Smith / Pencils: Howard Bender / Inks: Rudy Lapick / Letters: Bill Yoshida

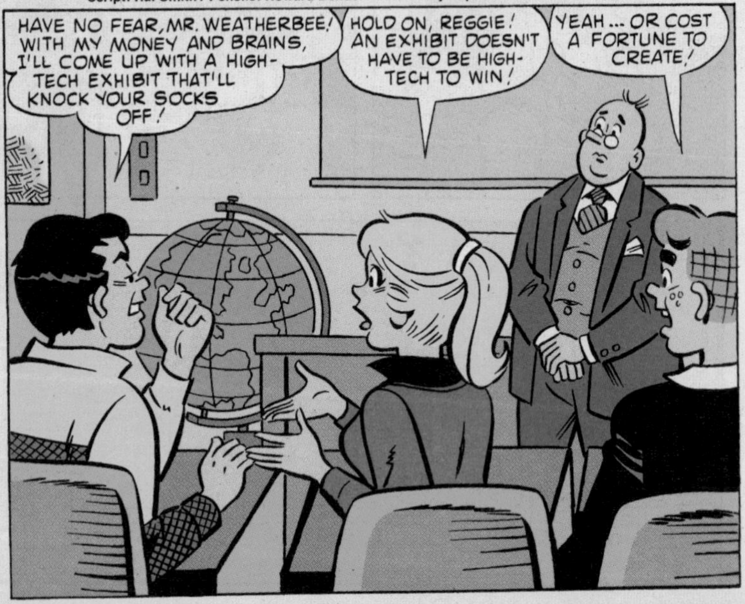
HAVE NO FEAR, MR. WEATHERBEE! WITH MY MONEY AND BRAINS, I'LL COME UP WITH A HIGH-TECH EXHIBIT THAT'LL KNOCK YOUR SOCKS OFF!
HOLD ON, REGGIE! AN EXHIBIT DOESN'T HAVE TO BE HIGH-TECH TO WIN!
YEAH ... OR COST A FORTUNE TO CREATE!

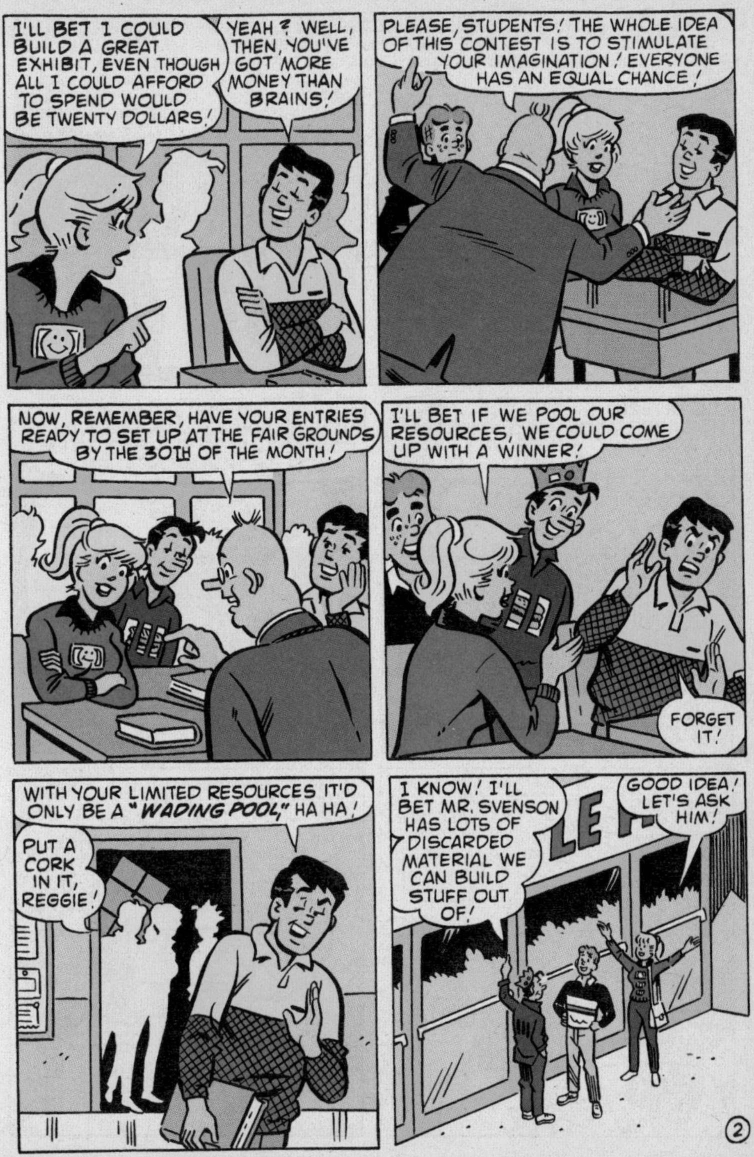

I'LL BET I COULD BUILD A GREAT EXHIBIT, EVEN THOUGH ALL I COULD AFFORD TO SPEND WOULD BE TWENTY DOLLARS!
YEAH? WELL, THEN, YOU'VE GOT MORE MONEY THAN BRAINS!
PLEASE, STUDENTS! THE WHOLE IDEA OF THIS CONTEST IS TO STIMULATE YOUR IMAGINATION! EVERYONE HAS AN EQUAL CHANCE!
NOW, REMEMBER, HAVE YOUR ENTRIES READY TO SET UP AT THE FAIR GROUNDS BY THE 30TH OF THE MONTH!
I'LL BET IF WE POOL OUR RESOURCES, WE COULD COME UP WITH A WINNER!
FORGET IT!
WITH YOUR LIMITED RESOURCES IT'D ONLY BE A "WADING POOL," HA HA!
PUT A CORK IN IT, REGGIE!
I KNOW! I'LL BET MR. SVENSON HAS LOTS OF DISCARDED MATERIAL WE CAN BUILD STUFF OUT OF!
GOOD IDEA! LET'S ASK HIM!
2

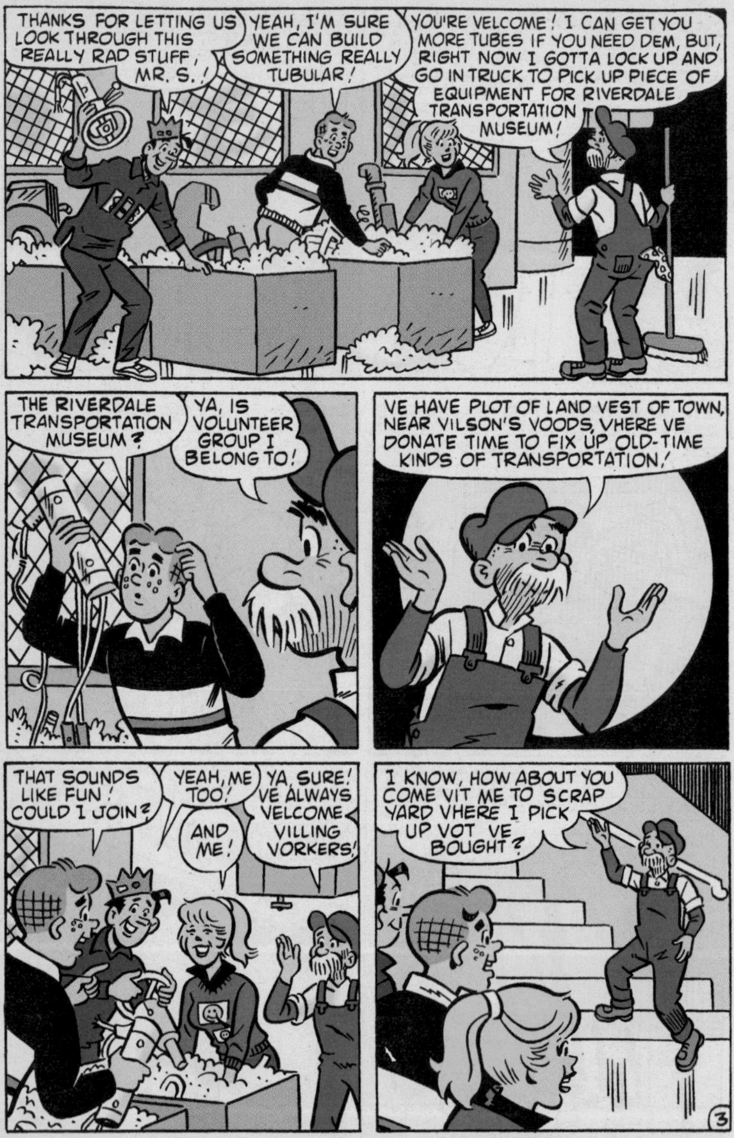

THANKS FOR LETTING US LOOK THROUGH THIS REALLY RAD STUFF, MR. S.!
YEAH, I'M SURE WE CAN BUILD SOMETHING REALLY TUBULAR!
YOU'RE VELCOME! I CAN GET YOU MORE TUBES IF YOU NEED DEM, BUT, RIGHT NOW I GOTTA LOCK UP AND GO IN TRUCK TO PICK UP PIECE OF EQUIPMENT FOR RIVERDALE TRANSPORTATION MUSEUM!
THE RIVERDALE TRANSPORTATION MUSEUM?
YA, IS VOLUNTEER GROUP I BELONG TO!
VE HAVE PLOT OF LAND VEST OF TOWN, NEAR VILSON'S VOODS, VHERE VE DONATE TIME TO FIX UP OLD-TIME KINDS OF TRANSPORTATION!
THAT SOUNDS LIKE FUN! COULD I JOIN?
YEAH, ME TOO!
AND ME!
YA, SURE! VE ALWAYS VELCOME VILLING VORKERS!
I KNOW, HOW ABOUT YOU COME VIT ME TO SCRAP YARD VHERE I PICK UP VOT VE BOUGHT?
3

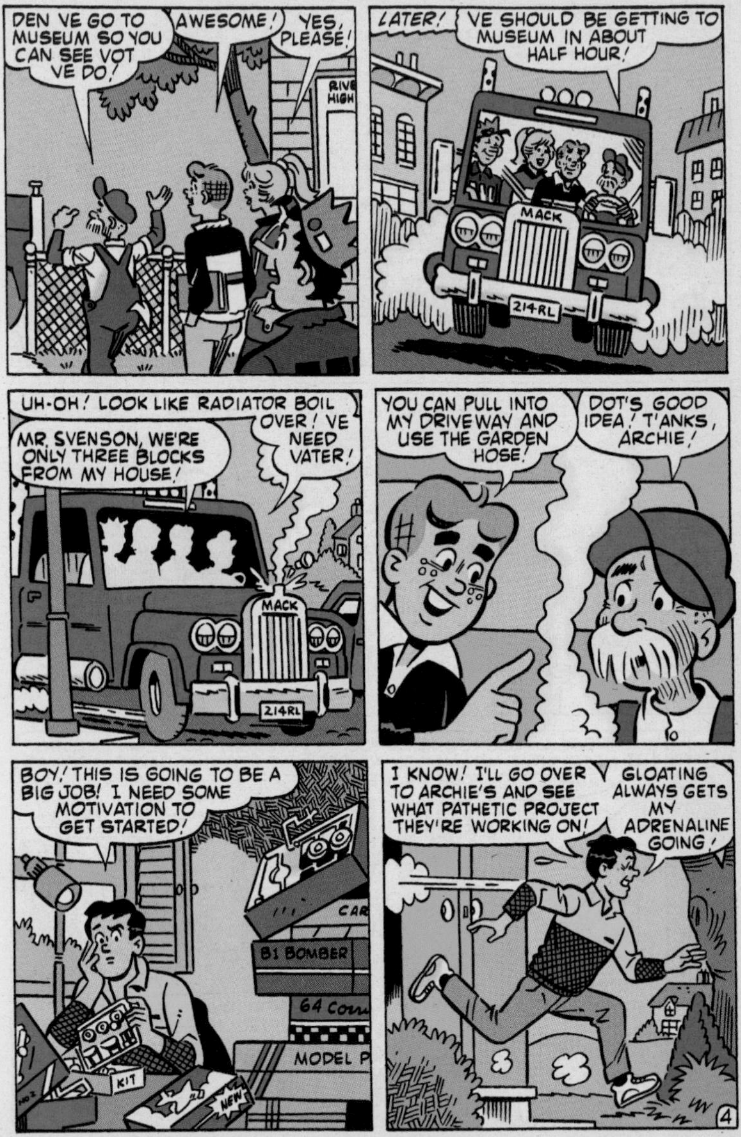
DEN VE GO TO MUSEUM SO YOU CAN SEE VOT VE DO!
AWESOME!
YES, PLEASE!
RIVE HIGH
LATER!
VE SHOULD BE GETTING TO MUSEUM IN ABOUT HALF HOUR!
MACK
214RL
UH-OH! LOOK LIKE RADIATOR BOIL OVER! VE NEED VATER!
MR. SVENSON, WE'RE ONLY THREE BLOCKS FROM MY HOUSE!
MACK
214RL
YOU CAN PULL INTO MY DRIVEWAY AND USE THE GARDEN HOSE!
DOT'S GOOD IDEA! T'ANKS, ARCHIE!
BOY! THIS IS GOING TO BE A BIG JOB! I NEED SOME MOTIVATION TO GET STARTED!
B1 BOMBER
KIT
NEW
MODEL P
I KNOW! I'LL GO OVER TO ARCHIE'S AND SEE WHAT PATHETIC PROJECT THEY'RE WORKING ON!
GLOATING ALWAYS GETS MY ADRENALINE GOING!
4

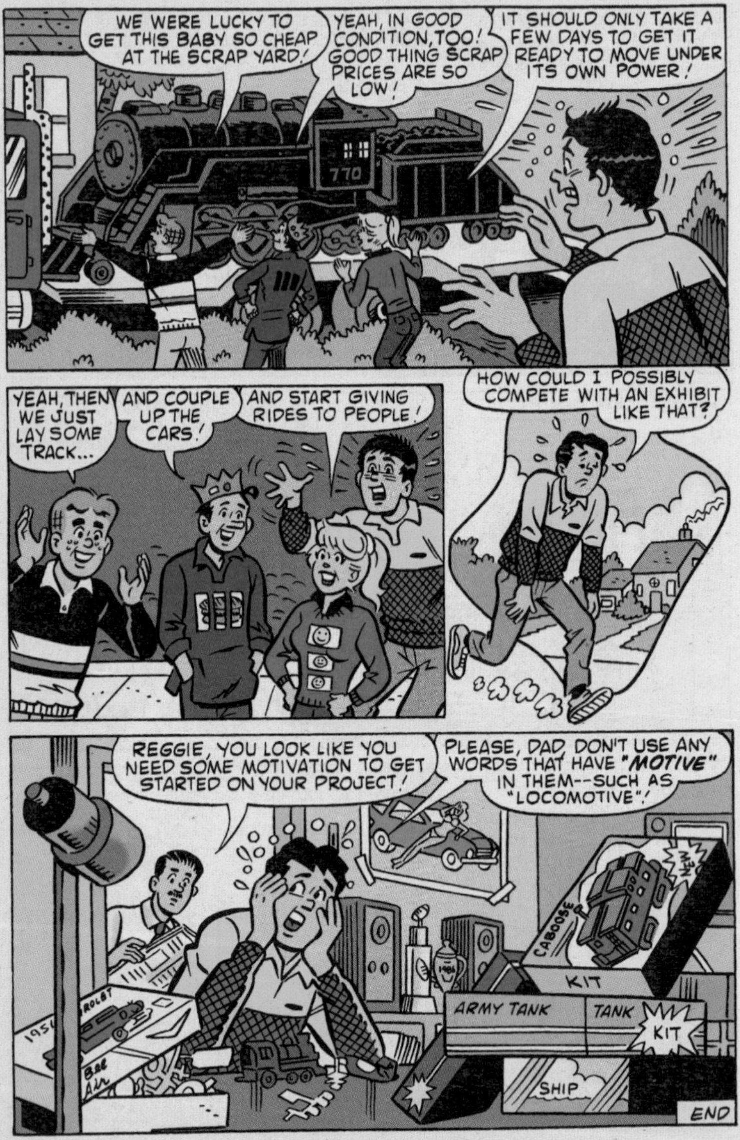
WE WERE LUCKY TO GET THIS BABY SO CHEAP AT THE SCRAP YARD!
YEAH, IN GOOD CONDITION, TOO! GOOD THING SCRAP PRICES ARE SO LOW!
IT SHOULD ONLY TAKE A FEW DAYS TO GET IT READY TO MOVE UNDER ITS OWN POWER!
770
YEAH, THEN WE JUST LAY SOME TRACK...
AND COUPLE UP THE CARS!
AND START GIVING RIDES TO PEOPLE!
HOW COULD I POSSIBLY COMPETE WITH AN EXHIBIT LIKE THAT?
REGGIE, YOU LOOK LIKE YOU NEED SOME MOTIVATION TO GET STARTED ON YOUR PROJECT!
PLEASE, DAD, DON'T USE ANY WORDS THAT HAVE "MOTIVE" IN THEM--SUCH AS "LOCOMOTIVE"!
NEW
CABOOSE
KIT
ARMY TANK
TANK
KIT
SHIP
END

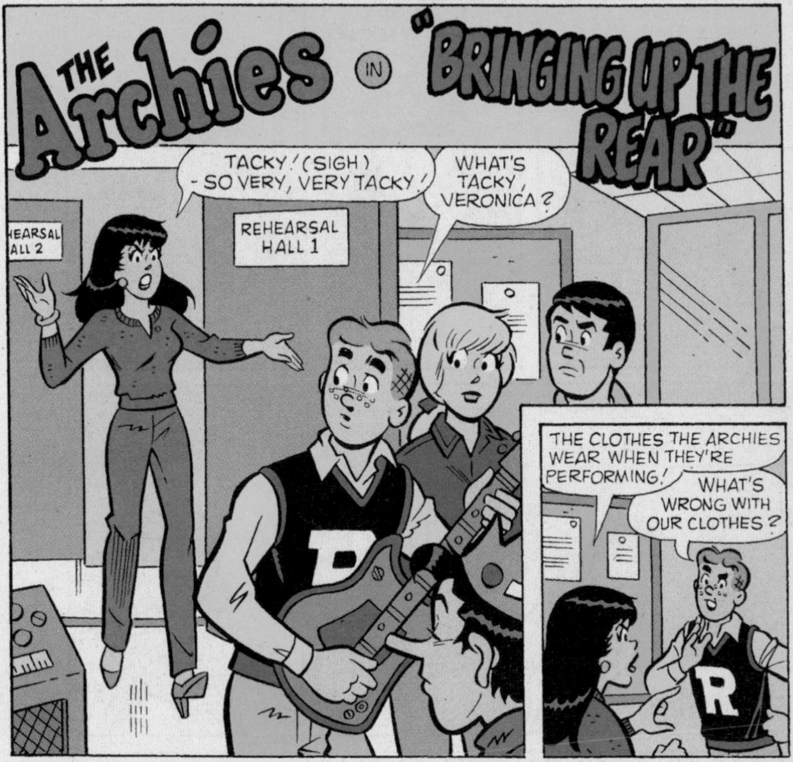
THE Archies
IN
"BRINGING UP THE REAR"
TACKY! (SIGH) - SO VERY, VERY TACKY!
WHAT'S TACKY, VERONICA?
REHEARSAL HALL 1
EARSAL ALL 2
THE CLOTHES THE ARCHIES WEAR WHEN THEY'RE PERFORMING!
WHAT'S WRONG WITH OUR CLOTHES?

Script: Frank Doyle / Pencils: Stan Goldberg / Inks: Rudy Lapick / Letters: Bill Yoshida / Colors: Barry Grossman

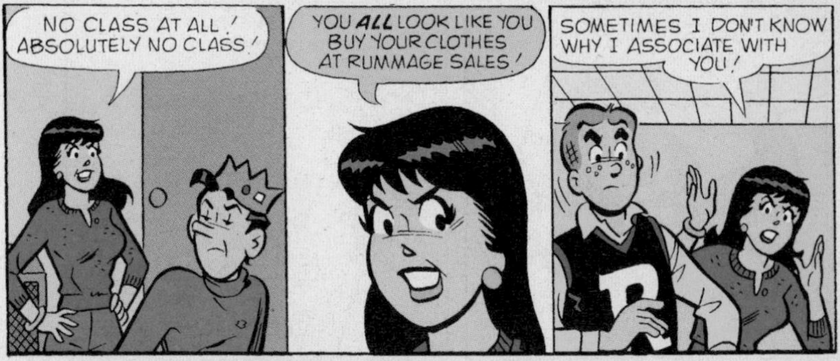
NO CLASS AT ALL! ABSOLUTELY NO CLASS!
YOU ALL LOOK LIKE YOU BUY YOUR CLOTHES AT RUMMAGE SALES!
SOMETIMES I DON'T KNOW WHY I ASSOCIATE WITH YOU!

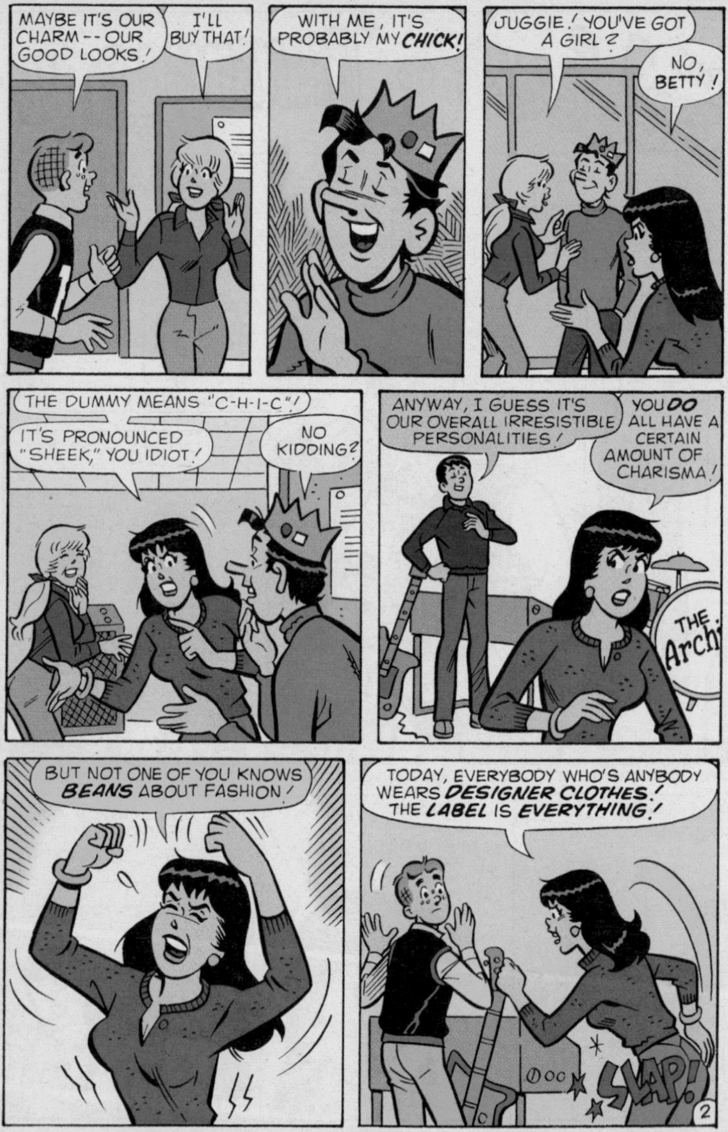
MAYBE IT'S OUR CHARM -- OUR GOOD LOOKS!
I'LL BUY THAT!
WITH ME, IT'S PROBABLY MY CHICK!
JUGGIE! YOU'VE GOT A GIRL?
NO, BETTY!
THE DUMMY MEANS "C-H-I-C"!
IT'S PRONOUNCED "SHEEK," YOU IDIOT!
NO KIDDING?
ANYWAY, I GUESS IT'S OUR OVERALL IRRESISTIBLE PERSONALITIES!
YOU DO ALL HAVE A CERTAIN AMOUNT OF CHARISMA!
BUT NOT ONE OF YOU KNOWS BEANS ABOUT FASHION!
TODAY, EVERYBODY WHO'S ANYBODY WEARS DESIGNER CLOTHES! THE LABEL IS EVERYTHING!
SLAP!
2

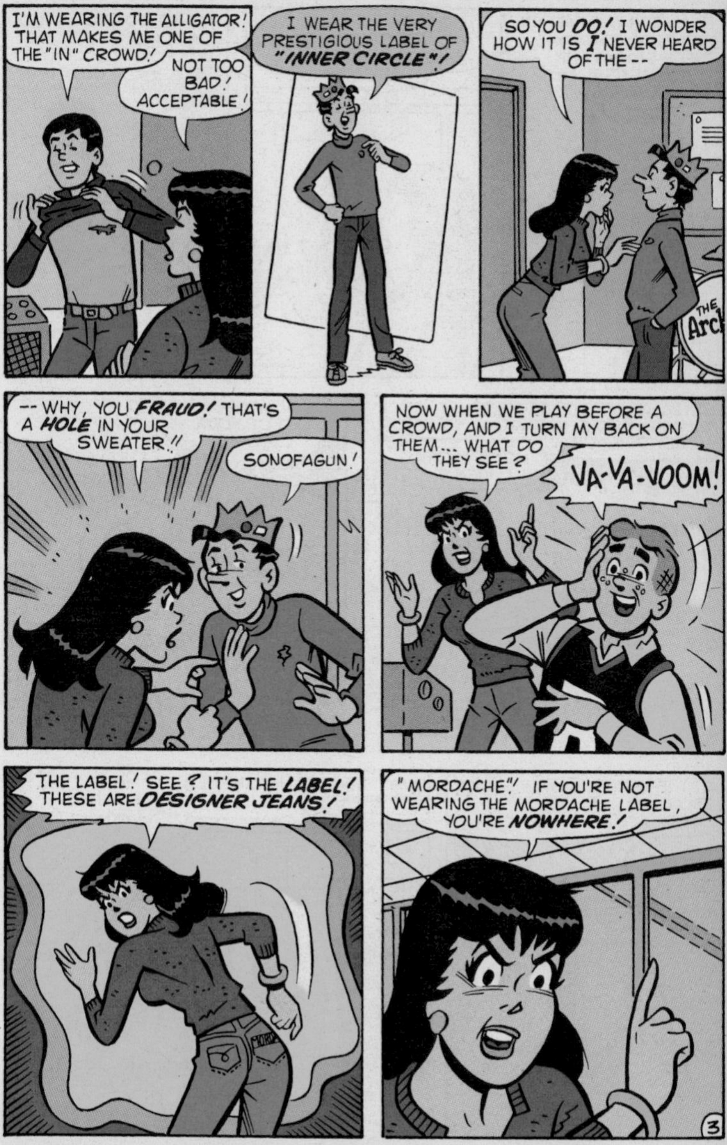

I'M WEARING THE ALLIGATOR! THAT MAKES ME ONE OF THE "IN" CROWD!
NOT TOO BAD! ACCEPTABLE!
I WEAR THE VERY PRESTIGIOUS LABEL OF "INNER CIRCLE"!
SO YOU DO! I WONDER HOW IT IS I NEVER HEARD OF THE --
THE Arc
-- WHY, YOU FRAUD! THAT'S A HOLE IN YOUR SWEATER!!
SONOFAGUN!
NOW WHEN WE PLAY BEFORE A CROWD, AND I TURN MY BACK ON THEM... WHAT DO THEY SEE?
VA-VA-VOOM!
THE LABEL! SEE? IT'S THE LABEL! THESE ARE DESIGNER JEANS!
"MORDACHE"! IF YOU'RE NOT WEARING THE MORDACHE LABEL, YOU'RE NOWHERE!
3

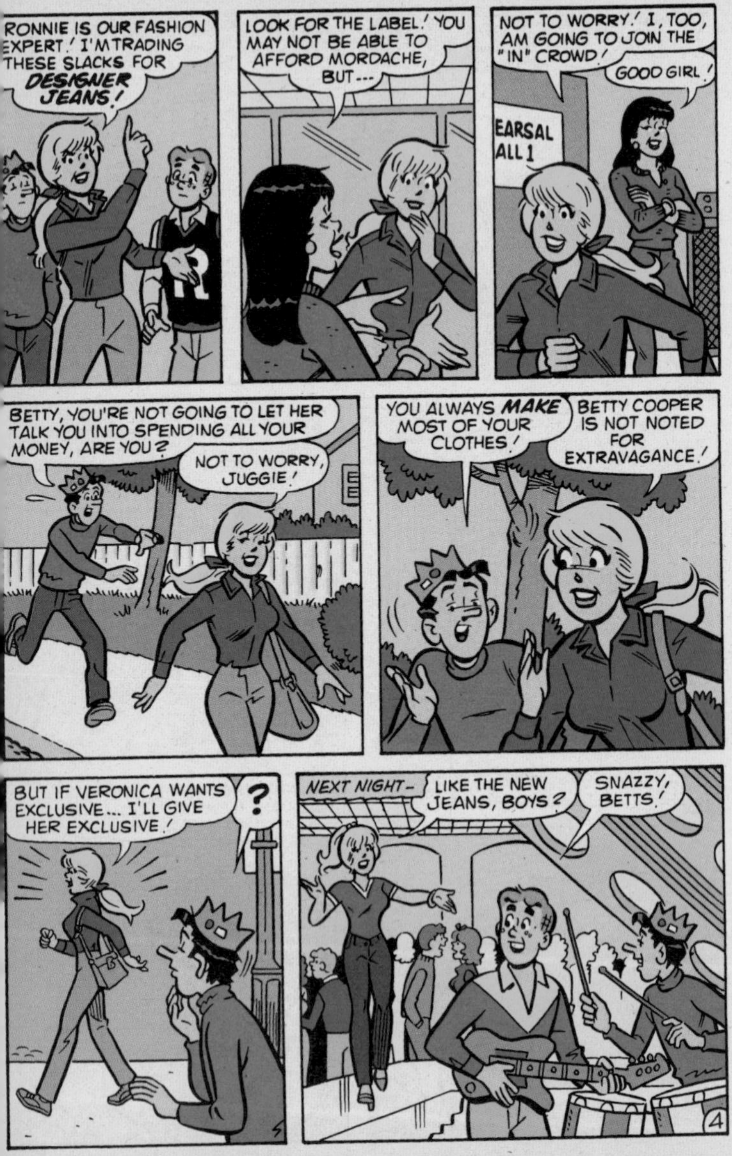
RONNIE IS OUR FASHION EXPERT! I'M TRADING THESE SLACKS FOR DESIGNER JEANS!
LOOK FOR THE LABEL! YOU MAY NOT BE ABLE TO AFFORD MORDACHE, BUT---
NOT TO WORRY! I, TOO, AM GOING TO JOIN THE "IN" CROWD!
GOOD GIRL!
EARSAL
ALL 1
BETTY, YOU'RE NOT GOING TO LET HER TALK YOU INTO SPENDING ALL YOUR MONEY, ARE YOU?
NOT TO WORRY, JUGGIE!
YOU ALWAYS MAKE MOST OF YOUR CLOTHES!
BETTY COOPER IS NOT NOTED FOR EXTRAVAGANCE!
BUT IF VERONICA WANTS EXCLUSIVE... I'LL GIVE HER EXCLUSIVE!
?
NEXT NIGHT-
LIKE THE NEW JEANS, BOYS?
SNAZZY, BETTS!
4

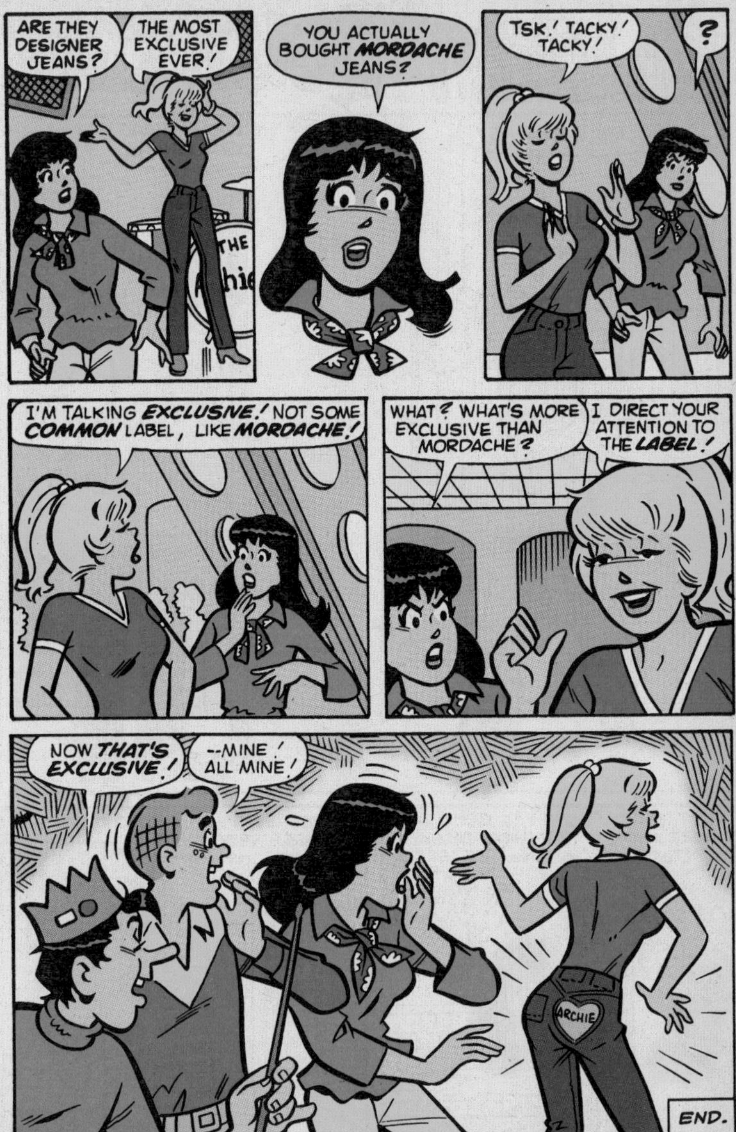
ARE THEY DESIGNER JEANS?
THE MOST EXCLUSIVE EVER!
THE
YOU ACTUALLY BOUGHT MORDACHE JEANS?
TSK! TACKY! TACKY!
?
I'M TALKING EXCLUSIVE! NOT SOME COMMON LABEL, LIKE MORDACHE!
WHAT? WHAT'S MORE EXCLUSIVE THAN MORDACHE?
I DIRECT YOUR ATTENTION TO THE LABEL!
NOW THAT'S EXCLUSIVE!
--MINE! ALL MINE!
ARCHIE
END.

Mr. Andrews in "QUICK STUDY"

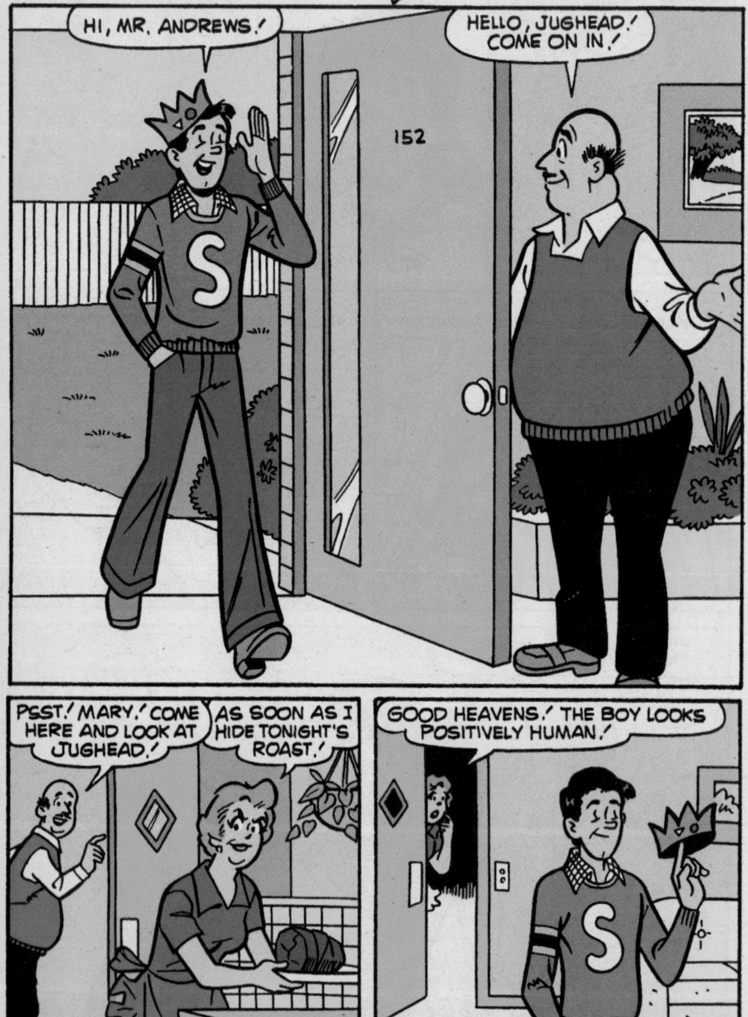
HI, MR. ANDREWS!
HELLO, JUGHEAD! COME ON IN!
152
PSST! MARY! COME HERE AND LOOK AT JUGHEAD!
AS SOON AS I HIDE TONIGHT'S ROAST!
GOOD HEAVENS! THE BOY LOOKS POSITIVELY HUMAN!

Script: Frank Doyle / Pencils: Dan DeCarlo Jr. / Inks: Jimmy DeCarlo / Letters: Bill Yoshida / Colors: Barry Grossman

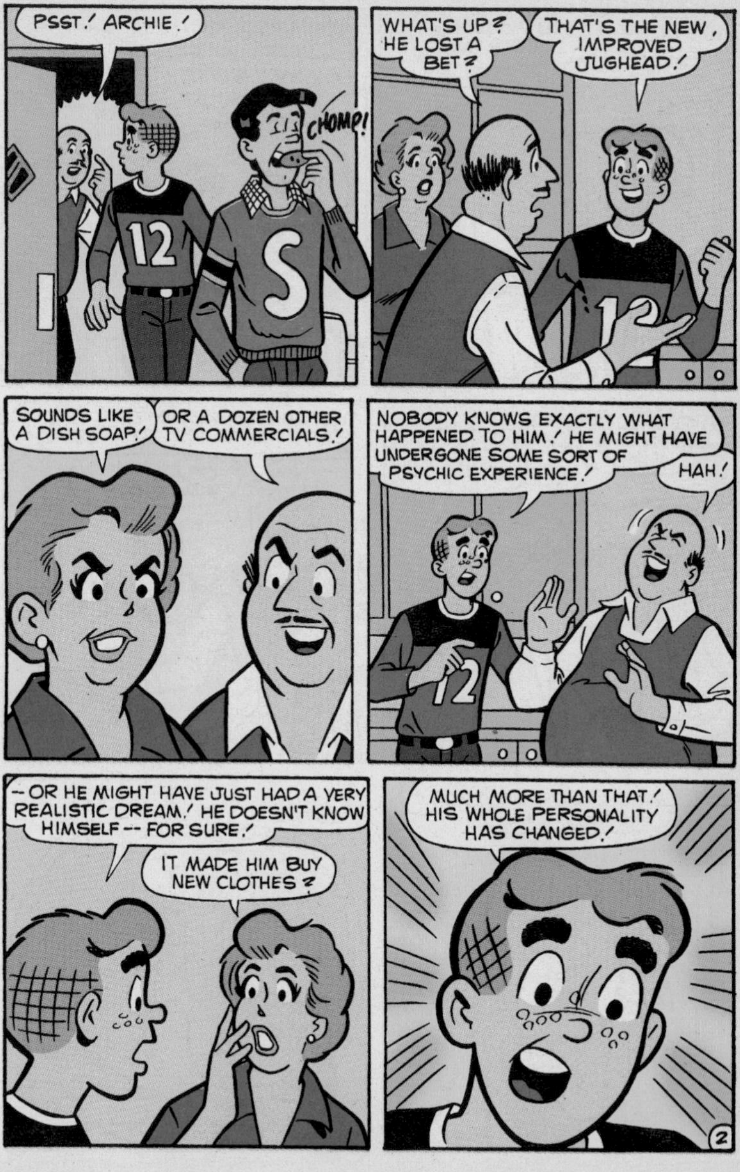
PSST! ARCHIE!
CHOMP!
WHAT'S UP? HE LOST A BET?
THAT'S THE NEW, IMPROVED JUGHEAD!
SOUNDS LIKE A DISH SOAP!
OR A DOZEN OTHER TV COMMERCIALS!
NOBODY KNOWS EXACTLY WHAT HAPPENED TO HIM! HE MIGHT HAVE UNDERGONE SOME SORT OF PSYCHIC EXPERIENCE!
HAH!
--OR HE MIGHT HAVE JUST HAD A VERY REALISTIC DREAM! HE DOESN'T KNOW HIMSELF -- FOR SURE!
IT MADE HIM BUY NEW CLOTHES?
MUCH MORE THAN THAT! HIS WHOLE PERSONALITY HAS CHANGED!
2

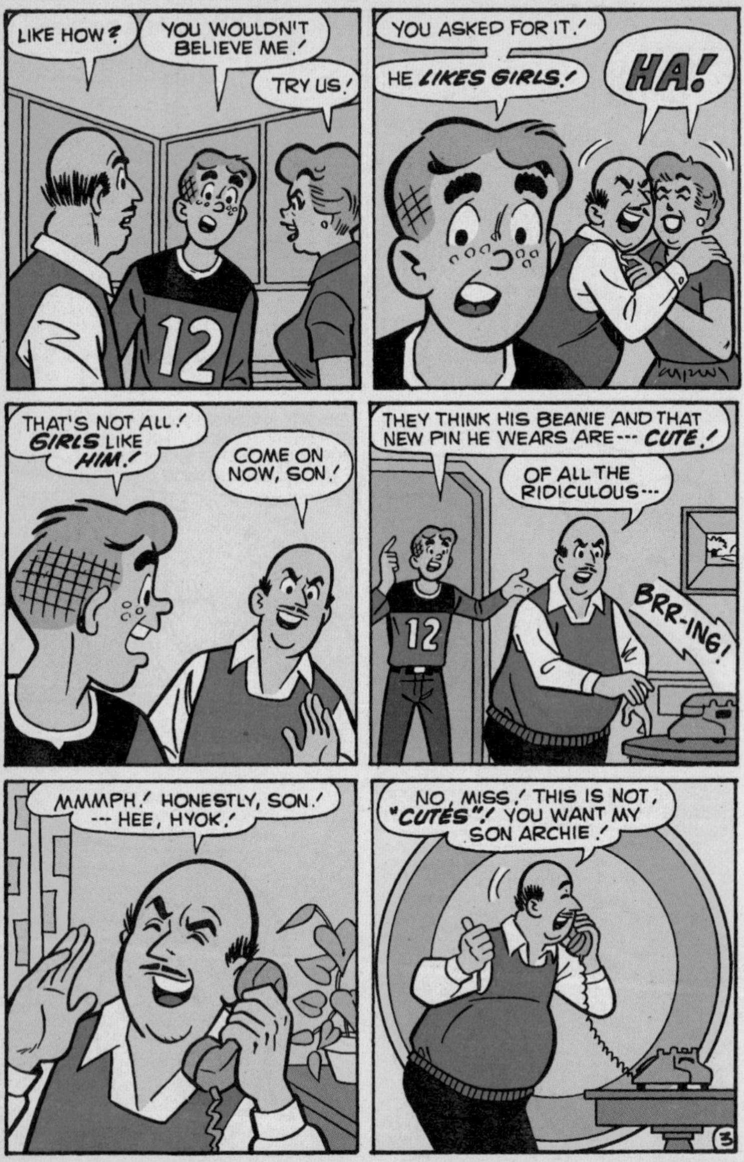
LIKE HOW?
YOU WOULDN'T BELIEVE ME!
TRY US!
YOU ASKED FOR IT!
HE LIKES GIRLS!
HA!
THAT'S NOT ALL! GIRLS LIKE HIM!
COME ON NOW, SON!
THEY THINK HIS BEANIE AND THAT NEW PIN HE WEARS ARE--- CUTE!
OF ALL THE RIDICULOUS---
BRR-ING!
MMMPH! HONESTLY, SON! --- HEE, HYOK!
NO, MISS! THIS IS NOT "CUTES"! YOU WANT MY SON ARCHIE!

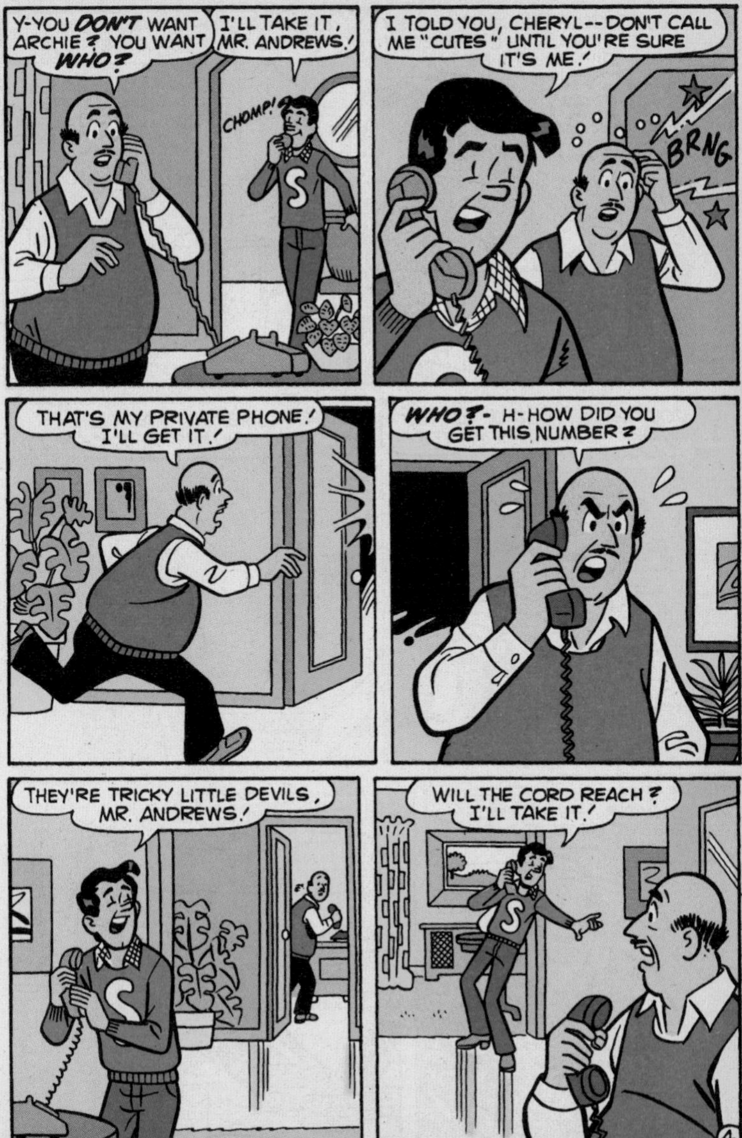

Y-YOU DON'T WANT ARCHIE? YOU WANT WHO?
I'LL TAKE IT, MR. ANDREWS!
CHOMP!
I TOLD YOU, CHERYL--DON'T CALL ME "CUTES" UNTIL YOU'RE SURE IT'S ME!
BRNG
THAT'S MY PRIVATE PHONE! I'LL GET IT!
WHO?- H-HOW DID YOU GET THIS NUMBER?
THEY'RE TRICKY LITTLE DEVILS, MR. ANDREWS!
WILL THE CORD REACH? I'LL TAKE IT!
4

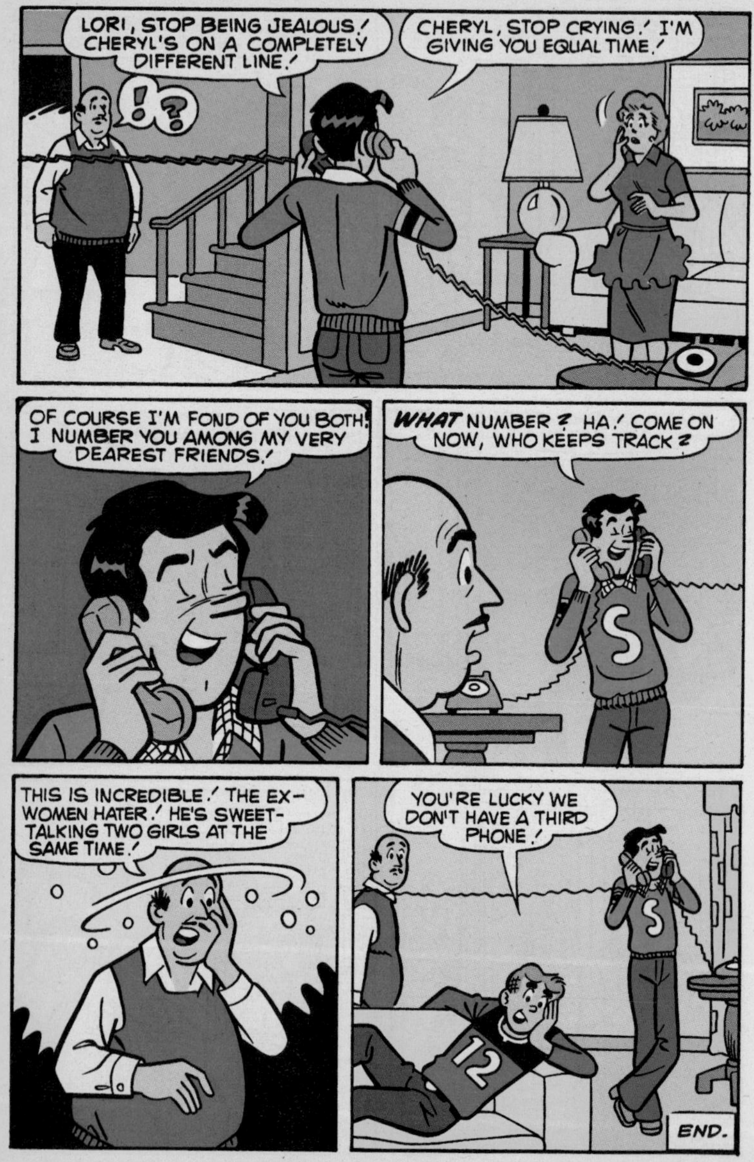
LORI, STOP BEING JEALOUS! CHERYL'S ON A COMPLETELY DIFFERENT LINE!
!?
CHERYL, STOP CRYING! I'M GIVING YOU EQUAL TIME!
OF COURSE I'M FOND OF YOU BOTH! I NUMBER YOU AMONG MY VERY DEAREST FRIENDS!
WHAT NUMBER? HA! COME ON NOW, WHO KEEPS TRACK?
THIS IS INCREDIBLE! THE EX-WOMEN HATER! HE'S SWEET-TALKING TWO GIRLS AT THE SAME TIME!
YOU'RE LUCKY WE DON'T HAVE A THIRD PHONE!
S
12
END.

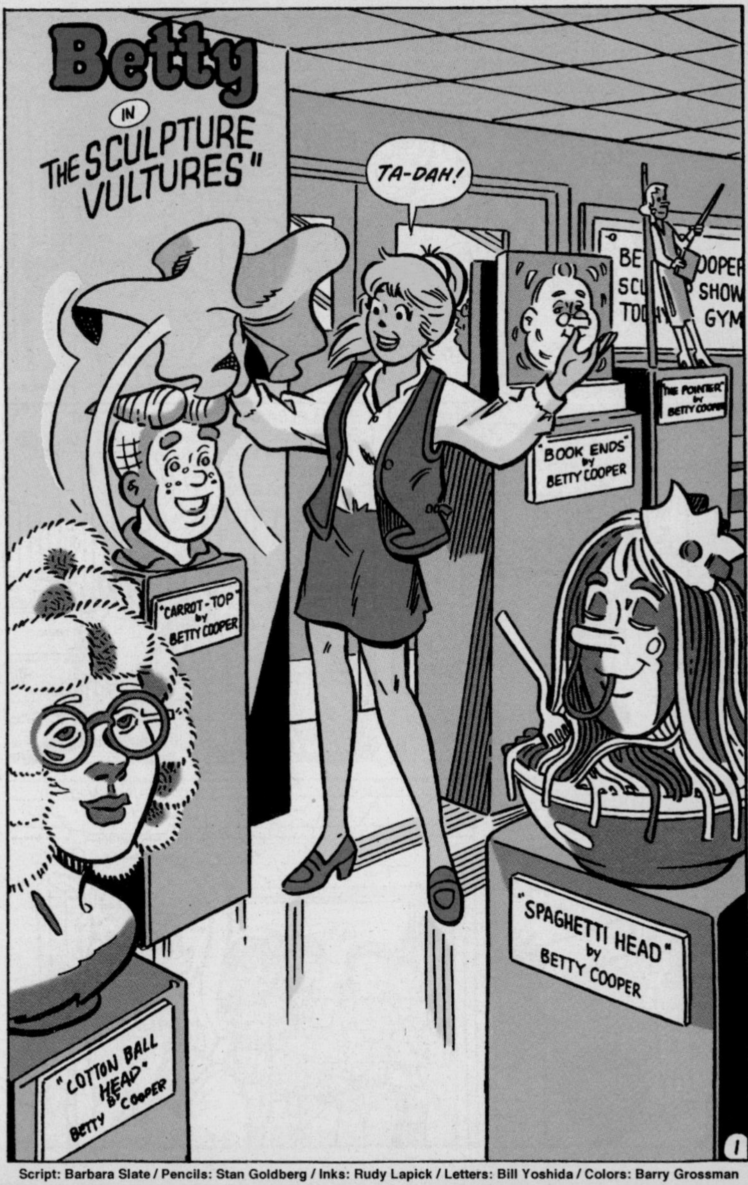
Betty
IN
"THE SCULPTURE VULTURES"
TA-DAH!
BETTY COOPER SCULPTURE SHOW TODAY GYM
"THE POINTER" by BETTY COOPER
"BOOK ENDS" by BETTY COOPER
"CARROT-TOP" by BETTY COOPER
"SPAGHETTI HEAD" by BETTY COOPER
"COTTON BALL HEAD" BY BETTY COOPER
1

Script: Barbara Slate / Pencils: Stan Goldberg / Inks: Rudy Lapick / Letters: Bill Yoshida / Colors: Barry Grossman

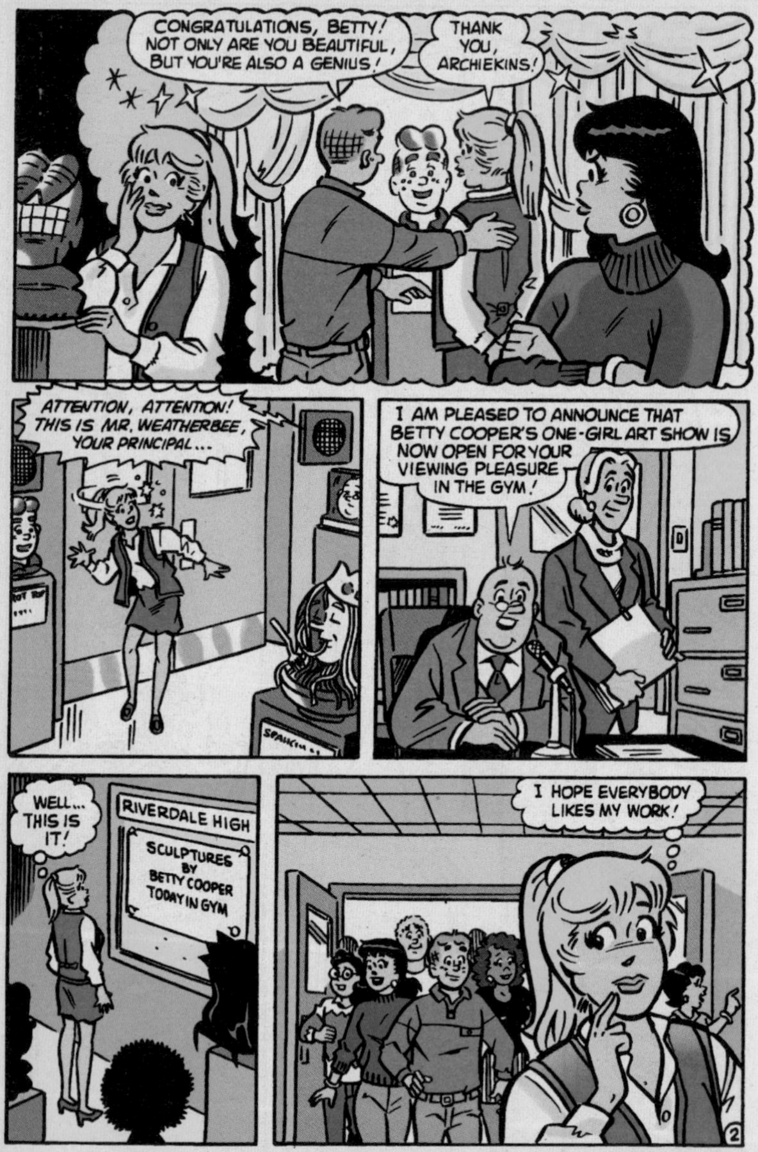
CONGRATULATIONS, BETTY! NOT ONLY ARE YOU BEAUTIFUL, BUT YOU'RE ALSO A GENIUS!
THANK YOU, ARCHIEKINS!
ATTENTION, ATTENTION! THIS IS MR. WEATHERBEE, YOUR PRINCIPAL...
I AM PLEASED TO ANNOUNCE THAT BETTY COOPER'S ONE-GIRL ART SHOW IS NOW OPEN FOR YOUR VIEWING PLEASURE IN THE GYM!
WELL... THIS IS IT!
RIVERDALE HIGH
SCULPTURES BY BETTY COOPER TODAY IN GYM
I HOPE EVERYBODY LIKES MY WORK!
2

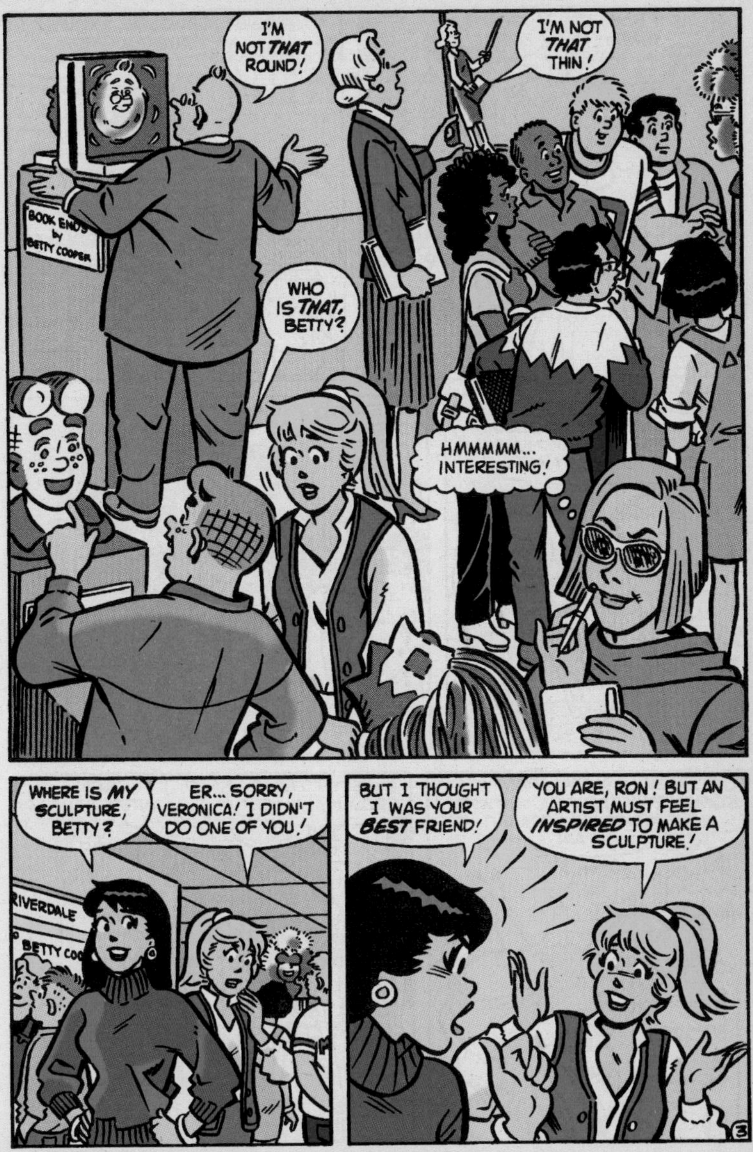

I'M NOT THAT ROUND!
BOOK ENDS by BETTY COOPER
I'M NOT THAT THIN!
WHO IS THAT, BETTY?
HMMMMM... INTERESTING!
WHERE IS MY SCULPTURE, BETTY?
ER... SORRY, VERONICA! I DIDN'T DO ONE OF YOU!
RIVERDALE
BETTY COO
BUT I THOUGHT I WAS YOUR BEST FRIEND!
YOU ARE, RON! BUT AN ARTIST MUST FEEL INSPIRED TO MAKE A SCULPTURE!

AS IF I AM NOT *WORTHY* OF INSPIRATION!

HEY, BETTY!

HUMPF!

HI, REGGIE!

OBVIOUSLY, YOU HAVEN'T CAUGHT MY PROFILE!

RIVERDALE

TTY COOP
TURE SHO
AYIN GYM

BECAUSE HAD YOU *BOTHERED* TO STUDY MY *CLASSIC* GOOD LOOKS THEN YOU WOULD HAVE CHOSEN TO SCULPT *ME*...

INSTEAD OF THAT!

YUMMY! THAT LOOKS DELICIOUS!

HEAD PAPER

COTTON BALLS?! HOW *DARE* YOU *SLANDER* MY BEAUTIFUL HAIR WITH YOUR NONSENSE NO TALENT NON-ART!

COTTONBALL
HEAD
BETTY PAPER

EXPECT TO HEAR FROM MY LAWYER!

!

VERY INTERESTING!

4

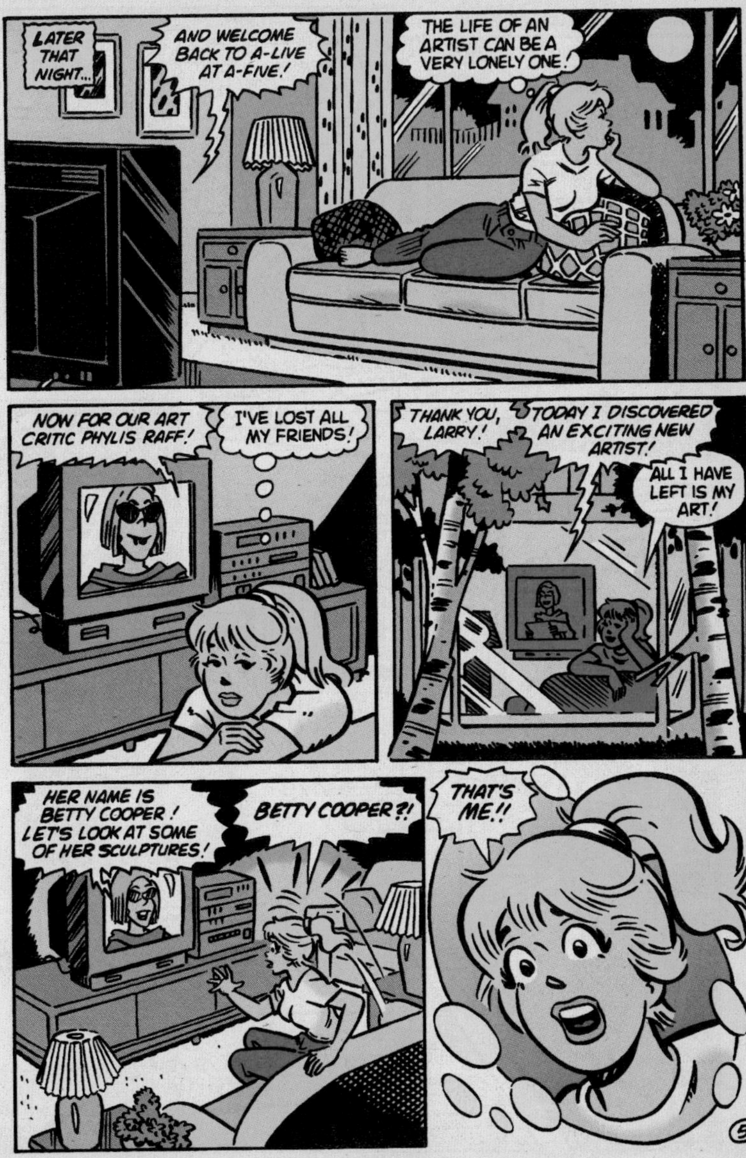
LATER THAT NIGHT...
AND WELCOME BACK TO A-LIVE AT A-FIVE!
THE LIFE OF AN ARTIST CAN BE A VERY LONELY ONE!
NOW FOR OUR ART CRITIC PHYLIS RAFF!
I'VE LOST ALL MY FRIENDS!
THANK YOU, LARRY!
TODAY I DISCOVERED AN EXCITING NEW ARTIST!
ALL I HAVE LEFT IS MY ART!
HER NAME IS BETTY COOPER! LET'S LOOK AT SOME OF HER SCULPTURES!
BETTY COOPER?!
THAT'S ME!!
5

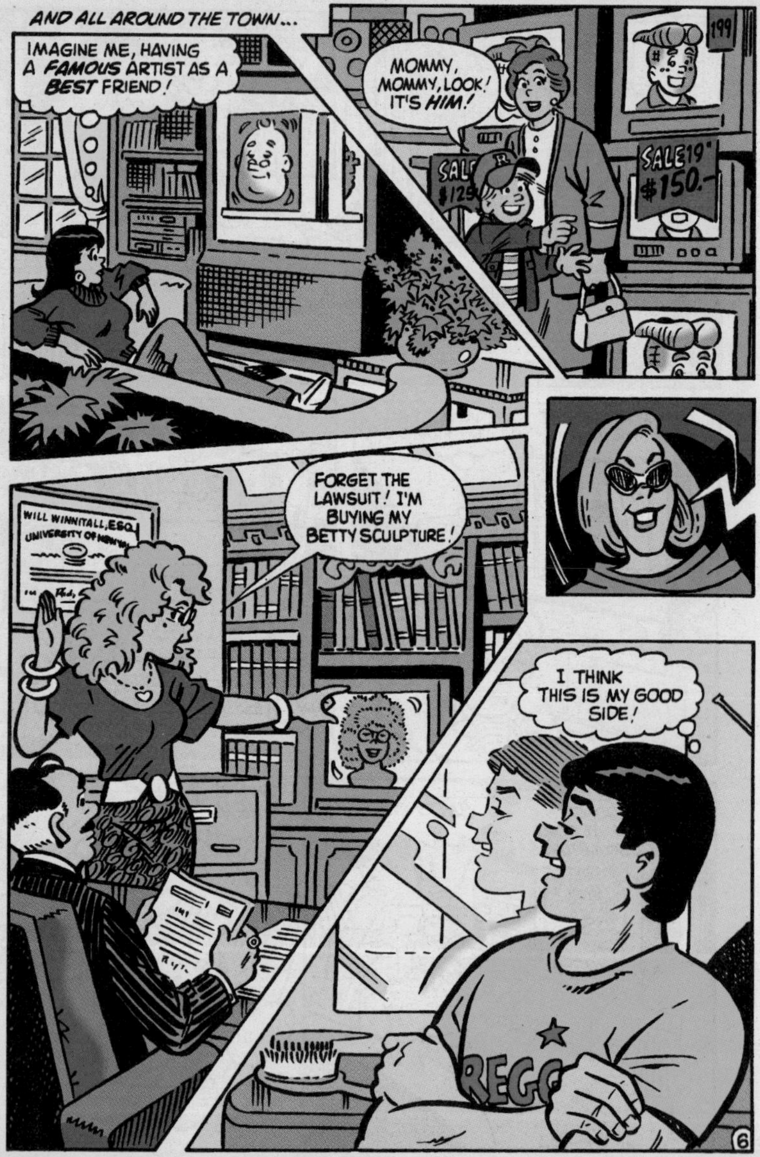
AND ALL AROUND THE TOWN...
IMAGINE ME, HAVING A FAMOUS ARTIST AS A BEST FRIEND!
MOMMY, MOMMY, LOOK! IT'S HIM!
199
SALE $125
SALE 19" $150.-
WILL WINNITALL, ESQ.
FORGET THE LAWSUIT! I'M BUYING MY BETTY SCULPTURE!
I THINK THIS IS MY GOOD SIDE!
REGG
6

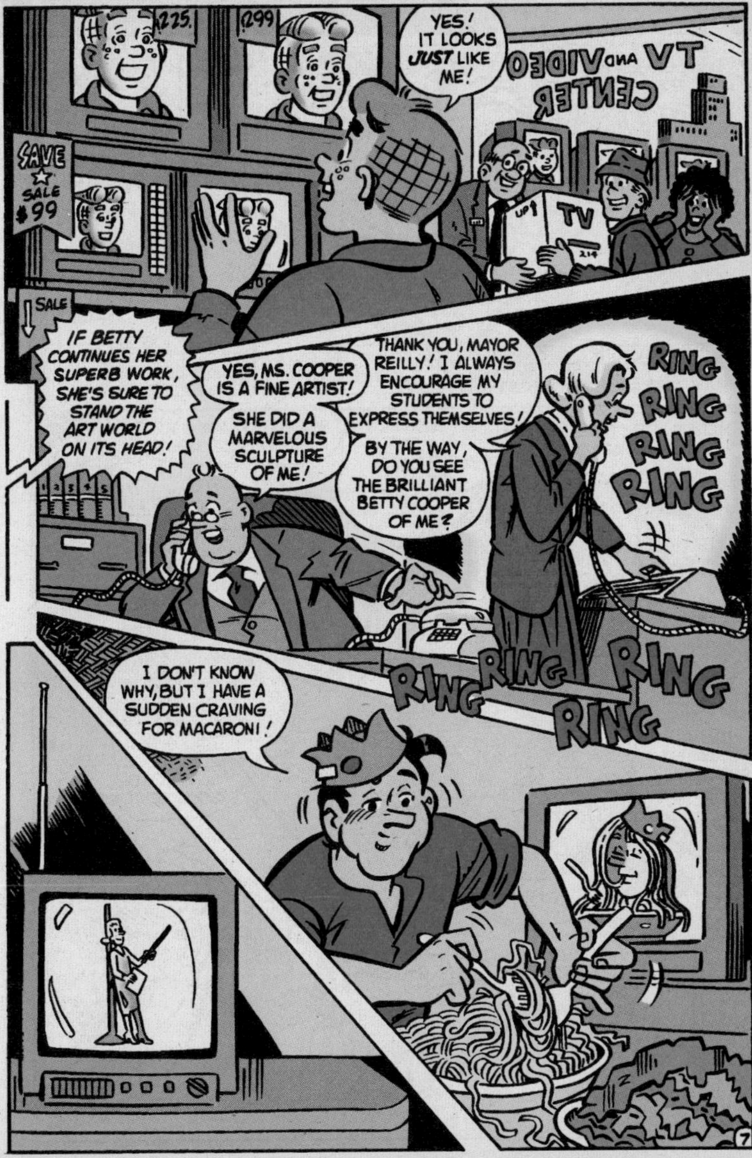

225.
299
YES! IT LOOKS JUST LIKE ME!
TV AND VIDEO CENTER
SAVE ☆ SALE $99
TV
UP
SALE
IF BETTY CONTINUES HER SUPERB WORK, SHE'S SURE TO STAND THE ART WORLD ON ITS HEAD!
YES, MS. COOPER IS A FINE ARTIST!
SHE DID A MARVELOUS SCULPTURE OF ME!
THANK YOU, MAYOR REILLY! I ALWAYS ENCOURAGE MY STUDENTS TO EXPRESS THEMSELVES!
BY THE WAY, DO YOU SEE THE BRILLIANT BETTY COOPER OF ME?
RING RING RING RING
RING RING RING RING
I DON'T KNOW WHY, BUT I HAVE A SUDDEN CRAVING FOR MACARONI!

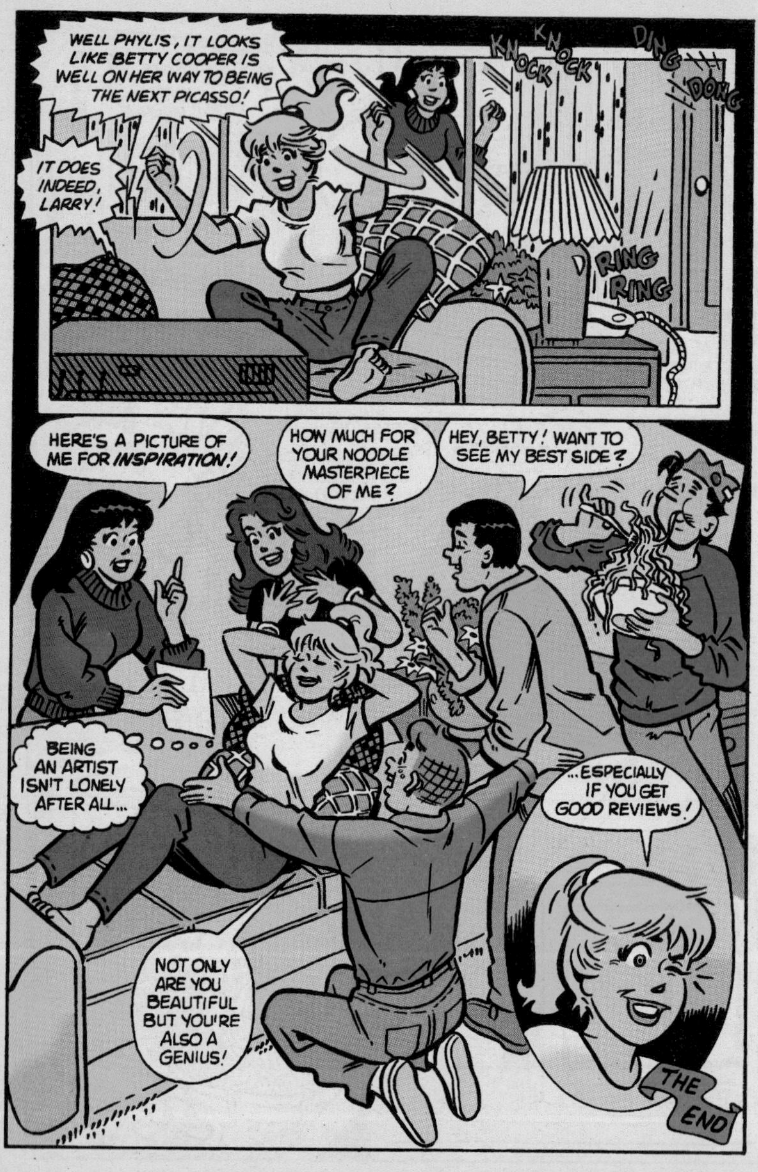
WELL PHYLIS, IT LOOKS LIKE BETTY COOPER IS WELL ON HER WAY TO BEING THE NEXT PICASSO!
IT DOES INDEED, LARRY!
KNOCK KNOCK
DING DONG
RING RING
HERE'S A PICTURE OF ME FOR *INSPIRATION*!
HOW MUCH FOR YOUR NOODLE MASTERPIECE OF ME?
HEY, BETTY! WANT TO SEE MY BEST SIDE?
BEING AN ARTIST ISN'T LONELY AFTER ALL...
...ESPECIALLY IF YOU GET GOOD REVIEWS!
NOT ONLY ARE YOU BEAUTIFUL BUT YOU'RE ALSO A GENIUS!
THE END

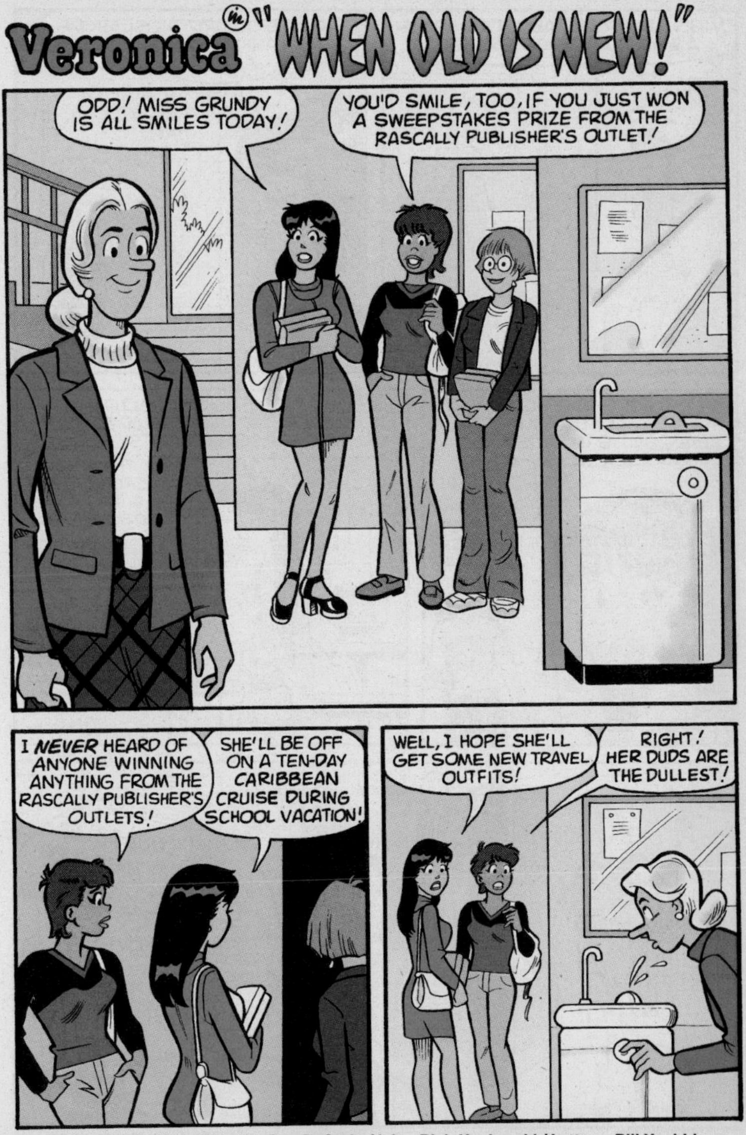
Veronica in "WHEN OLD IS NEW!"
ODD! MISS GRUNDY IS ALL SMILES TODAY!
YOU'D SMILE, TOO, IF YOU JUST WON A SWEEPSTAKES PRIZE FROM THE RASCALLY PUBLISHER'S OUTLET!
I NEVER HEARD OF ANYONE WINNING ANYTHING FROM THE RASCALLY PUBLISHER'S OUTLETS!
SHE'LL BE OFF ON A TEN-DAY CARIBBEAN CRUISE DURING SCHOOL VACATION!
WELL, I HOPE SHE'LL GET SOME NEW TRAVEL OUTFITS!
RIGHT! HER DUDS ARE THE DULLEST!

Script: Bob Bolling / Pencils: Dan DeCarlo / Inks: Rich Koslowski / Letters: Bill Yoshida

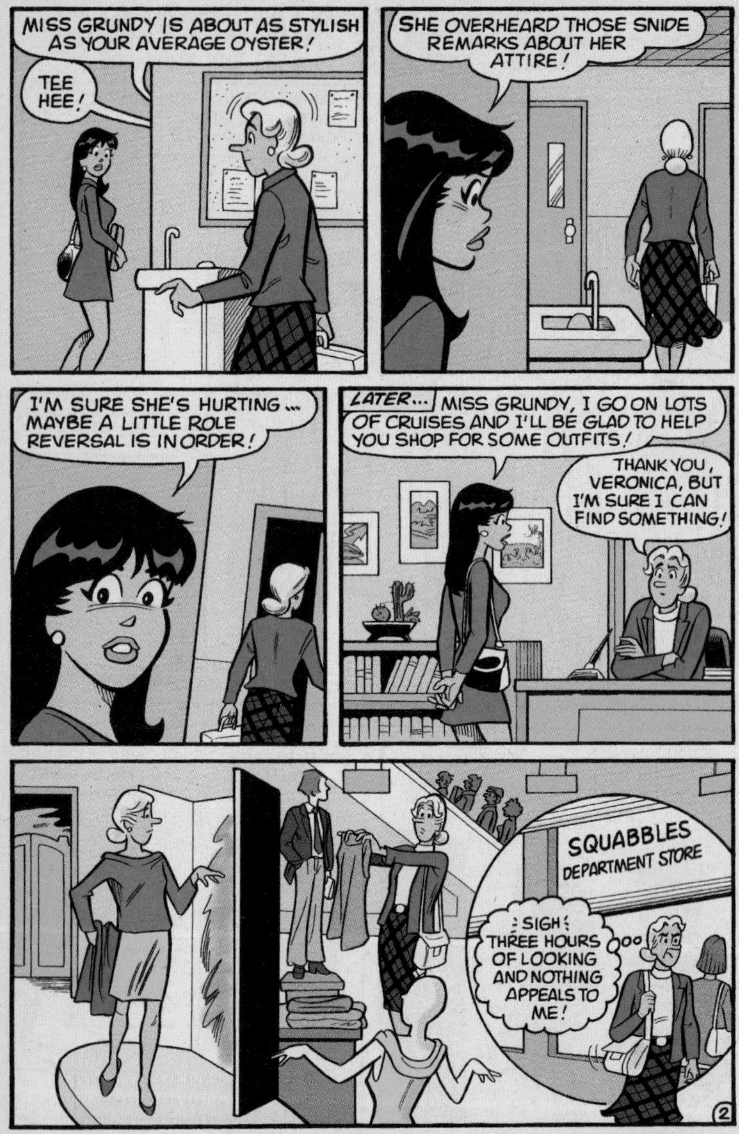

MISS GRUNDY IS ABOUT AS STYLISH AS YOUR AVERAGE OYSTER!
TEE HEE!
SHE OVERHEARD THOSE SNIDE REMARKS ABOUT HER ATTIRE!
I'M SURE SHE'S HURTING ... MAYBE A LITTLE ROLE REVERSAL IS IN ORDER!
LATER...
MISS GRUNDY, I GO ON LOTS OF CRUISES AND I'LL BE GLAD TO HELP YOU SHOP FOR SOME OUTFITS!
THANK YOU, VERONICA, BUT I'M SURE I CAN FIND SOMETHING!
SQUABBLES DEPARTMENT STORE
SIGH THREE HOURS OF LOOKING AND NOTHING APPEALS TO ME!
2

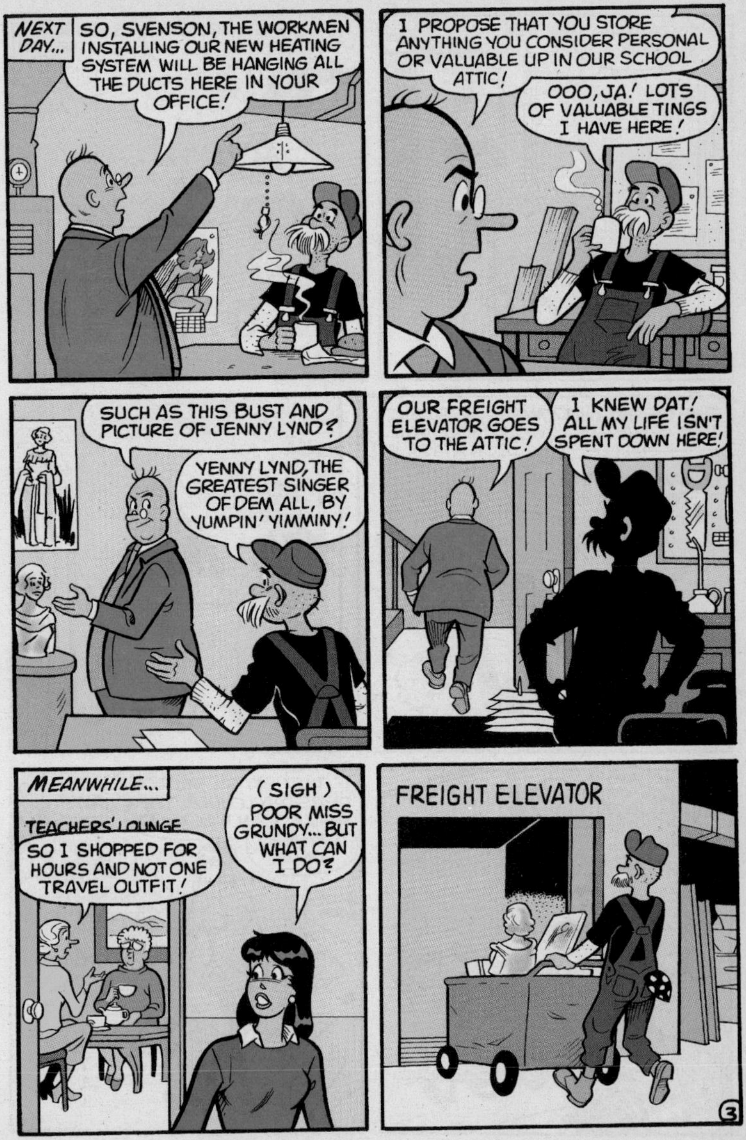
NEXT DAY...
SO, SVENSON, THE WORKMEN INSTALLING OUR NEW HEATING SYSTEM WILL BE HANGING ALL THE DUCTS HERE IN YOUR OFFICE!
I PROPOSE THAT YOU STORE ANYTHING YOU CONSIDER PERSONAL OR VALUABLE UP IN OUR SCHOOL ATTIC!
OOO, JA! LOTS OF VALUABLE TINGS I HAVE HERE!
SUCH AS THIS BUST AND PICTURE OF JENNY LYND?
YENNY LYND, THE GREATEST SINGER OF DEM ALL, BY YUMPIN' YIMMINY!
OUR FREIGHT ELEVATOR GOES TO THE ATTIC!
I KNEW DAT! ALL MY LIFE ISN'T SPENT DOWN HERE!
MEANWHILE...
TEACHERS' LOUNGE
SO I SHOPPED FOR HOURS AND NOT ONE TRAVEL OUTFIT!
(SIGH) POOR MISS GRUNDY... BUT WHAT CAN I DO?
FREIGHT ELEVATOR
3

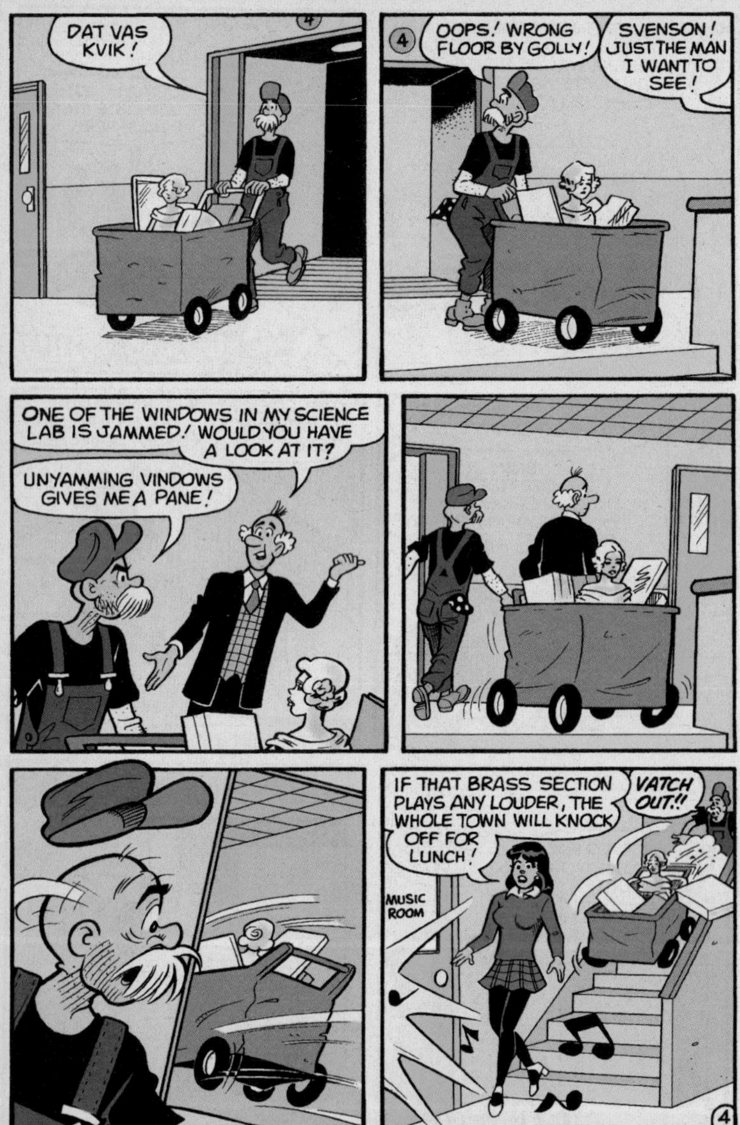

4
DAT VAS KVIK!
4
OOPS! WRONG FLOOR BY GOLLY!
SVENSON! JUST THE MAN I WANT TO SEE!
ONE OF THE WINDOWS IN MY SCIENCE LAB IS JAMMED! WOULD YOU HAVE A LOOK AT IT?
UNYAMMING VINDOWS GIVES ME A PANE!
IF THAT BRASS SECTION PLAYS ANY LOUDER, THE WHOLE TOWN WILL KNOCK OFF FOR LUNCH!
VATCH OUT!!
MUSIC ROOM
4

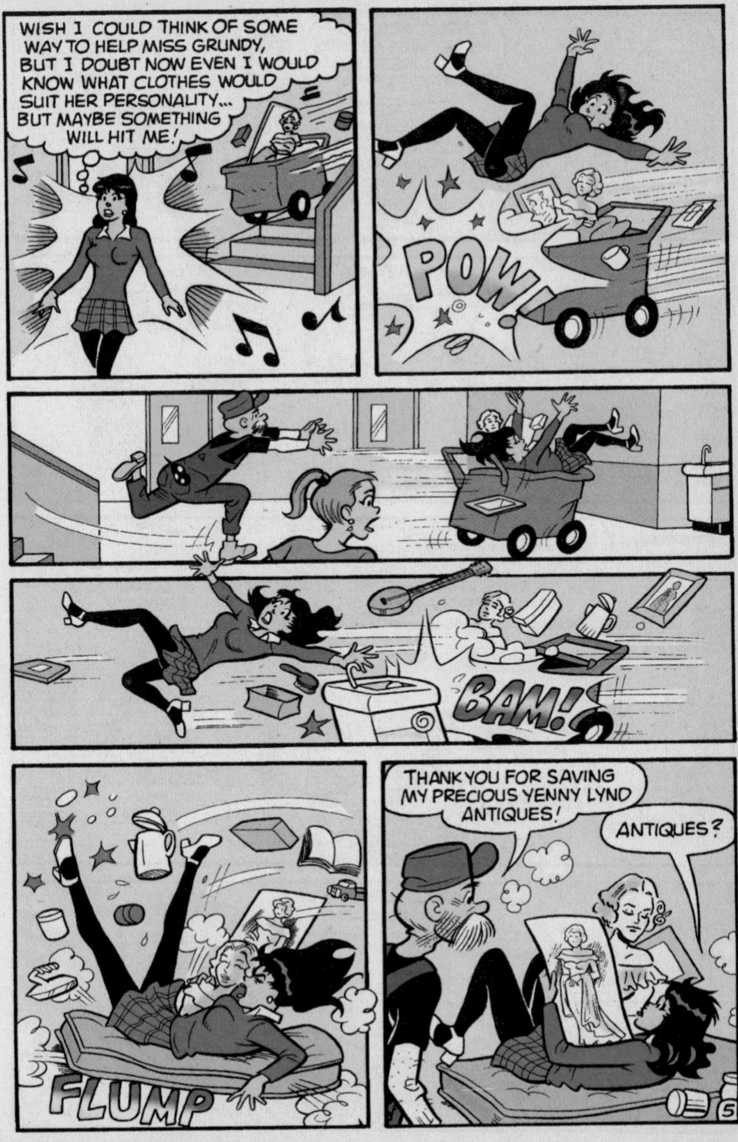
WISH I COULD THINK OF SOME WAY TO HELP MISS GRUNDY, BUT I DOUBT NOW EVEN I WOULD KNOW WHAT CLOTHES WOULD SUIT HER PERSONALITY... BUT MAYBE SOMETHING WILL HIT ME!
POW!
BAM!
FLUMP
THANK YOU FOR SAVING MY PRECIOUS YENNY LYND ANTIQUES!
ANTIQUES?
5

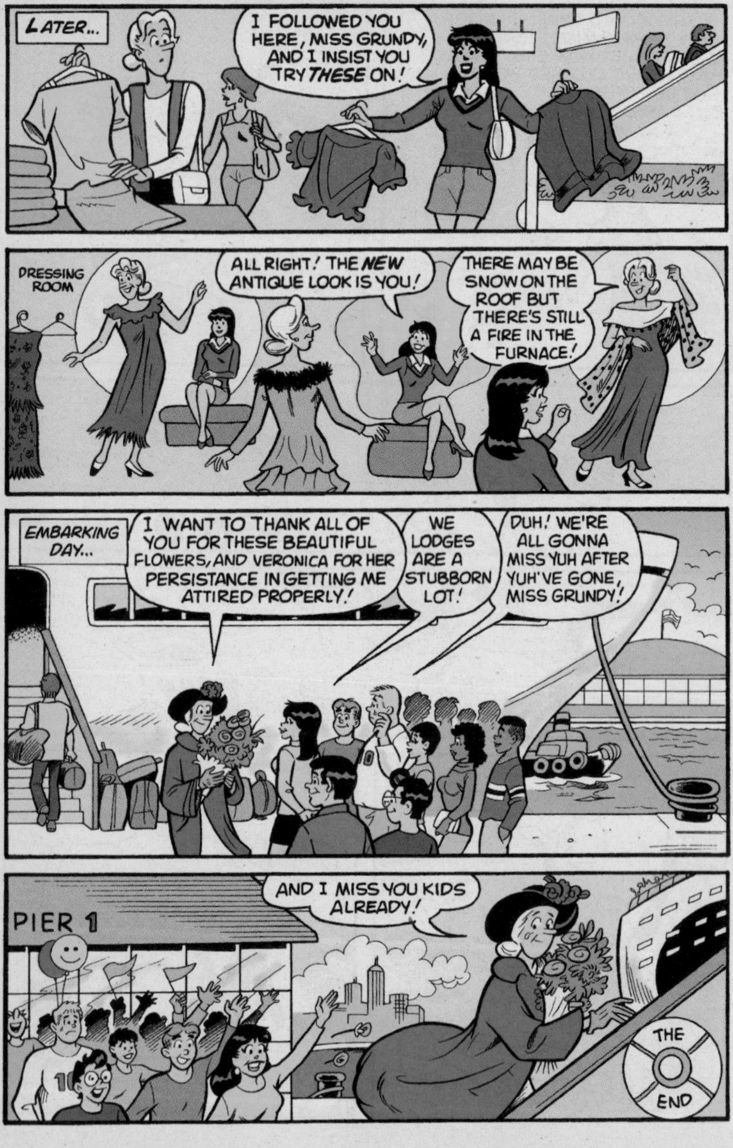
LATER...
I FOLLOWED YOU HERE, MISS GRUNDY, AND I INSIST YOU TRY THESE ON!
DRESSING ROOM
ALL RIGHT! THE NEW ANTIQUE LOOK IS YOU!
THERE MAY BE SNOW ON THE ROOF BUT THERE'S STILL A FIRE IN THE FURNACE!
EMBARKING DAY...
I WANT TO THANK ALL OF YOU FOR THESE BEAUTIFUL FLOWERS, AND VERONICA FOR HER PERSISTANCE IN GETTING ME ATTIRED PROPERLY!
WE LODGES ARE A STUBBORN LOT!
DUH! WE'RE ALL GONNA MISS YUH AFTER YUH'VE GONE, MISS GRUNDY!
AND I MISS YOU KIDS ALREADY!
PIER 1
THE END

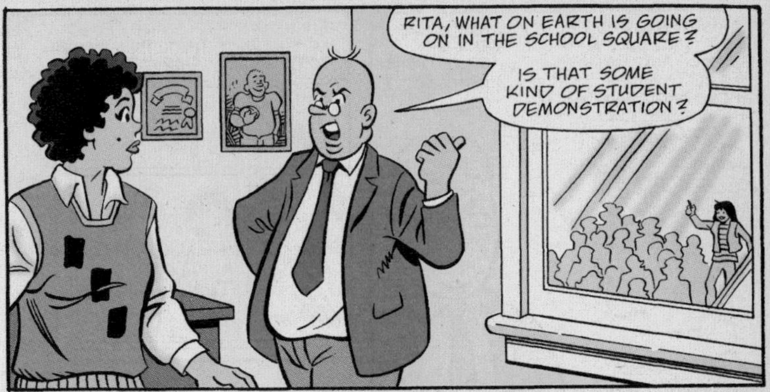

RITA, WHAT ON EARTH IS GOING ON IN THE SCHOOL SQUARE?
IS THAT SOME KIND OF STUDENT DEMONSTRATION?

Betty and Veronica® in The BIG EXAM!

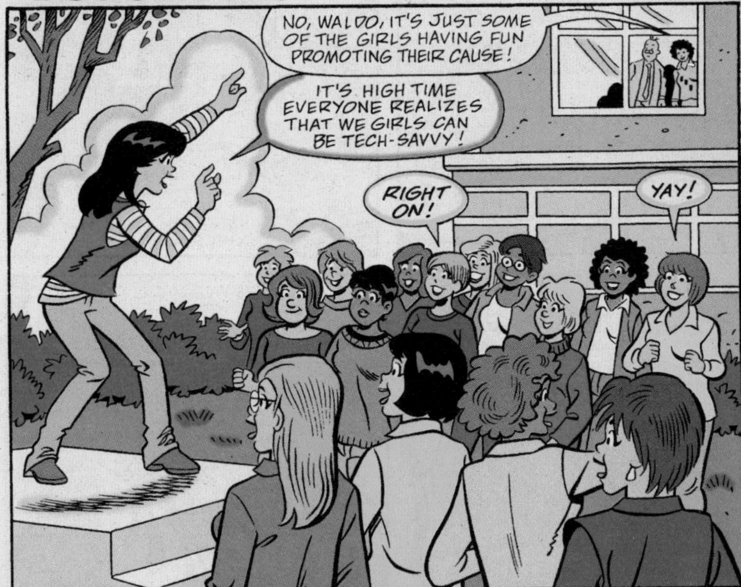

NO, WALDO, IT'S JUST SOME OF THE GIRLS HAVING FUN PROMOTING THEIR CAUSE!
IT'S HIGH TIME EVERYONE REALIZES THAT WE GIRLS CAN BE TECH-SAVVY!
RIGHT ON!
YAY!

Script: GEORGE GLADIR	Pencils: JEFF SHULTZ	Inks: AL MILGROM	Letters: PHIL FELIX	Colors: JOE MORCIGLIO

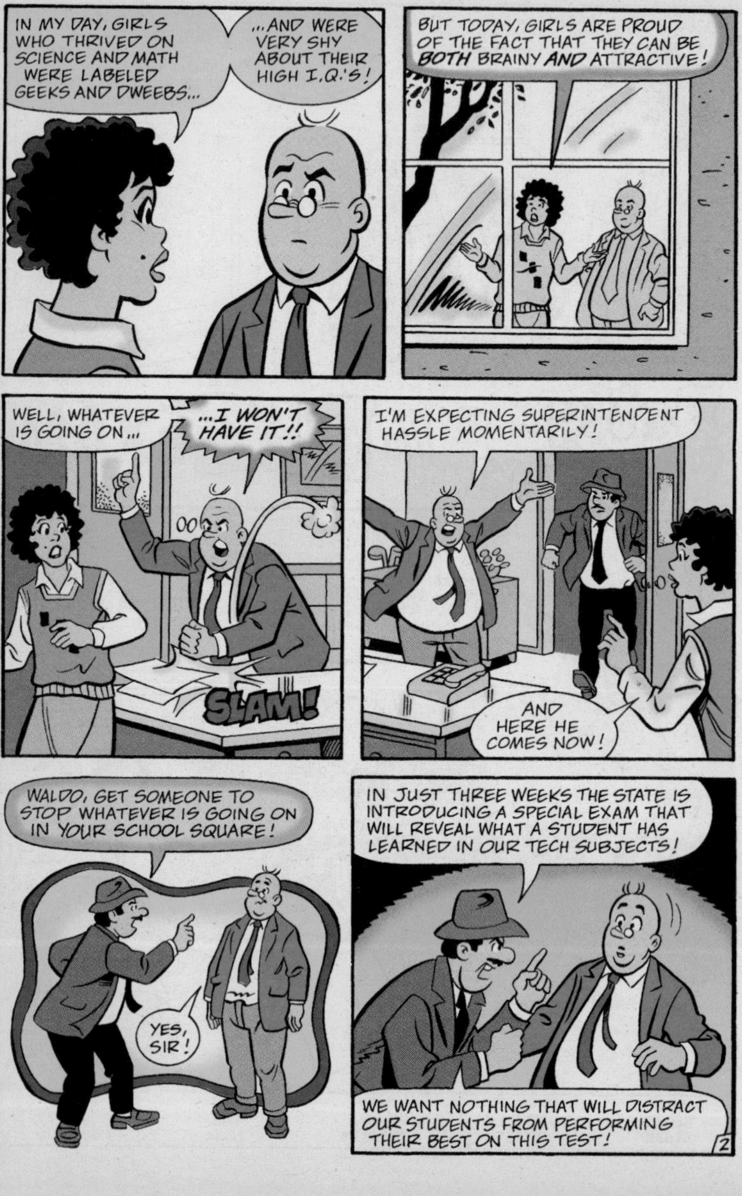
IN MY DAY, GIRLS WHO THRIVED ON SCIENCE AND MATH WERE LABELED GEEKS AND DWEEBS...
...AND WERE VERY SHY ABOUT THEIR HIGH I.Q.'S!
BUT TODAY, GIRLS ARE PROUD OF THE FACT THAT THEY CAN BE **BOTH** BRAINY **AND** ATTRACTIVE!
WELL, WHATEVER IS GOING ON...
...I WON'T HAVE IT!!
SLAM!
I'M EXPECTING SUPERINTENDENT HASSLE MOMENTARILY!
AND HERE HE COMES NOW!
WALDO, GET SOMEONE TO STOP WHATEVER IS GOING ON IN YOUR SCHOOL SQUARE!
YES, SIR!
IN JUST THREE WEEKS THE STATE IS INTRODUCING A SPECIAL EXAM THAT WILL REVEAL WHAT A STUDENT HAS LEARNED IN OUR TECH SUBJECTS!
WE WANT NOTHING THAT WILL DISTRACT OUR STUDENTS FROM PERFORMING THEIR BEST ON THIS TEST!
2

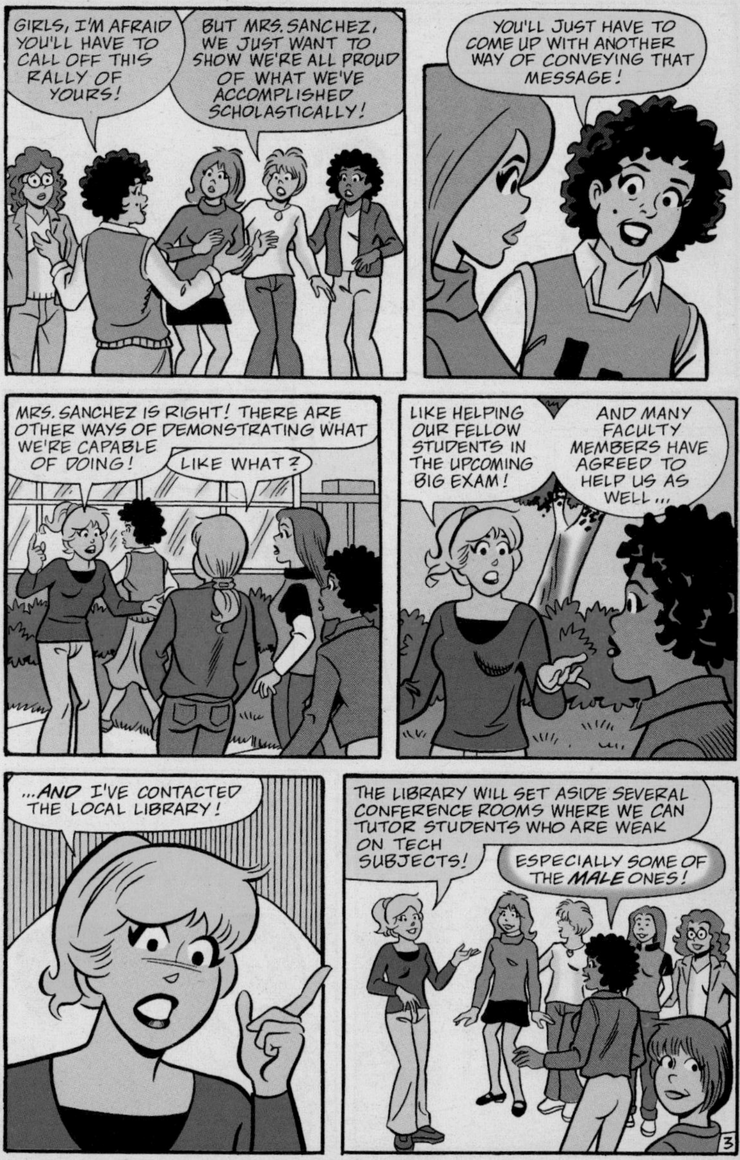
GIRLS, I'M AFRAID YOU'LL HAVE TO CALL OFF THIS RALLY OF YOURS!
BUT MRS. SANCHEZ, WE JUST WANT TO SHOW WE'RE ALL PROUD OF WHAT WE'VE ACCOMPLISHED SCHOLASTICALLY!
YOU'LL JUST HAVE TO COME UP WITH ANOTHER WAY OF CONVEYING THAT MESSAGE!
MRS. SANCHEZ IS RIGHT! THERE ARE OTHER WAYS OF DEMONSTRATING WHAT WE'RE CAPABLE OF DOING!
LIKE WHAT?
LIKE HELPING OUR FELLOW STUDENTS IN THE UPCOMING BIG EXAM!
AND MANY FACULTY MEMBERS HAVE AGREED TO HELP US AS WELL...
...AND I'VE CONTACTED THE LOCAL LIBRARY!
THE LIBRARY WILL SET ASIDE SEVERAL CONFERENCE ROOMS WHERE WE CAN TUTOR STUDENTS WHO ARE WEAK ON TECH SUBJECTS!
ESPECIALLY SOME OF THE MALE ONES!
3

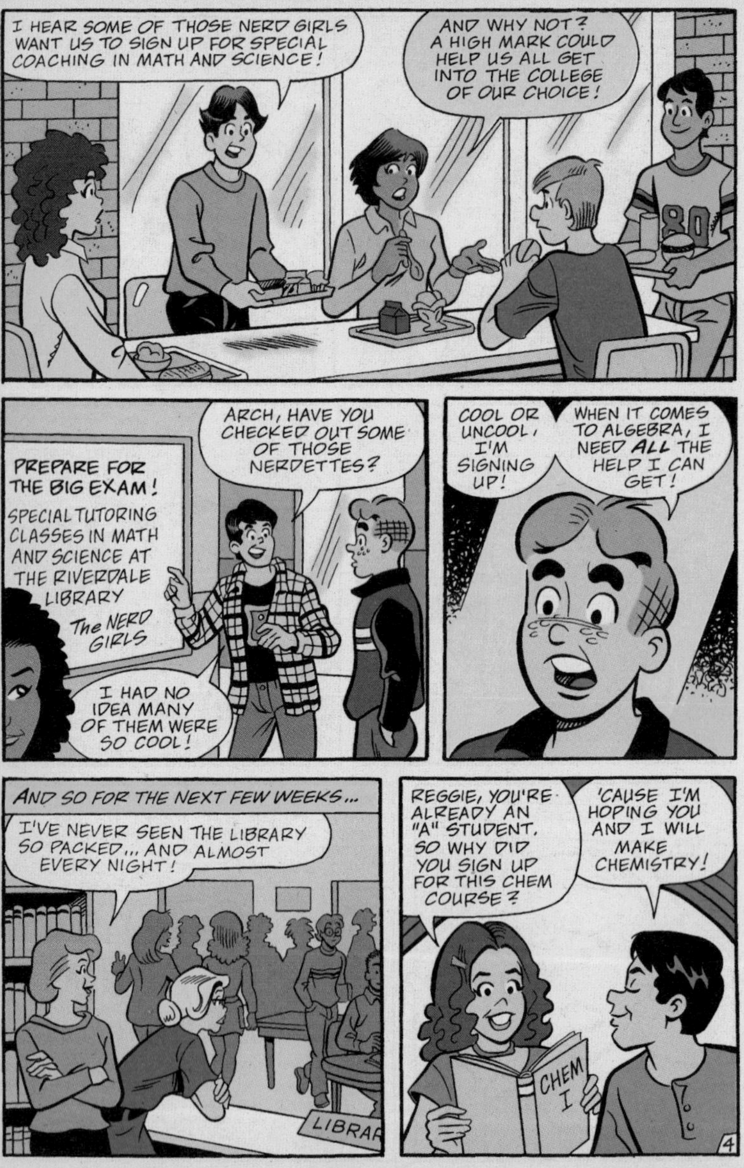
I HEAR SOME OF THOSE NERD GIRLS WANT US TO SIGN UP FOR SPECIAL COACHING IN MATH AND SCIENCE!
AND WHY NOT? A HIGH MARK COULD HELP US ALL GET INTO THE COLLEGE OF OUR CHOICE!
PREPARE FOR THE BIG EXAM! SPECIAL TUTORING CLASSES IN MATH AND SCIENCE AT THE RIVERDALE LIBRARY The NERD GIRLS
ARCH, HAVE YOU CHECKED OUT SOME OF THOSE NERDETTES?
I HAD NO IDEA MANY OF THEM WERE SO COOL!
COOL OR UNCOOL, I'M SIGNING UP!
WHEN IT COMES TO ALGEBRA, I NEED ALL THE HELP I CAN GET!
AND SO FOR THE NEXT FEW WEEKS...
I'VE NEVER SEEN THE LIBRARY SO PACKED... AND ALMOST EVERY NIGHT!
LIBRAR
REGGIE, YOU'RE ALREADY AN "A" STUDENT, SO WHY DID YOU SIGN UP FOR THIS CHEM COURSE?
'CAUSE I'M HOPING YOU AND I WILL MAKE CHEMISTRY!
CHEM I
4

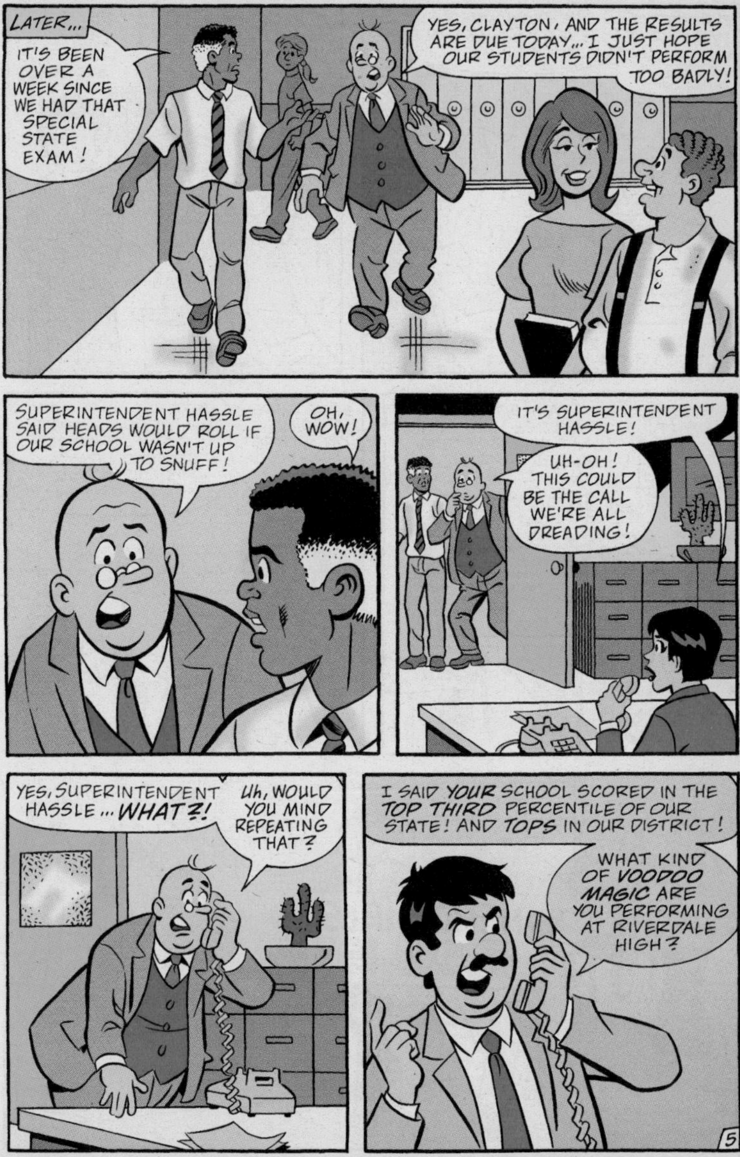
LATER...
IT'S BEEN OVER A WEEK SINCE WE HAD THAT SPECIAL STATE EXAM!
YES, CLAYTON, AND THE RESULTS ARE DUE TODAY... I JUST HOPE OUR STUDENTS DIDN'T PERFORM TOO BADLY!
SUPERINTENDENT HASSLE SAID HEADS WOULD ROLL IF OUR SCHOOL WASN'T UP TO SNUFF!
OH, WOW!
IT'S SUPERINTENDENT HASSLE!
UH-OH! THIS COULD BE THE CALL WE'RE ALL DREADING!
YES, SUPERINTENDENT HASSLE... WHAT?!
Uh, WOULD YOU MIND REPEATING THAT?
I SAID YOUR SCHOOL SCORED IN THE TOP THIRD PERCENTILE OF OUR STATE! AND TOPS IN OUR DISTRICT!
WHAT KIND OF VOODOO MAGIC ARE YOU PERFORMING AT RIVERDALE HIGH?
5

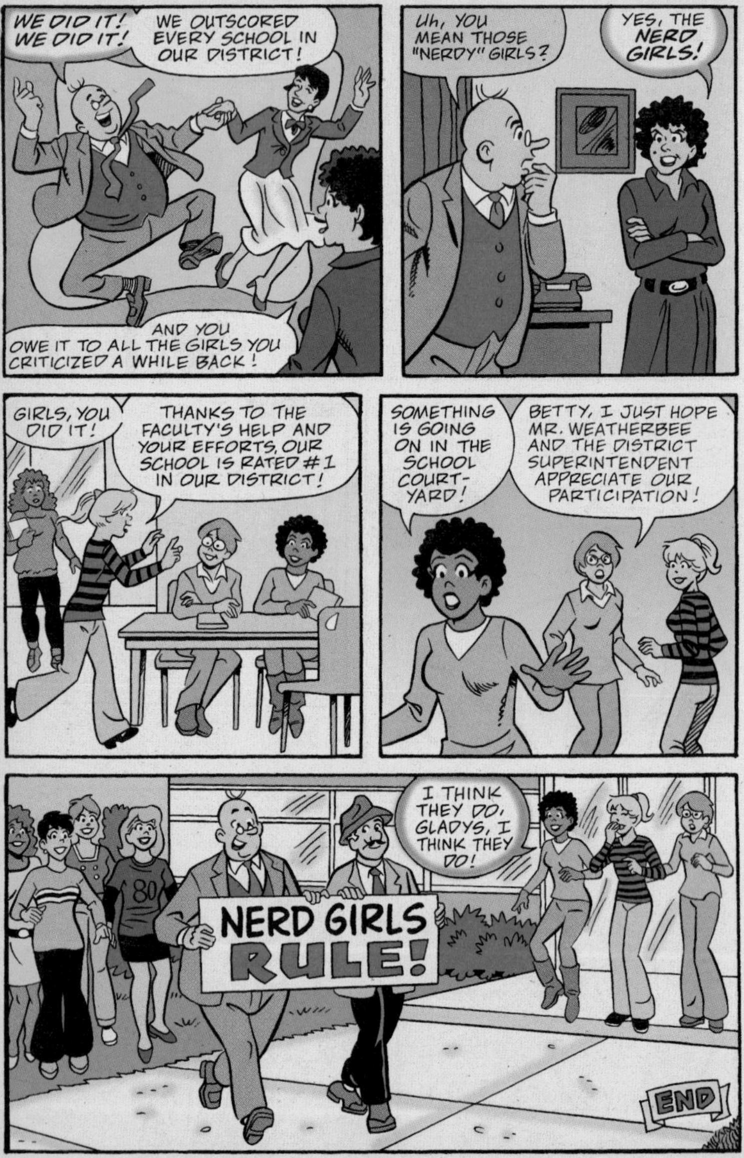
WE DID IT! WE DID IT!
WE OUTSCORED EVERY SCHOOL IN OUR DISTRICT!
AND YOU OWE IT TO ALL THE GIRLS YOU CRITICIZED A WHILE BACK!
UH, YOU MEAN THOSE "NERDY" GIRLS?
YES, THE NERD GIRLS!
GIRLS, YOU DID IT!
THANKS TO THE FACULTY'S HELP AND YOUR EFFORTS, OUR SCHOOL IS RATED #1 IN OUR DISTRICT!
SOMETHING IS GOING ON IN THE SCHOOL COURT-YARD!
BETTY, I JUST HOPE MR. WEATHERBEE AND THE DISTRICT SUPERINTENDENT APPRECIATE OUR PARTICIPATION!
I THINK THEY DO, GLADYS, I THINK THEY DO!
NERD GIRLS RULE!
80
END

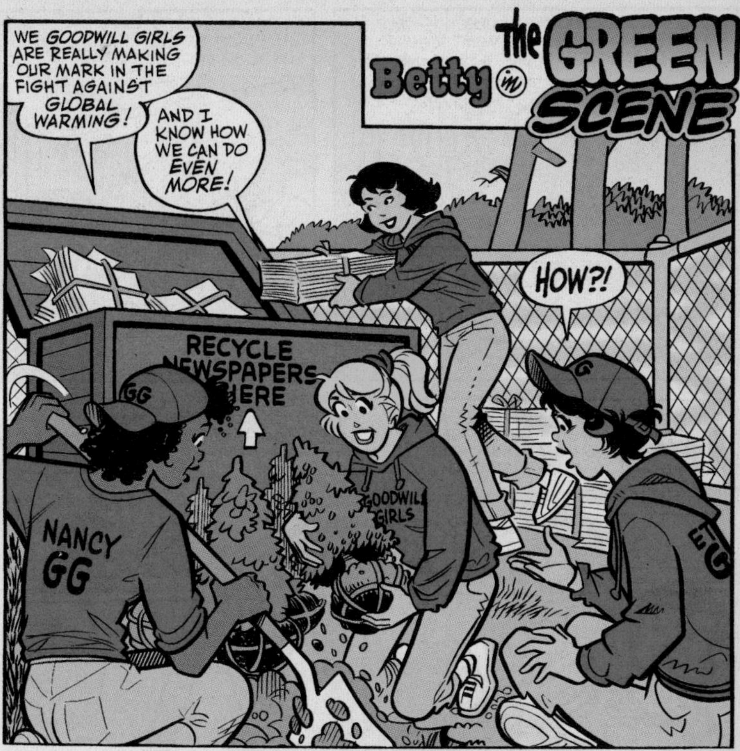
Betty in The GREEN SCENE
WE GOODWILL GIRLS ARE REALLY MAKING OUR MARK IN THE FIGHT AGAINST GLOBAL WARMING!
AND I KNOW HOW WE CAN DO EVEN MORE!
HOW?!
RECYCLE NEWSPAPERS HERE
NANCY GG
GOODWILL GIRLS

SCRIPT: GEORGE GLADIR PENCILS: STAN GOLDBERG INKING: RICH KOSLOWSKI LETTERING: JACK MORELLI COLORING: BARRY GROSSMAN

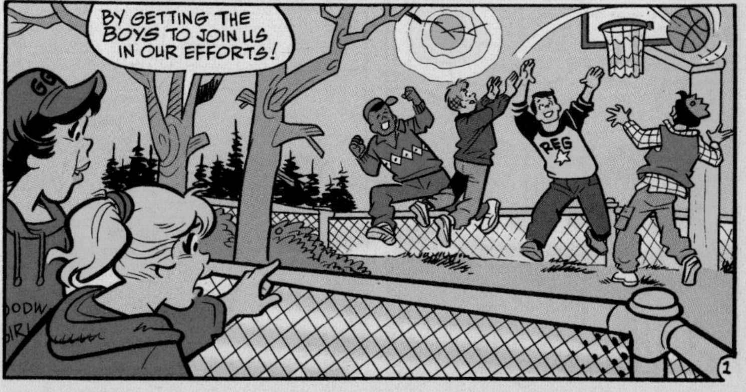
BY GETTING THE BOYS TO JOIN US IN OUR EFFORTS!
REG

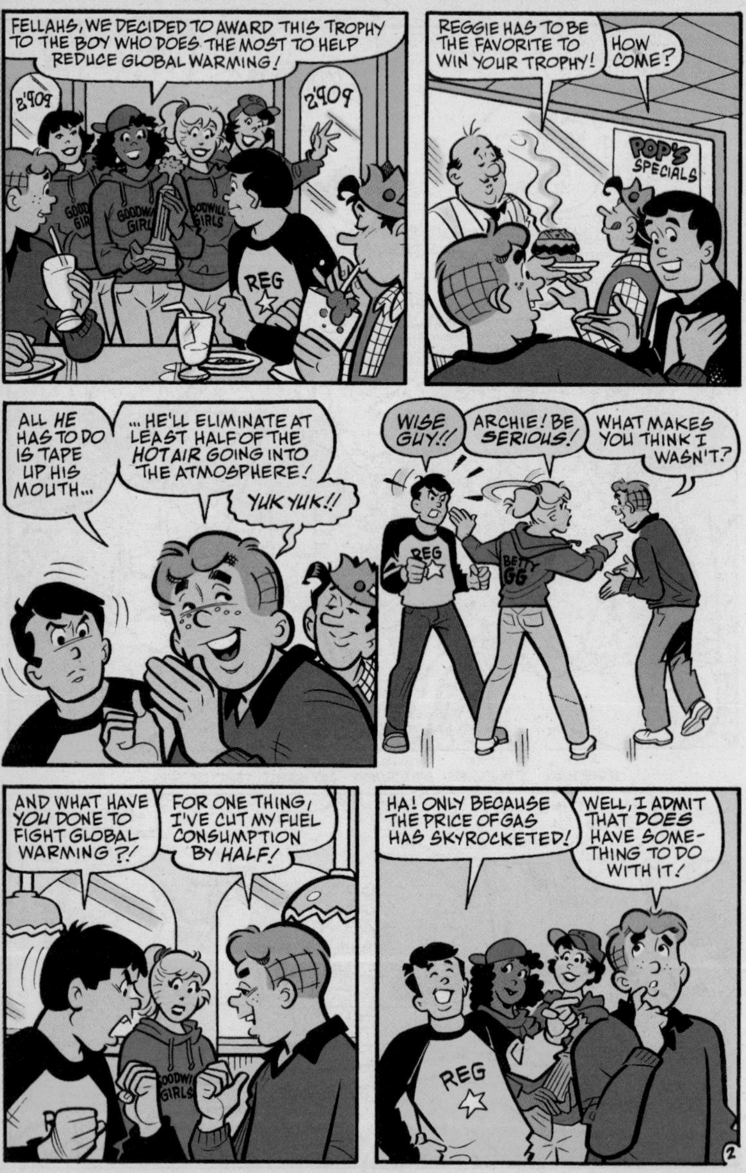
FELLAHS, WE DECIDED TO AWARD THIS TROPHY TO THE BOY WHO DOES THE MOST TO HELP REDUCE GLOBAL WARMING!
POP'S
POP'S
GOODWILL GIRLS
REG
REGGIE HAS TO BE THE FAVORITE TO WIN YOUR TROPHY!
HOW COME?
POP'S SPECIALS
ALL HE HAS TO DO IS TAPE UP HIS MOUTH...
... HE'LL ELIMINATE AT LEAST HALF OF THE HOT AIR GOING INTO THE ATMOSPHERE!
YUK YUK!!
WISE GUY!!
ARCHIE! BE SERIOUS!
WHAT MAKES YOU THINK I WASN'T?
REG
BETTY GG
AND WHAT HAVE YOU DONE TO FIGHT GLOBAL WARMING?!
FOR ONE THING, I'VE CUT MY FUEL CONSUMPTION BY HALF!
HA! ONLY BECAUSE THE PRICE OF GAS HAS SKYROCKETED!
WELL, I ADMIT THAT DOES HAVE SOME-THING TO DO WITH IT!
REG
2

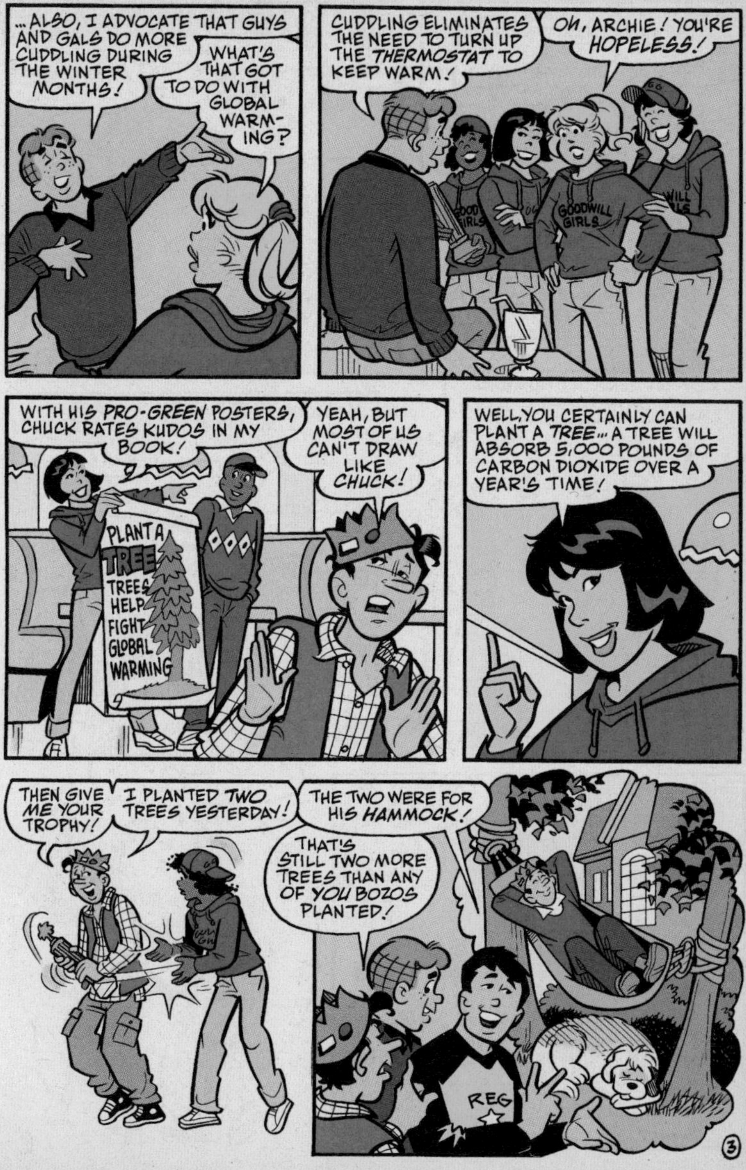
...ALSO, I ADVOCATE THAT GUYS AND GALS DO MORE CUDDLING DURING THE WINTER MONTHS!
WHAT'S THAT GOT TO DO WITH GLOBAL WARMING?
CUDDLING ELIMINATES THE NEED TO TURN UP THE THERMOSTAT TO KEEP WARM!
OH, ARCHIE! YOU'RE HOPELESS!
GOODWILL GIRLS
WITH HIS PRO-GREEN POSTERS, CHUCK RATES KUDOS IN MY BOOK!
PLANT A TREE
TREES HELP FIGHT GLOBAL WARMING
YEAH, BUT MOST OF US CAN'T DRAW LIKE CHUCK!
WELL, YOU CERTAINLY CAN PLANT A TREE... A TREE WILL ABSORB 5,000 POUNDS OF CARBON DIOXIDE OVER A YEAR'S TIME!
THEN GIVE ME YOUR TROPHY!
I PLANTED TWO TREES YESTERDAY!
THE TWO WERE FOR HIS HAMMOCK!
THAT'S STILL TWO MORE TREES THAN ANY OF YOU BOZOS PLANTED!
REG

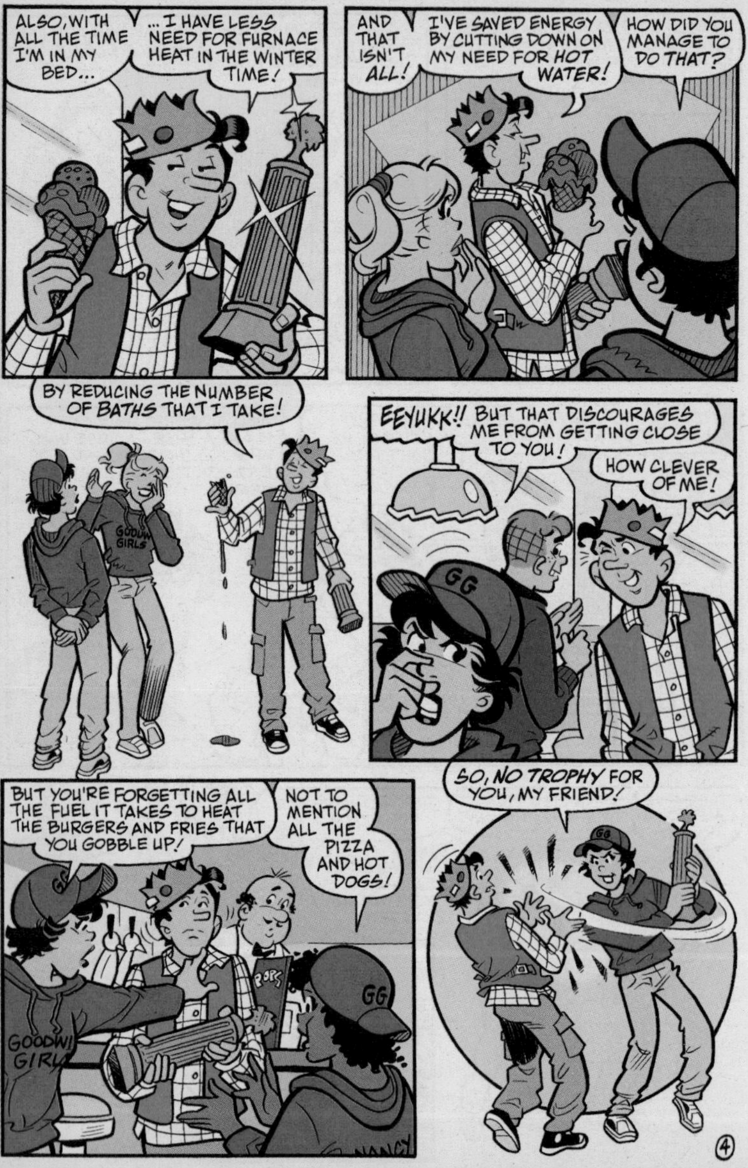

ALSO, WITH ALL THE TIME I'M IN MY BED...
... I HAVE LESS NEED FOR FURNACE HEAT IN THE WINTER TIME!
AND THAT ISN'T ALL!
I'VE SAVED ENERGY BY CUTTING DOWN ON MY NEED FOR HOT WATER!
HOW DID YOU MANAGE TO DO THAT?
BY REDUCING THE NUMBER OF BATHS THAT I TAKE!
GOODWI GIRLS
EEYUKK!! BUT THAT DISCOURAGES ME FROM GETTING CLOSE TO YOU!
HOW CLEVER OF ME!
GG
BUT YOU'RE FORGETTING ALL THE FUEL IT TAKES TO HEAT THE BURGERS AND FRIES THAT YOU GOBBLE UP!
NOT TO MENTION ALL THE PIZZA AND HOT DOGS!
POP'S
GG
GOODWI GIRL
SO, NO TROPHY FOR YOU, MY FRIEND!
GG
NANCY

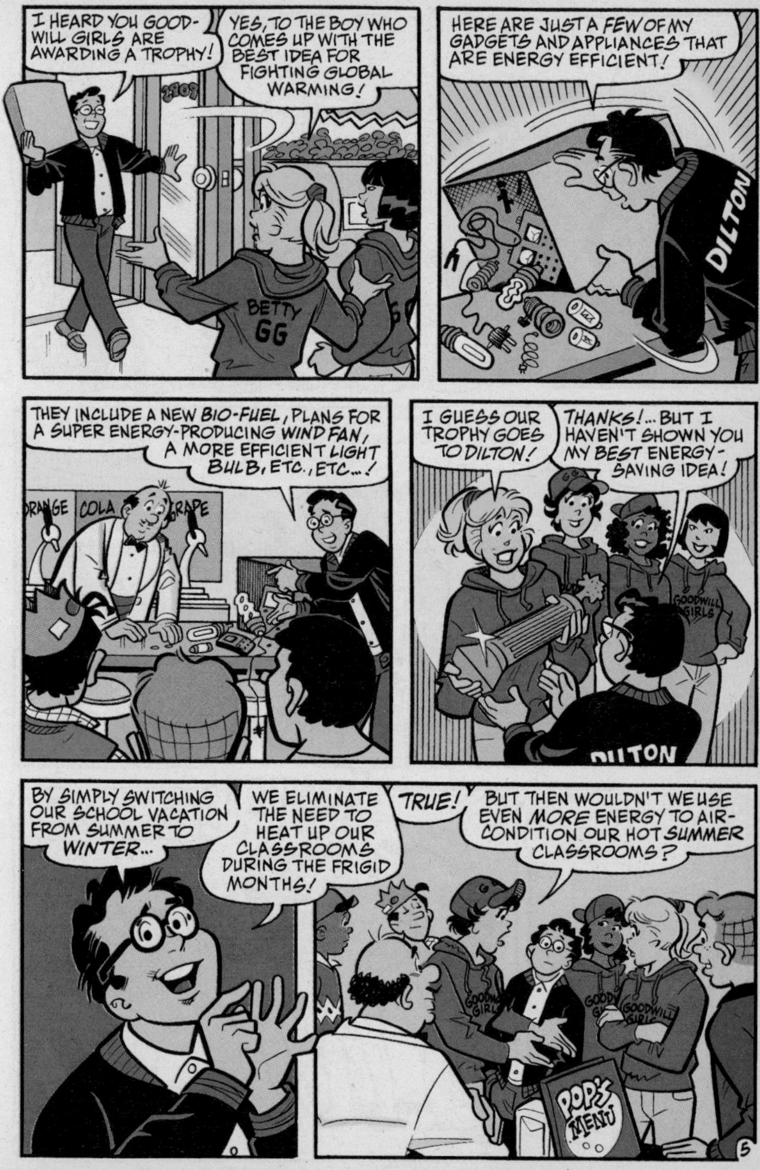

I HEARD YOU GOOD-WILL GIRLS ARE AWARDING A TROPHY!
YES, TO THE BOY WHO COMES UP WITH THE BEST IDEA FOR FIGHTING GLOBAL WARMING!
BETTY GG
HERE ARE JUST A FEW OF MY GADGETS AND APPLIANCES THAT ARE ENERGY EFFICIENT!
DILTON
THEY INCLUDE A NEW BIO-FUEL, PLANS FOR A SUPER ENERGY-PRODUCING WIND FAN, A MORE EFFICIENT LIGHT BULB, ETC., ETC...!
COLA
I GUESS OUR TROPHY GOES TO DILTON!
THANKS!... BUT I HAVEN'T SHOWN YOU MY BEST ENERGY-SAVING IDEA!
GOODWILL GIRLS
BY SIMPLY SWITCHING OUR SCHOOL VACATION FROM SUMMER TO WINTER...
WE ELIMINATE THE NEED TO HEAT UP OUR CLASSROOMS DURING THE FRIGID MONTHS!
TRUE!
BUT THEN WOULDN'T WE USE EVEN MORE ENERGY TO AIR-CONDITION OUR HOT SUMMER CLASSROOMS?
POP'S MENU
5

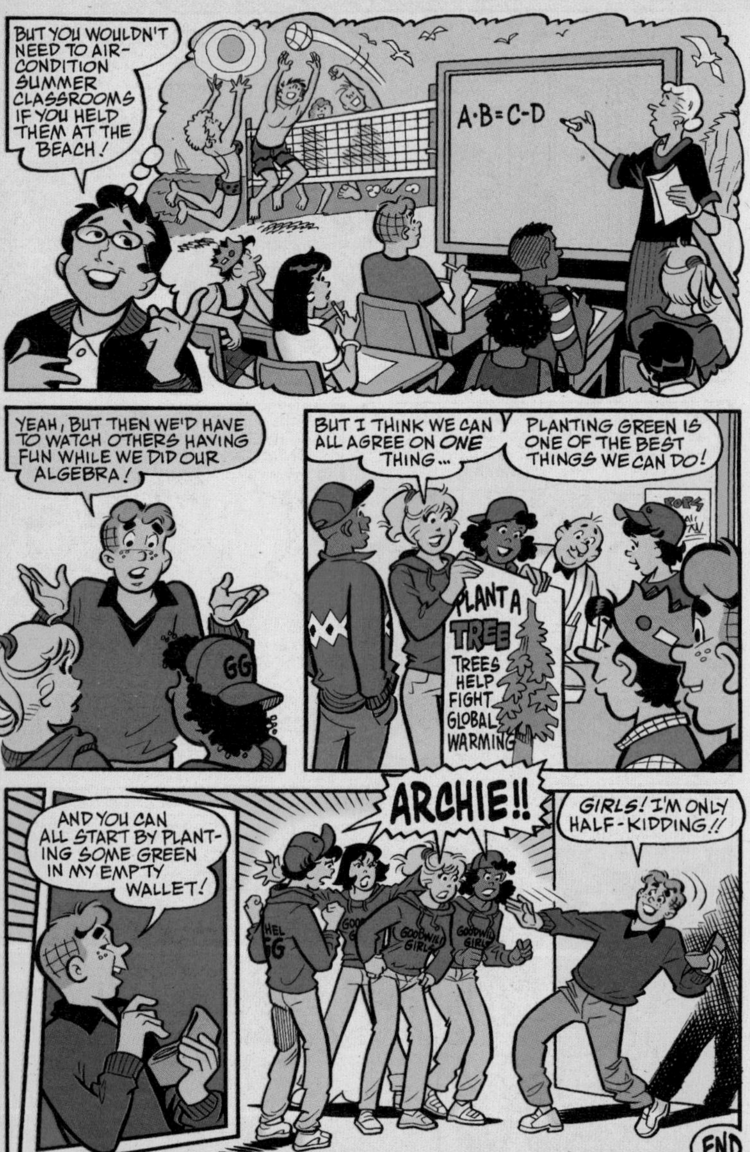
BUT YOU WOULDN'T NEED TO AIR-CONDITION SUMMER CLASSROOMS IF YOU HELD THEM AT THE BEACH!
A·B=C-D
YEAH, BUT THEN WE'D HAVE TO WATCH OTHERS HAVING FUN WHILE WE DID OUR ALGEBRA!
GG
BUT I THINK WE CAN ALL AGREE ON ONE THING...
PLANTING GREEN IS ONE OF THE BEST THINGS WE CAN DO!
PLANT A TREE
TREES HELP FIGHT GLOBAL WARMING
AND YOU CAN ALL START BY PLANTING SOME GREEN IN MY EMPTY WALLET!
ARCHIE!!
GIRLS! I'M ONLY HALF-KIDDING!!
GOODWILL GIRLS
END

Betty and Veronica *in* Dressing DOWN!

"SCHOOL SPIRIT" WEEK IS SO MUCH FUN!

SO FAR, WE'VE HAD "SCHOOL COLORS" DAY AND "CRAZY HATS" DAY!

WHAT'S ON FOR TOMORROW?

Script: Kathleen Webb / Pencils: Jeff Shultz / Inks: Henry Scarpelli / Letters: Vickie Williams / Colors: Barry Grossman

"MISMATCH DAY"! WE GET TO WEAR THE MOST MISMATCHED OUTFIT IN OUR WARDROBE!

THAT LETS RON OUT!

WARDROBE SPIRIT WEEK

MON.	SCHOOL COLORS
TUES.	HATS
WED.	MISMATCH DAY
THURS.	DRESS DOWN
FRI.	DRESS UP

I DOUBT OUR RESIDENT FASHION QUEEN WOULD ALLOW HERSELF TO BE SEEN IN SUCH AN *UNCOORDINATED* MANNER!

I WOULD, TOO!

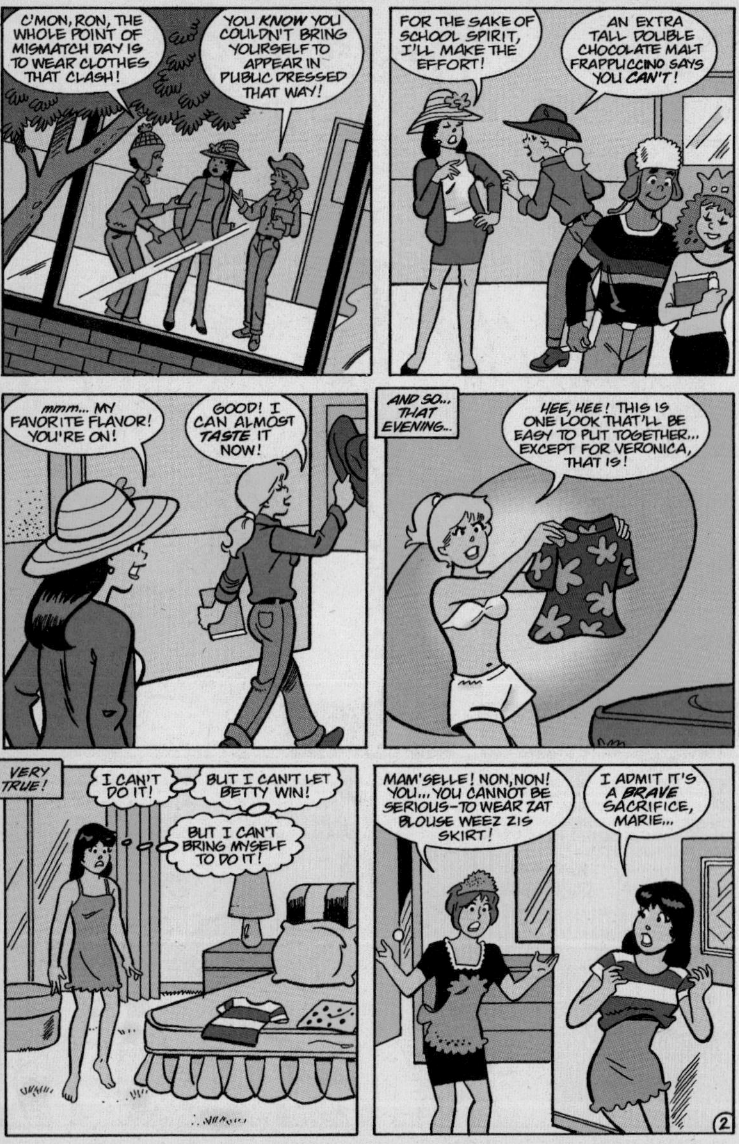
C'MON, RON, THE WHOLE POINT OF MISMATCH DAY IS TO WEAR CLOTHES THAT CLASH!
YOU KNOW YOU COULDN'T BRING YOURSELF TO APPEAR IN PUBLIC DRESSED THAT WAY!
FOR THE SAKE OF SCHOOL SPIRIT, I'LL MAKE THE EFFORT!
AN EXTRA TALL DOUBLE CHOCOLATE MALT FRAPPUCCINO SAYS YOU CAN'T!
mmm... MY FAVORITE FLAVOR! YOU'RE ON!
GOOD! I CAN ALMOST TASTE IT NOW!
AND SO... THAT EVENING...
HEE, HEE! THIS IS ONE LOOK THAT'LL BE EASY TO PUT TOGETHER... EXCEPT FOR VERONICA, THAT IS!
VERY TRUE!
I CAN'T DO IT!
BUT I CAN'T LET BETTY WIN!
BUT I CAN'T BRING MYSELF TO DO IT!
MAM'SELLE! NON, NON! YOU... YOU CANNOT BE SERIOUS–TO WEAR ZAT BLOUSE WEEZ ZIS SKIRT!
I ADMIT IT'S A BRAVE SACRIFICE, MARIE...
2

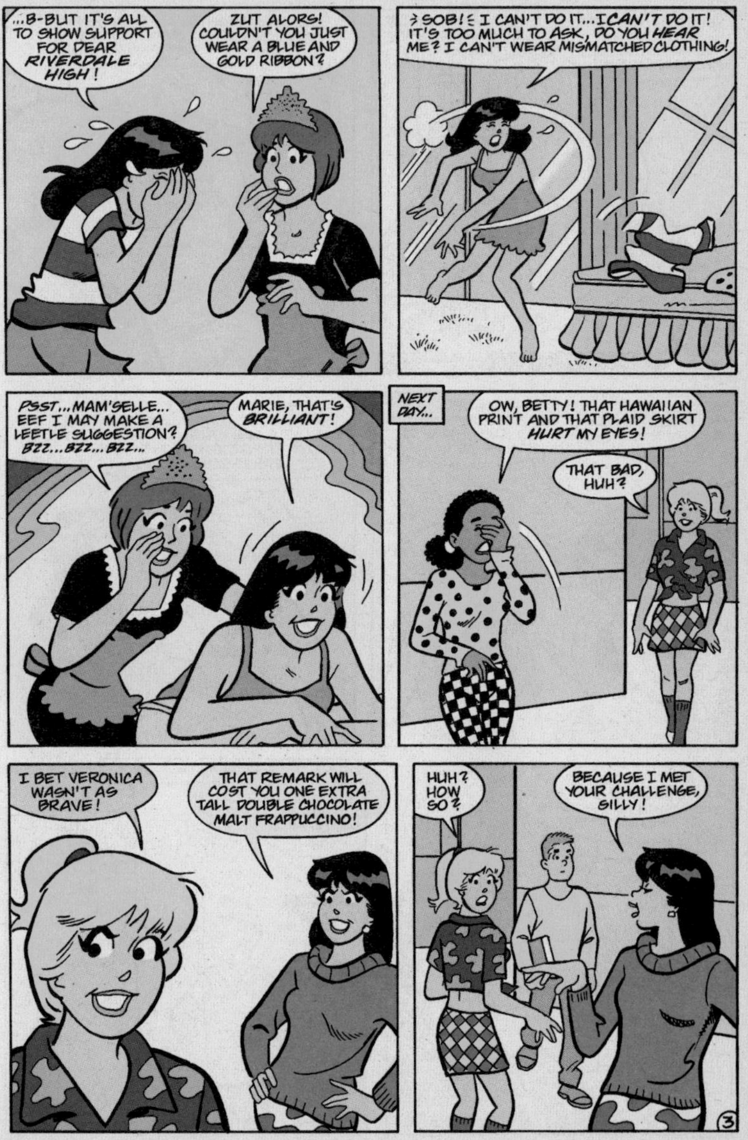
...B-BUT IT'S ALL TO SHOW SUPPORT FOR DEAR RIVERDALE HIGH!
ZUT ALORS! COULDN'T YOU JUST WEAR A BLUE AND GOLD RIBBON?
SOB! I CAN'T DO IT...I CAN'T DO IT! IT'S TOO MUCH TO ASK, DO YOU HEAR ME? I CAN'T WEAR MISMATCHED CLOTHING!
PSST...MAM'SELLE... EEF I MAY MAKE A LEETLE SUGGESTION? BZZ...BZZ...BZZ...
MARIE, THAT'S BRILLIANT!
NEXT DAY...
OW, BETTY! THAT HAWAIIAN PRINT AND THAT PLAID SKIRT HURT MY EYES!
THAT BAD, HUH?
I BET VERONICA WASN'T AS BRAVE!
THAT REMARK WILL COST YOU ONE EXTRA TALL DOUBLE CHOCOLATE MALT FRAPPUCCINO!
HUH? HOW SO?
BECAUSE I MET YOUR CHALLENGE, SILLY!
3

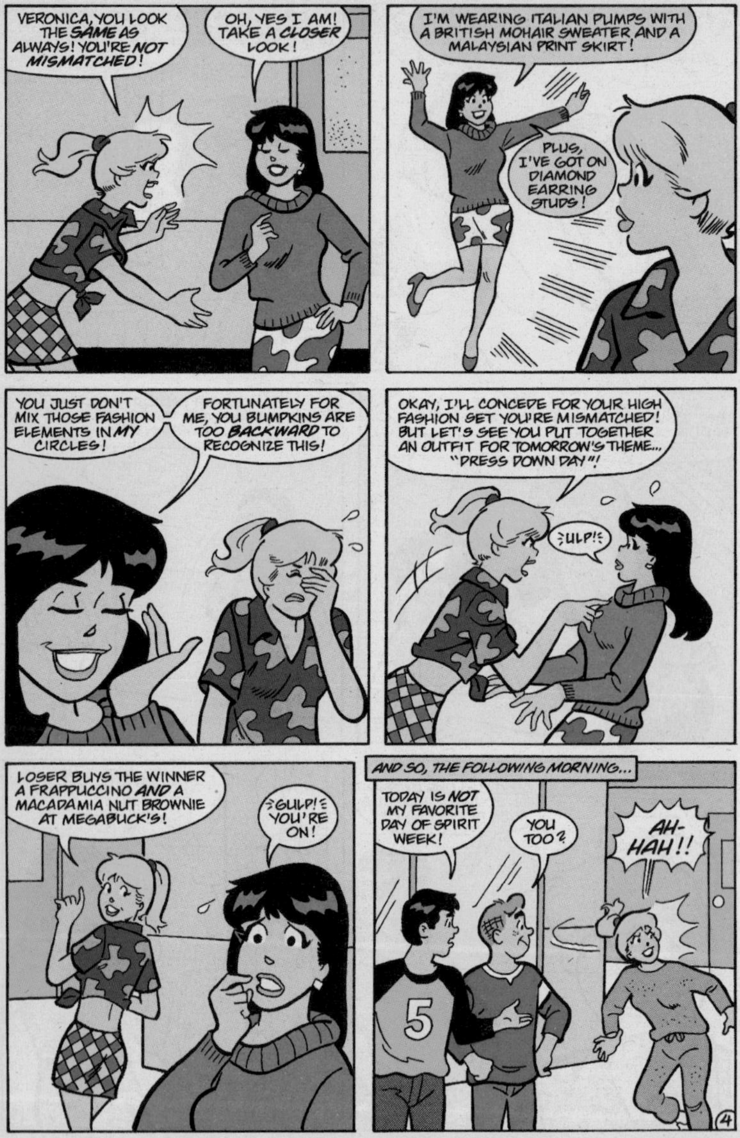

VERONICA, YOU LOOK THE *SAME* AS ALWAYS! YOU'RE *NOT MISMATCHED*!
OH, YES I AM! TAKE A *CLOSER* LOOK!
I'M WEARING ITALIAN PUMPS WITH A BRITISH MOHAIR SWEATER AND A MALAYSIAN PRINT SKIRT!
PLUS, I'VE GOT ON DIAMOND EARRING STUDS!
YOU JUST DON'T MIX THOSE FASHION ELEMENTS IN *MY* CIRCLES!
FORTUNATELY FOR ME, YOU BUMPKINS ARE TOO *BACKWARD* TO RECOGNIZE THIS!
OKAY, I'LL CONCEDE FOR YOUR HIGH FASHION SET YOU'RE MISMATCHED! BUT LET'S SEE YOU PUT TOGETHER AN OUTFIT FOR TOMORROW'S THEME... "DRESS DOWN DAY"!
ULP!
LOSER BUYS THE WINNER A FRAPPUCCINO *AND* A MACADAMIA NUT BROWNIE AT MEGABUCK'S!
GULP! YOU'RE ON!
AND SO, THE FOLLOWING MORNING...
TODAY IS *NOT* MY FAVORITE DAY OF SPIRIT WEEK!
YOU TOO?
AH-HAH!!
5
4

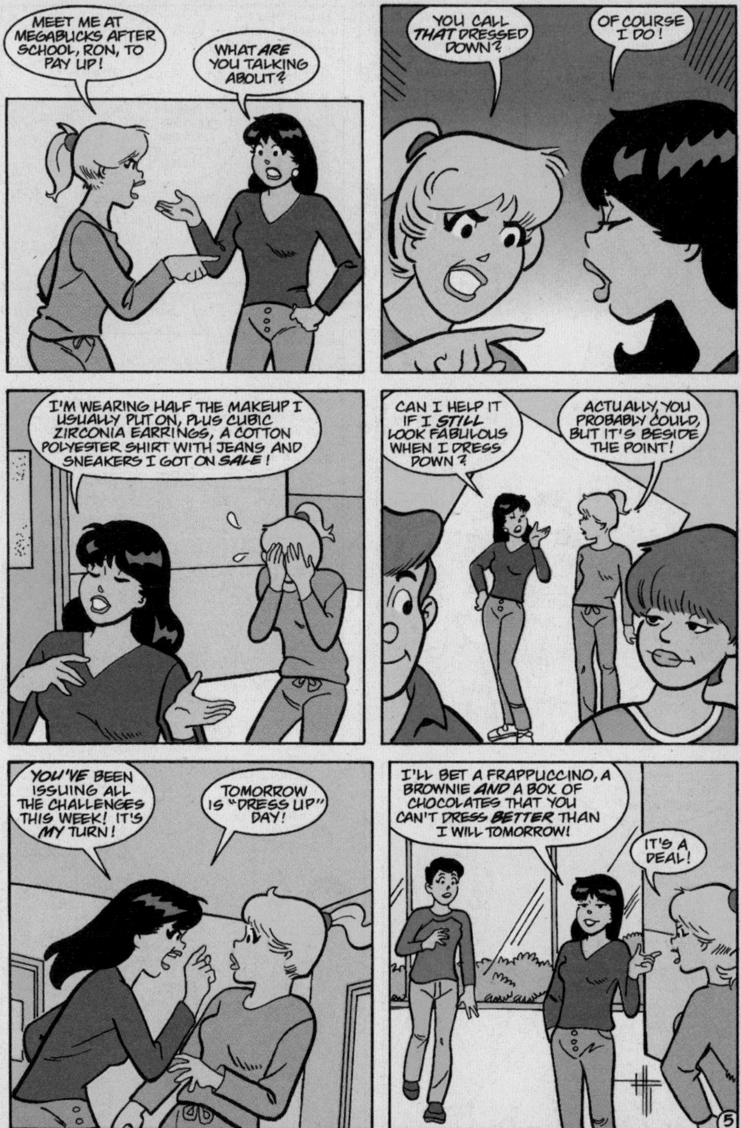
MEET ME AT MEGABUCKS AFTER SCHOOL, RON, TO PAY UP!
WHAT *ARE* YOU TALKING ABOUT?
YOU CALL *THAT* DRESSED DOWN?
OF COURSE I DO!
I'M WEARING HALF THE MAKEUP I USUALLY PUT ON, PLUS CUBIC ZIRCONIA EARRINGS, A COTTON POLYESTER SHIRT WITH JEANS AND SNEAKERS I GOT ON *SALE*!
CAN I HELP IT IF I *STILL* LOOK FABULOUS WHEN I DRESS DOWN?
ACTUALLY, YOU PROBABLY COULD, BUT IT'S BESIDE THE POINT!
YOU'VE BEEN ISSUING ALL THE CHALLENGES THIS WEEK! IT'S *MY* TURN!
TOMORROW IS "DRESS UP" DAY!
I'LL BET A FRAPPUCCINO, A BROWNIE *AND* A BOX OF CHOCOLATES THAT YOU CAN'T DRESS *BETTER* THAN I WILL TOMORROW!
IT'S A DEAL!
5

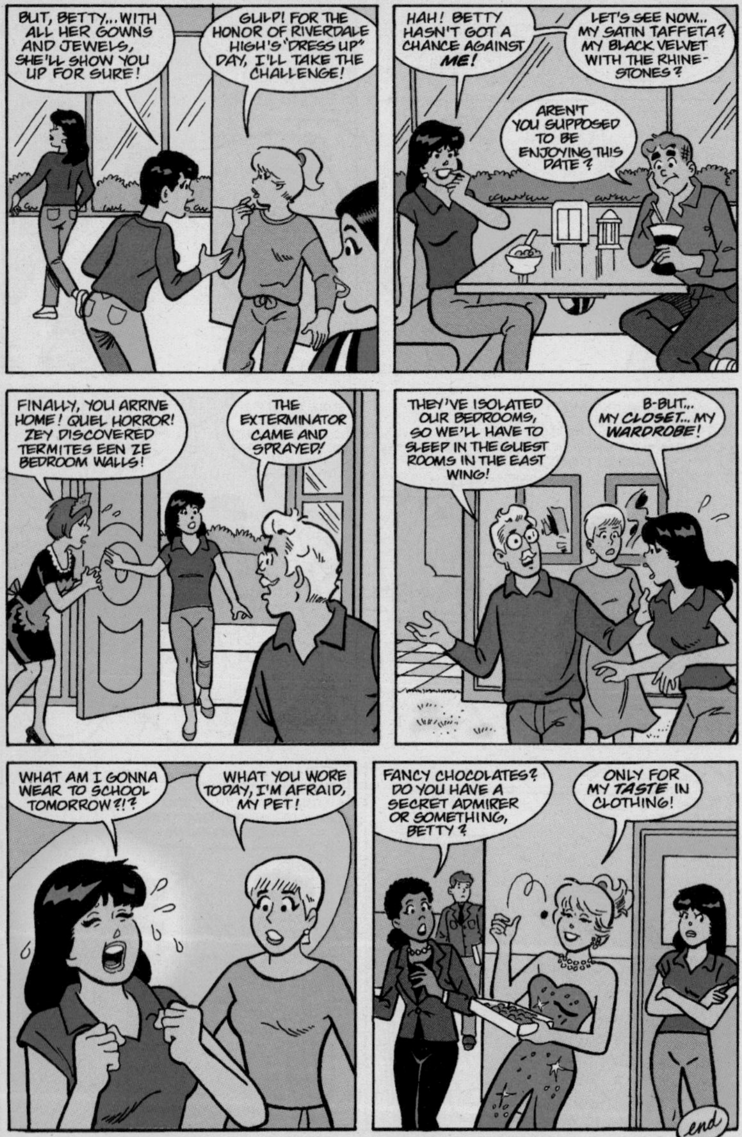
BUT, BETTY... WITH ALL HER GOWNS AND JEWELS, SHE'LL SHOW YOU UP FOR SURE!
GULP! FOR THE HONOR OF RIVERDALE HIGH'S "DRESS UP" DAY, I'LL TAKE THE CHALLENGE!
HAH! BETTY HASN'T GOT A CHANCE AGAINST ME!
LET'S SEE NOW... MY SATIN TAFFETA? MY BLACK VELVET WITH THE RHINE-STONES?
AREN'T YOU SUPPOSED TO BE ENJOYING THIS DATE?
FINALLY, YOU ARRIVE HOME! QUEL HORROR! ZEY DISCOVERED TERMITES EEN ZE BEDROOM WALLS!
THE EXTERMINATOR CAME AND SPRAYED!
THEY'VE ISOLATED OUR BEDROOMS, SO WE'LL HAVE TO SLEEP IN THE GUEST ROOMS IN THE EAST WING!
B-BUT... MY CLOSET... MY WARDROBE!
WHAT AM I GONNA WEAR TO SCHOOL TOMORROW?!?
WHAT YOU WORE TODAY, I'M AFRAID, MY PET!
FANCY CHOCOLATES? DO YOU HAVE A SECRET ADMIRER OR SOMETHING, BETTY?
ONLY FOR MY TASTE IN CLOTHING!
end

Archie -in- "I SAW HIM FIRST"

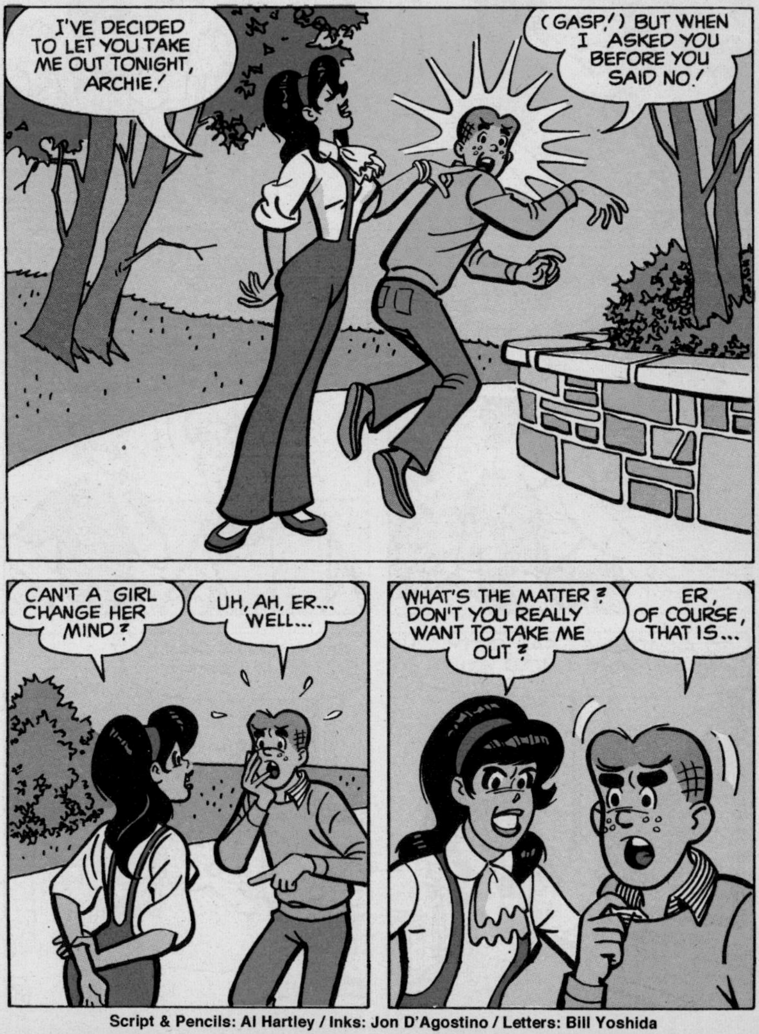

I'VE DECIDED TO LET YOU TAKE ME OUT TONIGHT, ARCHIE!
(GASP!) BUT WHEN I ASKED YOU BEFORE YOU SAID NO!
CAN'T A GIRL CHANGE HER MIND?
UH, AH, ER... WELL...
WHAT'S THE MATTER? DON'T YOU REALLY WANT TO TAKE ME OUT?
ER, OF COURSE, THAT IS...

Script & Pencils: Al Hartley / Inks: Jon D'Agostino / Letters: Bill Yoshida

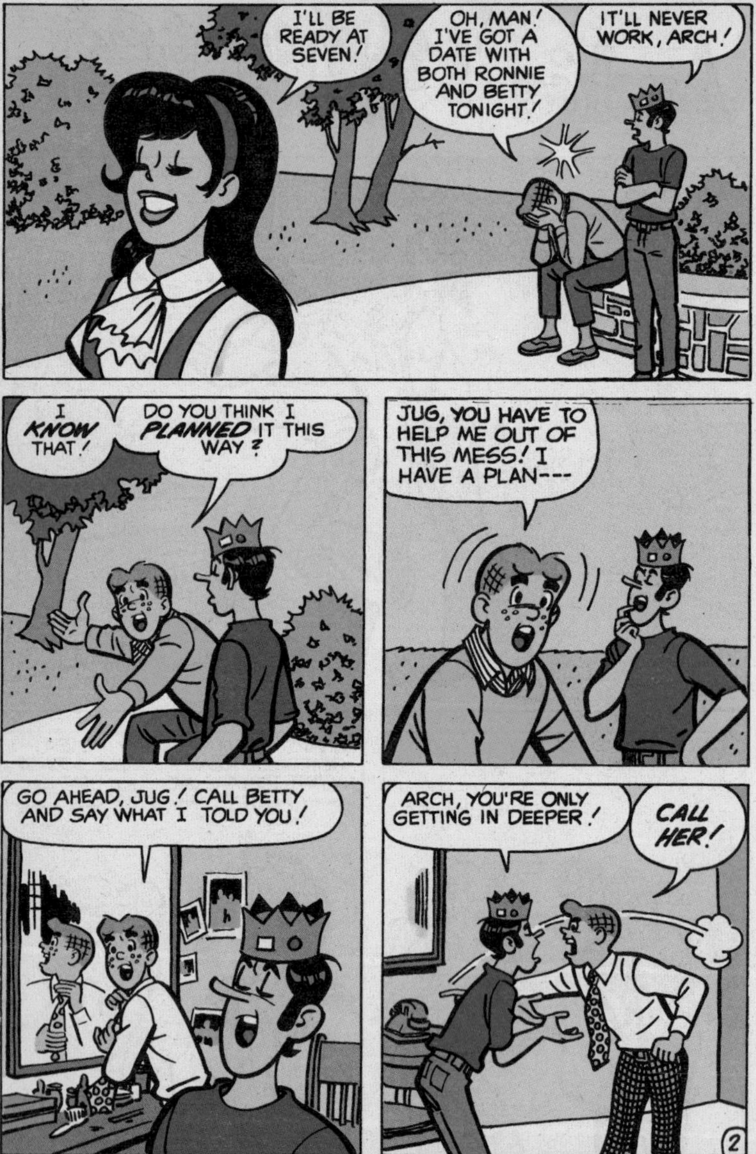
I'LL BE READY AT SEVEN!
OH, MAN! I'VE GOT A DATE WITH BOTH RONNIE AND BETTY TONIGHT!
IT'LL NEVER WORK, ARCH!
I KNOW THAT!
DO YOU THINK I PLANNED IT THIS WAY?
JUG, YOU HAVE TO HELP ME OUT OF THIS MESS! I HAVE A PLAN---
GO AHEAD, JUG! CALL BETTY AND SAY WHAT I TOLD YOU!
ARCH, YOU'RE ONLY GETTING IN DEEPER!
CALL HER!
2

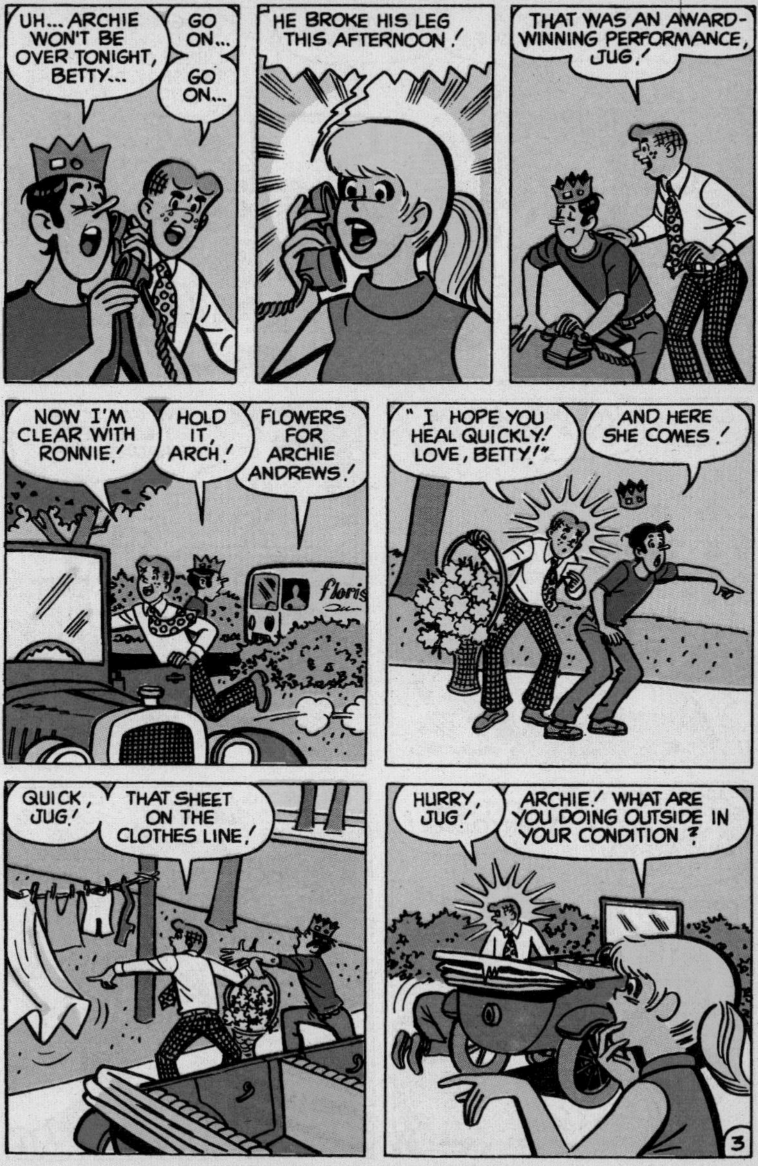

UH... ARCHIE WON'T BE OVER TONIGHT, BETTY...
GO ON...
GO ON...
HE BROKE HIS LEG THIS AFTERNOON!
THAT WAS AN AWARD-WINNING PERFORMANCE, JUG!
NOW I'M CLEAR WITH RONNIE!
HOLD IT, ARCH!
FLOWERS FOR ARCHIE ANDREWS!
floris
" I HOPE YOU HEAL QUICKLY! LOVE, BETTY!"
AND HERE SHE COMES!
QUICK, JUG!
THAT SHEET ON THE CLOTHES LINE!
HURRY, JUG!
ARCHIE! WHAT ARE YOU DOING OUTSIDE IN YOUR CONDITION?

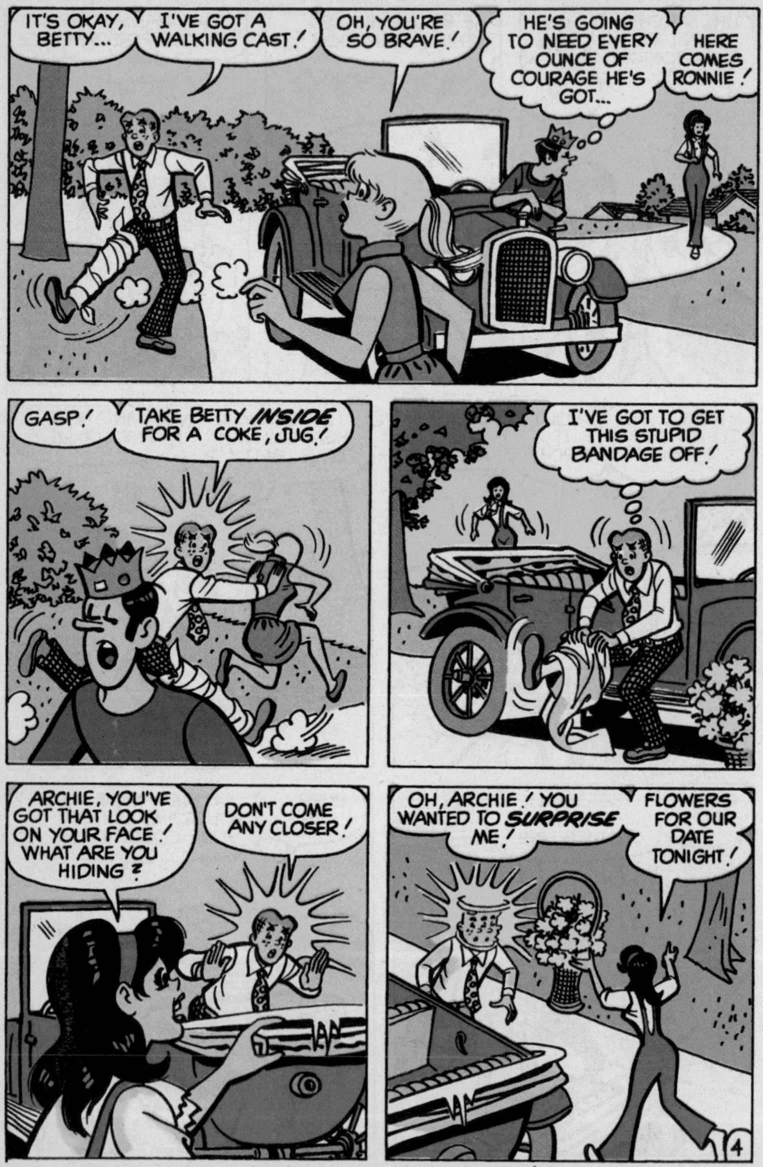
IT'S OKAY, BETTY...
I'VE GOT A WALKING CAST!
OH, YOU'RE SO BRAVE!
HE'S GOING TO NEED EVERY OUNCE OF COURAGE HE'S GOT...
HERE COMES RONNIE!
GASP!
TAKE BETTY *INSIDE* FOR A COKE, JUG!
I'VE GOT TO GET THIS STUPID BANDAGE OFF!
ARCHIE, YOU'VE GOT THAT LOOK ON YOUR FACE! WHAT ARE YOU HIDING?
DON'T COME ANY CLOSER!
OH, ARCHIE! YOU WANTED TO *SURPRISE* ME!
FLOWERS FOR OUR DATE TONIGHT!
4

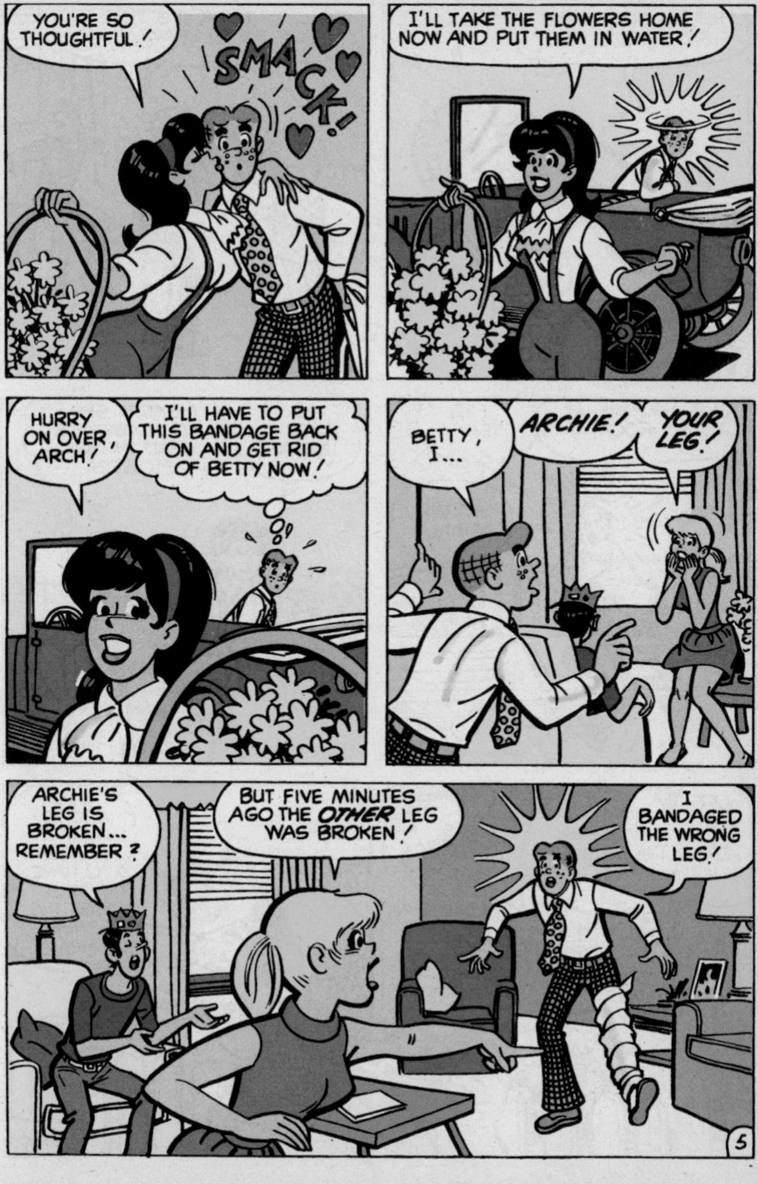
YOU'RE SO THOUGHTFUL!
SMACK!
I'LL TAKE THE FLOWERS HOME NOW AND PUT THEM IN WATER!
HURRY ON OVER, ARCH!
I'LL HAVE TO PUT THIS BANDAGE BACK ON AND GET RID OF BETTY NOW!
BETTY, I...
ARCHIE!
YOUR LEG!
ARCHIE'S LEG IS BROKEN... REMEMBER?
BUT FIVE MINUTES AGO THE OTHER LEG WAS BROKEN!
I BANDAGED THE WRONG LEG!
5

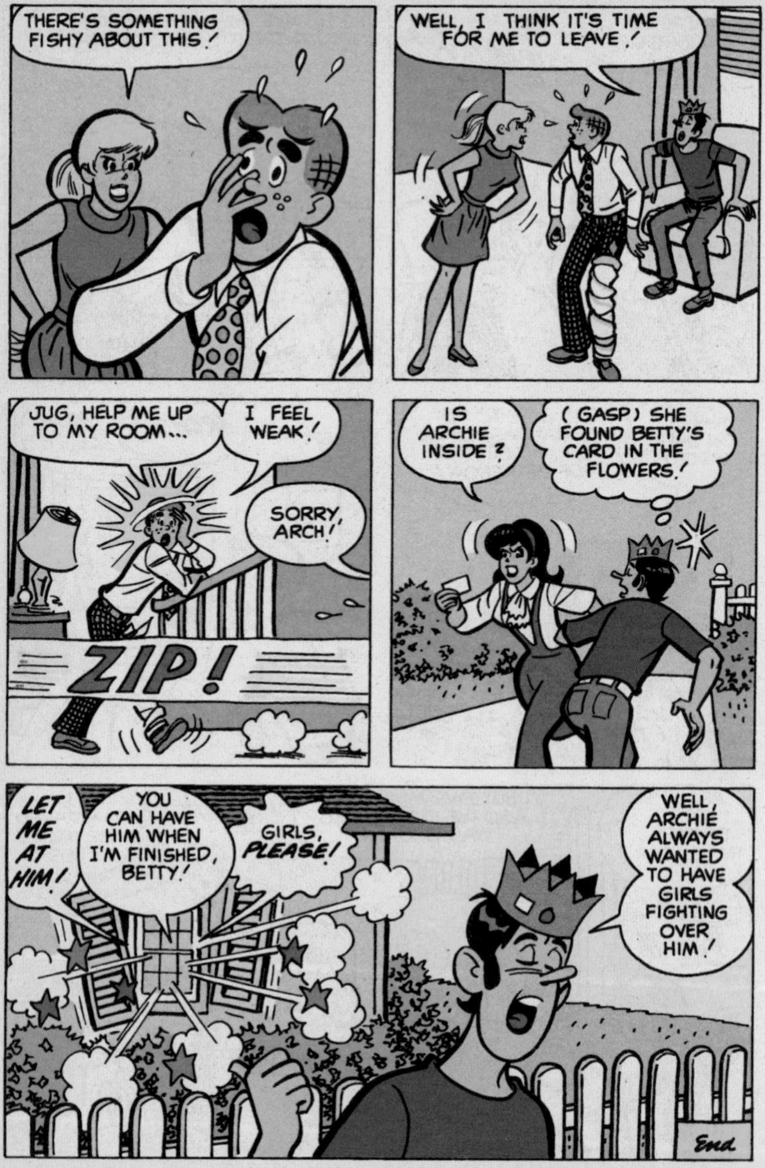

THERE'S SOMETHING FISHY ABOUT THIS!
WELL, I THINK IT'S TIME FOR ME TO LEAVE!
JUG, HELP ME UP TO MY ROOM...
I FEEL WEAK!
SORRY, ARCH!
ZIP!
IS ARCHIE INSIDE?
(GASP) SHE FOUND BETTY'S CARD IN THE FLOWERS!
LET ME AT HIM!
YOU CAN HAVE HIM WHEN I'M FINISHED, BETTY!
GIRLS, PLEASE!
WELL, ARCHIE ALWAYS WANTED TO HAVE GIRLS FIGHTING OVER HIM!
End

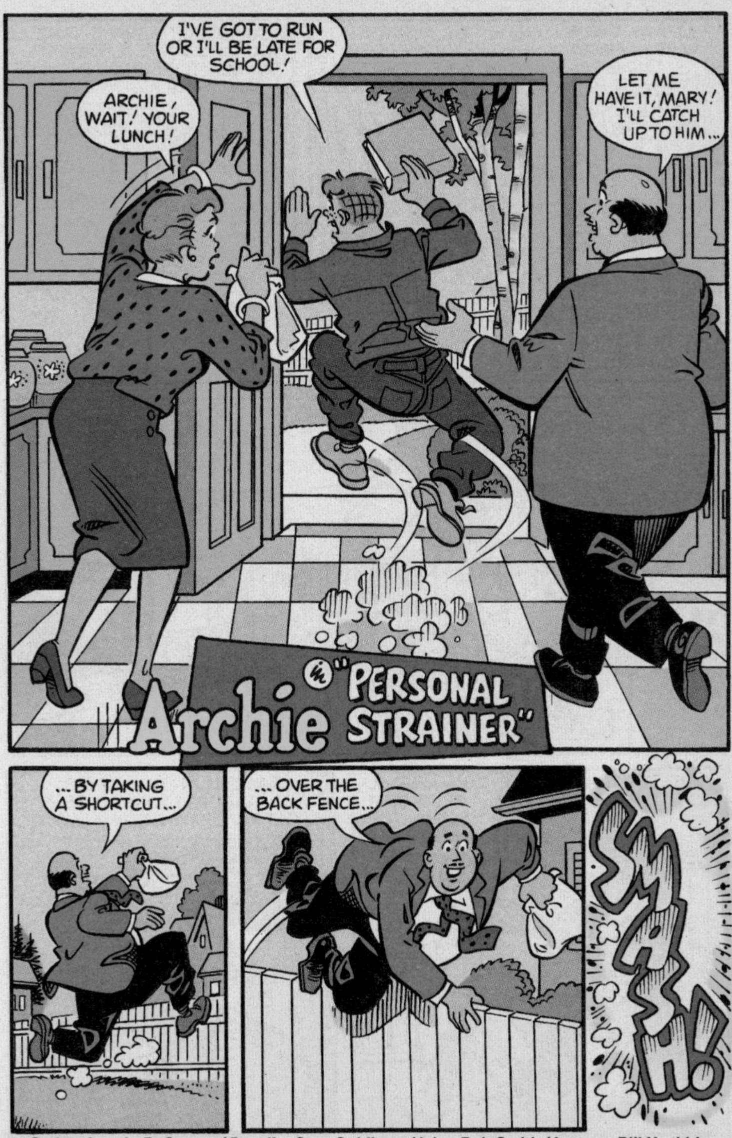
ARCHIE, WAIT! YOUR LUNCH!
I'VE GOT TO RUN OR I'LL BE LATE FOR SCHOOL!
LET ME HAVE IT, MARY! I'LL CATCH UP TO HIM...
Archie in "PERSONAL STRAINER"
...BY TAKING A SHORTCUT...
...OVER THE BACK FENCE...
SMASH!

Script: Angelo DeCesare / Pencils: Stan Goldberg / Inks: Bob Smith / Letters: Bill Yoshida

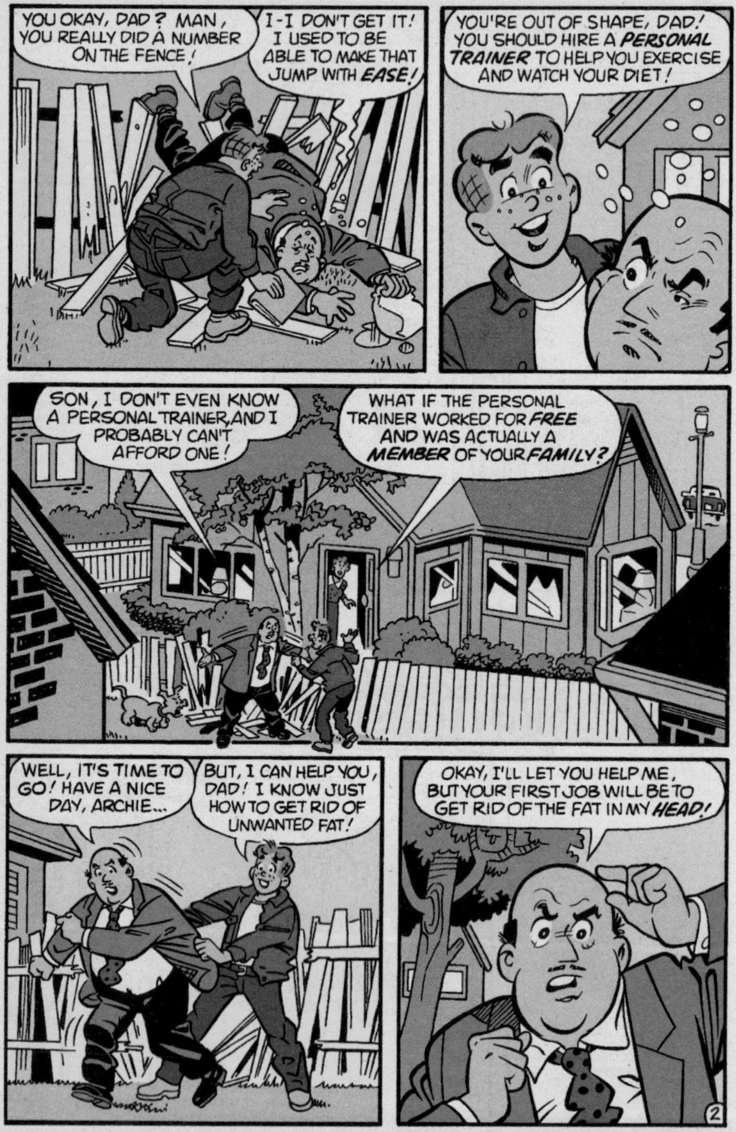
YOU OKAY, DAD? MAN, YOU REALLY DID A NUMBER ON THE FENCE!
I-I DON'T GET IT! I USED TO BE ABLE TO MAKE THAT JUMP WITH *EASE*!
YOU'RE OUT OF SHAPE, DAD! YOU SHOULD HIRE A ***PERSONAL TRAINER*** TO HELP YOU EXERCISE AND WATCH YOUR DIET!
SON, I DON'T EVEN KNOW A PERSONAL TRAINER, AND I PROBABLY CAN'T AFFORD ONE!
WHAT IF THE PERSONAL TRAINER WORKED FOR *FREE* AND WAS ACTUALLY A ***MEMBER*** OF YOUR *FAMILY*?
WELL, IT'S TIME TO GO! HAVE A NICE DAY, ARCHIE...
BUT, I CAN HELP YOU, DAD! I KNOW JUST HOW TO GET RID OF UNWANTED FAT!
OKAY, I'LL LET YOU HELP ME, BUT YOUR FIRST JOB WILL BE TO GET RID OF THE FAT IN MY *HEAD*!
2

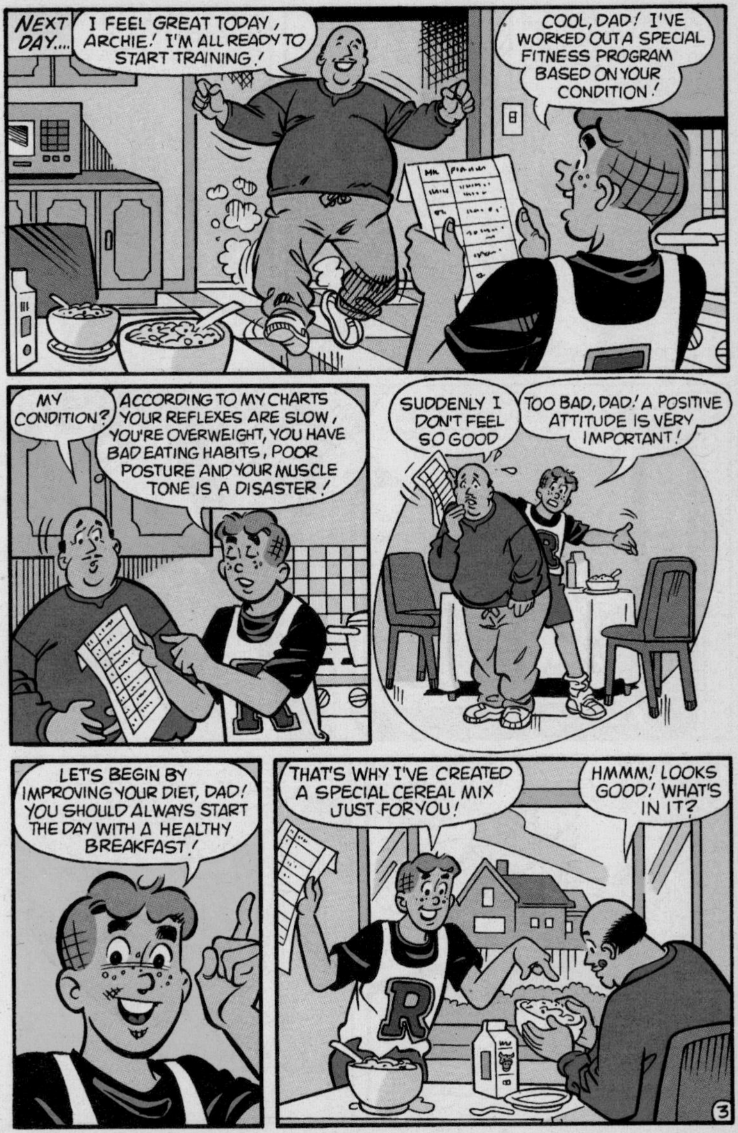
NEXT DAY....
I FEEL GREAT TODAY, ARCHIE! I'M ALL READY TO START TRAINING!
COOL, DAD! I'VE WORKED OUT A SPECIAL FITNESS PROGRAM BASED ON YOUR CONDITION!
MY CONDITION?
ACCORDING TO MY CHARTS YOUR REFLEXES ARE SLOW, YOU'RE OVERWEIGHT, YOU HAVE BAD EATING HABITS, POOR POSTURE AND YOUR MUSCLE TONE IS A DISASTER!
SUDDENLY I DON'T FEEL SO GOOD
TOO BAD, DAD! A POSITIVE ATTITUDE IS VERY IMPORTANT!
LET'S BEGIN BY IMPROVING YOUR DIET, DAD! YOU SHOULD ALWAYS START THE DAY WITH A HEALTHY BREAKFAST!
THAT'S WHY I'VE CREATED A SPECIAL CEREAL MIX JUST FOR YOU!
HMMM! LOOKS GOOD! WHAT'S IN IT?
3

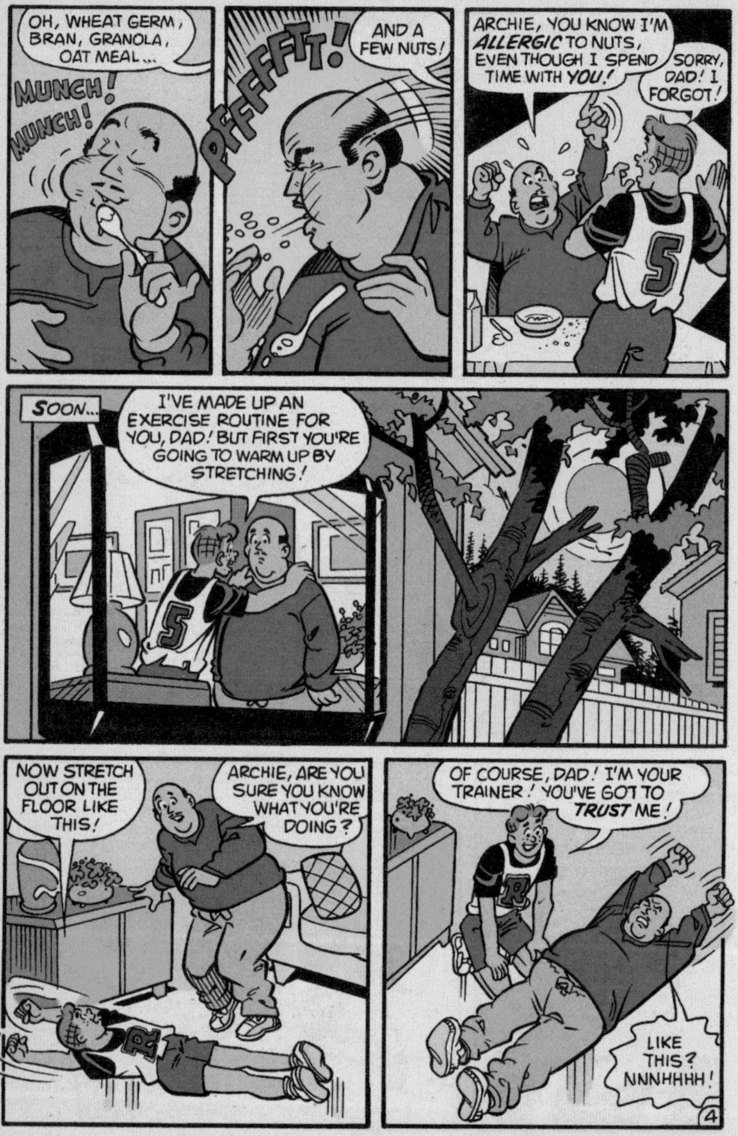
OH, WHEAT GERM, BRAN, GRANOLA, OAT MEAL...
MUNCH! MUNCH!
PFFFFFTTT!
AND A FEW NUTS!
ARCHIE, YOU KNOW I'M ALLERGIC TO NUTS, EVEN THOUGH I SPEND TIME WITH YOU!
SORRY, DAD! I FORGOT!
SOON...
I'VE MADE UP AN EXERCISE ROUTINE FOR YOU, DAD! BUT FIRST YOU'RE GOING TO WARM UP BY STRETCHING!
NOW STRETCH OUT ON THE FLOOR LIKE THIS!
ARCHIE, ARE YOU SURE YOU KNOW WHAT YOU'RE DOING?
OF COURSE, DAD! I'M YOUR TRAINER! YOU'VE GOT TO TRUST ME!
LIKE THIS? NNNHHHH!
4

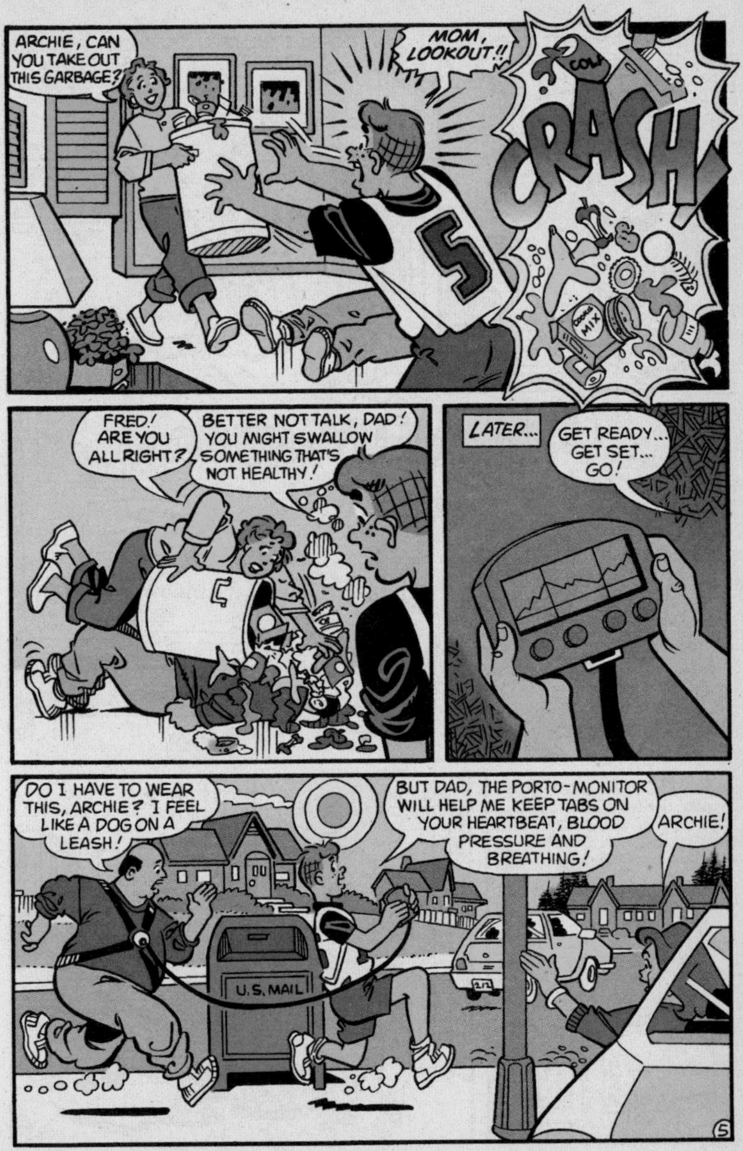
ARCHIE, CAN YOU TAKE OUT THIS GARBAGE?
MOM, LOOKOUT!!
COLA
CRASH
COOKIE MIX
FRED! ARE YOU ALL RIGHT?
BETTER NOT TALK, DAD! YOU MIGHT SWALLOW SOMETHING THAT'S NOT HEALTHY!
LATER...
GET READY... GET SET... GO!
DO I HAVE TO WEAR THIS, ARCHIE? I FEEL LIKE A DOG ON A LEASH!
BUT DAD, THE PORTO-MONITOR WILL HELP ME KEEP TABS ON YOUR HEARTBEAT, BLOOD PRESSURE AND BREATHING!
ARCHIE!
U.S. MAIL
5

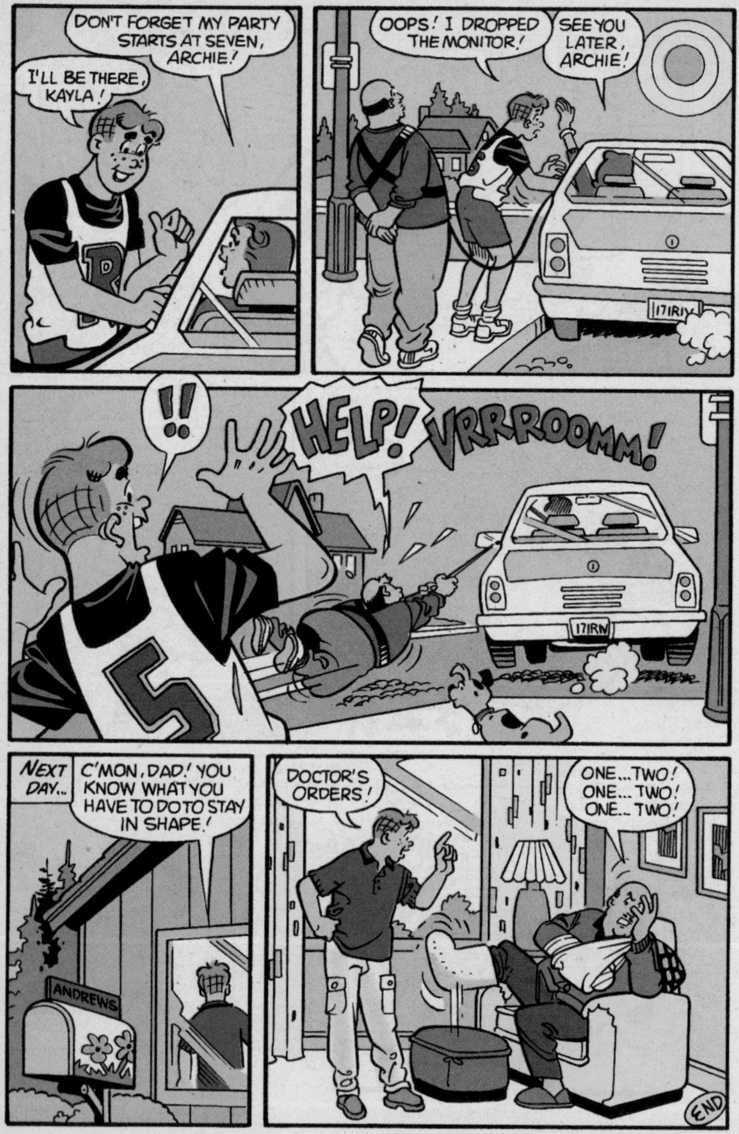
DON'T FORGET MY PARTY STARTS AT SEVEN, ARCHIE!
I'LL BE THERE, KAYLA!
OOPS! I DROPPED THE MONITOR!
SEE YOU LATER, ARCHIE!
17IRIY
!!
HELP!
VRRROOMM!
17IRIY
NEXT DAY...
C'MON, DAD! YOU KNOW WHAT YOU HAVE TO DO TO STAY IN SHAPE!
ANDREWS
DOCTOR'S ORDERS!
ONE...TWO! ONE...TWO! ONE...TWO!
END

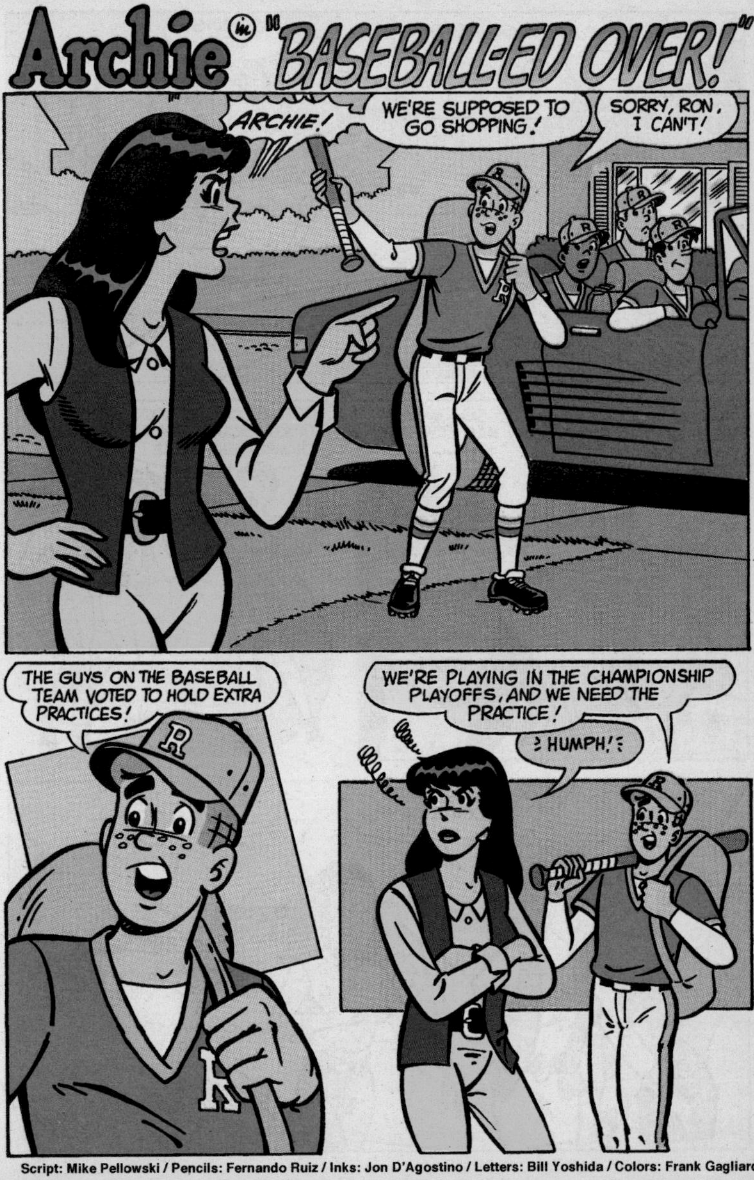
Archie in "BASEBALL-ED OVER!"
ARCHIE!
WE'RE SUPPOSED TO GO SHOPPING!
SORRY, RON, I CAN'T!
THE GUYS ON THE BASEBALL TEAM VOTED TO HOLD EXTRA PRACTICES!
WE'RE PLAYING IN THE CHAMPIONSHIP PLAYOFFS, AND WE NEED THE PRACTICE!
HUMPH!

Script: Mike Pellowski / Pencils: Fernando Ruiz / Inks: Jon D'Agostino / Letters: Bill Yoshida / Colors: Frank Gagliardo

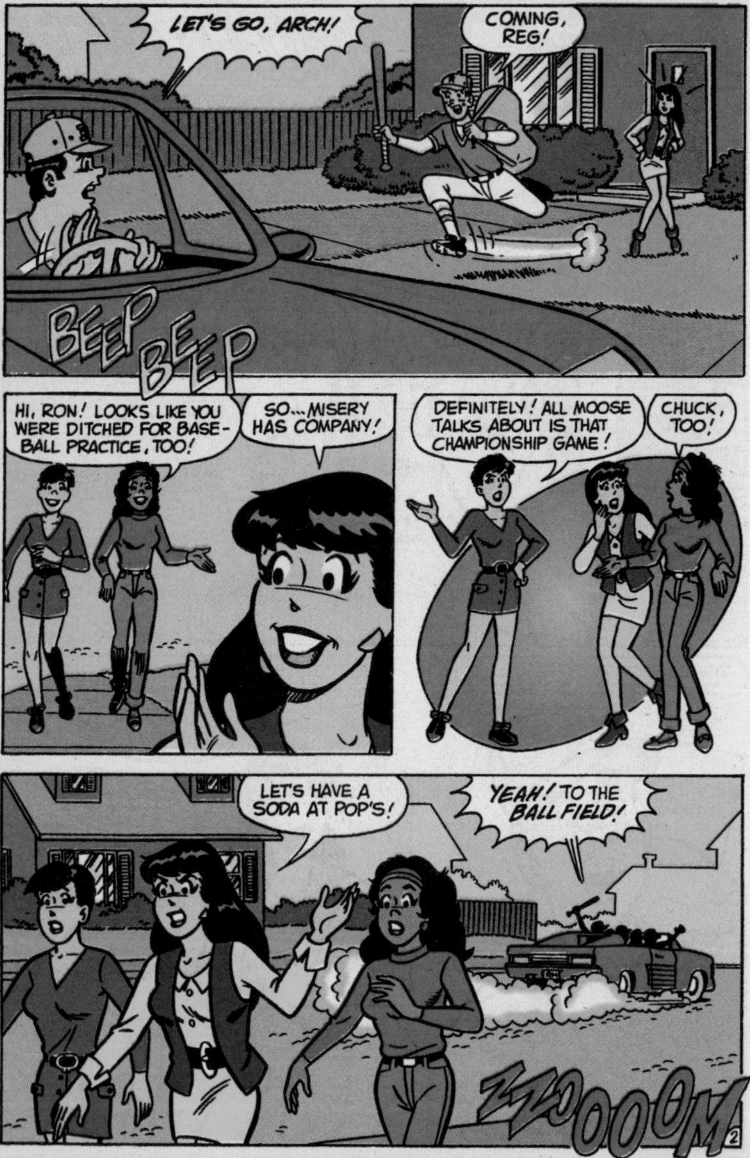

LET'S GO, ARCH!
COMING, REG!
BEEP BEEP
HI, RON! LOOKS LIKE YOU WERE DITCHED FOR BASE-BALL PRACTICE, TOO!
SO...MISERY HAS COMPANY!
DEFINITELY! ALL MOOSE TALKS ABOUT IS THAT CHAMPIONSHIP GAME!
CHUCK, TOO!
LET'S HAVE A SODA AT POP'S!
YEAH! TO THE BALL FIELD!
ZZOOOOOM
2

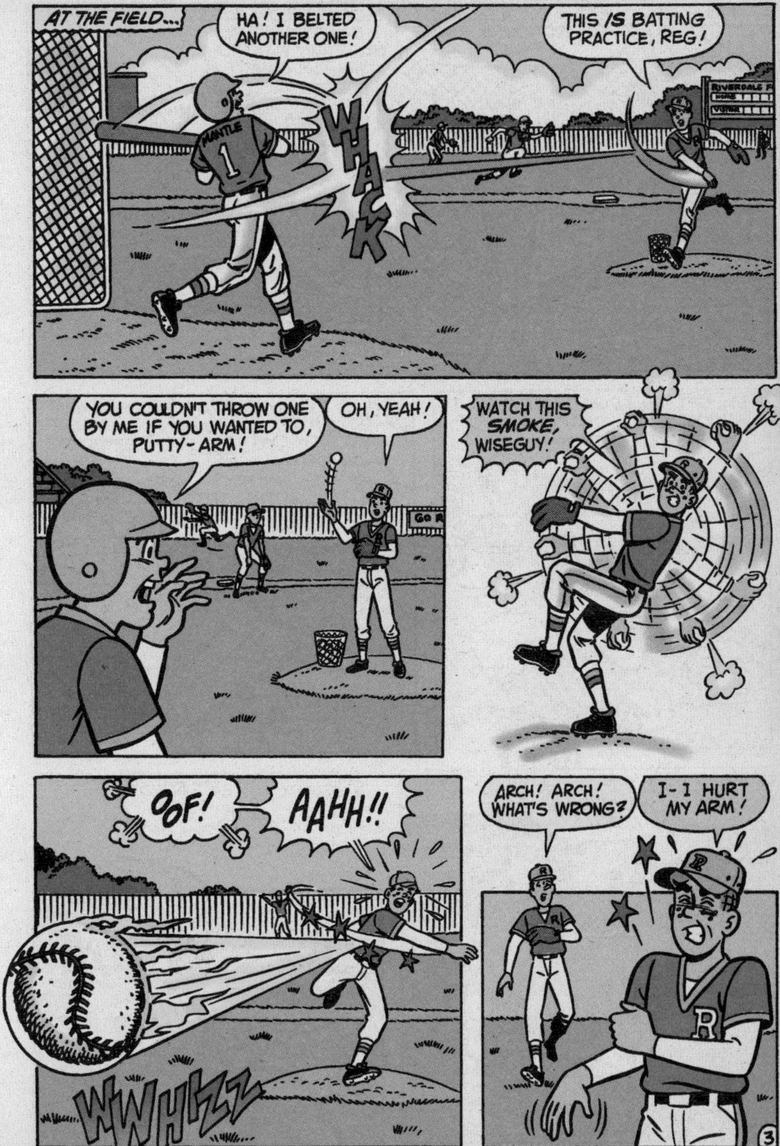

AT THE FIELD...
HA! I BELTED ANOTHER ONE!
THIS IS BATTING PRACTICE, REG!
WHACK
MANTLE
1
YOU COULDN'T THROW ONE BY ME IF YOU WANTED TO, PUTTY-ARM!
OH, YEAH!
WATCH THIS SMOKE, WISEGUY!
OOF!
AAHH!!
WWHIZZ
ARCH! ARCH! WHAT'S WRONG?
I- I HURT MY ARM!

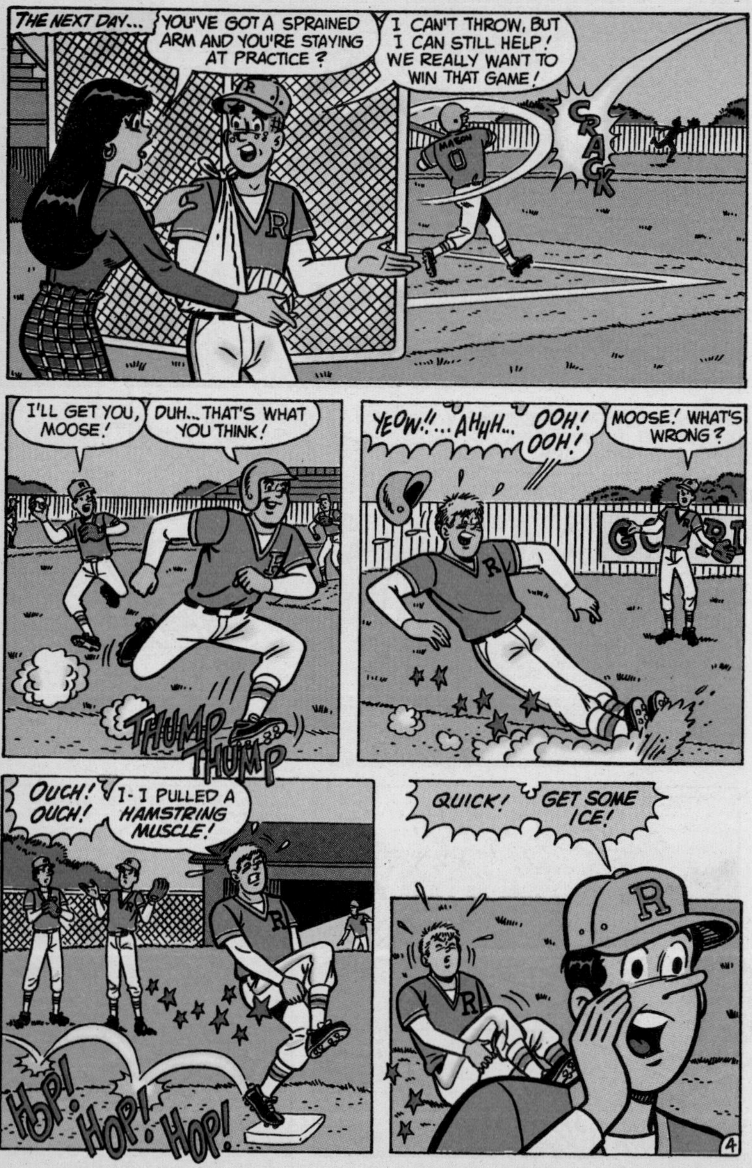

THE NEXT DAY...
YOU'VE GOT A SPRAINED ARM AND YOU'RE STAYING AT PRACTICE ?
I CAN'T THROW, BUT I CAN STILL HELP! WE REALLY WANT TO WIN THAT GAME!
CRACK
MASON
0
I'LL GET YOU, MOOSE!
DUH... THAT'S WHAT YOU THINK!
THUMP
THUMP
YEOW!!... AHHH...
OOH! OOH!
MOOSE! WHAT'S WRONG ?
OUCH! OUCH!
I- I PULLED A HAMSTRING MUSCLE!
HOP! HOP! HOP!
QUICK! GET SOME ICE!
4

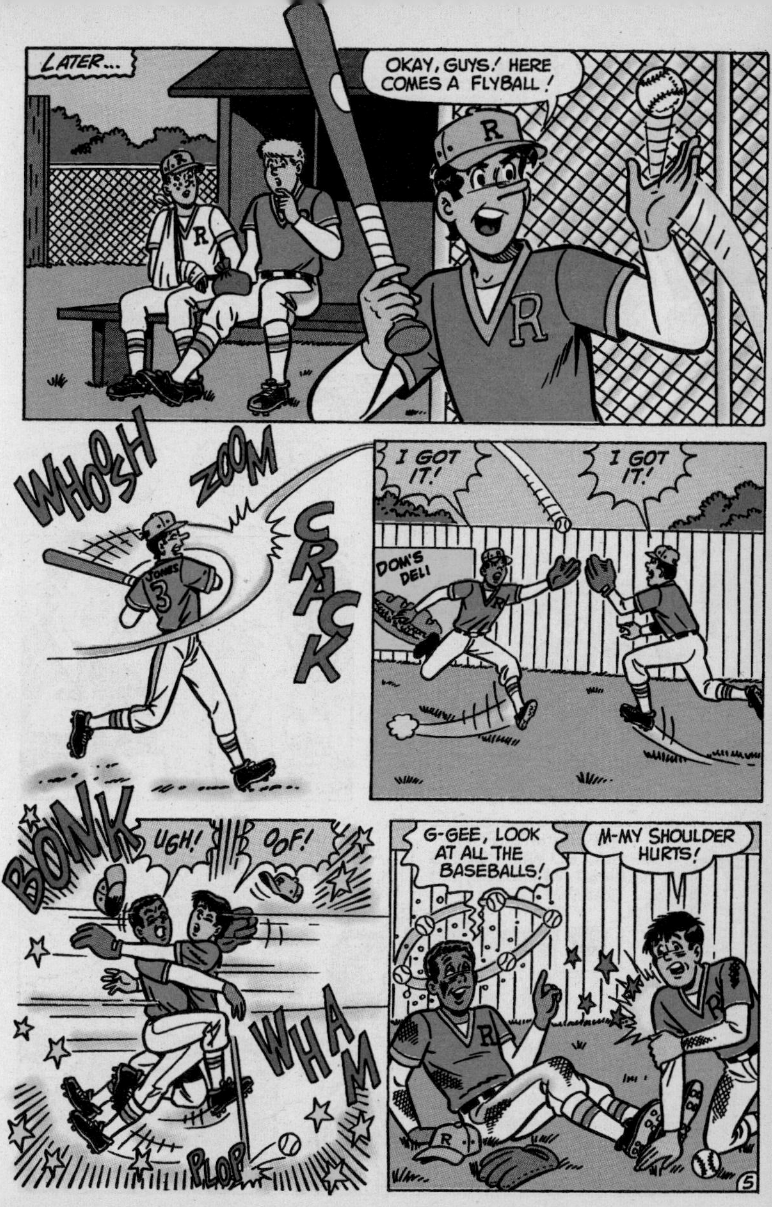
LATER...
OKAY, GUYS! HERE COMES A FLYBALL!
WHOOSH
ZOOM
CRACK
JONES
3
I GOT IT!
I GOT IT!
DOM'S DELI
BONK
UGH!
OOF!
WHAM
PLOP
G-GEE, LOOK AT ALL THE BASEBALLS!
M-MY SHOULDER HURTS!
5

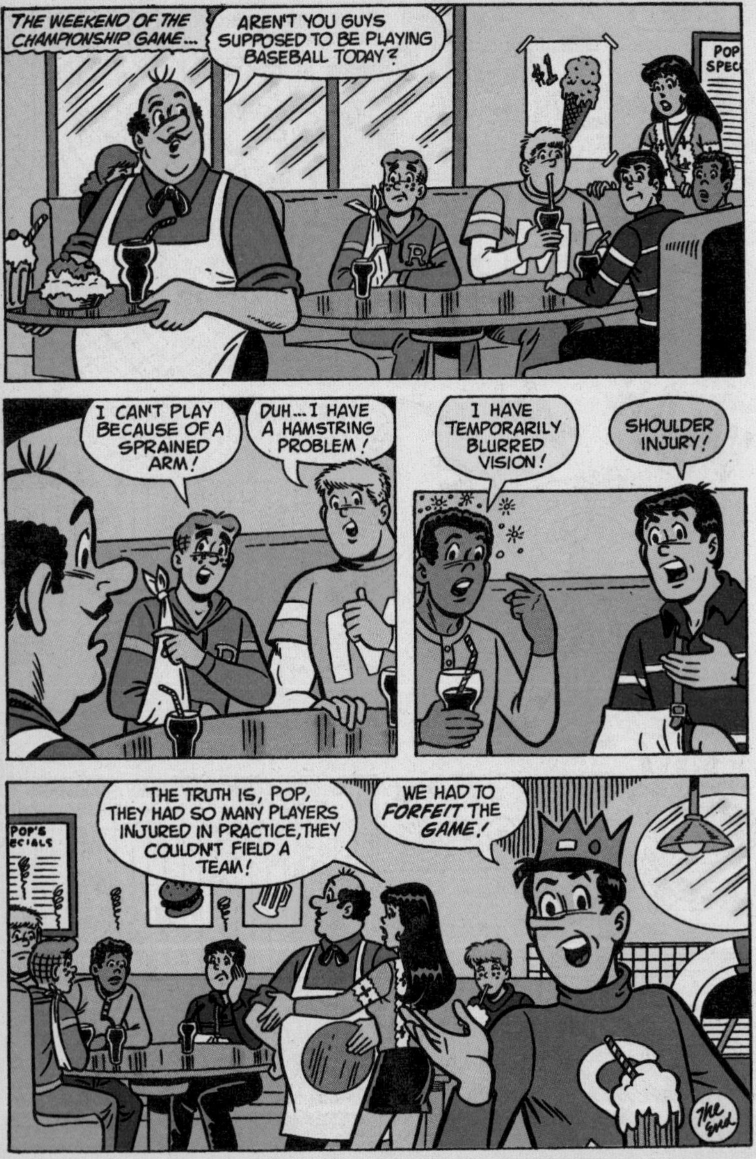
THE WEEKEND OF THE CHAMPIONSHIP GAME...
AREN'T YOU GUYS SUPPOSED TO BE PLAYING BASEBALL TODAY?
#1
POP SPEC
I CAN'T PLAY BECAUSE OF A SPRAINED ARM!
DUH... I HAVE A HAMSTRING PROBLEM!
I HAVE TEMPORARILY BLURRED VISION!
SHOULDER INJURY!
THE TRUTH IS, POP, THEY HAD SO MANY PLAYERS INJURED IN PRACTICE, THEY COULDN'T FIELD A TEAM!
WE HAD TO *FORFEIT* THE *GAME*!
POP'S ECIALS
The End

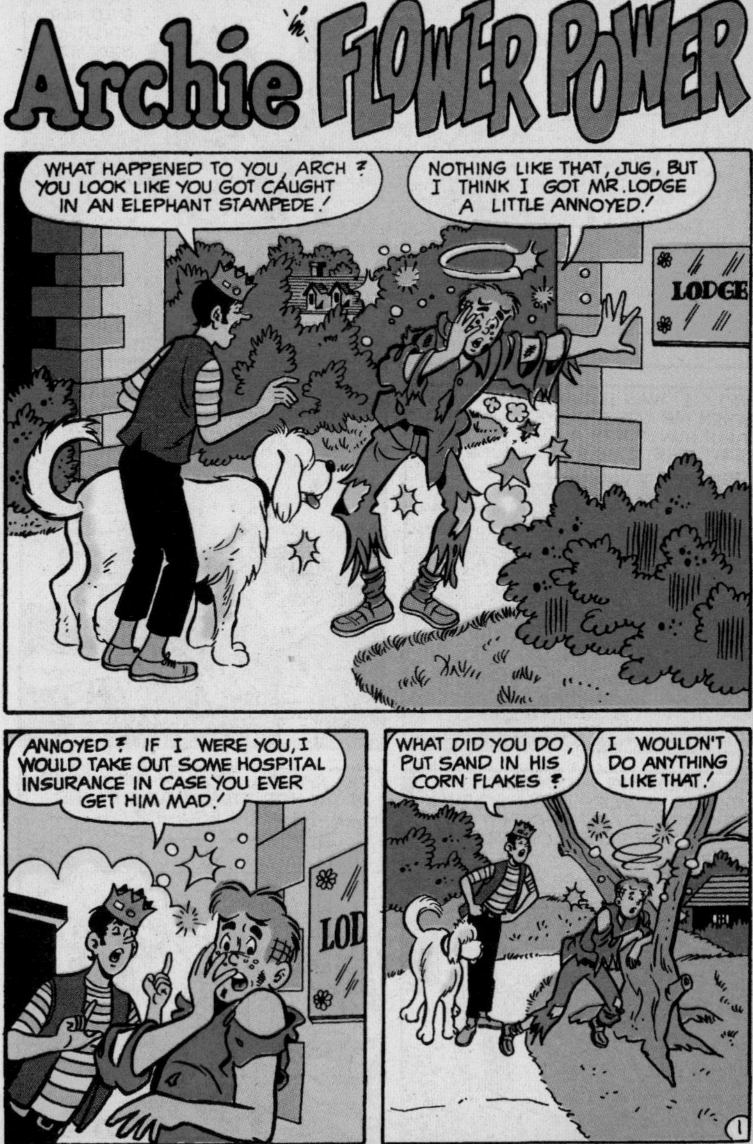

Archie in FLOWER POWER
WHAT HAPPENED TO YOU, ARCH ? YOU LOOK LIKE YOU GOT CAUGHT IN AN ELEPHANT STAMPEDE!
NOTHING LIKE THAT, JUG, BUT I THINK I GOT MR. LODGE A LITTLE ANNOYED!
LODGE
ANNOYED? IF I WERE YOU, I WOULD TAKE OUT SOME HOSPITAL INSURANCE IN CASE YOU EVER GET HIM MAD!
LOD
WHAT DID YOU DO, PUT SAND IN HIS CORN FLAKES ?
I WOULDN'T DO ANYTHING LIKE THAT!
1

Script & Pencils: Al Hartley / Inks: Jon D'Agostino / Letters: Bill Yoshida

RONNIE SAID SHE DIDN'T WANT TO SEE ME ANYMORE BECAUSE SHE SAYS I DON'T REALLY APPRECIATE HER!

SO SHE TOLD HER FATHER TO BEAT YOU UP?

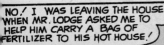

NO! I WAS LEAVING THE HOUSE WHEN MR. LODGE ASKED ME TO HELP HIM CARRY A BAG OF FERTILIZER TO HIS HOT HOUSE!

THEN HE BEAT YOU UP?

NO! I SPOTTED THIS BEAUTIFUL FLOWER AND I ASKED HIM WHAT KIND IT WAS!

THIS, ARCHIE, IS AN ORCHID! NO FLOWER IS MORE BEAUTIFUL THAN THE ORCHID AND VERY FEW CUT FLOWERS LAST LONGER!

THE NATURAL HOME OF THE ORCHID IS THE HOT, STEAMY JUNGLE LAND NEAR THE EQUATOR!

2

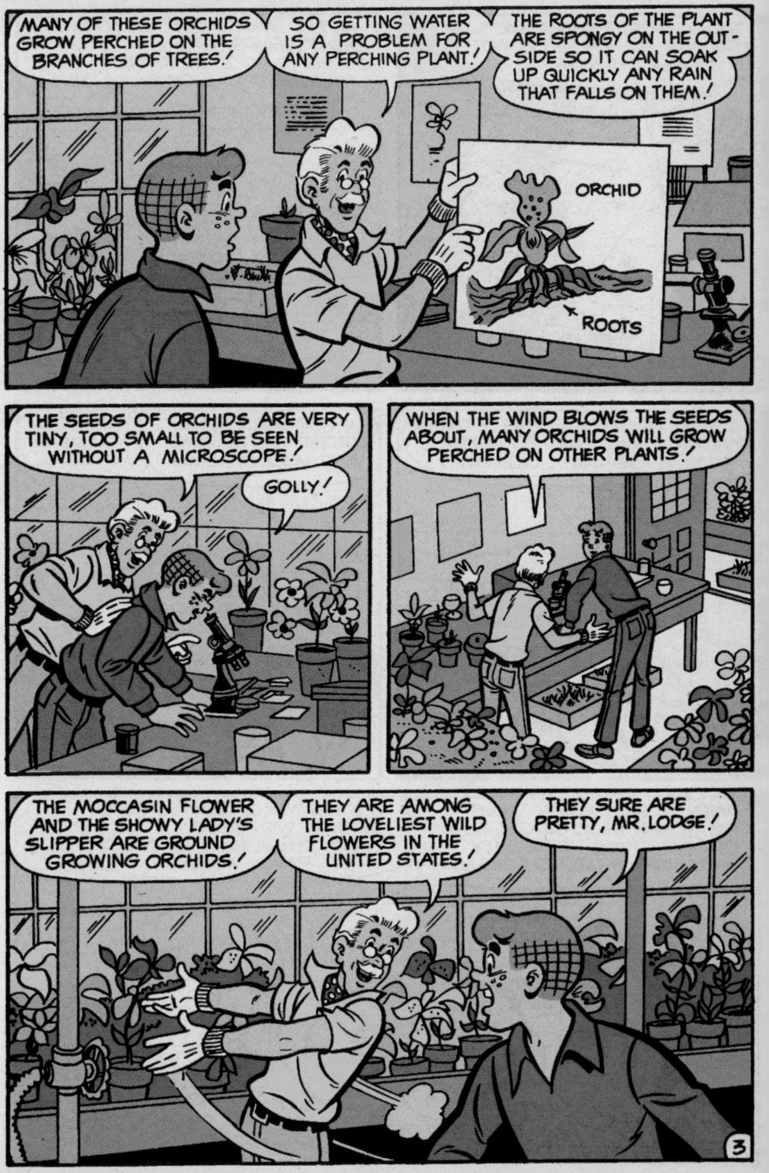
MANY OF THESE ORCHIDS GROW PERCHED ON THE BRANCHES OF TREES.!
SO GETTING WATER IS A PROBLEM FOR ANY PERCHING PLANT.!
THE ROOTS OF THE PLANT ARE SPONGY ON THE OUT-SIDE SO IT CAN SOAK UP QUICKLY ANY RAIN THAT FALLS ON THEM.!
ORCHID
ROOTS
THE SEEDS OF ORCHIDS ARE VERY TINY, TOO SMALL TO BE SEEN WITHOUT A MICROSCOPE.!
GOLLY!
WHEN THE WIND BLOWS THE SEEDS ABOUT, MANY ORCHIDS WILL GROW PERCHED ON OTHER PLANTS.!
THE MOCCASIN FLOWER AND THE SHOWY LADY'S SLIPPER ARE GROUND GROWING ORCHIDS.!
THEY ARE AMONG THE LOVELIEST WILD FLOWERS IN THE UNITED STATES.!
THEY SURE ARE PRETTY, MR. LODGE!
3

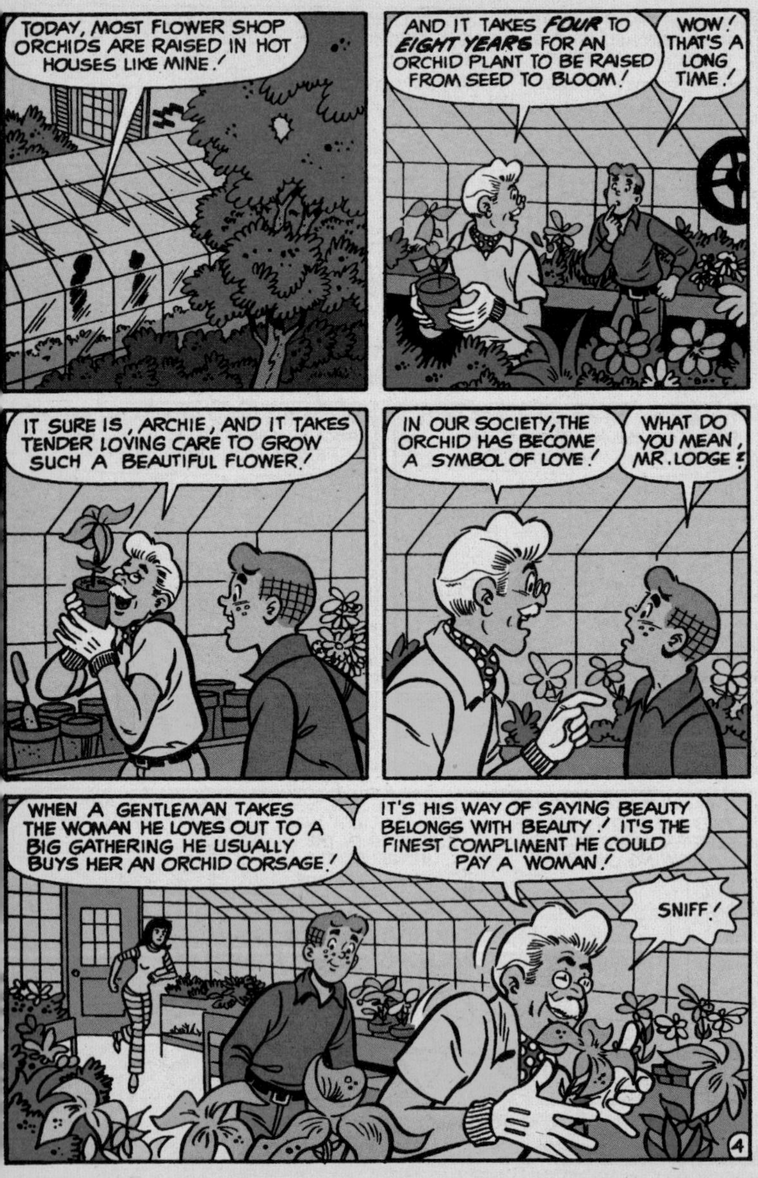
TODAY, MOST FLOWER SHOP ORCHIDS ARE RAISED IN HOT HOUSES LIKE MINE!
AND IT TAKES FOUR TO EIGHT YEARS FOR AN ORCHID PLANT TO BE RAISED FROM SEED TO BLOOM!
WOW! THAT'S A LONG TIME!
IT SURE IS, ARCHIE, AND IT TAKES TENDER LOVING CARE TO GROW SUCH A BEAUTIFUL FLOWER!
IN OUR SOCIETY, THE ORCHID HAS BECOME A SYMBOL OF LOVE!
WHAT DO YOU MEAN, MR. LODGE?
WHEN A GENTLEMAN TAKES THE WOMAN HE LOVES OUT TO A BIG GATHERING HE USUALLY BUYS HER AN ORCHID CORSAGE!
IT'S HIS WAY OF SAYING BEAUTY BELONGS WITH BEAUTY! IT'S THE FINEST COMPLIMENT HE COULD PAY A WOMAN!
SNIFF!
4

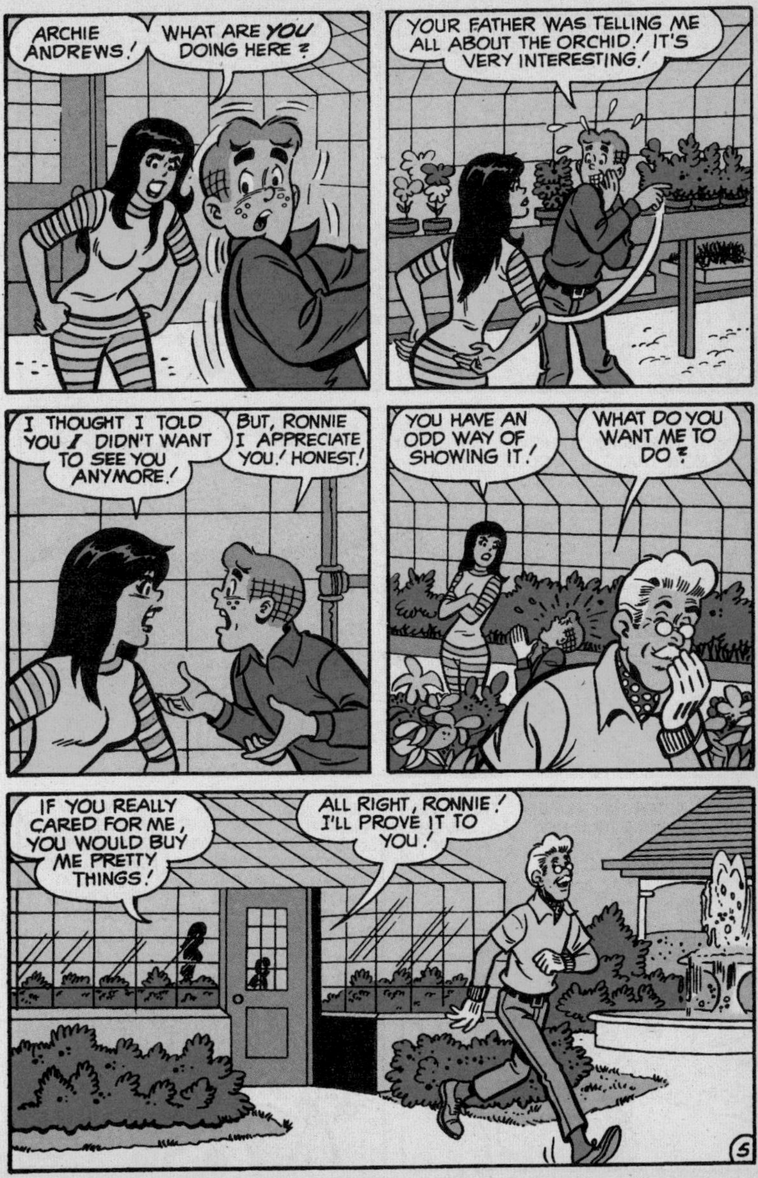
ARCHIE ANDREWS!
WHAT ARE YOU DOING HERE?
YOUR FATHER WAS TELLING ME ALL ABOUT THE ORCHID! IT'S VERY INTERESTING!
I THOUGHT I TOLD YOU I DIDN'T WANT TO SEE YOU ANYMORE!
BUT, RONNIE I APPRECIATE YOU! HONEST!
YOU HAVE AN ODD WAY OF SHOWING IT!
WHAT DO YOU WANT ME TO DO?
IF YOU REALLY CARED FOR ME, YOU WOULD BUY ME PRETTY THINGS!
ALL RIGHT, RONNIE! I'LL PROVE IT TO YOU!
5

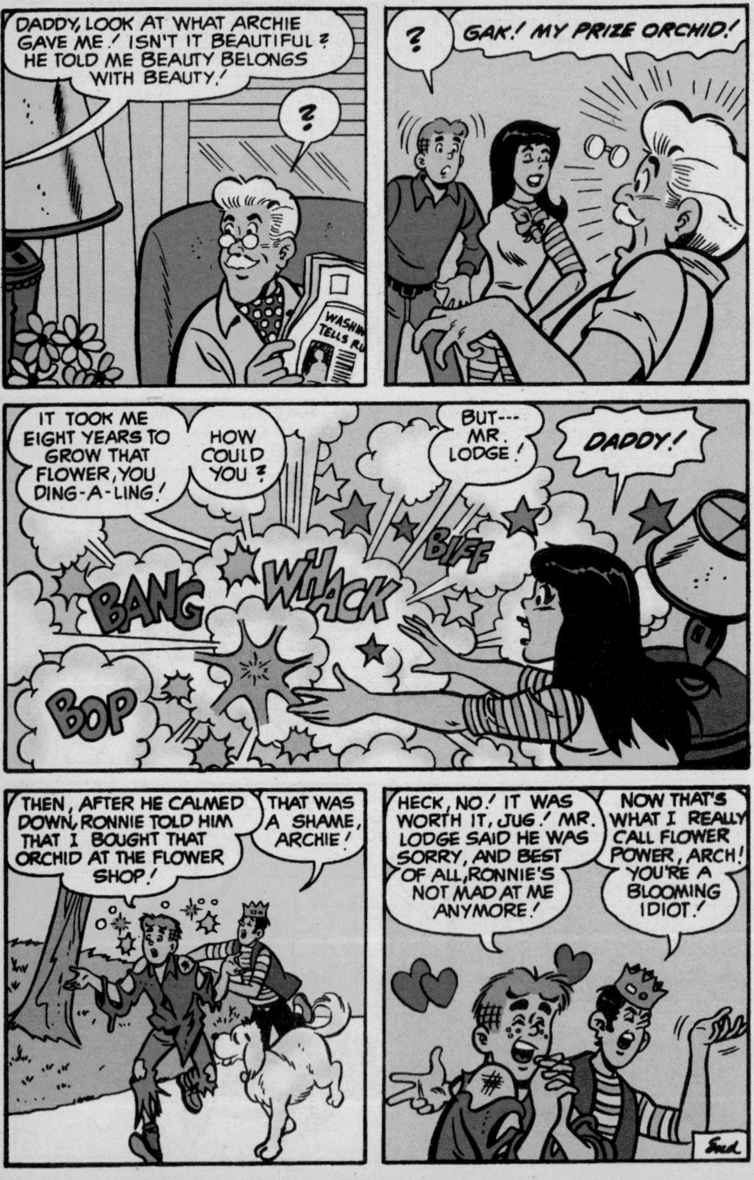
DADDY, LOOK AT WHAT ARCHIE GAVE ME! ISN'T IT BEAUTIFUL? HE TOLD ME BEAUTY BELONGS WITH BEAUTY!
?
?
GAK! MY PRIZE ORCHID!
IT TOOK ME EIGHT YEARS TO GROW THAT FLOWER, YOU DING-A-LING!
HOW COULD YOU?
BUT--- MR. LODGE!
DADDY!
BIFF
BANG
WHACK
BOP
THEN, AFTER HE CALMED DOWN, RONNIE TOLD HIM THAT I BOUGHT THAT ORCHID AT THE FLOWER SHOP!
THAT WAS A SHAME, ARCHIE!
HECK, NO! IT WAS WORTH IT, JUG! MR. LODGE SAID HE WAS SORRY, AND BEST OF ALL, RONNIE'S NOT MAD AT ME ANYMORE!
NOW THAT'S WHAT I REALLY CALL FLOWER POWER, ARCH! YOU'RE A BLOOMING IDIOT!
End

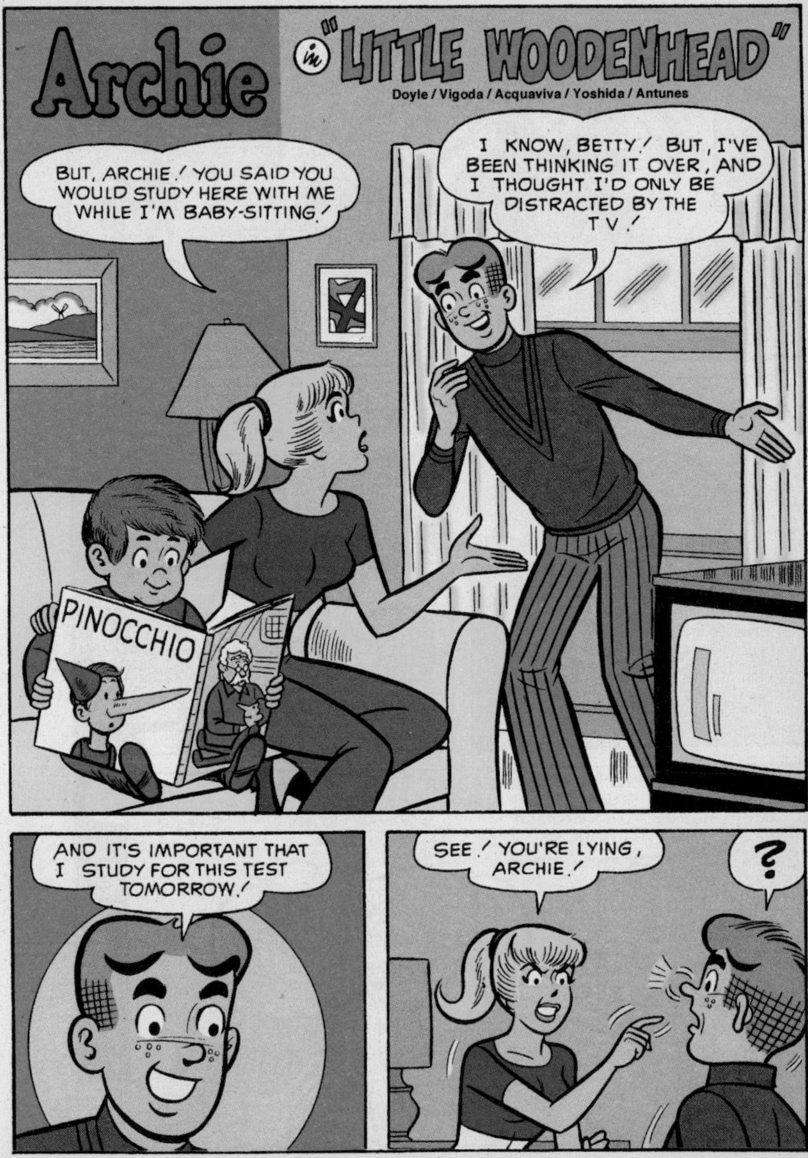
Archie in "LITTLE WOODENHEAD"
Doyle / Vigoda / Acquaviva / Yoshida / Antunes
BUT, ARCHIE! YOU SAID YOU WOULD STUDY HERE WITH ME WHILE I'M BABY-SITTING!
I KNOW, BETTY! BUT, I'VE BEEN THINKING IT OVER, AND I THOUGHT I'D ONLY BE DISTRACTED BY THE TV!
PINOCCHIO
AND IT'S IMPORTANT THAT I STUDY FOR THIS TEST TOMORROW!
SEE! YOU'RE LYING, ARCHIE!
?

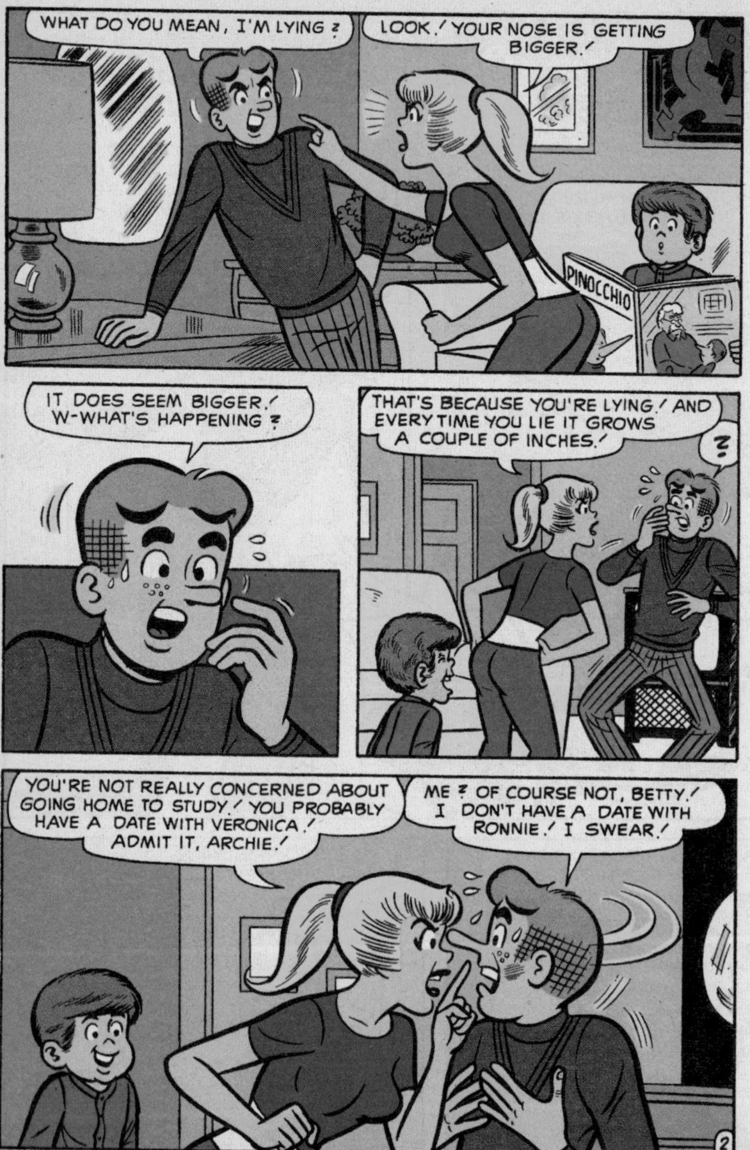
WHAT DO YOU MEAN, I'M LYING ?
LOOK.! YOUR NOSE IS GETTING BIGGER.!
PINOCCHIO
IT DOES SEEM BIGGER.! W-WHAT'S HAPPENING ?
THAT'S BECAUSE YOU'RE LYING.! AND EVERY TIME YOU LIE IT GROWS A COUPLE OF INCHES.!
?
YOU'RE NOT REALLY CONCERNED ABOUT GOING HOME TO STUDY.! YOU PROBABLY HAVE A DATE WITH VERONICA.! ADMIT IT, ARCHIE.!
ME ? OF COURSE NOT, BETTY.! I DON'T HAVE A DATE WITH RONNIE.! I SWEAR.!
2

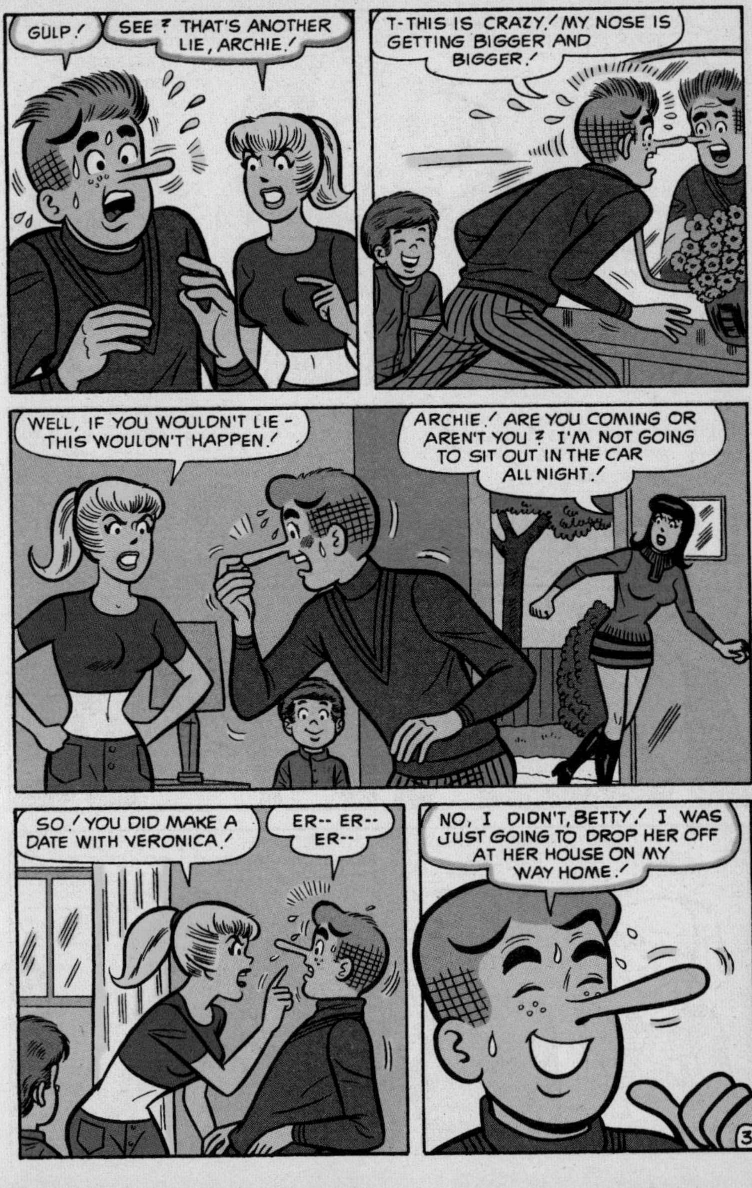
GULP!
SEE? THAT'S ANOTHER LIE, ARCHIE!
T-THIS IS CRAZY! MY NOSE IS GETTING BIGGER AND BIGGER!
WELL, IF YOU WOULDN'T LIE - THIS WOULDN'T HAPPEN!
ARCHIE! ARE YOU COMING OR AREN'T YOU? I'M NOT GOING TO SIT OUT IN THE CAR ALL NIGHT!
SO! YOU DID MAKE A DATE WITH VERONICA!
ER-- ER-- ER--
NO, I DIDN'T, BETTY! I WAS JUST GOING TO DROP HER OFF AT HER HOUSE ON MY WAY HOME!
3

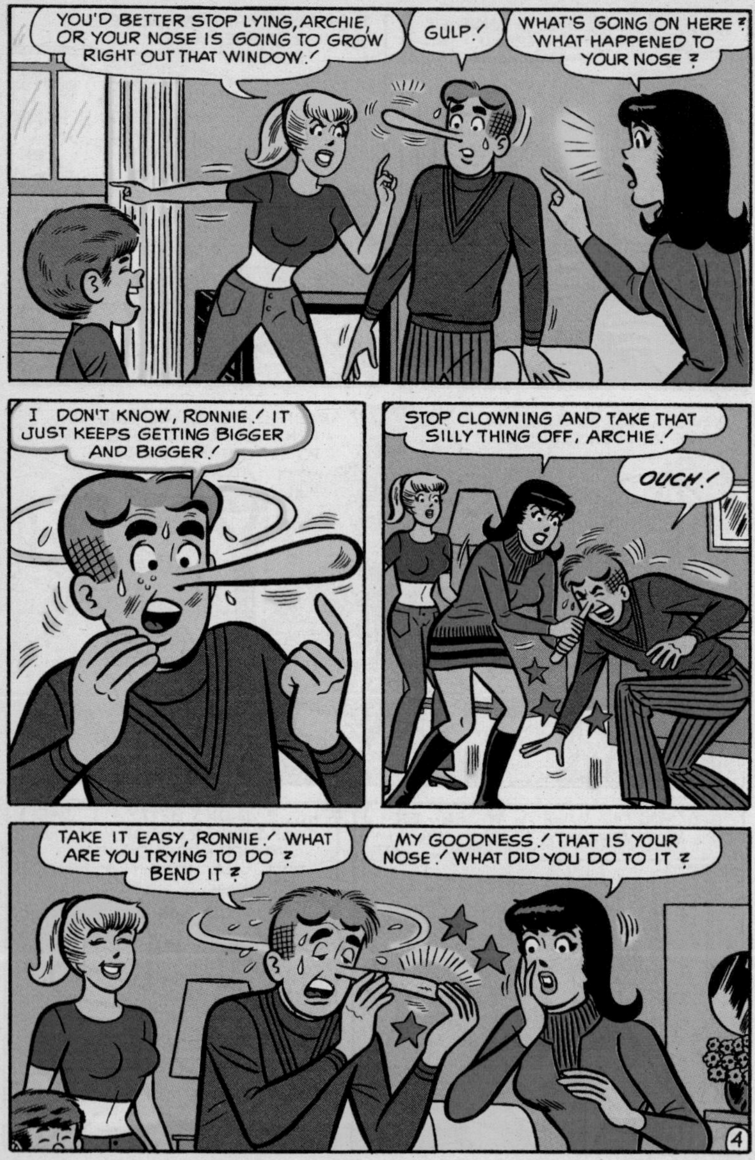

YOU'D BETTER STOP LYING, ARCHIE, OR YOUR NOSE IS GOING TO GROW RIGHT OUT THAT WINDOW!
GULP!
WHAT'S GOING ON HERE? WHAT HAPPENED TO YOUR NOSE?
I DON'T KNOW, RONNIE! IT JUST KEEPS GETTING BIGGER AND BIGGER!
STOP CLOWNING AND TAKE THAT SILLY THING OFF, ARCHIE!
OUCH!
TAKE IT EASY, RONNIE! WHAT ARE YOU TRYING TO DO? BEND IT?
MY GOODNESS! THAT IS YOUR NOSE! WHAT DID YOU DO TO IT?
4

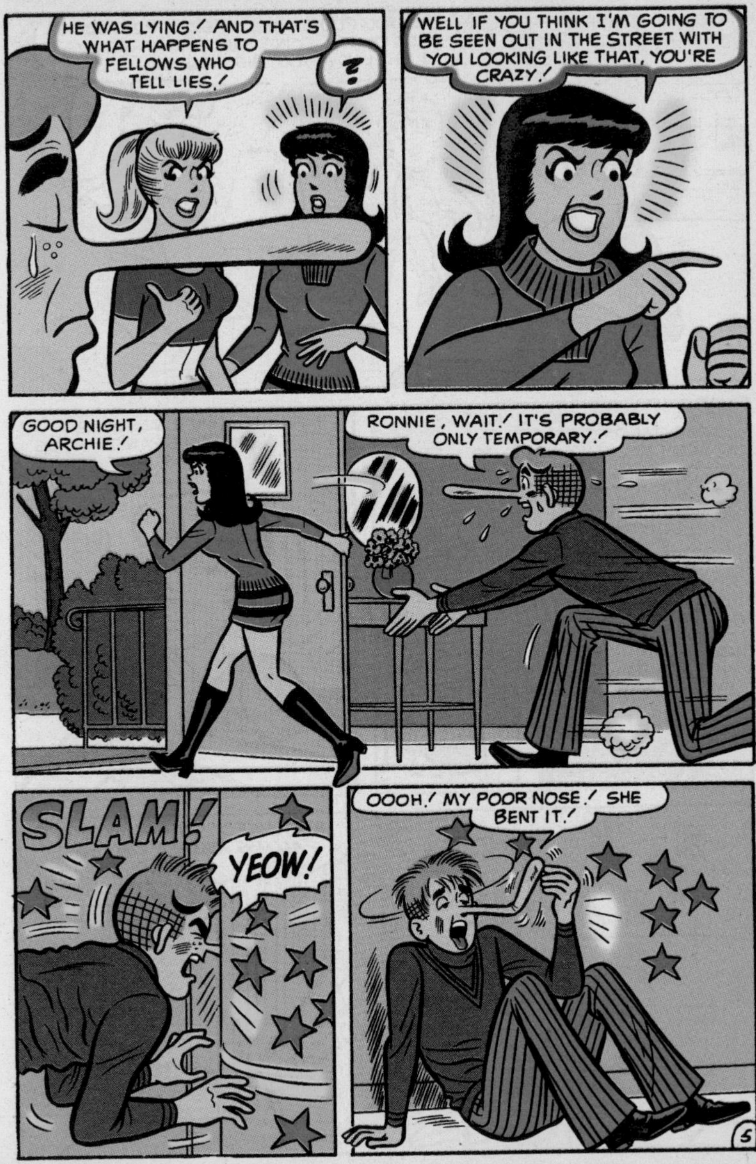
HE WAS LYING! AND THAT'S WHAT HAPPENS TO FELLOWS WHO TELL LIES!
?
WELL IF YOU THINK I'M GOING TO BE SEEN OUT IN THE STREET WITH YOU LOOKING LIKE THAT, YOU'RE CRAZY!
GOOD NIGHT, ARCHIE!
RONNIE, WAIT! IT'S PROBABLY ONLY TEMPORARY!
SLAM!
YEOW!
OOOH! MY POOR NOSE! SHE BENT IT!
5

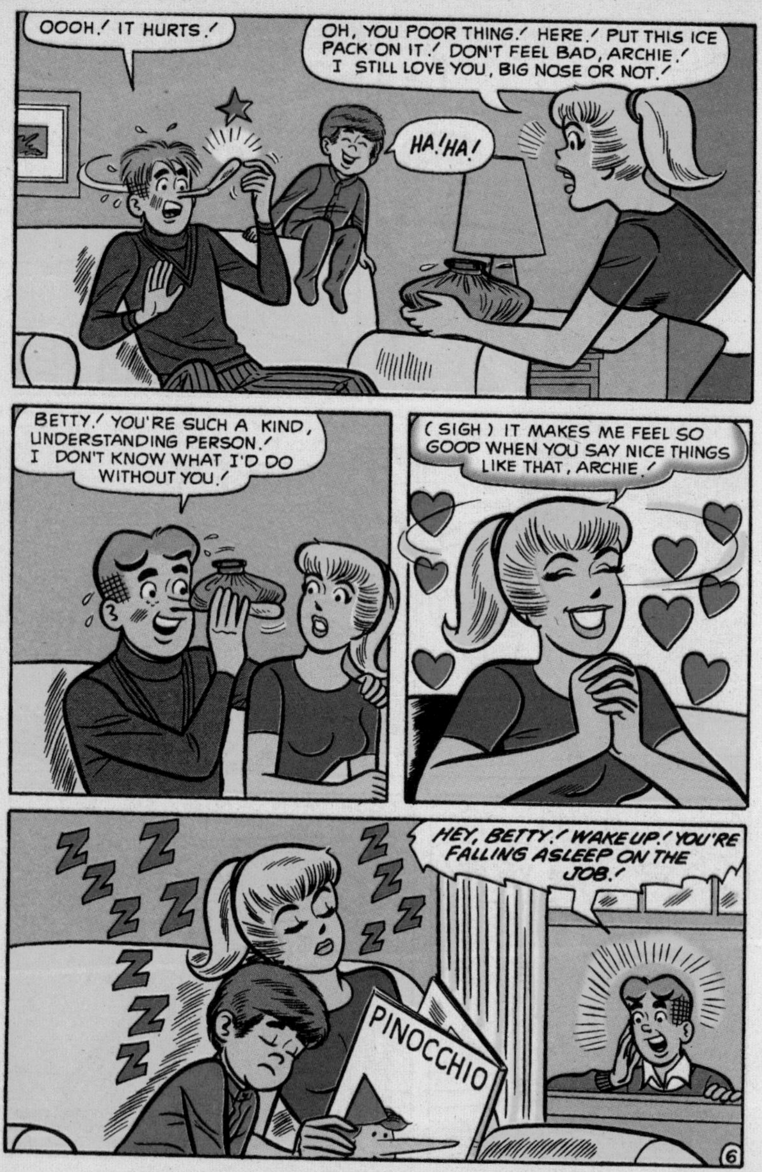

OOOH.! IT HURTS.!
OH, YOU POOR THING.! HERE.! PUT THIS ICE PACK ON IT.! DON'T FEEL BAD, ARCHIE.! I STILL LOVE YOU, BIG NOSE OR NOT.!
HA!HA!
BETTY.! YOU'RE SUCH A KIND, UNDERSTANDING PERSON.! I DON'T KNOW WHAT I'D DO WITHOUT YOU.!
(SIGH) IT MAKES ME FEEL SO GOOD WHEN YOU SAY NICE THINGS LIKE THAT, ARCHIE.!
Z Z Z Z Z Z Z Z
Z Z Z Z
HEY, BETTY.! WAKE UP.! YOU'RE FALLING ASLEEP ON THE JOB.!
PINOCCHIO
6

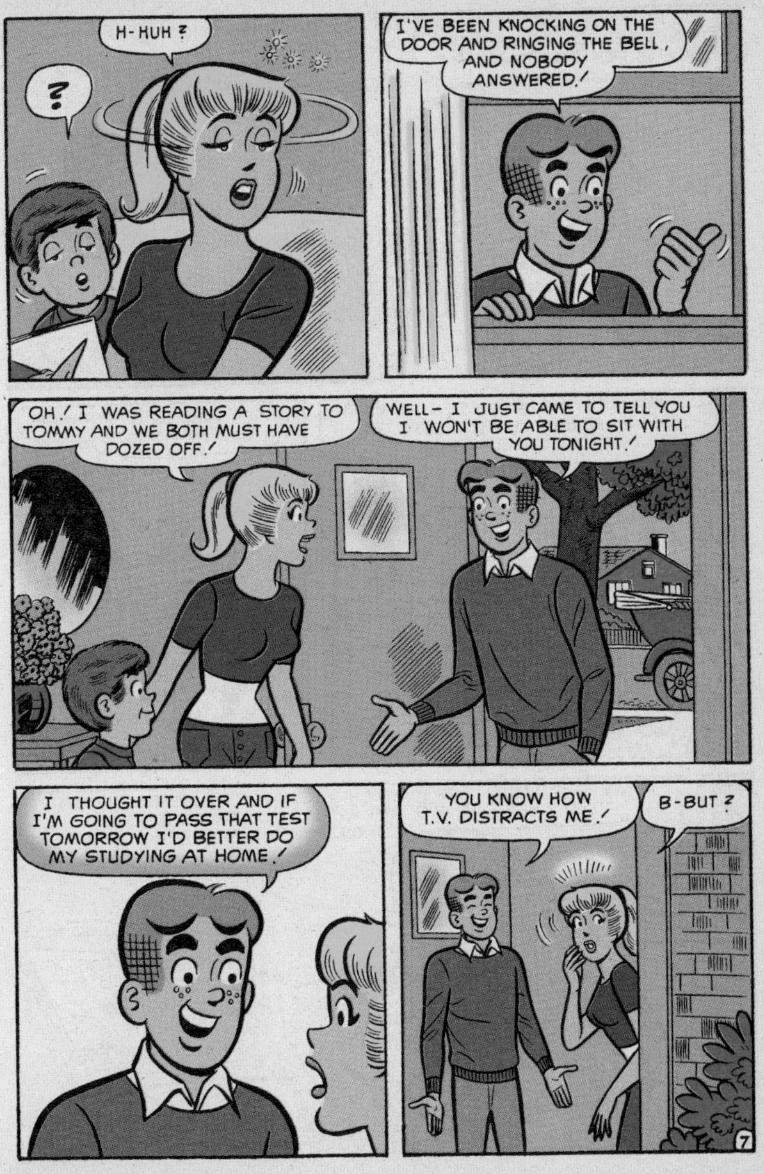
H-HUH ?
?
I'VE BEEN KNOCKING ON THE DOOR AND RINGING THE BELL, AND NOBODY ANSWERED!
OH! I WAS READING A STORY TO TOMMY AND WE BOTH MUST HAVE DOZED OFF!
WELL- I JUST CAME TO TELL YOU I WON'T BE ABLE TO SIT WITH YOU TONIGHT!
I THOUGHT IT OVER AND IF I'M GOING TO PASS THAT TEST TOMORROW I'D BETTER DO MY STUDYING AT HOME!
YOU KNOW HOW T.V. DISTRACTS ME!
B-BUT ?
7

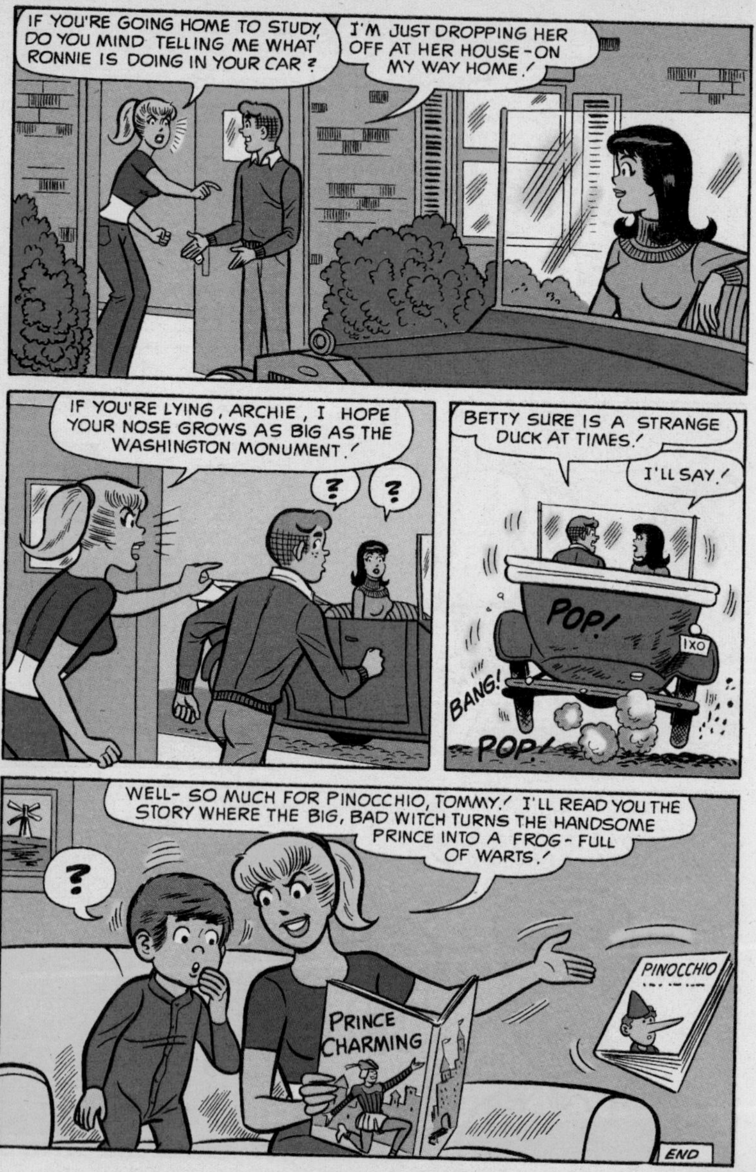
IF YOU'RE GOING HOME TO STUDY, DO YOU MIND TELLING ME WHAT RONNIE IS DOING IN YOUR CAR ?
I'M JUST DROPPING HER OFF AT HER HOUSE - ON MY WAY HOME !
IF YOU'RE LYING, ARCHIE, I HOPE YOUR NOSE GROWS AS BIG AS THE WASHINGTON MONUMENT !
?
?
BETTY SURE IS A STRANGE DUCK AT TIMES !
I'LL SAY !
POP!
1XO
BANG!
POP!
WELL- SO MUCH FOR PINOCCHIO, TOMMY ! I'LL READ YOU THE STORY WHERE THE BIG, BAD WITCH TURNS THE HANDSOME PRINCE INTO A FROG - FULL OF WARTS !
?
PRINCE CHARMING
PINOCCHIO
END

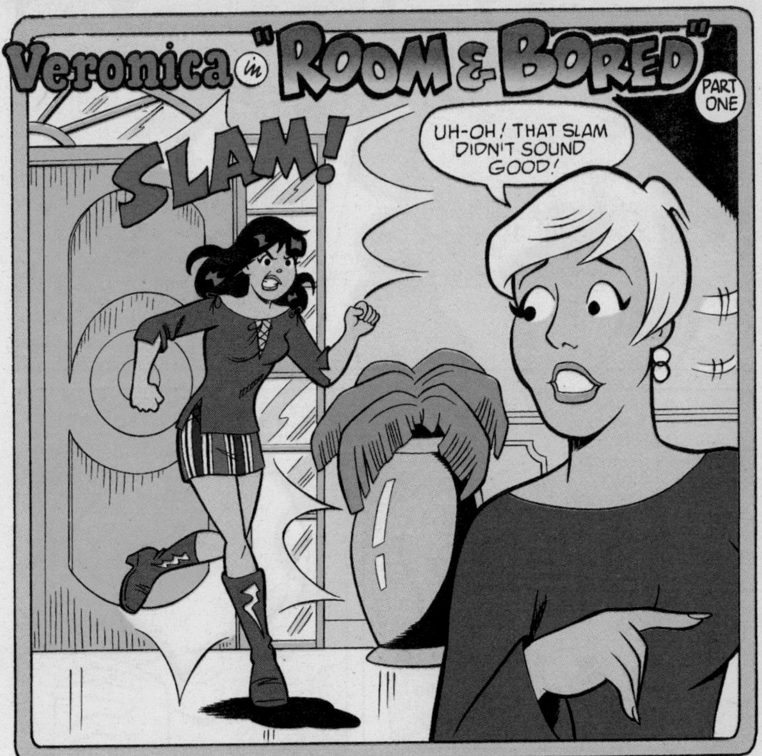
Veronica in "ROOM & BORED"
PART ONE
SLAM!
UH-OH! THAT SLAM DIDN'T SOUND GOOD!

Script & Pencils: Dan Parent / Inks: Jim Amash / Letters: Bill Yoshida / Colors: Barry Grossman

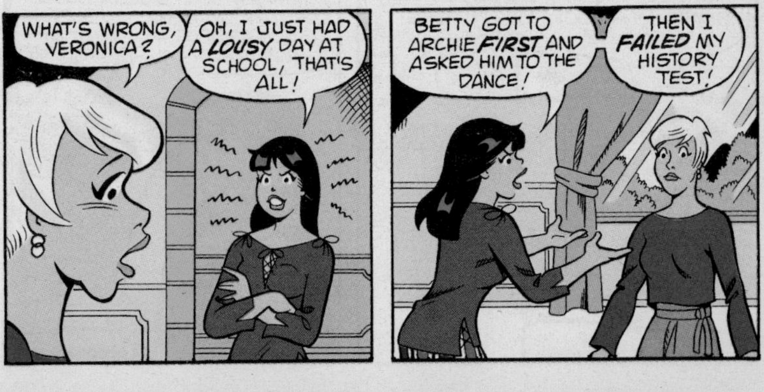
WHAT'S WRONG, VERONICA?
OH, I JUST HAD A LOUSY DAY AT SCHOOL, THAT'S ALL!
BETTY GOT TO ARCHIE FIRST AND ASKED HIM TO THE DANCE!
THEN I FAILED MY HISTORY TEST!

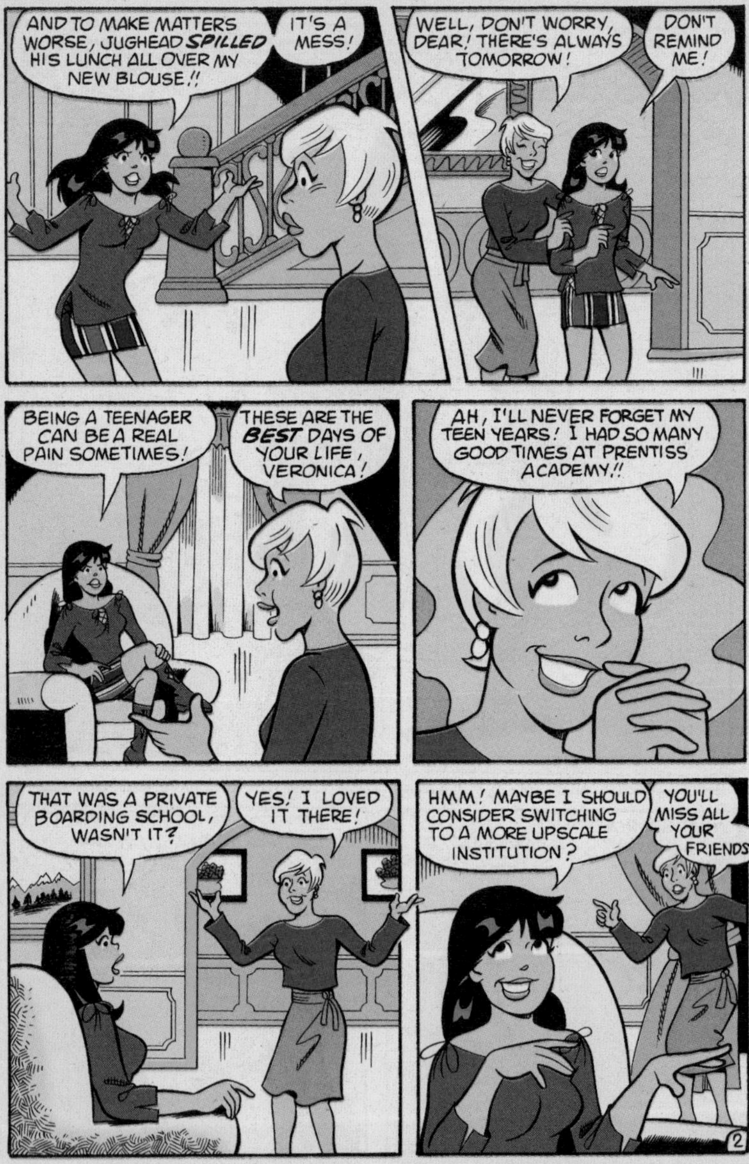
AND TO MAKE MATTERS WORSE, JUGHEAD SPILLED HIS LUNCH ALL OVER MY NEW BLOUSE!!
IT'S A MESS!
WELL, DON'T WORRY, DEAR! THERE'S ALWAYS TOMORROW!
DON'T REMIND ME!
BEING A TEENAGER CAN BE A REAL PAIN SOMETIMES!
THESE ARE THE BEST DAYS OF YOUR LIFE, VERONICA!
AH, I'LL NEVER FORGET MY TEEN YEARS! I HAD SO MANY GOOD TIMES AT PRENTISS ACADEMY!!
THAT WAS A PRIVATE BOARDING SCHOOL, WASN'T IT?
YES! I LOVED IT THERE!
HMM! MAYBE I SHOULD CONSIDER SWITCHING TO A MORE UPSCALE INSTITUTION?
YOU'LL MISS ALL YOUR FRIENDS!!
2

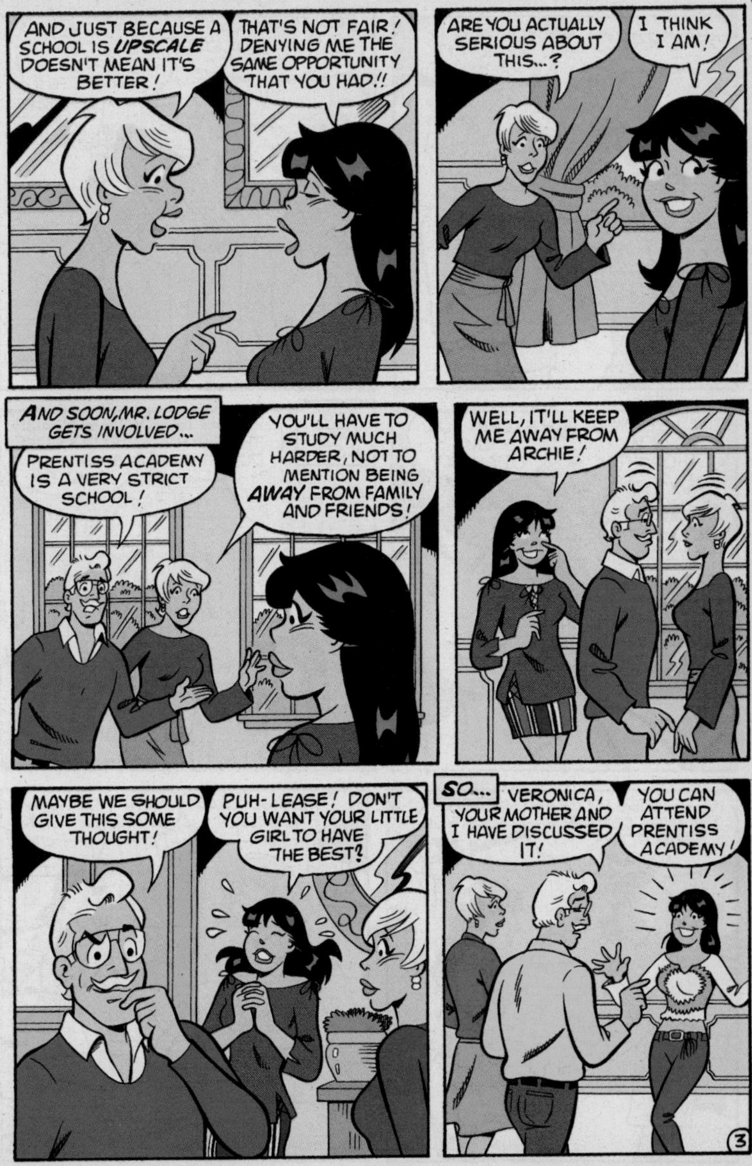
AND JUST BECAUSE A SCHOOL IS *UPSCALE* DOESN'T MEAN IT'S BETTER!
THAT'S NOT FAIR! DENYING ME THE SAME OPPORTUNITY THAT YOU HAD!!
ARE YOU ACTUALLY SERIOUS ABOUT THIS...?
I THINK I AM!
AND SOON, MR. LODGE GETS INVOLVED...
PRENTISS ACADEMY IS A VERY STRICT SCHOOL!
YOU'LL HAVE TO STUDY MUCH HARDER, NOT TO MENTION BEING *AWAY* FROM FAMILY AND FRIENDS!
WELL, IT'LL KEEP ME AWAY FROM ARCHIE!
MAYBE WE SHOULD GIVE THIS SOME THOUGHT!
PUH-LEASE! DON'T YOU WANT YOUR LITTLE GIRL TO HAVE THE BEST?
SO...
VERONICA, YOUR MOTHER AND I HAVE DISCUSSED IT!
YOU CAN ATTEND PRENTISS ACADEMY!
3

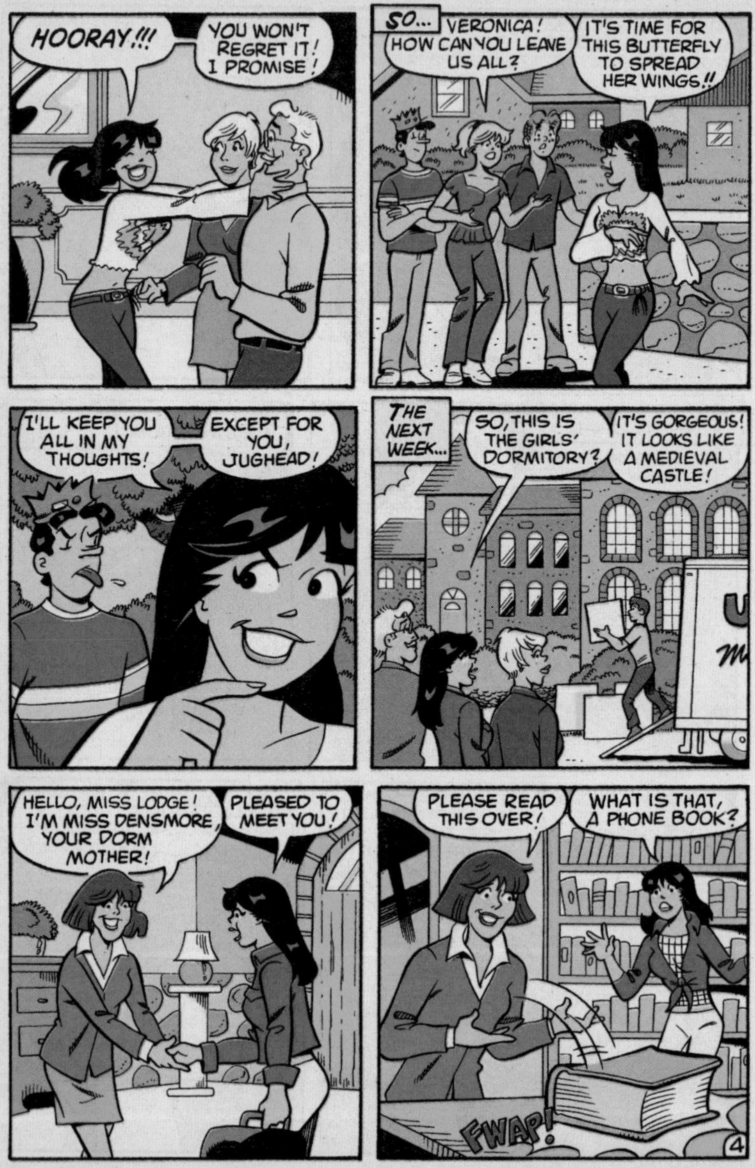
HOORAY!!!
YOU WON'T REGRET IT! I PROMISE!
SO...
VERONICA! HOW CAN YOU LEAVE US ALL?
IT'S TIME FOR THIS BUTTERFLY TO SPREAD HER WINGS!!
I'LL KEEP YOU ALL IN MY THOUGHTS!
EXCEPT FOR YOU, JUGHEAD!
THE NEXT WEEK...
SO, THIS IS THE GIRLS' DORMITORY?
IT'S GORGEOUS! IT LOOKS LIKE A MEDIEVAL CASTLE!
HELLO, MISS LODGE! I'M MISS DENSMORE, YOUR DORM MOTHER!
PLEASED TO MEET YOU!
PLEASE READ THIS OVER!
WHAT IS THAT, A PHONE BOOK?
FWAP!
4

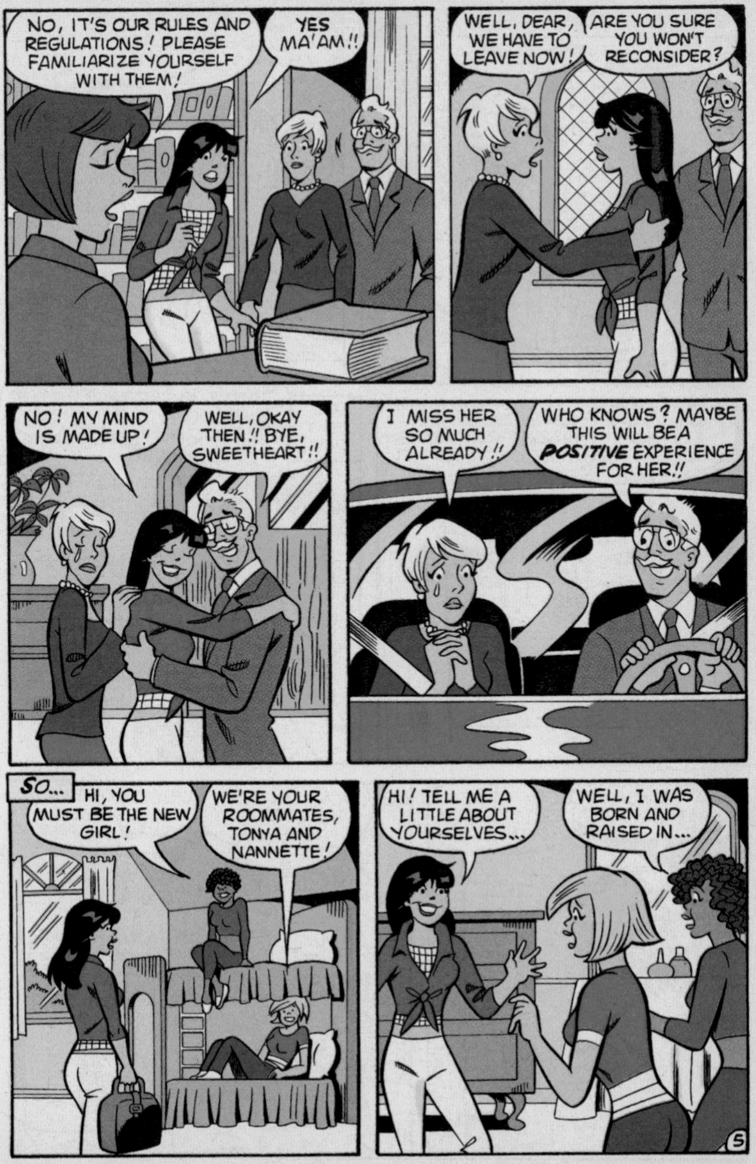
NO, IT'S OUR RULES AND REGULATIONS! PLEASE FAMILIARIZE YOURSELF WITH THEM!
YES MA'AM!!
WELL, DEAR, WE HAVE TO LEAVE NOW!
ARE YOU SURE YOU WON'T RECONSIDER?
NO! MY MIND IS MADE UP!
WELL, OKAY THEN!! BYE, SWEETHEART!!
I MISS HER SO MUCH ALREADY!!
WHO KNOWS? MAYBE THIS WILL BE A POSITIVE EXPERIENCE FOR HER!!
SO...
HI, YOU MUST BE THE NEW GIRL!
WE'RE YOUR ROOMMATES, TONYA AND NANNETTE!
HI! TELL ME A LITTLE ABOUT YOURSELVES...
WELL, I WAS BORN AND RAISED IN...
5

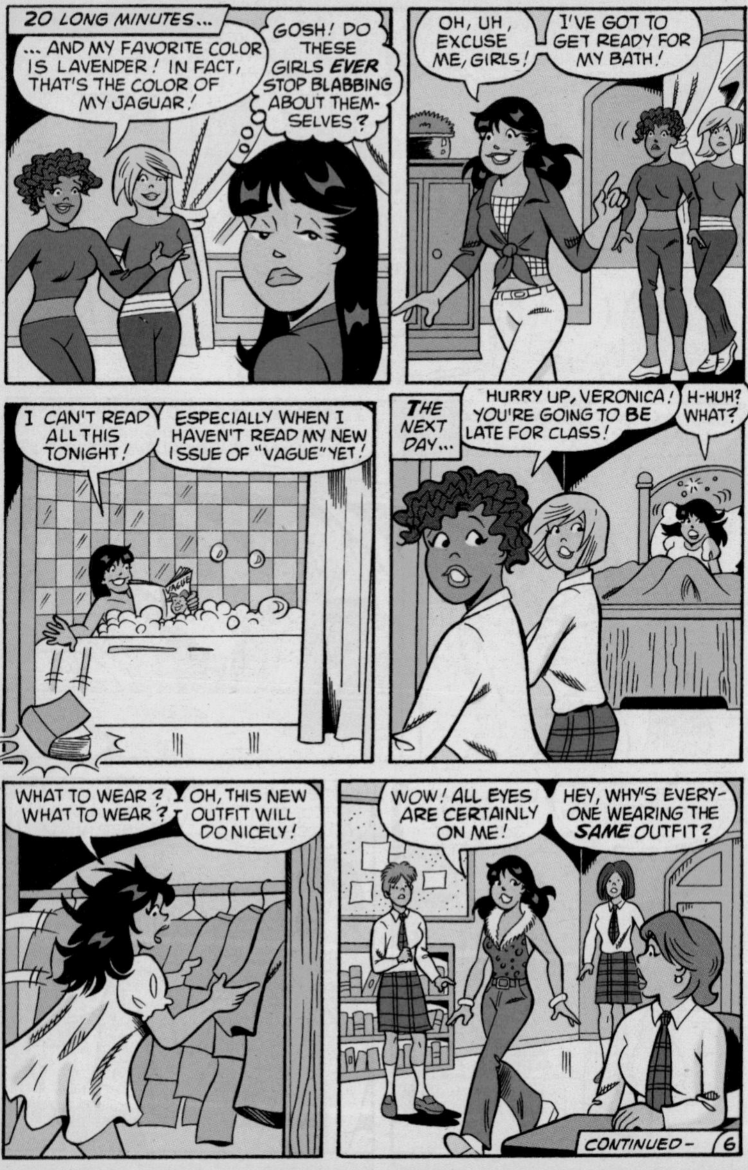
20 LONG MINUTES...
... AND MY FAVORITE COLOR IS LAVENDER! IN FACT, THAT'S THE COLOR OF MY JAGUAR!
GOSH! DO THESE GIRLS EVER STOP BLABBING ABOUT THEM-SELVES?
OH, UH, EXCUSE ME, GIRLS!
I'VE GOT TO GET READY FOR MY BATH!
I CAN'T READ ALL THIS TONIGHT!
ESPECIALLY WHEN I HAVEN'T READ MY NEW ISSUE OF "VAGUE" YET!
VAGUE
THE NEXT DAY...
HURRY UP, VERONICA! YOU'RE GOING TO BE LATE FOR CLASS!
H-HUH? WHAT?
WHAT TO WEAR? WHAT TO WEAR?
OH, THIS NEW OUTFIT WILL DO NICELY!
WOW! ALL EYES ARE CERTAINLY ON ME!
HEY, WHY'S EVERY-ONE WEARING THE SAME OUTFIT?
CONTINUED-
6

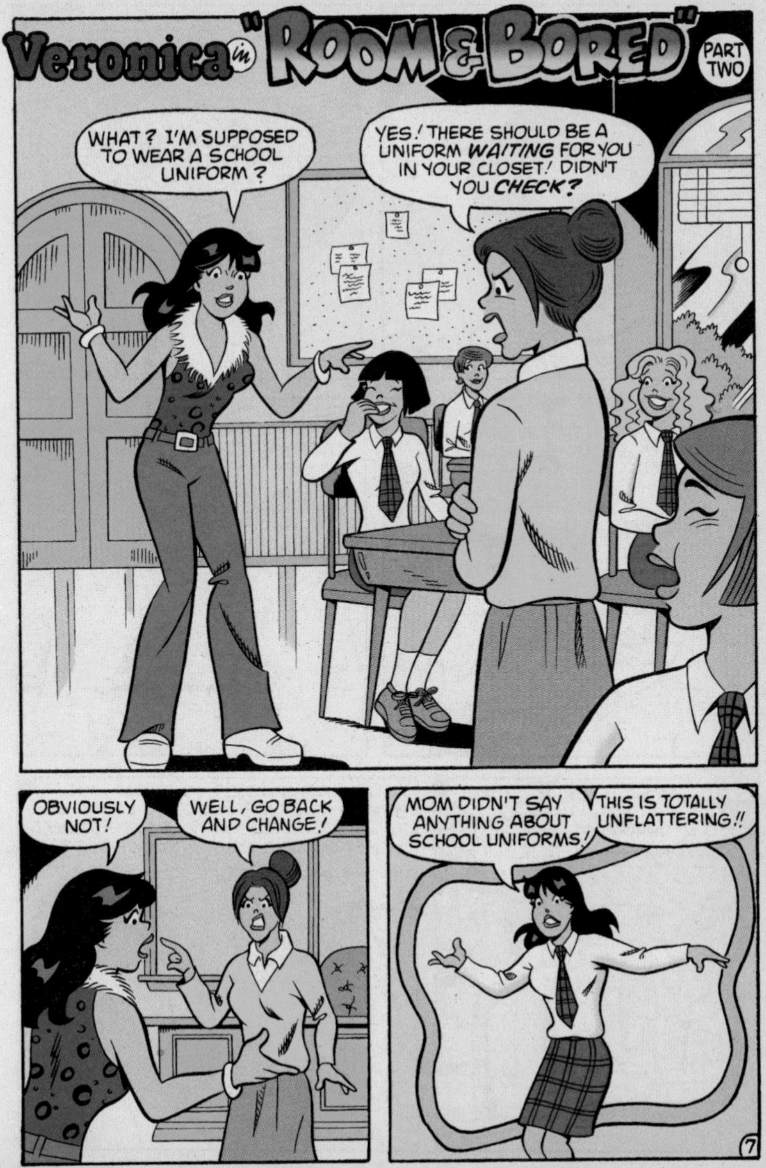
Veronica in "ROOM & BORED" PART TWO
WHAT? I'M SUPPOSED TO WEAR A SCHOOL UNIFORM?
YES! THERE SHOULD BE A UNIFORM *WAITING* FOR YOU IN YOUR CLOSET! DIDN'T YOU *CHECK?*
OBVIOUSLY NOT!
WELL, GO BACK AND CHANGE!
MOM DIDN'T SAY ANYTHING ABOUT SCHOOL UNIFORMS!
THIS IS TOTALLY UNFLATTERING!!
7

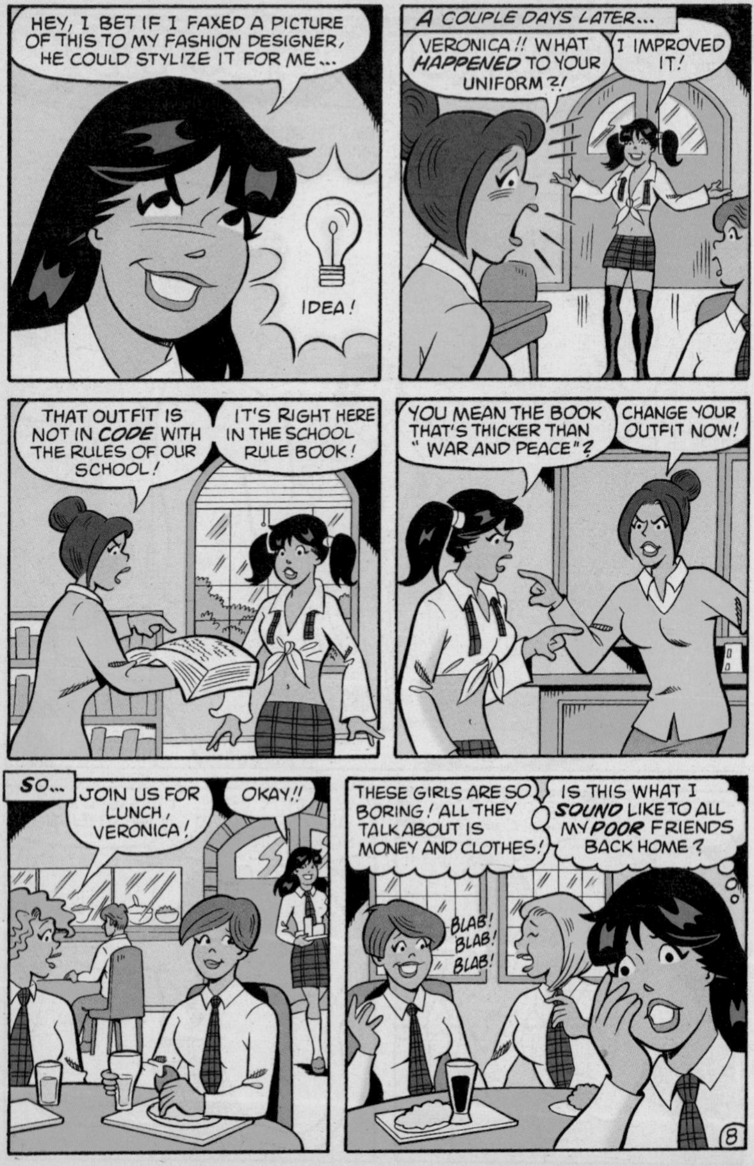

HEY, I BET IF I FAXED A PICTURE OF THIS TO MY FASHION DESIGNER, HE COULD STYLIZE IT FOR ME...
IDEA!
A COUPLE DAYS LATER...
VERONICA!! WHAT HAPPENED TO YOUR UNIFORM?!
I IMPROVED IT!
THAT OUTFIT IS NOT IN CODE WITH THE RULES OF OUR SCHOOL!
IT'S RIGHT HERE IN THE SCHOOL RULE BOOK!
YOU MEAN THE BOOK THAT'S THICKER THAN "WAR AND PEACE"?
CHANGE YOUR OUTFIT NOW!
SO...
JOIN US FOR LUNCH, VERONICA!
OKAY!!
THESE GIRLS ARE SO BORING! ALL THEY TALK ABOUT IS MONEY AND CLOTHES!
IS THIS WHAT I SOUND LIKE TO ALL MY POOR FRIENDS BACK HOME?
BLAB! BLAB! BLAB!

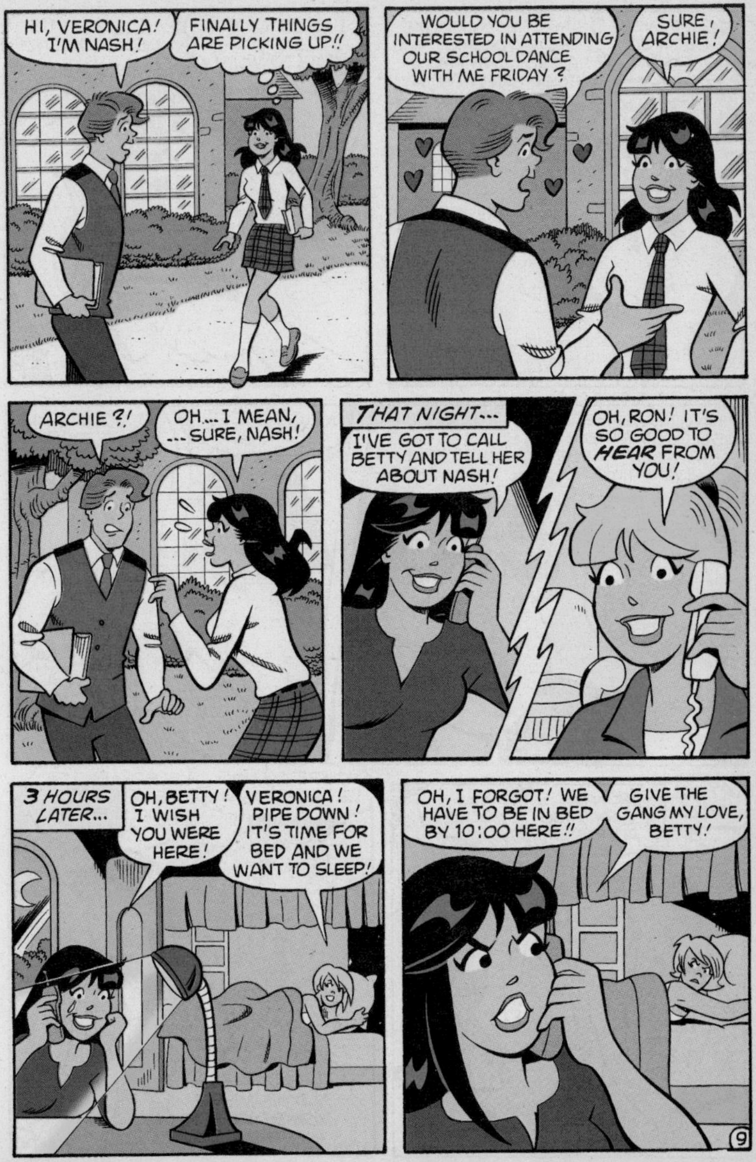
HI, VERONICA! I'M NASH!
FINALLY THINGS ARE PICKING UP!!
WOULD YOU BE INTERESTED IN ATTENDING OUR SCHOOL DANCE WITH ME FRIDAY?
SURE, ARCHIE!
ARCHIE?!
OH... I MEAN, ... SURE, NASH!
THAT NIGHT...
I'VE GOT TO CALL BETTY AND TELL HER ABOUT NASH!
OH, RON! IT'S SO GOOD TO HEAR FROM YOU!
3 HOURS LATER...
OH, BETTY! I WISH YOU WERE HERE!
VERONICA! PIPE DOWN! IT'S TIME FOR BED AND WE WANT TO SLEEP!
OH, I FORGOT! WE HAVE TO BE IN BED BY 10:00 HERE!!
GIVE THE GANG MY LOVE, BETTY!
9

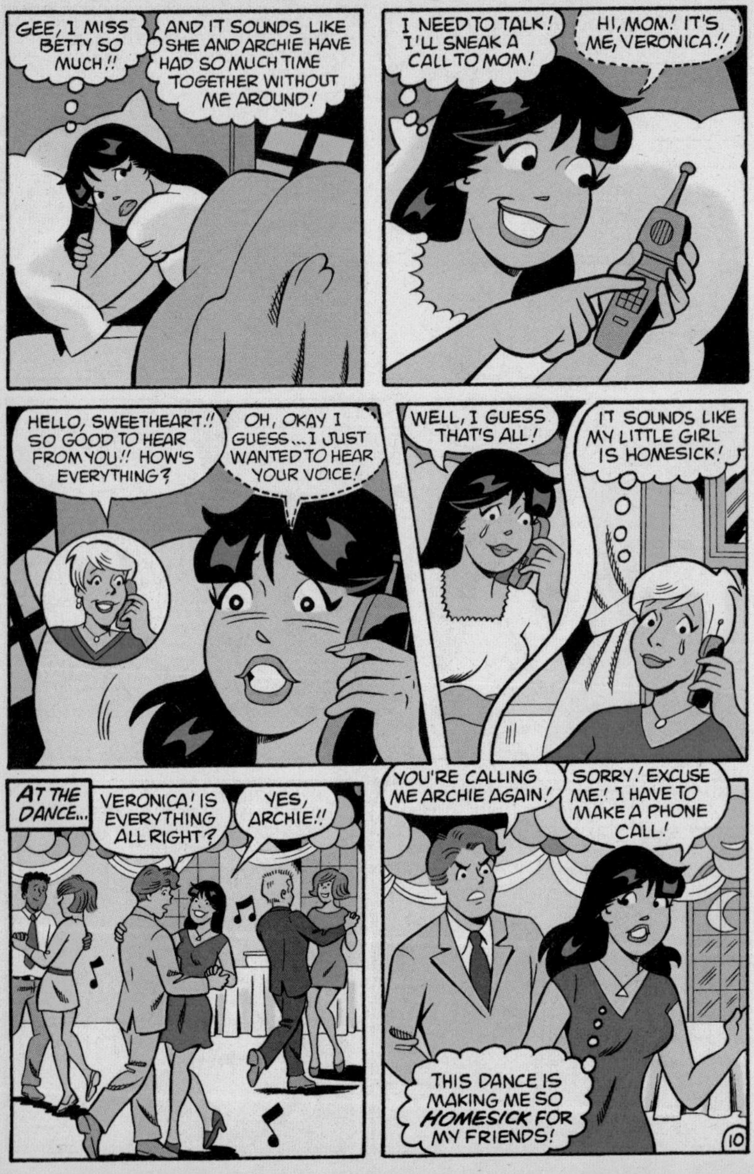

GEE, I MISS BETTY SO MUCH!!
AND IT SOUNDS LIKE SHE AND ARCHIE HAVE HAD SO MUCH TIME TOGETHER WITHOUT ME AROUND!
I NEED TO TALK! I'LL SNEAK A CALL TO MOM!
HI, MOM! IT'S ME, VERONICA!!
HELLO, SWEETHEART!! SO GOOD TO HEAR FROM YOU!! HOW'S EVERYTHING?
OH, OKAY I GUESS... I JUST WANTED TO HEAR YOUR VOICE!
WELL, I GUESS THAT'S ALL!
IT SOUNDS LIKE MY LITTLE GIRL IS HOMESICK!
AT THE DANCE...
VERONICA! IS EVERYTHING ALL RIGHT?
YES, ARCHIE!!
YOU'RE CALLING ME ARCHIE AGAIN!
SORRY! EXCUSE ME! I HAVE TO MAKE A PHONE CALL!
THIS DANCE IS MAKING ME SO HOMESICK FOR MY FRIENDS!
10

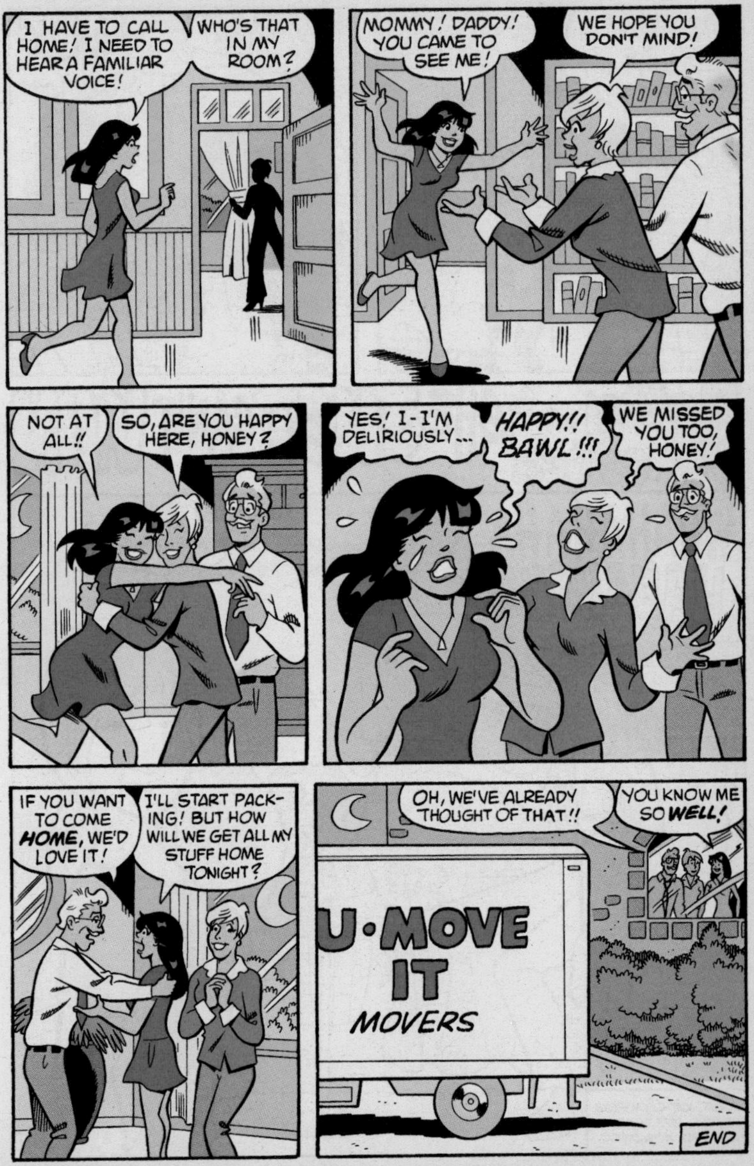

I HAVE TO CALL HOME! I NEED TO HEAR A FAMILIAR VOICE!
WHO'S THAT IN MY ROOM?
MOMMY! DADDY! YOU CAME TO SEE ME!
WE HOPE YOU DON'T MIND!
NOT AT ALL!!
SO, ARE YOU HAPPY HERE, HONEY?
YES! I-I'M DELIRIOUSLY...
HAPPY!! BAWL!!!
WE MISSED YOU TOO, HONEY!
IF YOU WANT TO COME HOME, WE'D LOVE IT!
I'LL START PACK-ING! BUT HOW WILL WE GET ALL MY STUFF HOME TONIGHT?
OH, WE'VE ALREADY THOUGHT OF THAT!!
YOU KNOW ME SO WELL!
U·MOVE IT MOVERS
END

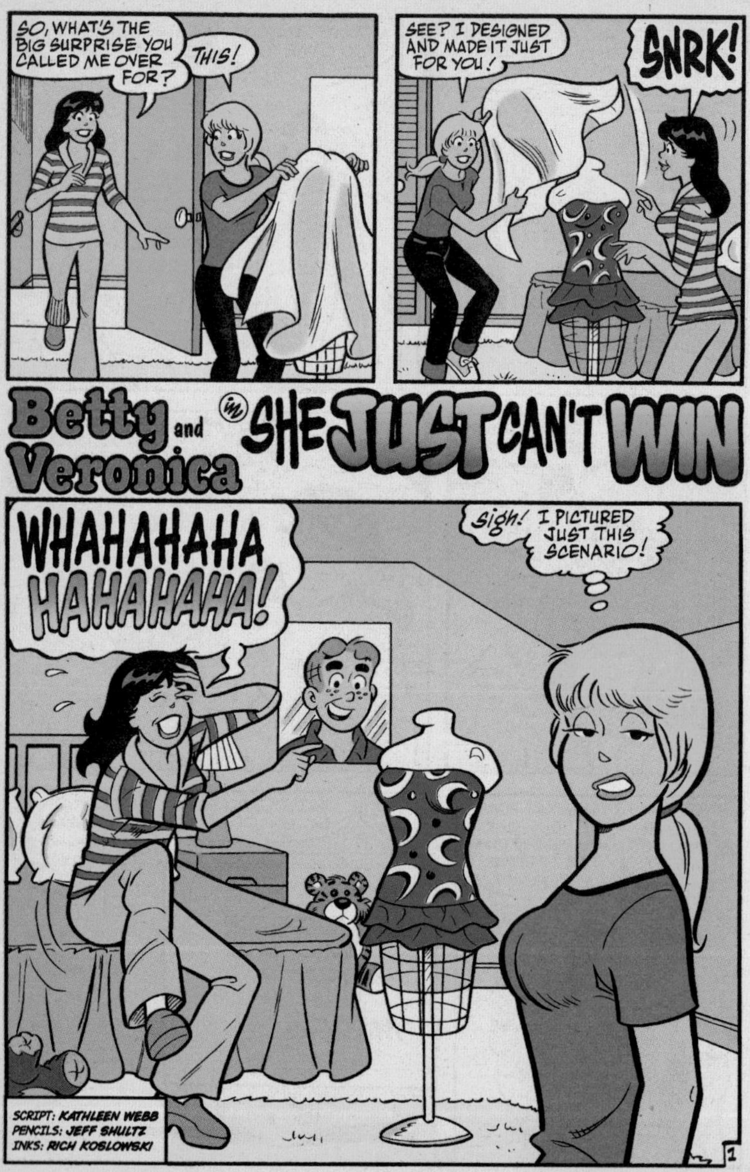

SO, WHAT'S THE BIG SURPRISE YOU CALLED ME OVER FOR?
THIS!
SEE? I DESIGNED AND MADE IT JUST FOR YOU!
SNRK!
Betty and Veronica in SHE JUST CAN'T WIN
WHAHAHAHA HAHAHAHA!
sigh! I PICTURED JUST THIS SCENARIO!
SCRIPT: KATHLEEN WEBB
PENCILS: JEFF SHULTZ
INKS: RICH KOSLOWSKI
1

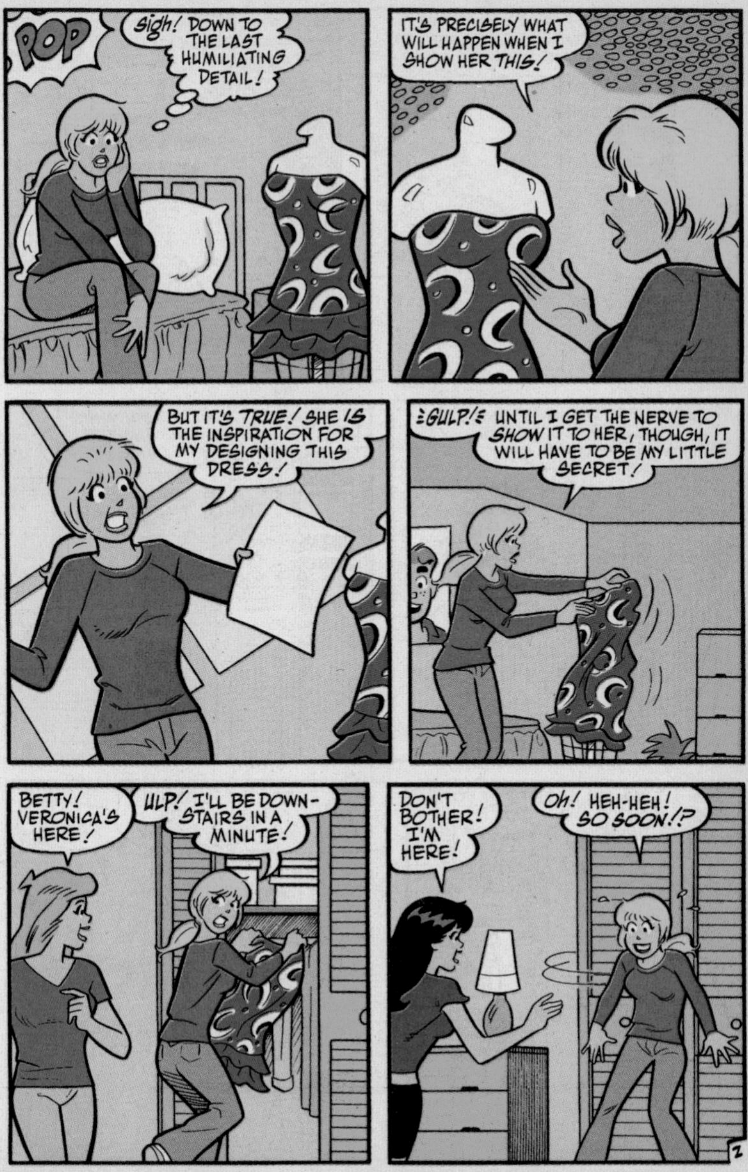
POP
Sigh! DOWN TO THE LAST HUMILIATING DETAIL!
IT'S PRECISELY WHAT WILL HAPPEN WHEN I SHOW HER THIS!
BUT IT'S TRUE! SHE IS THE INSPIRATION FOR MY DESIGNING THIS DRESS!
GULP! UNTIL I GET THE NERVE TO SHOW IT TO HER, THOUGH, IT WILL HAVE TO BE MY LITTLE SECRET!
BETTY! VERONICA'S HERE!
ULP! I'LL BE DOWN-STAIRS IN A MINUTE!
DON'T BOTHER! I'M HERE!
Oh! HEH-HEH! SO SOON!?

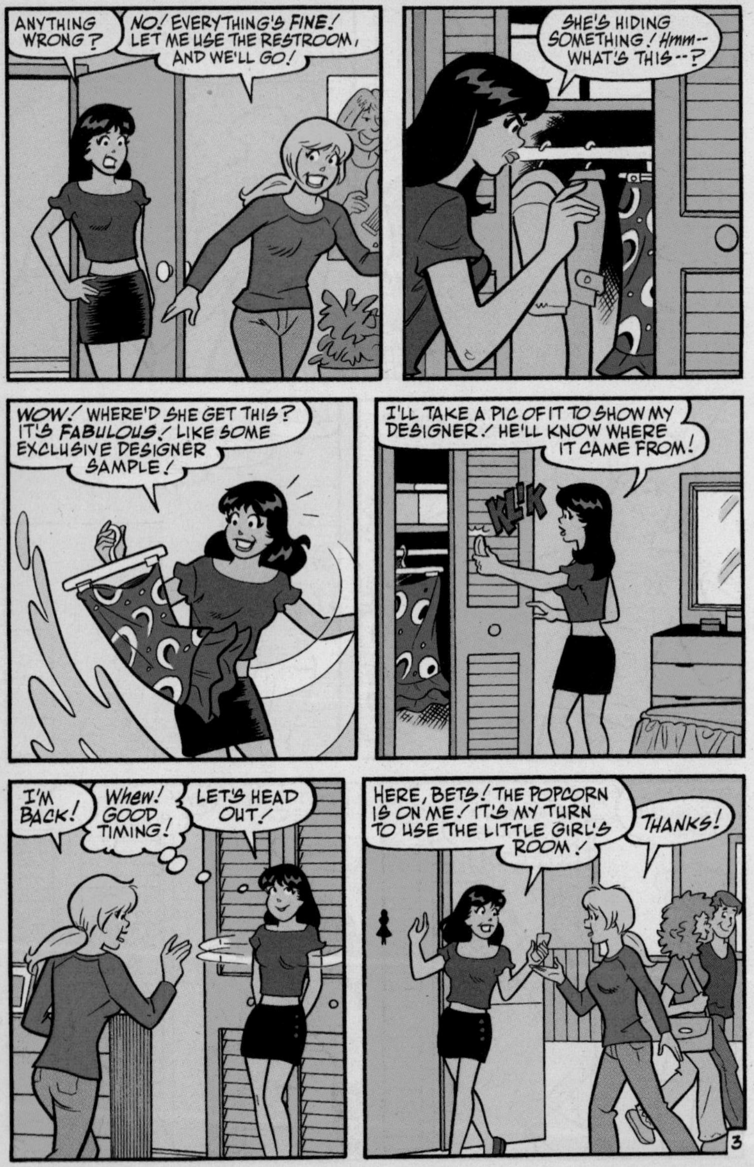
ANYTHING WRONG?
NO! EVERYTHING'S FINE! LET ME USE THE RESTROOM, AND WE'LL GO!
SHE'S HIDING SOMETHING! Hmm-- WHAT'S THIS--?
WOW! WHERE'D SHE GET THIS? IT'S FABULOUS! LIKE SOME EXCLUSIVE DESIGNER SAMPLE!
I'LL TAKE A PIC OF IT TO SHOW MY DESIGNER! HE'LL KNOW WHERE IT CAME FROM!
KLIK
I'M BACK!
Whew! GOOD TIMING!
LET'S HEAD OUT!
HERE, BETS! THE POPCORN IS ON ME! IT'S MY TURN TO USE THE LITTLE GIRL'S ROOM!
THANKS!

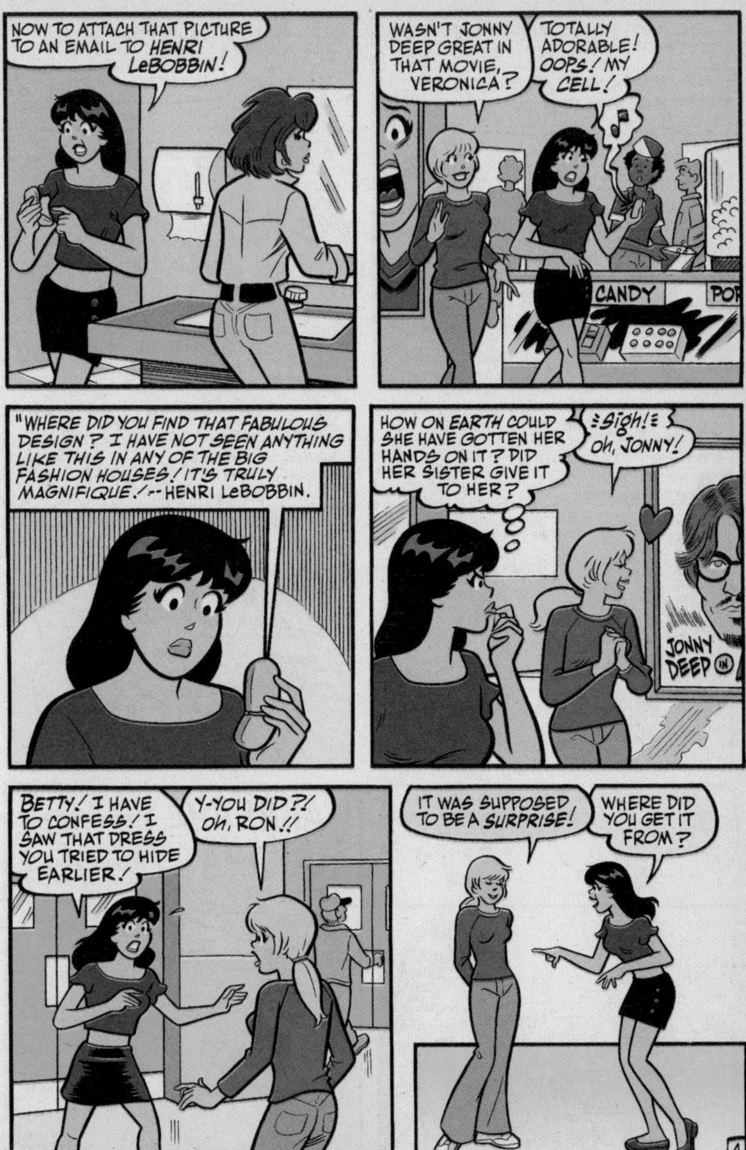
NOW TO ATTACH THAT PICTURE TO AN EMAIL TO HENRI LeBOBBIN!
WASN'T JONNY DEEP GREAT IN THAT MOVIE, VERONICA?
TOTALLY ADORABLE! OOPS! MY CELL!
CANDY
POP
"WHERE DID YOU FIND THAT FABULOUS DESIGN? I HAVE NOT SEEN ANYTHING LIKE THIS IN ANY OF THE BIG FASHION HOUSES! IT'S TRULY MAGNIFIQUE!" -- HENRI LeBOBBIN.
HOW ON EARTH COULD SHE HAVE GOTTEN HER HANDS ON IT? DID HER SISTER GIVE IT TO HER?
Sigh! oh, JONNY!
JONNY DEEP IN
BETTY! I HAVE TO CONFESS! I SAW THAT DRESS YOU TRIED TO HIDE EARLIER!
Y-YOU DID?! oh, RON!!
IT WAS SUPPOSED TO BE A SURPRISE!
WHERE DID YOU GET IT FROM?
4

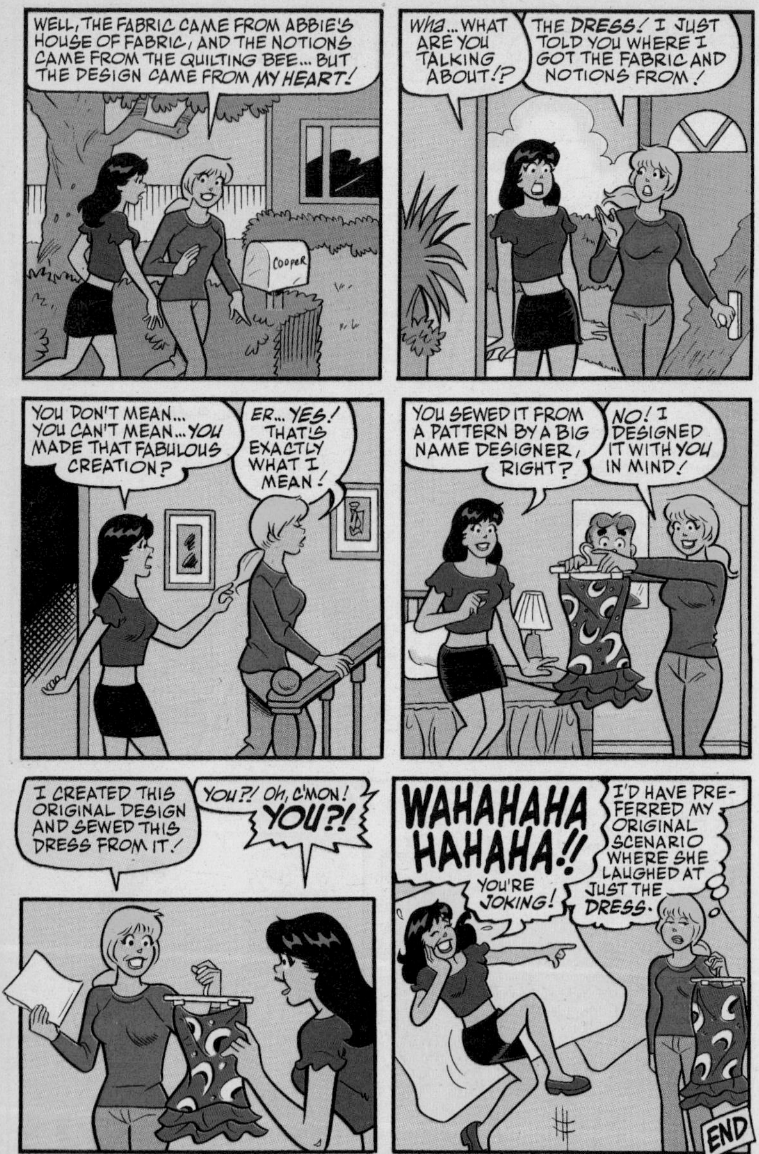

WELL, THE FABRIC CAME FROM ABBIE'S HOUSE OF FABRIC, AND THE NOTIONS CAME FROM THE QUILTING BEE... BUT THE DESIGN CAME FROM MY HEART!
COOPER
WHA... WHAT ARE YOU TALKING ABOUT!?
THE DRESS! I JUST TOLD YOU WHERE I GOT THE FABRIC AND NOTIONS FROM!
YOU DON'T MEAN... YOU CAN'T MEAN... YOU MADE THAT FABULOUS CREATION?
ER... YES! THAT'S EXACTLY WHAT I MEAN!
YOU SEWED IT FROM A PATTERN BY A BIG NAME DESIGNER, RIGHT?
NO! I DESIGNED IT WITH YOU IN MIND!
I CREATED THIS ORIGINAL DESIGN AND SEWED THIS DRESS FROM IT!
YOU?! OH, C'MON! YOU?!
WAHAHAHA HAHAHA!!
YOU'RE JOKING!
I'D HAVE PREFERRED MY ORIGINAL SCENARIO WHERE SHE LAUGHED AT JUST THE DRESS.
END

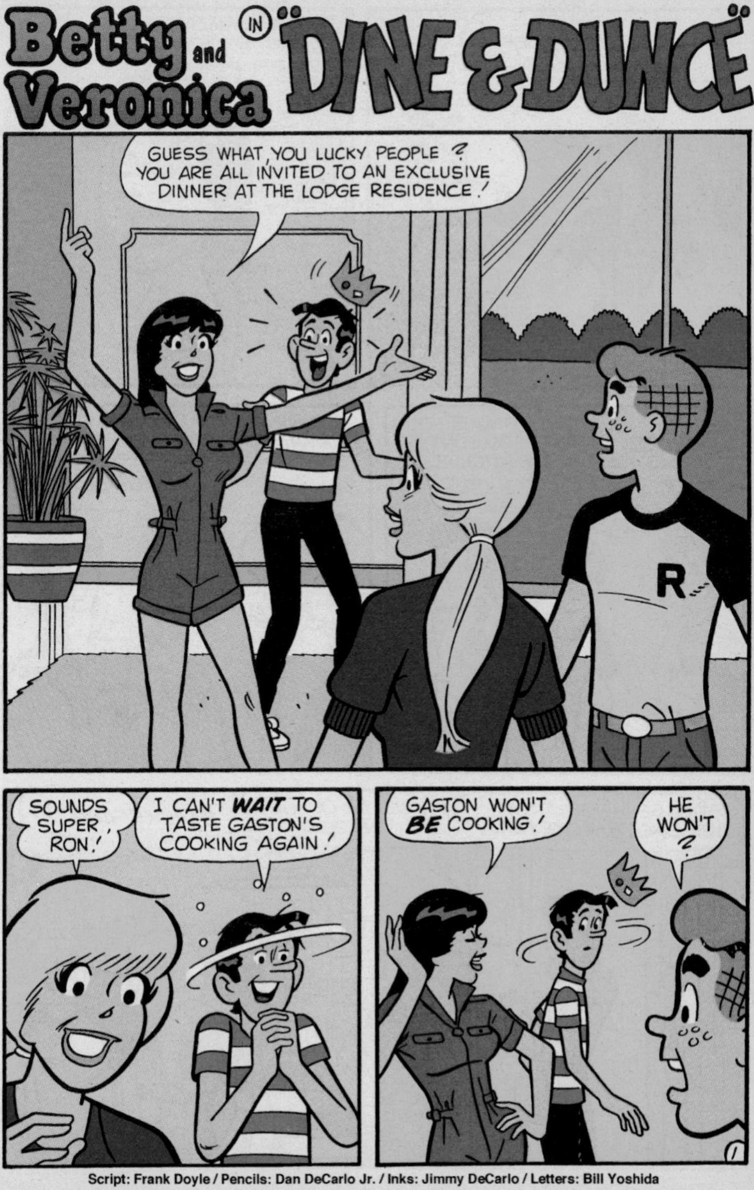
Betty and Veronica
IN "DINE & DUNCE"
GUESS WHAT, YOU LUCKY PEOPLE ? YOU ARE ALL INVITED TO AN EXCLUSIVE DINNER AT THE LODGE RESIDENCE !
R
SOUNDS SUPER, RON !
I CAN'T WAIT TO TASTE GASTON'S COOKING AGAIN !
GASTON WON'T BE COOKING !
HE WON'T ?
1

Script: Frank Doyle / Pencils: Dan DeCarlo Jr. / Inks: Jimmy DeCarlo / Letters: Bill Yoshida

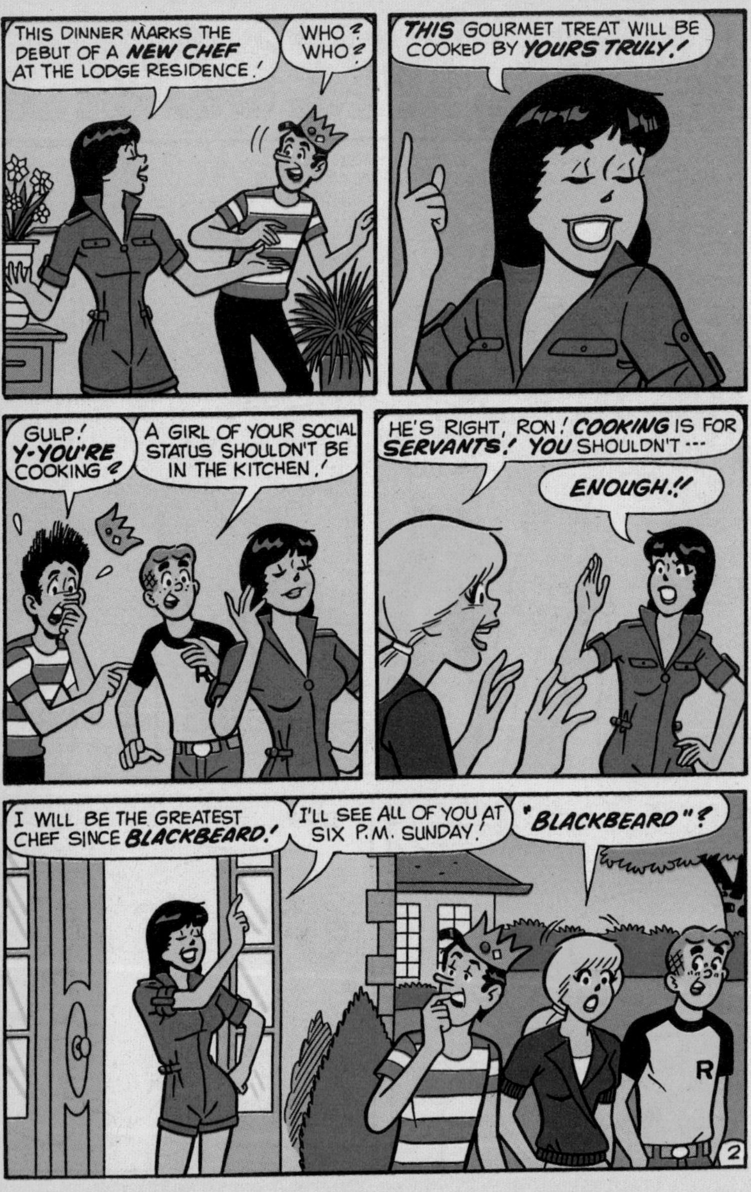

THIS DINNER MARKS THE DEBUT OF A **NEW CHEF** AT THE LODGE RESIDENCE!
WHO? WHO?
THIS GOURMET TREAT WILL BE COOKED BY **YOURS TRULY!**
GULP! **Y-YOU'RE** COOKING?
A GIRL OF YOUR SOCIAL STATUS SHOULDN'T BE IN THE KITCHEN!
HE'S RIGHT, RON! **COOKING** IS FOR **SERVANTS! YOU** SHOULDN'T ---
ENOUGH!!
I WILL BE THE GREATEST CHEF SINCE **BLACKBEARD!**
I'LL SEE ALL OF YOU AT SIX P.M. SUNDAY!
"BLACKBEARD"?
2

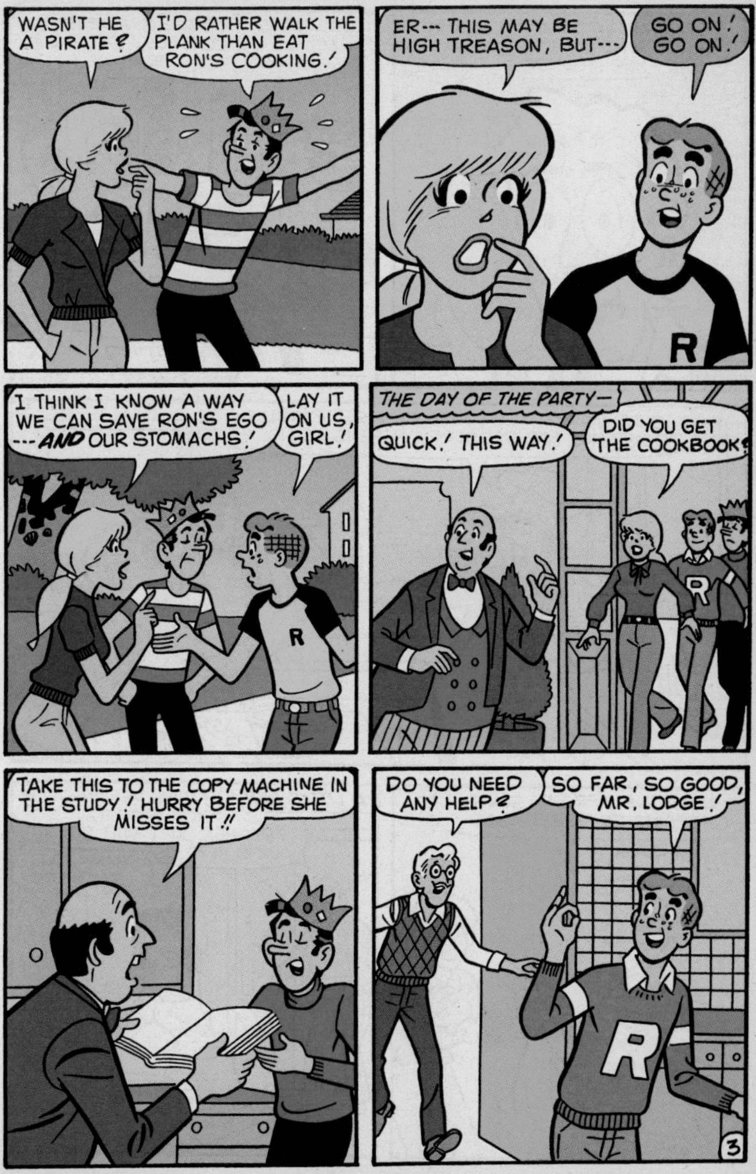
WASN'T HE A PIRATE?
I'D RATHER WALK THE PLANK THAN EAT RON'S COOKING!
ER--- THIS MAY BE HIGH TREASON, BUT---
GO ON! GO ON!
I THINK I KNOW A WAY WE CAN SAVE RON'S EGO ---AND OUR STOMACHS!
LAY IT ON US, GIRL!
THE DAY OF THE PARTY—
QUICK! THIS WAY!
DID YOU GET THE COOKBOOK?
TAKE THIS TO THE COPY MACHINE IN THE STUDY! HURRY BEFORE SHE MISSES IT!!
DO YOU NEED ANY HELP?
SO FAR, SO GOOD, MR. LODGE!
3

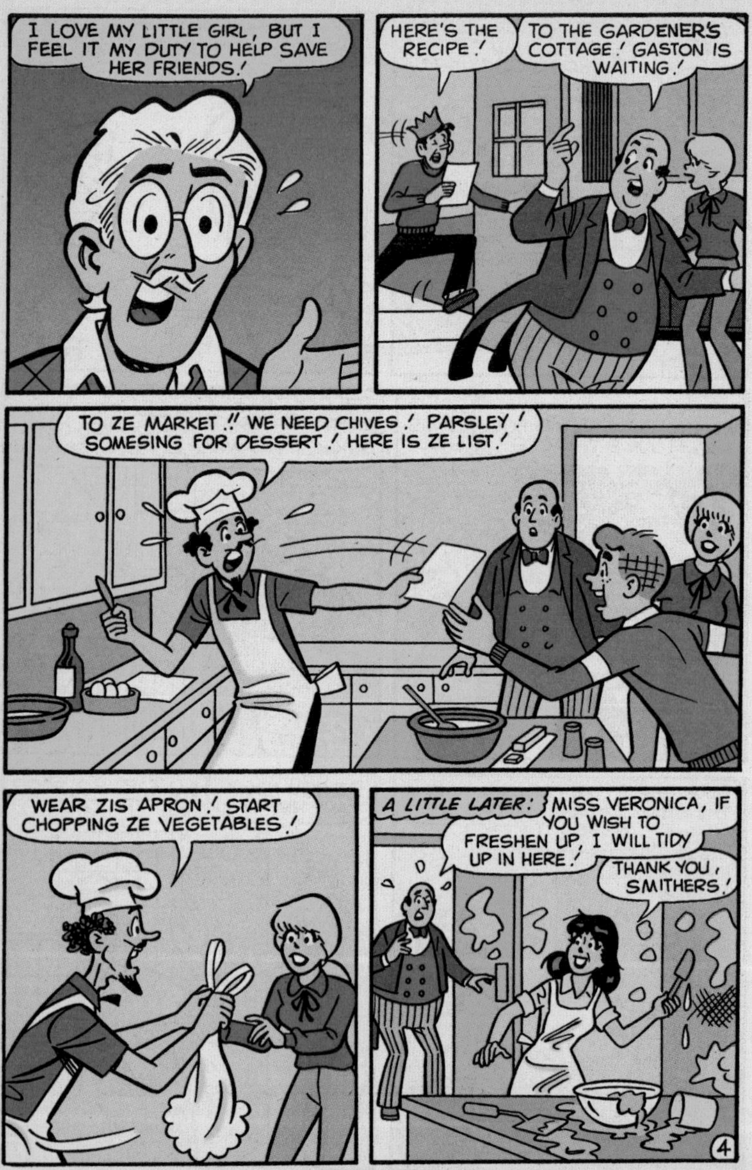
I LOVE MY LITTLE GIRL, BUT I FEEL IT MY DUTY TO HELP SAVE HER FRIENDS!
HERE'S THE RECIPE!
TO THE GARDENER'S COTTAGE! GASTON IS WAITING!
TO ZE MARKET!! WE NEED CHIVES! PARSLEY! SOMESING FOR DESSERT! HERE IS ZE LIST!
WEAR ZIS APRON! START CHOPPING ZE VEGETABLES!
A LITTLE LATER:
MISS VERONICA, IF YOU WISH TO FRESHEN UP, I WILL TIDY UP IN HERE!
THANK YOU, SMITHERS!
4

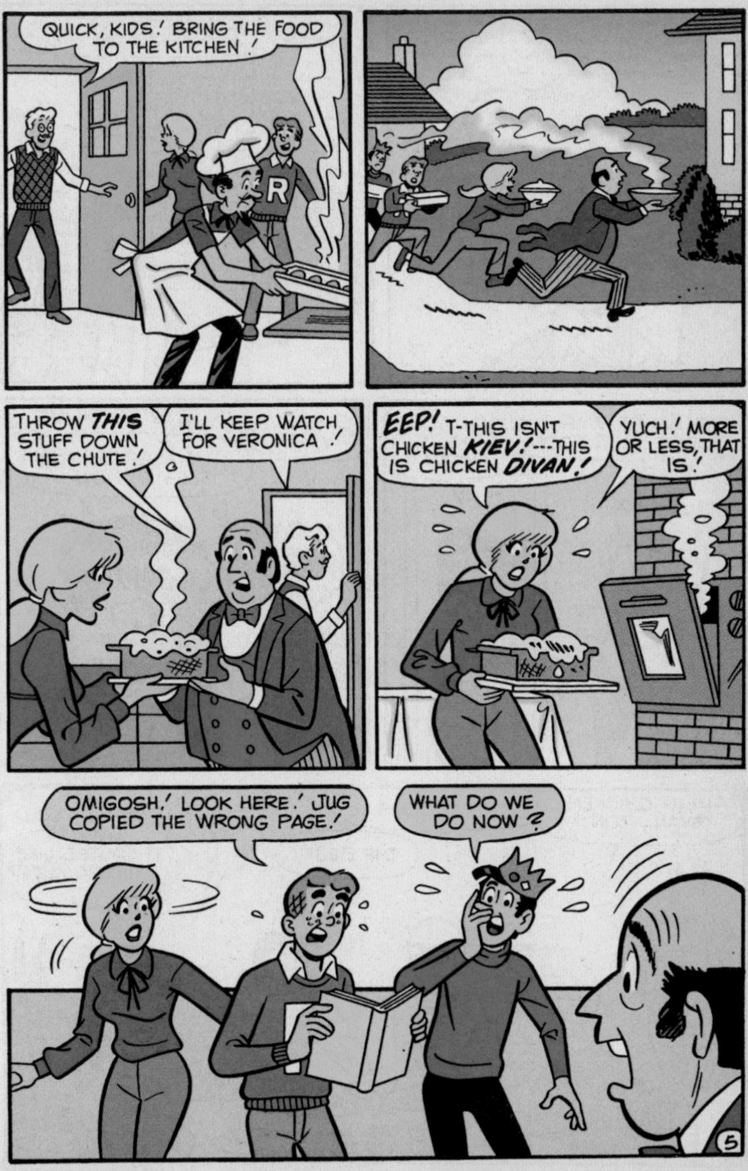
QUICK, KIDS! BRING THE FOOD TO THE KITCHEN!
THROW THIS STUFF DOWN THE CHUTE!
I'LL KEEP WATCH FOR VERONICA!
EEP! T-THIS ISN'T CHICKEN KIEV!---THIS IS CHICKEN DIVAN!
YUCH! MORE OR LESS, THAT IS!
OMIGOSH! LOOK HERE! JUG COPIED THE WRONG PAGE!
WHAT DO WE DO NOW?
5

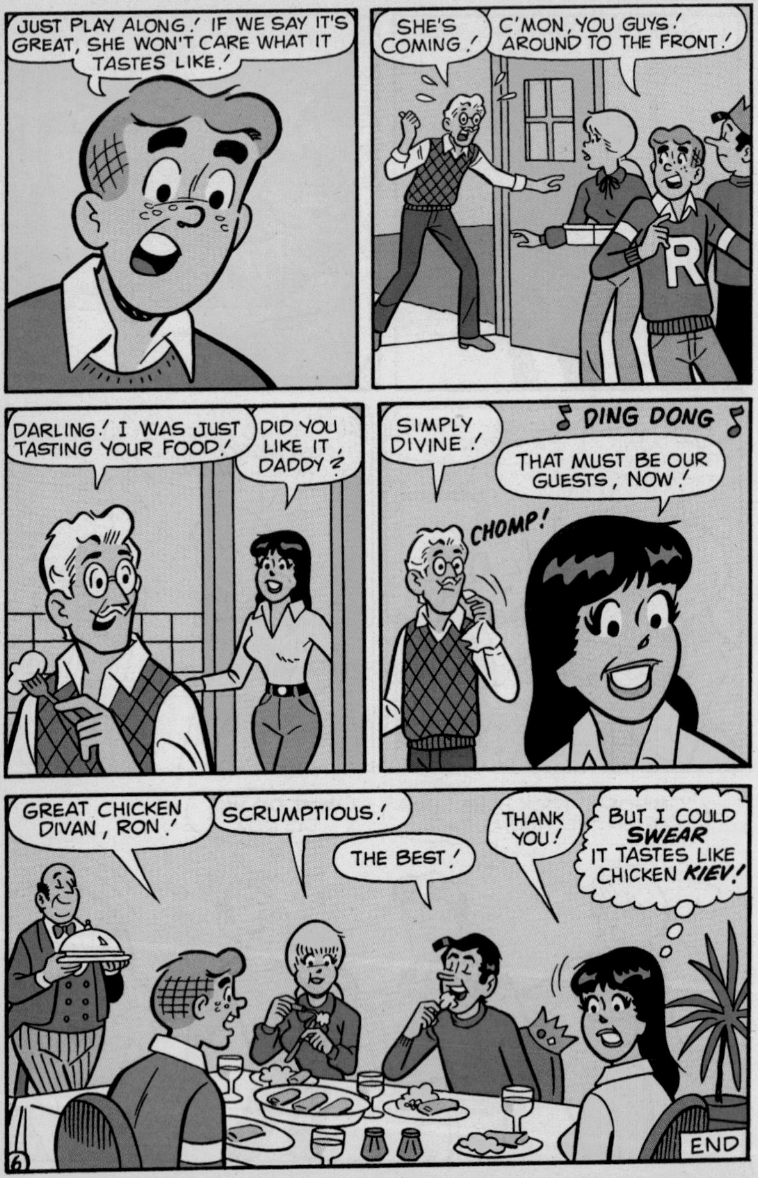
JUST PLAY ALONG! IF WE SAY IT'S GREAT, SHE WON'T CARE WHAT IT TASTES LIKE!
SHE'S COMING!
C'MON, YOU GUYS! AROUND TO THE FRONT!
DARLING! I WAS JUST TASTING YOUR FOOD!
DID YOU LIKE IT, DADDY?
SIMPLY DIVINE!
DING DONG
THAT MUST BE OUR GUESTS, NOW!
CHOMP!
GREAT CHICKEN DIVAN, RON!
SCRUMPTIOUS!
THE BEST!
THANK YOU!
BUT I COULD SWEAR IT TASTES LIKE CHICKEN KIEV!
END
6

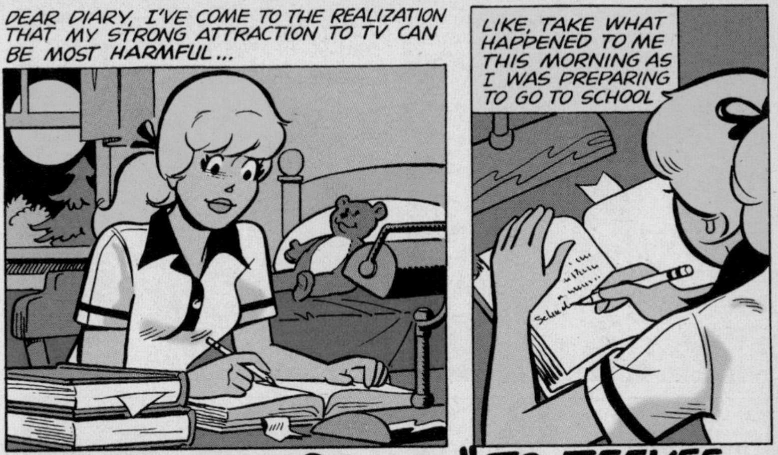
DEAR DIARY, I'VE COME TO THE REALIZATION THAT MY STRONG ATTRACTION TO TV CAN BE MOST HARMFUL...
LIKE, TAKE WHAT HAPPENED TO ME THIS MORNING AS I WAS PREPARING TO GO TO SCHOOL

Betty's Diary

"TO TEEVEE OR NOT TO TEEVEE"

Script: George Gladir / Pencils: Bob Bolling / Inks: Hy Eisman / Letters: Bill Yoshida

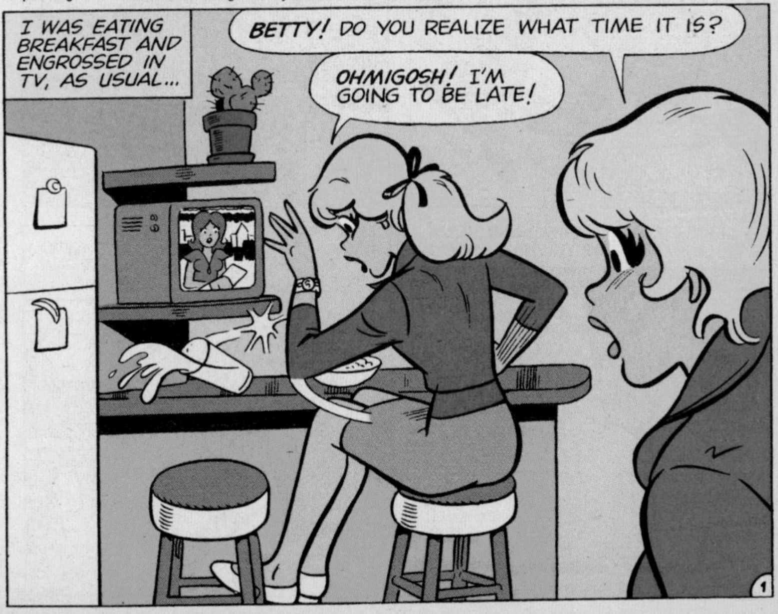
I WAS EATING BREAKFAST AND ENGROSSED IN TV, AS USUAL...
BETTY! DO YOU REALIZE WHAT TIME IT IS?
OHMIGOSH! I'M GOING TO BE LATE!

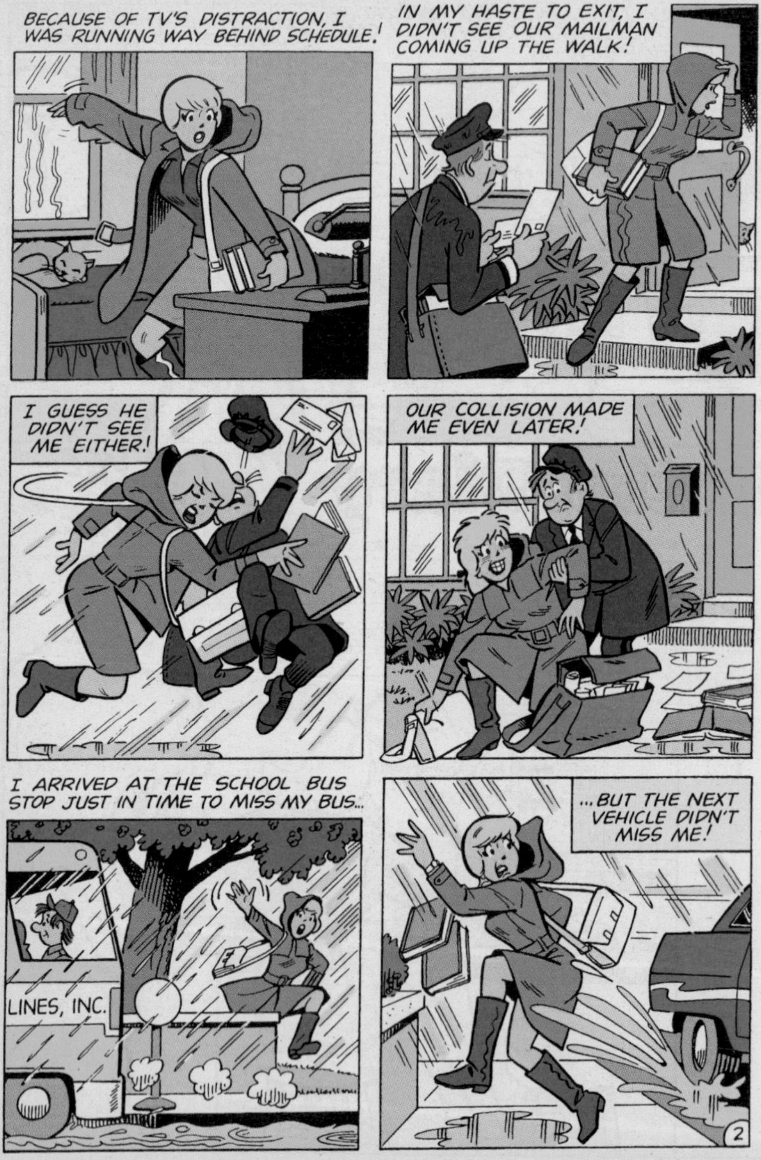
BECAUSE OF TV'S DISTRACTION, I WAS RUNNING WAY BEHIND SCHEDULE!
IN MY HASTE TO EXIT, I DIDN'T SEE OUR MAILMAN COMING UP THE WALK!
I GUESS HE DIDN'T SEE ME EITHER!
OUR COLLISION MADE ME EVEN LATER!
I ARRIVED AT THE SCHOOL BUS STOP JUST IN TIME TO MISS MY BUS...
LINES, INC.
...BUT THE NEXT VEHICLE DIDN'T MISS ME!
2

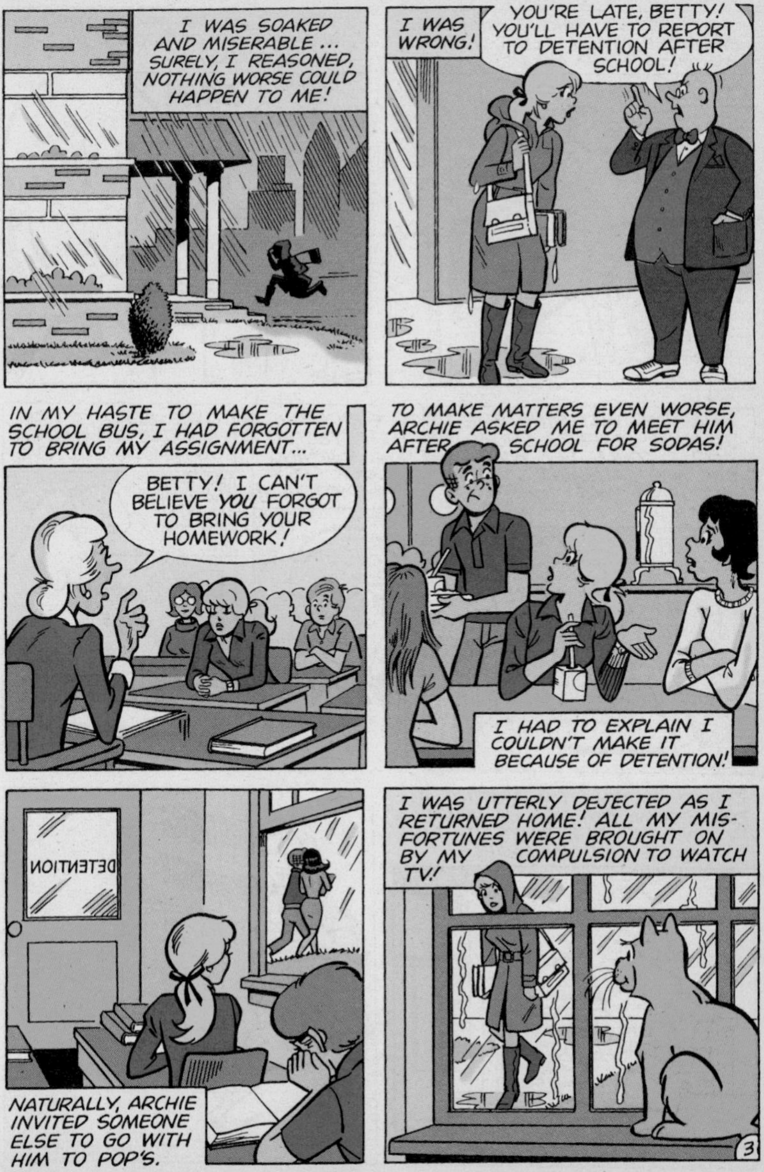

I WAS SOAKED AND MISERABLE ... SURELY, I REASONED, NOTHING WORSE COULD HAPPEN TO ME!
I WAS WRONG!
YOU'RE LATE, BETTY! YOU'LL HAVE TO REPORT TO DETENTION AFTER SCHOOL!
IN MY HASTE TO MAKE THE SCHOOL BUS, I HAD FORGOTTEN TO BRING MY ASSIGNMENT...
BETTY! I CAN'T BELIEVE YOU FORGOT TO BRING YOUR HOMEWORK!
TO MAKE MATTERS EVEN WORSE, ARCHIE ASKED ME TO MEET HIM AFTER SCHOOL FOR SODAS!
I HAD TO EXPLAIN I COULDN'T MAKE IT BECAUSE OF DETENTION!
DETENTION
NATURALLY, ARCHIE INVITED SOMEONE ELSE TO GO WITH HIM TO POP'S.
I WAS UTTERLY DEJECTED AS I RETURNED HOME! ALL MY MISFORTUNES WERE BROUGHT ON BY MY COMPULSION TO WATCH TV!

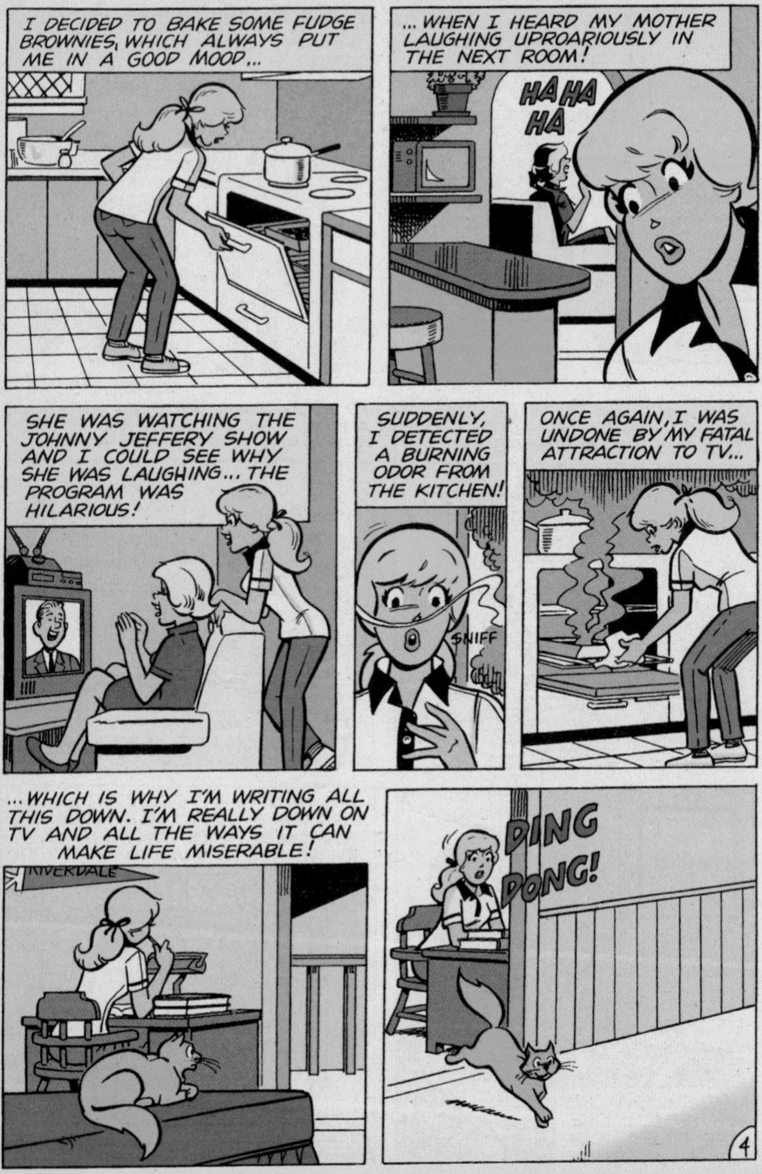

I DECIDED TO BAKE SOME FUDGE BROWNIES, WHICH ALWAYS PUT ME IN A GOOD MOOD...
...WHEN I HEARD MY MOTHER LAUGHING UPROARIOUSLY IN THE NEXT ROOM!
HA HA HA
SHE WAS WATCHING THE JOHNNY JEFFERY SHOW AND I COULD SEE WHY SHE WAS LAUGHING... THE PROGRAM WAS HILARIOUS!
SUDDENLY, I DETECTED A BURNING ODOR FROM THE KITCHEN!
SNIFF
ONCE AGAIN, I WAS UNDONE BY MY FATAL ATTRACTION TO TV...
...WHICH IS WHY I'M WRITING ALL THIS DOWN. I'M REALLY DOWN ON TV AND ALL THE WAYS IT CAN MAKE LIFE MISERABLE!
RIVERDALE
DING DONG!

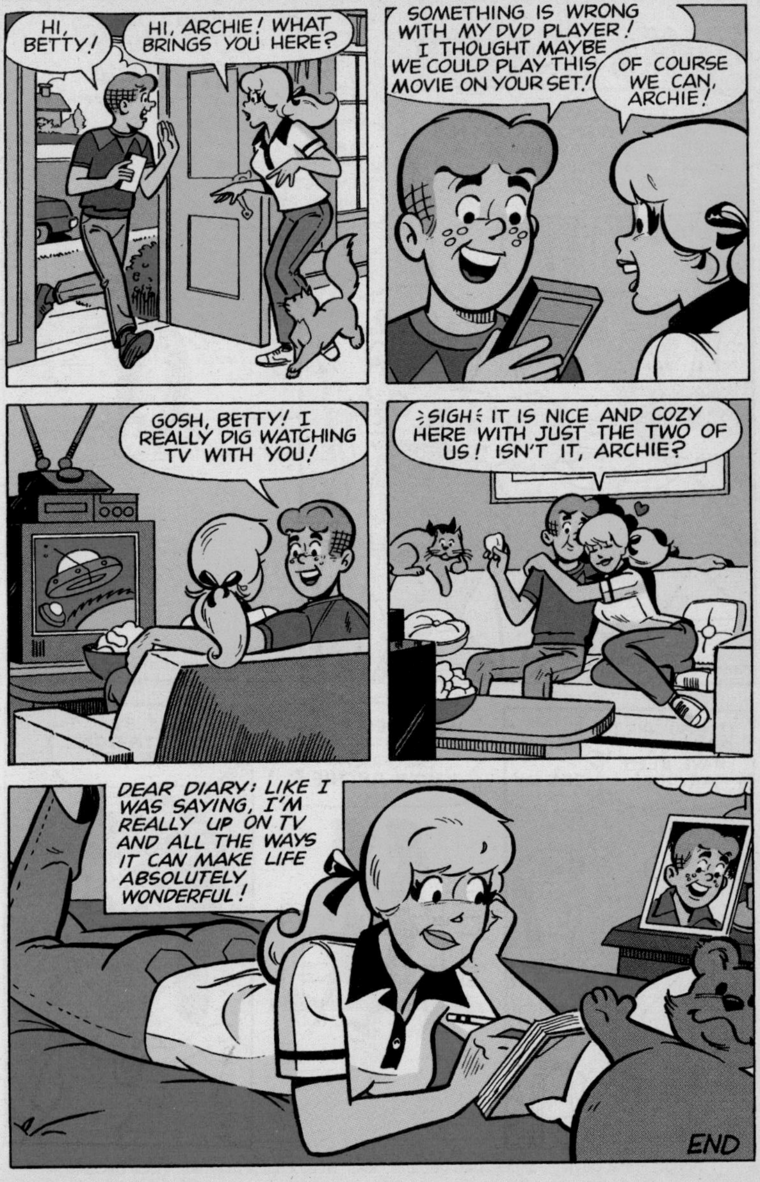
HI, BETTY!
HI, ARCHIE! WHAT BRINGS YOU HERE?
SOMETHING IS WRONG WITH MY DVD PLAYER! I THOUGHT MAYBE WE COULD PLAY THIS MOVIE ON YOUR SET!
OF COURSE WE CAN, ARCHIE!
GOSH, BETTY! I REALLY DIG WATCHING TV WITH YOU!
SIGH IT IS NICE AND COZY HERE WITH JUST THE TWO OF US! ISN'T IT, ARCHIE?
DEAR DIARY: LIKE I WAS SAYING, I'M REALLY UP ON TV AND ALL THE WAYS IT CAN MAKE LIFE ABSOLUTELY WONDERFUL!
END

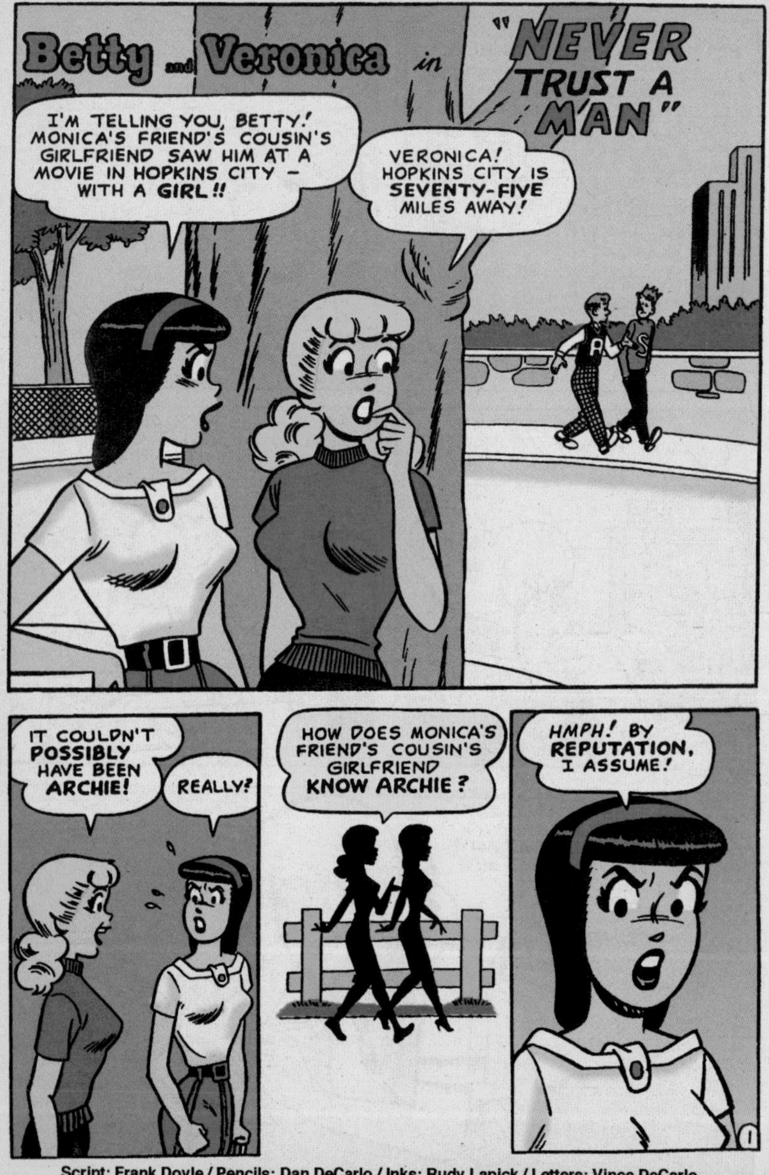
Betty and Veronica in
"NEVER TRUST A MAN"
I'M TELLING YOU, BETTY! MONICA'S FRIEND'S COUSIN'S GIRLFRIEND SAW HIM AT A MOVIE IN HOPKINS CITY – WITH A GIRL!!
VERONICA! HOPKINS CITY IS SEVENTY-FIVE MILES AWAY!
IT COULDN'T POSSIBLY HAVE BEEN ARCHIE!
REALLY?
HOW DOES MONICA'S FRIEND'S COUSIN'S GIRLFRIEND KNOW ARCHIE?
HMPH! BY REPUTATION, I ASSUME!
1

Script: Frank Doyle / Pencils: Dan DeCarlo / Inks: Rudy Lapick / Letters: Vince DeCarlo

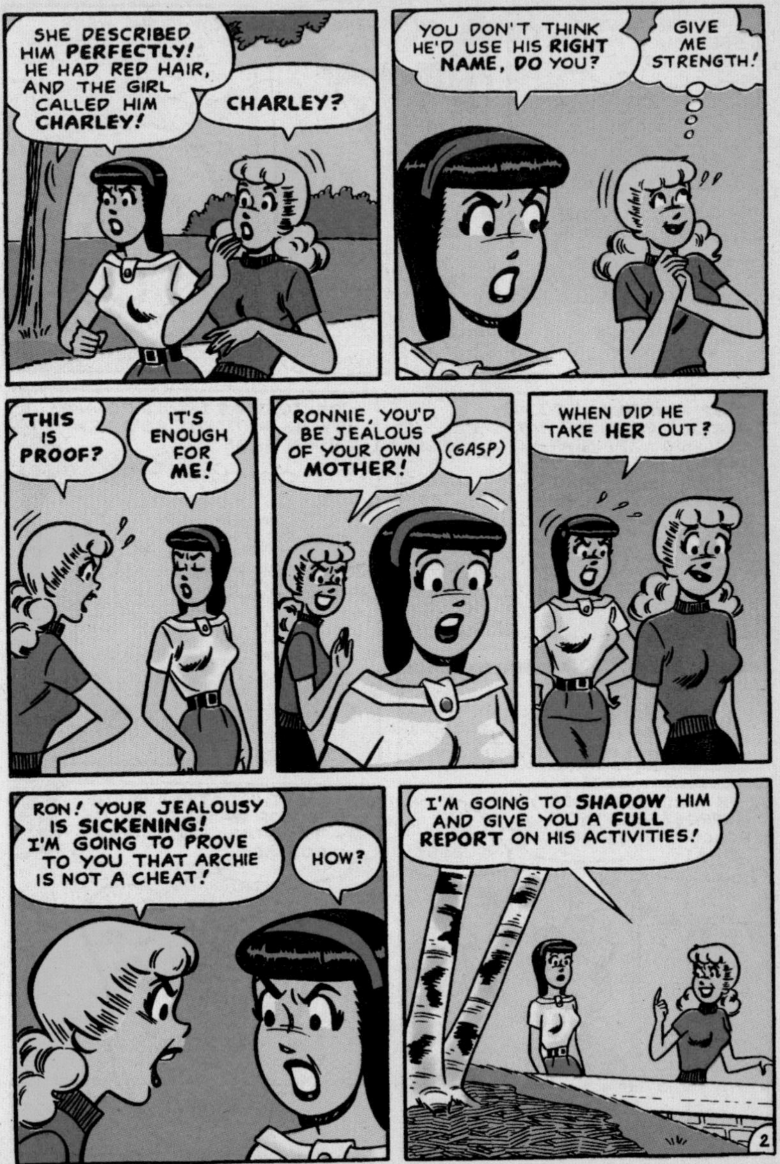
SHE DESCRIBED HIM PERFECTLY! HE HAD RED HAIR, AND THE GIRL CALLED HIM CHARLEY!
CHARLEY?
YOU DON'T THINK HE'D USE HIS RIGHT NAME, DO YOU?
GIVE ME STRENGTH!
THIS IS PROOF?
IT'S ENOUGH FOR ME!
RONNIE, YOU'D BE JEALOUS OF YOUR OWN MOTHER!
(GASP)
WHEN DID HE TAKE HER OUT?
RON! YOUR JEALOUSY IS SICKENING! I'M GOING TO PROVE TO YOU THAT ARCHIE IS NOT A CHEAT!
HOW?
I'M GOING TO SHADOW HIM AND GIVE YOU A FULL REPORT ON HIS ACTIVITIES!
2

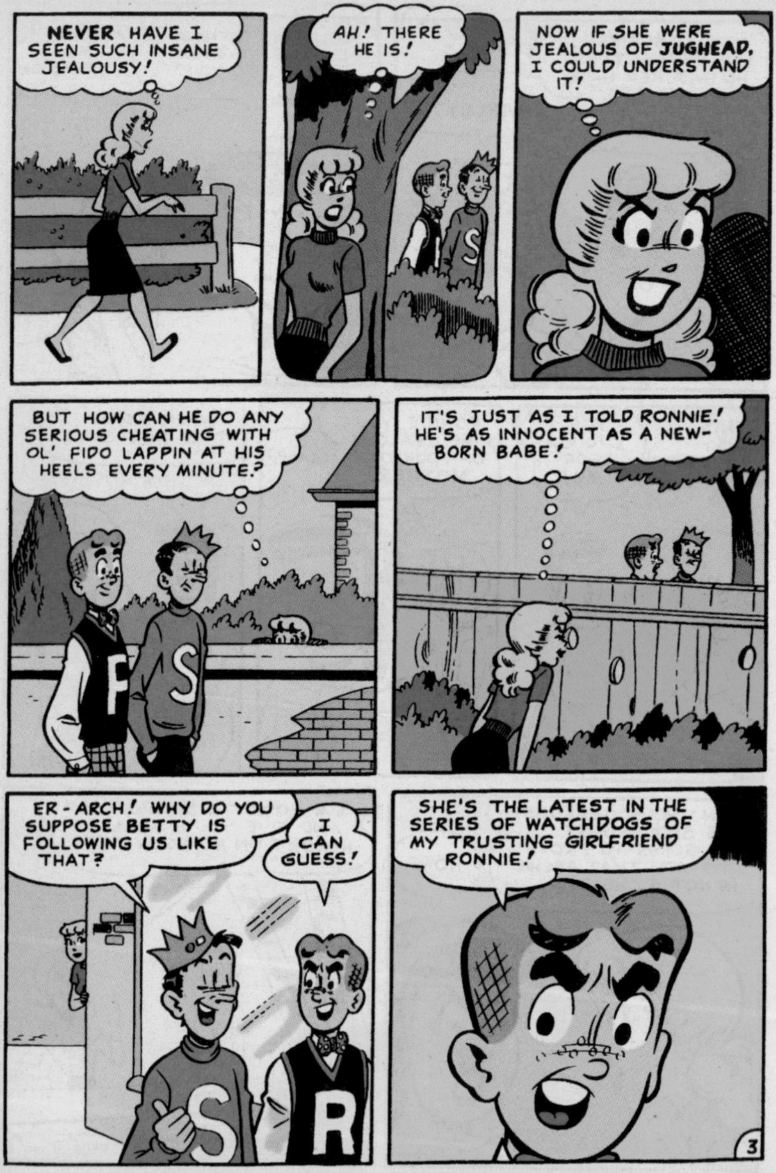

NEVER HAVE I SEEN SUCH INSANE JEALOUSY!
AH! THERE HE IS!
NOW IF SHE WERE JEALOUS OF JUGHEAD, I COULD UNDERSTAND IT!
BUT HOW CAN HE DO ANY SERIOUS CHEATING WITH OL' FIDO LAPPIN AT HIS HEELS EVERY MINUTE?
IT'S JUST AS I TOLD RONNIE! HE'S AS INNOCENT AS A NEW-BORN BABE!
ER-ARCH! WHY DO YOU SUPPOSE BETTY IS FOLLOWING US LIKE THAT?
I CAN GUESS!
SHE'S THE LATEST IN THE SERIES OF WATCHDOGS OF MY TRUSTING GIRLFRIEND RONNIE!
3

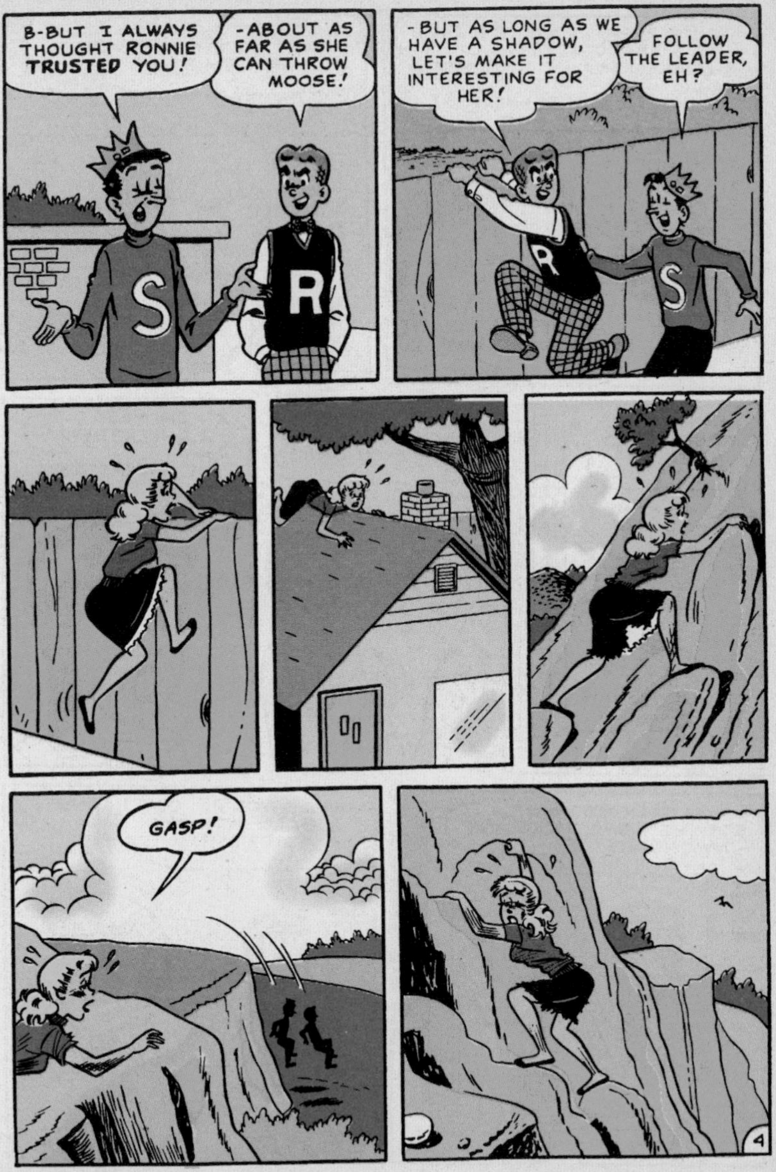
B-BUT I ALWAYS THOUGHT RONNIE TRUSTED YOU!
-ABOUT AS FAR AS SHE CAN THROW MOOSE!
-BUT AS LONG AS WE HAVE A SHADOW, LET'S MAKE IT INTERESTING FOR HER!
FOLLOW THE LEADER, EH?
GASP!
4

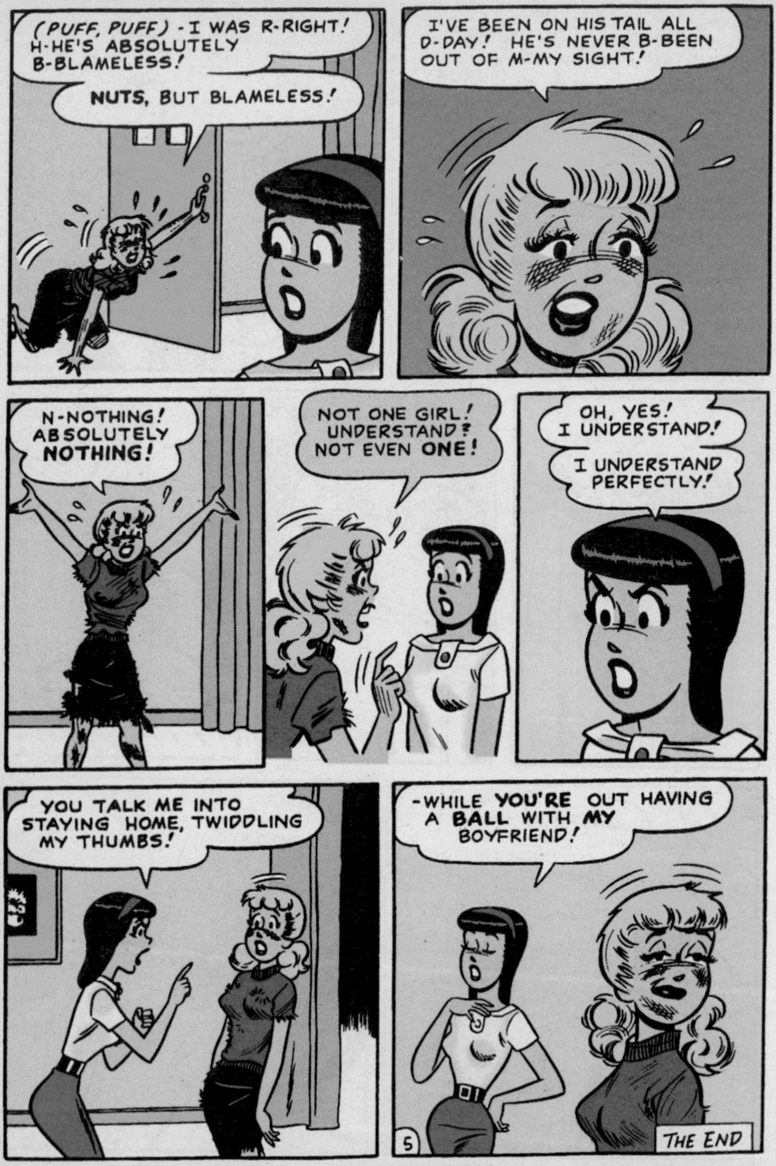
(PUFF, PUFF) - I WAS R-RIGHT! H-HE'S ABSOLUTELY B-BLAMELESS!
NUTS, BUT BLAMELESS!
I'VE BEEN ON HIS TAIL ALL D-DAY! HE'S NEVER B-BEEN OUT OF M-MY SIGHT!
N-NOTHING! ABSOLUTELY NOTHING!
NOT ONE GIRL! UNDERSTAND? NOT EVEN ONE!
OH, YES! I UNDERSTAND!
I UNDERSTAND PERFECTLY!
YOU TALK ME INTO STAYING HOME, TWIDDLING MY THUMBS!
-WHILE YOU'RE OUT HAVING A BALL WITH MY BOYFRIEND!
5
THE END

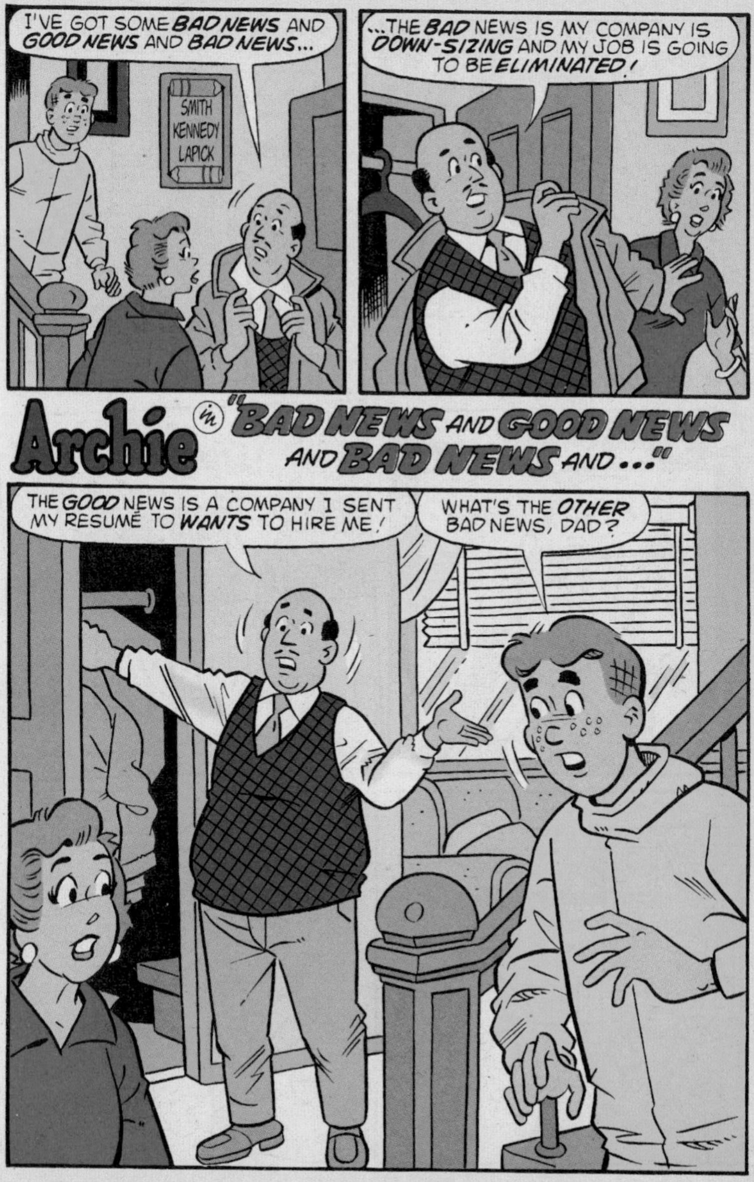
I'VE GOT SOME BAD NEWS AND GOOD NEWS AND BAD NEWS...
SMITH KENNEDY LAPICK
...THE BAD NEWS IS MY COMPANY IS DOWN-SIZING AND MY JOB IS GOING TO BE ELIMINATED!
Archie in "BAD NEWS AND GOOD NEWS AND BAD NEWS AND..."
THE GOOD NEWS IS A COMPANY I SENT MY RESUMÉ TO WANTS TO HIRE ME!
WHAT'S THE OTHER BAD NEWS, DAD?

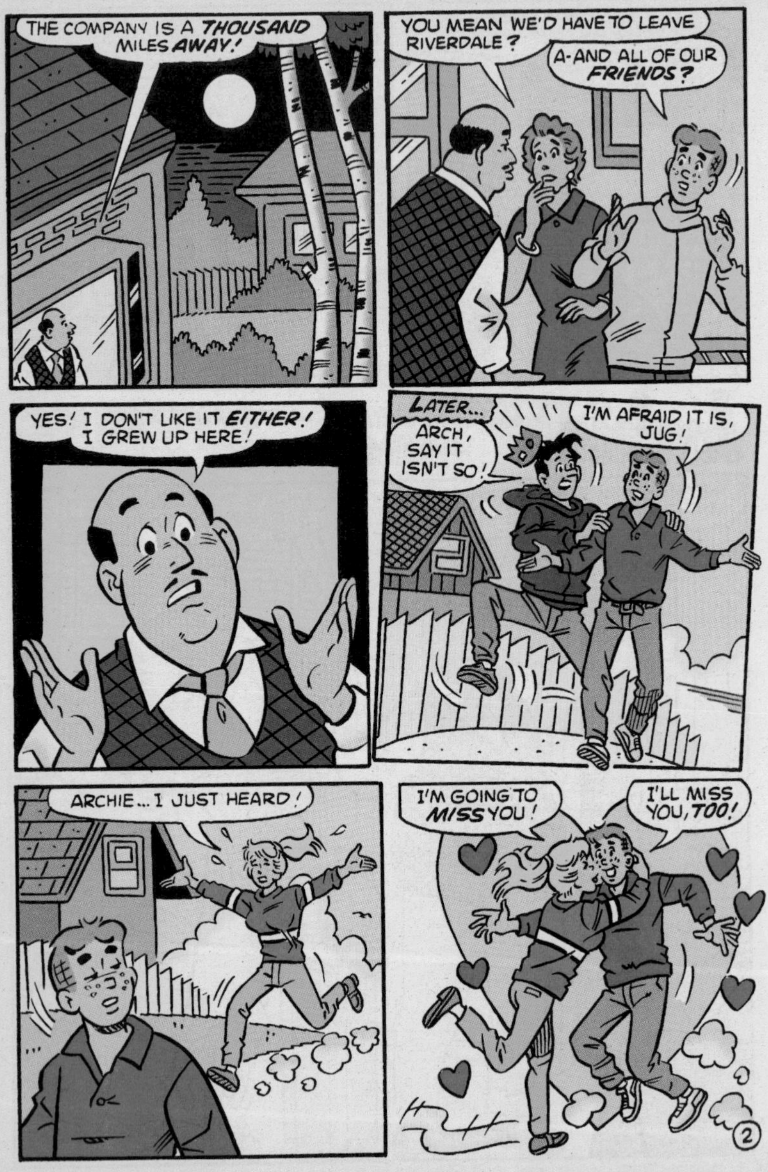
THE COMPANY IS A THOUSAND MILES AWAY!
YOU MEAN WE'D HAVE TO LEAVE RIVERDALE?
A-AND ALL OF OUR FRIENDS?
YES! I DON'T LIKE IT EITHER! I GREW UP HERE!
LATER...
ARCH, SAY IT ISN'T SO!
I'M AFRAID IT IS, JUG!
ARCHIE... I JUST HEARD!
I'M GOING TO MISS YOU!
I'LL MISS YOU, TOO!
2

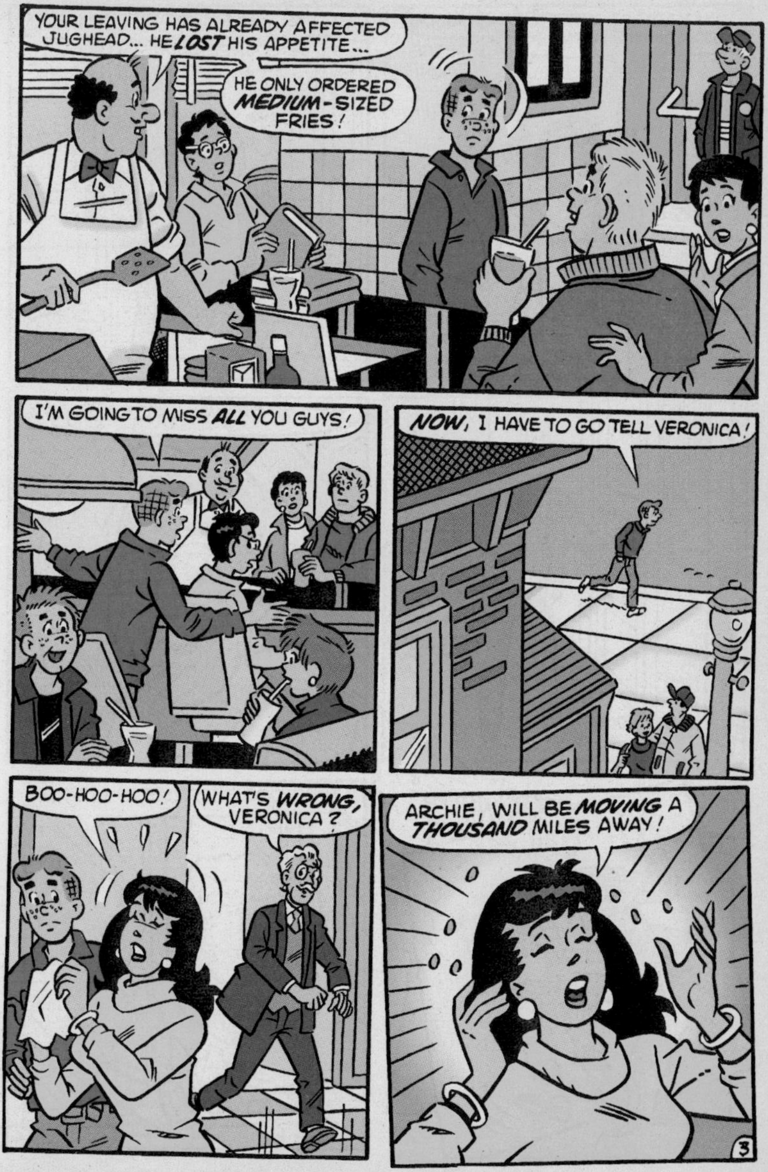
YOUR LEAVING HAS ALREADY AFFECTED JUGHEAD... HE LOST HIS APPETITE...
HE ONLY ORDERED MEDIUM-SIZED FRIES!
I'M GOING TO MISS ALL YOU GUYS!
NOW, I HAVE TO GO TELL VERONICA!
BOO-HOO-HOO!
WHAT'S WRONG, VERONICA?
ARCHIE, WILL BE MOVING A THOUSAND MILES AWAY!

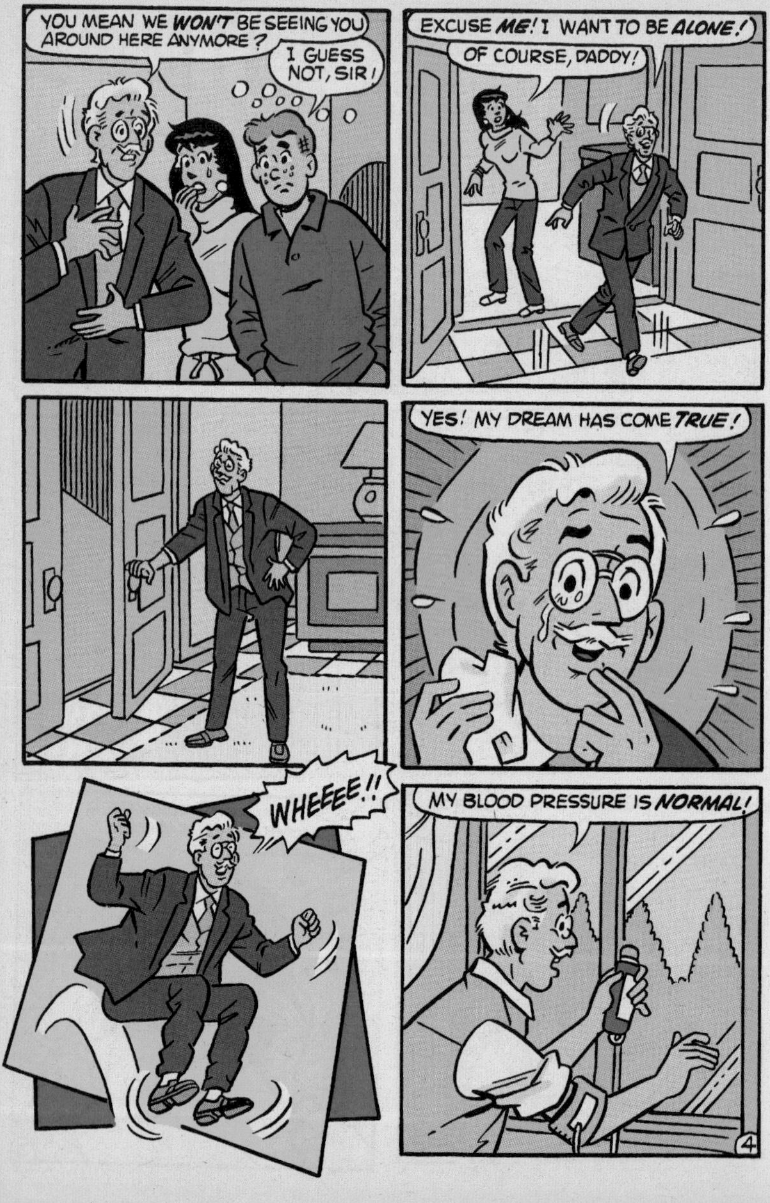
YOU MEAN WE WON'T BE SEEING YOU AROUND HERE ANYMORE?
I GUESS NOT, SIR!
EXCUSE ME! I WANT TO BE ALONE!
OF COURSE, DADDY!
YES! MY DREAM HAS COME TRUE!
WHEEEE!!
MY BLOOD PRESSURE IS NORMAL!
4

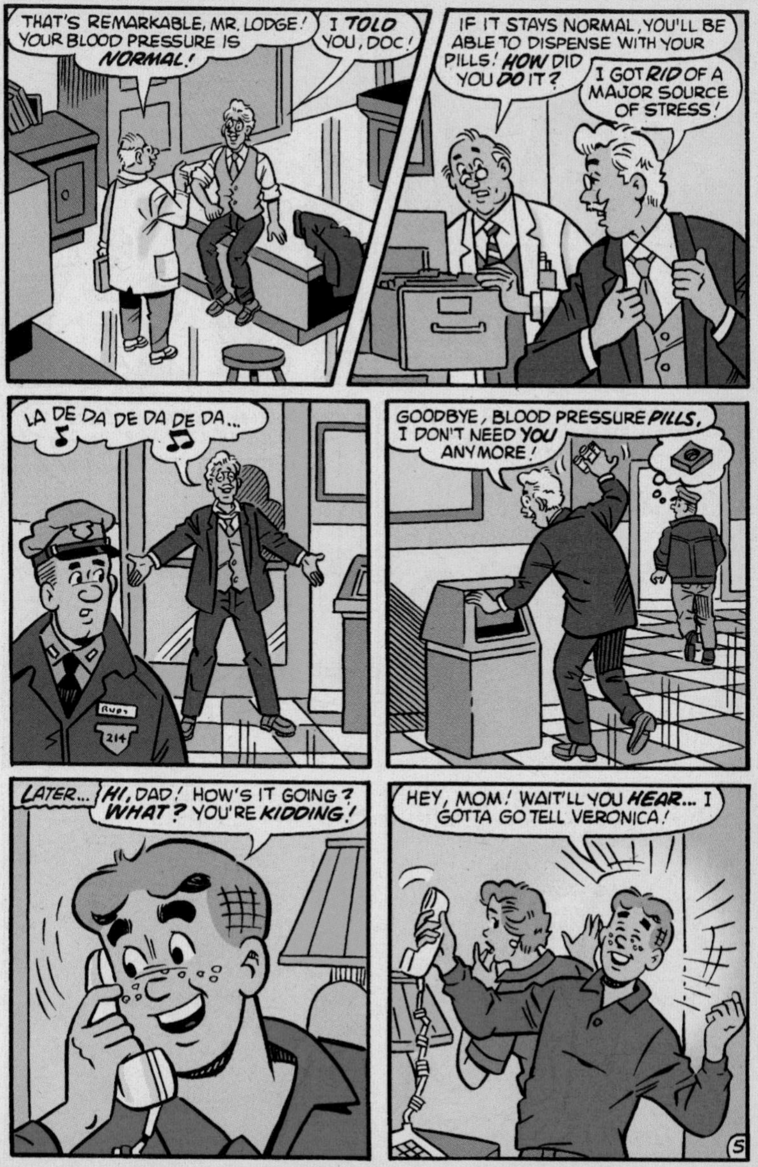
THAT'S REMARKABLE, MR. LODGE! YOUR BLOOD PRESSURE IS NORMAL!
I TOLD YOU, DOC!
IF IT STAYS NORMAL, YOU'LL BE ABLE TO DISPENSE WITH YOUR PILLS! HOW DID YOU DO IT?
I GOT RID OF A MAJOR SOURCE OF STRESS!
LA DE DA DE DA DE DA...
RUPY
214
GOODBYE, BLOOD PRESSURE PILLS, I DON'T NEED YOU ANYMORE!
LATER...
HI, DAD! HOW'S IT GOING? WHAT? YOU'RE KIDDING!
HEY, MOM! WAIT'LL YOU HEAR... I GOTTA GO TELL VERONICA!
5

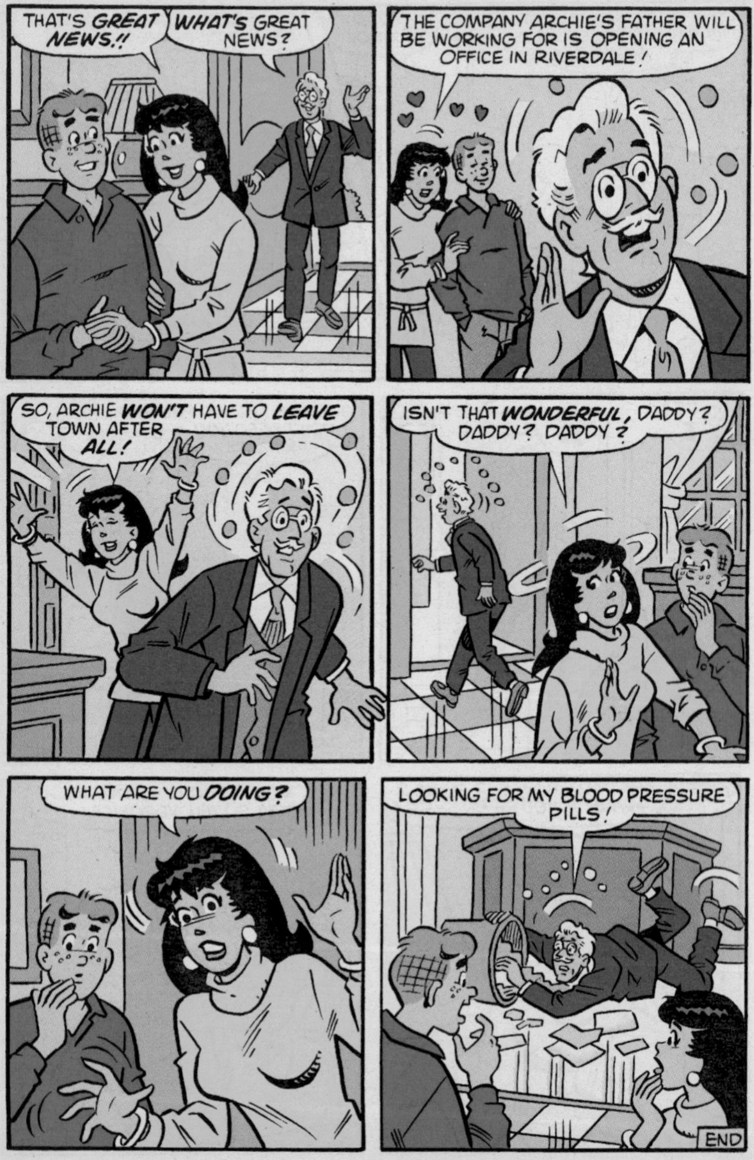
THAT'S GREAT NEWS.!!
WHAT'S GREAT NEWS?
THE COMPANY ARCHIE'S FATHER WILL BE WORKING FOR IS OPENING AN OFFICE IN RIVERDALE!
SO, ARCHIE WON'T HAVE TO LEAVE TOWN AFTER ALL!
ISN'T THAT WONDERFUL, DADDY? DADDY? DADDY?
WHAT ARE YOU DOING?
LOOKING FOR MY BLOOD PRESSURE PILLS!
END

Archie in "WHEN TIME STOOD STILL"

Doyle / Goldberg / D'Agostino / Yoshida

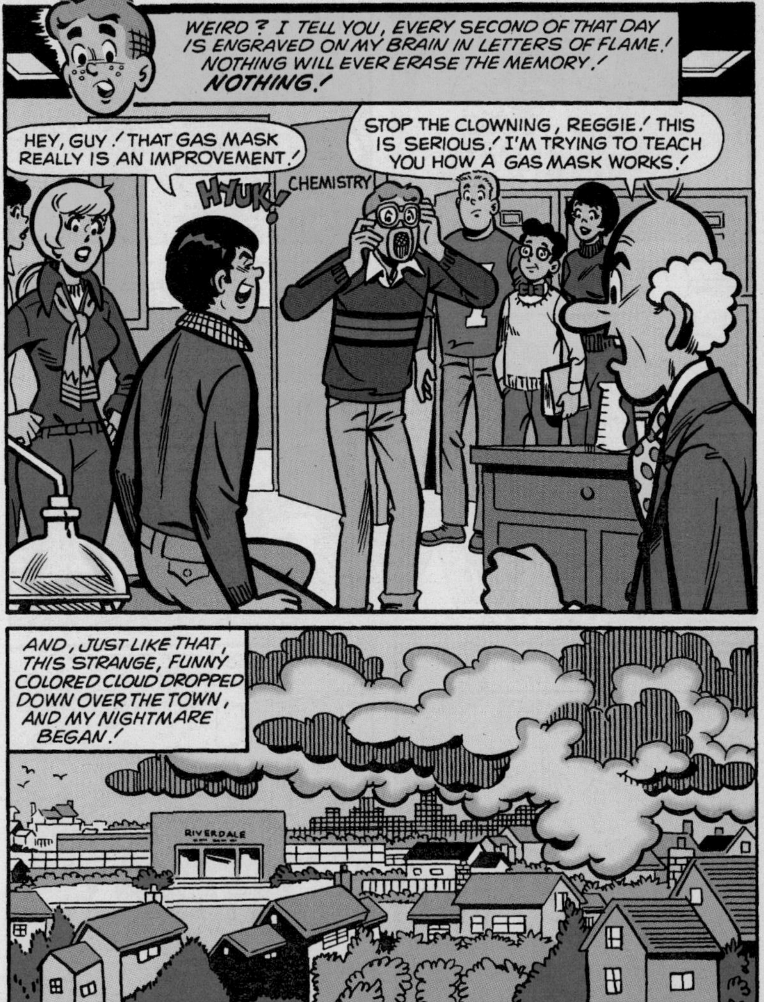
WEIRD? I TELL YOU, EVERY SECOND OF THAT DAY IS ENGRAVED ON MY BRAIN IN LETTERS OF FLAME! NOTHING WILL EVER ERASE THE MEMORY! NOTHING!
HEY, GUY! THAT GAS MASK REALLY IS AN IMPROVEMENT!
HYUK!
CHEMISTRY
STOP THE CLOWNING, REGGIE! THIS IS SERIOUS! I'M TRYING TO TEACH YOU HOW A GAS MASK WORKS!
AND, JUST LIKE THAT, THIS STRANGE, FUNNY COLORED CLOUD DROPPED DOWN OVER THE TOWN, AND MY NIGHTMARE BEGAN!
RIVERDALE

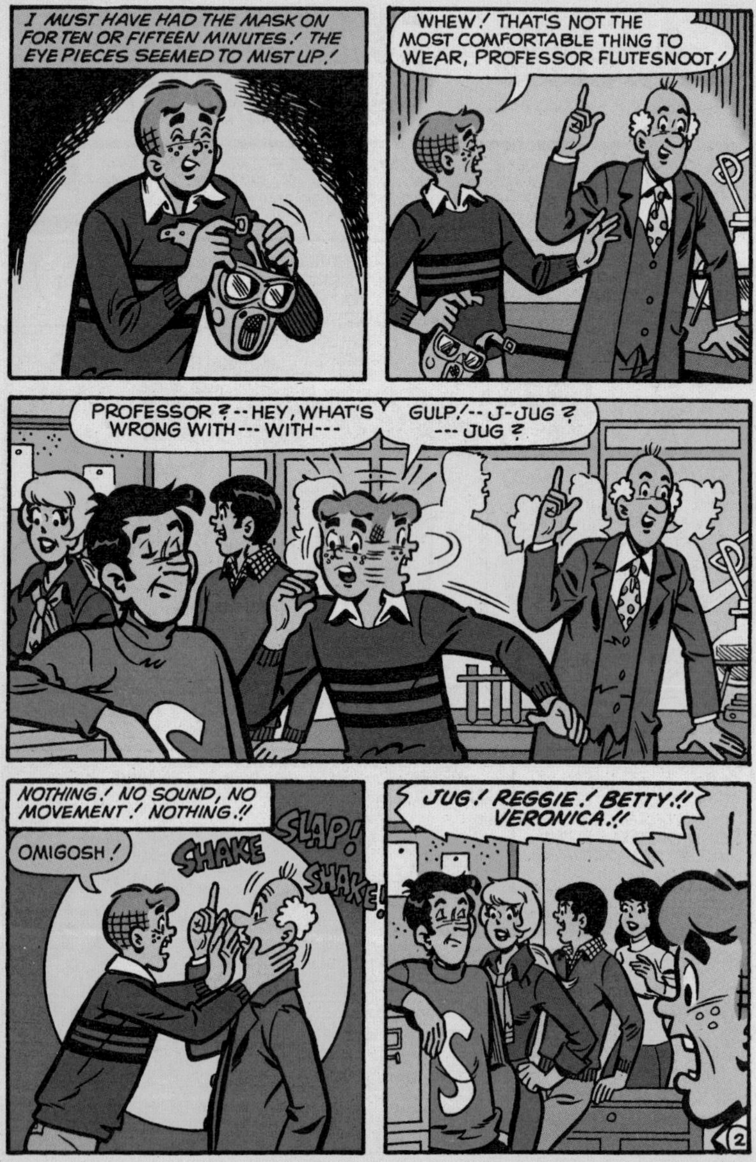
I MUST HAVE HAD THE MASK ON FOR TEN OR FIFTEEN MINUTES! THE EYE PIECES SEEMED TO MIST UP!
WHEW! THAT'S NOT THE MOST COMFORTABLE THING TO WEAR, PROFESSOR FLUTESNOOT!
PROFESSOR?--HEY, WHAT'S WRONG WITH--- WITH---
GULP!-- J-JUG? ---JUG?
NOTHING! NO SOUND, NO MOVEMENT! NOTHING!!
OMIGOSH!
SHAKE
SLAP!
SHAKE!
JUG! REGGIE! BETTY!! VERONICA!!
2

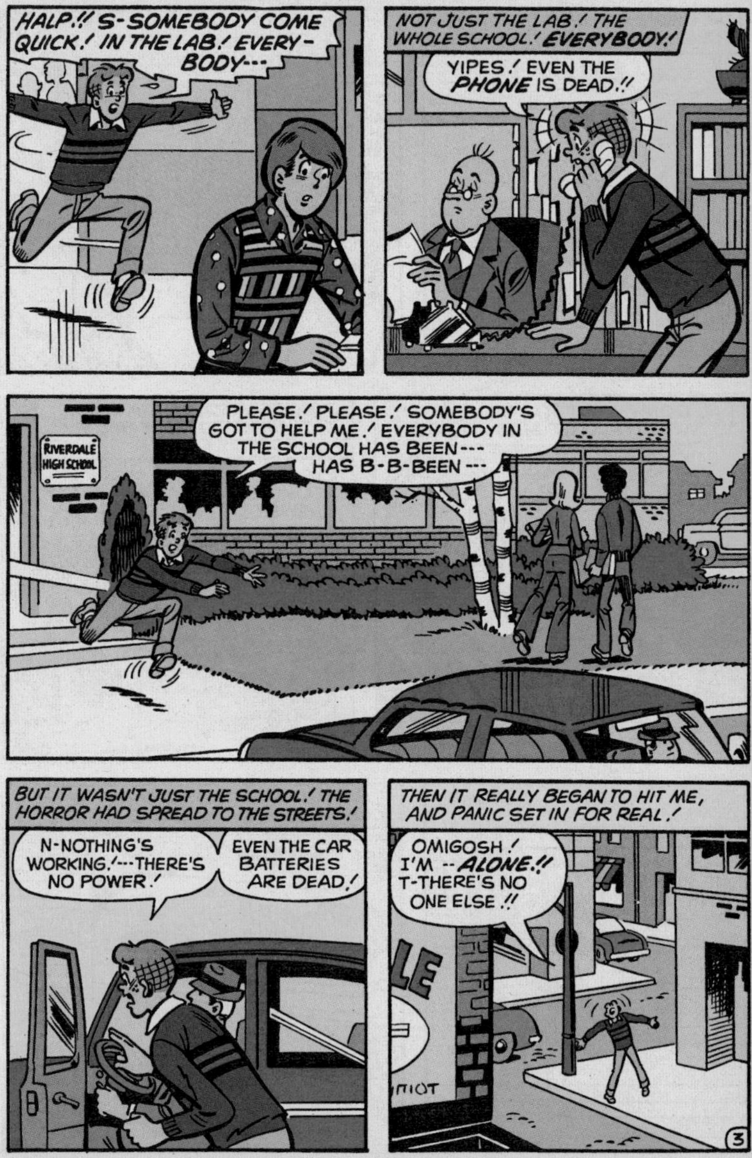

HALP!! S-SOMEBODY COME QUICK! IN THE LAB! EVERY-BODY---
NOT JUST THE LAB! THE WHOLE SCHOOL! EVERYBODY!
YIPES! EVEN THE PHONE IS DEAD!!
RIVERDALE HIGH SCHOOL
PLEASE! PLEASE! SOMEBODY'S GOT TO HELP ME! EVERYBODY IN THE SCHOOL HAS BEEN--- HAS B-B-BEEN ---
BUT IT WASN'T JUST THE SCHOOL! THE HORROR HAD SPREAD TO THE STREETS!
N-NOTHING'S WORKING!---THERE'S NO POWER!
EVEN THE CAR BATTERIES ARE DEAD!
THEN IT REALLY BEGAN TO HIT ME, AND PANIC SET IN FOR REAL!
OMIGOSH! I'M --ALONE!! T-THERE'S NO ONE ELSE!!
3

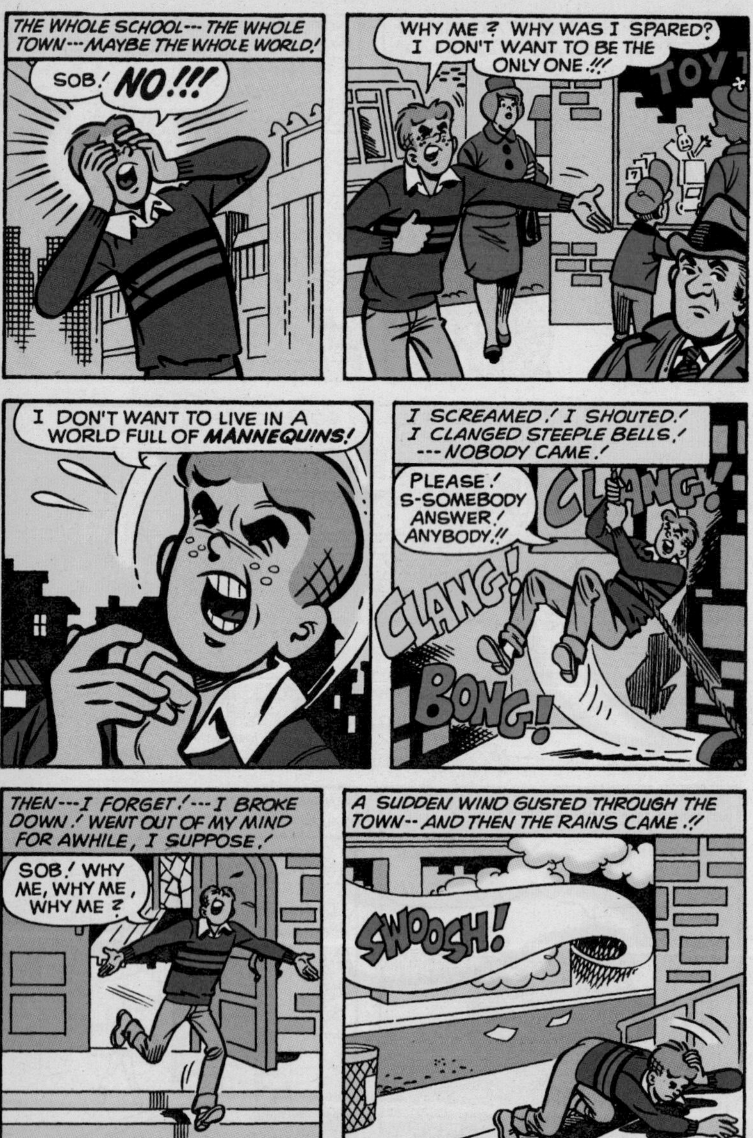
THE WHOLE SCHOOL--- THE WHOLE TOWN---MAYBE THE WHOLE WORLD!
SOB! NO!!!
WHY ME? WHY WAS I SPARED? I DON'T WANT TO BE THE ONLY ONE.!!!
TOY
I DON'T WANT TO LIVE IN A WORLD FULL OF MANNEQUINS!
I SCREAMED! I SHOUTED! I CLANGED STEEPLE BELLS! ---NOBODY CAME!
PLEASE! S-SOMEBODY ANSWER! ANYBODY!!
CLANG!
CLANG!
BONG!
THEN---I FORGET!---I BROKE DOWN! WENT OUT OF MY MIND FOR AWHILE, I SUPPOSE!
SOB! WHY ME, WHY ME, WHY ME?
A SUDDEN WIND GUSTED THROUGH THE TOWN-- AND THEN THE RAINS CAME!!
SWOOSH!
4

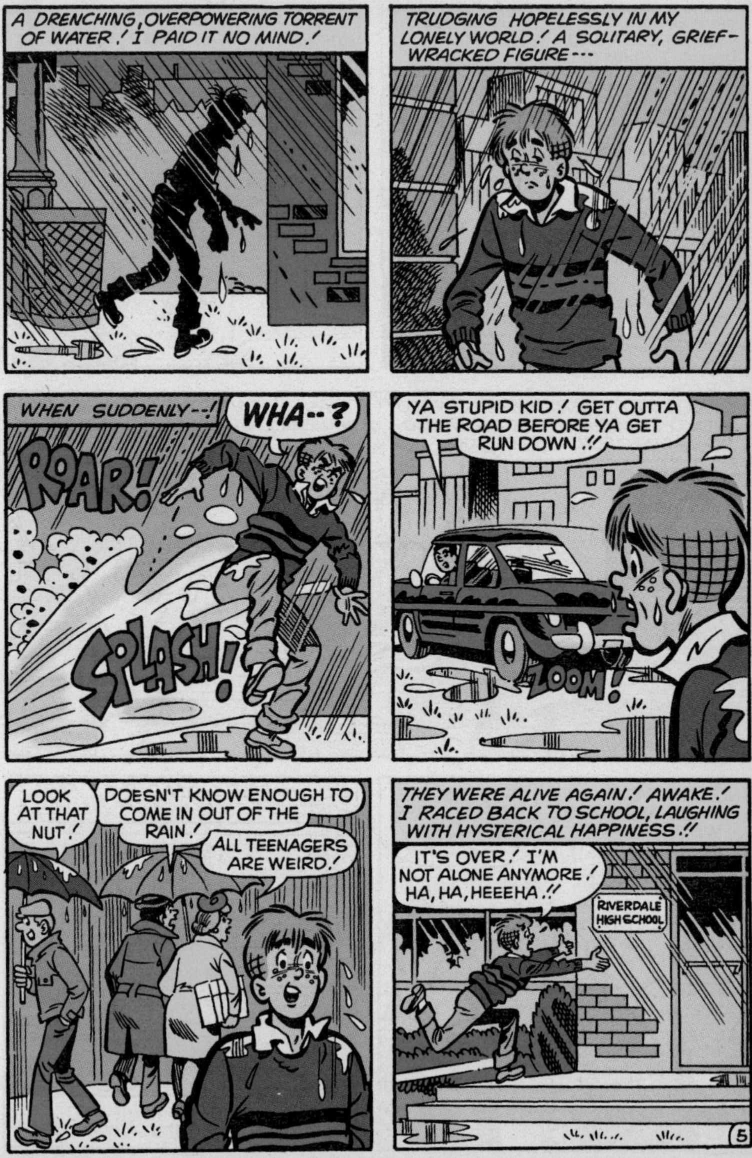
A DRENCHING, OVERPOWERING TORRENT OF WATER! I PAID IT NO MIND!
TRUDGING HOPELESSLY IN MY LONELY WORLD! A SOLITARY, GRIEF-WRACKED FIGURE---
WHEN SUDDENLY--!
WHA--?
ROAR!
SPLASH!
YA STUPID KID! GET OUTTA THE ROAD BEFORE YA GET RUN DOWN!!
ZOOM!
LOOK AT THAT NUT!
DOESN'T KNOW ENOUGH TO COME IN OUT OF THE RAIN!
ALL TEENAGERS ARE WEIRD!
THEY WERE ALIVE AGAIN! AWAKE! I RACED BACK TO SCHOOL, LAUGHING WITH HYSTERICAL HAPPINESS!!
IT'S OVER! I'M NOT ALONE ANYMORE! HA, HA, HEEEHA!!
RIVERDALE HIGH SCHOOL
5

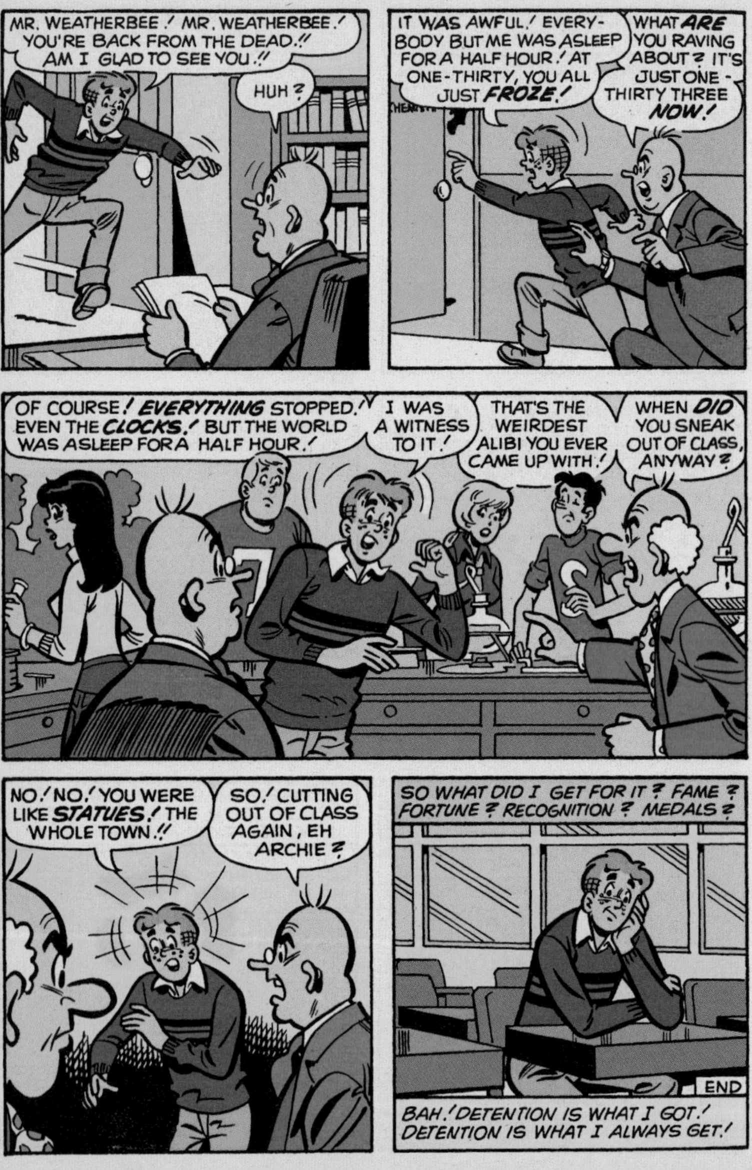
MR. WEATHERBEE! MR. WEATHERBEE! YOU'RE BACK FROM THE DEAD!! AM I GLAD TO SEE YOU!!
HUH?
IT WAS AWFUL! EVERY-BODY BUT ME WAS ASLEEP FOR A HALF HOUR! AT ONE-THIRTY, YOU ALL JUST FROZE!
WHAT ARE YOU RAVING ABOUT? IT'S JUST ONE-THIRTY THREE NOW!
OF COURSE! EVERYTHING STOPPED! EVEN THE CLOCKS! BUT THE WORLD WAS ASLEEP FOR A HALF HOUR!
I WAS A WITNESS TO IT!
THAT'S THE WEIRDEST ALIBI YOU EVER CAME UP WITH!
WHEN DID YOU SNEAK OUT OF CLASS, ANYWAY?
NO! NO! YOU WERE LIKE STATUES! THE WHOLE TOWN!!
SO! CUTTING OUT OF CLASS AGAIN, EH ARCHIE?
SO WHAT DID I GET FOR IT? FAME? FORTUNE? RECOGNITION? MEDALS?
END
BAH! DETENTION IS WHAT I GOT! DETENTION IS WHAT I ALWAYS GET!

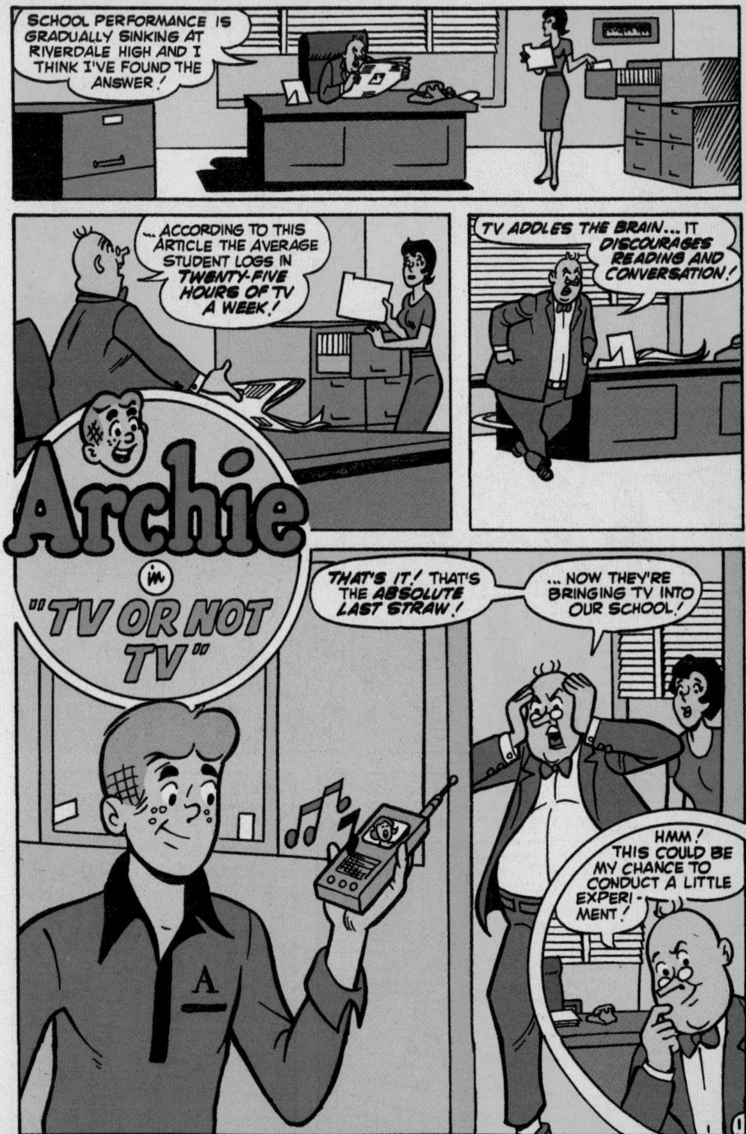
SCHOOL PERFORMANCE IS GRADUALLY SINKING AT RIVERDALE HIGH AND I THINK I'VE FOUND THE ANSWER!
...ACCORDING TO THIS ARTICLE THE AVERAGE STUDENT LOGS IN TWENTY-FIVE HOURS OF TV A WEEK!
TV ADDLES THE BRAIN... IT DISCOURAGES READING AND CONVERSATION!
Archie
in
"TV OR NOT TV"
THAT'S IT! THAT'S THE ABSOLUTE LAST STRAW!
...NOW THEY'RE BRINGING TV INTO OUR SCHOOL!
HMM! THIS COULD BE MY CHANCE TO CONDUCT A LITTLE EXPERI-MENT!
A
1

Script: George Gladir / Pencils: Bob Bolling / Inks: Chic Stone / Letters: Bill Yoshida / Colors: Barry Grossman

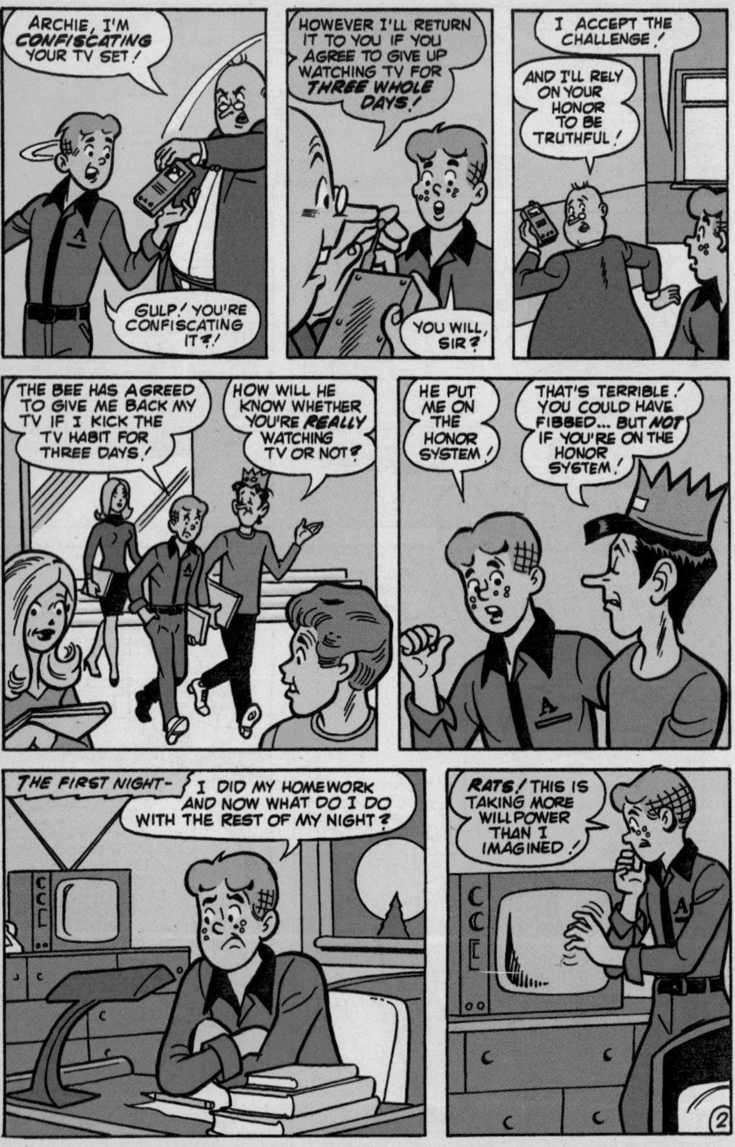
ARCHIE, I'M CONFISCATING YOUR TV SET!
GULP! YOU'RE CONFISCATING IT?!
HOWEVER I'LL RETURN IT TO YOU IF YOU AGREE TO GIVE UP WATCHING TV FOR THREE WHOLE DAYS!
YOU WILL, SIR?
I ACCEPT THE CHALLENGE!
AND I'LL RELY ON YOUR HONOR TO BE TRUTHFUL!
THE BEE HAS AGREED TO GIVE ME BACK MY TV IF I KICK THE TV HABIT FOR THREE DAYS!
HOW WILL HE KNOW WHETHER YOU'RE REALLY WATCHING TV OR NOT?
HE PUT ME ON THE HONOR SYSTEM!
THAT'S TERRIBLE! YOU COULD HAVE FIBBED... BUT NOT IF YOU'RE ON THE HONOR SYSTEM!
THE FIRST NIGHT-
I DID MY HOMEWORK AND NOW WHAT DO I DO WITH THE REST OF MY NIGHT?
RATS! THIS IS TAKING MORE WILLPOWER THAN I IMAGINED!
2

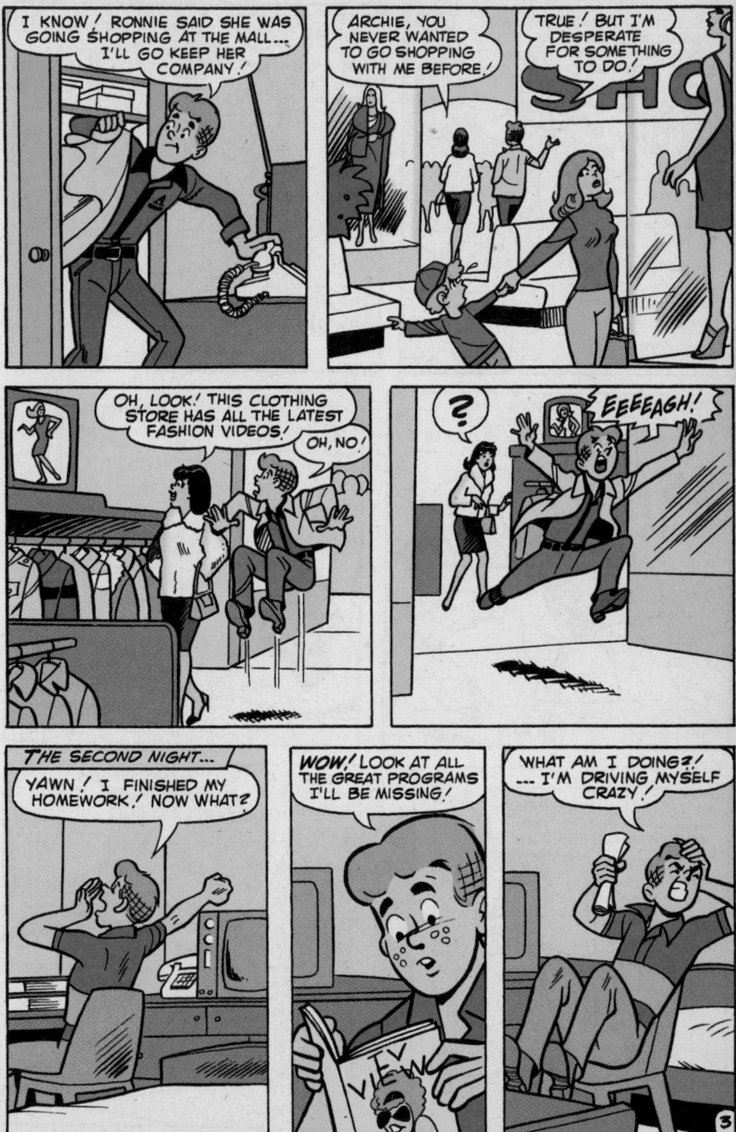
I KNOW! RONNIE SAID SHE WAS GOING SHOPPING AT THE MALL... I'LL GO KEEP HER COMPANY!
ARCHIE, YOU NEVER WANTED TO GO SHOPPING WITH ME BEFORE!
TRUE! BUT I'M DESPERATE FOR SOMETHING TO DO!
SHO
OH, LOOK! THIS CLOTHING STORE HAS ALL THE LATEST FASHION VIDEOS!
OH, NO!
?
EEEEAGH!
THE SECOND NIGHT...
YAWN! I FINISHED MY HOMEWORK! NOW WHAT?
WOW! LOOK AT ALL THE GREAT PROGRAMS I'LL BE MISSING!
TV VIEW
WHAT AM I DOING?! --- I'M DRIVING MYSELF CRAZY!

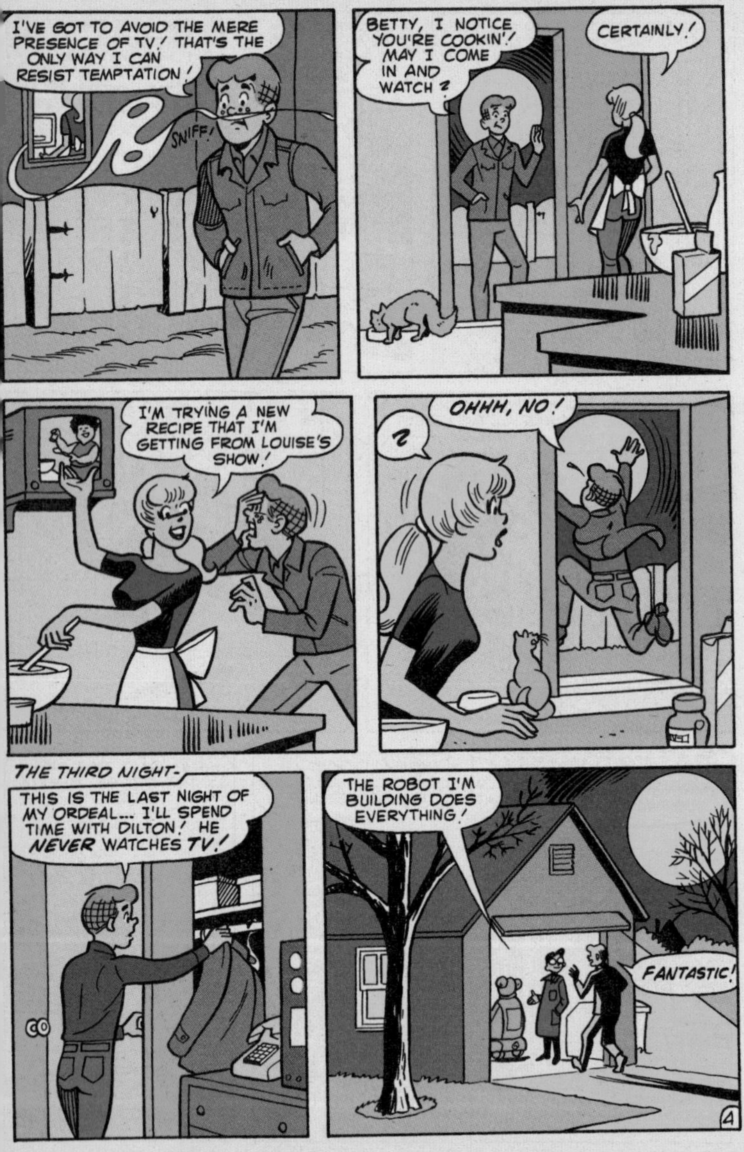
I'VE GOT TO AVOID THE MERE PRESENCE OF TV! THAT'S THE ONLY WAY I CAN RESIST TEMPTATION!
SNIFF!
BETTY, I NOTICE YOU'RE COOKIN'! MAY I COME IN AND WATCH?
CERTAINLY!
I'M TRYING A NEW RECIPE THAT I'M GETTING FROM LOUISE'S SHOW!
?
OHHH, NO!
THE THIRD NIGHT-
THIS IS THE LAST NIGHT OF MY ORDEAL... I'LL SPEND TIME WITH DILTON! HE NEVER WATCHES TV!
THE ROBOT I'M BUILDING DOES EVERYTHING!
FANTASTIC!
4

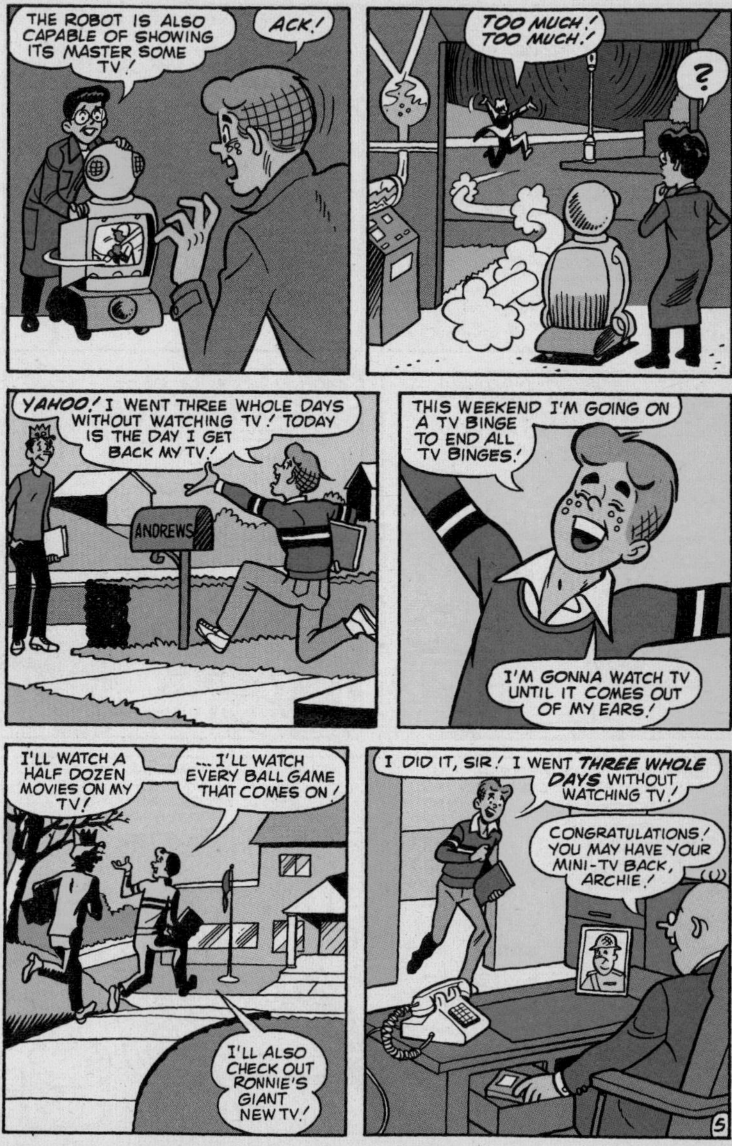
THE ROBOT IS ALSO CAPABLE OF SHOWING ITS MASTER SOME TV!
ACK!
TOO MUCH! TOO MUCH!
?
YAHOO! I WENT THREE WHOLE DAYS WITHOUT WATCHING TV! TODAY IS THE DAY I GET BACK MY TV!
ANDREWS
THIS WEEKEND I'M GOING ON A TV BINGE TO END ALL TV BINGES!
I'M GONNA WATCH TV UNTIL IT COMES OUT OF MY EARS!
I'LL WATCH A HALF DOZEN MOVIES ON MY TV!
... I'LL WATCH EVERY BALL GAME THAT COMES ON!
I'LL ALSO CHECK OUT RONNIE'S GIANT NEW TV!
I DID IT, SIR! I WENT THREE WHOLE DAYS WITHOUT WATCHING TV!
CONGRATULATIONS! YOU MAY HAVE YOUR MINI-TV BACK, ARCHIE!
5

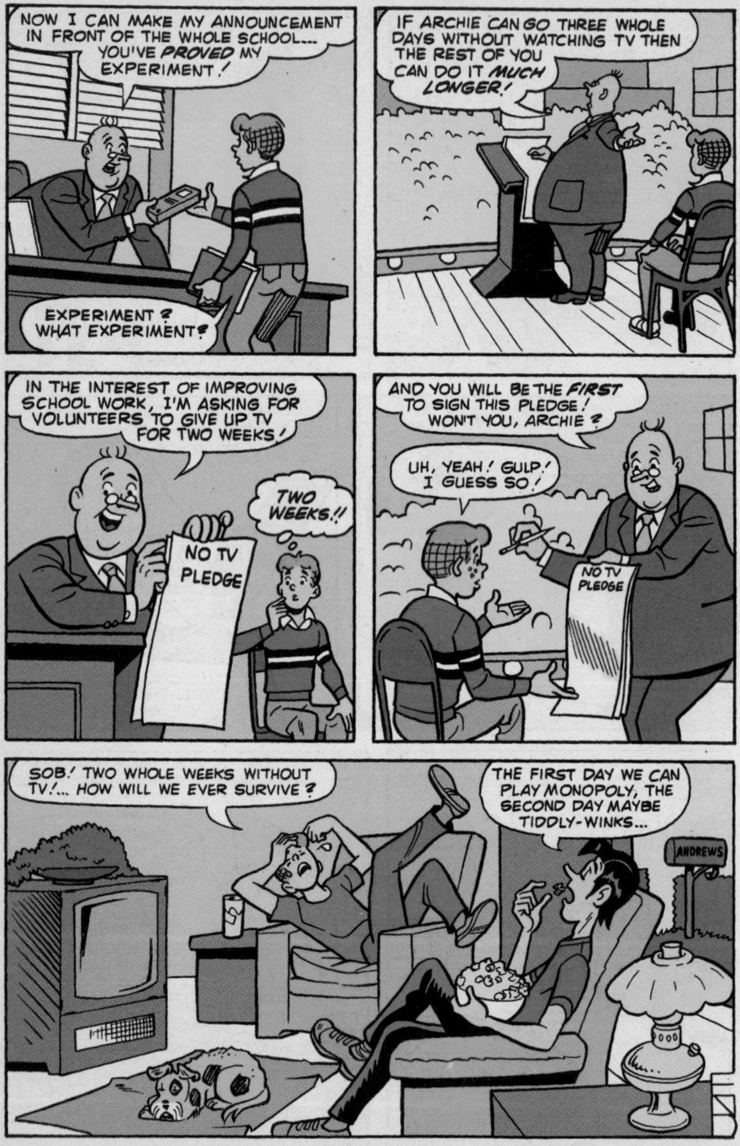
NOW I CAN MAKE MY ANNOUNCEMENT IN FRONT OF THE WHOLE SCHOOL... YOU'VE PROVED MY EXPERIMENT!
EXPERIMENT? WHAT EXPERIMENT?
IF ARCHIE CAN GO THREE WHOLE DAYS WITHOUT WATCHING TV THEN THE REST OF YOU CAN DO IT MUCH LONGER!
IN THE INTEREST OF IMPROVING SCHOOL WORK, I'M ASKING FOR VOLUNTEERS TO GIVE UP TV FOR TWO WEEKS!
NO TV PLEDGE
TWO WEEKS!!
AND YOU WILL BE THE FIRST TO SIGN THIS PLEDGE! WON'T YOU, ARCHIE?
UH, YEAH! GULP! I GUESS SO!
NO TV PLEDGE
SOB! TWO WHOLE WEEKS WITHOUT TV!... HOW WILL WE EVER SURVIVE?
THE FIRST DAY WE CAN PLAY MONOPOLY, THE SECOND DAY MAYBE TIDDLY-WINKS...
ANDREWS

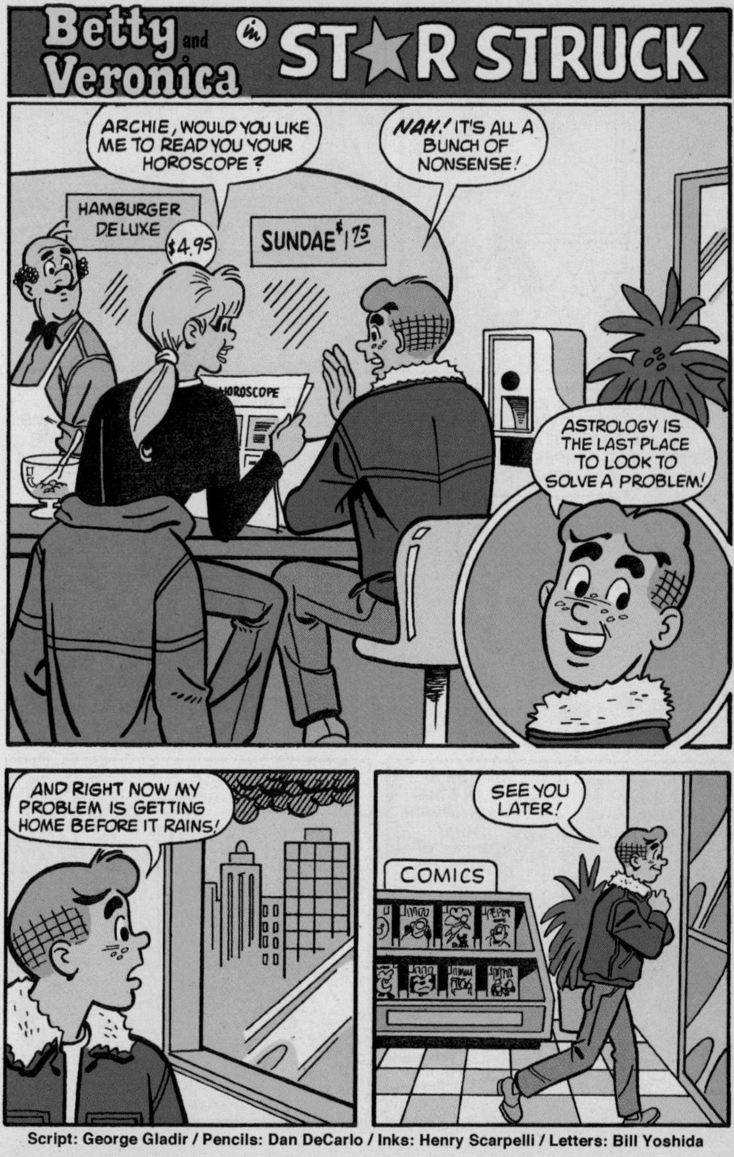

Betty and Veronica in STAR STRUCK
ARCHIE, WOULD YOU LIKE ME TO READ YOU YOUR HOROSCOPE?
NAH! IT'S ALL A BUNCH OF NONSENSE!
HAMBURGER DELUXE
$4.95
SUNDAE $1.75
HOROSCOPE
ASTROLOGY IS THE LAST PLACE TO LOOK TO SOLVE A PROBLEM!
AND RIGHT NOW MY PROBLEM IS GETTING HOME BEFORE IT RAINS!
SEE YOU LATER!
COMICS

Script: George Gladir / Pencils: Dan DeCarlo / Inks: Henry Scarpelli / Letters: Bill Yoshida

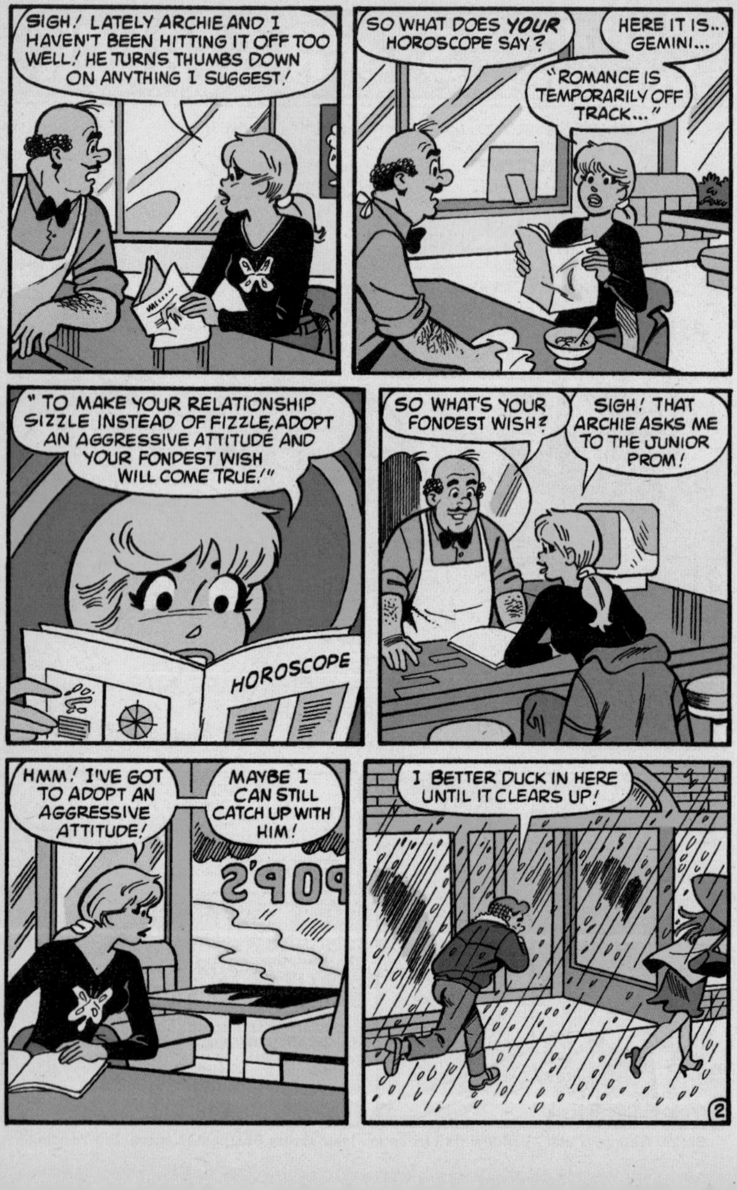
SIGH! LATELY ARCHIE AND I HAVEN'T BEEN HITTING IT OFF TOO WELL! HE TURNS THUMBS DOWN ON ANYTHING I SUGGEST!
SO WHAT DOES YOUR HOROSCOPE SAY?
HERE IT IS... GEMINI...
"ROMANCE IS TEMPORARILY OFF TRACK..."
"TO MAKE YOUR RELATIONSHIP SIZZLE INSTEAD OF FIZZLE, ADOPT AN AGGRESSIVE ATTITUDE AND YOUR FONDEST WISH WILL COME TRUE!"
HOROSCOPE
SO WHAT'S YOUR FONDEST WISH?
SIGH! THAT ARCHIE ASKS ME TO THE JUNIOR PROM!
HMM! I'VE GOT TO ADOPT AN AGGRESSIVE ATTITUDE!
MAYBE I CAN STILL CATCH UP WITH HIM!
I BETTER DUCK IN HERE UNTIL IT CLEARS UP!
2

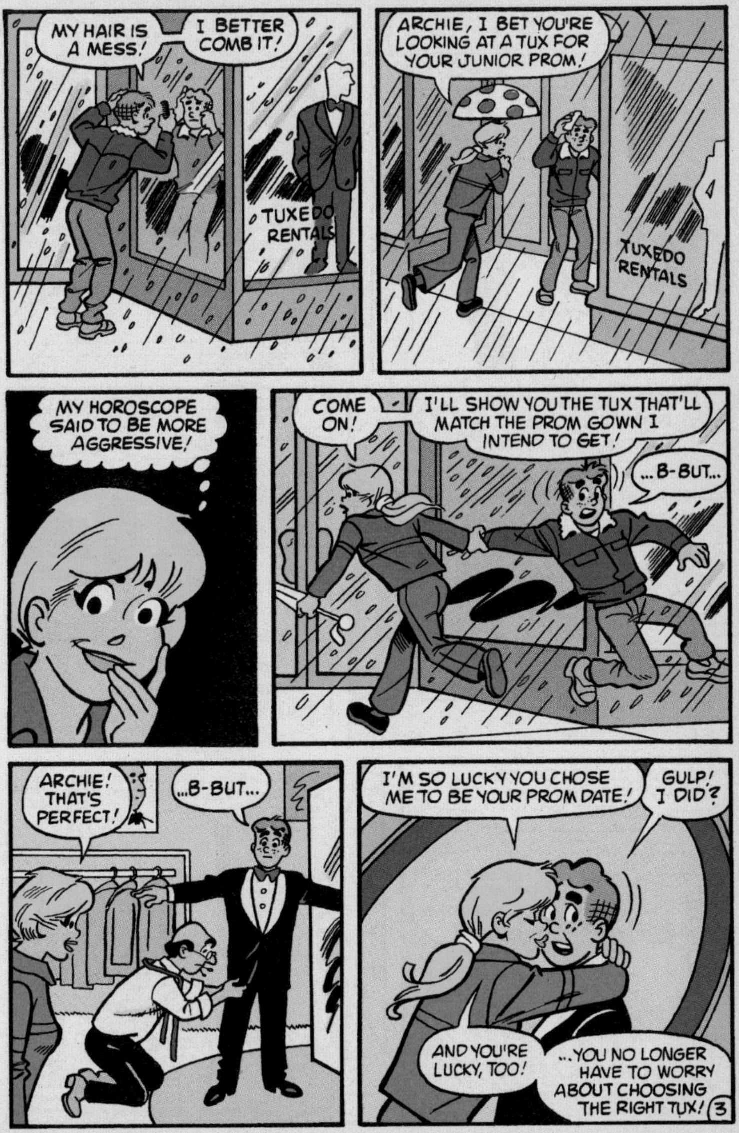
MY HAIR IS A MESS!
I BETTER COMB IT!
TUXEDO RENTALS
ARCHIE, I BET YOU'RE LOOKING AT A TUX FOR YOUR JUNIOR PROM!
TUXEDO RENTALS
MY HOROSCOPE SAID TO BE MORE AGGRESSIVE!
COME ON!
I'LL SHOW YOU THE TUX THAT'LL MATCH THE PROM GOWN I INTEND TO GET!
...B-BUT...
ARCHIE! THAT'S PERFECT!
...B-BUT...
I'M SO LUCKY YOU CHOSE ME TO BE YOUR PROM DATE!
GULP! I DID?
AND YOU'RE LUCKY, TOO!
...YOU NO LONGER HAVE TO WORRY ABOUT CHOOSING THE RIGHT TUX!
3

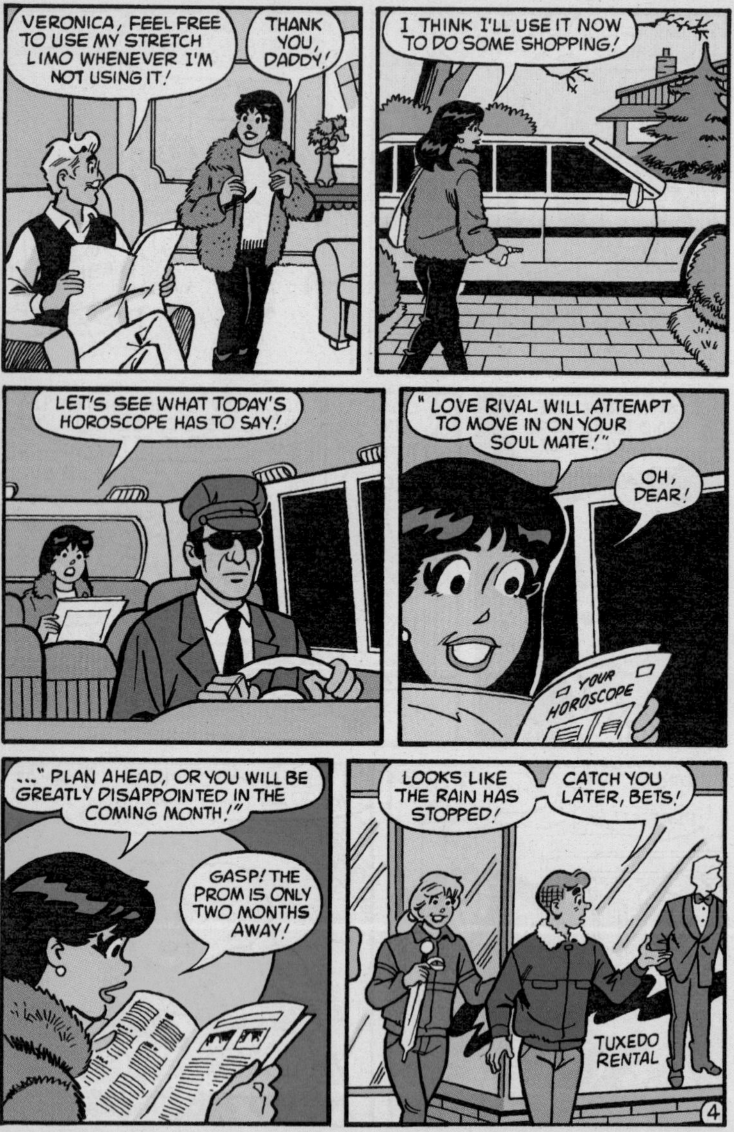
VERONICA, FEEL FREE TO USE MY STRETCH LIMO WHENEVER I'M NOT USING IT!
THANK YOU, DADDY!
I THINK I'LL USE IT NOW TO DO SOME SHOPPING!
LET'S SEE WHAT TODAY'S HOROSCOPE HAS TO SAY!
" LOVE RIVAL WILL ATTEMPT TO MOVE IN ON YOUR SOUL MATE!"
OH, DEAR!
YOUR HOROSCOPE
..." PLAN AHEAD, OR YOU WILL BE GREATLY DISAPPOINTED IN THE COMING MONTH!"
GASP! THE PROM IS ONLY TWO MONTHS AWAY!
LOOKS LIKE THE RAIN HAS STOPPED!
CATCH YOU LATER, BETS!
TUXEDO RENTAL
4

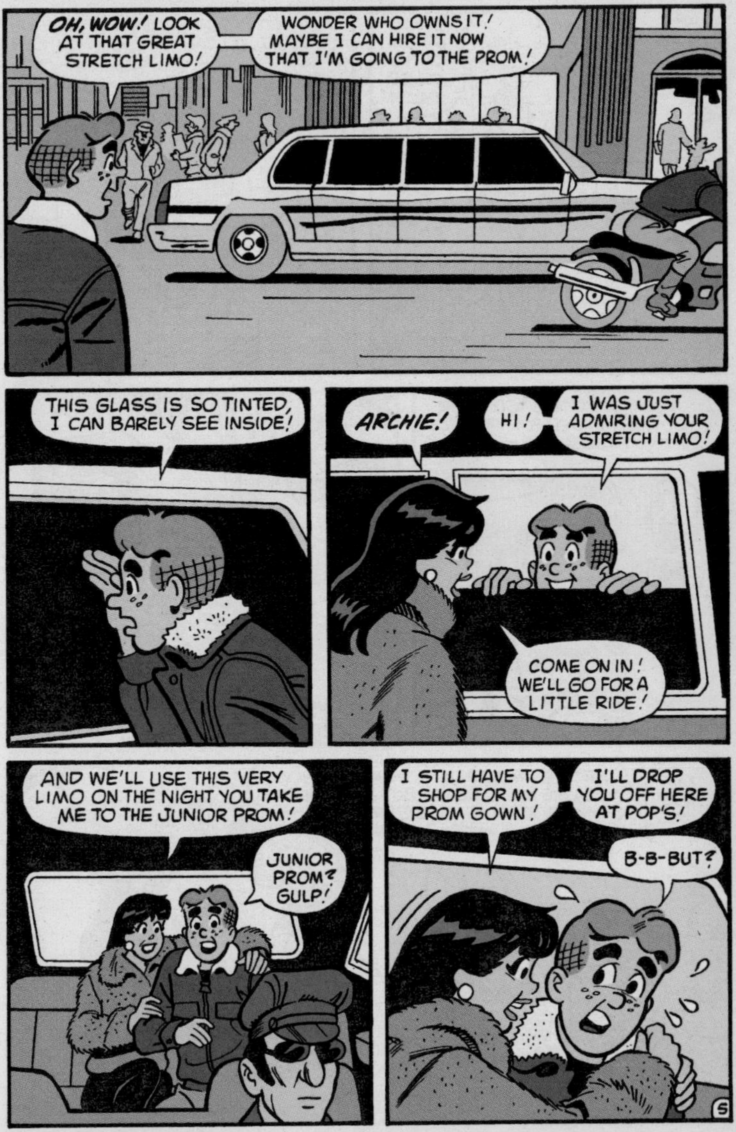
OH, WOW! LOOK AT THAT GREAT STRETCH LIMO!
WONDER WHO OWNS IT! MAYBE I CAN HIRE IT NOW THAT I'M GOING TO THE PROM!
THIS GLASS IS SO TINTED, I CAN BARELY SEE INSIDE!
ARCHIE!
HI!
I WAS JUST ADMIRING YOUR STRETCH LIMO!
COME ON IN! WE'LL GO FOR A LITTLE RIDE!
AND WE'LL USE THIS VERY LIMO ON THE NIGHT YOU TAKE ME TO THE JUNIOR PROM!
JUNIOR PROM? GULP!
I STILL HAVE TO SHOP FOR MY PROM GOWN!
I'LL DROP YOU OFF HERE AT POP'S!
B-B-BUT?
5

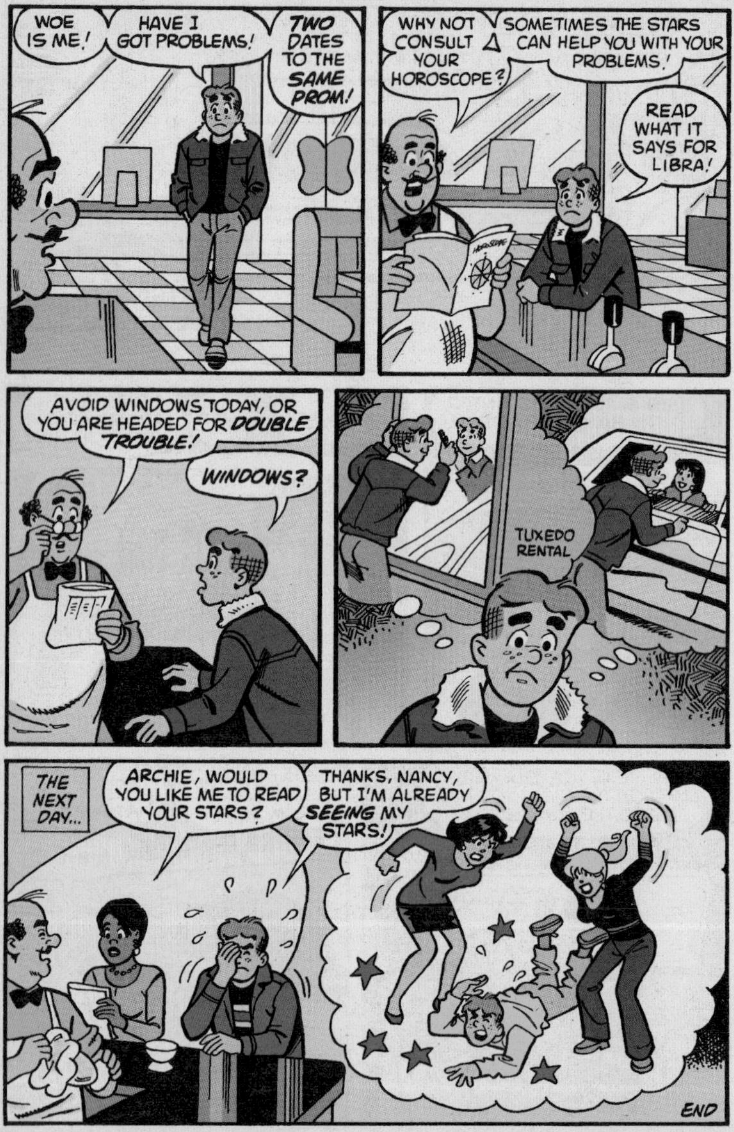
WOE IS ME!
HAVE I GOT PROBLEMS!
TWO DATES TO THE SAME PROM!
WHY NOT CONSULT YOUR HOROSCOPE?
SOMETIMES THE STARS CAN HELP YOU WITH YOUR PROBLEMS!
READ WHAT IT SAYS FOR LIBRA!
AVOID WINDOWS TODAY, OR YOU ARE HEADED FOR DOUBLE TROUBLE!
WINDOWS?
TUXEDO RENTAL
THE NEXT DAY...
ARCHIE, WOULD YOU LIKE ME TO READ YOUR STARS?
THANKS, NANCY, BUT I'M ALREADY SEEING MY STARS!
END

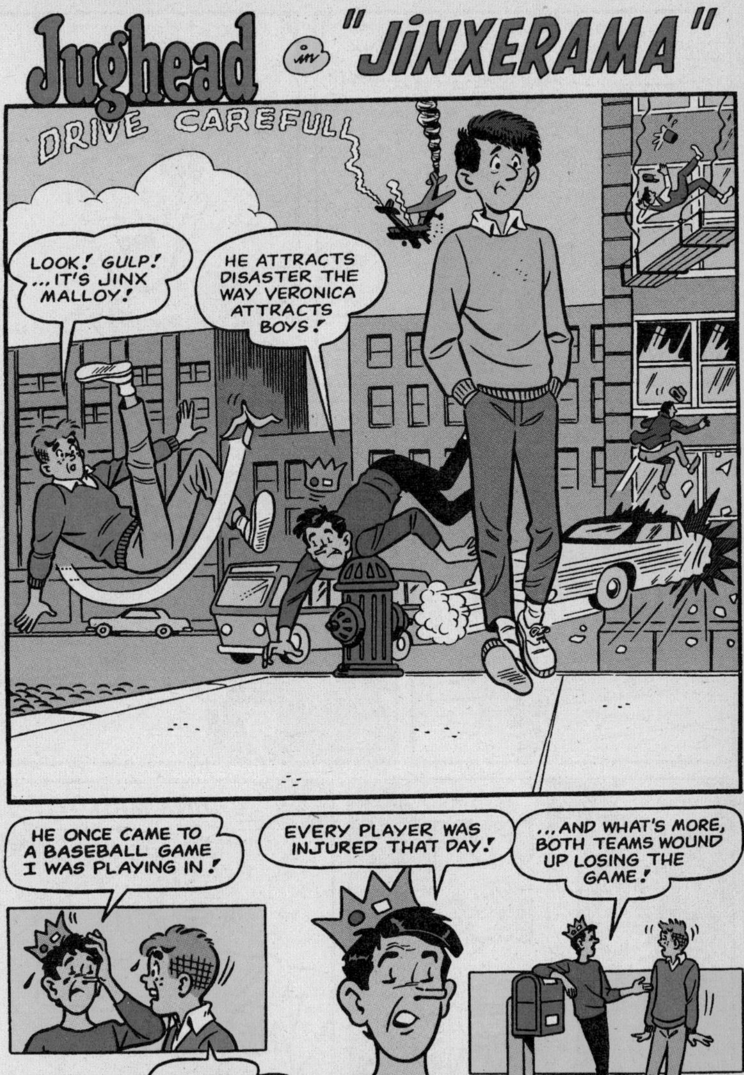
Jughead in "JINXERAMA"
DRIVE CAREFULL
LOOK! GULP! ...IT'S JINX MALLOY!
HE ATTRACTS DISASTER THE WAY VERONICA ATTRACTS BOYS!
HE ONCE CAME TO A BASEBALL GAME I WAS PLAYING IN!
WHAT HAPPENED?
EVERY PLAYER WAS INJURED THAT DAY!
...AND WHAT'S MORE, BOTH TEAMS WOUND UP LOSING THE GAME!

Script: F. Doyle / Pencils: B.Vigoda / Inks & Letters: V. DeCarlo

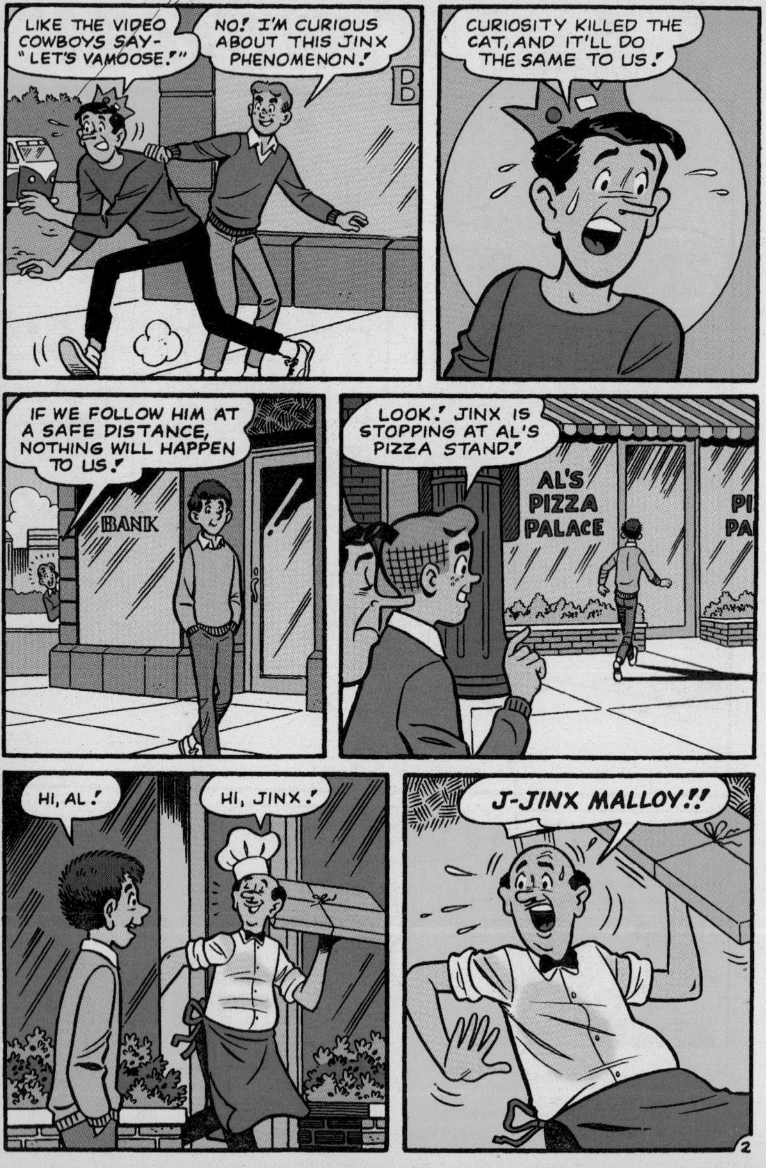
LIKE THE VIDEO COWBOYS SAY- "LET'S VAMOOSE!"
NO! I'M CURIOUS ABOUT THIS JINX PHENOMENON!
B
CURIOSITY KILLED THE CAT, AND IT'LL DO THE SAME TO US!
IF WE FOLLOW HIM AT A SAFE DISTANCE, NOTHING WILL HAPPEN TO US!
BANK
LOOK! JINX IS STOPPING AT AL'S PIZZA STAND!
AL'S PIZZA PALACE
HI, AL!
HI, JINX!
J-JINX MALLOY!!
2

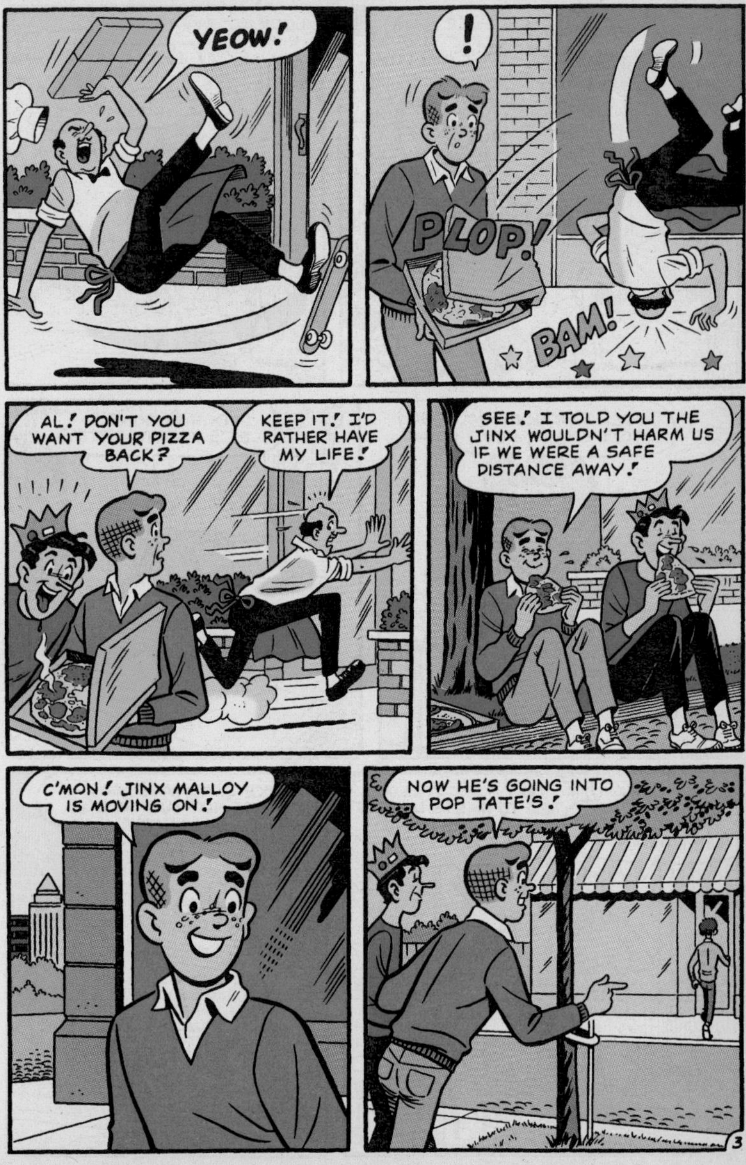

YEOW!
!
PLOP!
BAM!
AL! DON'T YOU WANT YOUR PIZZA BACK?
KEEP IT! I'D RATHER HAVE MY LIFE!
SEE! I TOLD YOU THE JINX WOULDN'T HARM US IF WE WERE A SAFE DISTANCE AWAY!
C'MON! JINX MALLOY IS MOVING ON!
NOW HE'S GOING INTO POP TATE'S!

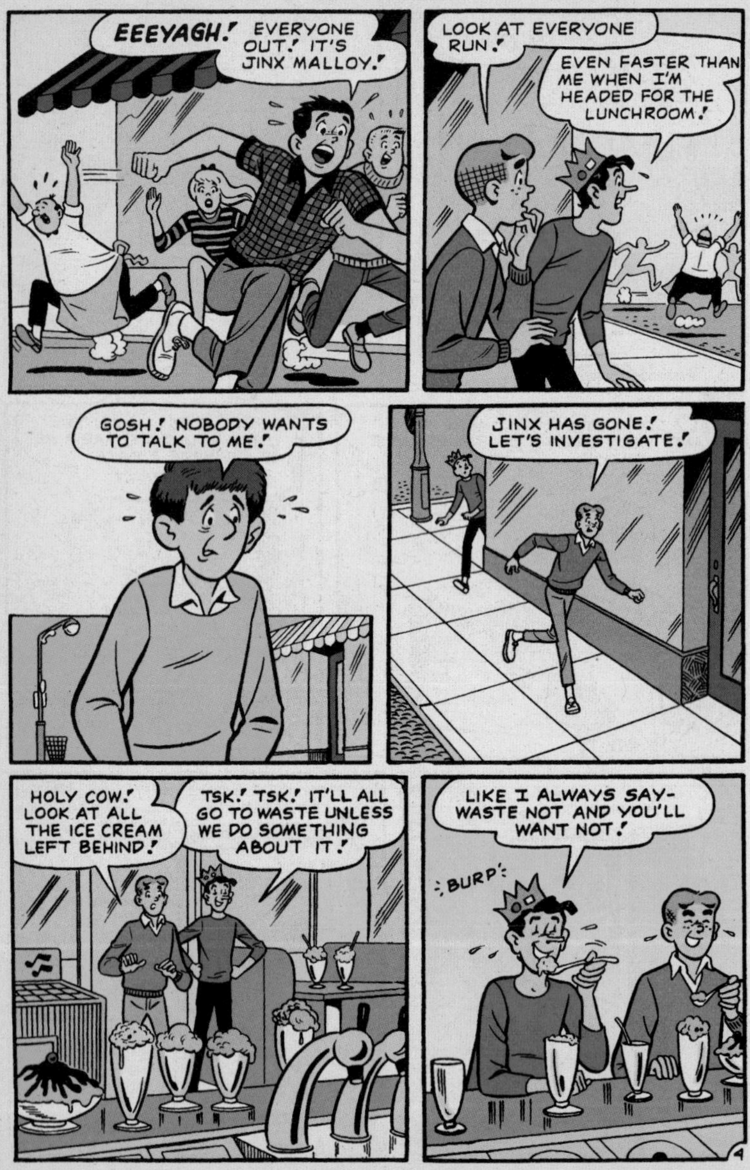
EEEYAGH! EVERYONE OUT! IT'S JINX MALLOY!
LOOK AT EVERYONE RUN!
EVEN FASTER THAN ME WHEN I'M HEADED FOR THE LUNCHROOM!
GOSH! NOBODY WANTS TO TALK TO ME!
JINX HAS GONE! LET'S INVESTIGATE!
HOLY COW! LOOK AT ALL THE ICE CREAM LEFT BEHIND!
TSK! TSK! IT'LL ALL GO TO WASTE UNLESS WE DO SOMETHING ABOUT IT!
LIKE I ALWAYS SAY- WASTE NOT AND YOU'LL WANT NOT!
BURP
4

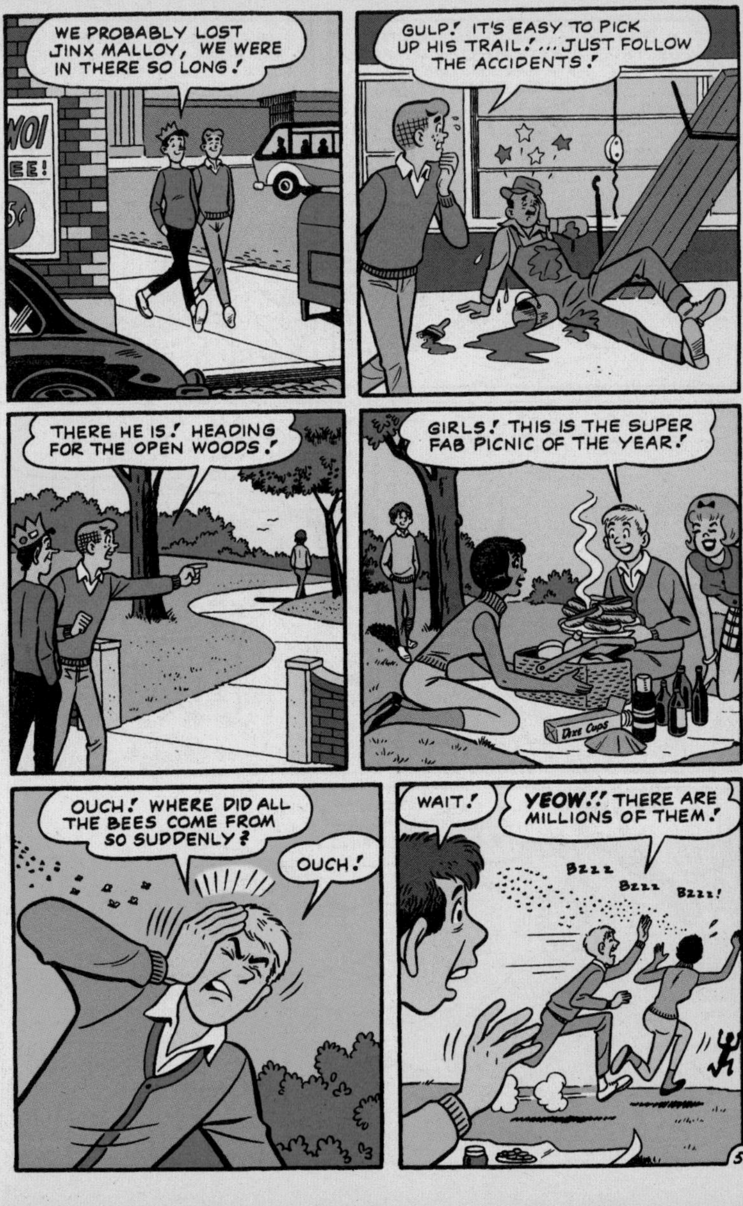

WE PROBABLY LOST JINX MALLOY, WE WERE IN THERE SO LONG!
GULP! IT'S EASY TO PICK UP HIS TRAIL!... JUST FOLLOW THE ACCIDENTS!
THERE HE IS! HEADING FOR THE OPEN WOODS!
GIRLS! THIS IS THE SUPER FAB PICNIC OF THE YEAR!
Dixie Cups
OUCH! WHERE DID ALL THE BEES COME FROM SO SUDDENLY?
OUCH!
WAIT!
YEOW!! THERE ARE MILLIONS OF THEM!
Bzzz
Bzzz
Bzzz!

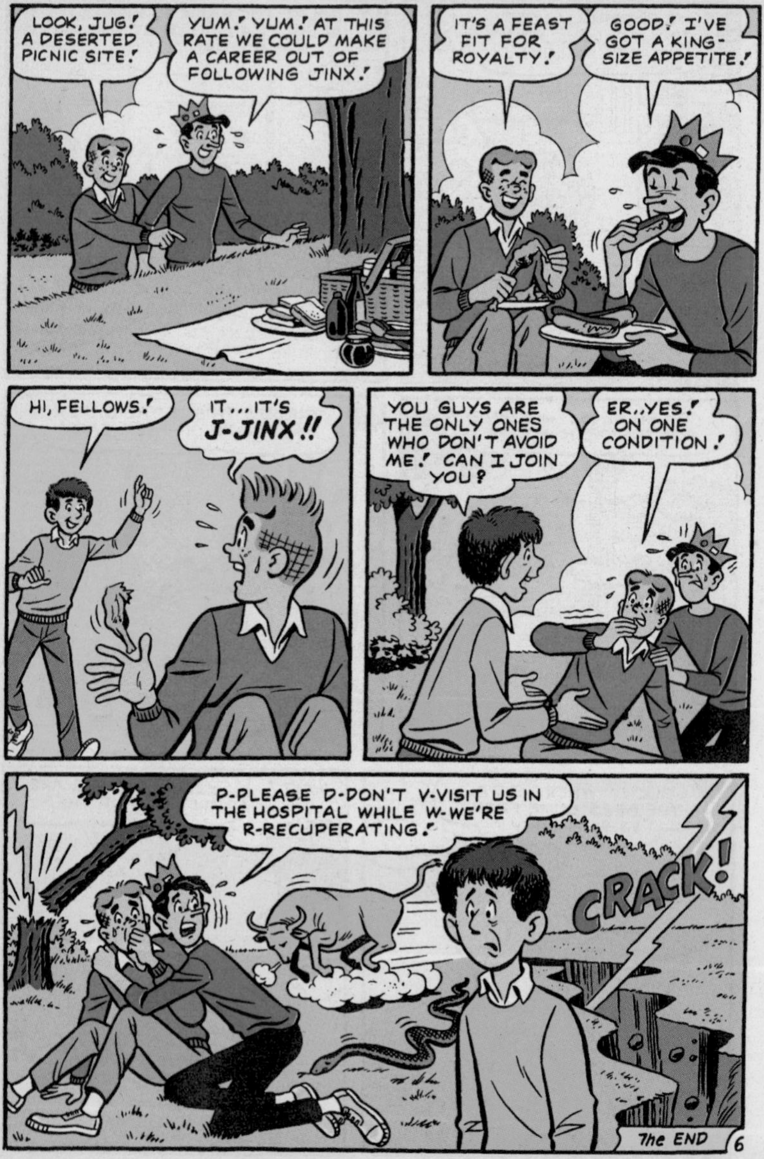
LOOK, JUG! A DESERTED PICNIC SITE!
YUM! YUM! AT THIS RATE WE COULD MAKE A CAREER OUT OF FOLLOWING JINX!
IT'S A FEAST FIT FOR ROYALTY!
GOOD! I'VE GOT A KING-SIZE APPETITE!
HI, FELLOWS!
IT... IT'S J-JINX!!
YOU GUYS ARE THE ONLY ONES WHO DON'T AVOID ME! CAN I JOIN YOU?
ER..YES! ON ONE CONDITION!
P-PLEASE D-DON'T V-VISIT US IN THE HOSPITAL WHILE W-WE'RE R-RECUPERATING!
CRACK!
The END
6

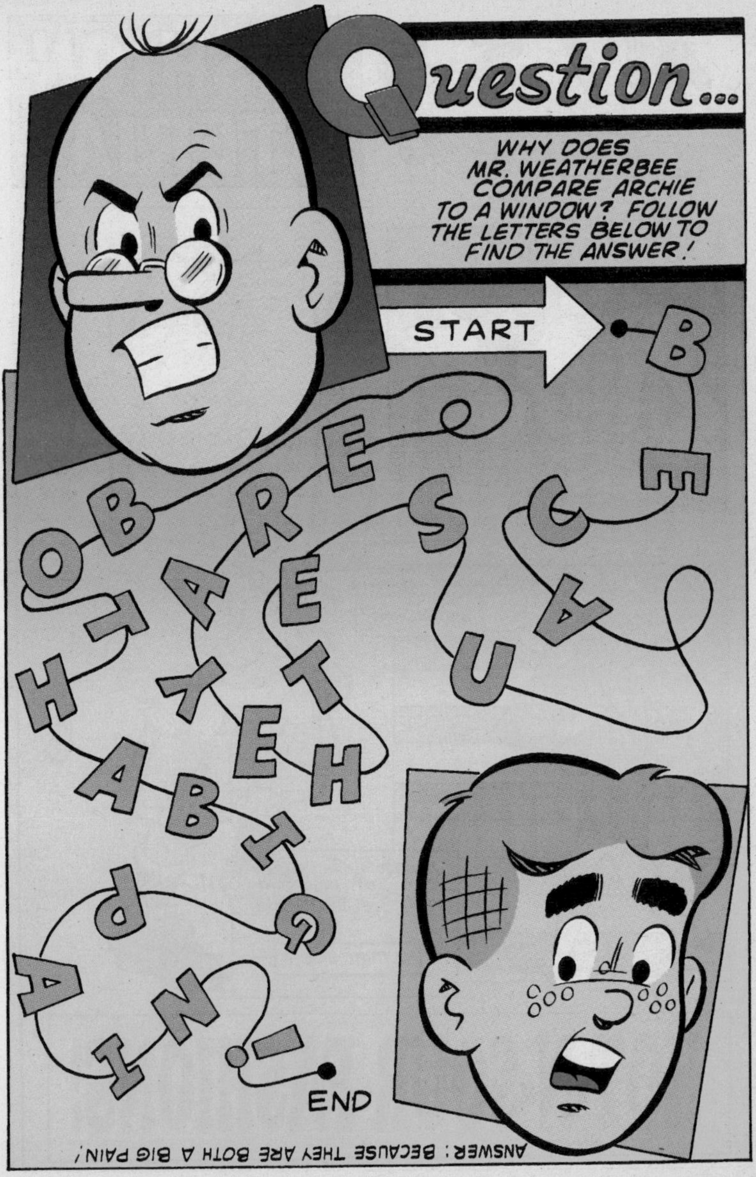
Question...
WHY DOES MR. WEATHERBEE COMPARE ARCHIE TO A WINDOW? FOLLOW THE LETTERS BELOW TO FIND THE ANSWER!
START
END
ANSWER: BECAUSE THEY ARE BOTH A BIG PAIN!

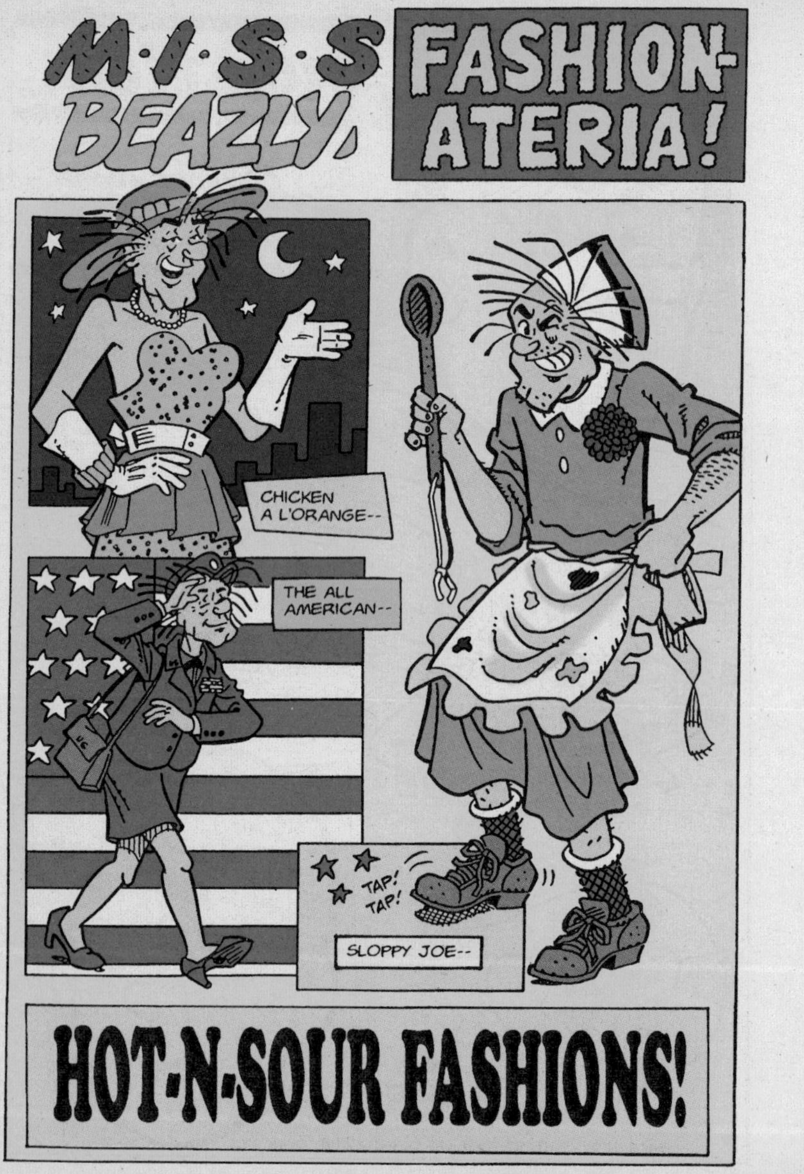
MISS BEAZLY
FASHION-ATERIA!
CHICKEN A L'ORANGE--
THE ALL AMERICAN--
TAP! TAP!
SLOPPY JOE--
HOT-N-SOUR FASHIONS!

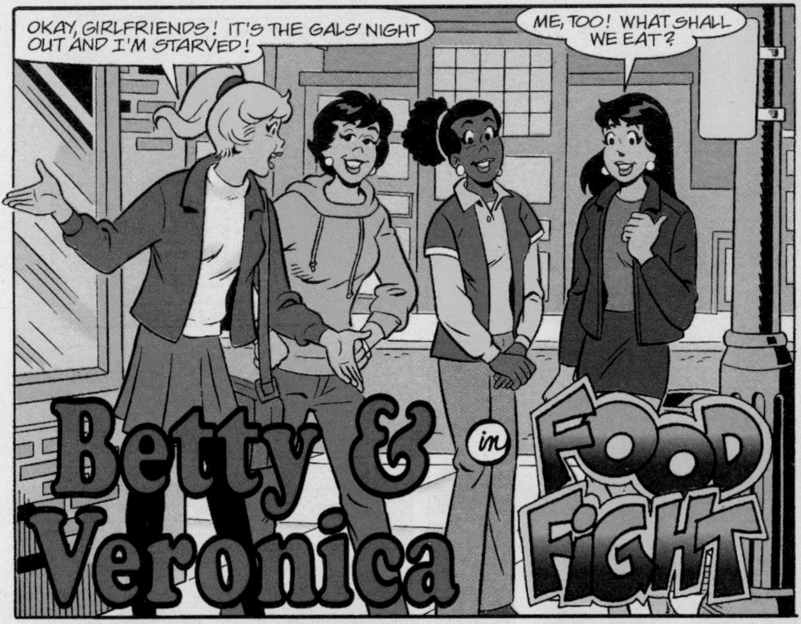
OKAY, GIRLFRIENDS! IT'S THE GALS' NIGHT OUT AND I'M STARVED!
ME, TOO! WHAT SHALL WE EAT?
Betty & Veronica
in
FOOD FIGHT

SCRIPT: MIKE PELLOWSKI PENCILS: TIM KENNEDY INKS: JON D'AGOSTINO
COLORS: BARRY GROSSMAN LETTERS: VICKIE WILLIAMS

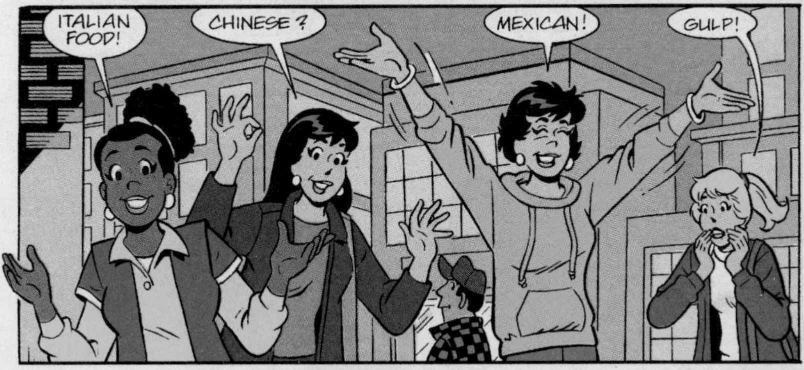
ITALIAN FOOD!
CHINESE?
MEXICAN!
GULP!

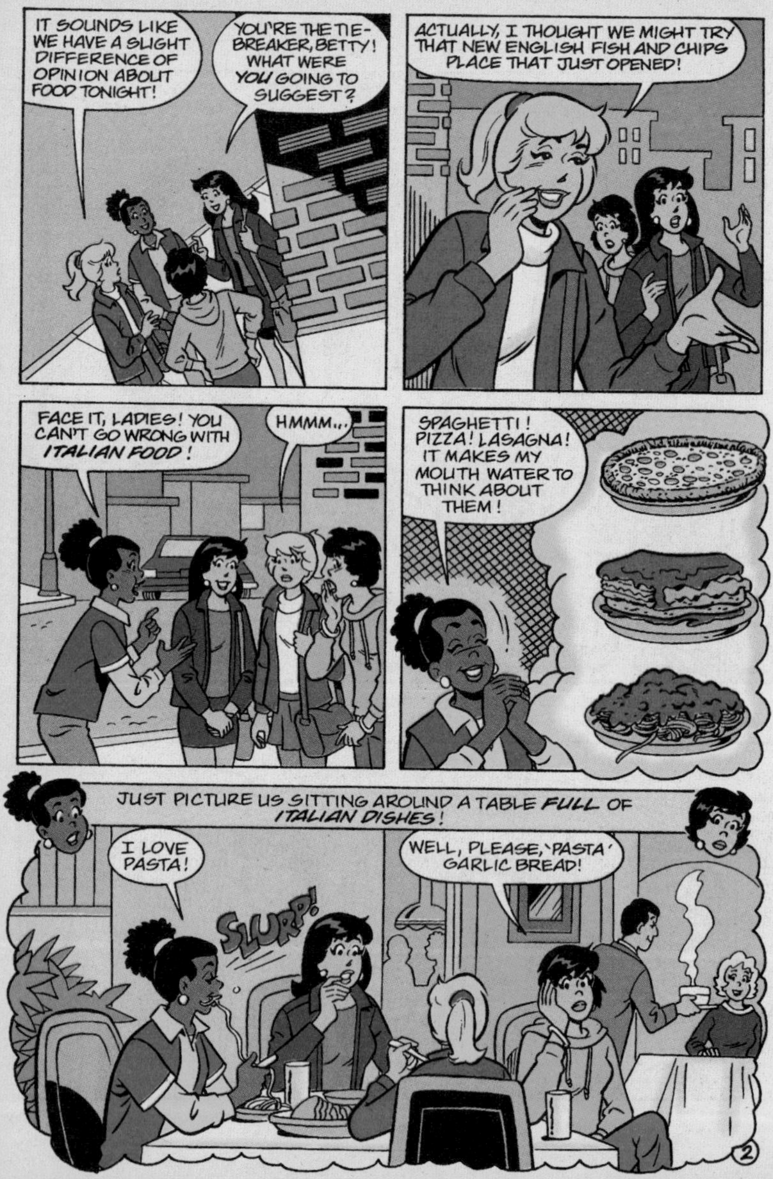
IT SOUNDS LIKE WE HAVE A SLIGHT DIFFERENCE OF OPINION ABOUT FOOD TONIGHT!
YOU'RE THE TIE-BREAKER, BETTY! WHAT WERE YOU GOING TO SUGGEST?
ACTUALLY, I THOUGHT WE MIGHT TRY THAT NEW ENGLISH FISH AND CHIPS PLACE THAT JUST OPENED!
FACE IT, LADIES! YOU CAN'T GO WRONG WITH ITALIAN FOOD!
HMMM...
SPAGHETTI! PIZZA! LASAGNA! IT MAKES MY MOUTH WATER TO THINK ABOUT THEM!
JUST PICTURE US SITTING AROUND A TABLE FULL OF ITALIAN DISHES!
I LOVE PASTA!
SLURP!
WELL, PLEASE, 'PASTA' GARLIC BREAD!
2

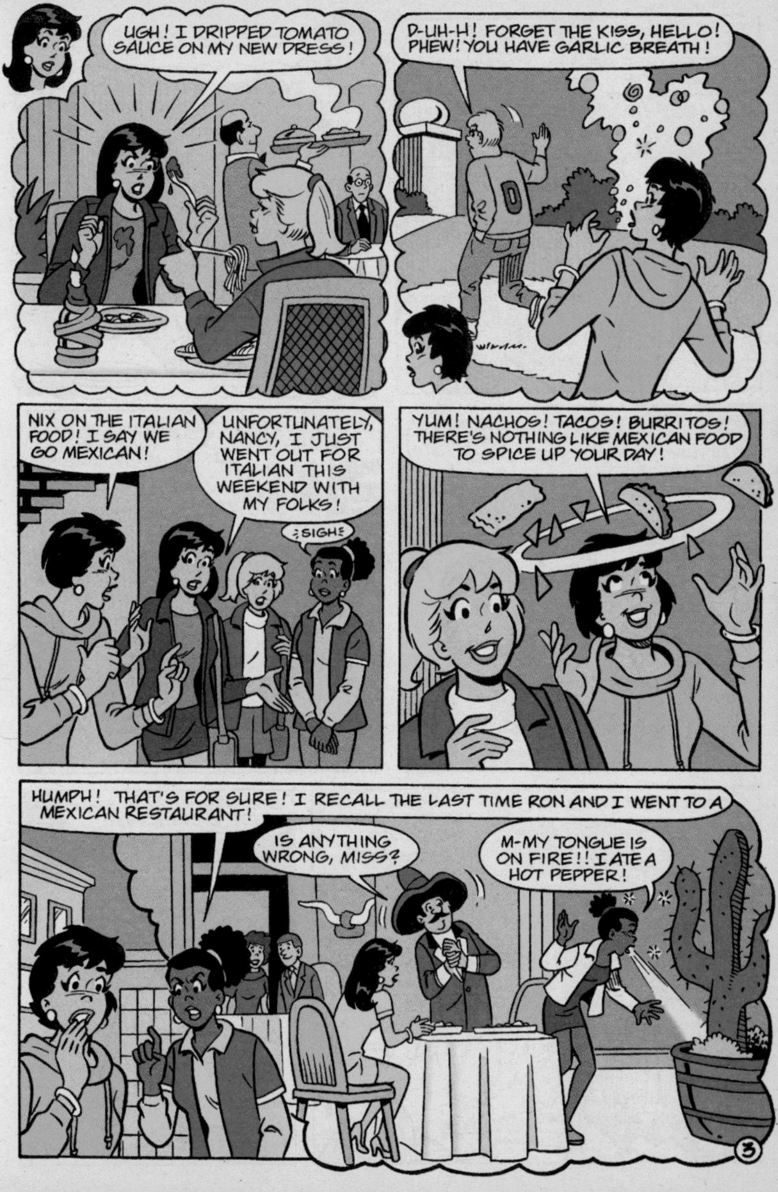
UGH! I DRIPPED TOMATO SAUCE ON MY NEW DRESS!
D-UH-H! FORGET THE KISS, HELLO! PHEW! YOU HAVE GARLIC BREATH!
NIX ON THE ITALIAN FOOD! I SAY WE GO MEXICAN!
UNFORTUNATELY, NANCY, I JUST WENT OUT FOR ITALIAN THIS WEEKEND WITH MY FOLKS!
SIGH
YUM! NACHOS! TACOS! BURRITOS! THERE'S NOTHING LIKE MEXICAN FOOD TO SPICE UP YOUR DAY!
HUMPH! THAT'S FOR SURE! I RECALL THE LAST TIME RON AND I WENT TO A MEXICAN RESTAURANT!
IS ANYTHING WRONG, MISS?
M-MY TONGUE IS ON FIRE!! I ATE A HOT PEPPER!
3

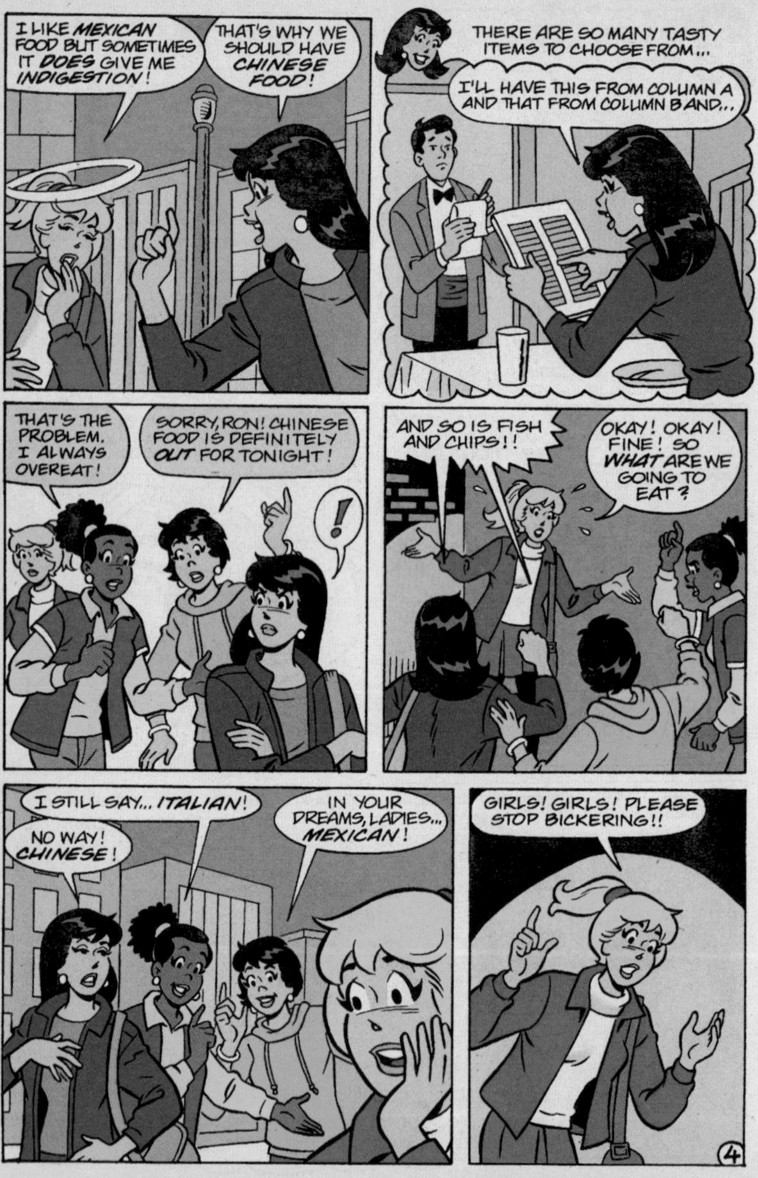
I LIKE MEXICAN FOOD BUT SOMETIMES IT DOES GIVE ME INDIGESTION!
THAT'S WHY WE SHOULD HAVE CHINESE FOOD!
THERE ARE SO MANY TASTY ITEMS TO CHOOSE FROM...
I'LL HAVE THIS FROM COLUMN A AND THAT FROM COLUMN B AND...
THAT'S THE PROBLEM. I ALWAYS OVEREAT!
SORRY, RON! CHINESE FOOD IS DEFINITELY OUT FOR TONIGHT!
!
AND SO IS FISH AND CHIPS!!
OKAY! OKAY! FINE! SO WHAT ARE WE GOING TO EAT?
I STILL SAY... ITALIAN!
NO WAY! CHINESE!
IN YOUR DREAMS, LADIES... MEXICAN!
GIRLS! GIRLS! PLEASE STOP BICKERING!!
4

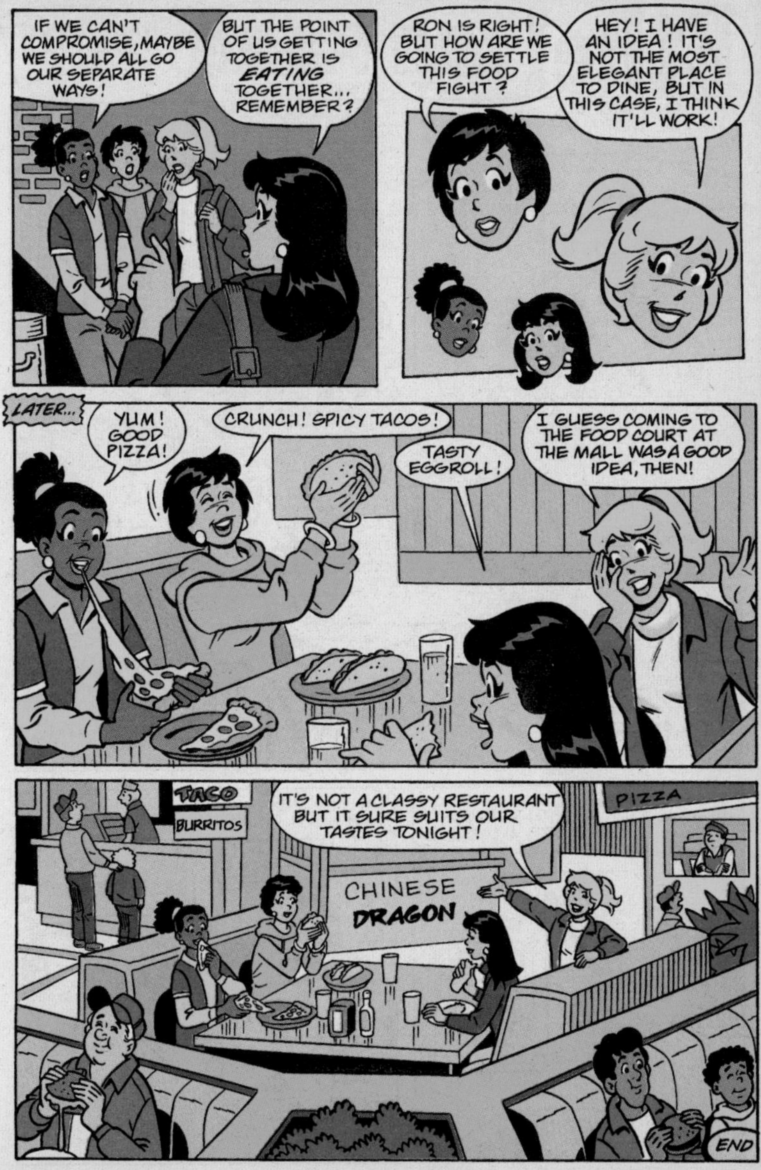
IF WE CAN'T COMPROMISE, MAYBE WE SHOULD ALL GO OUR SEPARATE WAYS!
BUT THE POINT OF US GETTING TOGETHER IS EATING TOGETHER... REMEMBER?
RON IS RIGHT! BUT HOW ARE WE GOING TO SETTLE THIS FOOD FIGHT?
HEY! I HAVE AN IDEA! IT'S NOT THE MOST ELEGANT PLACE TO DINE, BUT IN THIS CASE, I THINK IT'LL WORK!
LATER...
YUM! GOOD PIZZA!
CRUNCH! SPICY TACOS!
TASTY EGGROLL!
I GUESS COMING TO THE FOOD COURT AT THE MALL WAS A GOOD IDEA, THEN!
TACO
BURRITOS
IT'S NOT A CLASSY RESTAURANT BUT IT SURE SUITS OUR TASTES TONIGHT!
PIZZA
CHINESE DRAGON
END

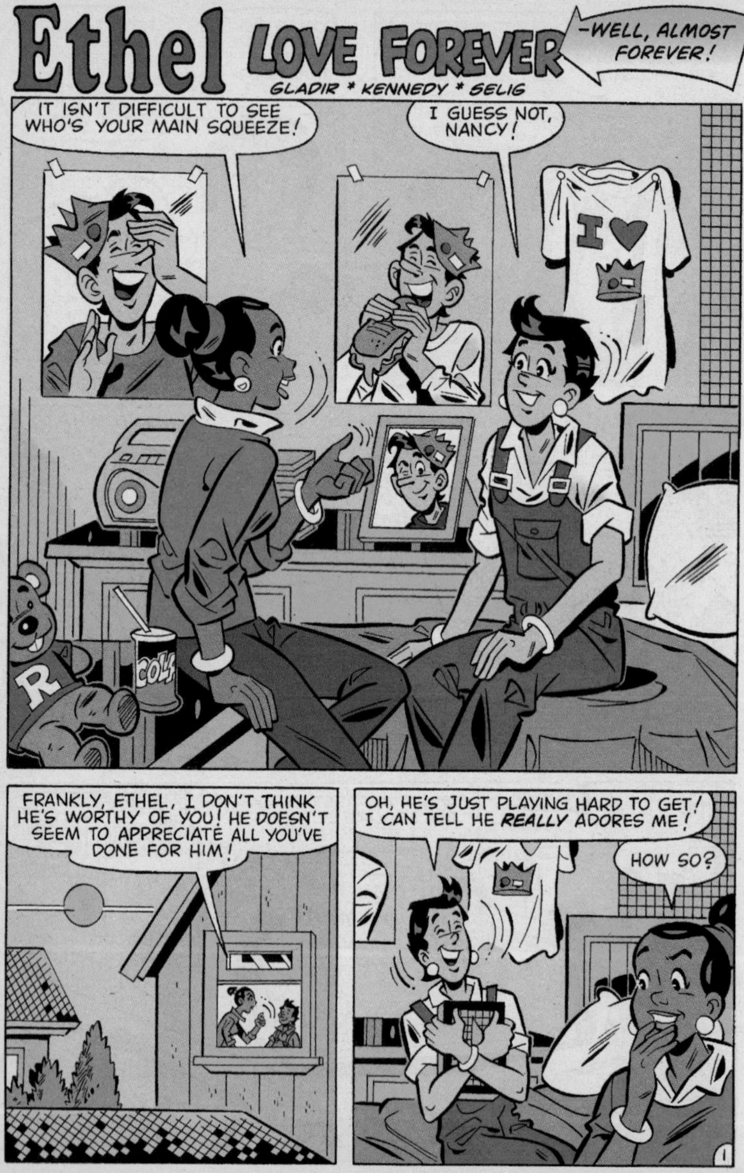
Ethel
LOVE FOREVER
-WELL, ALMOST FOREVER!
GLADIR * KENNEDY * SELIG
IT ISN'T DIFFICULT TO SEE WHO'S YOUR MAIN SQUEEZE!
I GUESS NOT, NANCY!
I ♥
COLA
R
FRANKLY, ETHEL, I DON'T THINK HE'S WORTHY OF YOU! HE DOESN'T SEEM TO APPRECIATE ALL YOU'VE DONE FOR HIM!
OH, HE'S JUST PLAYING HARD TO GET! I CAN TELL HE *REALLY* ADORES ME!
HOW SO?
1

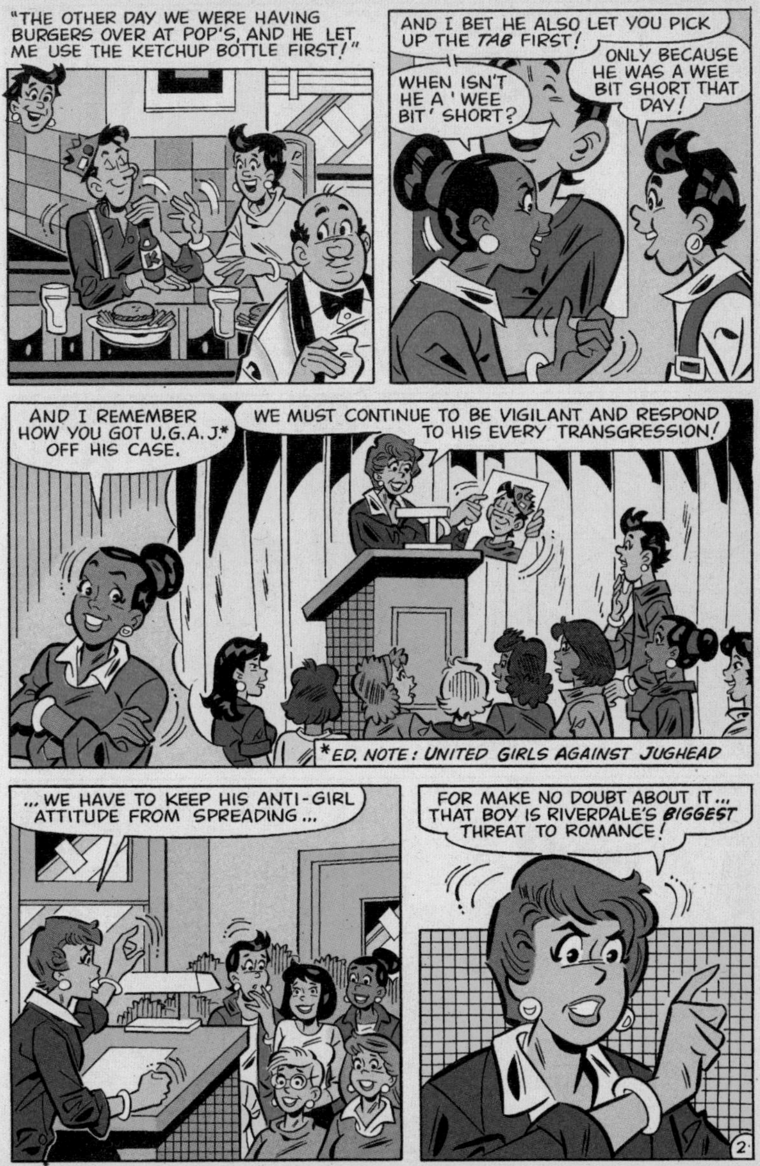

"THE OTHER DAY WE WERE HAVING BURGERS OVER AT POP'S, AND HE LET ME USE THE KETCHUP BOTTLE FIRST!"
AND I BET HE ALSO LET YOU PICK UP THE *TAB* FIRST!
WHEN ISN'T HE A 'WEE BIT' SHORT?
ONLY BECAUSE HE WAS A WEE BIT SHORT THAT DAY!
AND I REMEMBER HOW YOU GOT U.G.A.J.* OFF HIS CASE.
WE MUST CONTINUE TO BE VIGILANT AND RESPOND TO HIS EVERY TRANSGRESSION!
*ED. NOTE: UNITED GIRLS AGAINST JUGHEAD
...WE HAVE TO KEEP HIS ANTI-GIRL ATTITUDE FROM SPREADING...
FOR MAKE NO DOUBT ABOUT IT... THAT BOY IS RIVERDALE'S *BIGGEST* THREAT TO ROMANCE!
2

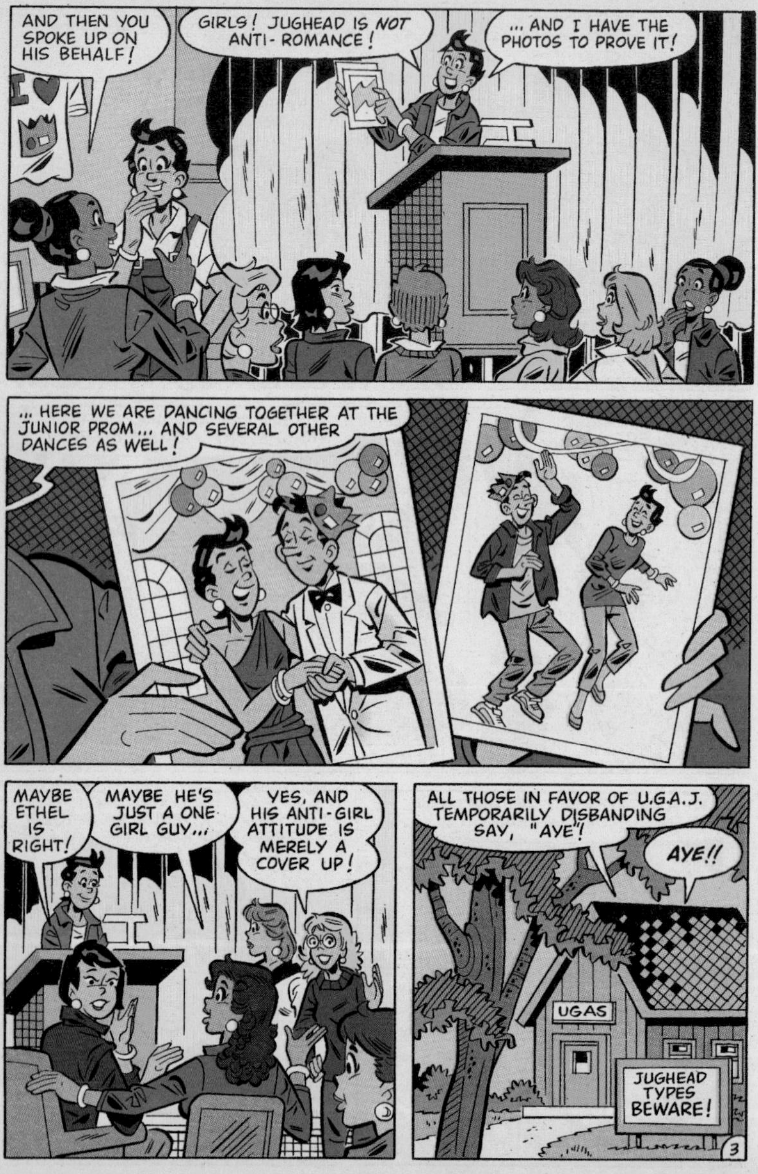
AND THEN YOU SPOKE UP ON HIS BEHALF!
GIRLS! JUGHEAD IS *NOT* ANTI-ROMANCE!
... AND I HAVE THE PHOTOS TO PROVE IT!
... HERE WE ARE DANCING TOGETHER AT THE JUNIOR PROM... AND SEVERAL OTHER DANCES AS WELL!
MAYBE ETHEL IS RIGHT!
MAYBE HE'S JUST A ONE GIRL GUY...
YES, AND HIS ANTI-GIRL ATTITUDE IS MERELY A COVER UP!
ALL THOSE IN FAVOR OF U.G.A.J. TEMPORARILY DISBANDING SAY, "AYE"!
AYE!!
UGAS
JUGHEAD TYPES BEWARE!
3

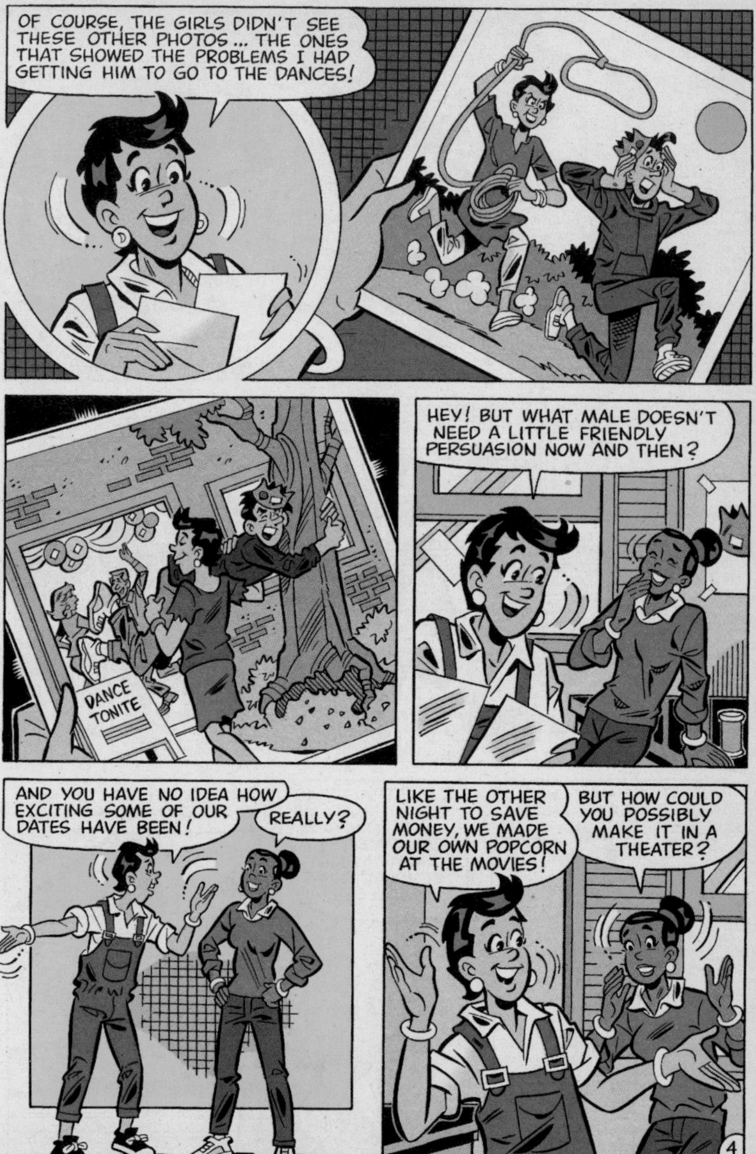
OF COURSE, THE GIRLS DIDN'T SEE THESE OTHER PHOTOS ... THE ONES THAT SHOWED THE PROBLEMS I HAD GETTING HIM TO GO TO THE DANCES!
DANCE TONITE
HEY! BUT WHAT MALE DOESN'T NEED A LITTLE FRIENDLY PERSUASION NOW AND THEN?
AND YOU HAVE NO IDEA HOW EXCITING SOME OF OUR DATES HAVE BEEN!
REALLY?
LIKE THE OTHER NIGHT TO SAVE MONEY, WE MADE OUR OWN POPCORN AT THE MOVIES!
BUT HOW COULD YOU POSSIBLY MAKE IT IN A THEATER?

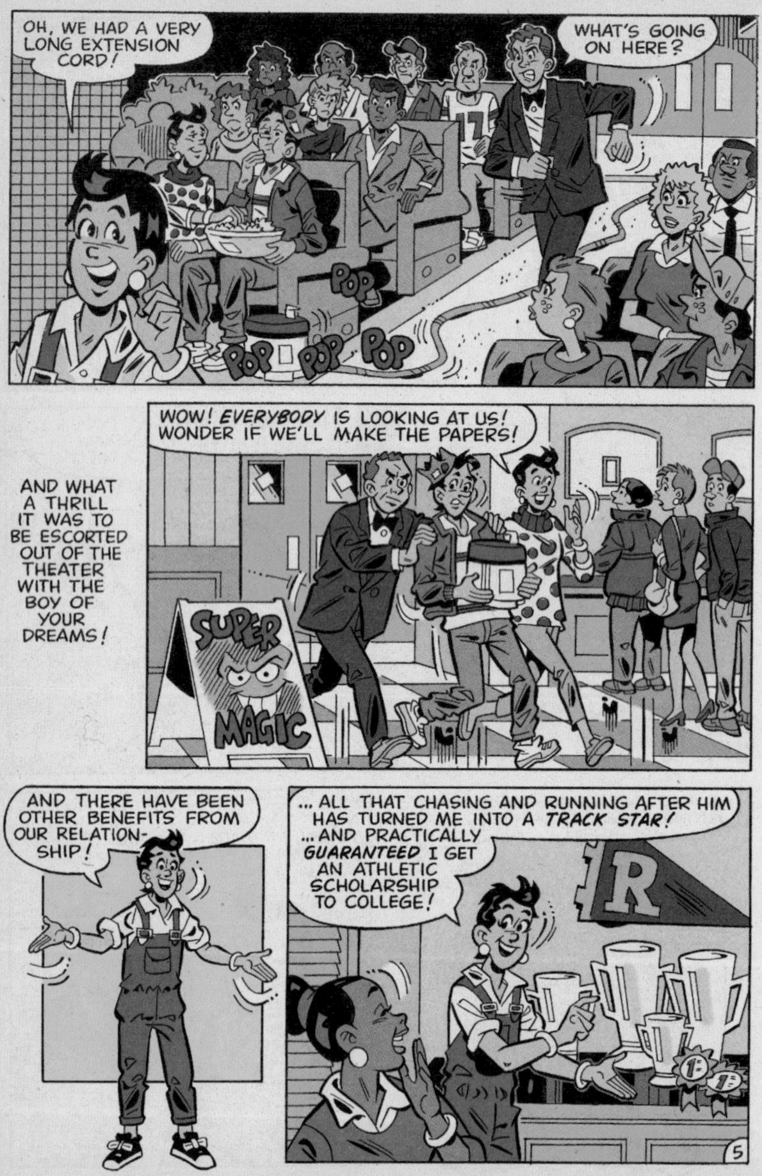

OH, WE HAD A VERY LONG EXTENSION CORD!
WHAT'S GOING ON HERE?
POP
POP
POP
POP
WOW! EVERYBODY IS LOOKING AT US! WONDER IF WE'LL MAKE THE PAPERS!
AND WHAT A THRILL IT WAS TO BE ESCORTED OUT OF THE THEATER WITH THE BOY OF YOUR DREAMS!
SUPER MAGIC
AND THERE HAVE BEEN OTHER BENEFITS FROM OUR RELATIONSHIP!
... ALL THAT CHASING AND RUNNING AFTER HIM HAS TURNED ME INTO A TRACK STAR! ... AND PRACTICALLY GUARANTEED I GET AN ATHLETIC SCHOLARSHIP TO COLLEGE!
R
5

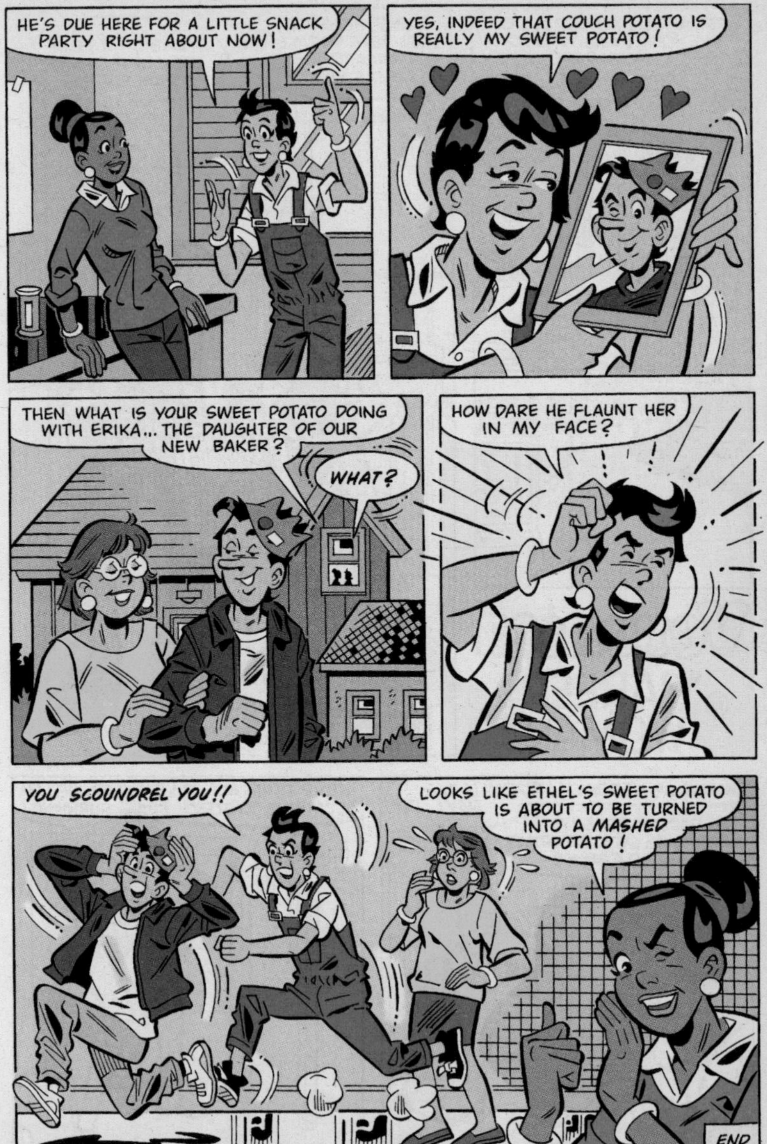
HE'S DUE HERE FOR A LITTLE SNACK PARTY RIGHT ABOUT NOW!
YES, INDEED THAT COUCH POTATO IS REALLY MY SWEET POTATO!
THEN WHAT IS YOUR SWEET POTATO DOING WITH ERIKA... THE DAUGHTER OF OUR NEW BAKER?
WHAT?
HOW DARE HE FLAUNT HER IN MY FACE?
YOU SCOUNDREL YOU!!
LOOKS LIKE ETHEL'S SWEET POTATO IS ABOUT TO BE TURNED INTO A MASHED POTATO!
END

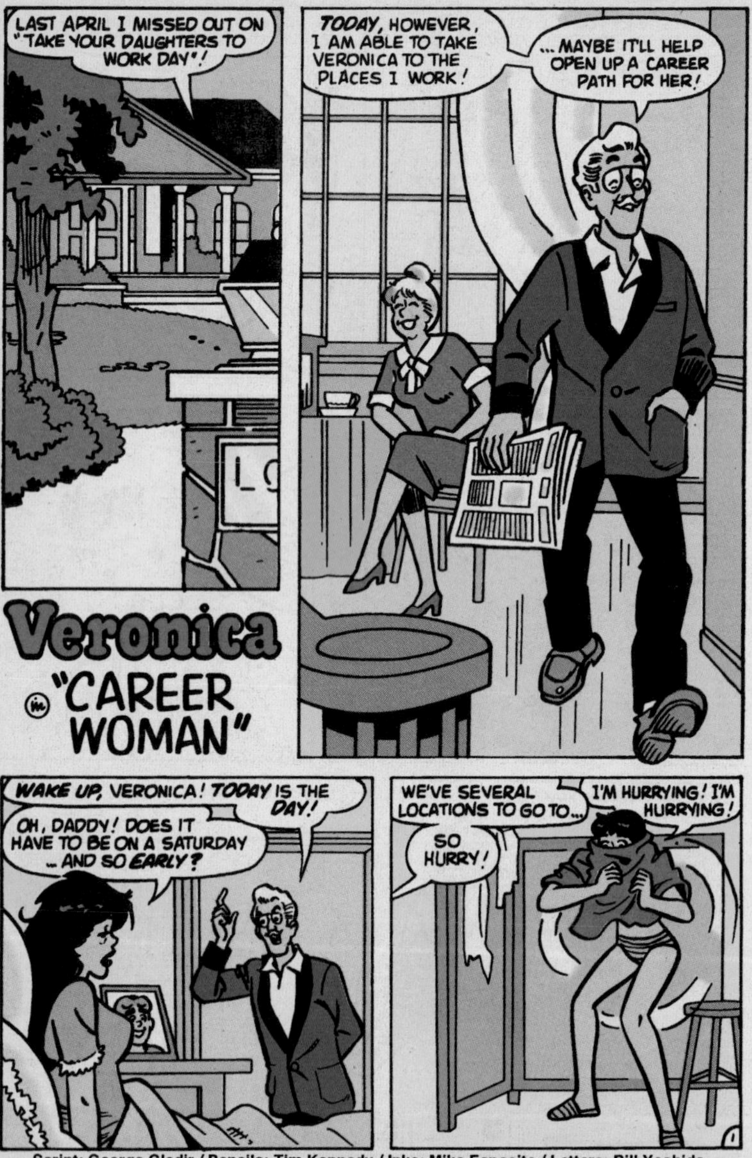
LAST APRIL I MISSED OUT ON "TAKE YOUR DAUGHTERS TO WORK DAY"!
TODAY, HOWEVER, I AM ABLE TO TAKE VERONICA TO THE PLACES I WORK!
...MAYBE IT'LL HELP OPEN UP A CAREER PATH FOR HER!
Veronica
in "CAREER WOMAN"
WAKE UP, VERONICA! TODAY IS THE DAY!
OH, DADDY! DOES IT HAVE TO BE ON A SATURDAY ...AND SO EARLY?
WE'VE SEVERAL LOCATIONS TO GO TO...
SO HURRY!
I'M HURRYING! I'M HURRYING!
1

Script: George Gladir / Pencils: Tim Kennedy / Inks: Mike Esposito / Letters: Bill Yoshida

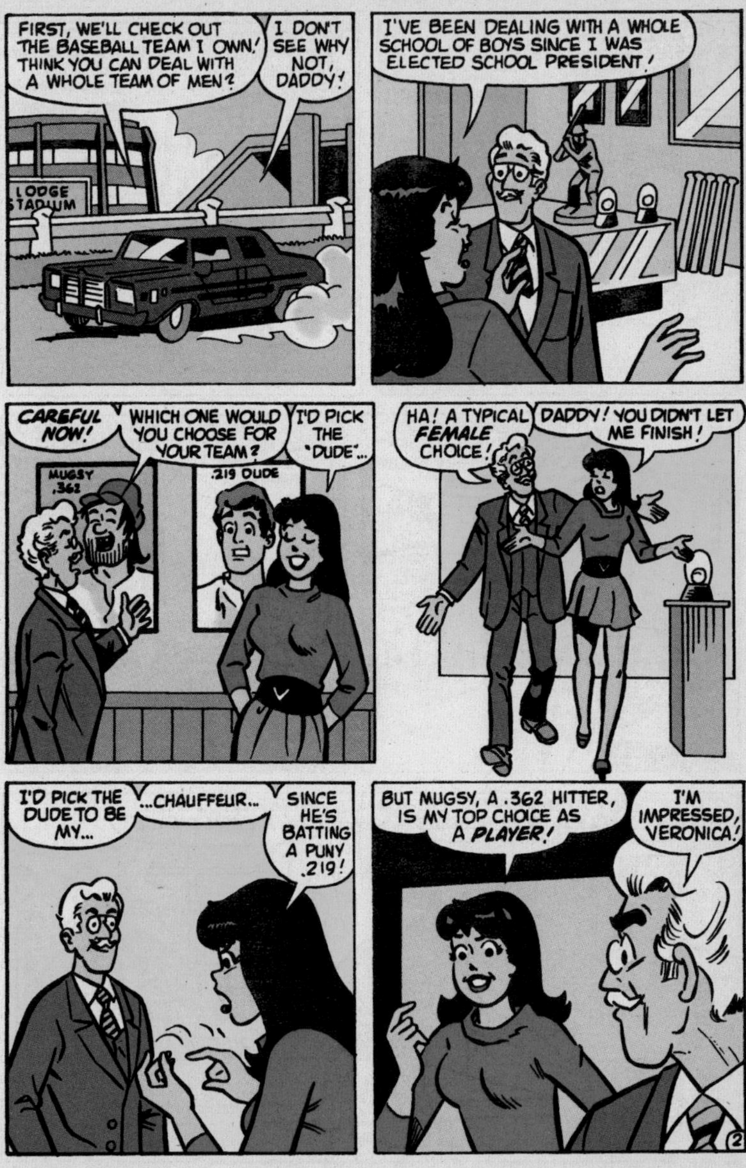
FIRST, WE'LL CHECK OUT THE BASEBALL TEAM I OWN! THINK YOU CAN DEAL WITH A WHOLE TEAM OF MEN?
I DON'T SEE WHY NOT, DADDY!
LODGE STADIUM
I'VE BEEN DEALING WITH A WHOLE SCHOOL OF BOYS SINCE I WAS ELECTED SCHOOL PRESIDENT!
CAREFUL NOW!
WHICH ONE WOULD YOU CHOOSE FOR YOUR TEAM?
I'D PICK THE "DUDE"...
MUGSY .362
.219 DUDE
HA! A TYPICAL FEMALE CHOICE!
DADDY! YOU DIDN'T LET ME FINISH!
I'D PICK THE DUDE TO BE MY...
...CHAUFFEUR...
SINCE HE'S BATTING A PUNY .219!
BUT MUGSY, A .362 HITTER, IS MY TOP CHOICE AS A PLAYER!
I'M IMPRESSED, VERONICA!
2

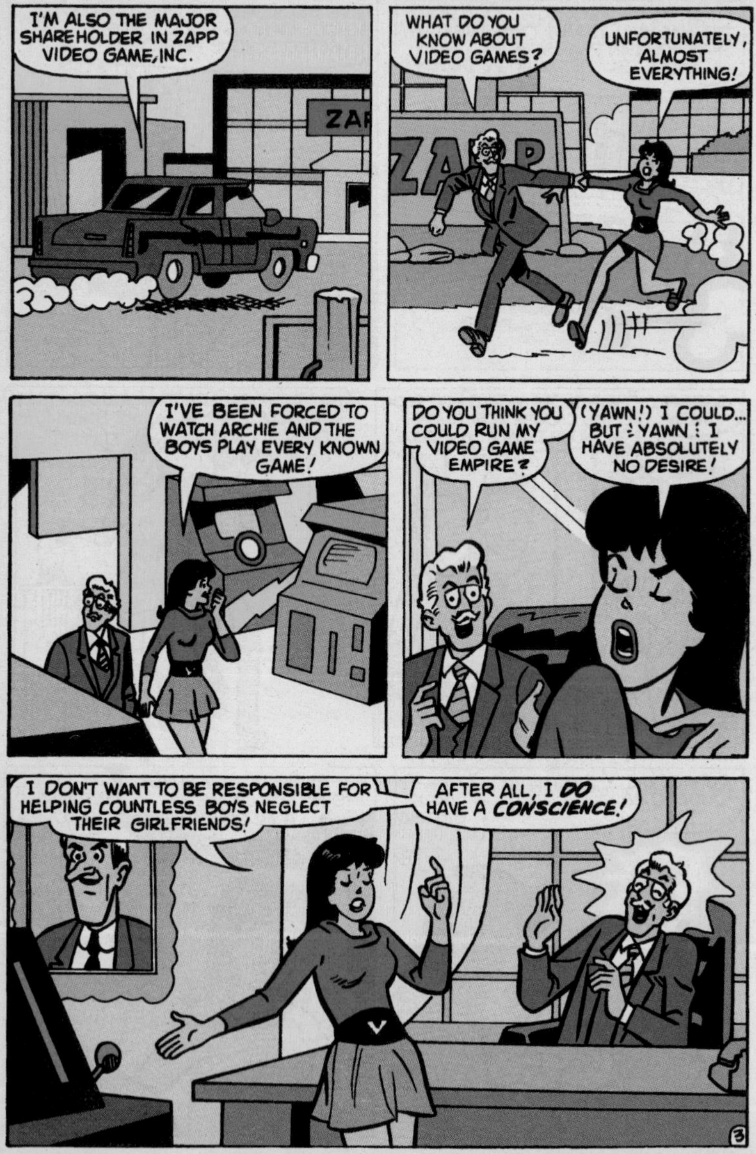

I'M ALSO THE MAJOR SHAREHOLDER IN ZAPP VIDEO GAME, INC.
ZAP
WHAT DO YOU KNOW ABOUT VIDEO GAMES?
UNFORTUNATELY, ALMOST EVERYTHING!
I'VE BEEN FORCED TO WATCH ARCHIE AND THE BOYS PLAY EVERY KNOWN GAME!
DO YOU THINK YOU COULD RUN MY VIDEO GAME EMPIRE?
(YAWN!) I COULD... BUT : YAWN : I HAVE ABSOLUTELY NO DESIRE!
I DON'T WANT TO BE RESPONSIBLE FOR HELPING COUNTLESS BOYS NEGLECT THEIR GIRLFRIENDS!
AFTER ALL, I *DO* HAVE A ***CONSCIENCE***!
3

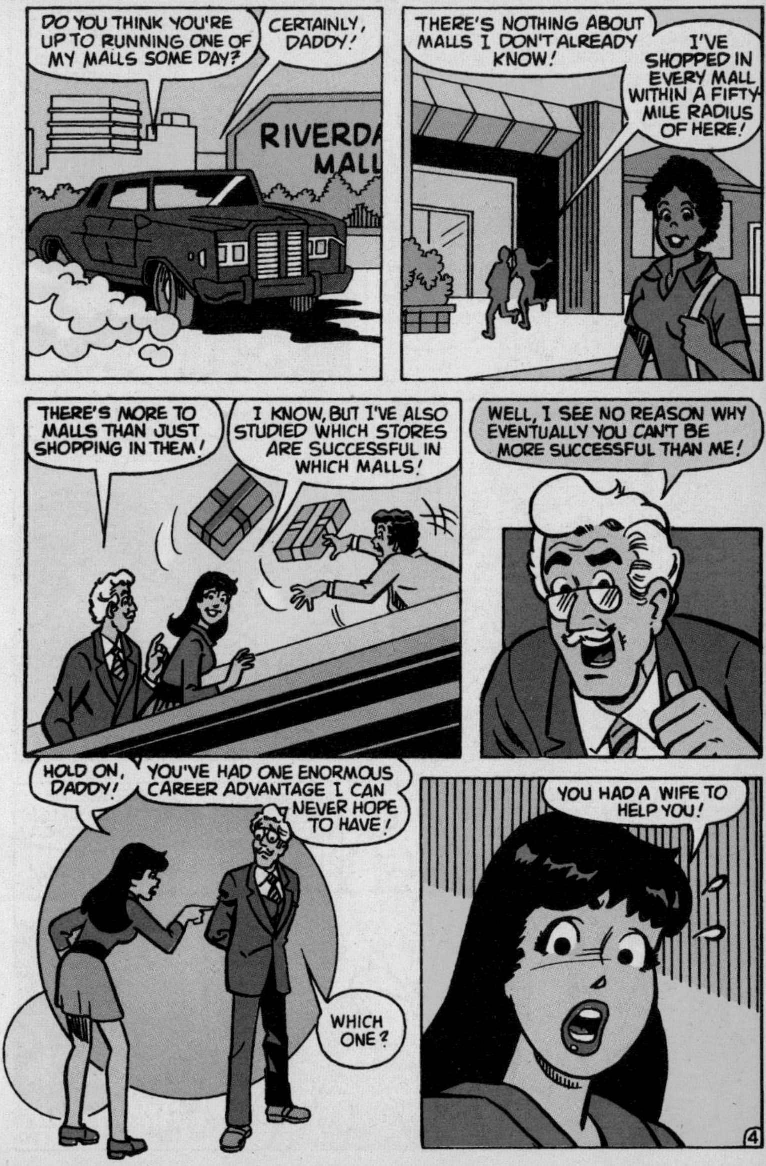
DO YOU THINK YOU'RE UP TO RUNNING ONE OF MY MALLS SOME DAY?
CERTAINLY, DADDY!
RIVERDA MALL
THERE'S NOTHING ABOUT MALLS I DON'T ALREADY KNOW!
I'VE SHOPPED IN EVERY MALL WITHIN A FIFTY-MILE RADIUS OF HERE!
THERE'S MORE TO MALLS THAN JUST SHOPPING IN THEM!
I KNOW, BUT I'VE ALSO STUDIED WHICH STORES ARE SUCCESSFUL IN WHICH MALLS!
WELL, I SEE NO REASON WHY EVENTUALLY YOU CAN'T BE MORE SUCCESSFUL THAN ME!
HOLD ON, DADDY!
YOU'VE HAD ONE ENORMOUS CAREER ADVANTAGE I CAN NEVER HOPE TO HAVE!
WHICH ONE?
YOU HAD A WIFE TO HELP YOU!
4

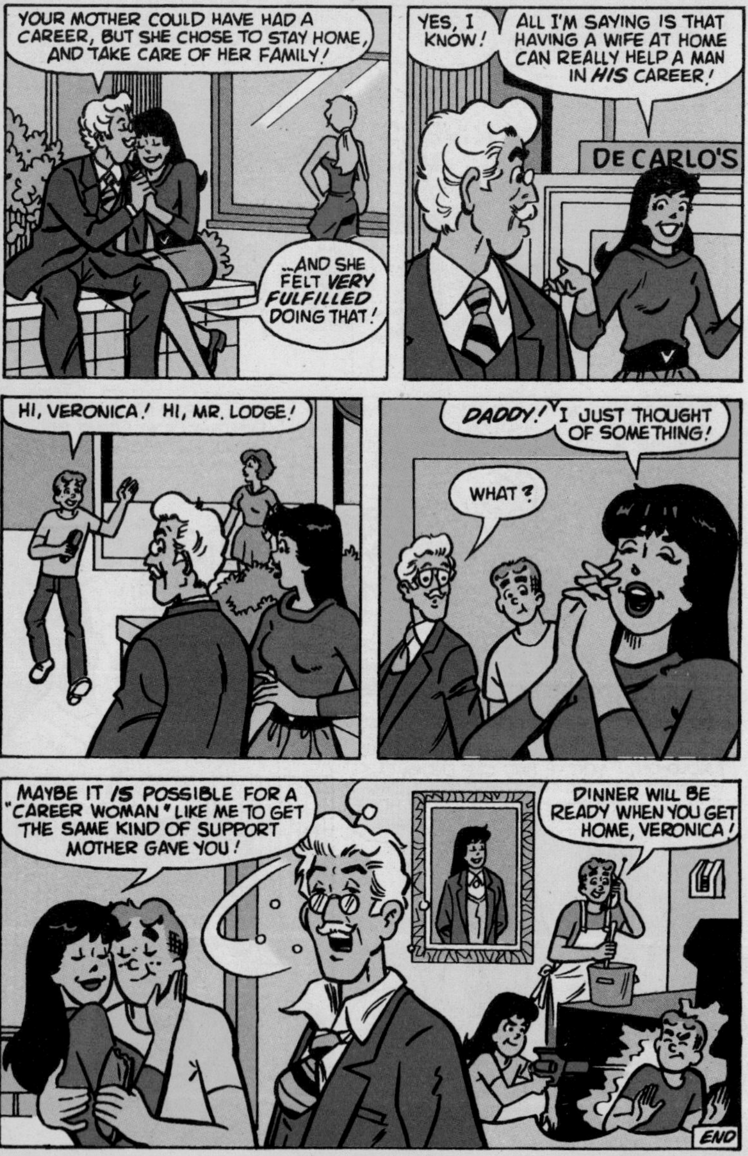

YOUR MOTHER COULD HAVE HAD A CAREER, BUT SHE CHOSE TO STAY HOME, AND TAKE CARE OF HER FAMILY!
...AND SHE FELT VERY FULFILLED DOING THAT!
YES, I KNOW!
ALL I'M SAYING IS THAT HAVING A WIFE AT HOME CAN REALLY HELP A MAN IN HIS CAREER!
DE CARLO'S
HI, VERONICA! HI, MR. LODGE!
DADDY!
I JUST THOUGHT OF SOMETHING!
WHAT?
MAYBE IT IS POSSIBLE FOR A "CAREER WOMAN" LIKE ME TO GET THE SAME KIND OF SUPPORT MOTHER GAVE YOU!
DINNER WILL BE READY WHEN YOU GET HOME, VERONICA!
END

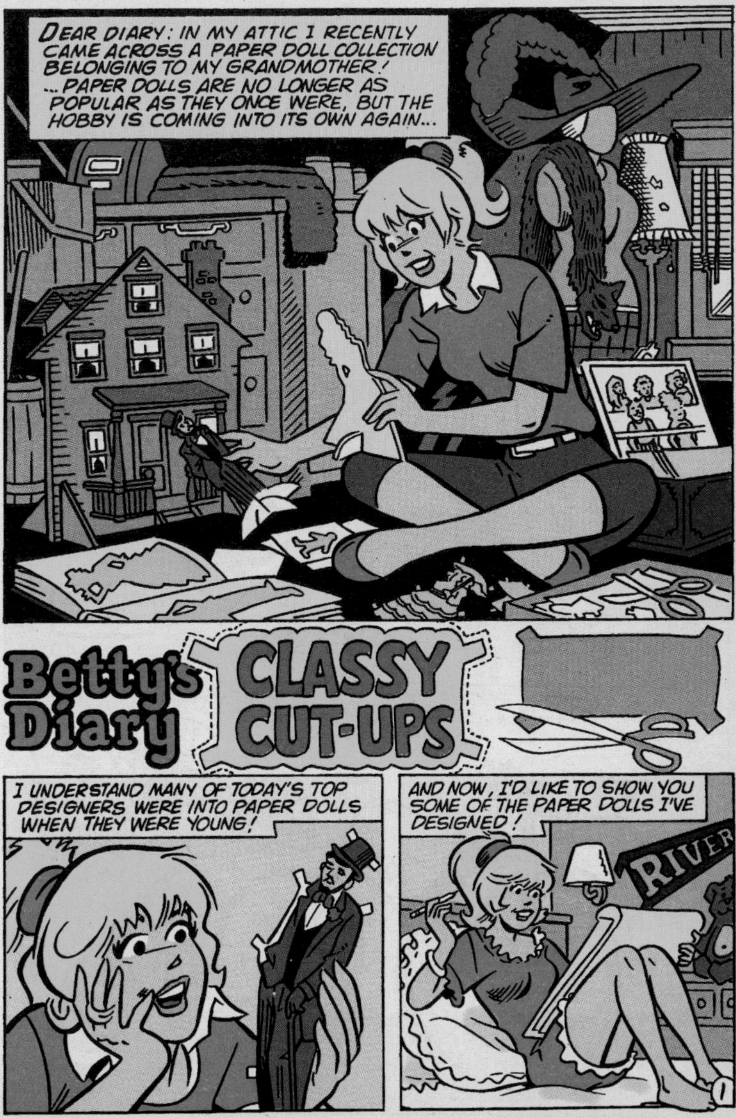
DEAR DIARY: IN MY ATTIC I RECENTLY CAME ACROSS A PAPER DOLL COLLECTION BELONGING TO MY GRANDMOTHER! ...PAPER DOLLS ARE NO LONGER AS POPULAR AS THEY ONCE WERE, BUT THE HOBBY IS COMING INTO ITS OWN AGAIN...
Betty's Diary
CLASSY CUT-UPS
I UNDERSTAND MANY OF TODAY'S TOP DESIGNERS WERE INTO PAPER DOLLS WHEN THEY WERE YOUNG!
AND NOW, I'D LIKE TO SHOW YOU SOME OF THE PAPER DOLLS I'VE DESIGNED!
RIVER
1

Script: Kathleen Webb / Pencils: Doug Crane / Inks: Rudy Lapick / Letters: Bill Yoshida / Colors: Barry Grossman

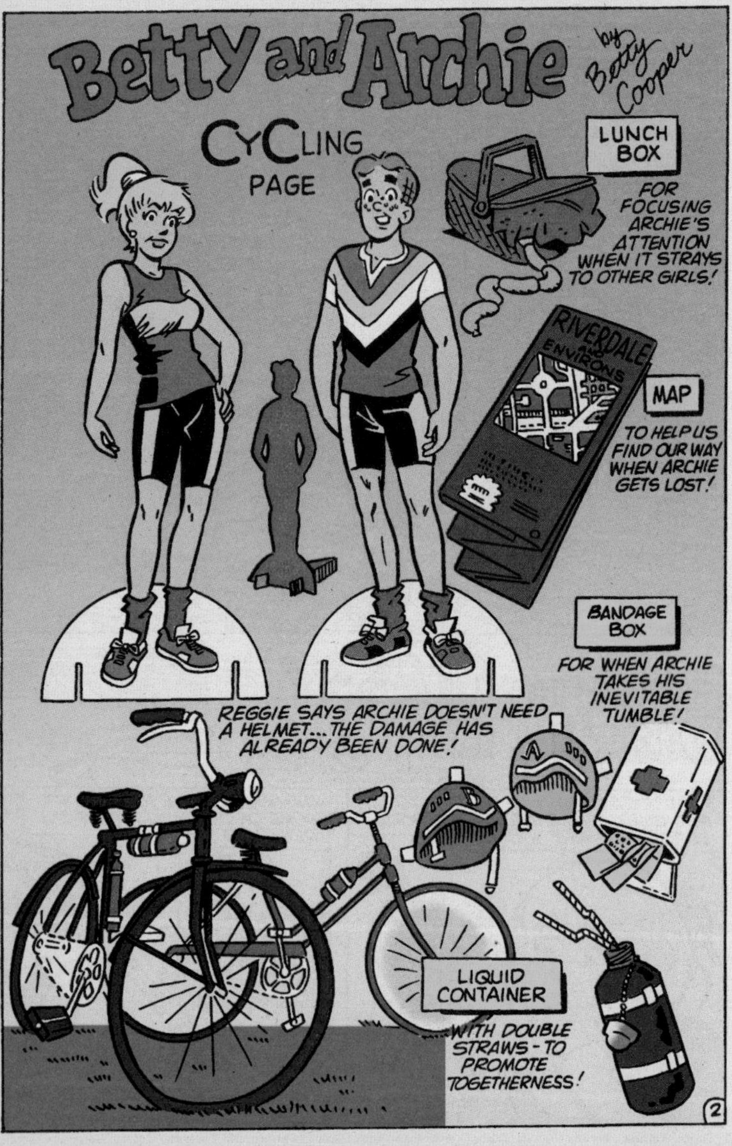

Betty and Archie
by Betty Cooper
CyCLING PAGE
LUNCH BOX
FOR FOCUSING ARCHIE'S ATTENTION WHEN IT STRAYS TO OTHER GIRLS!
RIVERDALE AND ENVIRONS
MAP
TO HELP US FIND OUR WAY WHEN ARCHIE GETS LOST!
BANDAGE BOX
FOR WHEN ARCHIE TAKES HIS INEVITABLE TUMBLE!
REGGIE SAYS ARCHIE DOESN'T NEED A HELMET... THE DAMAGE HAS ALREADY BEEN DONE!
LIQUID CONTAINER
WITH DOUBLE STRAWS - TO PROMOTE TOGETHERNESS!
2

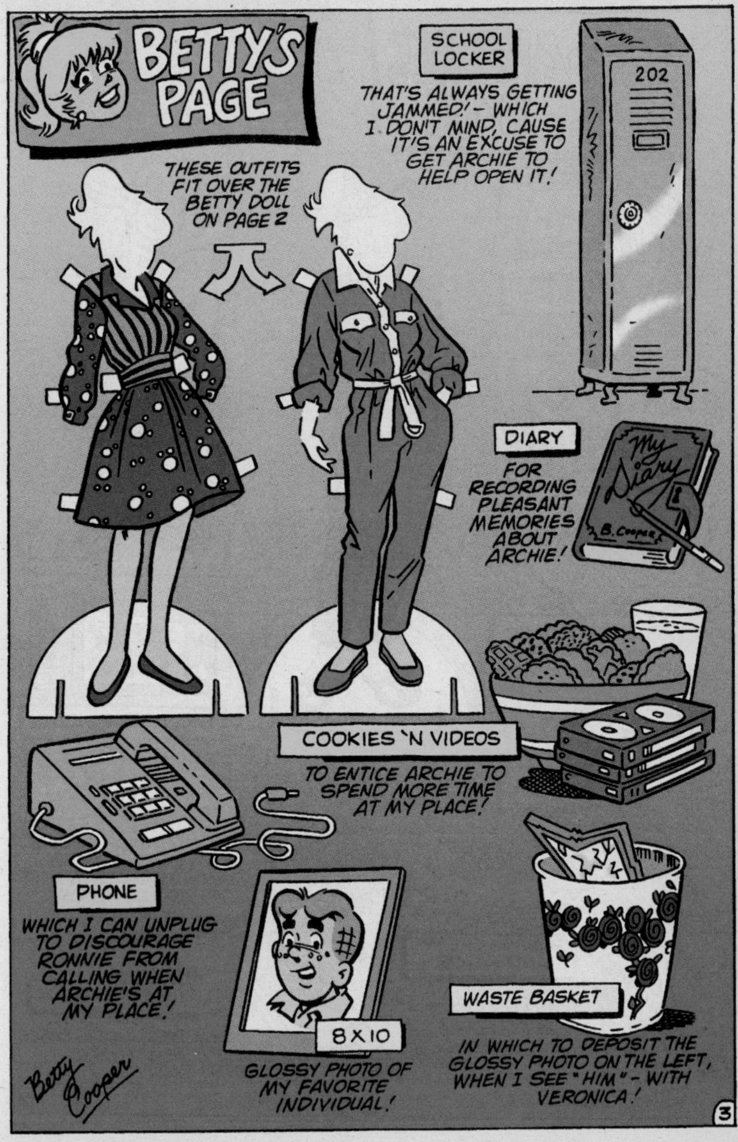

BETTY'S PAGE
SCHOOL LOCKER
THAT'S ALWAYS GETTING JAMMED! – WHICH I DON'T MIND, CAUSE IT'S AN EXCUSE TO GET ARCHIE TO HELP OPEN IT!
202
THESE OUTFITS FIT OVER THE BETTY DOLL ON PAGE 2
DIARY
FOR RECORDING PLEASANT MEMORIES ABOUT ARCHIE!
My Diary
B. Cooper
COOKIES 'N VIDEOS
TO ENTICE ARCHIE TO SPEND MORE TIME AT MY PLACE!
PHONE
WHICH I CAN UNPLUG TO DISCOURAGE RONNIE FROM CALLING WHEN ARCHIE'S AT MY PLACE!
8 X 10
GLOSSY PHOTO OF MY FAVORITE INDIVIDUAL!
WASTE BASKET
IN WHICH TO DEPOSIT THE GLOSSY PHOTO ON THE LEFT, WHEN I SEE "HIM" – WITH VERONICA!
Betty Cooper
3

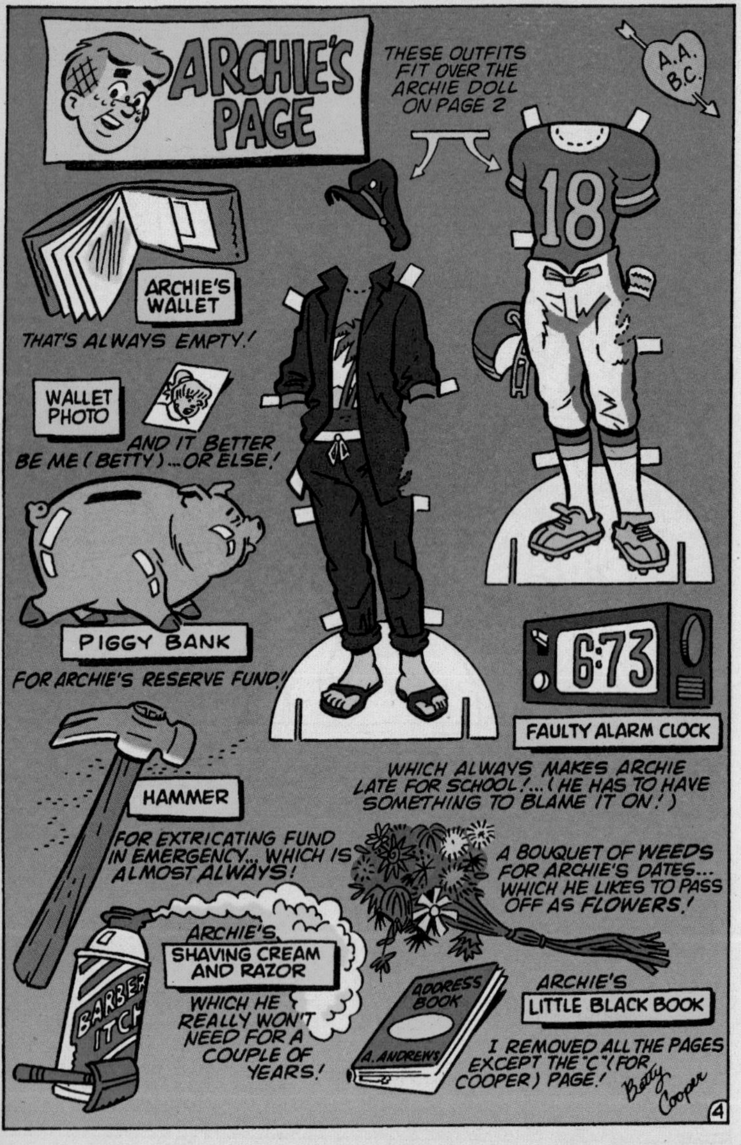

ARCHIE'S PAGE
THESE OUTFITS FIT OVER THE ARCHIE DOLL ON PAGE 2
A.A. B.C.
18
ARCHIE'S WALLET
THAT'S ALWAYS EMPTY!
WALLET PHOTO
AND IT BETTER BE ME (BETTY)...OR ELSE!
PIGGY BANK
FOR ARCHIE'S RESERVE FUND!
6:73
FAULTY ALARM CLOCK
WHICH ALWAYS MAKES ARCHIE LATE FOR SCHOOL!...(HE HAS TO HAVE SOMETHING TO BLAME IT ON!)
HAMMER
FOR EXTRICATING FUND IN EMERGENCY... WHICH IS ALMOST ALWAYS!
A BOUQUET OF WEEDS FOR ARCHIE'S DATES... WHICH HE LIKES TO PASS OFF AS FLOWERS!
ARCHIE'S
SHAVING CREAM AND RAZOR
WHICH HE REALLY WON'T NEED FOR A COUPLE OF YEARS!
BARBER ITCH
ADDRESS BOOK
A. ANDREWS
ARCHIE'S
LITTLE BLACK BOOK
I REMOVED ALL THE PAGES EXCEPT THE "C" (FOR COOPER) PAGE!
Betty Cooper

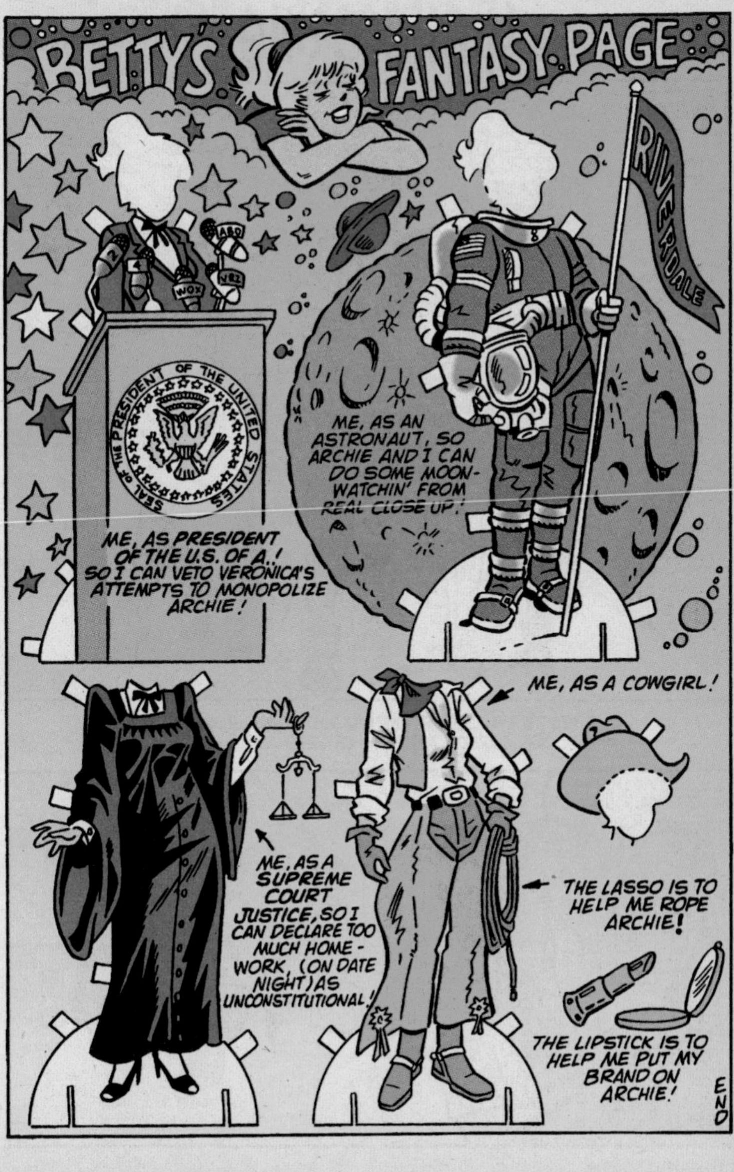
BETTY'S FANTASY PAGE
ME, AS PRESIDENT OF THE U.S. OF A.! SO I CAN VETO VERONICA'S ATTEMPTS TO MONOPOLIZE ARCHIE!
SEAL OF THE PRESIDENT OF THE UNITED STATES
ME, AS AN ASTRONAUT, SO ARCHIE AND I CAN DO SOME MOON-WATCHIN' FROM REAL CLOSE UP!
RIVERDALE
ME, AS A SUPREME COURT JUSTICE, SO I CAN DECLARE TOO MUCH HOME-WORK, (ON DATE NIGHT) AS UNCONSTITUTIONAL!
ME, AS A COWGIRL!
THE LASSO IS TO HELP ME ROPE ARCHIE!
THE LIPSTICK IS TO HELP ME PUT MY BRAND ON ARCHIE!
END

RAJ PATEL™ IN HIGH SCORING HIJINKS

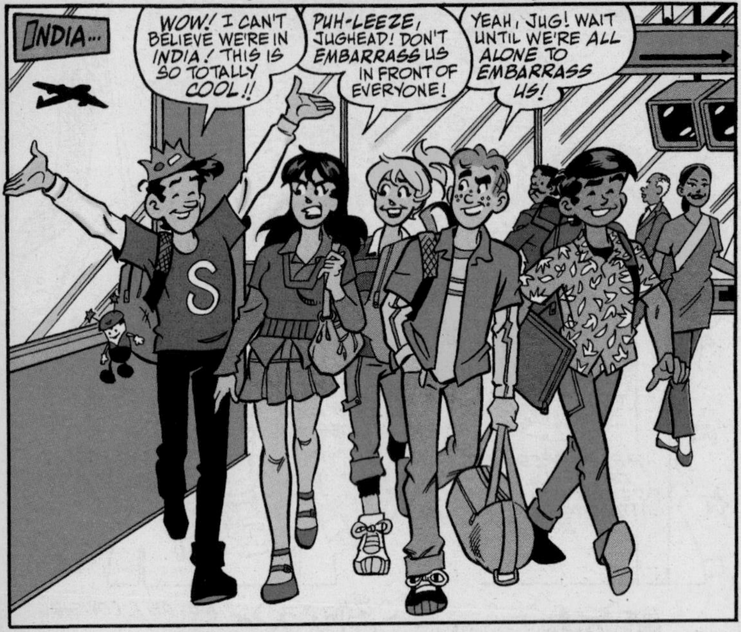
INDIA...
WOW! I CAN'T BELIEVE WE'RE IN INDIA! THIS IS SO TOTALLY COOL!!
PUH-LEEZE, JUGHEAD! DON'T EMBARRASS US IN FRONT OF EVERYONE!
YEAH, JUG! WAIT UNTIL WE'RE ALL ALONE TO EMBARRASS US!
S

SCRIPT & PENCILS: FERNANDO RUIZ INKS: BOB SMITH
COLORS: CARLOS ANTUNES LETTERS: JACK MORELLI

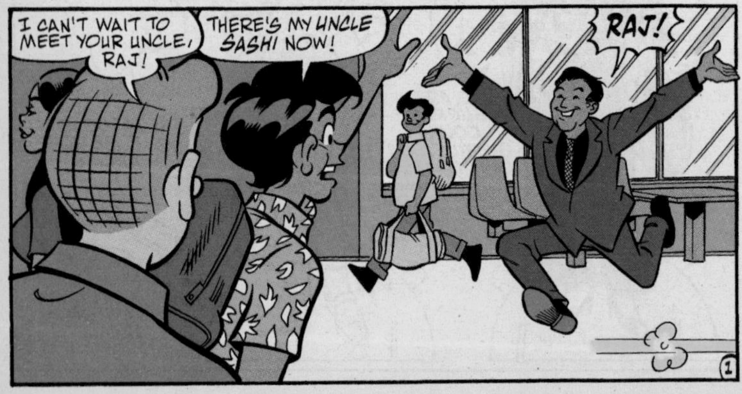
I CAN'T WAIT TO MEET YOUR UNCLE, RAJ!
THERE'S MY UNCLE SASHI NOW!
RAJ!
1

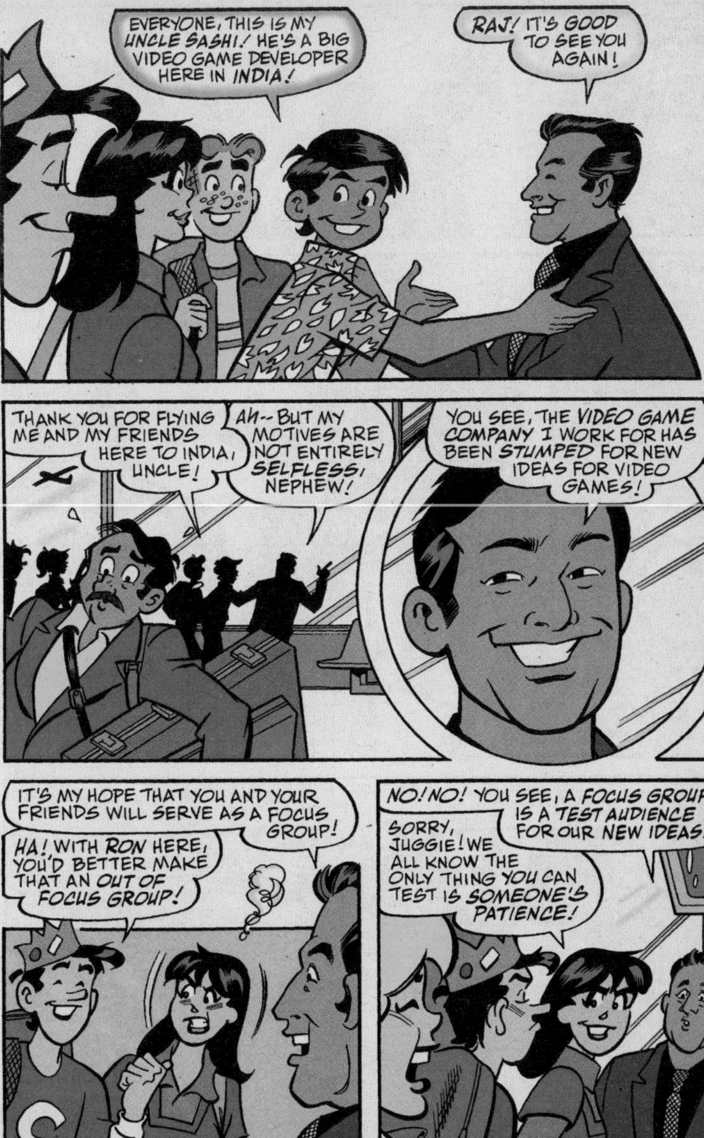
EVERYONE, THIS IS MY UNCLE SASHI! HE'S A BIG VIDEO GAME DEVELOPER HERE IN INDIA!
RAJ! IT'S GOOD TO SEE YOU AGAIN!
THANK YOU FOR FLYING ME AND MY FRIENDS HERE TO INDIA, UNCLE!
AH-- BUT MY MOTIVES ARE NOT ENTIRELY SELFLESS, NEPHEW!
YOU SEE, THE VIDEO GAME COMPANY I WORK FOR HAS BEEN STUMPED FOR NEW IDEAS FOR VIDEO GAMES!
IT'S MY HOPE THAT YOU AND YOUR FRIENDS WILL SERVE AS A FOCUS GROUP!
HA! WITH RON HERE, YOU'D BETTER MAKE THAT AN OUT OF FOCUS GROUP!
NO! NO! YOU SEE, A FOCUS GROUP IS A TEST AUDIENCE FOR OUR NEW IDEAS!
SORRY, JUGGIE! WE ALL KNOW THE ONLY THING YOU CAN TEST IS SOMEONE'S PATIENCE!
2

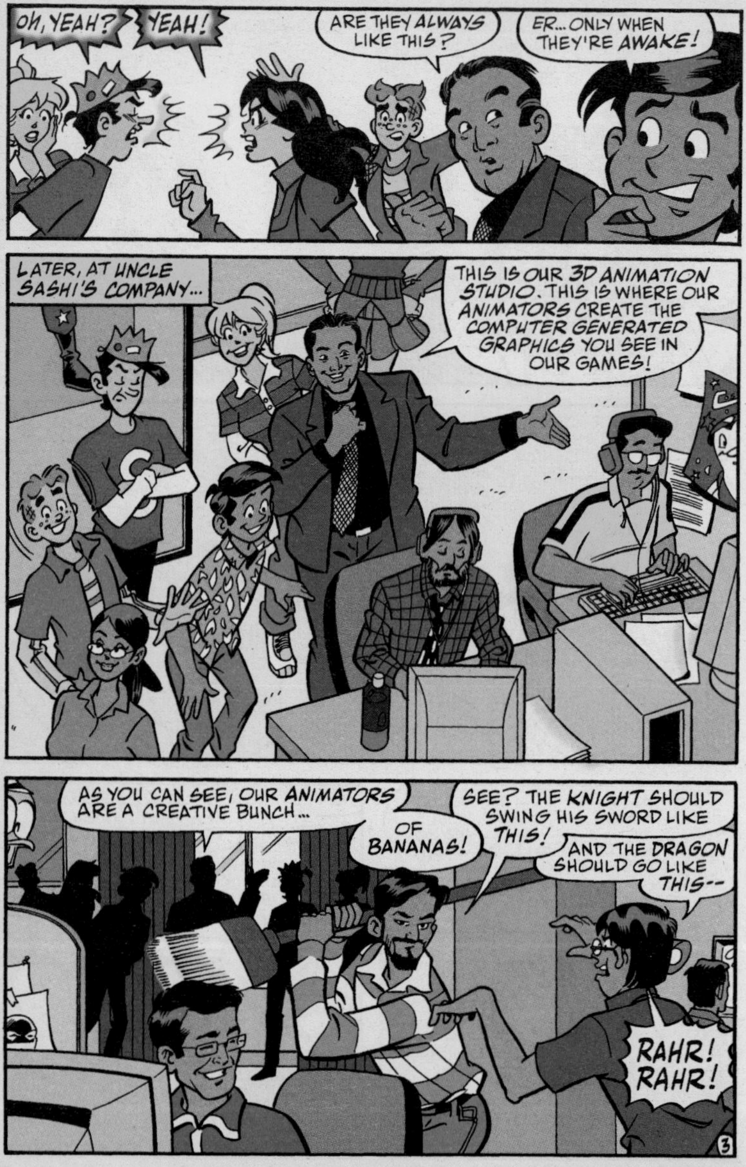
OH, YEAH?
YEAH!
ARE THEY ALWAYS LIKE THIS?
ER... ONLY WHEN THEY'RE AWAKE!
LATER, AT UNCLE SASHI'S COMPANY...
THIS IS OUR 3D ANIMATION STUDIO. THIS IS WHERE OUR ANIMATORS CREATE THE COMPUTER GENERATED GRAPHICS YOU SEE IN OUR GAMES!
AS YOU CAN SEE, OUR ANIMATORS ARE A CREATIVE BUNCH...
OF BANANAS!
SEE? THE KNIGHT SHOULD SWING HIS SWORD LIKE THIS!
AND THE DRAGON SHOULD GO LIKE THIS--
RAHR! RAHR!
3

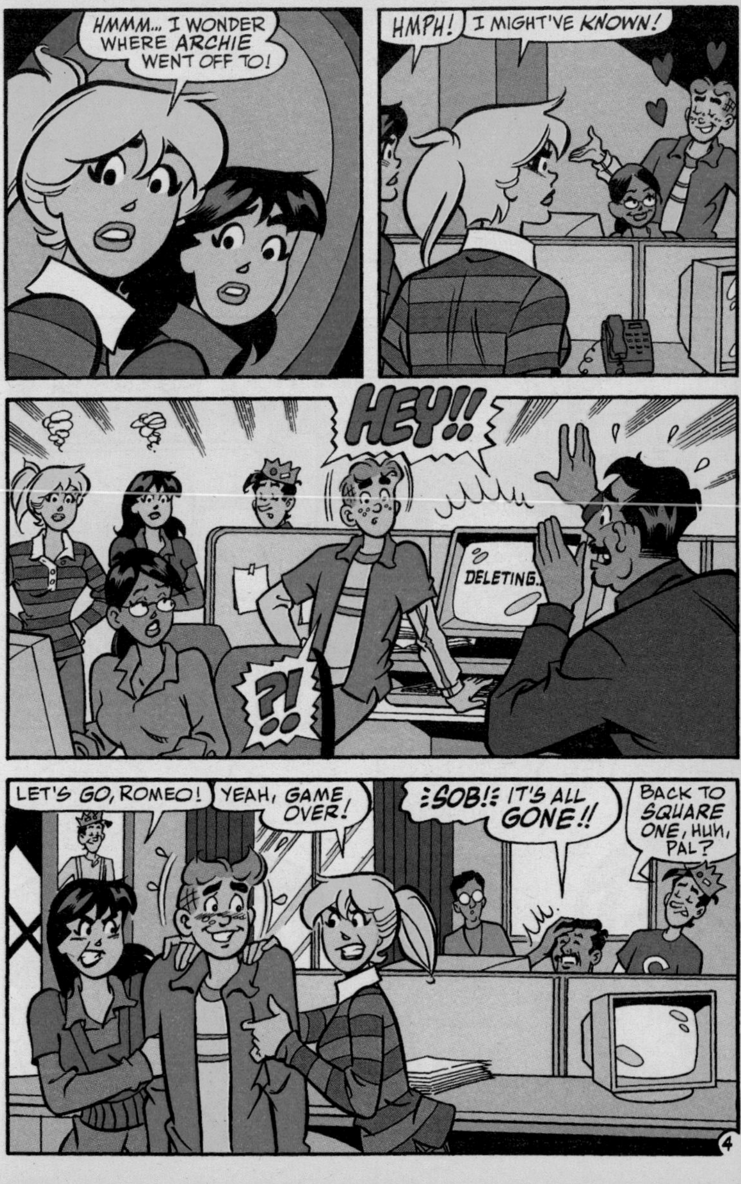
HMMM... I WONDER WHERE ARCHIE WENT OFF TO!
HMPH!
I MIGHT'VE KNOWN!
HEY!!
DELETING...
?!
LET'S GO, ROMEO!
YEAH, GAME OVER!
SOB! IT'S ALL GONE!!
BACK TO SQUARE ONE, HUH, PAL?

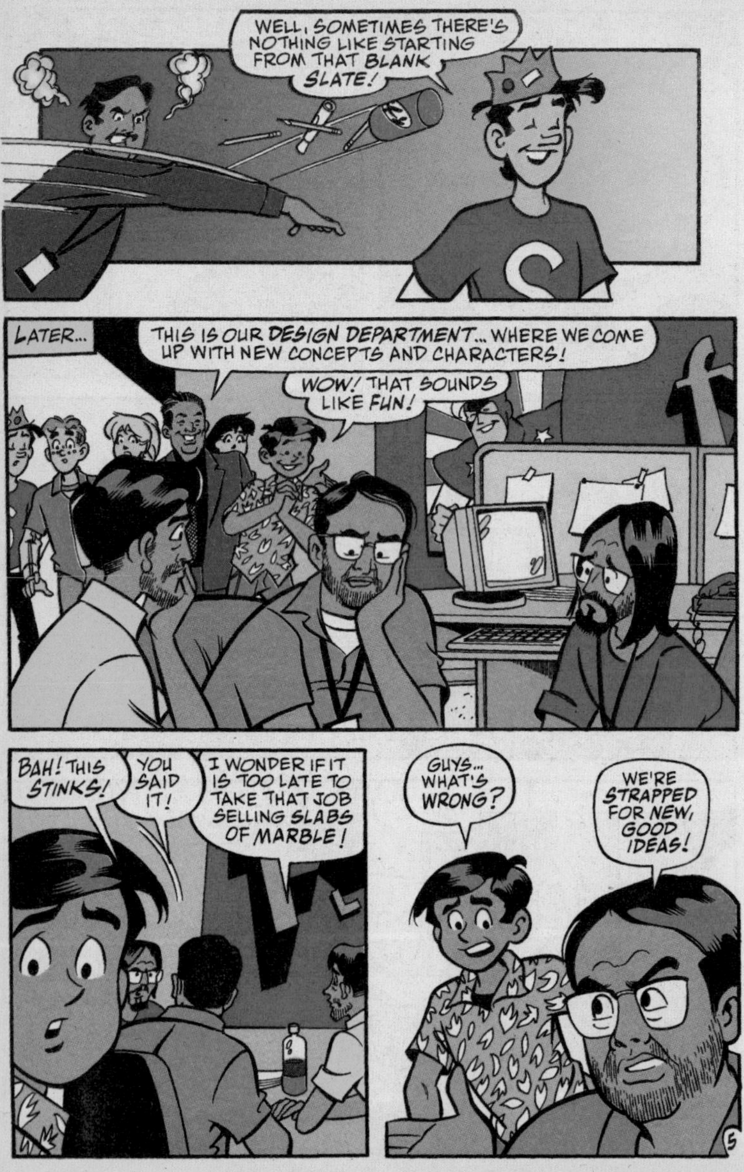

WELL, SOMETIMES THERE'S NOTHING LIKE STARTING FROM THAT BLANK SLATE!
LATER...
THIS IS OUR DESIGN DEPARTMENT... WHERE WE COME UP WITH NEW CONCEPTS AND CHARACTERS!
WOW! THAT SOUNDS LIKE FUN!
BAH! THIS STINKS!
YOU SAID IT!
I WONDER IF IT IS TOO LATE TO TAKE THAT JOB SELLING SLABS OF MARBLE!
GUYS... WHAT'S WRONG?
WE'RE STRAPPED FOR NEW, GOOD IDEAS!
5

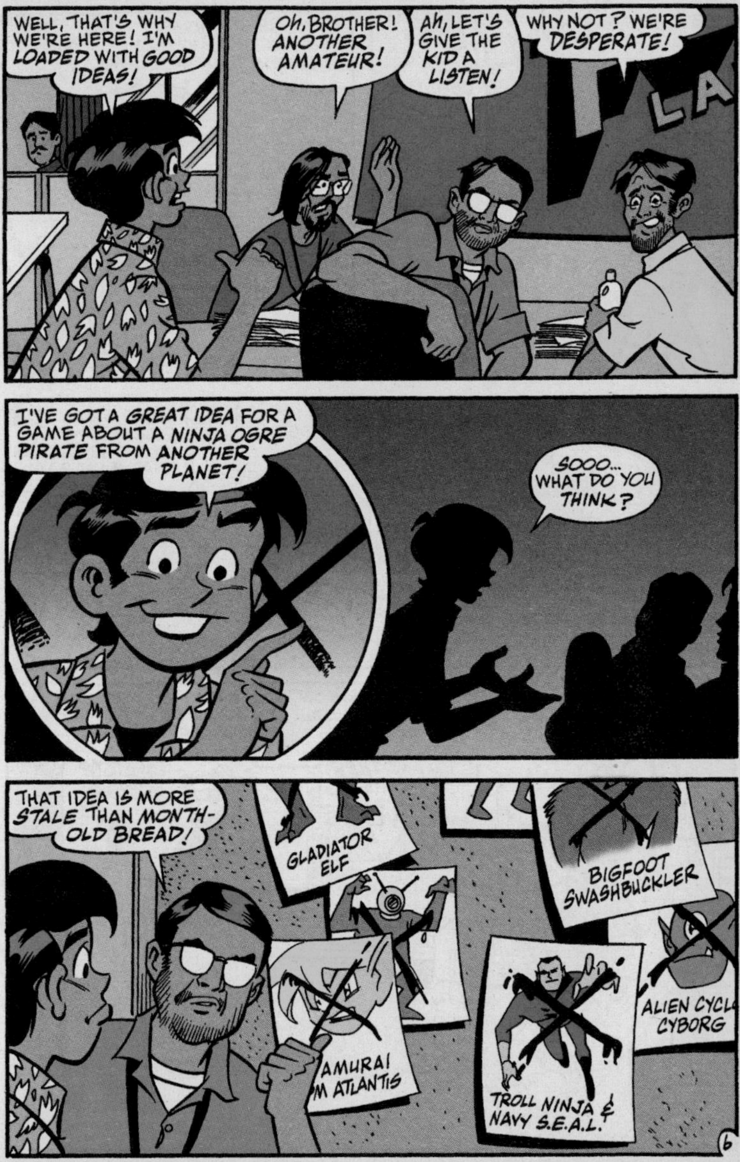
WELL, THAT'S WHY WE'RE HERE! I'M LOADED WITH GOOD IDEAS!
Oh, BROTHER! ANOTHER AMATEUR!
Ah, LET'S GIVE THE KID A LISTEN!
WHY NOT? WE'RE DESPERATE!
I'VE GOT A GREAT IDEA FOR A GAME ABOUT A NINJA OGRE PIRATE FROM ANOTHER PLANET!
SOOO... WHAT DO YOU THINK?
THAT IDEA IS MORE STALE THAN MONTH-OLD BREAD!
GLADIATOR ELF
BIGFOOT SWASHBUCKLER
ALIEN CYCL CYBORG
AMURAI M ATLANTIS
TROLL NINJA & NAVY S.E.A.L.
6

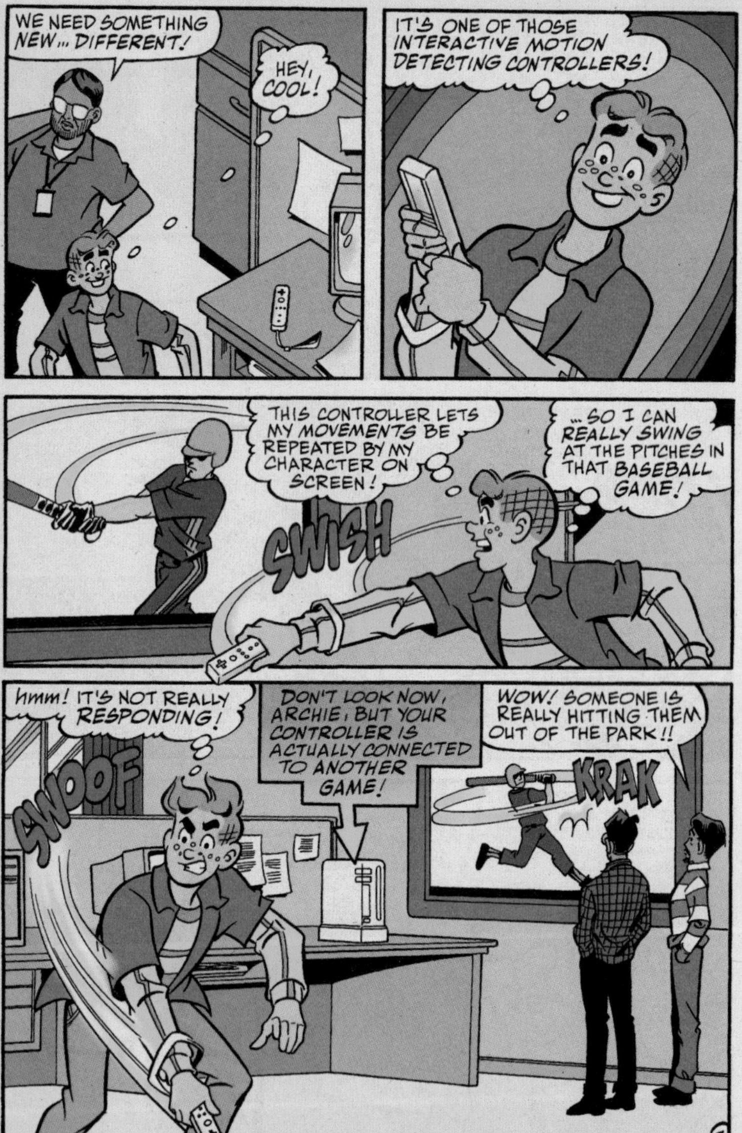
WE NEED SOMETHING NEW... DIFFERENT!
HEY, COOL!
IT'S ONE OF THOSE INTERACTIVE MOTION DETECTING CONTROLLERS!
THIS CONTROLLER LETS MY MOVEMENTS BE REPEATED BY MY CHARACTER ON SCREEN!
...SO I CAN REALLY SWING AT THE PITCHES IN THAT BASEBALL GAME!
SWISH
hmm! IT'S NOT REALLY RESPONDING!
SWOOF
DON'T LOOK NOW, ARCHIE, BUT YOUR CONTROLLER IS ACTUALLY CONNECTED TO ANOTHER GAME!
WOW! SOMEONE IS REALLY HITTING THEM OUT OF THE PARK!!
KRAK
7

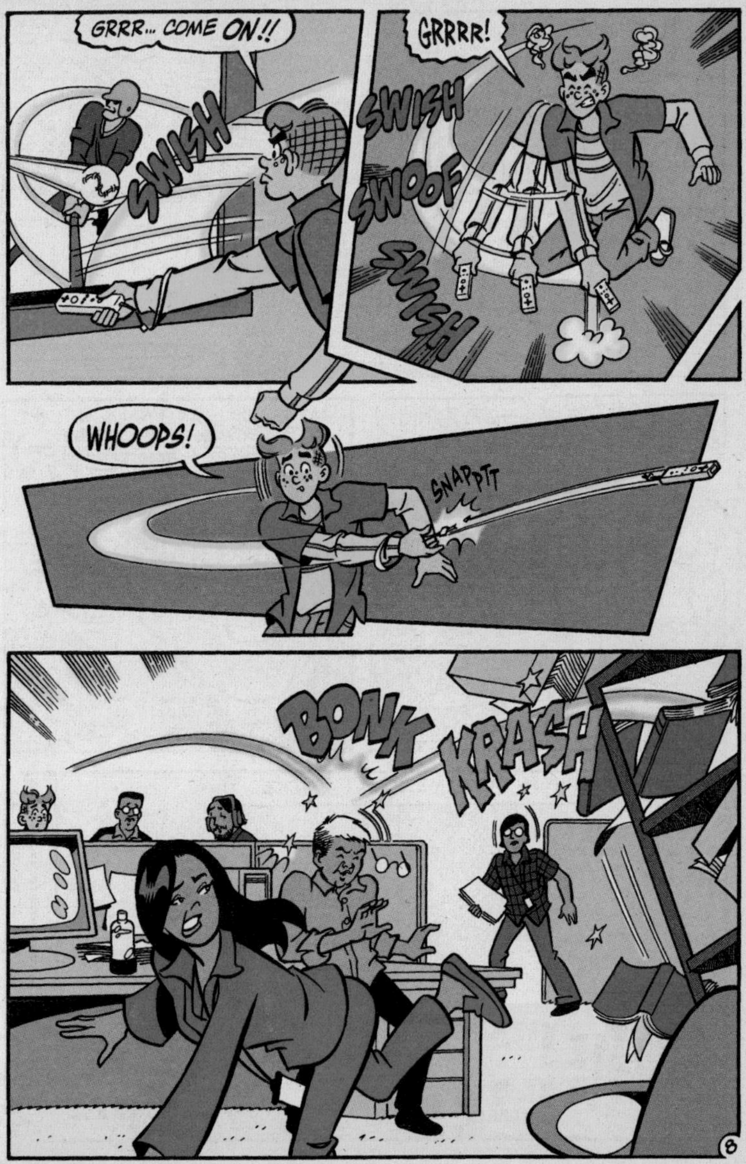

GRRR... COME ON!!
SWISH
GRRRR!
SWISH
SWOOF
SWISH
WHOOPS!
SNAPPTT
BONK
KRASH
8

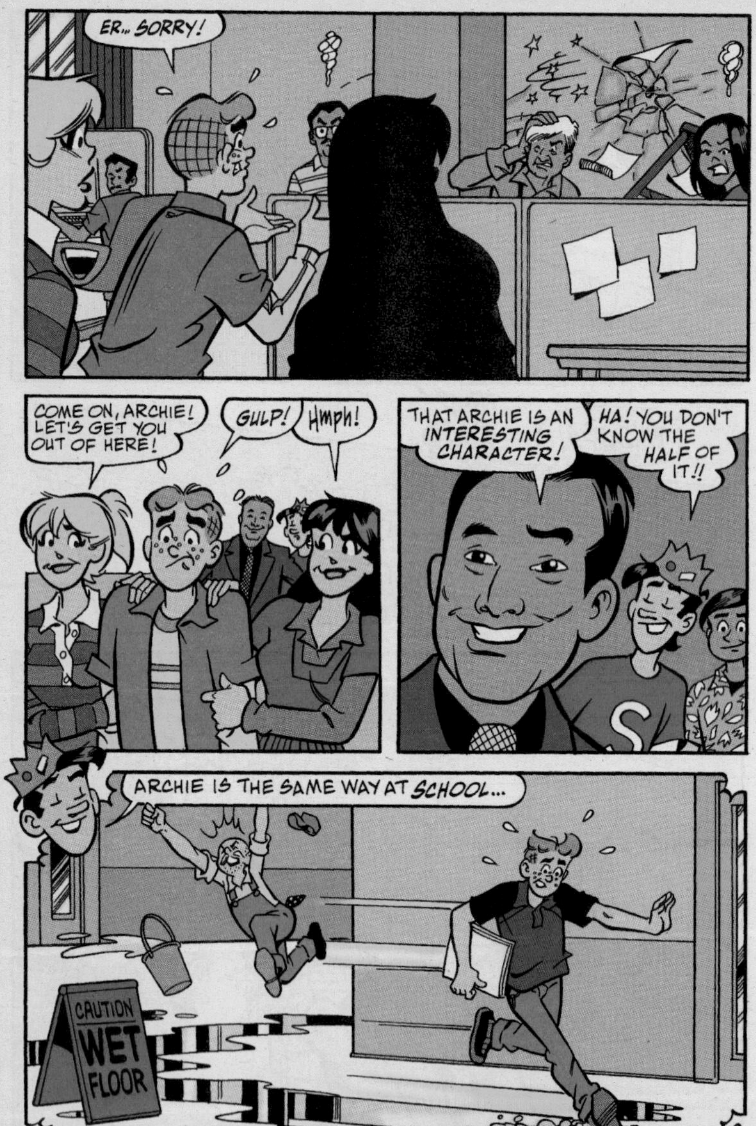
ER... SORRY!
COME ON, ARCHIE! LET'S GET YOU OUT OF HERE!
GULP!
Hmph!
THAT ARCHIE IS AN INTERESTING CHARACTER!
HA! YOU DON'T KNOW THE HALF OF IT!!
ARCHIE IS THE SAME WAY AT SCHOOL...
CAUTION
WET FLOOR

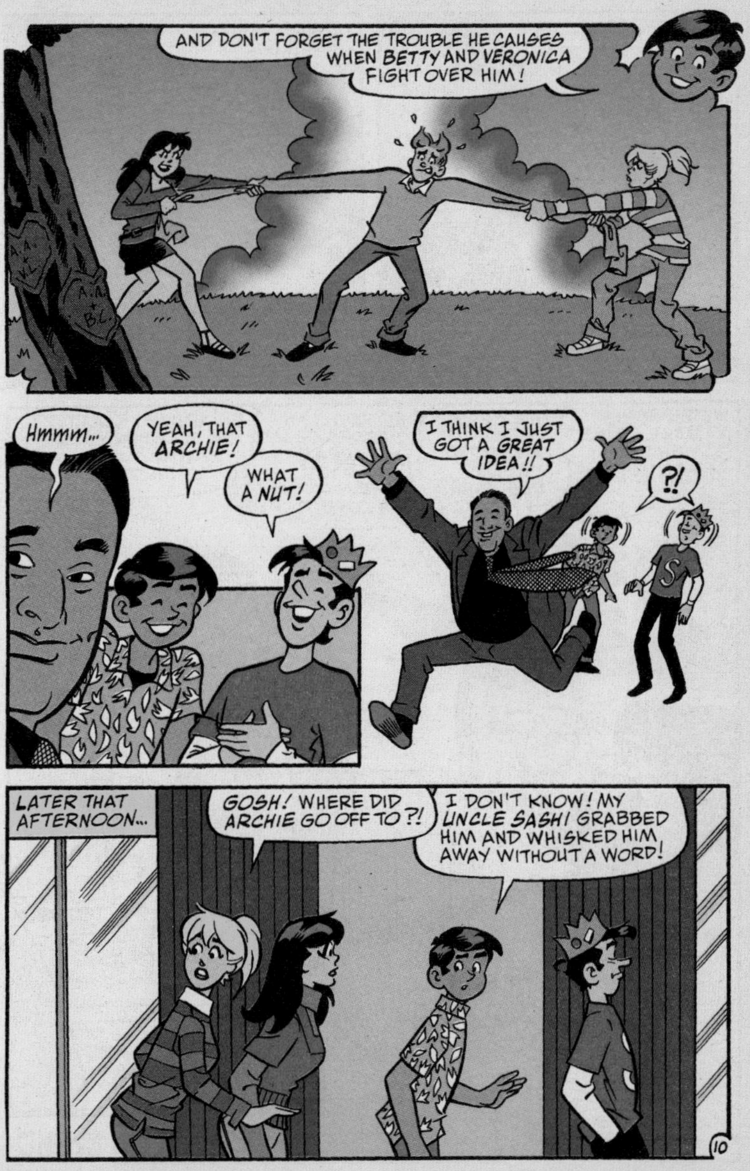

AND DON'T FORGET THE TROUBLE HE CAUSES WHEN BETTY AND VERONICA FIGHT OVER HIM!
Hmmm...
YEAH, THAT ARCHIE!
WHAT A NUT!
I THINK I JUST GOT A GREAT IDEA!!
?!
LATER THAT AFTERNOON...
GOSH! WHERE DID ARCHIE GO OFF TO?!
I DON'T KNOW! MY UNCLE SASHI GRABBED HIM AND WHISKED HIM AWAY WITHOUT A WORD!

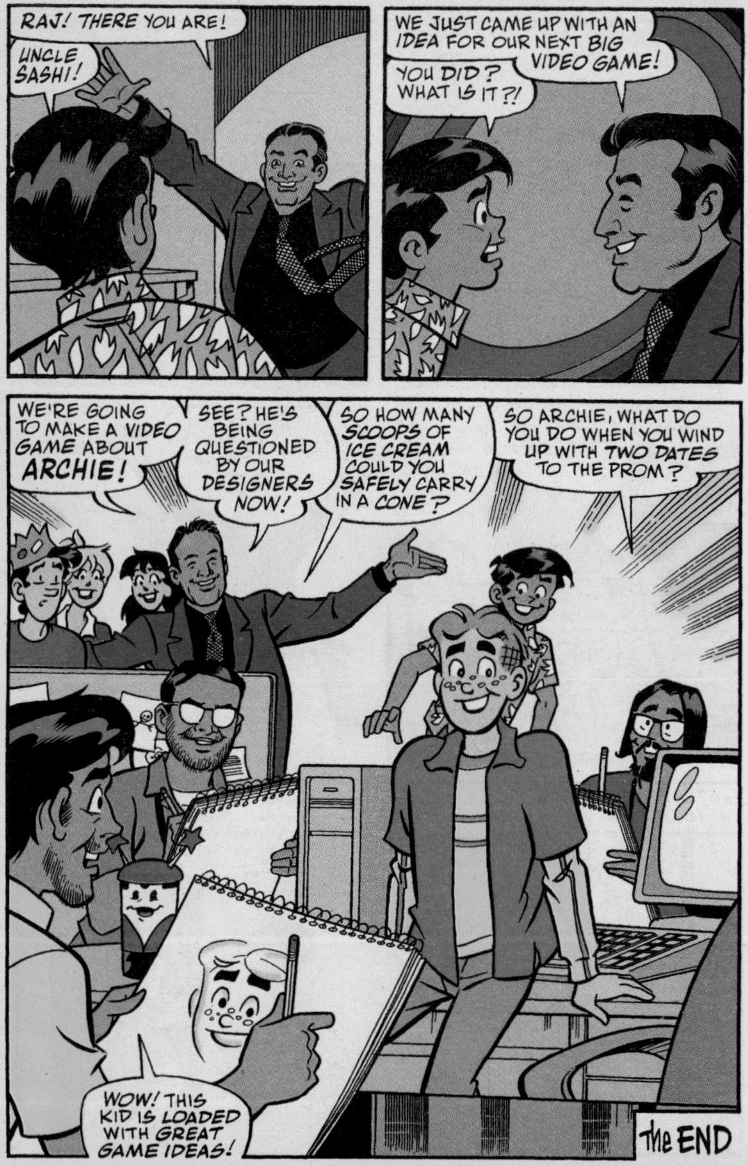
RAJ! THERE YOU ARE!
UNCLE SASHI!
WE JUST CAME UP WITH AN IDEA FOR OUR NEXT BIG VIDEO GAME!
YOU DID? WHAT IS IT?!
WE'RE GOING TO MAKE A VIDEO GAME ABOUT ARCHIE!
SEE? HE'S BEING QUESTIONED BY OUR DESIGNERS NOW!
SO HOW MANY SCOOPS OF ICE CREAM COULD YOU SAFELY CARRY IN A CONE?
SO ARCHIE, WHAT DO YOU DO WHEN YOU WIND UP WITH TWO DATES TO THE PROM?
WOW! THIS KID IS LOADED WITH GREAT GAME IDEAS!
The END

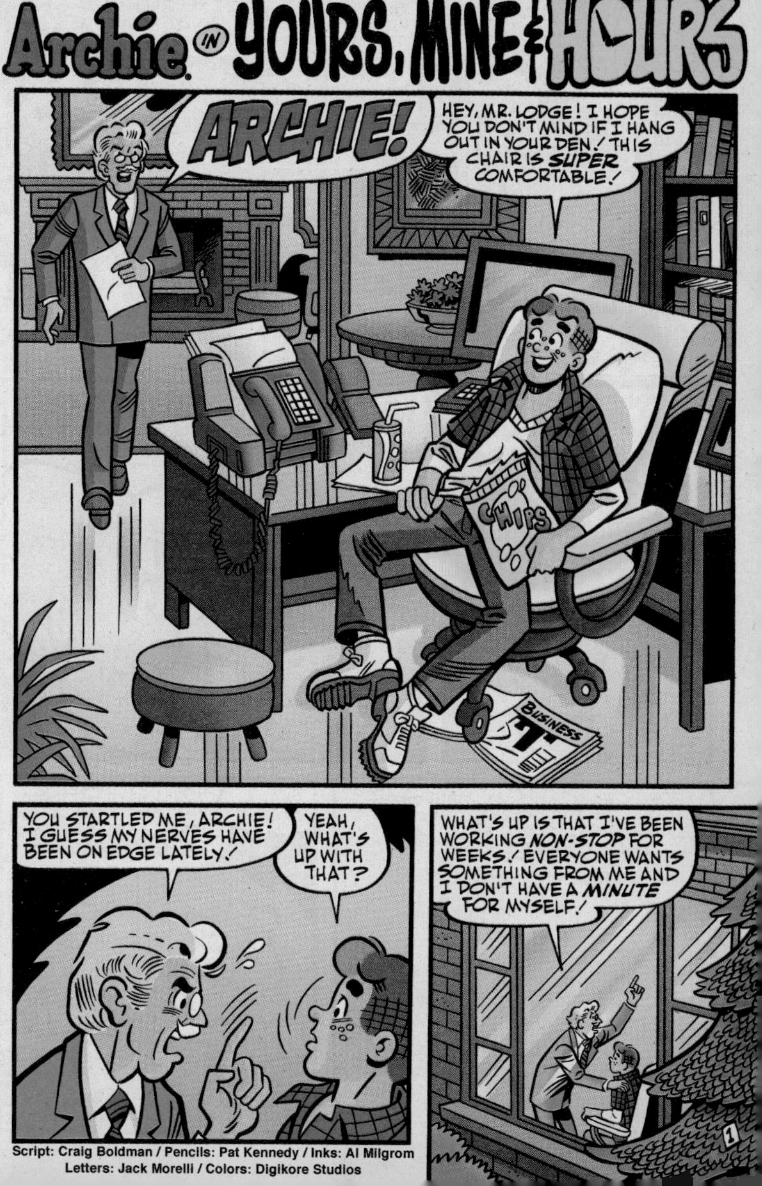
Archie IN YOURS, MINE & HOURS
ARCHIE!
HEY, MR. LODGE! I HOPE YOU DON'T MIND IF I HANG OUT IN YOUR DEN! THIS CHAIR IS SUPER COMFORTABLE!
CHIPS
BUSINESS
YOU STARTLED ME, ARCHIE! I GUESS MY NERVES HAVE BEEN ON EDGE LATELY!
YEAH, WHAT'S UP WITH THAT?
WHAT'S UP IS THAT I'VE BEEN WORKING NON-STOP FOR WEEKS! EVERYONE WANTS SOMETHING FROM ME AND I DON'T HAVE A MINUTE FOR MYSELF!
1

Script: Craig Boldman / Pencils: Pat Kennedy / Inks: Al Milgrom
Letters: Jack Morelli / Colors: Digikore Studios

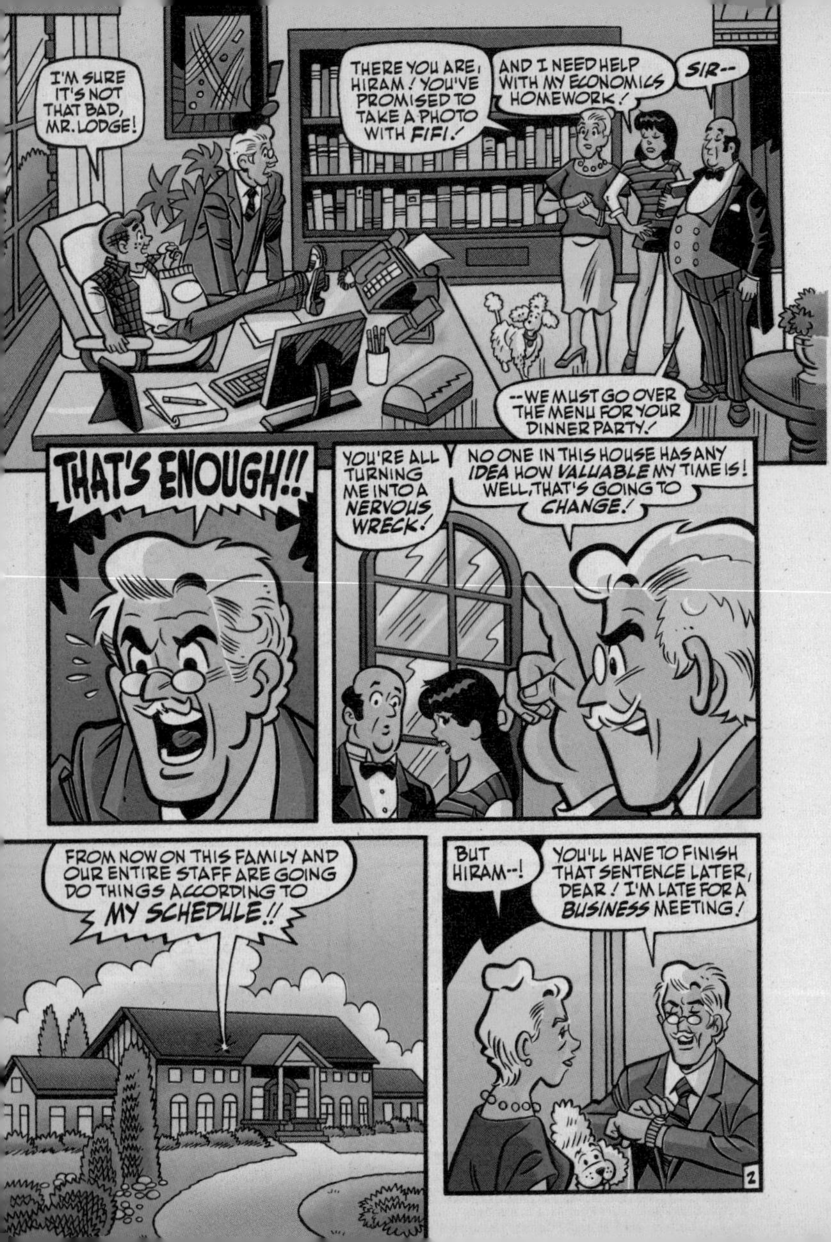
I'M SURE IT'S NOT THAT BAD, MR. LODGE!
THERE YOU ARE, HIRAM! YOU'VE PROMISED TO TAKE A PHOTO WITH FIFI!
AND I NEED HELP WITH MY ECONOMICS HOMEWORK!
SIR--
--WE MUST GO OVER THE MENU FOR YOUR DINNER PARTY!
THAT'S ENOUGH!!
YOU'RE ALL TURNING ME INTO A NERVOUS WRECK!
NO ONE IN THIS HOUSE HAS ANY IDEA HOW VALUABLE MY TIME IS! WELL, THAT'S GOING TO CHANGE!
FROM NOW ON THIS FAMILY AND OUR ENTIRE STAFF ARE GOING DO THINGS ACCORDING TO MY SCHEDULE!!
BUT HIRAM--!
YOU'LL HAVE TO FINISH THAT SENTENCE LATER, DEAR! I'M LATE FOR A BUSINESS MEETING!
2

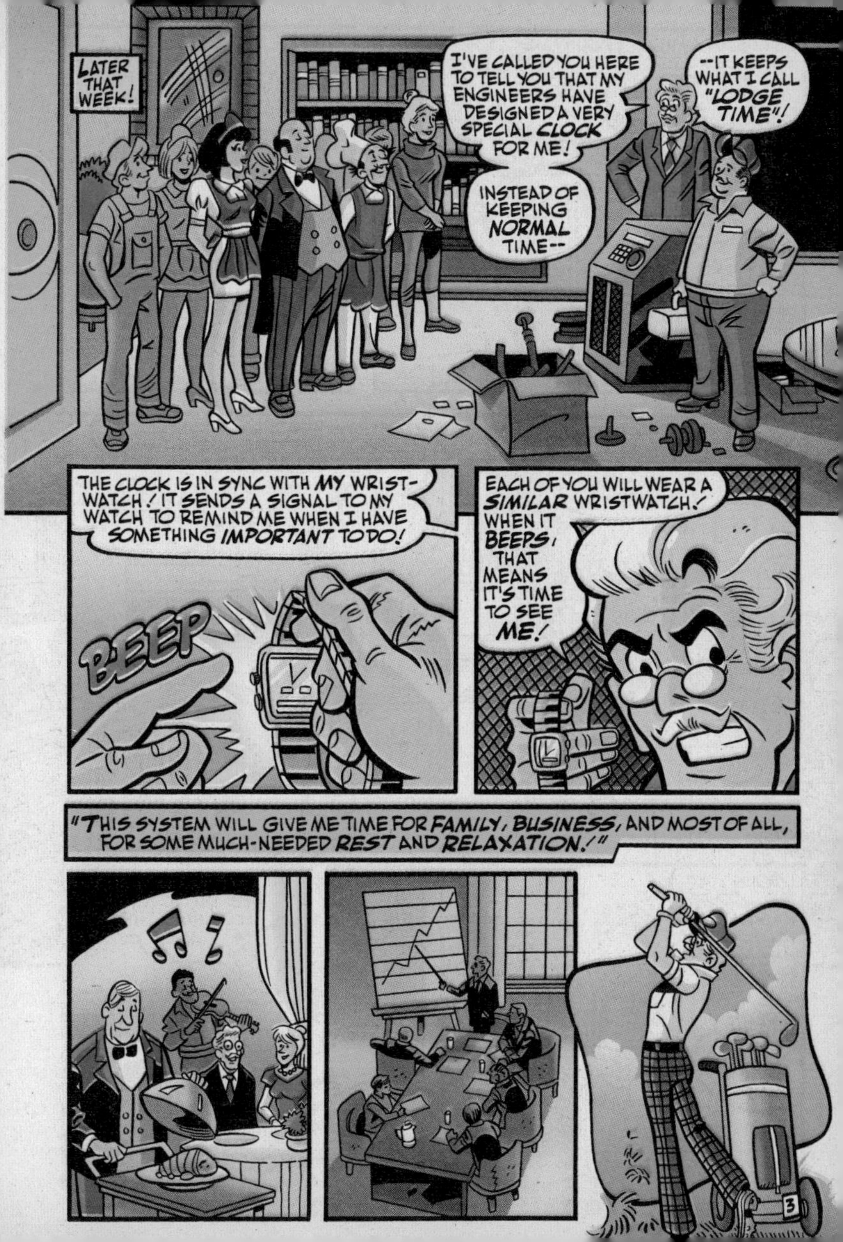

LATER THAT WEEK!
I'VE CALLED YOU HERE TO TELL YOU THAT MY ENGINEERS HAVE DESIGNED A VERY SPECIAL CLOCK FOR ME!
INSTEAD OF KEEPING NORMAL TIME--
--IT KEEPS WHAT I CALL "LODGE TIME"!
THE CLOCK IS IN SYNC WITH MY WRIST-WATCH! IT SENDS A SIGNAL TO MY WATCH TO REMIND ME WHEN I HAVE SOMETHING IMPORTANT TO DO!
BEEP
EACH OF YOU WILL WEAR A SIMILAR WRISTWATCH! WHEN IT BEEPS, THAT MEANS IT'S TIME TO SEE ME!
"THIS SYSTEM WILL GIVE ME TIME FOR FAMILY, BUSINESS, AND MOST OF ALL, FOR SOME MUCH-NEEDED REST AND RELAXATION!"
3

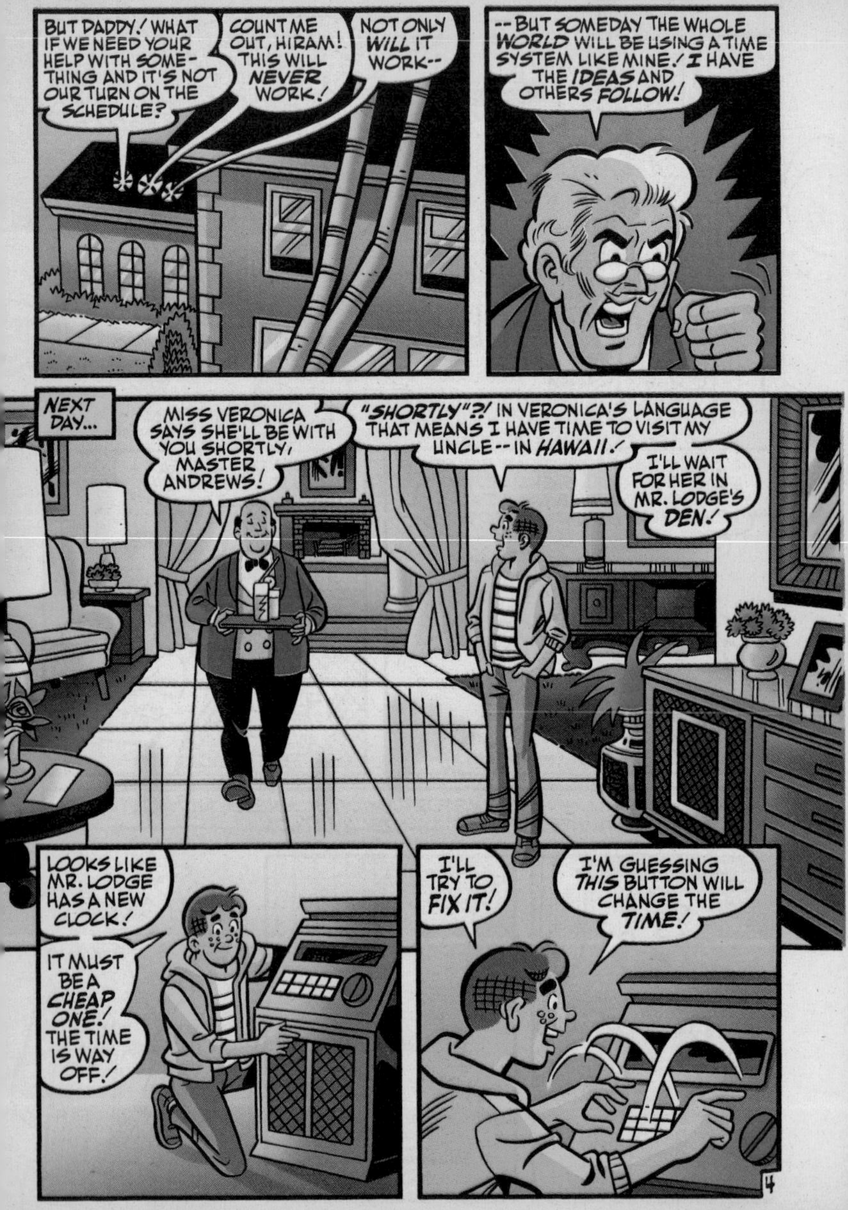
BUT DADDY! WHAT IF WE NEED YOUR HELP WITH SOME-THING AND IT'S NOT OUR TURN ON THE SCHEDULE?
COUNT ME OUT, HIRAM! THIS WILL NEVER WORK!
NOT ONLY WILL IT WORK--
--BUT SOMEDAY THE WHOLE WORLD WILL BE USING A TIME SYSTEM LIKE MINE! I HAVE THE IDEAS AND OTHERS FOLLOW!
NEXT DAY...
MISS VERONICA SAYS SHE'LL BE WITH YOU SHORTLY, MASTER ANDREWS!
"SHORTLY"?! IN VERONICA'S LANGUAGE THAT MEANS I HAVE TIME TO VISIT MY UNCLE-- IN HAWAII!
I'LL WAIT FOR HER IN MR. LODGE'S DEN!
LOOKS LIKE MR. LODGE HAS A NEW CLOCK!
IT MUST BE A CHEAP ONE! THE TIME IS WAY OFF!
I'LL TRY TO FIX IT!
I'M GUESSING THIS BUTTON WILL CHANGE THE TIME!

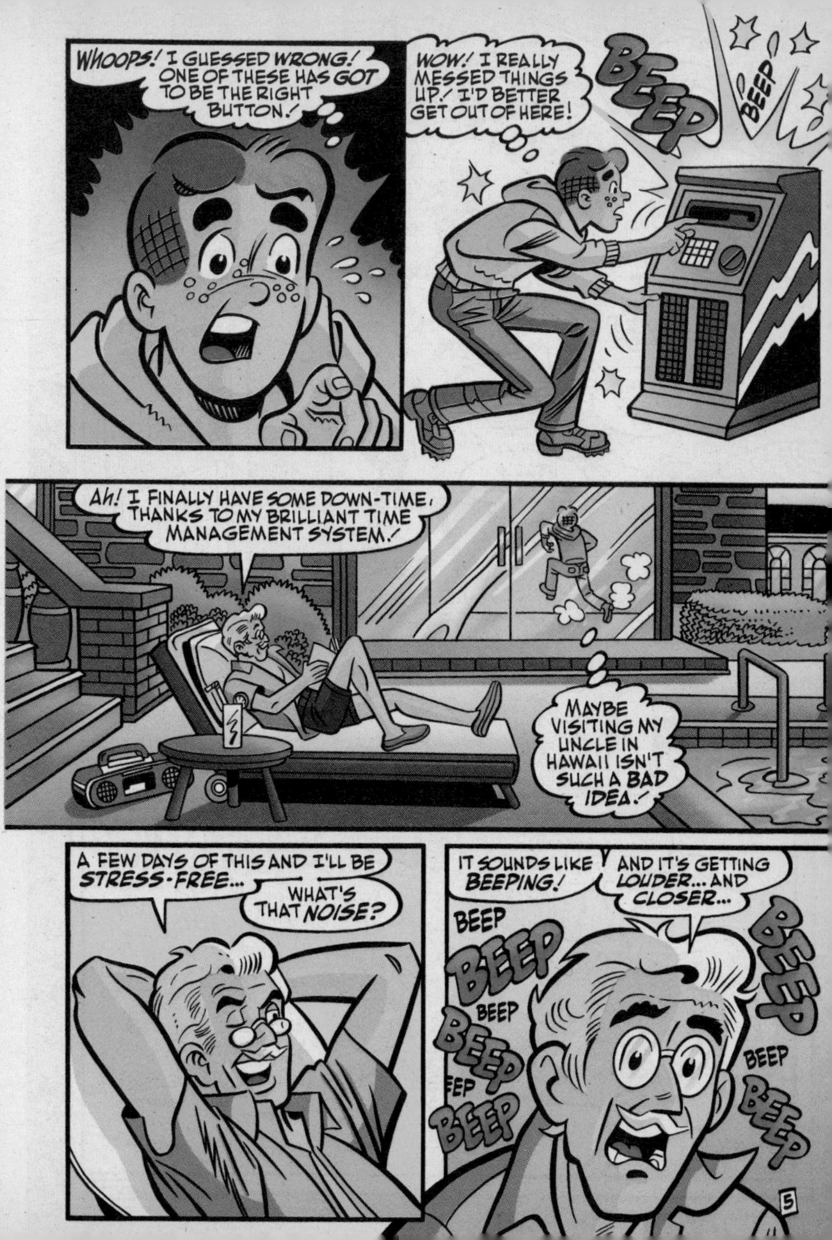

WHOOPS! I GUESSED WRONG! ONE OF THESE HAS GOT TO BE THE RIGHT BUTTON!
WOW! I REALLY MESSED THINGS UP! I'D BETTER GET OUT OF HERE!
BEEP
BEEP
AH! I FINALLY HAVE SOME DOWN-TIME, THANKS TO MY BRILLIANT TIME MANAGEMENT SYSTEM!
MAYBE VISITING MY UNCLE IN HAWAII ISN'T SUCH A BAD IDEA!
A FEW DAYS OF THIS AND I'LL BE STRESS-FREE...
WHAT'S THAT NOISE?
IT SOUNDS LIKE BEEPING!
AND IT'S GETTING LOUDER... AND CLOSER...
BEEP
BEEP
BEEP
BEEP
BEEP
BEEP
BEEP
BEEP
BEEP

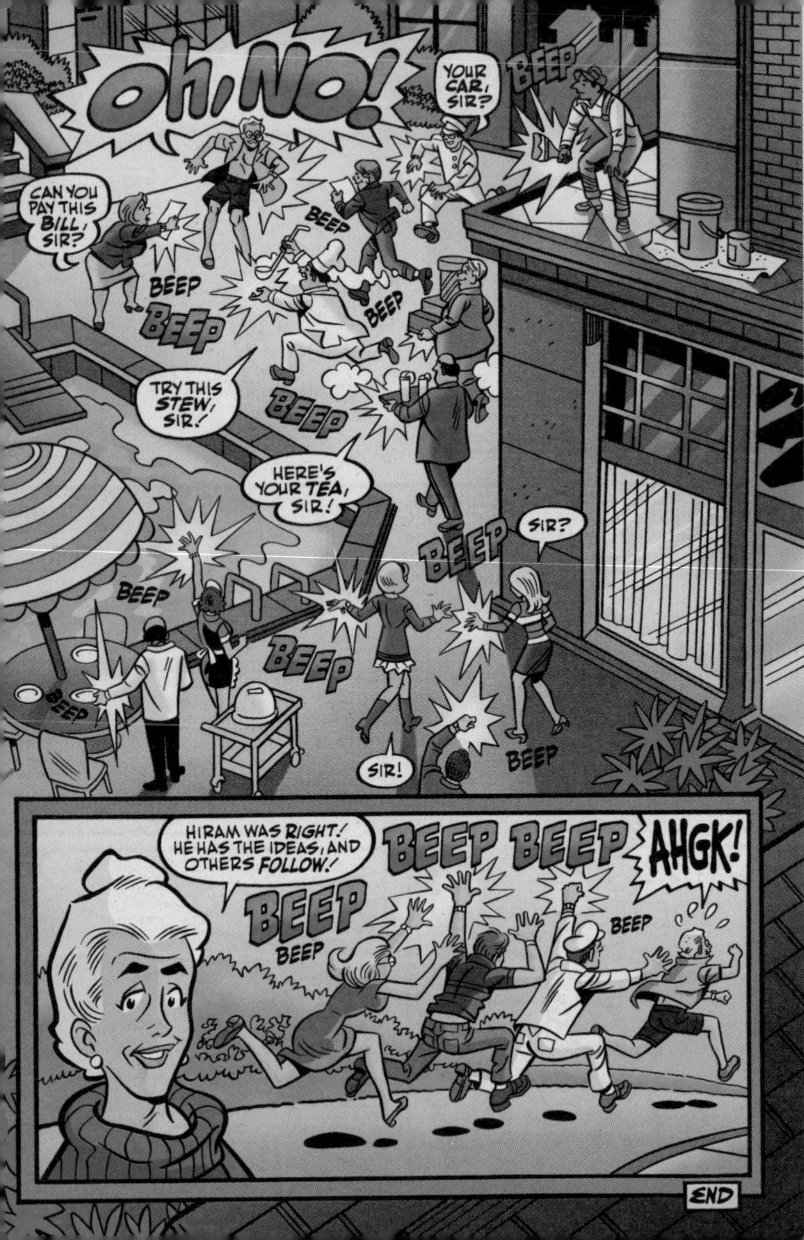
OH, NO!
YOUR CAR, SIR?
BEEP
CAN YOU PAY THIS BILL, SIR?
BEEP
BEEP
BEEP
BEEP
TRY THIS STEW, SIR!
BEEP
HERE'S YOUR TEA, SIR!
BEEP
SIR?
BEEP
BEEP
BEEP
SIR!
BEEP
HIRAM WAS RIGHT! HE HAS THE IDEAS, AND OTHERS FOLLOW!
BEEP BEEP
AHGK!
BEEP
BEEP
BEEP
END

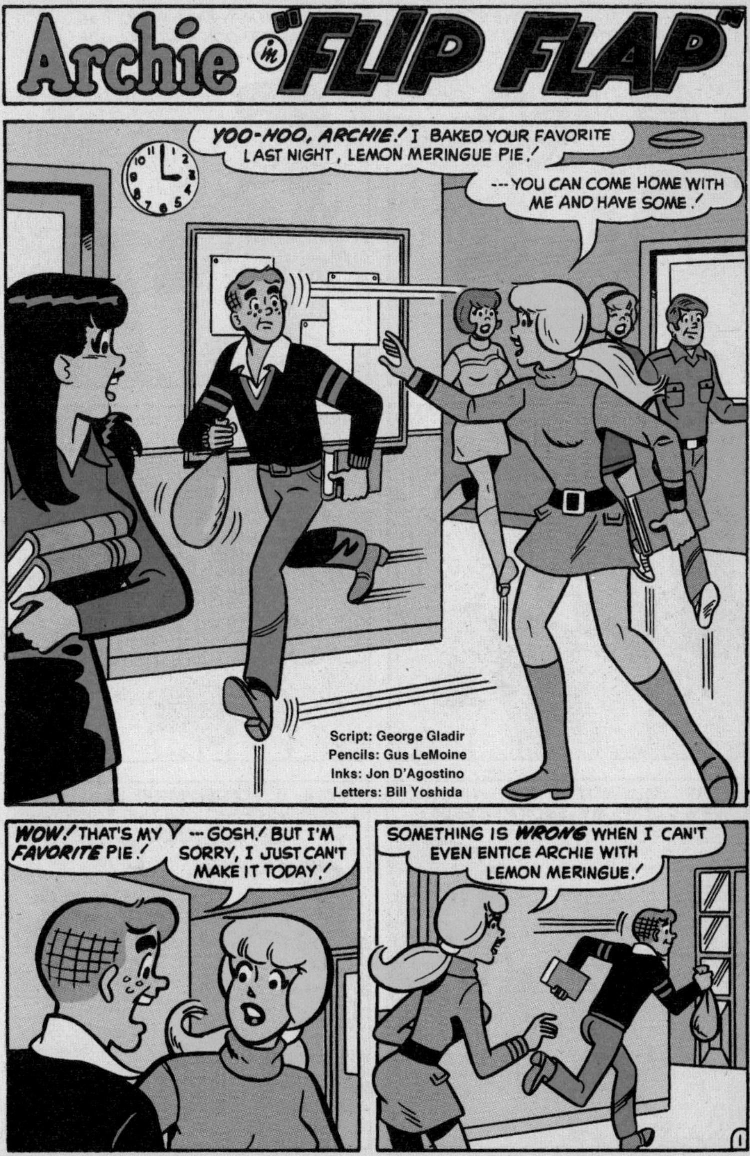

Archie in "FLIP FLAP"
YOO-HOO, ARCHIE! I BAKED YOUR FAVORITE LAST NIGHT, LEMON MERINGUE PIE!
--- YOU CAN COME HOME WITH ME AND HAVE SOME!
Script: George Gladir
Pencils: Gus LeMoine
Inks: Jon D'Agostino
Letters: Bill Yoshida
WOW! THAT'S MY FAVORITE PIE!
--- GOSH! BUT I'M SORRY, I JUST CAN'T MAKE IT TODAY!
SOMETHING IS WRONG WHEN I CAN'T EVEN ENTICE ARCHIE WITH LEMON MERINGUE!
1

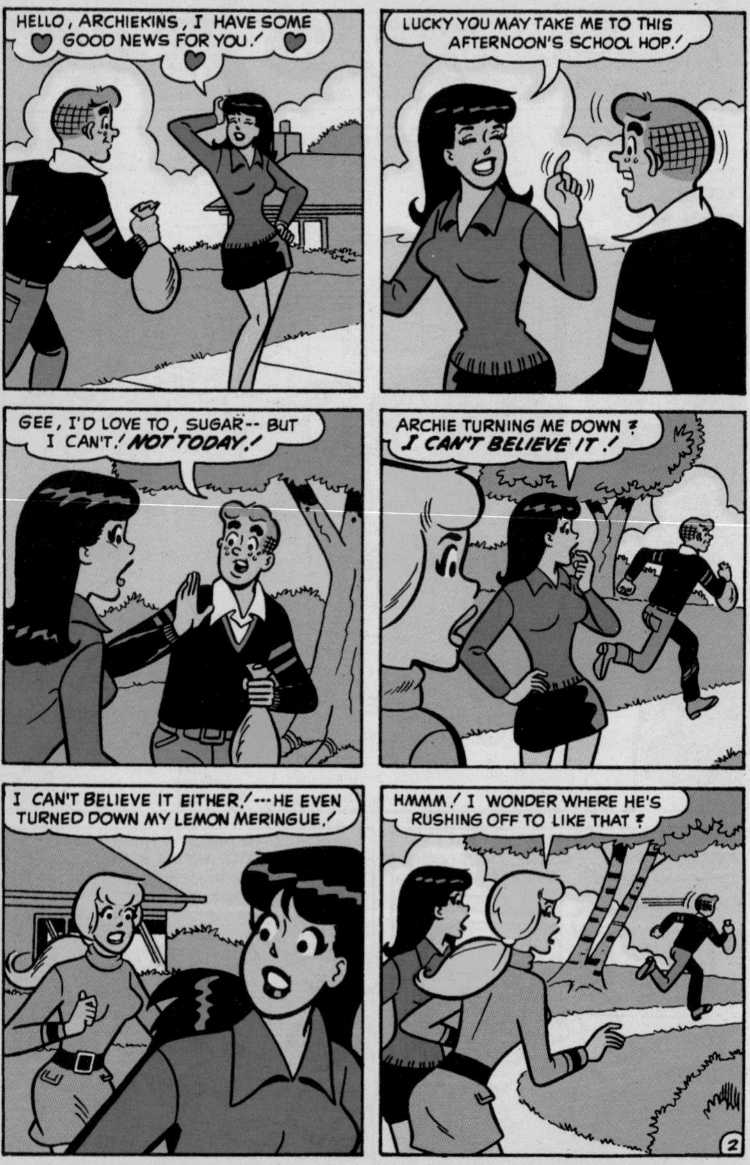
HELLO, ARCHIEKINS, I HAVE SOME GOOD NEWS FOR YOU!
LUCKY YOU MAY TAKE ME TO THIS AFTERNOON'S SCHOOL HOP!
GEE, I'D LOVE TO, SUGAR-- BUT I CAN'T! NOT TODAY!
ARCHIE TURNING ME DOWN? I CAN'T BELIEVE IT!
I CAN'T BELIEVE IT EITHER! --- HE EVEN TURNED DOWN MY LEMON MERINGUE!
HMMM! I WONDER WHERE HE'S RUSHING OFF TO LIKE THAT?
2

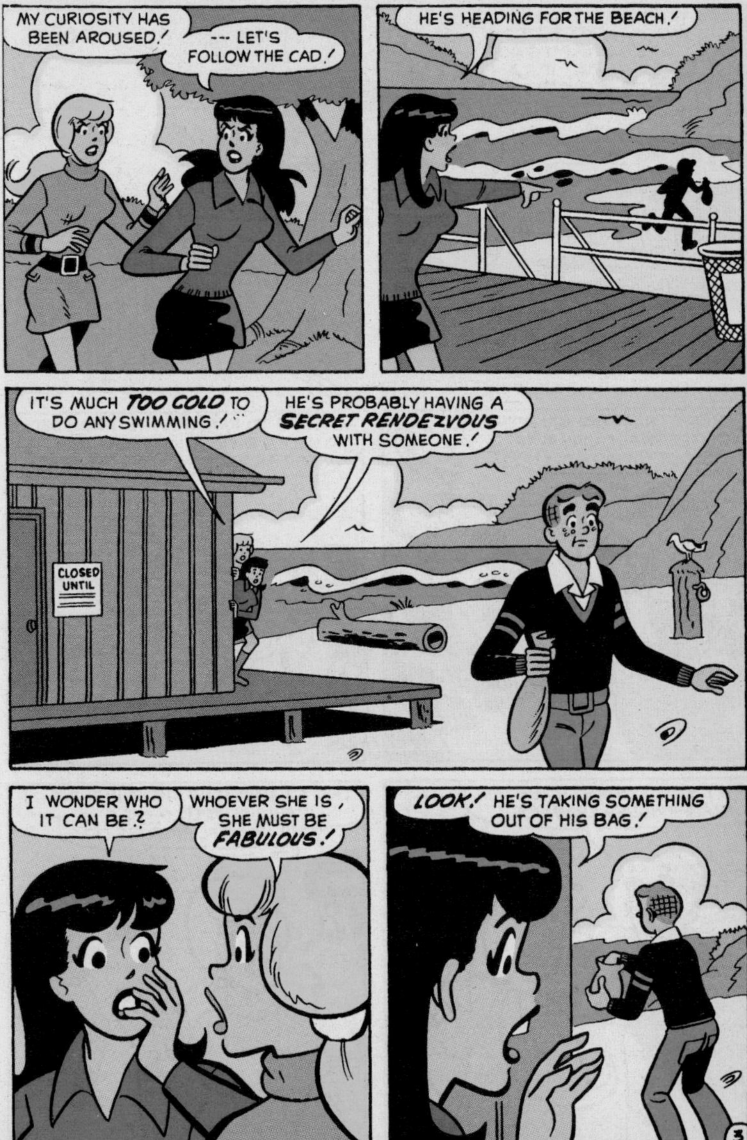

MY CURIOSITY HAS BEEN AROUSED!
--- LET'S FOLLOW THE CAD!
HE'S HEADING FOR THE BEACH!
IT'S MUCH TOO COLD TO DO ANY SWIMMING!
HE'S PROBABLY HAVING A SECRET RENDEZVOUS WITH SOMEONE!
CLOSED UNTIL
I WONDER WHO IT CAN BE?
WHOEVER SHE IS, SHE MUST BE FABULOUS!
LOOK! HE'S TAKING SOMETHING OUT OF HIS BAG!
3

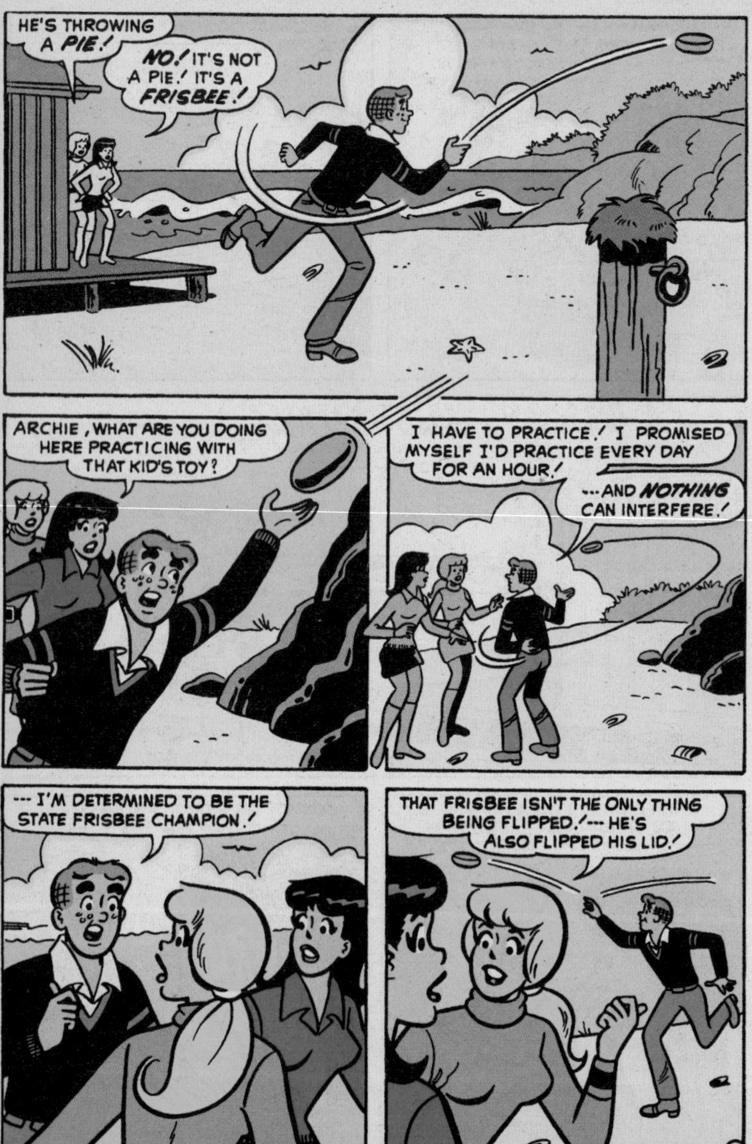
HE'S THROWING A PIE!
NO! IT'S NOT A PIE! IT'S A FRISBEE!
ARCHIE, WHAT ARE YOU DOING HERE PRACTICING WITH THAT KID'S TOY?
I HAVE TO PRACTICE! I PROMISED MYSELF I'D PRACTICE EVERY DAY FOR AN HOUR!
...AND NOTHING CAN INTERFERE!
--- I'M DETERMINED TO BE THE STATE FRISBEE CHAMPION!
THAT FRISBEE ISN'T THE ONLY THING BEING FLIPPED!--- HE'S ALSO FLIPPED HIS LID!
4

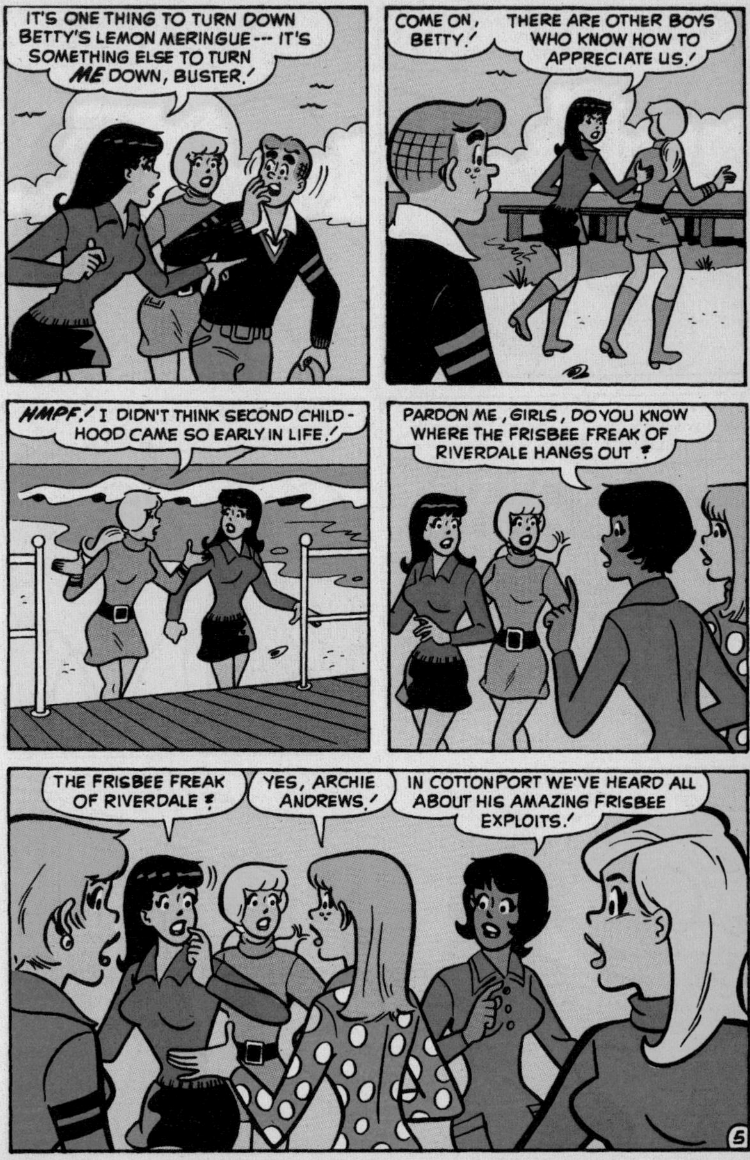
IT'S ONE THING TO TURN DOWN BETTY'S LEMON MERINGUE --- IT'S SOMETHING ELSE TO TURN ME DOWN, BUSTER!
COME ON, BETTY!
THERE ARE OTHER BOYS WHO KNOW HOW TO APPRECIATE US!
HMPF! I DIDN'T THINK SECOND CHILD-HOOD CAME SO EARLY IN LIFE!
PARDON ME, GIRLS, DO YOU KNOW WHERE THE FRISBEE FREAK OF RIVERDALE HANGS OUT?
THE FRISBEE FREAK OF RIVERDALE?
YES, ARCHIE ANDREWS!
IN COTTONPORT WE'VE HEARD ALL ABOUT HIS AMAZING FRISBEE EXPLOITS!
5

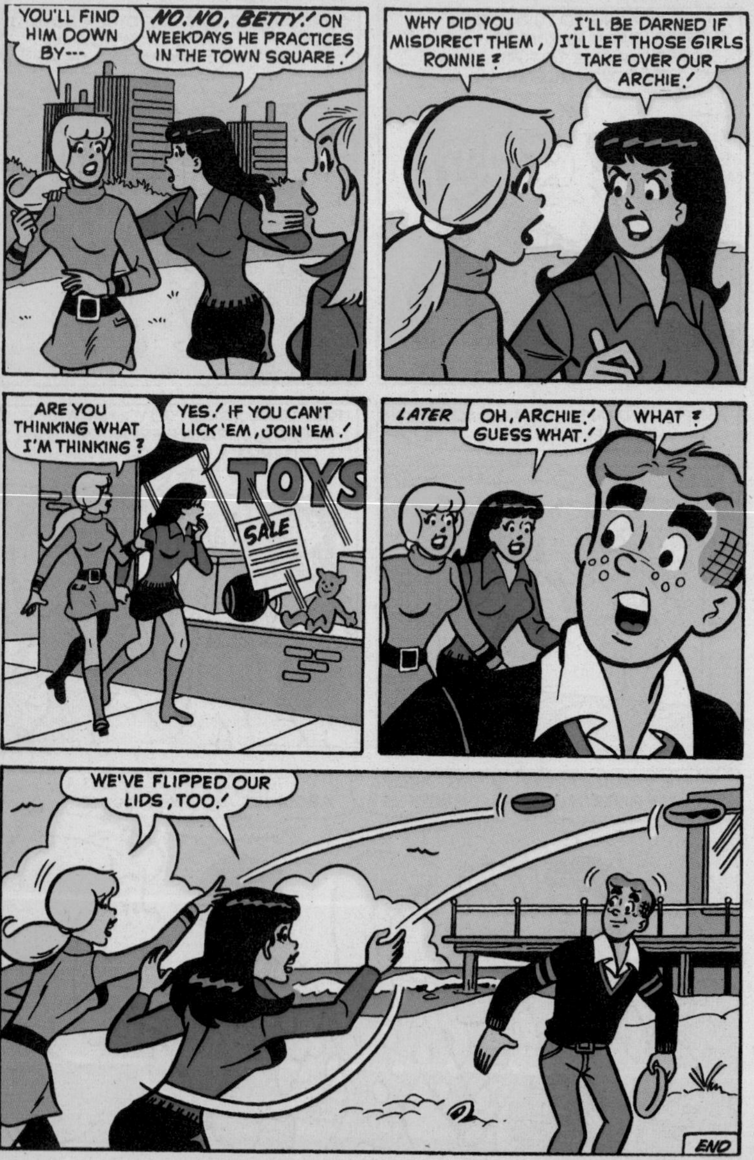

YOU'LL FIND HIM DOWN BY---
NO, NO, BETTY! ON WEEKDAYS HE PRACTICES IN THE TOWN SQUARE!
WHY DID YOU MISDIRECT THEM, RONNIE?
I'LL BE DARNED IF I'LL LET THOSE GIRLS TAKE OVER OUR ARCHIE!
ARE YOU THINKING WHAT I'M THINKING?
YES! IF YOU CAN'T LICK 'EM, JOIN 'EM!
TOYS
SALE
LATER
OH, ARCHIE! GUESS WHAT!
WHAT?
WE'VE FLIPPED OUR LIDS, TOO!
END

Archie in HIDE AND SEEK

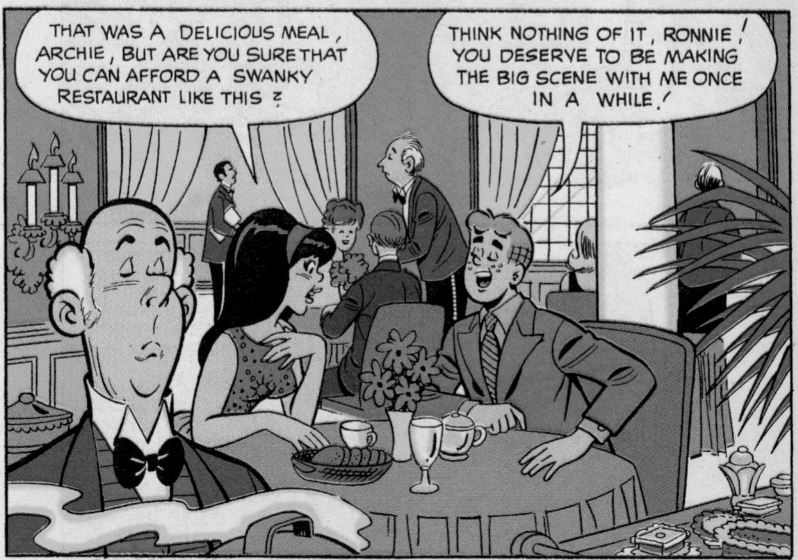
THAT WAS A DELICIOUS MEAL, ARCHIE, BUT ARE YOU SURE THAT YOU CAN AFFORD A SWANKY RESTAURANT LIKE THIS?
THINK NOTHING OF IT, RONNIE! YOU DESERVE TO BE MAKING THE BIG SCENE WITH ME ONCE IN A WHILE!

Script & Pencils: Al Hartley / Inks: Jon D'Agostino / Letters: Bill Yoshida / Colors: Carlos Antunes

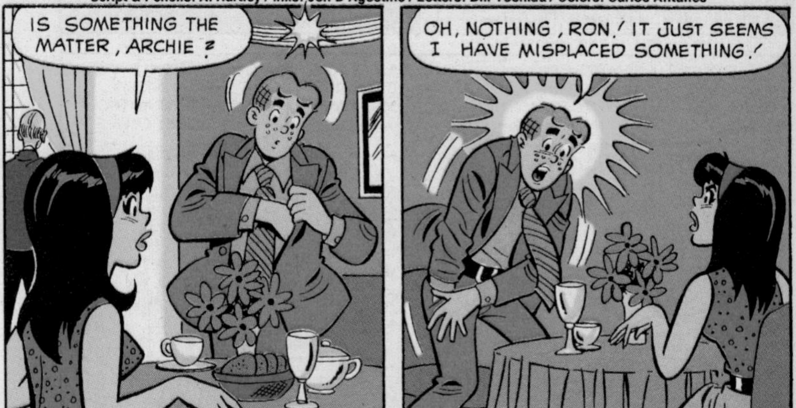
IS SOMETHING THE MATTER, ARCHIE?
OH, NOTHING, RON! IT JUST SEEMS I HAVE MISPLACED SOMETHING!

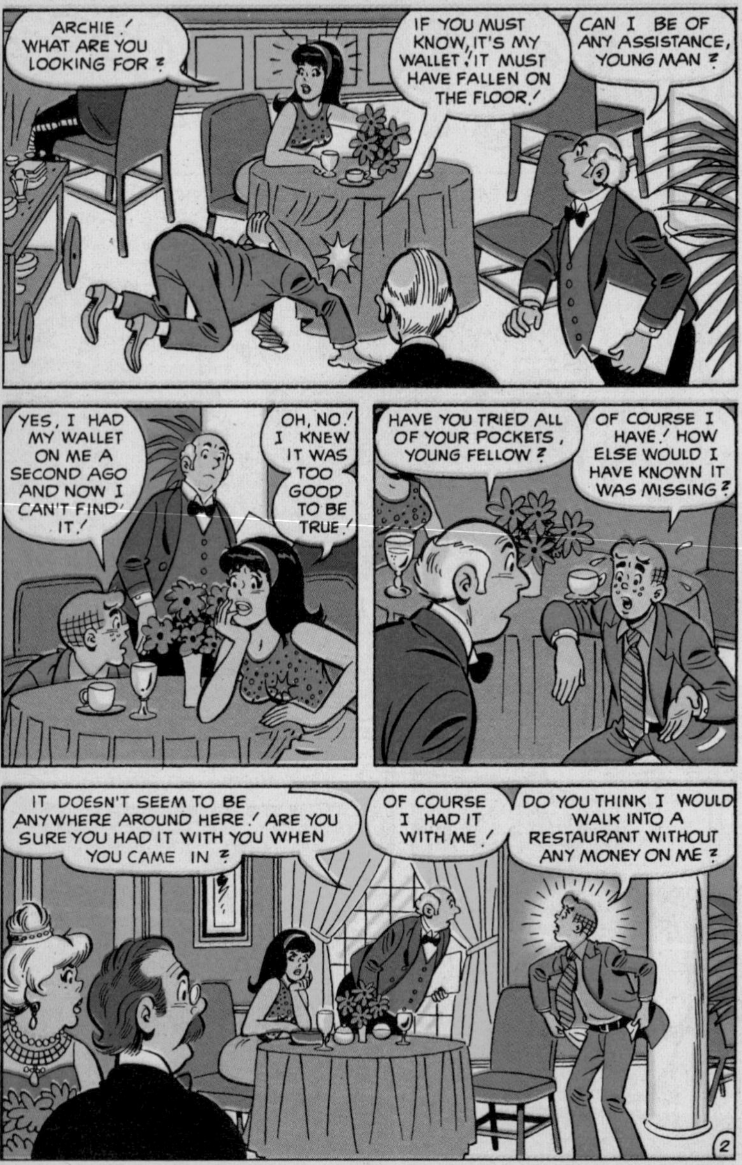
ARCHIE! WHAT ARE YOU LOOKING FOR?
IF YOU MUST KNOW, IT'S MY WALLET! IT MUST HAVE FALLEN ON THE FLOOR!
CAN I BE OF ANY ASSISTANCE, YOUNG MAN?
YES, I HAD MY WALLET ON ME A SECOND AGO AND NOW I CAN'T FIND IT!
OH, NO! I KNEW IT WAS TOO GOOD TO BE TRUE!
HAVE YOU TRIED ALL OF YOUR POCKETS, YOUNG FELLOW?
OF COURSE I HAVE! HOW ELSE WOULD I HAVE KNOWN IT WAS MISSING?
IT DOESN'T SEEM TO BE ANYWHERE AROUND HERE! ARE YOU SURE YOU HAD IT WITH YOU WHEN YOU CAME IN?
OF COURSE I HAD IT WITH ME!
DO YOU THINK I WOULD WALK INTO A RESTAURANT WITHOUT ANY MONEY ON ME?
2

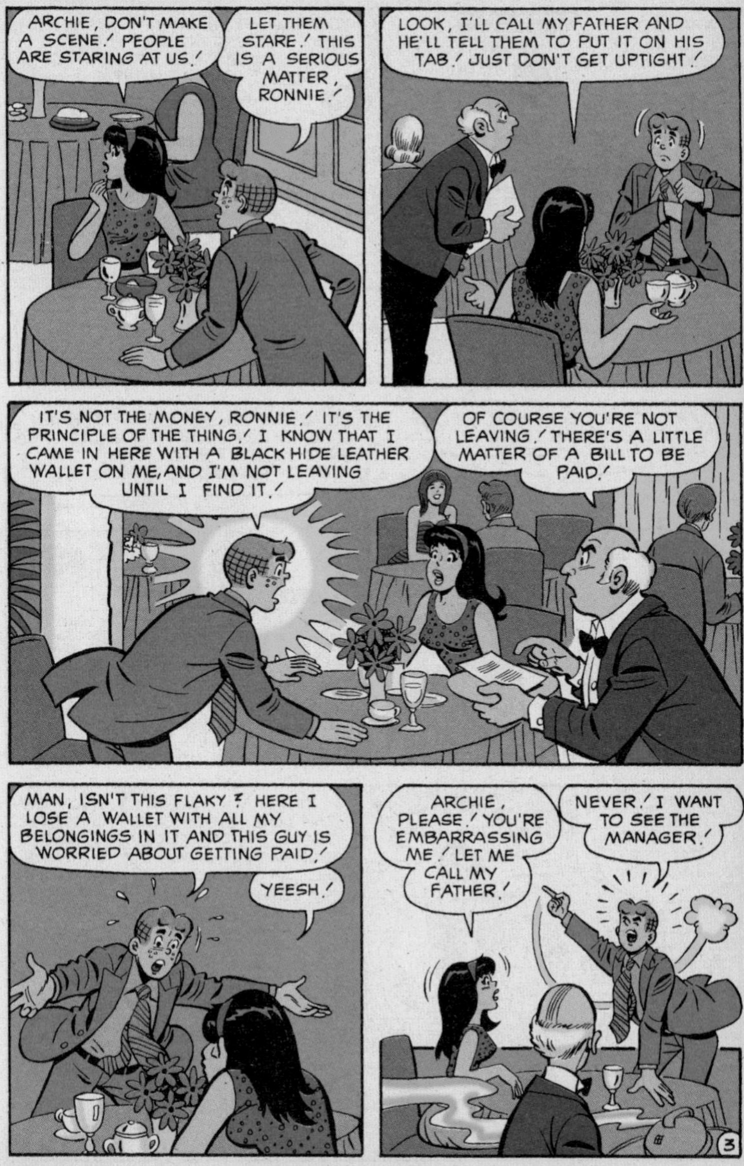
ARCHIE, DON'T MAKE A SCENE! PEOPLE ARE STARING AT US!
LET THEM STARE! THIS IS A SERIOUS MATTER, RONNIE!
LOOK, I'LL CALL MY FATHER AND HE'LL TELL THEM TO PUT IT ON HIS TAB! JUST DON'T GET UPTIGHT!
IT'S NOT THE MONEY, RONNIE! IT'S THE PRINCIPLE OF THE THING! I KNOW THAT I CAME IN HERE WITH A BLACK HIDE LEATHER WALLET ON ME, AND I'M NOT LEAVING UNTIL I FIND IT!
OF COURSE YOU'RE NOT LEAVING! THERE'S A LITTLE MATTER OF A BILL TO BE PAID!
MAN, ISN'T THIS FLAKY? HERE I LOSE A WALLET WITH ALL MY BELONGINGS IN IT AND THIS GUY IS WORRIED ABOUT GETTING PAID!
YEESH!
ARCHIE, PLEASE! YOU'RE EMBARRASSING ME! LET ME CALL MY FATHER!
NEVER! I WANT TO SEE THE MANAGER!
3

WHAT SEEMS TO BE THE TROUBLE, YOUNG MAN?

YOU'RE JUST THE MAN I WANT TO SEE! I CAME IN HERE WITH A BLACK HIDE LEATHER WALLET, AND NOW I CAN'T FIND IT!

GOOD GRIEF!

YOU'RE NOT SUGGESTING THAT ONE OF MY EMPLOYEES TOOK IT, ARE YOU?

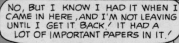

NO, BUT I KNOW I HAD IT WHEN I CAME IN HERE, AND I'M NOT LEAVING UNTIL I GET IT BACK! IT HAD A LOT OF IMPORTANT PAPERS IN IT!

WHAT KIND OF IMPORTANT PAPERS, ARCHIE?

I HAD A 75¢ I.O.U. FROM JUGHEAD...

MY LUNCH PASS CAFETERIA CARD...

AND A TORN AUTOGRAPHED PICTURE OF CUTIE-PIE HEATHERTON, THE BLUES SINGER!

4

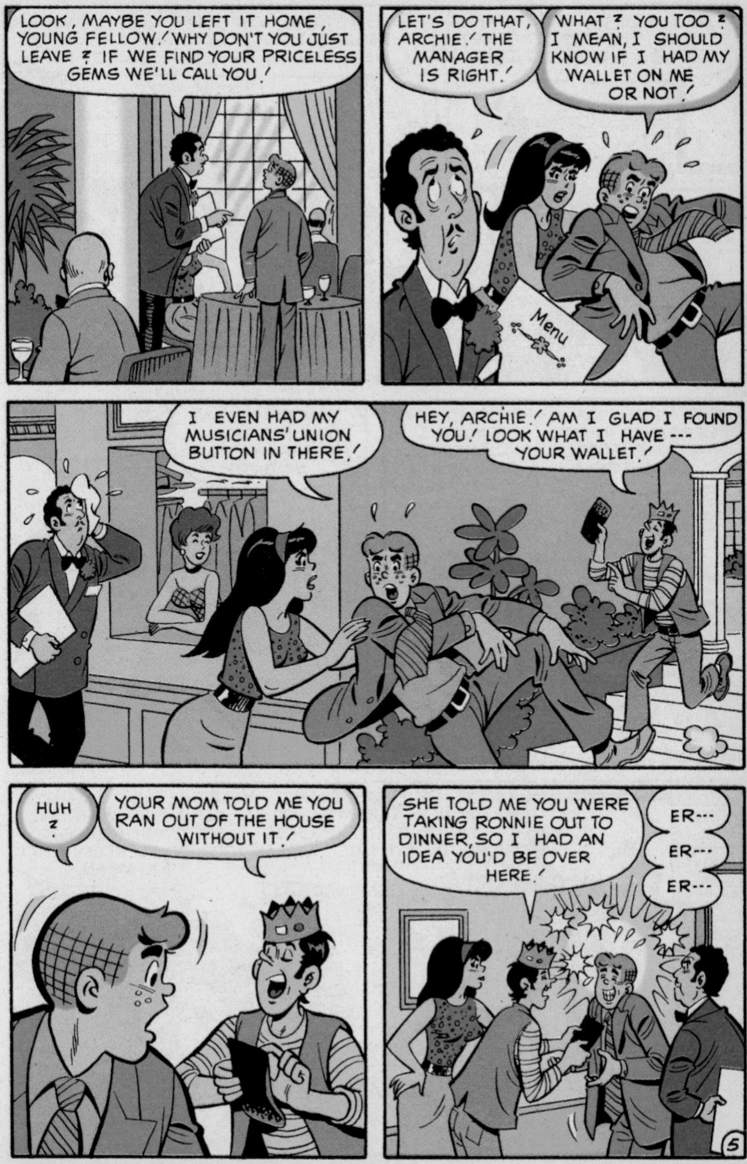

LOOK, MAYBE YOU LEFT IT HOME, YOUNG FELLOW! WHY DON'T YOU JUST LEAVE? IF WE FIND YOUR PRICELESS GEMS WE'LL CALL YOU!
LET'S DO THAT, ARCHIE! THE MANAGER IS RIGHT!
WHAT? YOU TOO? I MEAN, I SHOULD KNOW IF I HAD MY WALLET ON ME OR NOT!
Menu
I EVEN HAD MY MUSICIANS' UNION BUTTON IN THERE!
HEY, ARCHIE! AM I GLAD I FOUND YOU! LOOK WHAT I HAVE --- YOUR WALLET!
HUH?
YOUR MOM TOLD ME YOU RAN OUT OF THE HOUSE WITHOUT IT!
SHE TOLD ME YOU WERE TAKING RONNIE OUT TO DINNER, SO I HAD AN IDEA YOU'D BE OVER HERE!
ER---
ER---
ER---
5

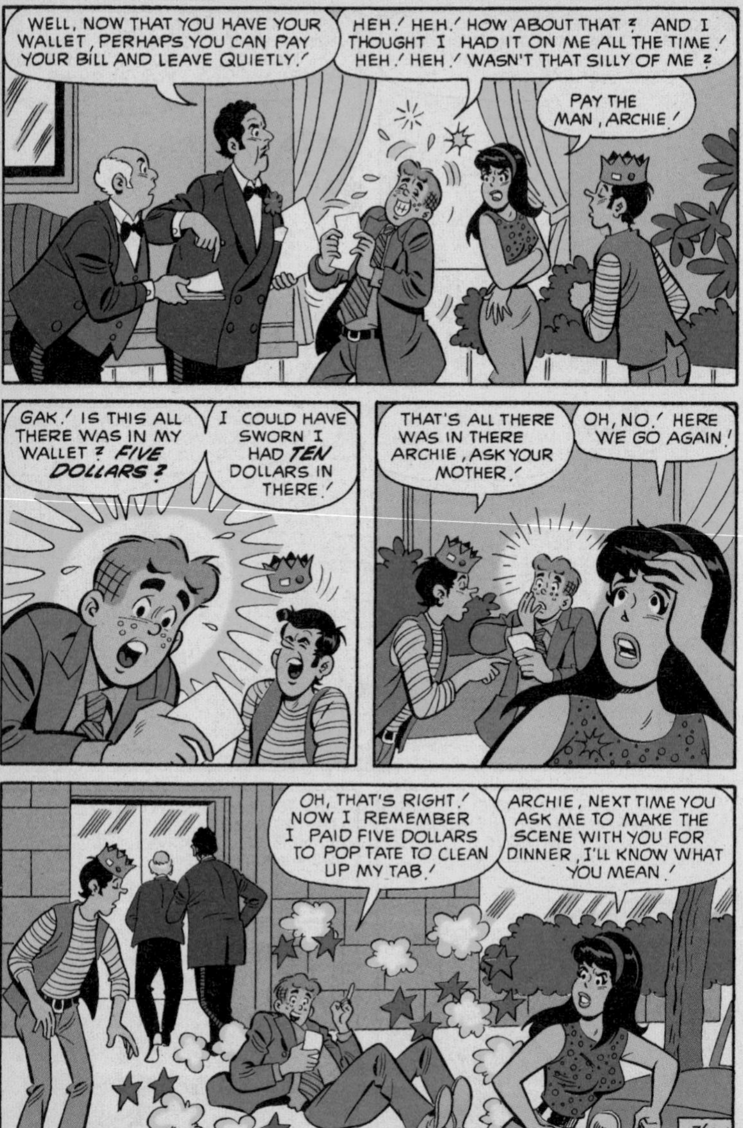
WELL, NOW THAT YOU HAVE YOUR WALLET, PERHAPS YOU CAN PAY YOUR BILL AND LEAVE QUIETLY!
HEH! HEH! HOW ABOUT THAT? AND I THOUGHT I HAD IT ON ME ALL THE TIME! HEH! HEH! WASN'T THAT SILLY OF ME?
PAY THE MAN, ARCHIE!
GAK! IS THIS ALL THERE WAS IN MY WALLET? FIVE DOLLARS?
I COULD HAVE SWORN I HAD TEN DOLLARS IN THERE!
THAT'S ALL THERE WAS IN THERE ARCHIE, ASK YOUR MOTHER!
OH, NO! HERE WE GO AGAIN!
OH, THAT'S RIGHT! NOW I REMEMBER I PAID FIVE DOLLARS TO POP TATE TO CLEAN UP MY TAB!
ARCHIE, NEXT TIME YOU ASK ME TO MAKE THE SCENE WITH YOU FOR DINNER, I'LL KNOW WHAT YOU MEAN!
The End

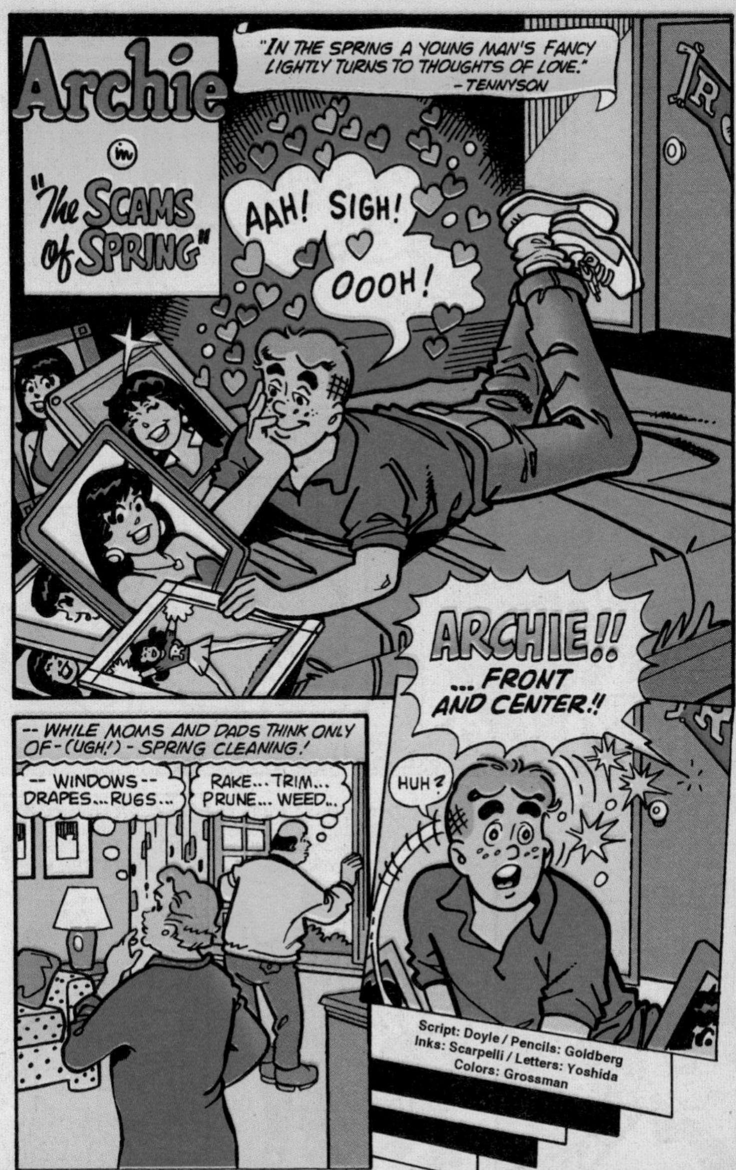
Archie
in
"The SCAMS of SPRING"
"IN THE SPRING A YOUNG MAN'S FANCY LIGHTLY TURNS TO THOUGHTS OF LOVE." –TENNYSON
AAH! SIGH! OOOH!
ARCHIE!! ...FRONT AND CENTER!!
-- WHILE MOMS AND DADS THINK ONLY OF - (UGH!) - SPRING CLEANING!
-- WINDOWS -- DRAPES... RUGS...
RAKE... TRIM... PRUNE... WEED...
HUH?
Script: Doyle / Pencils: Goldberg
Inks: Scarpelli / Letters: Yoshida
Colors: Grossman

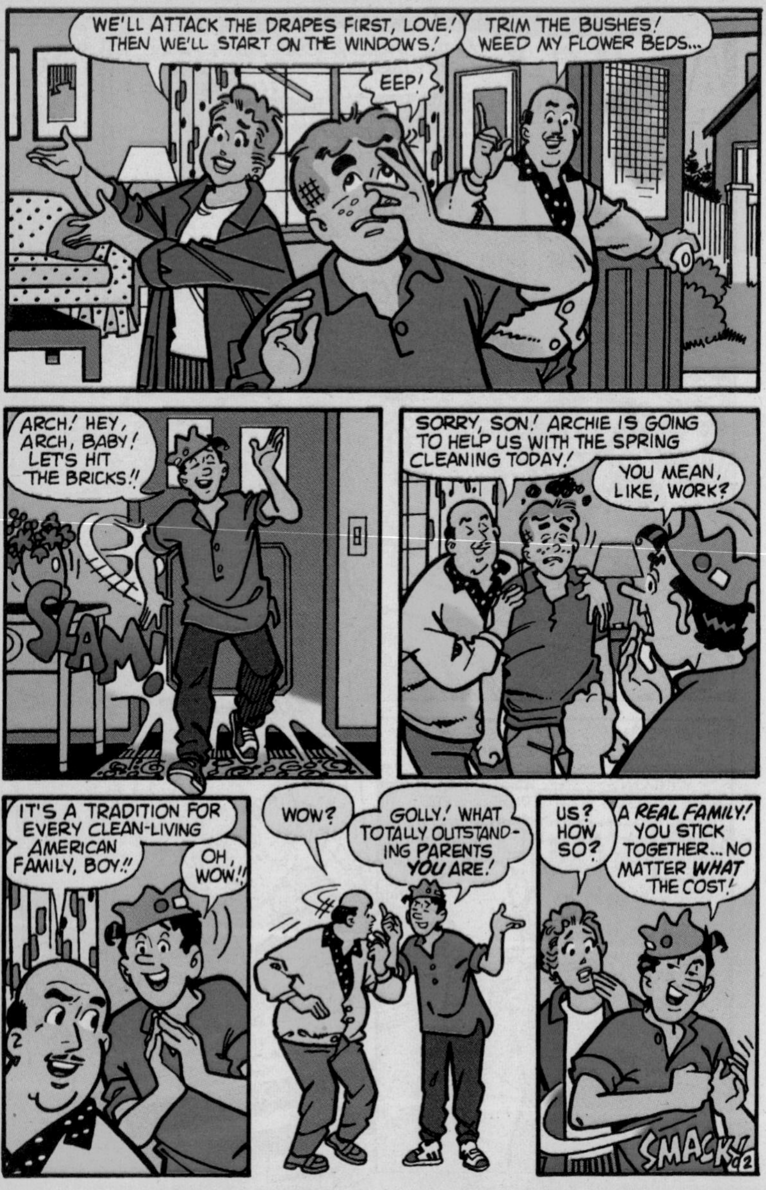

WE'LL ATTACK THE DRAPES FIRST, LOVE! THEN WE'LL START ON THE WINDOWS!
TRIM THE BUSHES! WEED MY FLOWER BEDS...
EEP!
ARCH! HEY, ARCH, BABY! LET'S HIT THE BRICKS!!
SLAM!
SORRY, SON! ARCHIE IS GOING TO HELP US WITH THE SPRING CLEANING TODAY!
YOU MEAN, LIKE, WORK?
IT'S A TRADITION FOR EVERY CLEAN-LIVING AMERICAN FAMILY, BOY!!
OH, WOW!!
WOW?
GOLLY! WHAT TOTALLY OUTSTAND-ING PARENTS YOU ARE!
US? HOW SO?
A REAL FAMILY! YOU STICK TOGETHER... NO MATTER WHAT THE COST!
SMACK!
2

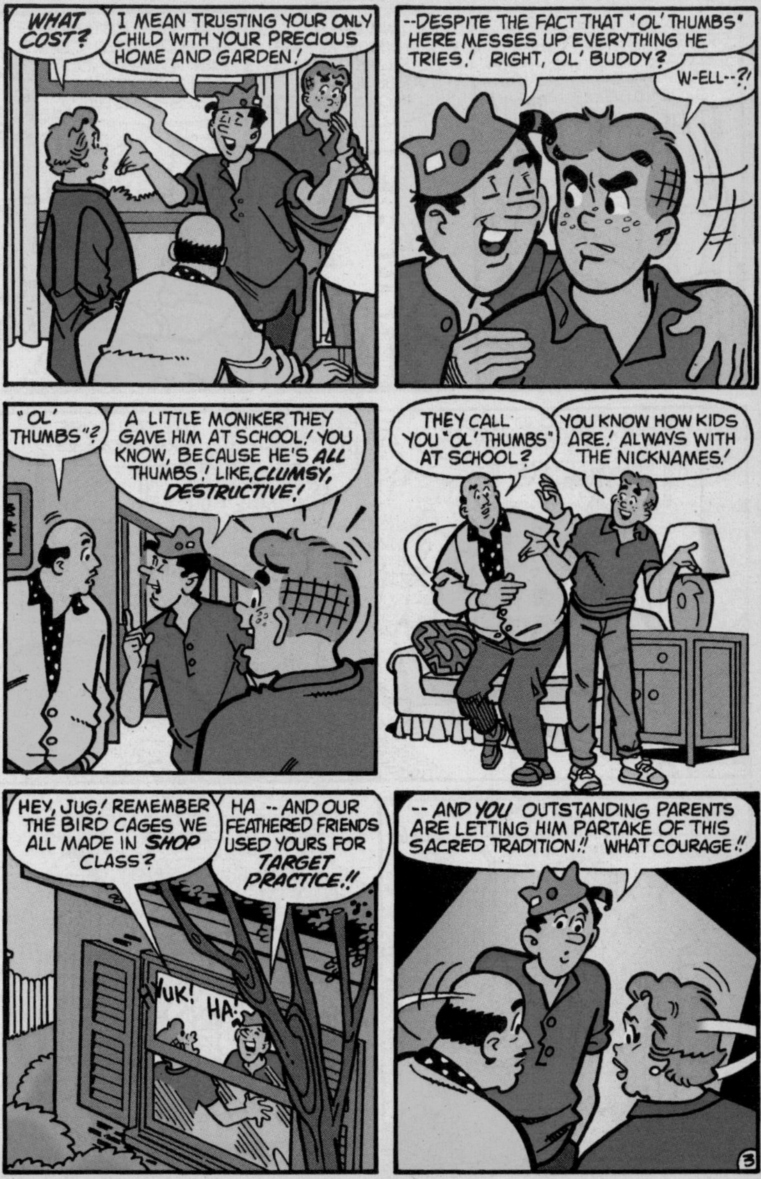
WHAT COST?
I MEAN TRUSTING YOUR ONLY CHILD WITH YOUR PRECIOUS HOME AND GARDEN!
--DESPITE THE FACT THAT "OL' THUMBS" HERE MESSES UP EVERYTHING HE TRIES! RIGHT, OL' BUDDY?
W-ELL--?!
"OL' THUMBS"?
A LITTLE MONIKER THEY GAVE HIM AT SCHOOL! YOU KNOW, BECAUSE HE'S ALL THUMBS! LIKE, CLUMSY, DESTRUCTIVE!
THEY CALL YOU "OL' THUMBS" AT SCHOOL?
YOU KNOW HOW KIDS ARE! ALWAYS WITH THE NICKNAMES!
HEY, JUG! REMEMBER THE BIRD CAGES WE ALL MADE IN SHOP CLASS?
HA --AND OUR FEATHERED FRIENDS USED YOURS FOR TARGET PRACTICE!!
HYUK!
HA!
-- AND YOU OUTSTANDING PARENTS ARE LETTING HIM PARTAKE OF THIS SACRED TRADITION!! WHAT COURAGE!!
3

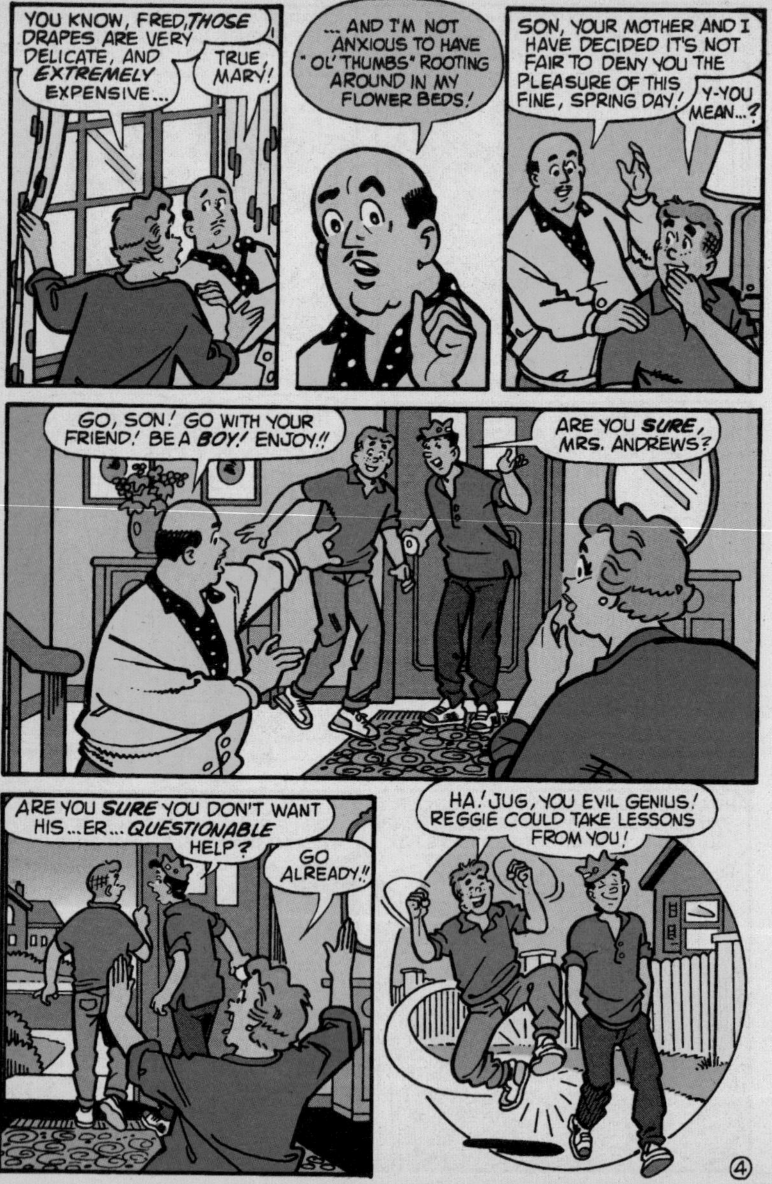
YOU KNOW, FRED, THOSE DRAPES ARE VERY DELICATE, AND EXTREMELY EXPENSIVE...
TRUE, MARY!
... AND I'M NOT ANXIOUS TO HAVE "OL' THUMBS" ROOTING AROUND IN MY FLOWER BEDS!
SON, YOUR MOTHER AND I HAVE DECIDED IT'S NOT FAIR TO DENY YOU THE PLEASURE OF THIS FINE, SPRING DAY!
Y-YOU MEAN...?
GO, SON! GO WITH YOUR FRIEND! BE A BOY! ENJOY!!
ARE YOU SURE, MRS. ANDREWS?
ARE YOU SURE YOU DON'T WANT HIS...ER...QUESTIONABLE HELP?
GO ALREADY!!
HA! JUG, YOU EVIL GENIUS! REGGIE COULD TAKE LESSONS FROM YOU!

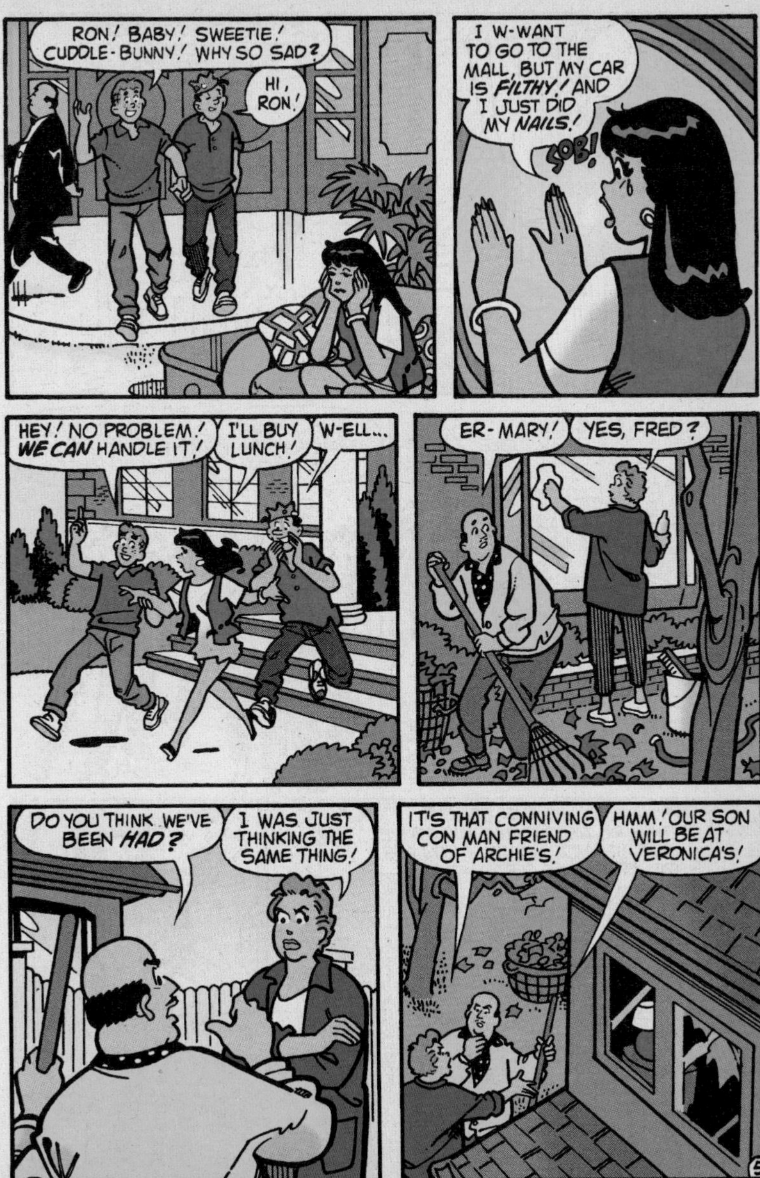
RON! BABY! SWEETIE! CUDDLE-BUNNY! WHY SO SAD?
HI, RON!
I W-WANT TO GO TO THE MALL, BUT MY CAR IS FILTHY! AND I JUST DID MY NAILS!
SOB!
HEY! NO PROBLEM! WE CAN HANDLE IT!
I'LL BUY LUNCH!
W-ELL...
ER-MARY!
YES, FRED?
DO YOU THINK WE'VE BEEN HAD?
I WAS JUST THINKING THE SAME THING!
IT'S THAT CONNIVING CON MAN FRIEND OF ARCHIE'S!
HMM! OUR SON WILL BE AT VERONICA'S!
5

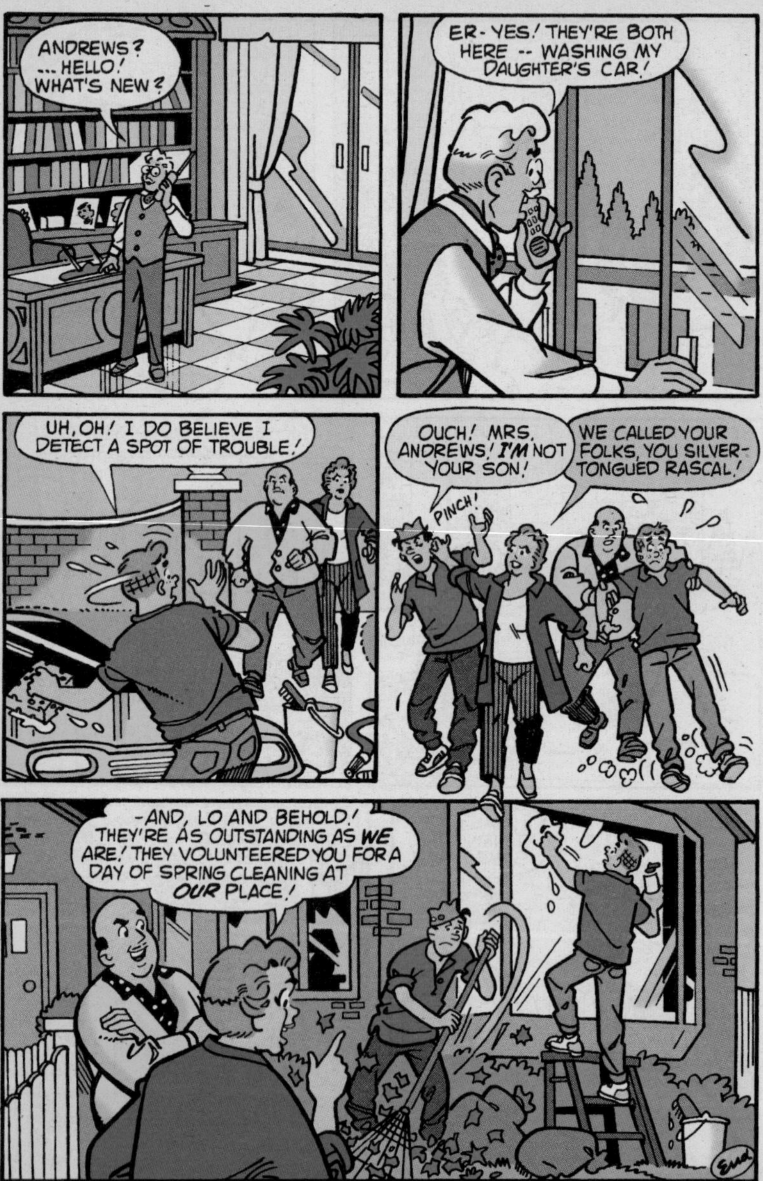
ANDREWS? ... HELLO! WHAT'S NEW?
ER-YES! THEY'RE BOTH HERE -- WASHING MY DAUGHTER'S CAR!
UH, OH! I DO BELIEVE I DETECT A SPOT OF TROUBLE!
OUCH! MRS. ANDREWS! I'M NOT YOUR SON!
PINCH!
WE CALLED YOUR FOLKS, YOU SILVER-TONGUED RASCAL!
-AND, LO AND BEHOLD! THEY'RE AS OUTSTANDING AS WE ARE! THEY VOLUNTEERED YOU FOR A DAY OF SPRING CLEANING AT OUR PLACE!
End

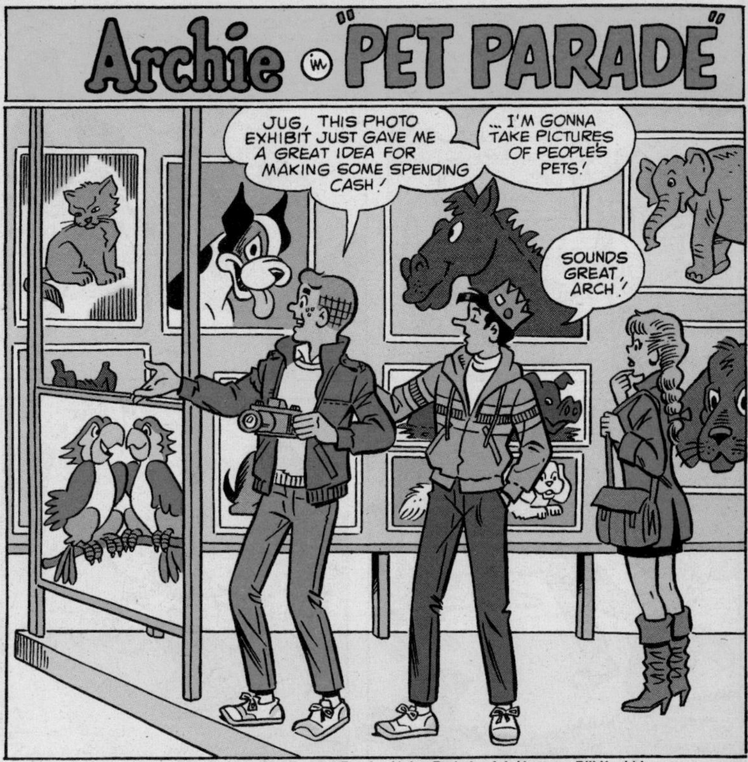
Archie in "PET PARADE"
JUG, THIS PHOTO EXHIBIT JUST GAVE ME A GREAT IDEA FOR MAKING SOME SPENDING CASH!
...I'M GONNA TAKE PICTURES OF PEOPLE'S PETS!
SOUNDS GREAT, ARCH!

Script: George Gladir / Pencils: Howard Bender / Inks: Rudy Lapick / Letters: Bill Yoshida

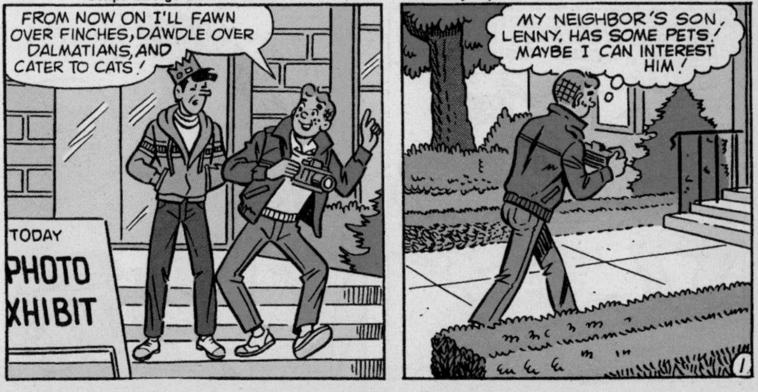
FROM NOW ON I'LL FAWN OVER FINCHES, DAWDLE OVER DALMATIANS, AND CATER TO CATS!
TODAY
PHOTO
XHIBIT
MY NEIGHBOR'S SON, LENNY, HAS SOME PETS! MAYBE I CAN INTEREST HIM!
1

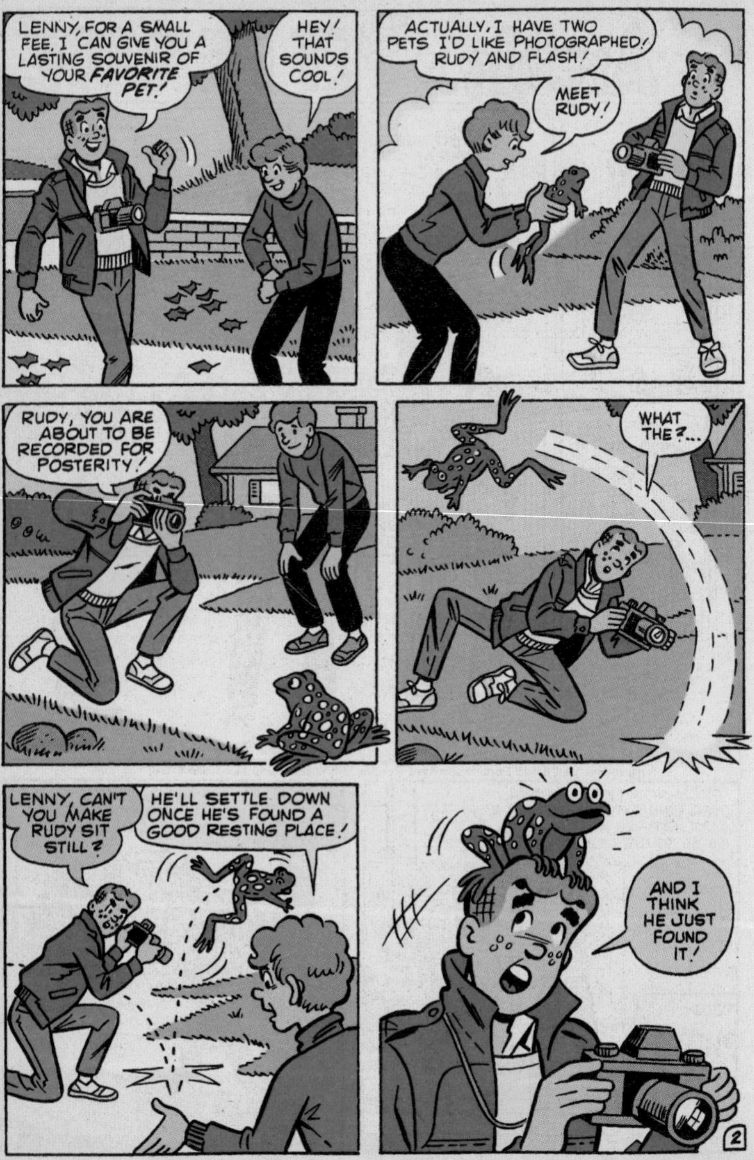
LENNY, FOR A SMALL FEE, I CAN GIVE YOU A LASTING SOUVENIR OF YOUR FAVORITE PET!
HEY! THAT SOUNDS COOL!
ACTUALLY, I HAVE TWO PETS I'D LIKE PHOTOGRAPHED! RUDY AND FLASH!
MEET RUDY!
RUDY, YOU ARE ABOUT TO BE RECORDED FOR POSTERITY!
WHAT THE?...
LENNY, CAN'T YOU MAKE RUDY SIT STILL?
HE'LL SETTLE DOWN ONCE HE'S FOUND A GOOD RESTING PLACE!
AND I THINK HE JUST FOUND IT!
2

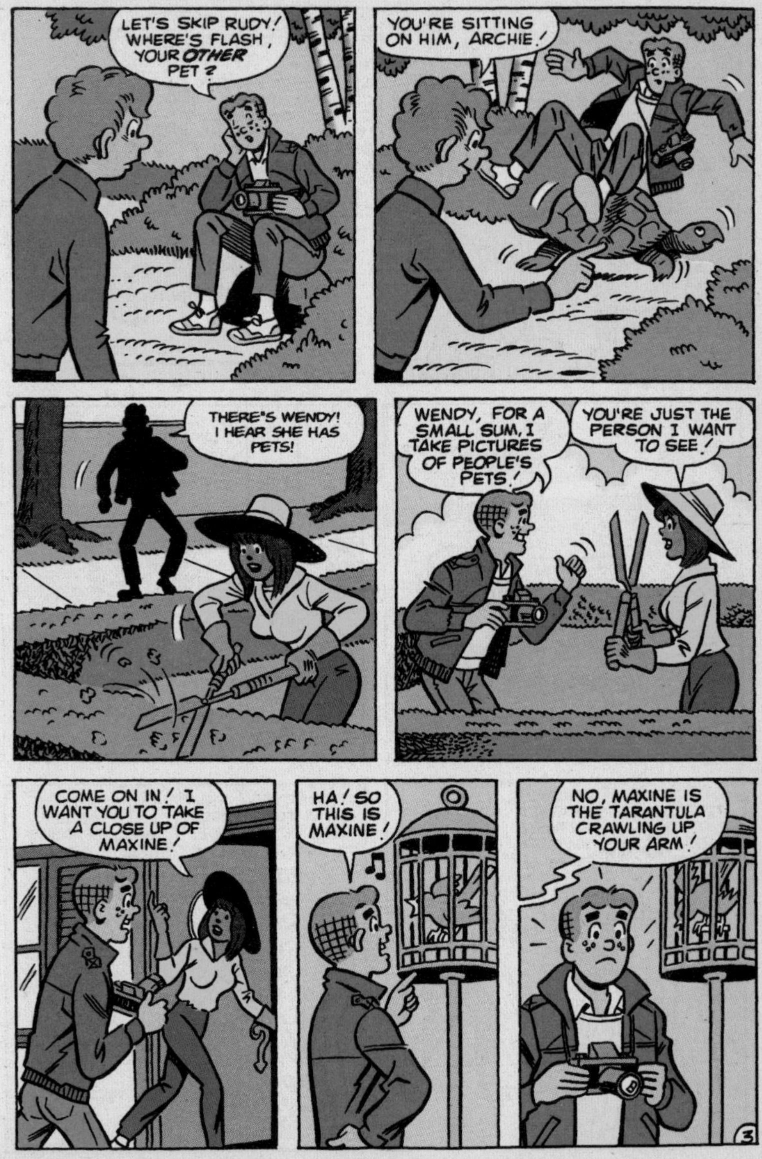
LET'S SKIP RUDY! WHERE'S FLASH, YOUR OTHER PET?
YOU'RE SITTING ON HIM, ARCHIE!
THERE'S WENDY! I HEAR SHE HAS PETS!
WENDY, FOR A SMALL SUM, I TAKE PICTURES OF PEOPLE'S PETS!
YOU'RE JUST THE PERSON I WANT TO SEE!
COME ON IN! I WANT YOU TO TAKE A CLOSE UP OF MAXINE!
HA! SO THIS IS MAXINE!
NO, MAXINE IS THE TARANTULA CRAWLING UP YOUR ARM!
3

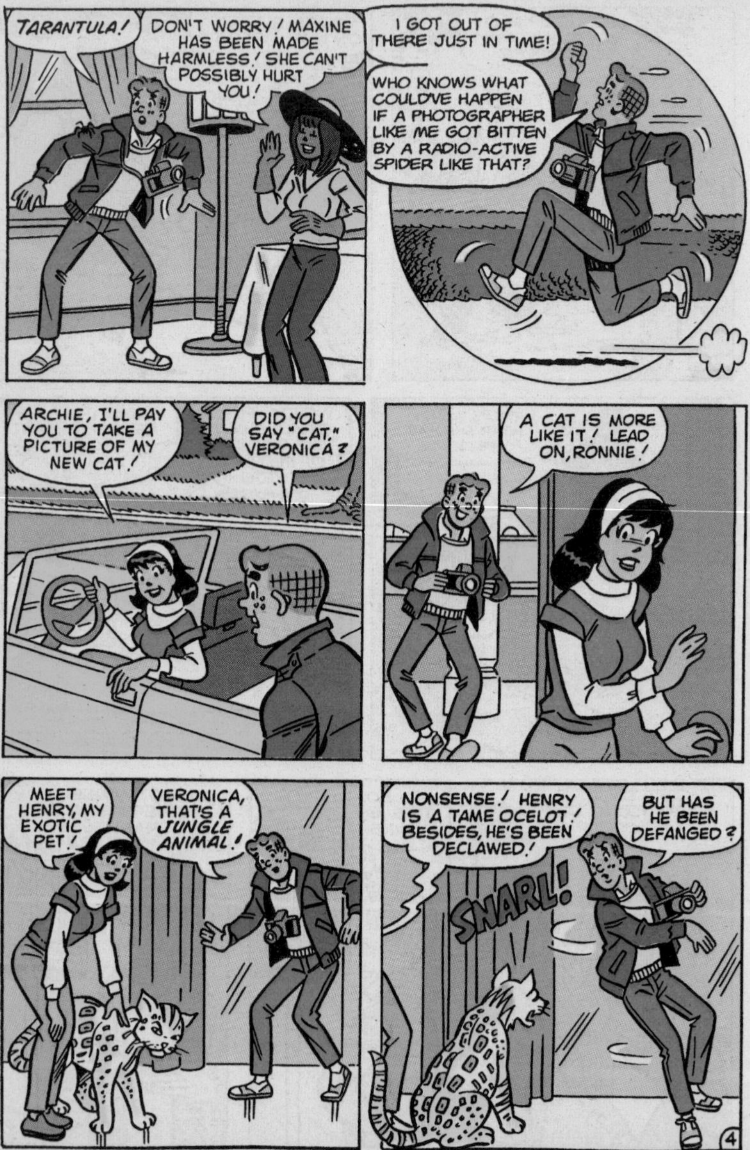
TARANTULA!
DON'T WORRY! MAXINE HAS BEEN MADE HARMLESS! SHE CAN'T POSSIBLY HURT YOU!
I GOT OUT OF THERE JUST IN TIME!
WHO KNOWS WHAT COULD'VE HAPPEN IF A PHOTOGRAPHER LIKE ME GOT BITTEN BY A RADIO-ACTIVE SPIDER LIKE THAT?
ARCHIE, I'LL PAY YOU TO TAKE A PICTURE OF MY NEW CAT!
DID YOU SAY "CAT," VERONICA?
A CAT IS MORE LIKE IT! LEAD ON, RONNIE!
MEET HENRY, MY EXOTIC PET!
VERONICA, THAT'S A JUNGLE ANIMAL!
NONSENSE! HENRY IS A TAME OCELOT! BESIDES, HE'S BEEN DECLAWED!
BUT HAS HE BEEN DEFANGED?
SNARL!
4

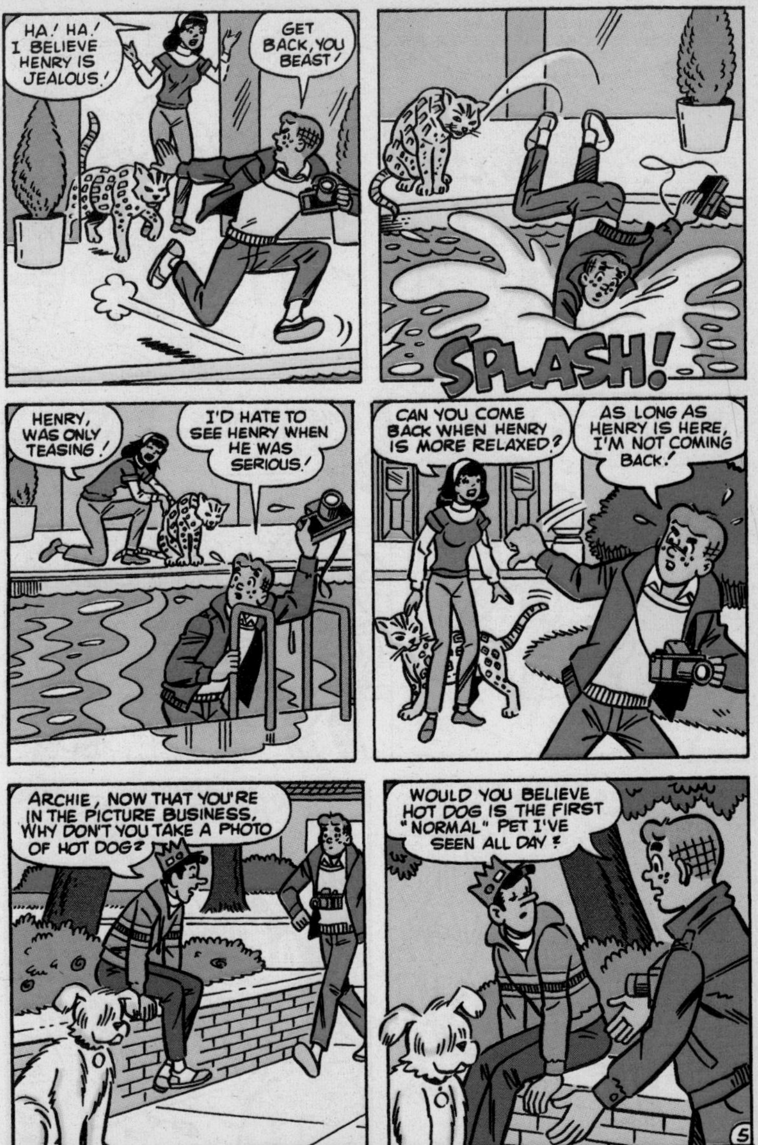
HA! HA! I BELIEVE HENRY IS JEALOUS!
GET BACK, YOU BEAST!
SPLASH!
HENRY, WAS ONLY TEASING!
I'D HATE TO SEE HENRY WHEN HE WAS SERIOUS!
CAN YOU COME BACK WHEN HENRY IS MORE RELAXED?
AS LONG AS HENRY IS HERE, I'M NOT COMING BACK!
ARCHIE, NOW THAT YOU'RE IN THE PICTURE BUSINESS, WHY DON'T YOU TAKE A PHOTO OF HOT DOG?
WOULD YOU BELIEVE HOT DOG IS THE FIRST "NORMAL" PET I'VE SEEN ALL DAY?
5

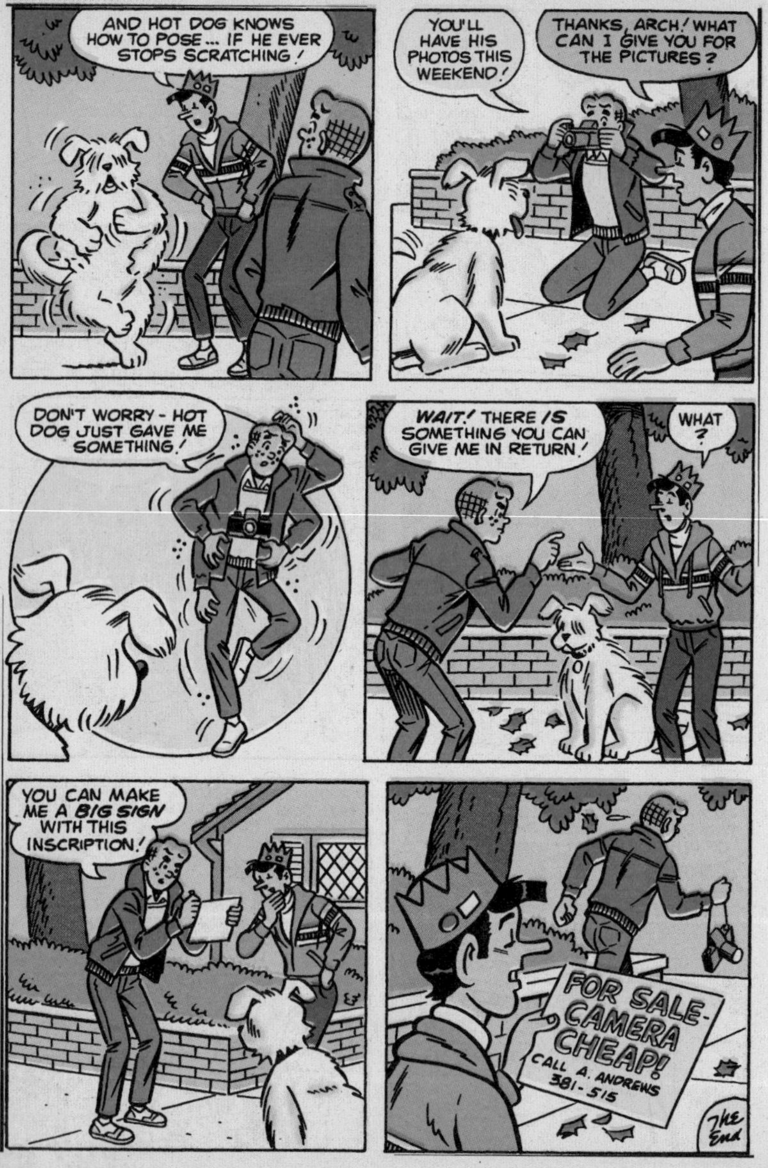
AND HOT DOG KNOWS HOW TO POSE... IF HE EVER STOPS SCRATCHING!
YOU'LL HAVE HIS PHOTOS THIS WEEKEND!
THANKS, ARCH! WHAT CAN I GIVE YOU FOR THE PICTURES?
DON'T WORRY - HOT DOG JUST GAVE ME SOMETHING!
WAIT! THERE IS SOMETHING YOU CAN GIVE ME IN RETURN!
WHAT?
YOU CAN MAKE ME A BIG SIGN WITH THIS INSCRIPTION!
FOR SALE-
CAMERA
CHEAP!
CALL A. ANDREWS
381-515
THE END

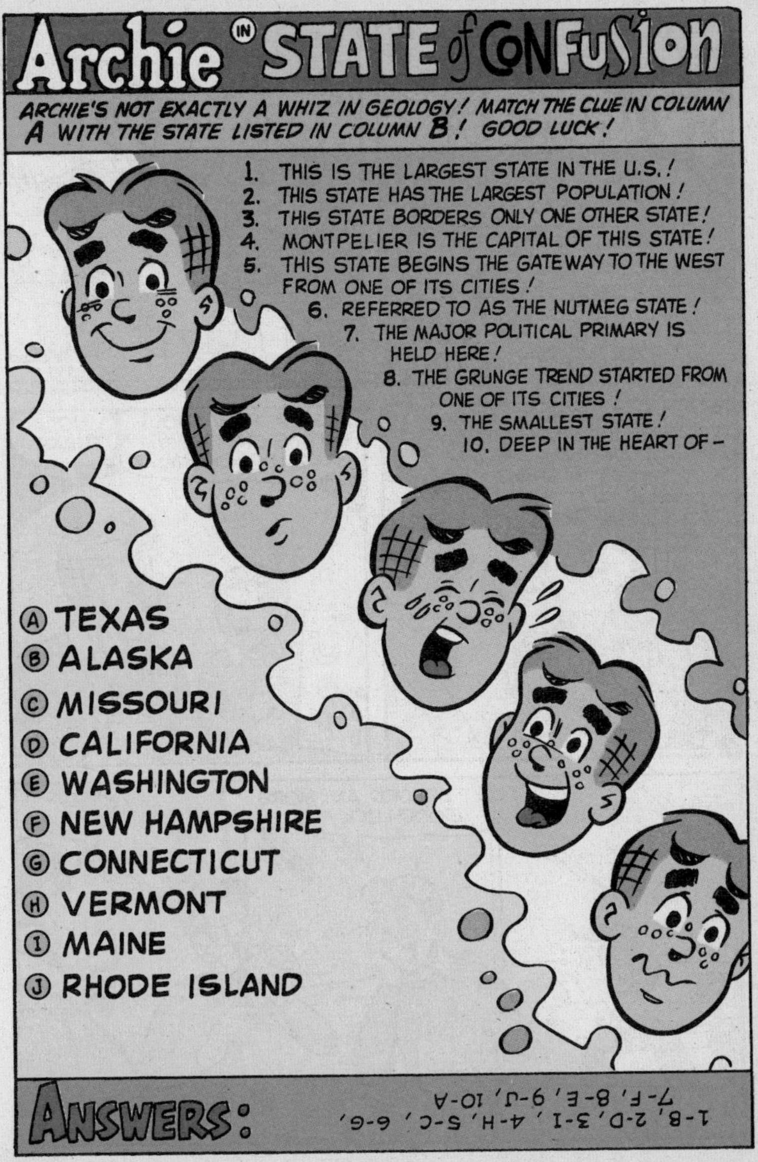
Archie IN STATE of CONFUSION
ARCHIE'S NOT EXACTLY A WHIZ IN GEOLOGY! MATCH THE CLUE IN COLUMN A WITH THE STATE LISTED IN COLUMN B! GOOD LUCK!
1. THIS IS THE LARGEST STATE IN THE U.S.!
2. THIS STATE HAS THE LARGEST POPULATION!
3. THIS STATE BORDERS ONLY ONE OTHER STATE!
4. MONTPELIER IS THE CAPITAL OF THIS STATE!
5. THIS STATE BEGINS THE GATEWAY TO THE WEST FROM ONE OF ITS CITIES!
6. REFERRED TO AS THE NUTMEG STATE!
7. THE MAJOR POLITICAL PRIMARY IS HELD HERE!
8. THE GRUNGE TREND STARTED FROM ONE OF ITS CITIES!
9. THE SMALLEST STATE!
10. DEEP IN THE HEART OF –
Ⓐ TEXAS
Ⓑ ALASKA
Ⓒ MISSOURI
Ⓓ CALIFORNIA
Ⓔ WASHINGTON
Ⓕ NEW HAMPSHIRE
Ⓖ CONNECTICUT
Ⓗ VERMONT
Ⓘ MAINE
Ⓙ RHODE ISLAND
ANSWERS:
1-B, 2-D, 3-I, 4-H, 5-C, 6-G, 7-F, 8-E, 9-J, 10-A

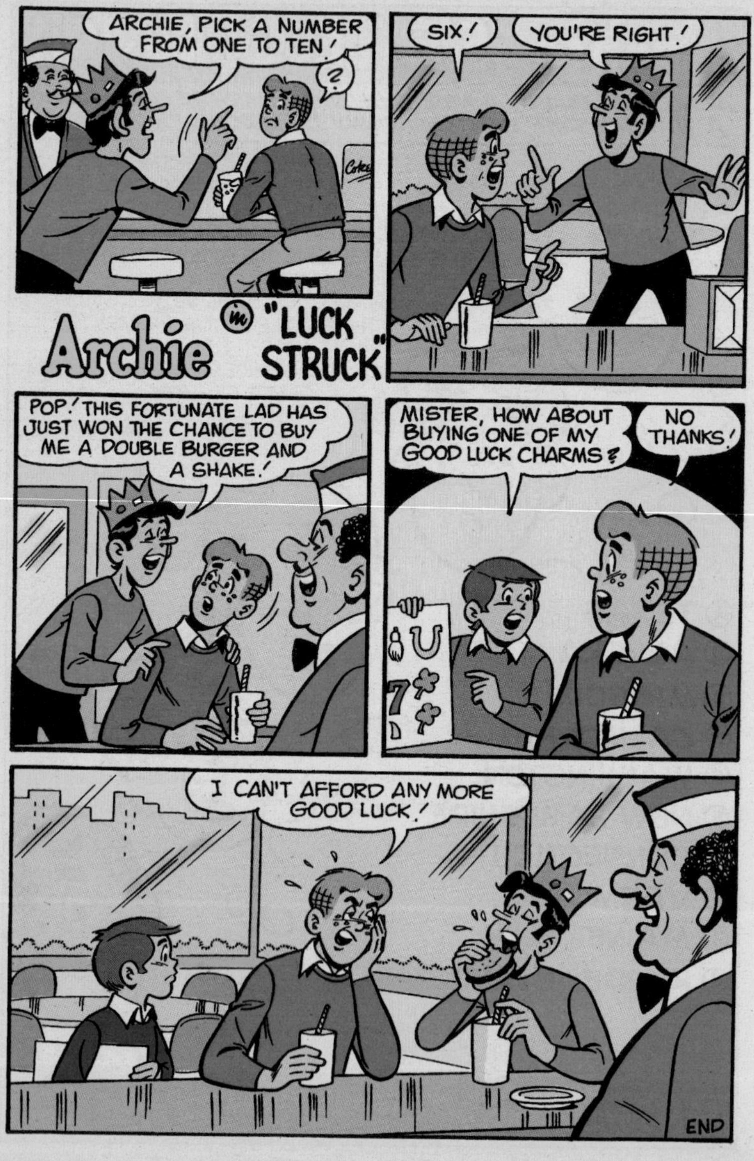
ARCHIE, PICK A NUMBER FROM ONE TO TEN!
?
SIX!
YOU'RE RIGHT!
Archie in "LUCK STRUCK"
POP! THIS FORTUNATE LAD HAS JUST WON THE CHANCE TO BUY ME A DOUBLE BURGER AND A SHAKE!
MISTER, HOW ABOUT BUYING ONE OF MY GOOD LUCK CHARMS?
NO THANKS!
I CAN'T AFFORD ANY MORE GOOD LUCK!
END

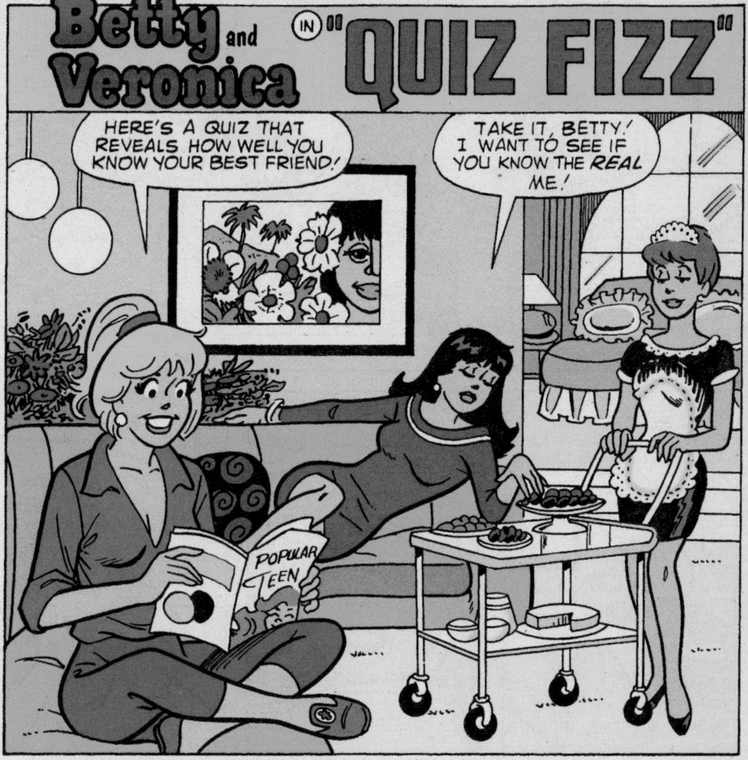
Betty and Veronica
IN "QUIZ FIZZ"
HERE'S A QUIZ THAT REVEALS HOW WELL YOU KNOW YOUR BEST FRIEND!
TAKE IT, BETTY! I WANT TO SEE IF YOU KNOW THE *REAL* ME!
POPULAR TEEN

Script: Gladir / Pencils: DeCarlo & Parent / Inks: Flood / Letters: Yoshida / Colors: Grossman

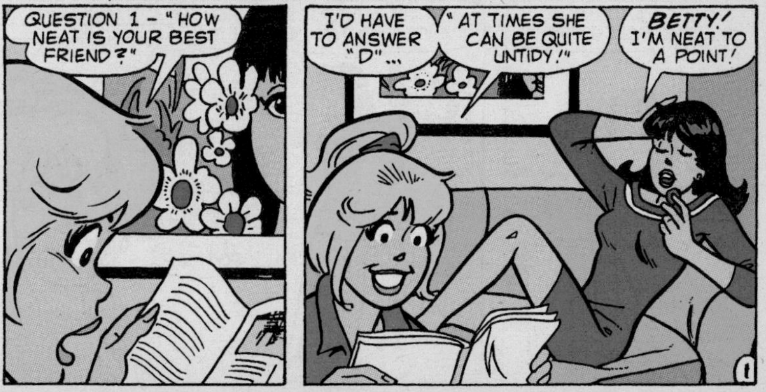
QUESTION 1 – "HOW NEAT IS YOUR BEST FRIEND?"
I'D HAVE TO ANSWER "D"...
"AT TIMES SHE CAN BE QUITE UNTIDY!"
BETTY! I'M NEAT TO A POINT!
1

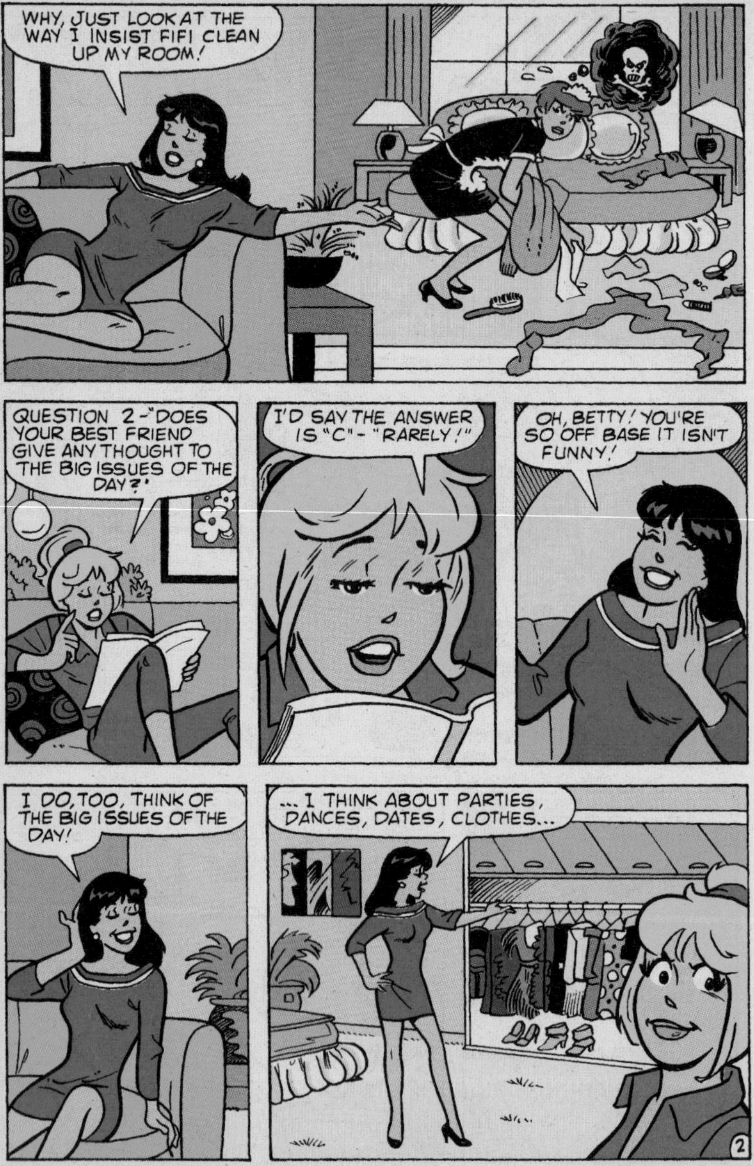
WHY, JUST LOOK AT THE WAY I INSIST FIFI CLEAN UP MY ROOM!
QUESTION 2-"DOES YOUR BEST FRIEND GIVE ANY THOUGHT TO THE BIG ISSUES OF THE DAY?"
I'D SAY THE ANSWER IS "C" - "RARELY!"
OH, BETTY! YOU'RE SO OFF BASE IT ISN'T FUNNY!
I DO, TOO, THINK OF THE BIG ISSUES OF THE DAY!
... I THINK ABOUT PARTIES, DANCES, DATES, CLOTHES...
2

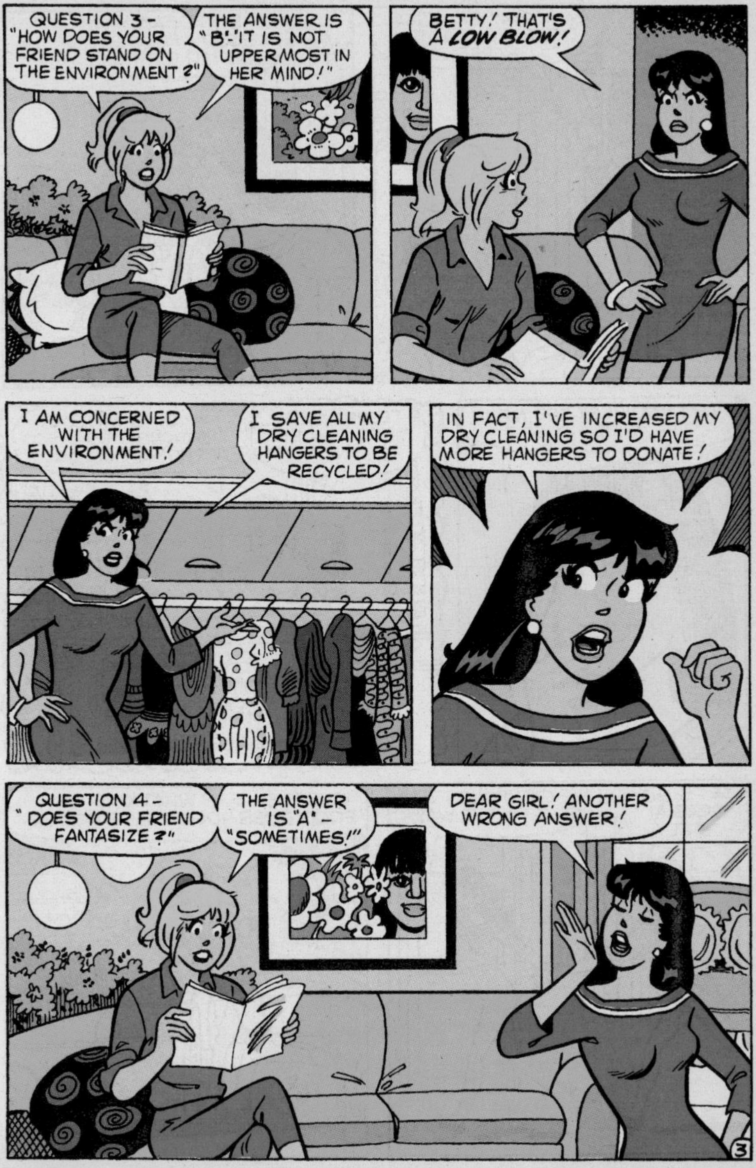
QUESTION 3 - "HOW DOES YOUR FRIEND STAND ON THE ENVIRONMENT ?"
THE ANSWER IS "B"-"IT IS NOT UPPERMOST IN HER MIND!"
BETTY! THAT'S A LOW BLOW!
I AM CONCERNED WITH THE ENVIRONMENT!
I SAVE ALL MY DRY CLEANING HANGERS TO BE RECYCLED!
IN FACT, I'VE INCREASED MY DRY CLEANING SO I'D HAVE MORE HANGERS TO DONATE!
QUESTION 4 - "DOES YOUR FRIEND FANTASIZE ?"
THE ANSWER IS "A" - "SOMETIMES!"
DEAR GIRL! ANOTHER WRONG ANSWER!
3

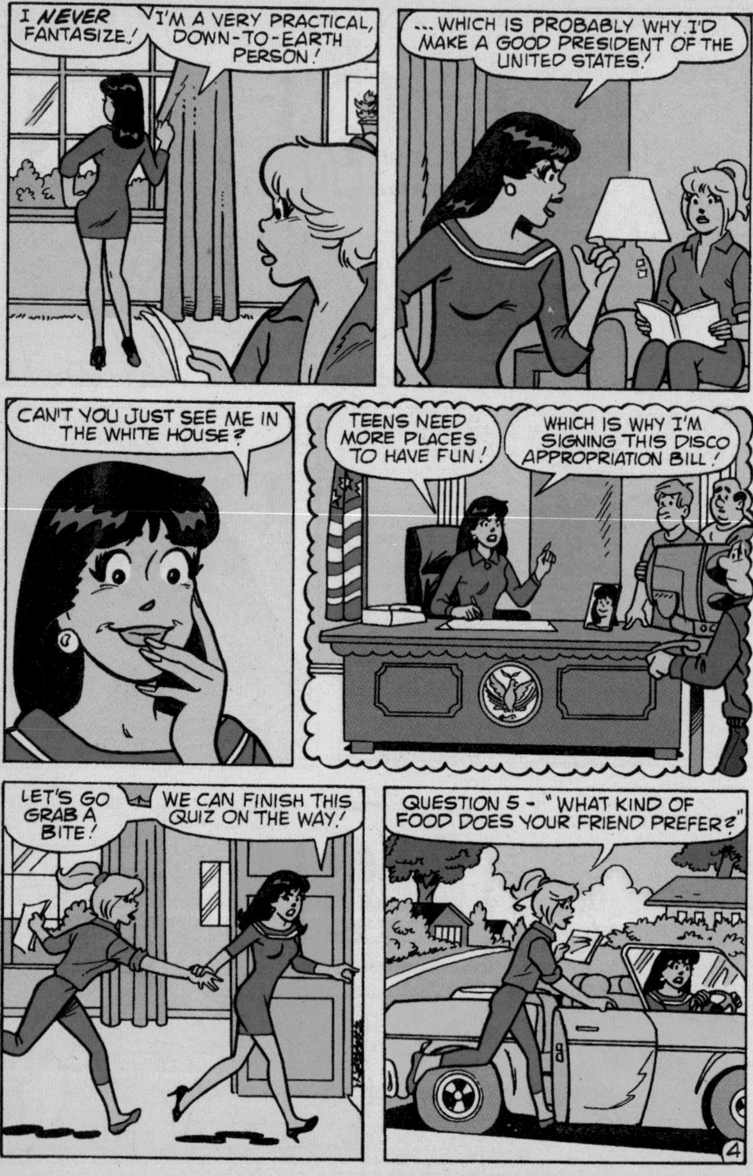
I NEVER FANTASIZE!
I'M A VERY PRACTICAL, DOWN-TO-EARTH PERSON!
...WHICH IS PROBABLY WHY I'D MAKE A GOOD PRESIDENT OF THE UNITED STATES!
CAN'T YOU JUST SEE ME IN THE WHITE HOUSE?
TEENS NEED MORE PLACES TO HAVE FUN!
WHICH IS WHY I'M SIGNING THIS DISCO APPROPRIATION BILL!
LET'S GO GRAB A BITE!
WE CAN FINISH THIS QUIZ ON THE WAY!
QUESTION 5 - "WHAT KIND OF FOOD DOES YOUR FRIEND PREFER?"
4

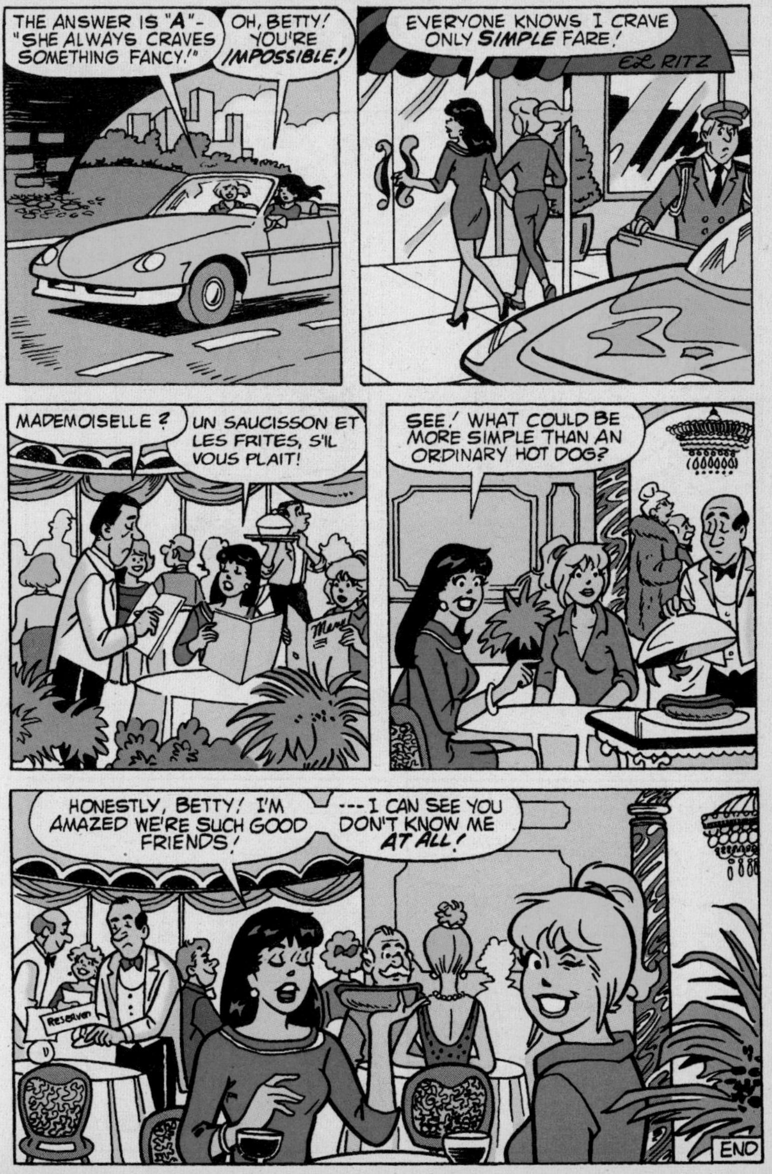
THE ANSWER IS "A"- "SHE ALWAYS CRAVES SOMETHING FANCY."
OH, BETTY! YOU'RE IMPOSSIBLE!
EVERYONE KNOWS I CRAVE ONLY SIMPLE FARE!
EL RITZ
MADEMOISELLE ?
UN SAUCISSON ET LES FRITES, S'IL VOUS PLAIT!
SEE! WHAT COULD BE MORE SIMPLE THAN AN ORDINARY HOT DOG?
HONESTLY, BETTY! I'M AMAZED WE'RE SUCH GOOD FRIENDS!
---I CAN SEE YOU DON'T KNOW ME AT ALL!
END

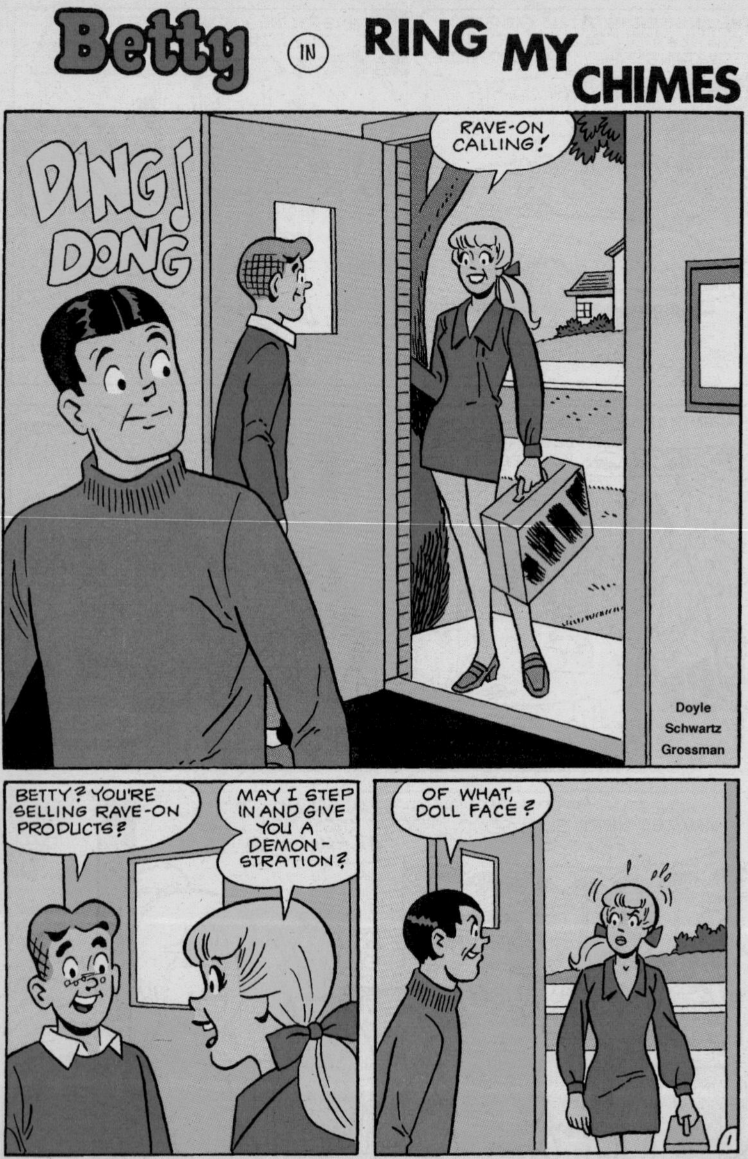
Betty IN RING MY CHIMES
DING DONG
RAVE-ON CALLING!
Doyle
Schwartz
Grossman
BETTY? YOU'RE SELLING RAVE-ON PRODUCTS?
MAY I STEP IN AND GIVE YOU A DEMON-STRATION?
OF WHAT, DOLL FACE?
1

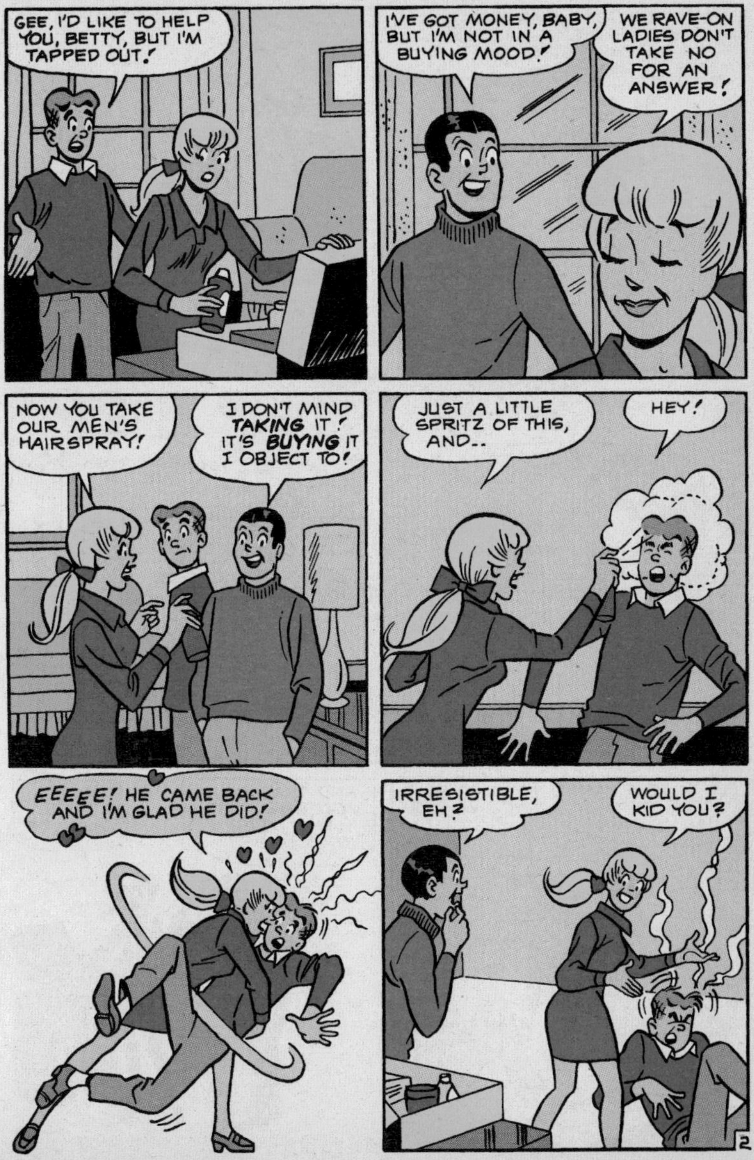
GEE, I'D LIKE TO HELP YOU, BETTY, BUT I'M TAPPED OUT!
I'VE GOT MONEY, BABY, BUT I'M NOT IN A BUYING MOOD!
WE RAVE-ON LADIES DON'T TAKE NO FOR AN ANSWER!
NOW YOU TAKE OUR MEN'S HAIRSPRAY!
I DON'T MIND TAKING IT! IT'S BUYING IT I OBJECT TO!
JUST A LITTLE SPRITZ OF THIS, AND..
HEY!
EEEEE! HE CAME BACK AND I'M GLAD HE DID!
IRRESISTIBLE, EH?
WOULD I KID YOU?

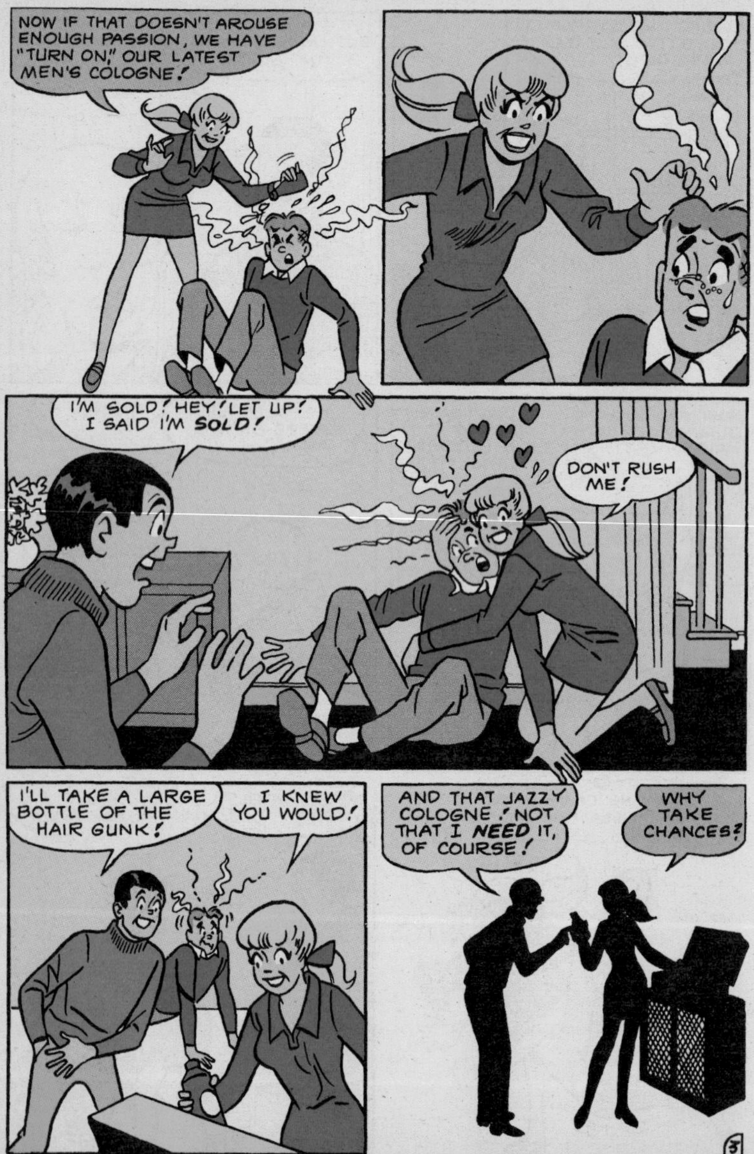
NOW IF THAT DOESN'T AROUSE ENOUGH PASSION, WE HAVE "TURN ON," OUR LATEST MEN'S COLOGNE!
I'M SOLD! HEY! LET UP! I SAID I'M SOLD!
DON'T RUSH ME!
I'LL TAKE A LARGE BOTTLE OF THE HAIR GUNK!
I KNEW YOU WOULD!
AND THAT JAZZY COLOGNE! NOT THAT I NEED IT, OF COURSE!
WHY TAKE CHANCES?
3

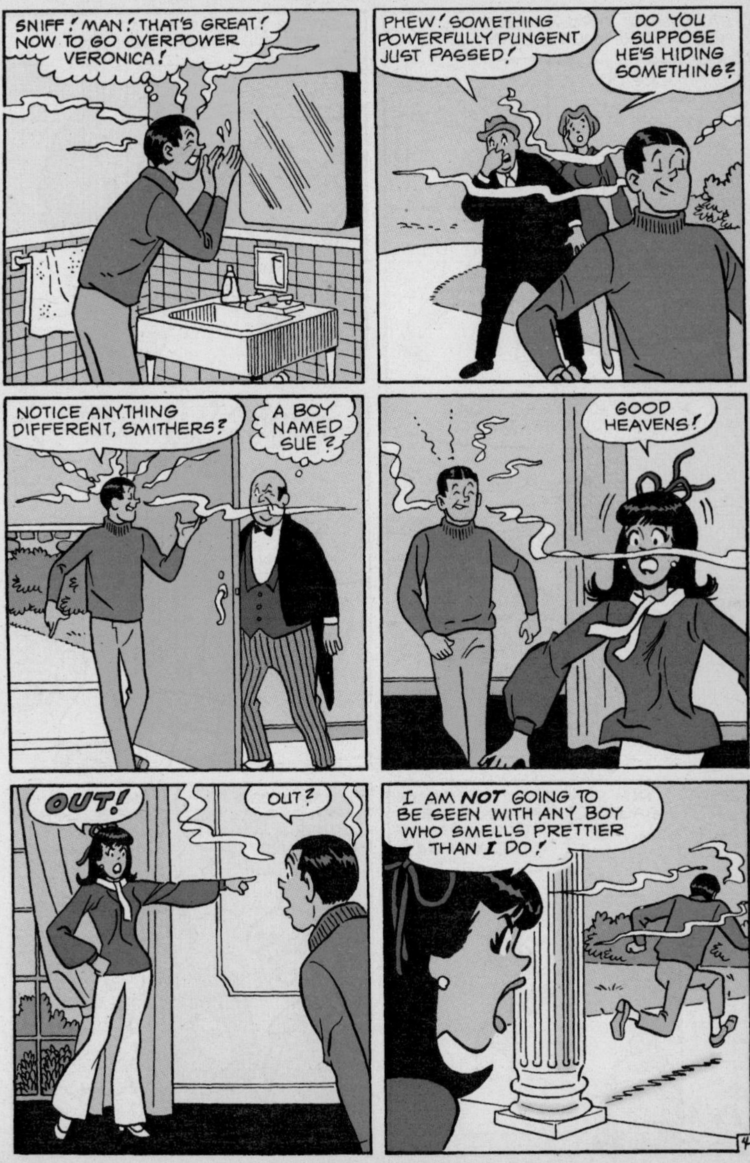
SNIFF! MAN! THAT'S GREAT! NOW TO GO OVERPOWER VERONICA!
PHEW! SOMETHING POWERFULLY PUNGENT JUST PASSED!
DO YOU SUPPOSE HE'S HIDING SOMETHING?
NOTICE ANYTHING DIFFERENT, SMITHERS?
A BOY NAMED SUE?
GOOD HEAVENS!
OUT!
OUT?
I AM NOT GOING TO BE SEEN WITH ANY BOY WHO SMELLS PRETTIER THAN I DO!
4

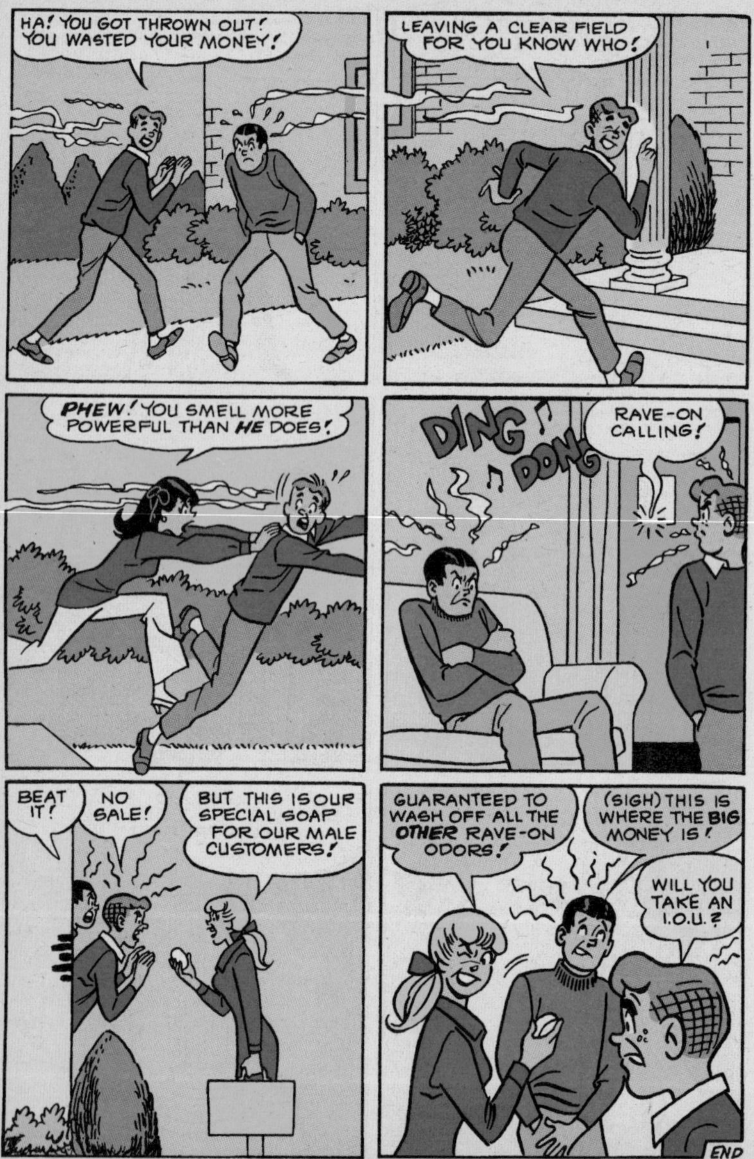
HA! YOU GOT THROWN OUT! YOU WASTED YOUR MONEY!
LEAVING A CLEAR FIELD FOR YOU KNOW WHO!
PHEW! YOU SMELL MORE POWERFUL THAN HE DOES!
DING DONG
RAVE-ON CALLING!
BEAT IT!
NO SALE!
BUT THIS IS OUR SPECIAL SOAP FOR OUR MALE CUSTOMERS!
GUARANTEED TO WASH OFF ALL THE OTHER RAVE-ON ODORS!
(SIGH) THIS IS WHERE THE BIG MONEY IS!
WILL YOU TAKE AN I.O.U.?
END

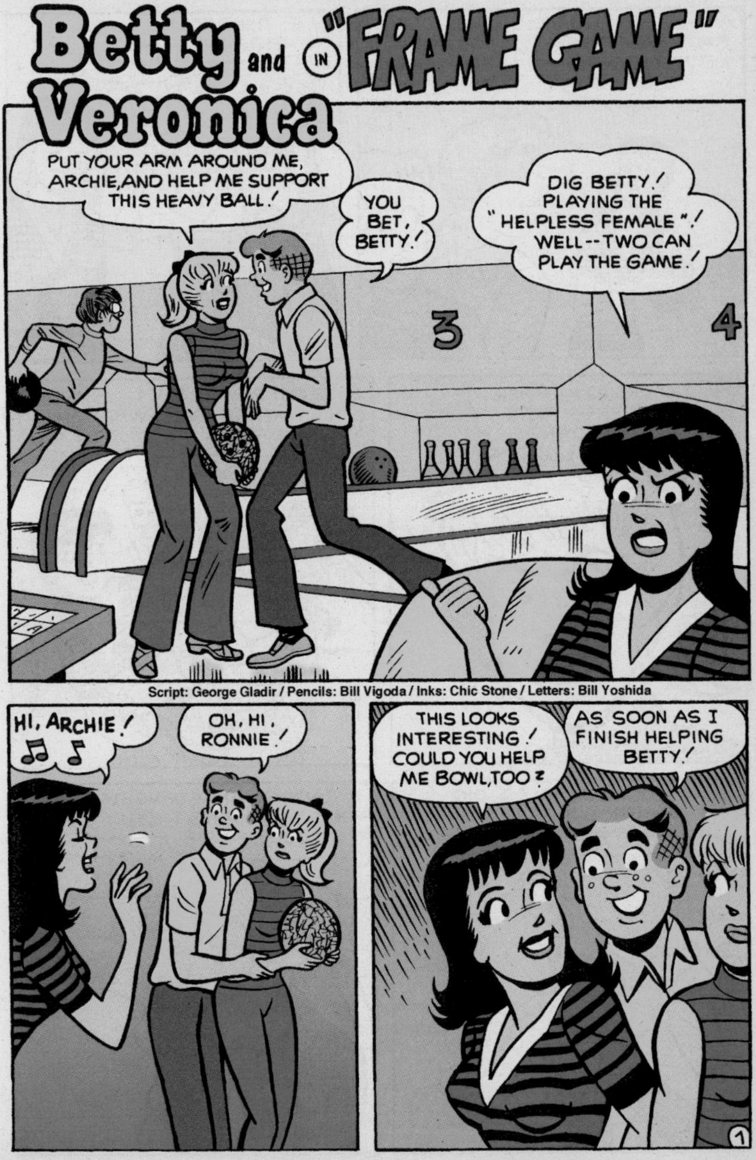
Betty and Veronica
IN "FRAME GAME"
PUT YOUR ARM AROUND ME, ARCHIE, AND HELP ME SUPPORT THIS HEAVY BALL!
YOU BET, BETTY!
DIG BETTY! PLAYING THE "HELPLESS FEMALE"! WELL--TWO CAN PLAY THE GAME!
3
4
Script: George Gladir / Pencils: Bill Vigoda / Inks: Chic Stone / Letters: Bill Yoshida
HI, ARCHIE!
OH, HI, RONNIE!
THIS LOOKS INTERESTING! COULD YOU HELP ME BOWL, TOO?
AS SOON AS I FINISH HELPING BETTY!
1

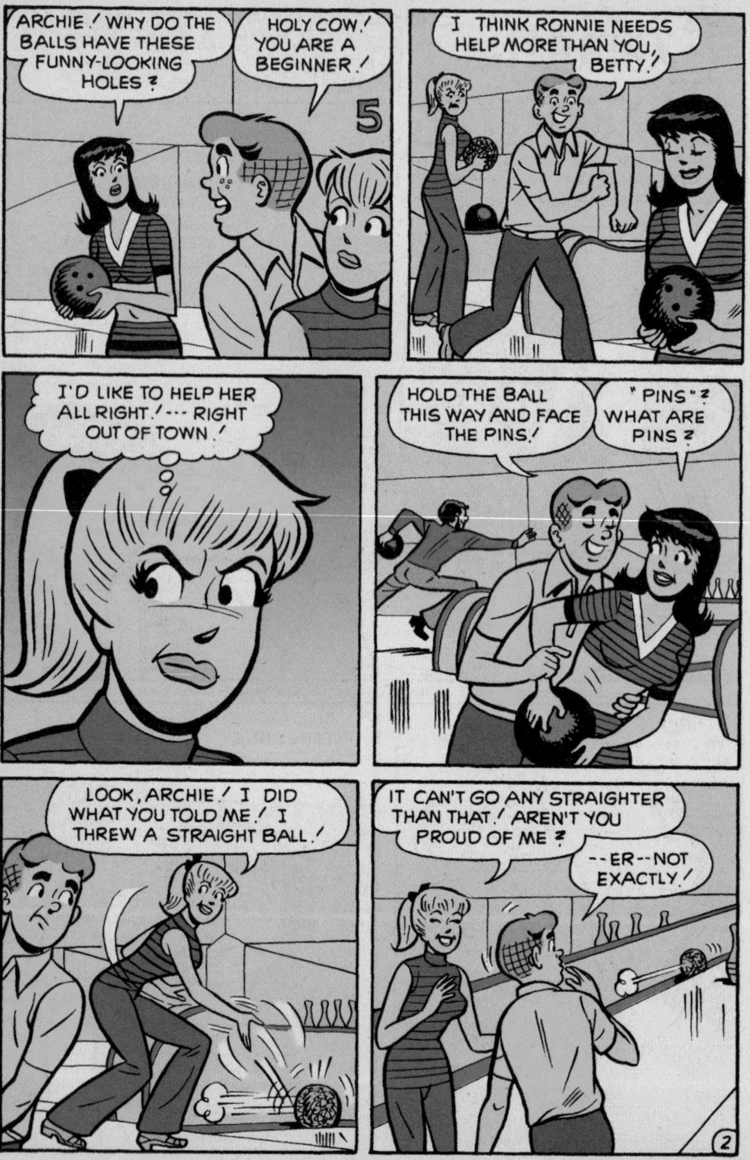

ARCHIE! WHY DO THE BALLS HAVE THESE FUNNY-LOOKING HOLES?
HOLY COW! YOU ARE A BEGINNER!
5
I THINK RONNIE NEEDS HELP MORE THAN YOU, BETTY!
I'D LIKE TO HELP HER ALL RIGHT! --- RIGHT OUT OF TOWN!
HOLD THE BALL THIS WAY AND FACE THE PINS!
"PINS"? WHAT ARE PINS?
LOOK, ARCHIE! I DID WHAT YOU TOLD ME! I THREW A STRAIGHT BALL!
IT CAN'T GO ANY STRAIGHTER THAN THAT! AREN'T YOU PROUD OF ME?
--ER--NOT EXACTLY!
2

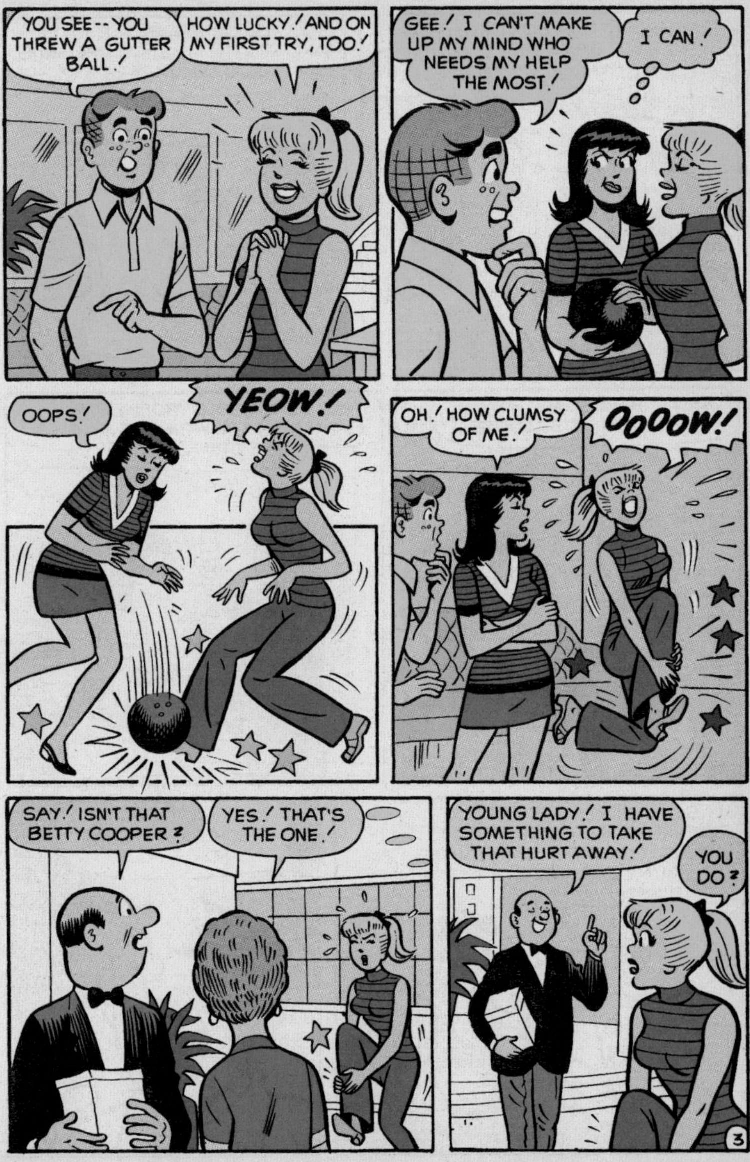
YOU SEE--YOU THREW A GUTTER BALL!
HOW LUCKY! AND ON MY FIRST TRY, TOO!
GEE! I CAN'T MAKE UP MY MIND WHO NEEDS MY HELP THE MOST!
I CAN!
OOPS!
YEOW!
OH! HOW CLUMSY OF ME!
OOOOW!
SAY! ISN'T THAT BETTY COOPER?
YES! THAT'S THE ONE!
YOUNG LADY! I HAVE SOMETHING TO TAKE THAT HURT AWAY!
YOU DO?
3

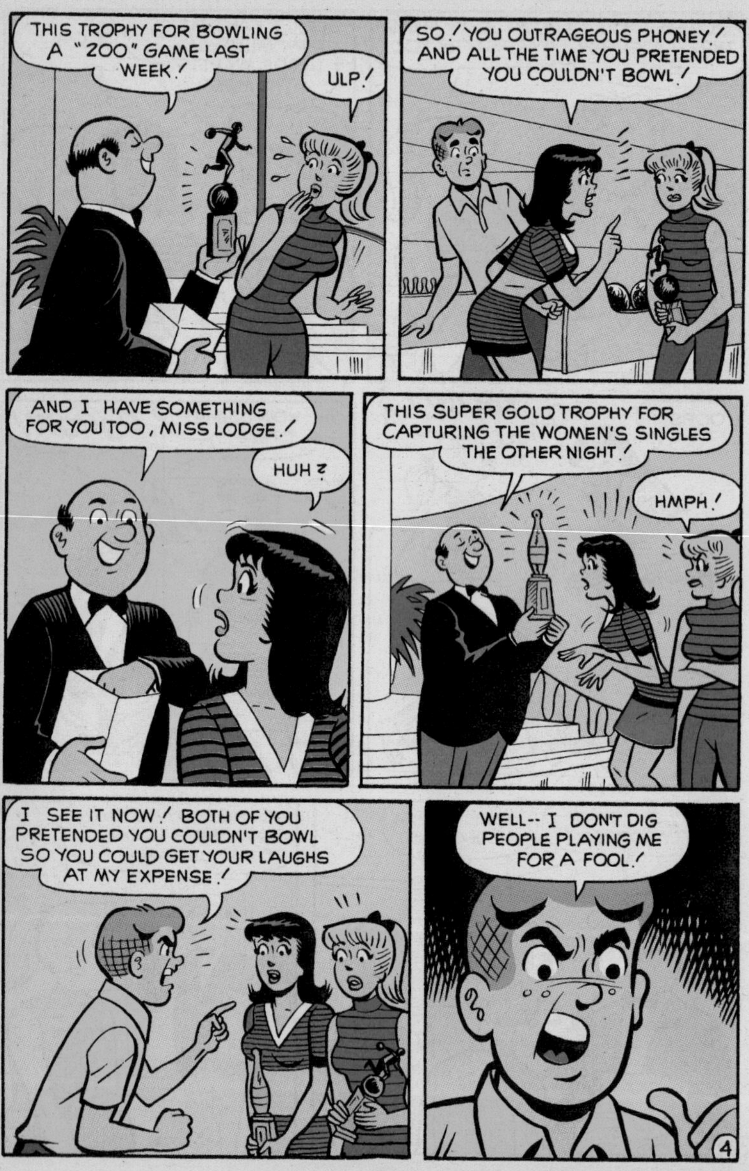
THIS TROPHY FOR BOWLING A "200" GAME LAST WEEK!
ULP!
SO! YOU OUTRAGEOUS PHONEY! AND ALL THE TIME YOU PRETENDED YOU COULDN'T BOWL!
AND I HAVE SOMETHING FOR YOU TOO, MISS LODGE!
HUH?
THIS SUPER GOLD TROPHY FOR CAPTURING THE WOMEN'S SINGLES THE OTHER NIGHT!
HMPH!
I SEE IT NOW! BOTH OF YOU PRETENDED YOU COULDN'T BOWL SO YOU COULD GET YOUR LAUGHS AT MY EXPENSE!
WELL-- I DON'T DIG PEOPLE PLAYING ME FOR A FOOL!
4

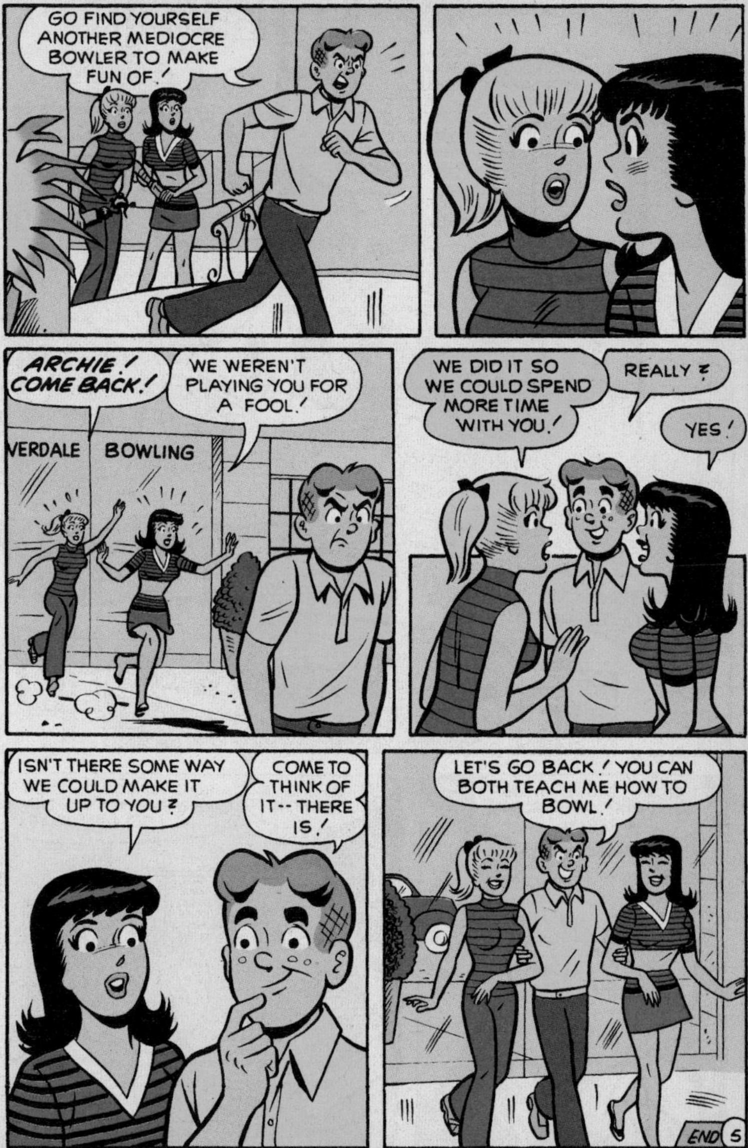
GO FIND YOURSELF ANOTHER MEDIOCRE BOWLER TO MAKE FUN OF!
ARCHIE! COME BACK!
WE WEREN'T PLAYING YOU FOR A FOOL!
VERDALE BOWLING
WE DID IT SO WE COULD SPEND MORE TIME WITH YOU!
REALLY?
YES!
ISN'T THERE SOME WAY WE COULD MAKE IT UP TO YOU?
COME TO THINK OF IT-- THERE IS!
LET'S GO BACK! YOU CAN BOTH TEACH ME HOW TO BOWL!
END
5

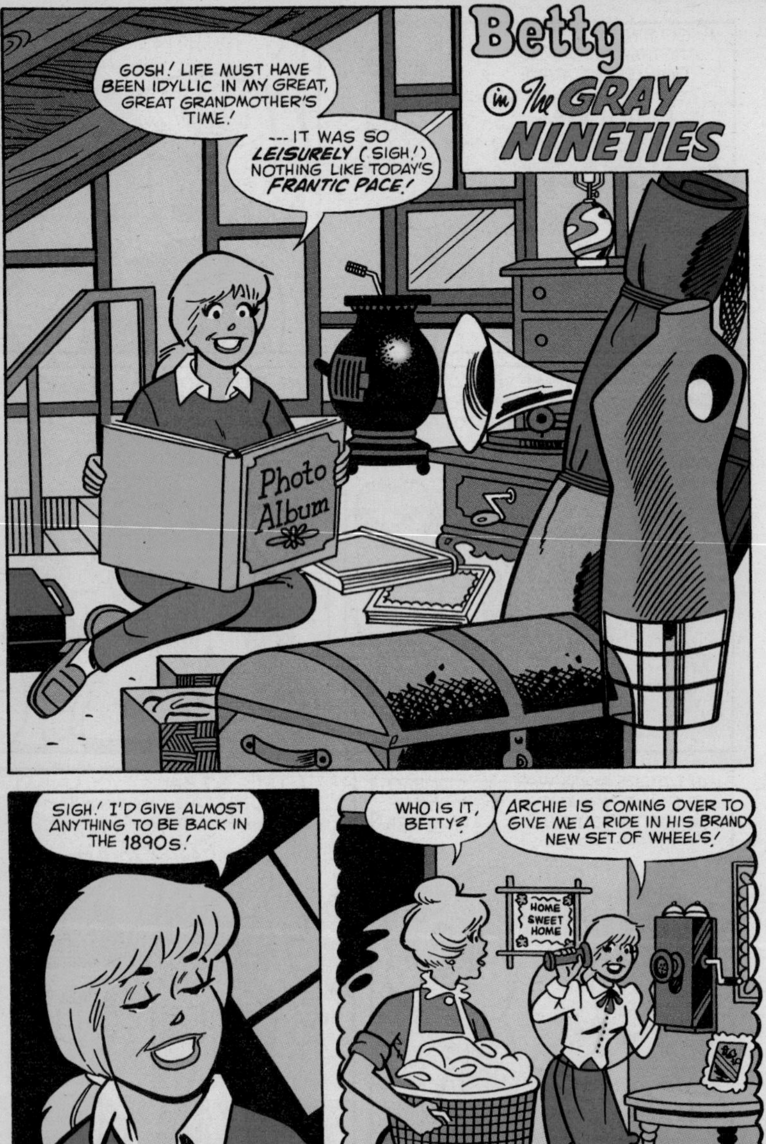
Betty in The GRAY NINETIES
GOSH! LIFE MUST HAVE BEEN IDYLLIC IN MY GREAT, GREAT GRANDMOTHER'S TIME!
--- IT WAS SO LEISURELY (SIGH!) NOTHING LIKE TODAY'S FRANTIC PACE!
Photo Album
SIGH! I'D GIVE ALMOST ANYTHING TO BE BACK IN THE 1890s!
WHO IS IT, BETTY?
ARCHIE IS COMING OVER TO GIVE ME A RIDE IN HIS BRAND NEW SET OF WHEELS!
HOME SWEET HOME

Script: Frank Doyle / Pencils: Dan DeCarlo Jr. / Inks: Jimmy DeCarlo / Letters: Bill Yoshida

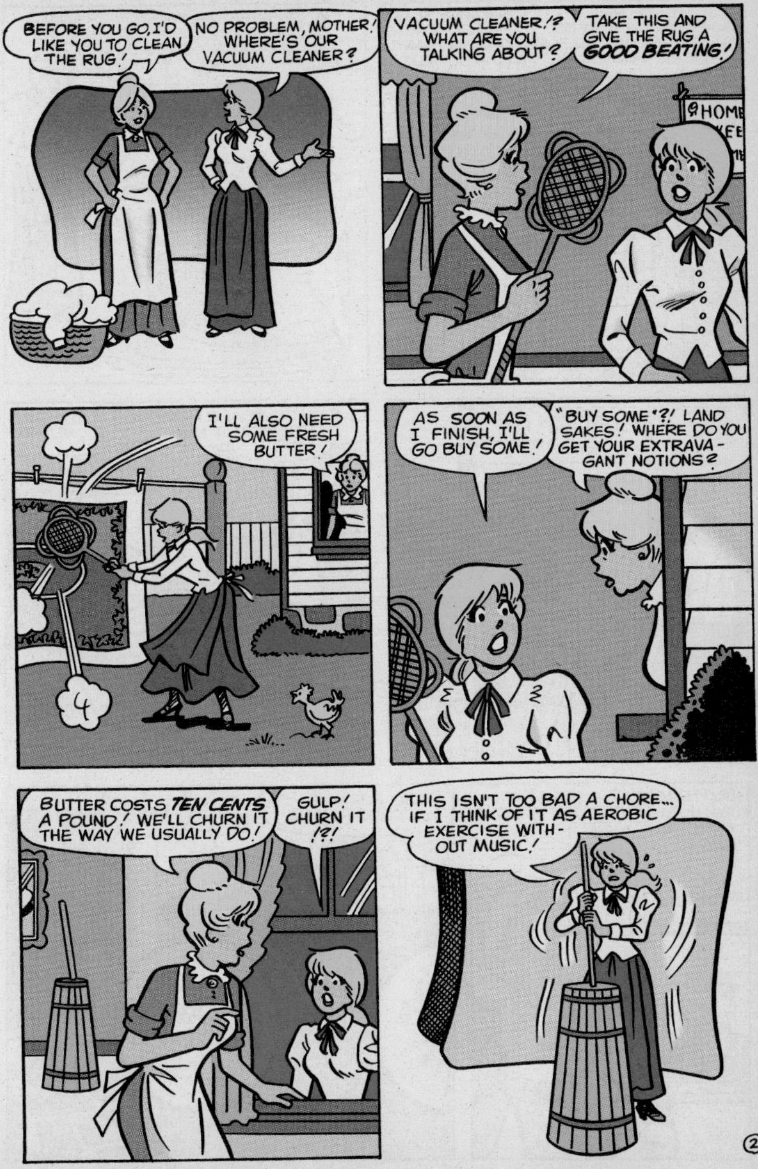
BEFORE YOU GO, I'D LIKE YOU TO CLEAN THE RUG!
NO PROBLEM, MOTHER! WHERE'S OUR VACUUM CLEANER?
VACUUM CLEANER!? WHAT ARE YOU TALKING ABOUT?
TAKE THIS AND GIVE THE RUG A GOOD BEATING!
HOME
I'LL ALSO NEED SOME FRESH BUTTER!
AS SOON AS I FINISH, I'LL GO BUY SOME!
"BUY SOME"?! LAND SAKES! WHERE DO YOU GET YOUR EXTRAVAGANT NOTIONS?
BUTTER COSTS TEN CENTS A POUND! WE'LL CHURN IT THE WAY WE USUALLY DO!
GULP! CHURN IT !?!
THIS ISN'T TOO BAD A CHORE... IF I THINK OF IT AS AEROBIC EXERCISE WITHOUT MUSIC!

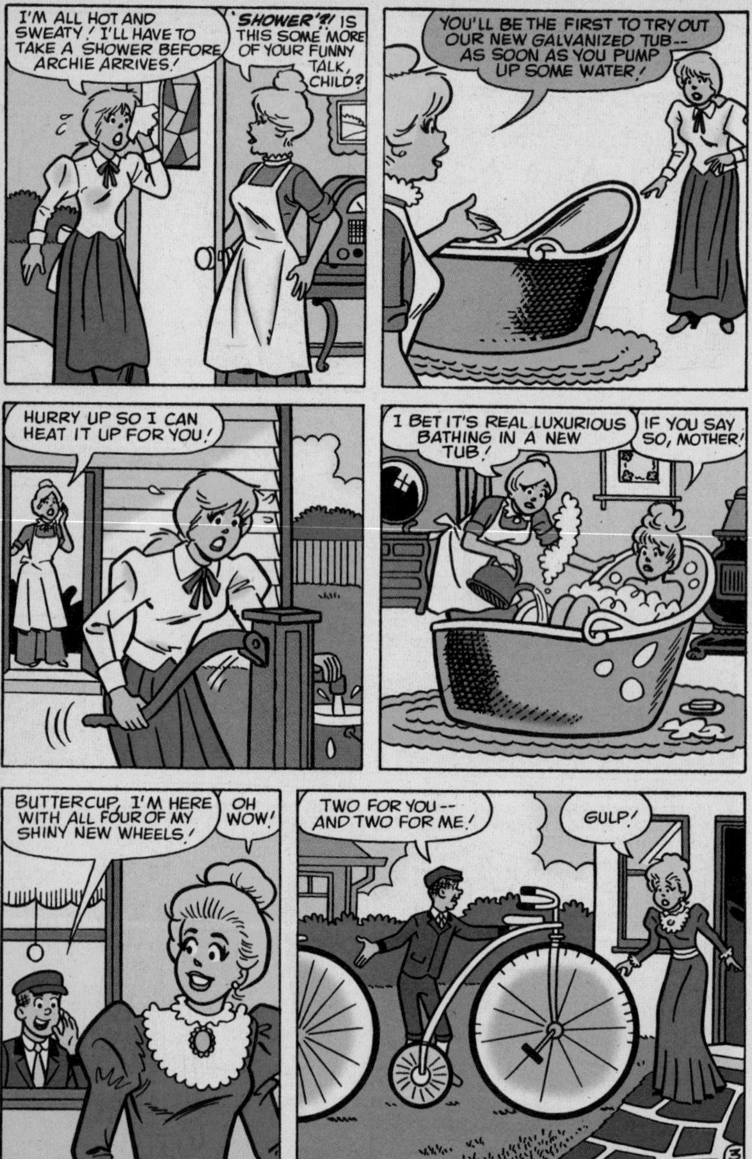
I'M ALL HOT AND SWEATY! I'LL HAVE TO TAKE A SHOWER BEFORE ARCHIE ARRIVES!
'SHOWER'?! IS THIS SOME MORE OF YOUR FUNNY TALK, CHILD?
YOU'LL BE THE FIRST TO TRY OUT OUR NEW GALVANIZED TUB-- AS SOON AS YOU PUMP UP SOME WATER!
HURRY UP SO I CAN HEAT IT UP FOR YOU!
I BET IT'S REAL LUXURIOUS BATHING IN A NEW TUB!
IF YOU SAY SO, MOTHER!
BUTTERCUP, I'M HERE WITH ALL FOUR OF MY SHINY NEW WHEELS!
OH WOW!
TWO FOR YOU -- AND TWO FOR ME!
GULP!
3

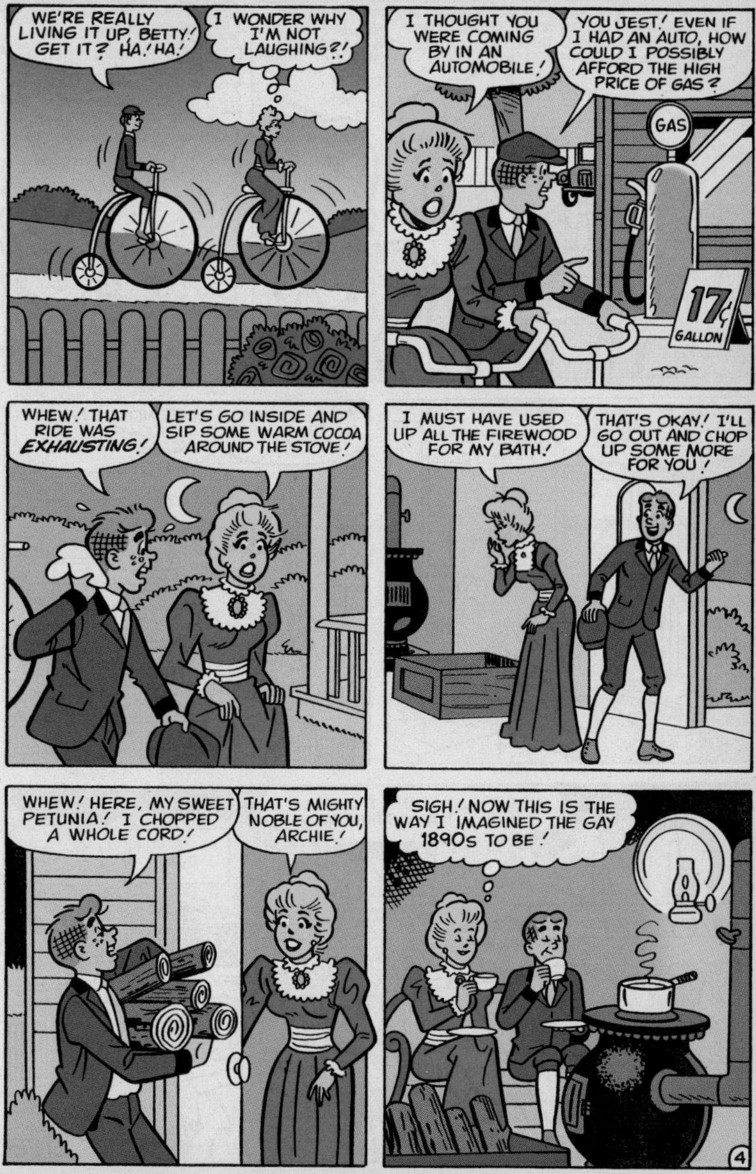
WE'RE REALLY LIVING IT UP, BETTY! GET IT? HA! HA!
I WONDER WHY I'M NOT LAUGHING?!
I THOUGHT YOU WERE COMING BY IN AN AUTOMOBILE!
YOU JEST! EVEN IF I HAD AN AUTO, HOW COULD I POSSIBLY AFFORD THE HIGH PRICE OF GAS?
GAS
17¢ GALLON
WHEW! THAT RIDE WAS EXHAUSTING!
LET'S GO INSIDE AND SIP SOME WARM COCOA AROUND THE STOVE!
I MUST HAVE USED UP ALL THE FIREWOOD FOR MY BATH!
THAT'S OKAY! I'LL GO OUT AND CHOP UP SOME MORE FOR YOU!
WHEW! HERE, MY SWEET PETUNIA! I CHOPPED A WHOLE CORD!
THAT'S MIGHTY NOBLE OF YOU, ARCHIE!
SIGH! NOW THIS IS THE WAY I IMAGINED THE GAY 1890s TO BE!
4

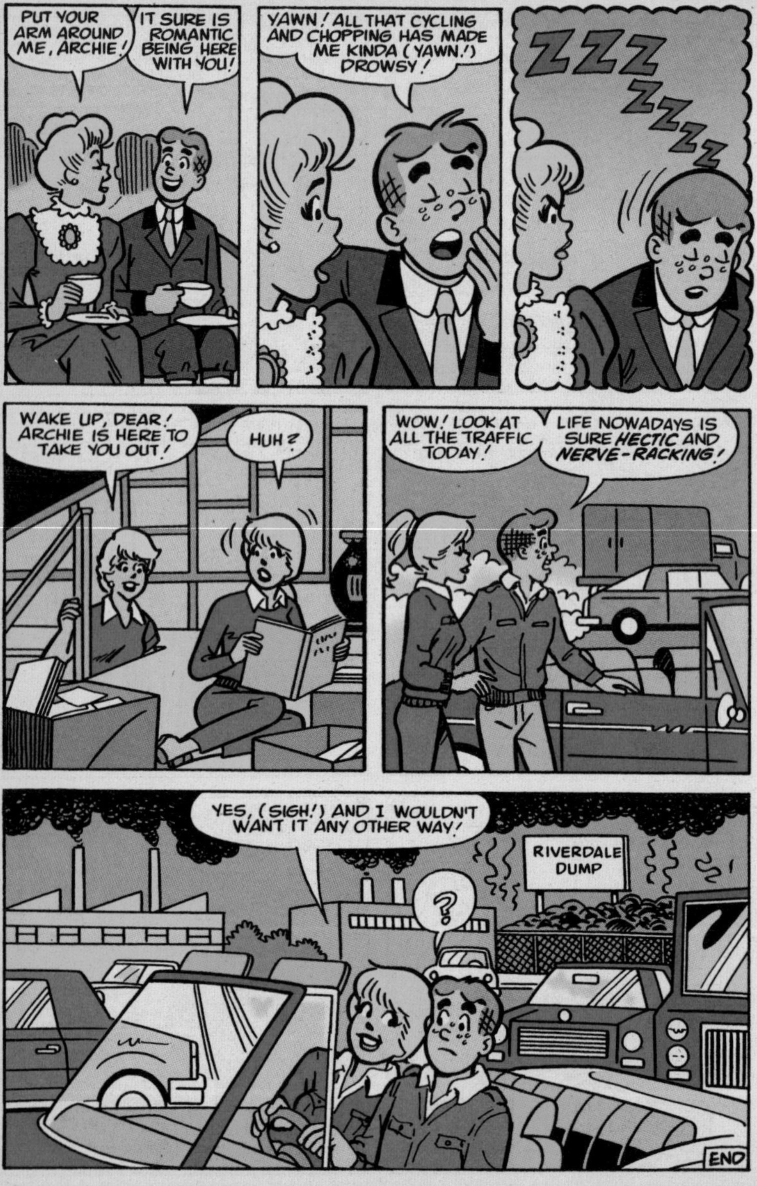
PUT YOUR ARM AROUND ME, ARCHIE!
IT SURE IS ROMANTIC BEING HERE WITH YOU!
YAWN! ALL THAT CYCLING AND CHOPPING HAS MADE ME KINDA (YAWN!) DROWSY!
ZZZ ZZZZ
WAKE UP, DEAR! ARCHIE IS HERE TO TAKE YOU OUT!
HUH?
WOW! LOOK AT ALL THE TRAFFIC TODAY!
LIFE NOWADAYS IS SURE HECTIC AND NERVE-RACKING!
YES, (SIGH!) AND I WOULDN'T WANT IT ANY OTHER WAY!
?
RIVERDALE DUMP
END

Betty and Veronica in "A TALE of TWO PAPERS"

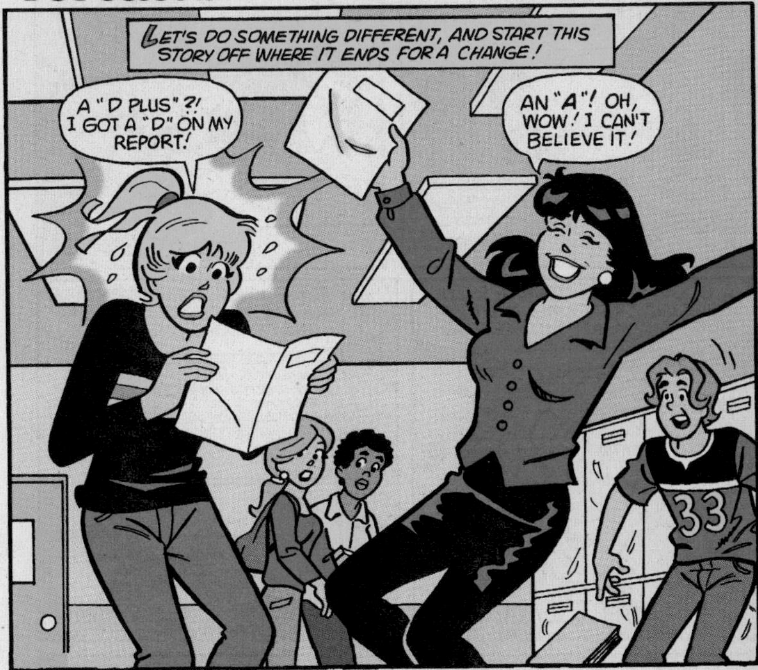
LET'S DO SOMETHING DIFFERENT, AND START THIS STORY OFF WHERE IT ENDS FOR A CHANGE!
A "D PLUS"?! I GOT A "D" ON MY REPORT!
AN "A"! OH, WOW! I CAN'T BELIEVE IT!
33

Script: Kathleen Webb / Pencils: Jeff Shultz / Inks: Henry Scarpelli / Letters: Bill Yoshida / Colors: Barry Grossman

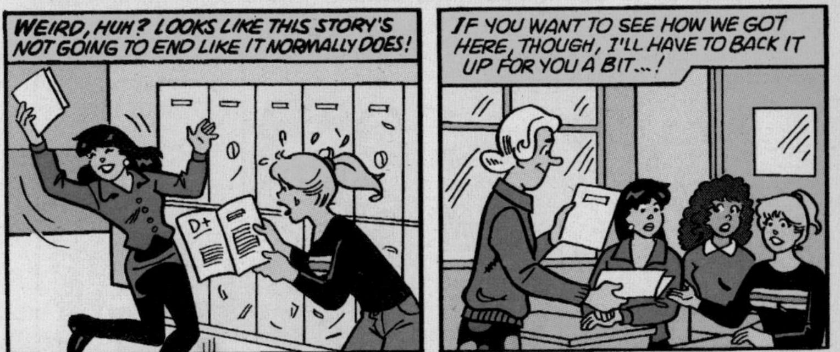
WEIRD, HUH? LOOKS LIKE THIS STORY'S NOT GOING TO END LIKE IT NORMALLY DOES!
D+
IF YOU WANT TO SEE HOW WE GOT HERE, THOUGH, I'LL HAVE TO BACK IT UP FOR YOU A BIT...!

IT ALL BEGAN WITH MISS GRUNDY ASSIGNING A REPORT ON A CERTAIN SUBJECT...

GARDENING ?!? WITH ALL DUE RESPECT, MISS GRUNDY, YOU'VE GOT TO BE KIDDING!

THIS IS WRITING CLASS, NOT BOTANY 101!

THAT'S EXACTLY WHY I'M ASSIGNING THE TOPIC!

A GOOD WRITER CAN TAKE EVEN A SUBJECT THAT BORES THEM TO TEARS AND MAKE IT INTERESTING TO OTHERS!

HERE ARE SEVERAL SUGGESTIONS FOR THE THEME OF YOUR PAPER! PICK ONE AND DEVELOP IT WELL!

EUROPEAN GARDENS
FAMOUS ANCIENT GARDENS
HYDROPONIC GARDENS
GREENHOUSE GARDENING
THE ORIGINS OF GARDENING

YOU HAVE TWO FULL WEEKS TO WORK ON IT!

SHE COULD GIVE ME TWO FULL CENTURIES...

BRIIING!

GARDENS
EAT GARDENS
GARDENS
GARDENS

...I STILL WOULDN'T BE ABLE TO COME UP WITH ANYTHING! GARDENING IS BORING!

I DON'T THINK SO!

2

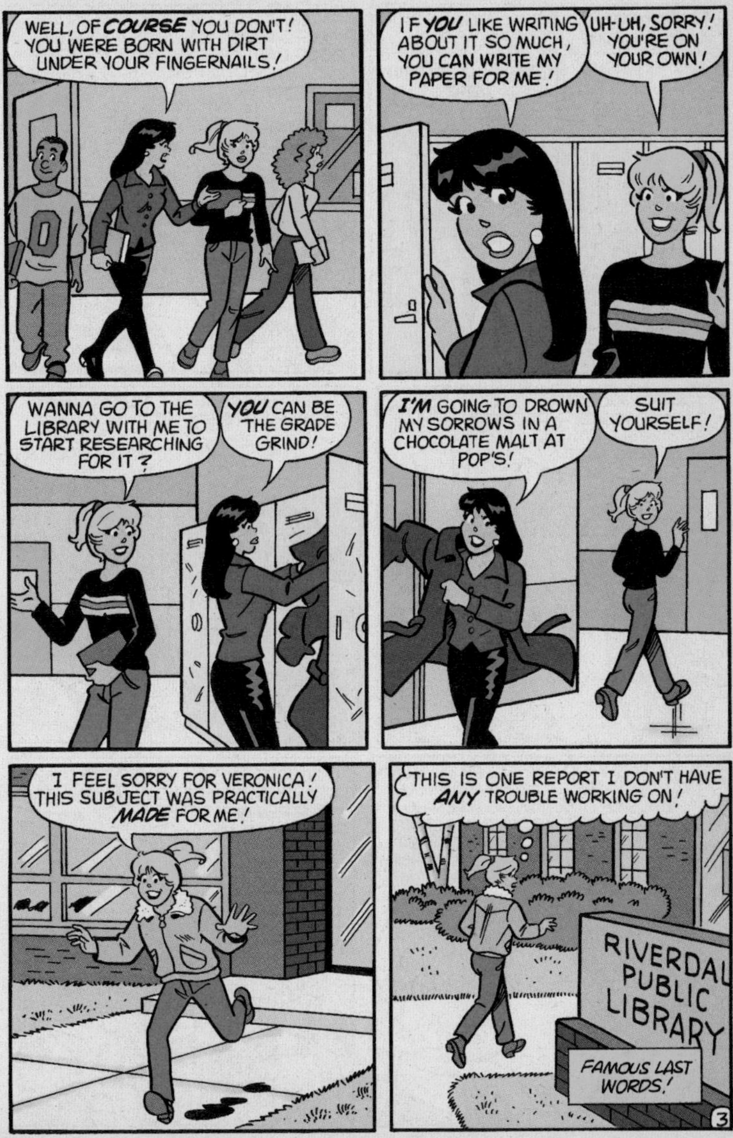

WELL, OF COURSE YOU DON'T! YOU WERE BORN WITH DIRT UNDER YOUR FINGERNAILS!
IF YOU LIKE WRITING ABOUT IT SO MUCH, YOU CAN WRITE MY PAPER FOR ME!
UH-UH, SORRY! YOU'RE ON YOUR OWN!
WANNA GO TO THE LIBRARY WITH ME TO START RESEARCHING FOR IT?
YOU CAN BE THE GRADE GRIND!
I'M GOING TO DROWN MY SORROWS IN A CHOCOLATE MALT AT POP'S!
SUIT YOURSELF!
I FEEL SORRY FOR VERONICA! THIS SUBJECT WAS PRACTICALLY MADE FOR ME!
THIS IS ONE REPORT I DON'T HAVE ANY TROUBLE WORKING ON!
RIVERDAL
PUBLIC
LIBRARY
FAMOUS LAST WORDS!
3

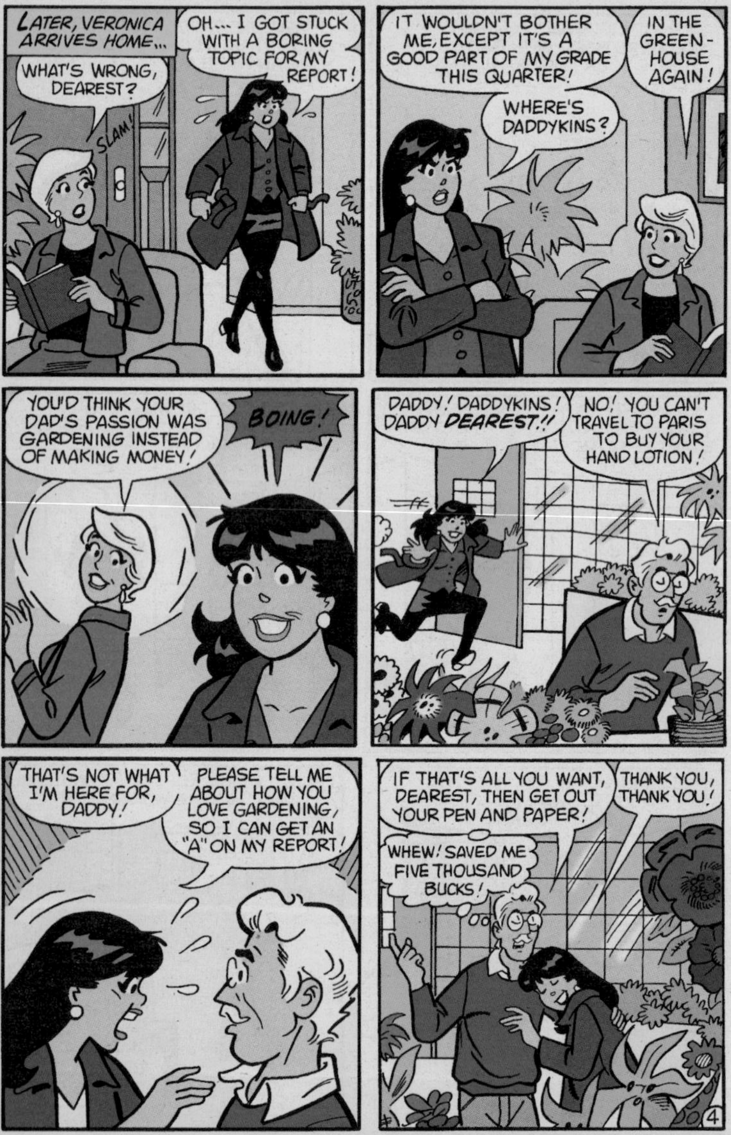
LATER, VERONICA ARRIVES HOME...
WHAT'S WRONG, DEAREST?
SLAM!
OH... I GOT STUCK WITH A BORING TOPIC FOR MY REPORT!
IT WOULDN'T BOTHER ME, EXCEPT IT'S A GOOD PART OF MY GRADE THIS QUARTER!
WHERE'S DADDYKINS?
IN THE GREEN-HOUSE AGAIN!
YOU'D THINK YOUR DAD'S PASSION WAS GARDENING INSTEAD OF MAKING MONEY!
BOING!
DADDY! DADDYKINS! DADDY DEAREST!!
NO! YOU CAN'T TRAVEL TO PARIS TO BUY YOUR HAND LOTION!
THAT'S NOT WHAT I'M HERE FOR, DADDY!
PLEASE TELL ME ABOUT HOW YOU LOVE GARDENING, SO I CAN GET AN "A" ON MY REPORT!
IF THAT'S ALL YOU WANT, DEAREST, THEN GET OUT YOUR PEN AND PAPER!
THANK YOU, THANK YOU!
WHEW! SAVED ME FIVE THOUSAND BUCKS!
4

AND WHILE VERONICA SOAKED UP HORTICULTURE, BETTY... WELL... SEE FOR YOURSELF!

WANNA GO OUT FOR PIZZA TONIGHT, BETS?

I THOUGHT YOU AND RON WERE GETTING TOGETHER!

SHHH!

SHE'S BUSY ON SOME PROJECT WITH HER DAD! YOU DON'T HAVE HOMEWORK, DO YOU?

NAW... NOTHING THAT'S REALLY HARD!

SO FOR THE NEXT TWO WEEKS, BETTY PLAYED WHILE RON ACTUALLY WORKED!

ALTHOUGH WHAT RON LEARNED WAS THAT SHE STILL DIDN'T LIKE GARDENING!

BUT AT LEAST NOW I CAN WRITE A DECENT REPORT ABOUT IT!

TAPPITY TAP!

THE NIGHT BEFORE THE REPORT WAS DUE IS WHEN BETTY REMEMBERED HERS!

AUGH! WHY DIDN'T I GET AT THIS TWO WEEKS AGO? WHERE ARE THOSE LIBRARY BOOKS? WHERE'S MOM'S GARDENING MAGAZINE?

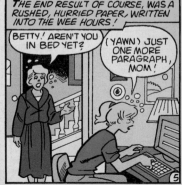

THE END RESULT OF COURSE, WAS A RUSHED, HURRIED PAPER, WRITTEN INTO THE WEE HOURS!

BETTY! AREN'T YOU IN BED YET?

(YAWN) JUST ONE MORE PARAGRAPH, MOM!

5

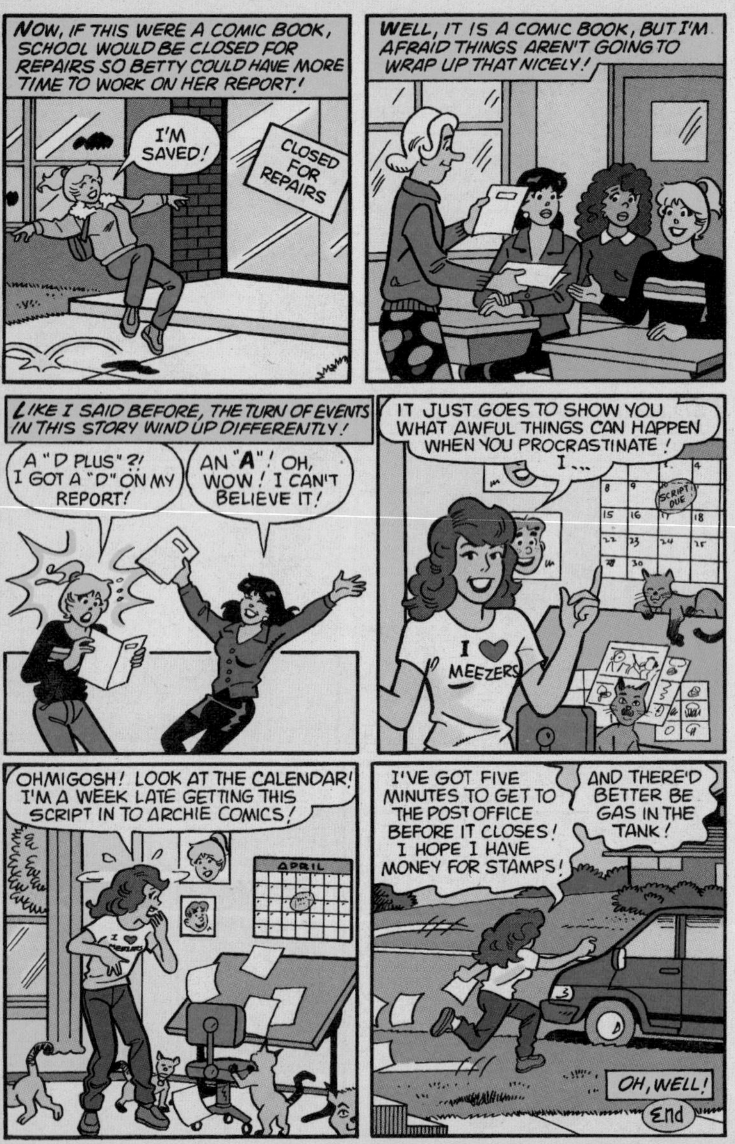
NOW, IF THIS WERE A COMIC BOOK, SCHOOL WOULD BE CLOSED FOR REPAIRS SO BETTY COULD HAVE MORE TIME TO WORK ON HER REPORT!
I'M SAVED!
CLOSED FOR REPAIRS
WELL, IT IS A COMIC BOOK, BUT I'M AFRAID THINGS AREN'T GOING TO WRAP UP THAT NICELY!
LIKE I SAID BEFORE, THE TURN OF EVENTS IN THIS STORY WIND UP DIFFERENTLY!
A "D PLUS"?! I GOT A "D" ON MY REPORT!
AN "A"! OH, WOW! I CAN'T BELIEVE IT!
IT JUST GOES TO SHOW YOU WHAT AWFUL THINGS CAN HAPPEN WHEN YOU PROCRASTINATE! I...
SCRIPT DUE
I ♥ MEEZERS
OHMIGOSH! LOOK AT THE CALENDAR! I'M A WEEK LATE GETTING THIS SCRIPT IN TO ARCHIE COMICS!
APRIL
I'VE GOT FIVE MINUTES TO GET TO THE POST OFFICE BEFORE IT CLOSES! I HOPE I HAVE MONEY FOR STAMPS!
AND THERE'D BETTER BE GAS IN THE TANK!
OH, WELL!
End

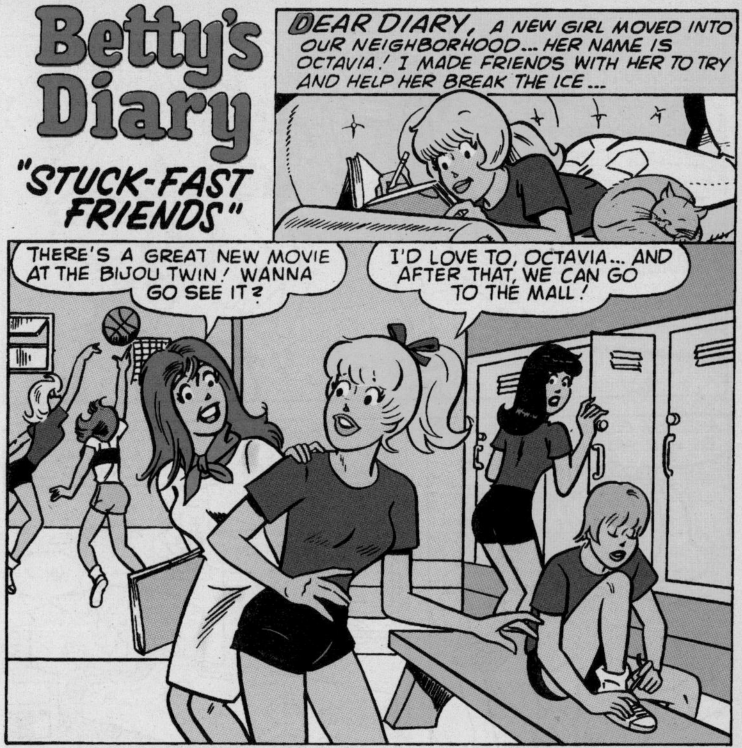

Betty's Diary
"STUCK-FAST FRIENDS"
DEAR DIARY, A NEW GIRL MOVED INTO OUR NEIGHBORHOOD... HER NAME IS OCTAVIA! I MADE FRIENDS WITH HER TO TRY AND HELP HER BREAK THE ICE...
THERE'S A GREAT NEW MOVIE AT THE BIJOU TWIN! WANNA GO SEE IT?
I'D LOVE TO, OCTAVIA... AND AFTER THAT, WE CAN GO TO THE MALL!

Script: Hal Smith / Pencils: Bob Bolling / Inks: Mike Esposito / Letters: Bill Yoshida / Colors: Barry Grossman

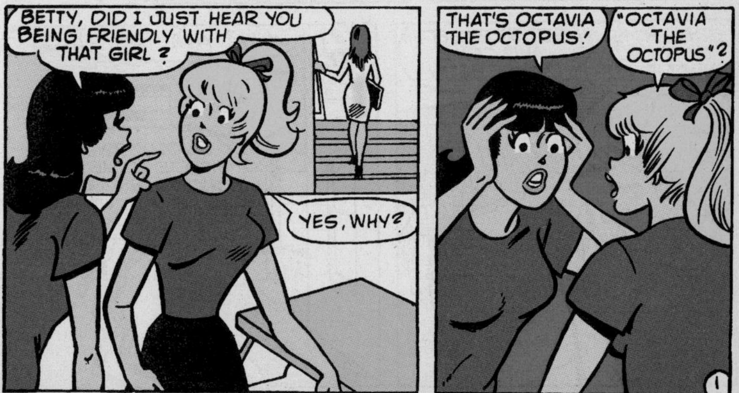

BETTY, DID I JUST HEAR YOU BEING FRIENDLY WITH THAT GIRL?
YES, WHY?
THAT'S OCTAVIA THE OCTOPUS!
"OCTAVIA THE OCTOPUS"?
1

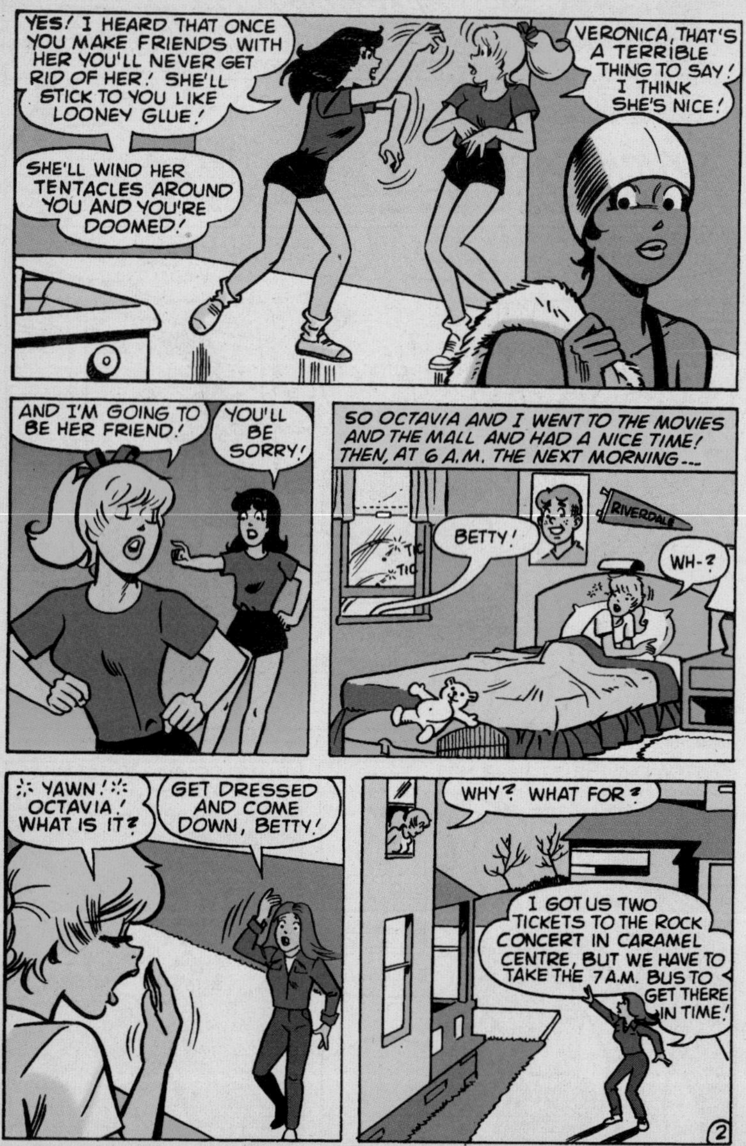

YES! I HEARD THAT ONCE YOU MAKE FRIENDS WITH HER YOU'LL NEVER GET RID OF HER! SHE'LL STICK TO YOU LIKE LOONEY GLUE!
SHE'LL WIND HER TENTACLES AROUND YOU AND YOU'RE DOOMED!
VERONICA, THAT'S A TERRIBLE THING TO SAY! I THINK SHE'S NICE!
AND I'M GOING TO BE HER FRIEND!
YOU'LL BE SORRY!
SO OCTAVIA AND I WENT TO THE MOVIES AND THE MALL AND HAD A NICE TIME! THEN, AT 6 A.M. THE NEXT MORNING---
RIVERDALE
TIC
TIC
BETTY!
WH-?
YAWN! OCTAVIA! WHAT IS IT?
GET DRESSED AND COME DOWN, BETTY!
WHY? WHAT FOR?
I GOT US TWO TICKETS TO THE ROCK CONCERT IN CARAMEL CENTRE, BUT WE HAVE TO TAKE THE 7 A.M. BUS TO GET THERE IN TIME!
2

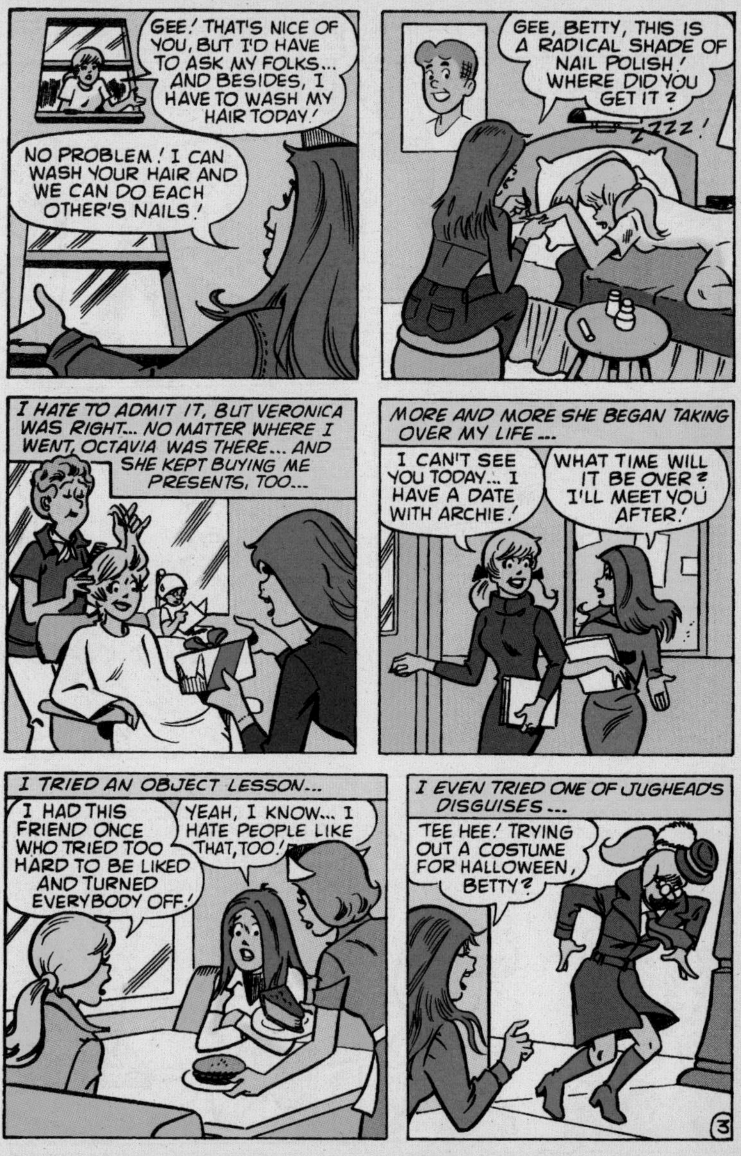
GEE! THAT'S NICE OF YOU, BUT I'D HAVE TO ASK MY FOLKS... AND BESIDES, I HAVE TO WASH MY HAIR TODAY!
NO PROBLEM! I CAN WASH YOUR HAIR AND WE CAN DO EACH OTHER'S NAILS!
GEE, BETTY, THIS IS A RADICAL SHADE OF NAIL POLISH! WHERE DID YOU GET IT?
ZZZZ!
I HATE TO ADMIT IT, BUT VERONICA WAS RIGHT... NO MATTER WHERE I WENT, OCTAVIA WAS THERE... AND SHE KEPT BUYING ME PRESENTS, TOO...
MORE AND MORE SHE BEGAN TAKING OVER MY LIFE ...
I CAN'T SEE YOU TODAY... I HAVE A DATE WITH ARCHIE!
WHAT TIME WILL IT BE OVER? I'LL MEET YOU AFTER!
I TRIED AN OBJECT LESSON...
I HAD THIS FRIEND ONCE WHO TRIED TOO HARD TO BE LIKED AND TURNED EVERYBODY OFF!
YEAH, I KNOW... I HATE PEOPLE LIKE THAT, TOO!
I EVEN TRIED ONE OF JUGHEAD'S DISGUISES ...
TEE HEE! TRYING OUT A COSTUME FOR HALLOWEEN, BETTY?
3

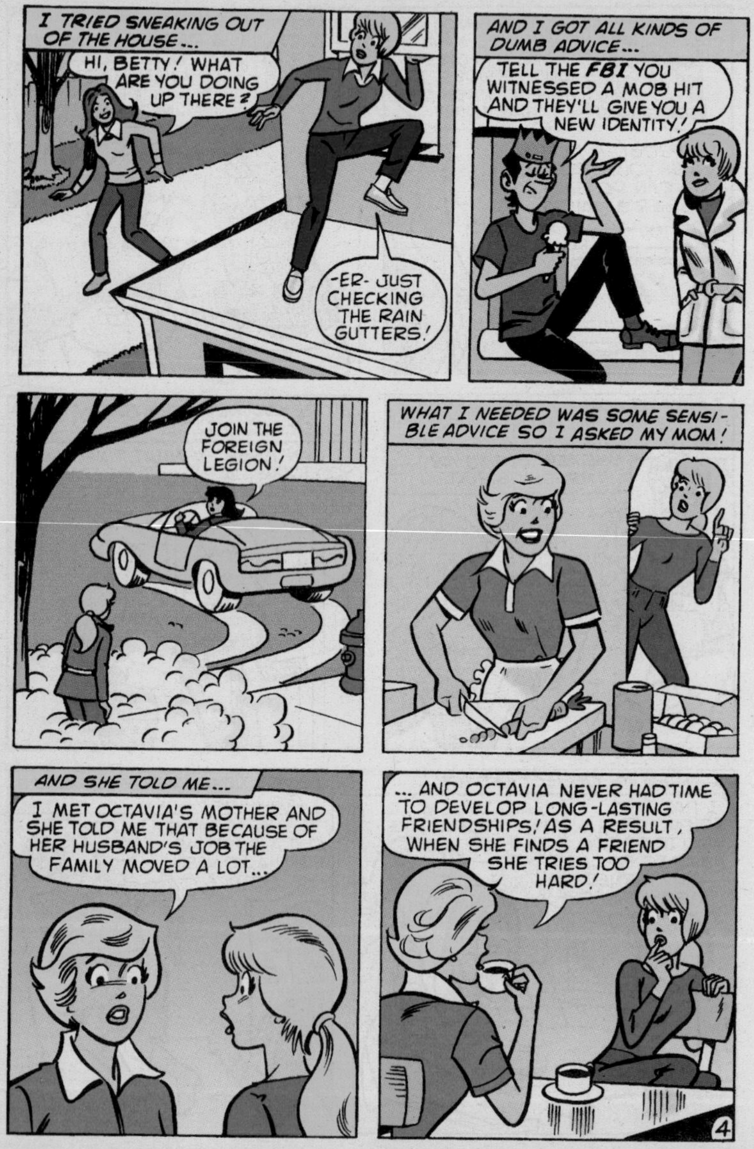
I TRIED SNEAKING OUT OF THE HOUSE...
HI, BETTY! WHAT ARE YOU DOING UP THERE?
-ER- JUST CHECKING THE RAIN GUTTERS!
AND I GOT ALL KINDS OF DUMB ADVICE...
TELL THE FBI YOU WITNESSED A MOB HIT AND THEY'LL GIVE YOU A NEW IDENTITY!
JOIN THE FOREIGN LEGION!
WHAT I NEEDED WAS SOME SENSIBLE ADVICE SO I ASKED MY MOM!
AND SHE TOLD ME...
I MET OCTAVIA'S MOTHER AND SHE TOLD ME THAT BECAUSE OF HER HUSBAND'S JOB THE FAMILY MOVED A LOT...
... AND OCTAVIA NEVER HAD TIME TO DEVELOP LONG-LASTING FRIENDSHIPS! AS A RESULT, WHEN SHE FINDS A FRIEND SHE TRIES TOO HARD!
4

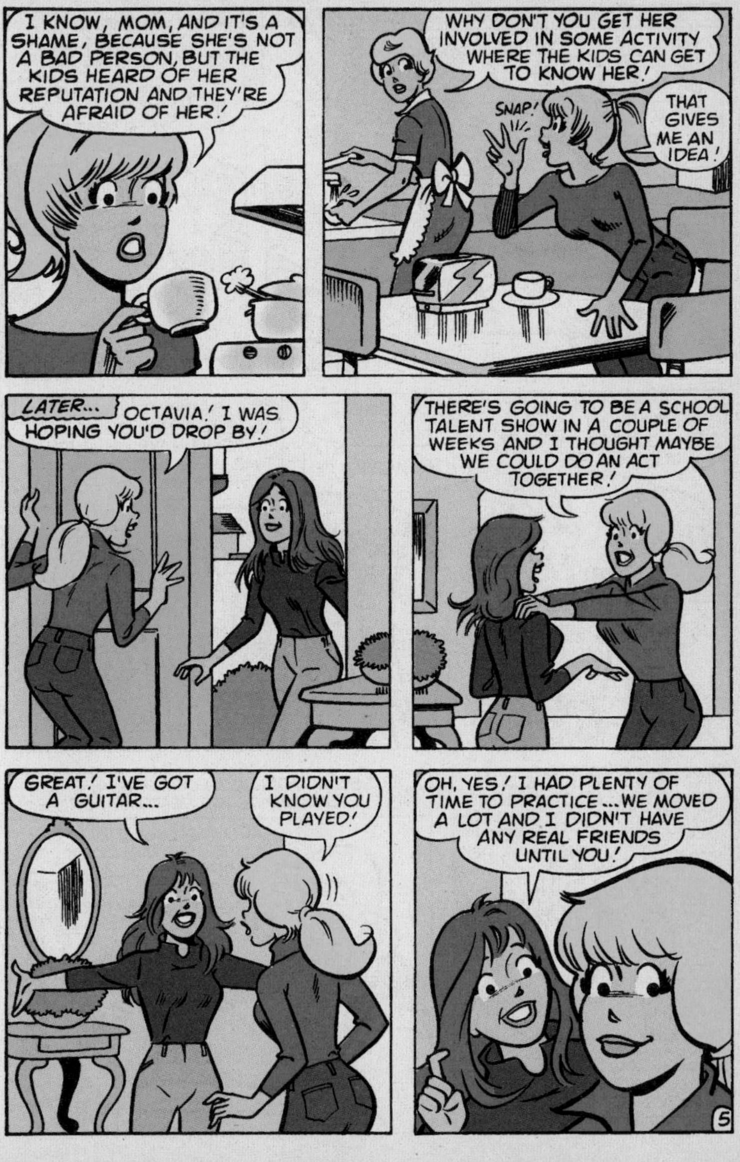
I KNOW, MOM, AND IT'S A SHAME, BECAUSE SHE'S NOT A BAD PERSON, BUT THE KIDS HEARD OF HER REPUTATION AND THEY'RE AFRAID OF HER!
WHY DON'T YOU GET HER INVOLVED IN SOME ACTIVITY WHERE THE KIDS CAN GET TO KNOW HER!
SNAP!
THAT GIVES ME AN IDEA!
LATER...
OCTAVIA! I WAS HOPING YOU'D DROP BY!
THERE'S GOING TO BE A SCHOOL TALENT SHOW IN A COUPLE OF WEEKS AND I THOUGHT MAYBE WE COULD DO AN ACT TOGETHER!
GREAT! I'VE GOT A GUITAR...
I DIDN'T KNOW YOU PLAYED!
OH, YES! I HAD PLENTY OF TIME TO PRACTICE ... WE MOVED A LOT AND I DIDN'T HAVE ANY REAL FRIENDS UNTIL YOU!
5

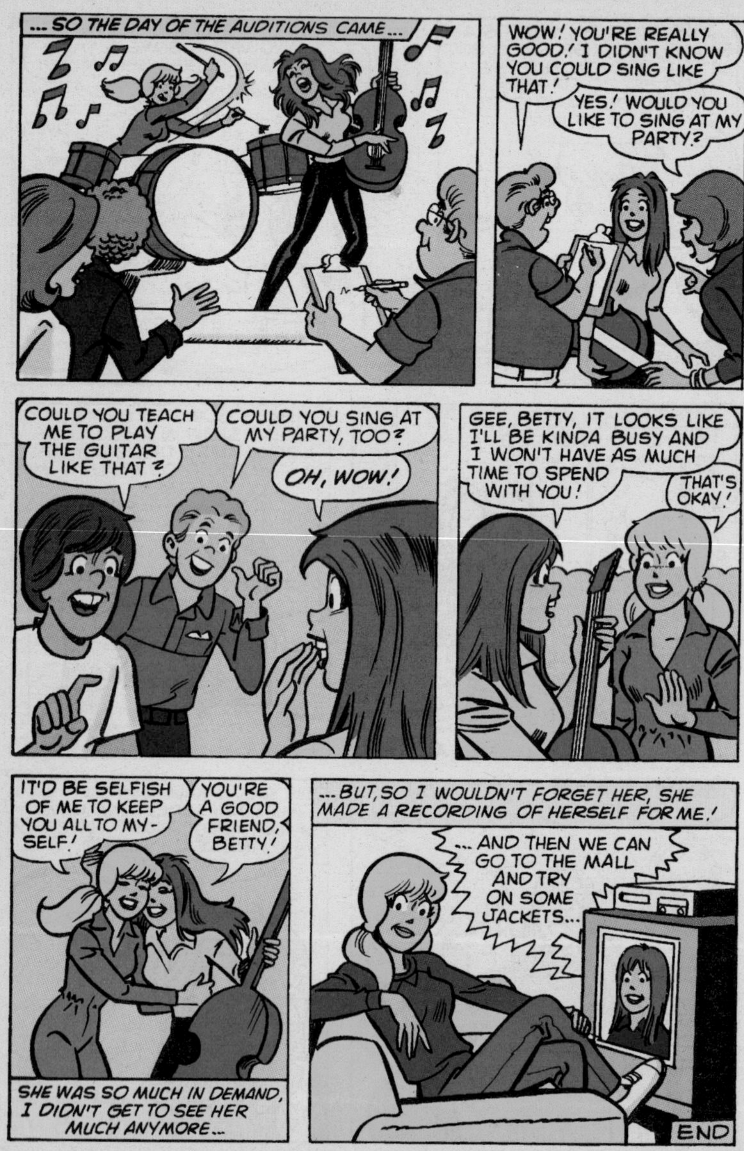
... SO THE DAY OF THE AUDITIONS CAME...
WOW! YOU'RE REALLY GOOD! I DIDN'T KNOW YOU COULD SING LIKE THAT!
YES! WOULD YOU LIKE TO SING AT MY PARTY?
COULD YOU TEACH ME TO PLAY THE GUITAR LIKE THAT?
COULD YOU SING AT MY PARTY, TOO?
OH, WOW!
GEE, BETTY, IT LOOKS LIKE I'LL BE KINDA BUSY AND I WON'T HAVE AS MUCH TIME TO SPEND WITH YOU!
THAT'S OKAY!
IT'D BE SELFISH OF ME TO KEEP YOU ALL TO MY-SELF!
YOU'RE A GOOD FRIEND, BETTY!
SHE WAS SO MUCH IN DEMAND, I DIDN'T GET TO SEE HER MUCH ANYMORE...
...BUT, SO I WOULDN'T FORGET HER, SHE MADE A RECORDING OF HERSELF FOR ME!
... AND THEN WE CAN GO TO THE MALL AND TRY ON SOME JACKETS...
END

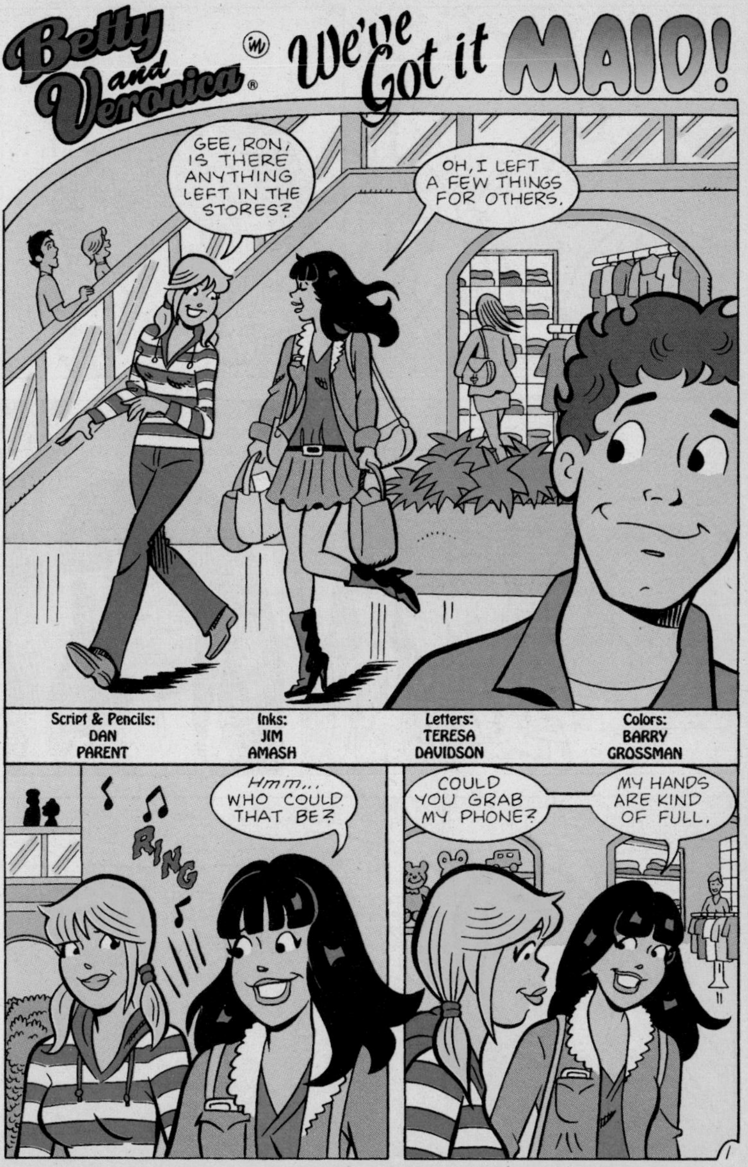
Betty and Veronica® in We've Got it MAID!
GEE, RON, IS THERE ANYTHING LEFT IN THE STORES?
OH, I LEFT A FEW THINGS FOR OTHERS.
Script & Pencils: DAN PARENT
Inks: JIM AMASH
Letters: TERESA DAVIDSON
Colors: BARRY GROSSMAN
RING
Hmm... WHO COULD THAT BE?
COULD YOU GRAB MY PHONE?
MY HANDS ARE KIND OF FULL.
1

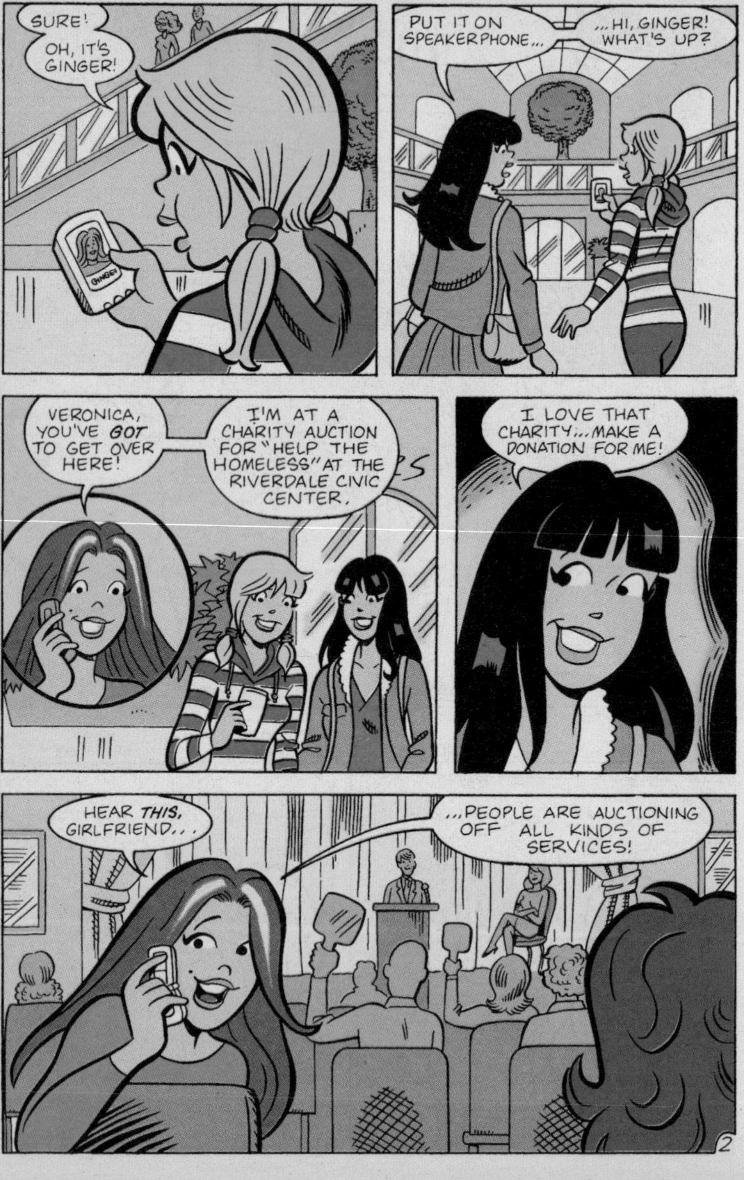
SURE!
OH, IT'S GINGER!
GINGER
PUT IT ON SPEAKERPHONE...
...HI, GINGER! WHAT'S UP?
VERONICA, YOU'VE *GOT* TO GET OVER HERE!
I'M AT A CHARITY AUCTION FOR "HELP THE HOMELESS" AT THE RIVERDALE CIVIC CENTER.
I LOVE THAT CHARITY...MAKE A DONATION FOR ME!
HEAR *THIS*, GIRLFRIEND...
...PEOPLE ARE AUCTIONING OFF ALL KINDS OF SERVICES!

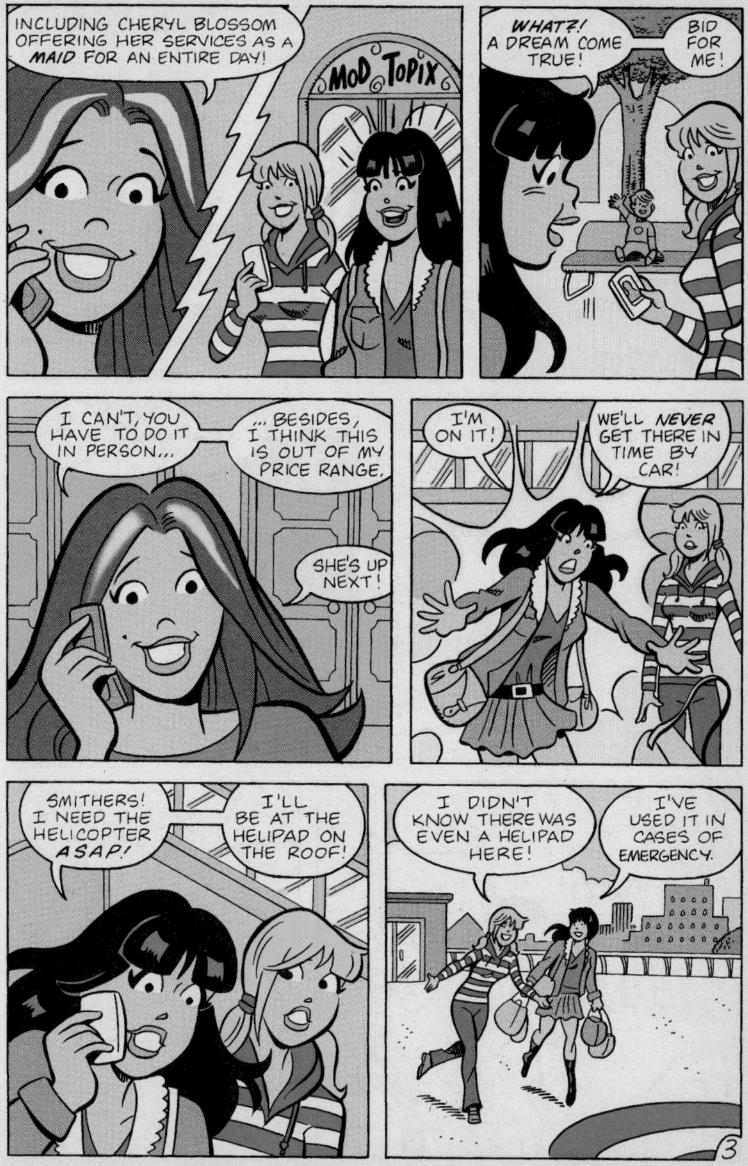
INCLUDING CHERYL BLOSSOM OFFERING HER SERVICES AS A MAID FOR AN ENTIRE DAY!
MOD TOPIX
WHAT?! A DREAM COME TRUE!
BID FOR ME!
I CAN'T, YOU HAVE TO DO IT IN PERSON...
... BESIDES, I THINK THIS IS OUT OF MY PRICE RANGE.
SHE'S UP NEXT!
I'M ON IT!
WE'LL NEVER GET THERE IN TIME BY CAR!
SMITHERS! I NEED THE HELICOPTER ASAP!
I'LL BE AT THE HELIPAD ON THE ROOF!
I DIDN'T KNOW THERE WAS EVEN A HELIPAD HERE!
I'VE USED IT IN CASES OF EMERGENCY.

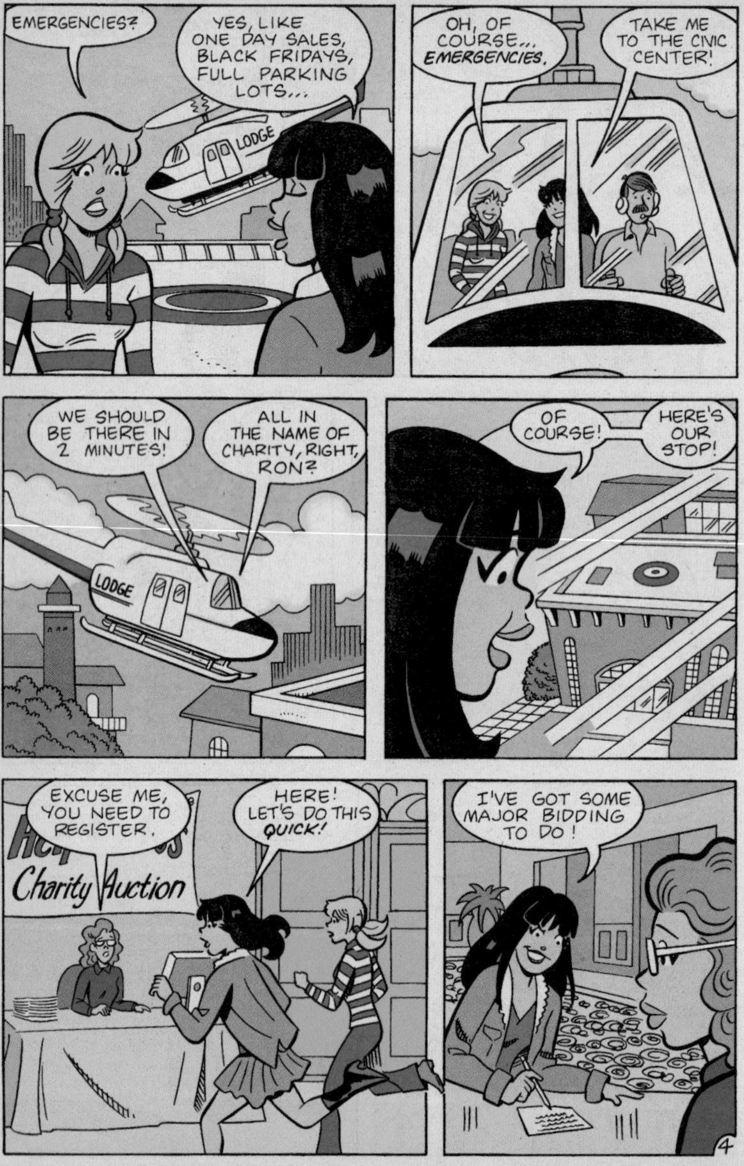
EMERGENCIES?
YES, LIKE ONE DAY SALES, BLACK FRIDAYS, FULL PARKING LOTS...
LODGE
OH, OF COURSE... EMERGENCIES.
TAKE ME TO THE CIVIC CENTER!
WE SHOULD BE THERE IN 2 MINUTES!
ALL IN THE NAME OF CHARITY, RIGHT, RON?
LODGE
OF COURSE!
HERE'S OUR STOP!
Charity Auction
EXCUSE ME, YOU NEED TO REGISTER.
HERE! LET'S DO THIS QUICK!
I'VE GOT SOME MAJOR BIDDING TO DO!
4

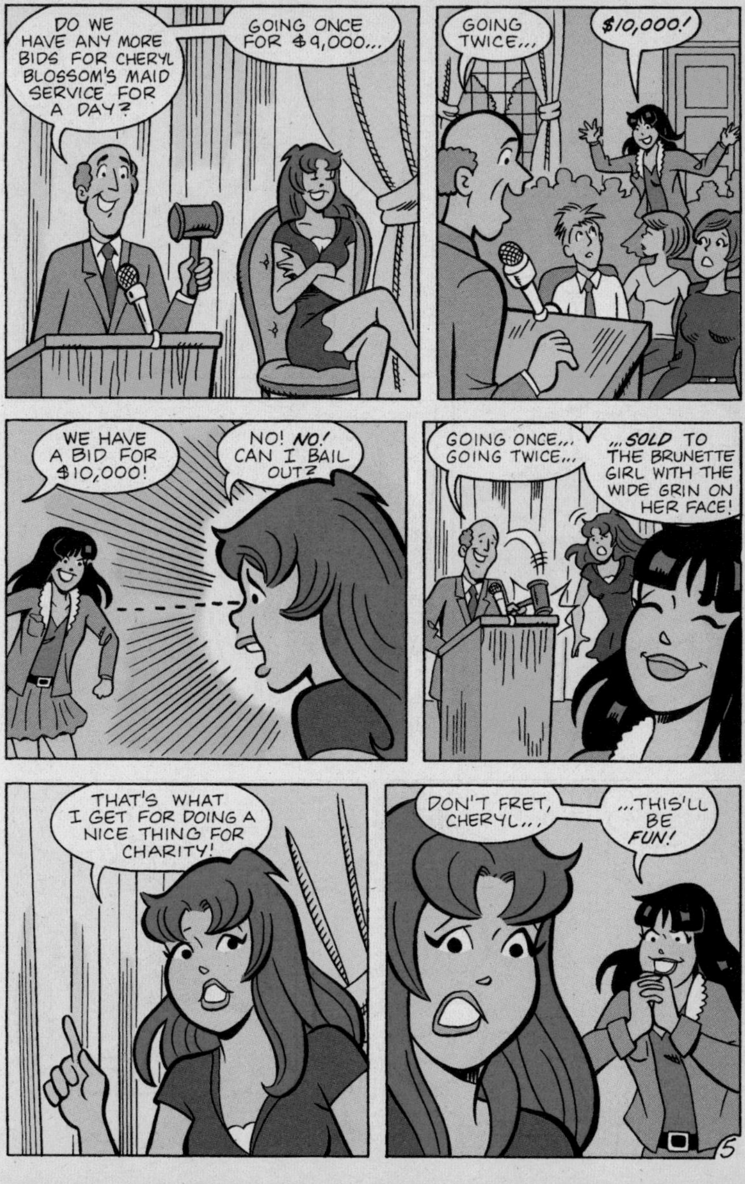
DO WE HAVE ANY MORE BIDS FOR CHERYL BLOSSOM'S MAID SERVICE FOR A DAY?
GOING ONCE FOR $9,000...
GOING TWICE...
$10,000!
WE HAVE A BID FOR $10,000!
NO! NO! CAN I BAIL OUT?
GOING ONCE... GOING TWICE...
...SOLD TO THE BRUNETTE GIRL WITH THE WIDE GRIN ON HER FACE!
THAT'S WHAT I GET FOR DOING A NICE THING FOR CHARITY!
DON'T FRET, CHERYL...
...THIS'LL BE FUN!

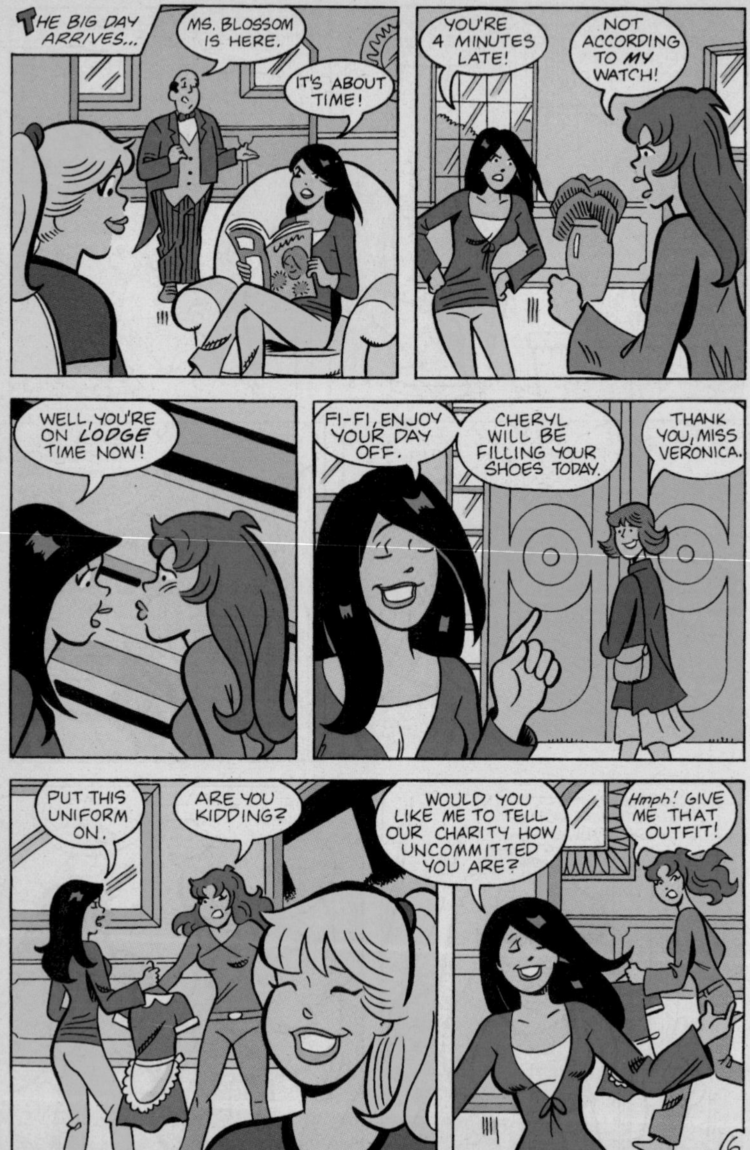
THE BIG DAY ARRIVES...
MS. BLOSSOM IS HERE.
IT'S ABOUT TIME!
YOU'RE 4 MINUTES LATE!
NOT ACCORDING TO MY WATCH!
WELL, YOU'RE ON LODGE TIME NOW!
FI-FI, ENJOY YOUR DAY OFF.
CHERYL WILL BE FILLING YOUR SHOES TODAY.
THANK YOU, MISS VERONICA.
PUT THIS UNIFORM ON.
ARE YOU KIDDING?
WOULD YOU LIKE ME TO TELL OUR CHARITY HOW UNCOMMITTED YOU ARE?
Hmph! GIVE ME THAT OUTFIT!
6

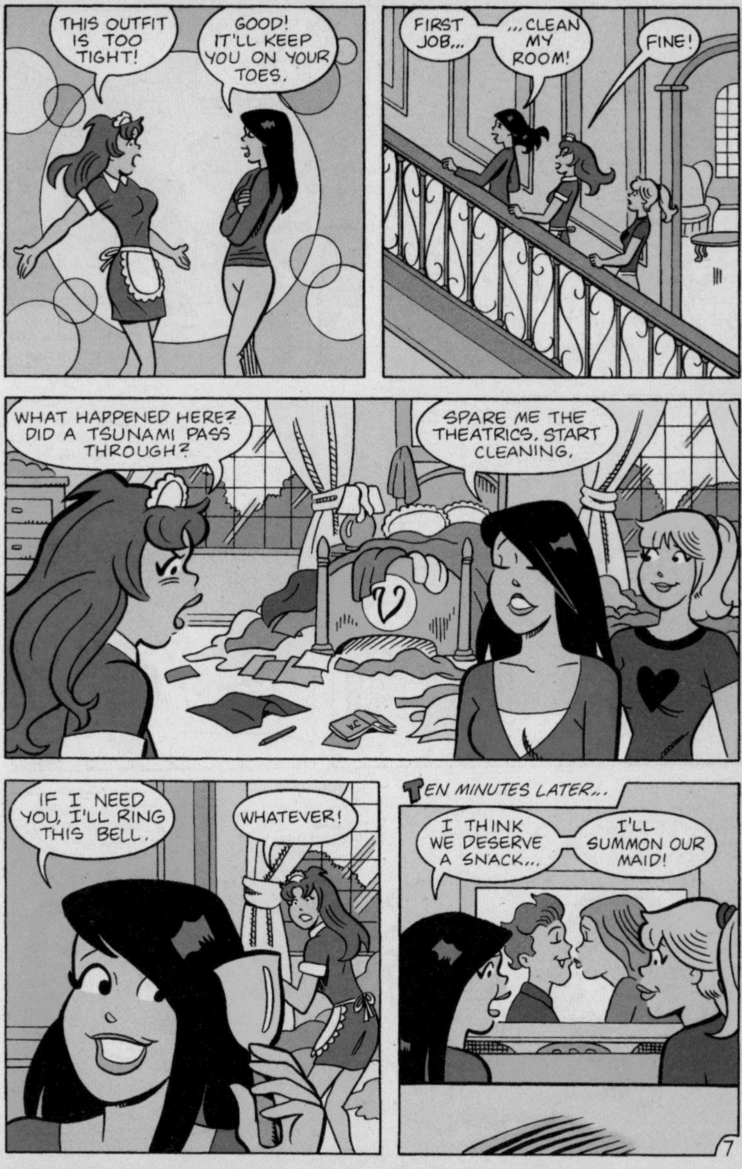
THIS OUTFIT IS TOO TIGHT!
GOOD! IT'LL KEEP YOU ON YOUR TOES.
FIRST JOB...
...CLEAN MY ROOM!
FINE!
WHAT HAPPENED HERE? DID A TSUNAMI PASS THROUGH?
SPARE ME THE THEATRICS. START CLEANING.
IF I NEED YOU, I'LL RING THIS BELL.
WHATEVER!
TEN MINUTES LATER...
I THINK WE DESERVE A SNACK...
I'LL SUMMON OUR MAID!

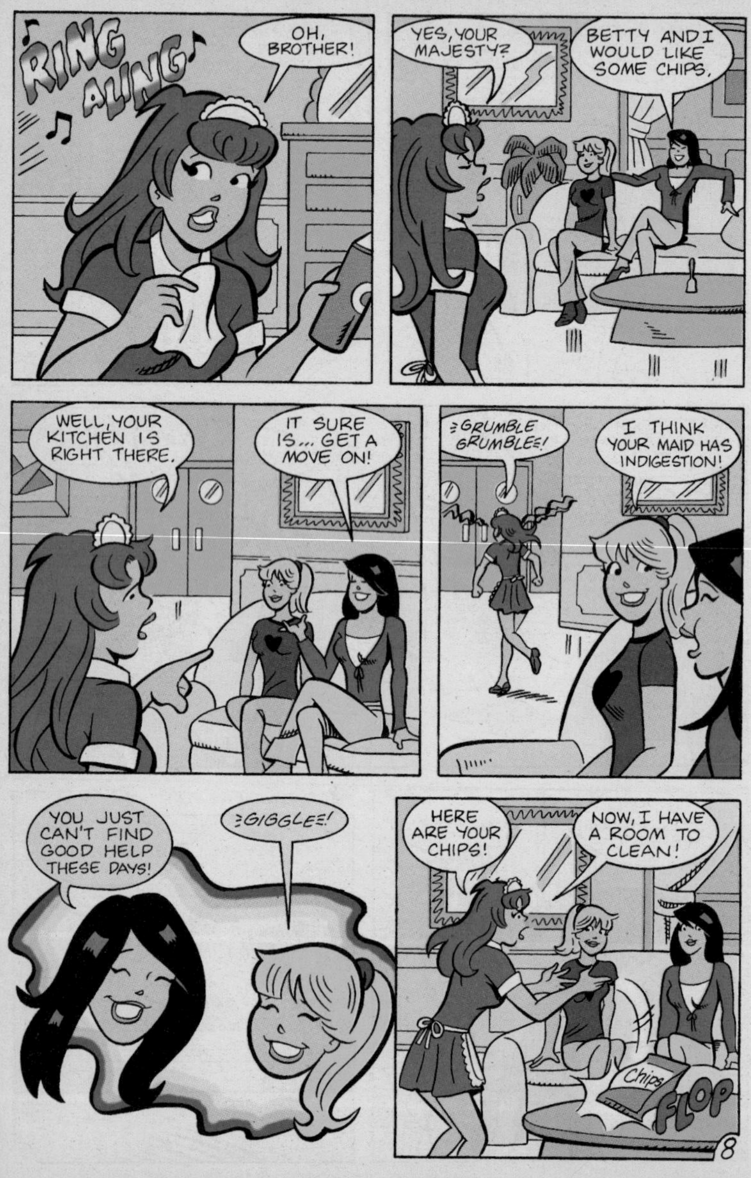
RING A-LING
OH, BROTHER!
YES, YOUR MAJESTY?
BETTY AND I WOULD LIKE SOME CHIPS.
WELL, YOUR KITCHEN IS RIGHT THERE.
IT SURE IS... GET A MOVE ON!
GRUMBLE GRUMBLE!
I THINK YOUR MAID HAS INDIGESTION!
YOU JUST CAN'T FIND GOOD HELP THESE DAYS!
GIGGLE!
HERE ARE YOUR CHIPS!
NOW, I HAVE A ROOM TO CLEAN!
Chips
FLOP

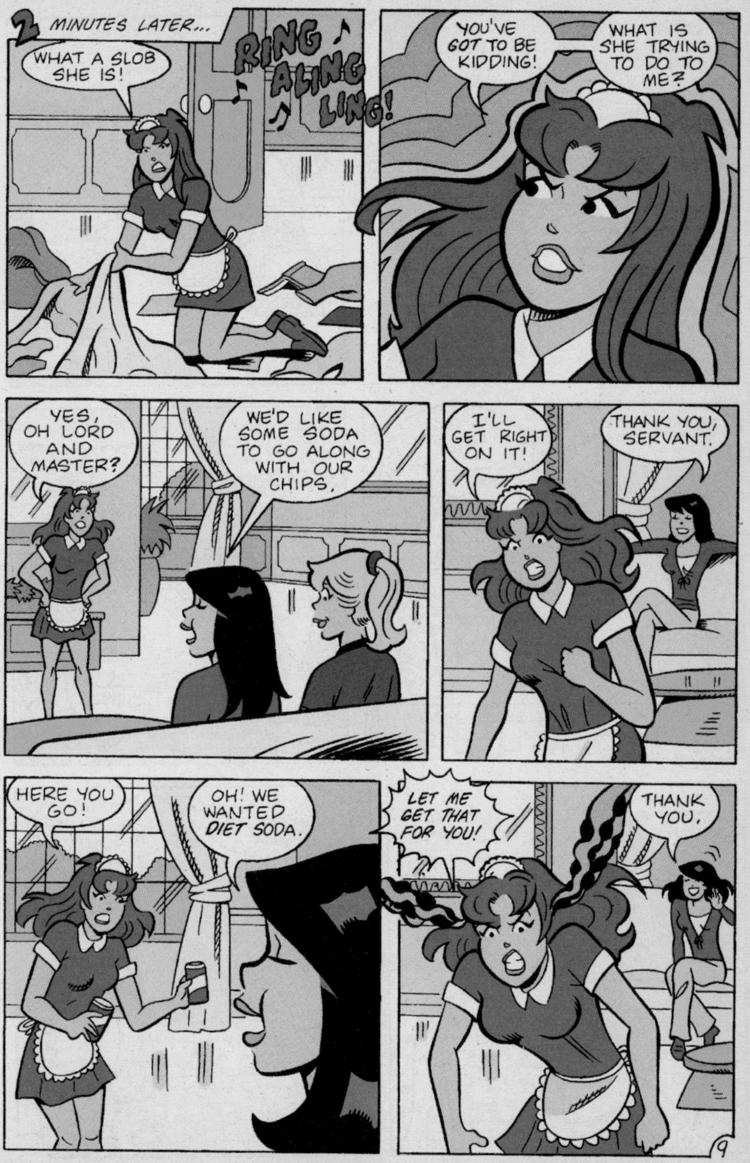
2 MINUTES LATER...
WHAT A SLOB SHE IS!
RING ALING LING!
YOU'VE GOT TO BE KIDDING!
WHAT IS SHE TRYING TO DO TO ME?
YES, OH LORD AND MASTER?
WE'D LIKE SOME SODA TO GO ALONG WITH OUR CHIPS.
I'LL GET RIGHT ON IT!
THANK YOU, SERVANT.
HERE YOU GO!
OH! WE WANTED DIET SODA.
LET ME GET THAT FOR YOU!
THANK YOU.
9

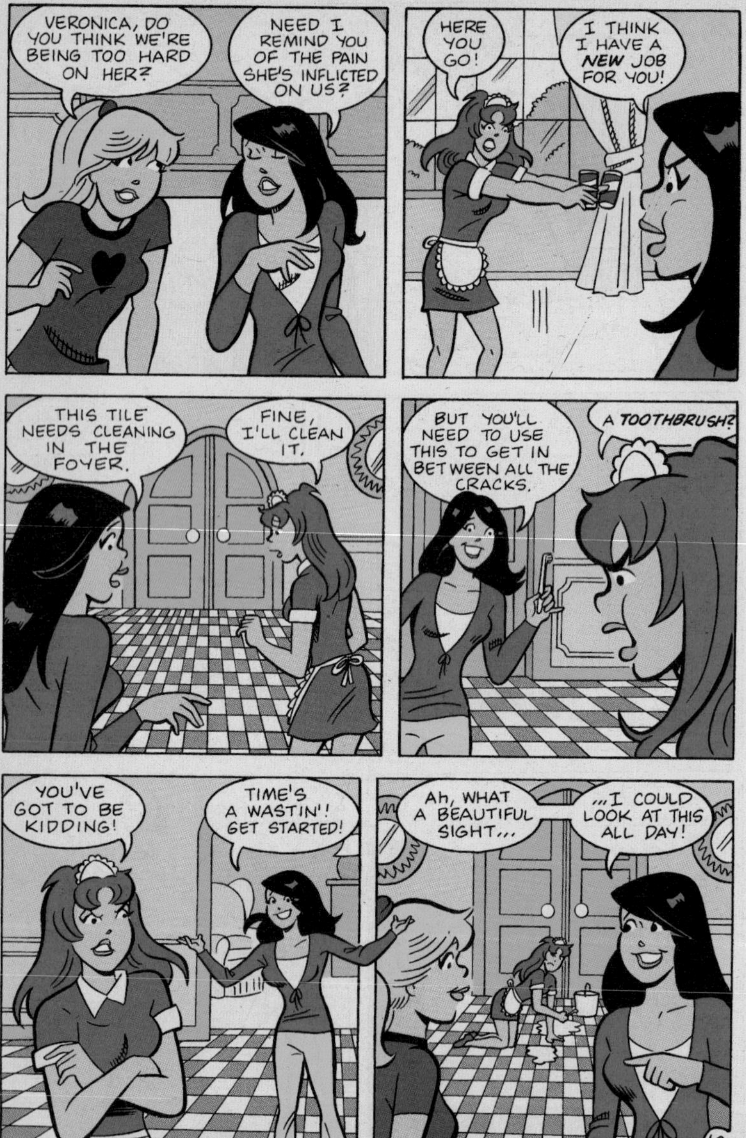

VERONICA, DO YOU THINK WE'RE BEING TOO HARD ON HER?
NEED I REMIND YOU OF THE PAIN SHE'S INFLICTED ON US?
HERE YOU GO!
I THINK I HAVE A NEW JOB FOR YOU!
THIS TILE NEEDS CLEANING IN THE FOYER.
FINE, I'LL CLEAN IT.
BUT YOU'LL NEED TO USE THIS TO GET IN BETWEEN ALL THE CRACKS.
A TOOTHBRUSH?
YOU'VE GOT TO BE KIDDING!
TIME'S A WASTIN'! GET STARTED!
Ah, WHAT A BEAUTIFUL SIGHT...
...I COULD LOOK AT THIS ALL DAY!

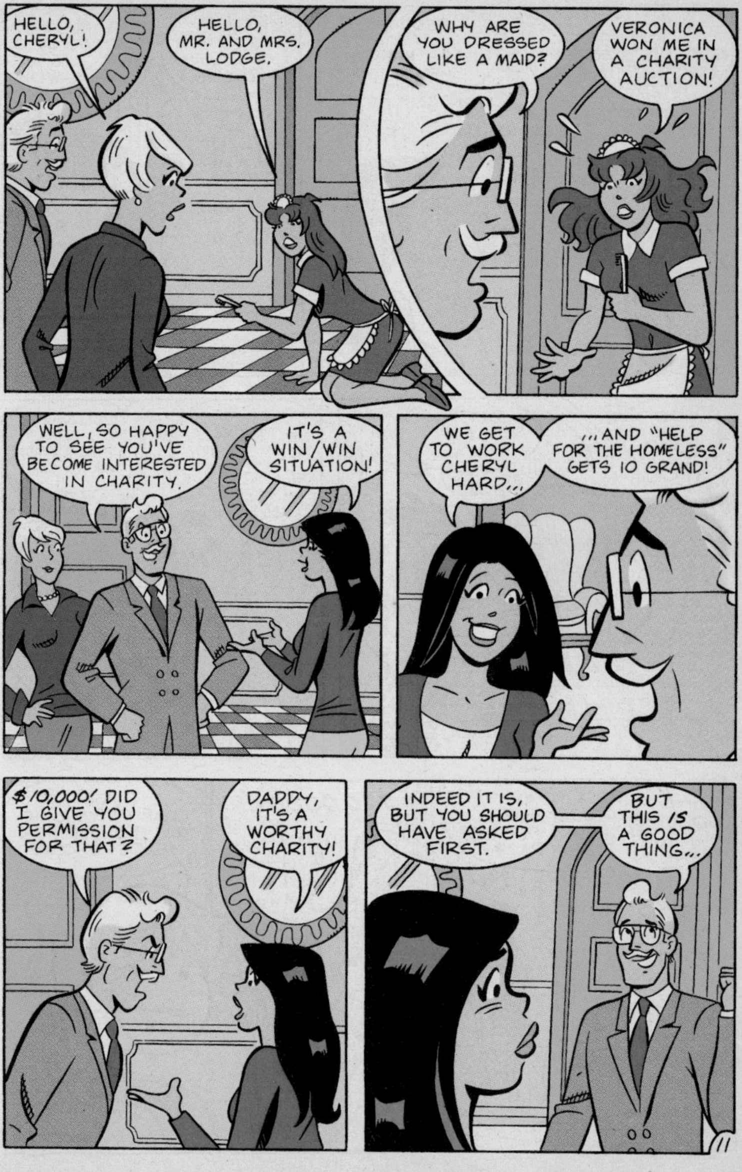
HELLO, CHERYL!
HELLO, MR. AND MRS. LODGE.
WHY ARE YOU DRESSED LIKE A MAID?
VERONICA WON ME IN A CHARITY AUCTION!
WELL, SO HAPPY TO SEE YOU'VE BECOME INTERESTED IN CHARITY.
IT'S A WIN/WIN SITUATION!
WE GET TO WORK CHERYL HARD...
...AND "HELP FOR THE HOMELESS" GETS 10 GRAND!
$10,000! DID I GIVE YOU PERMISSION FOR THAT?
DADDY, IT'S A WORTHY CHARITY!
INDEED IT IS, BUT YOU SHOULD HAVE ASKED FIRST.
BUT THIS IS A GOOD THING...

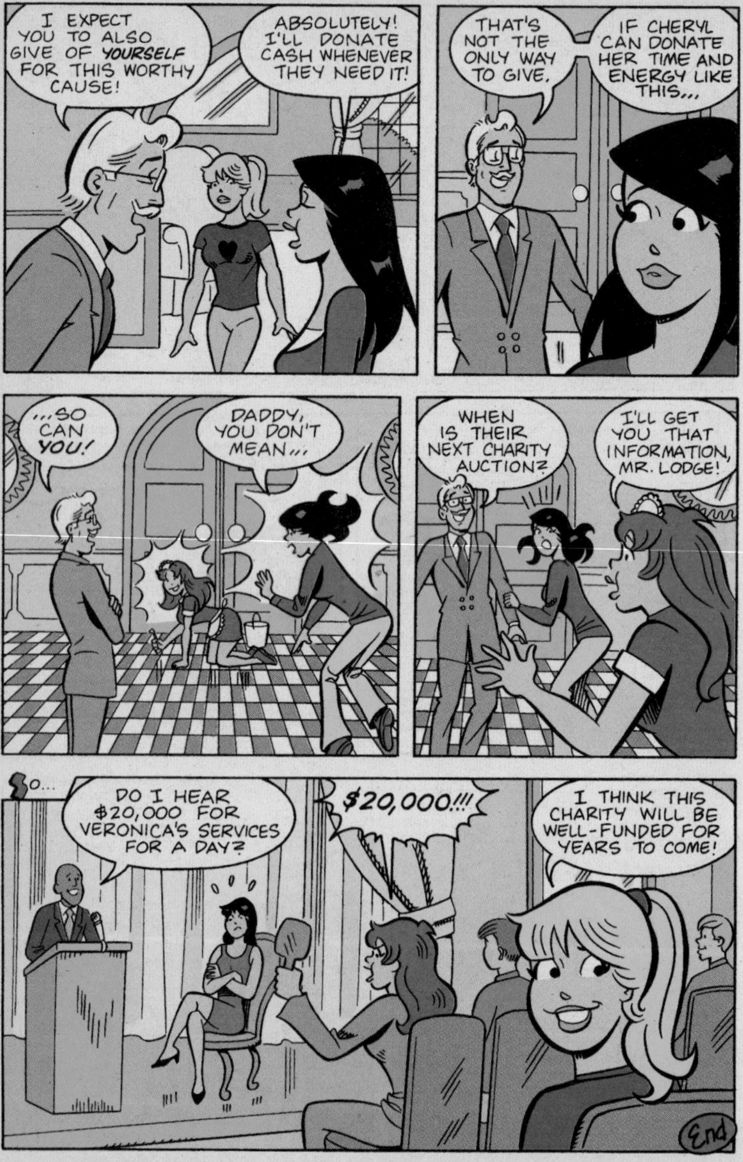

I EXPECT YOU TO ALSO GIVE OF *YOURSELF* FOR THIS WORTHY CAUSE!
ABSOLUTELY! I'LL DONATE CASH WHENEVER THEY NEED IT!
THAT'S NOT THE ONLY WAY TO GIVE.
IF CHERYL CAN DONATE HER TIME AND ENERGY LIKE THIS...
...SO CAN *YOU!*
DADDY, YOU DON'T MEAN...
WHEN IS THEIR NEXT CHARITY AUCTION?
I'LL GET YOU THAT INFORMATION, MR. LODGE!
SO...
DO I HEAR $20,000 FOR VERONICA'S SERVICES FOR A DAY?
$20,000!!!
I THINK THIS CHARITY WILL BE WELL-FUNDED FOR YEARS TO COME!
End

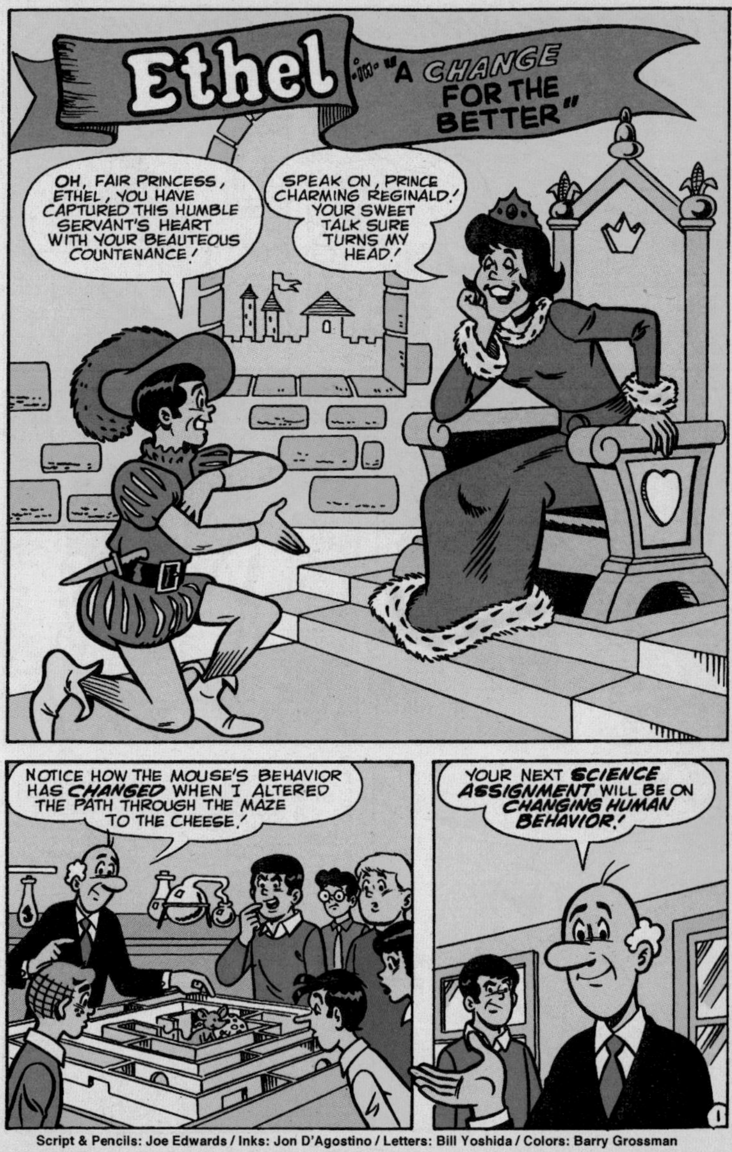
Ethel in "A CHANGE FOR THE BETTER"
OH, FAIR PRINCESS, ETHEL, YOU HAVE CAPTURED THIS HUMBLE SERVANT'S HEART WITH YOUR BEAUTEOUS COUNTENANCE!
SPEAK ON, PRINCE CHARMING REGINALD! YOUR SWEET TALK SURE TURNS MY HEAD!
NOTICE HOW THE MOUSE'S BEHAVIOR HAS CHANGED WHEN I ALTERED THE PATH THROUGH THE MAZE TO THE CHEESE!
YOUR NEXT SCIENCE ASSIGNMENT WILL BE ON CHANGING HUMAN BEHAVIOR!
1

Script & Pencils: Joe Edwards / Inks: Jon D'Agostino / Letters: Bill Yoshida / Colors: Barry Grossman

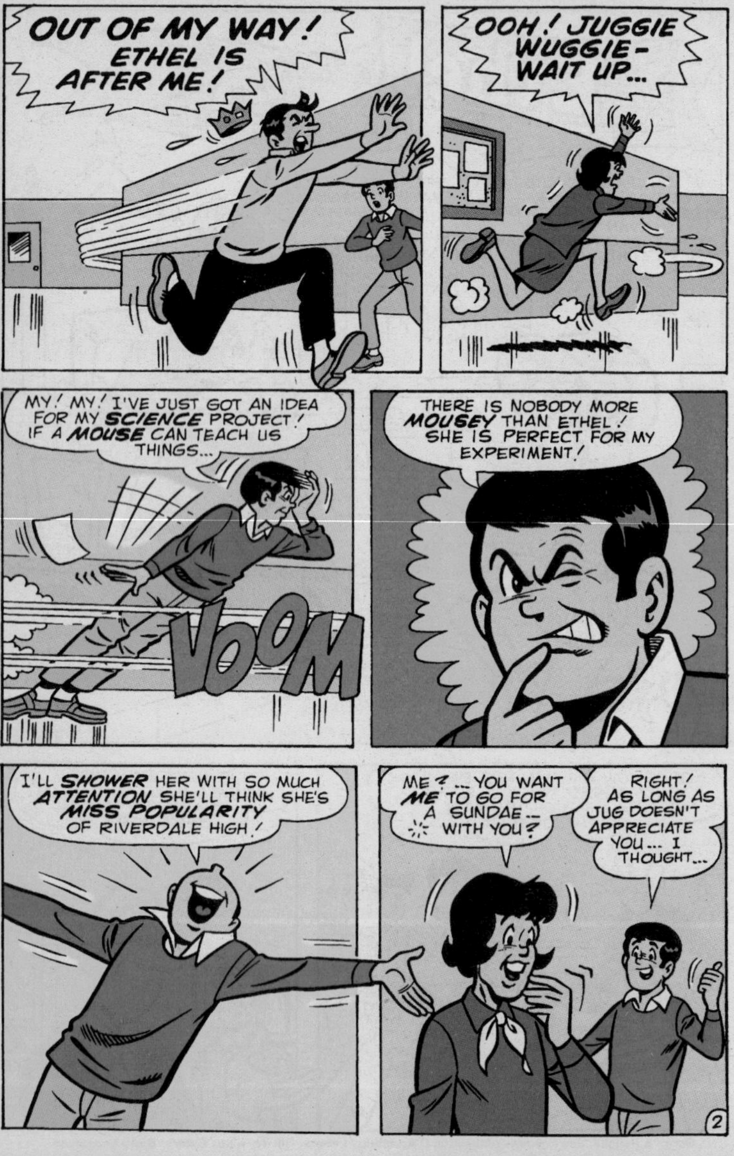
OUT OF MY WAY! ETHEL IS AFTER ME!
OOH! JUGGIE WUGGIE- WAIT UP...
MY! MY! I'VE JUST GOT AN IDEA FOR MY SCIENCE PROJECT! IF A MOUSE CAN TEACH US THINGS...
VOOM
THERE IS NOBODY MORE MOUSEY THAN ETHEL! SHE IS PERFECT FOR MY EXPERIMENT!
I'LL SHOWER HER WITH SO MUCH ATTENTION SHE'LL THINK SHE'S MISS POPULARITY OF RIVERDALE HIGH!
ME? ... YOU WANT ME TO GO FOR A SUNDAE... WITH YOU?
RIGHT! AS LONG AS JUG DOESN'T APPRECIATE YOU... I THOUGHT...
2

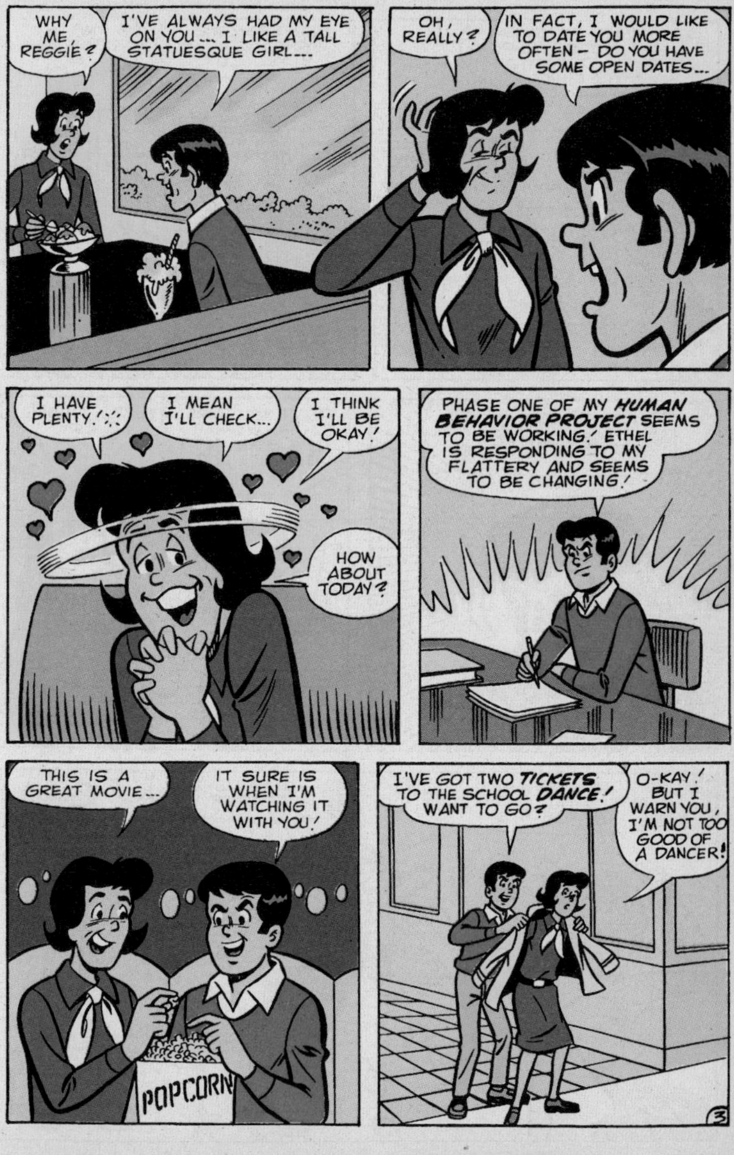
WHY ME, REGGIE?
I'VE ALWAYS HAD MY EYE ON YOU ... I LIKE A TALL STATUESQUE GIRL...
OH, REALLY?
IN FACT, I WOULD LIKE TO DATE YOU MORE OFTEN – DO YOU HAVE SOME OPEN DATES...
I HAVE PLENTY!
I MEAN I'LL CHECK...
I THINK I'LL BE OKAY!
HOW ABOUT TODAY?
PHASE ONE OF MY *HUMAN BEHAVIOR PROJECT* SEEMS TO BE WORKING! ETHEL IS RESPONDING TO MY FLATTERY AND SEEMS TO BE CHANGING!
THIS IS A GREAT MOVIE...
IT SURE IS WHEN I'M WATCHING IT WITH YOU!
POPCORN
I'VE GOT TWO *TICKETS* TO THE SCHOOL *DANCE*! WANT TO GO?
O-KAY! BUT I WARN YOU, I'M NOT TOO GOOD OF A DANCER!
3

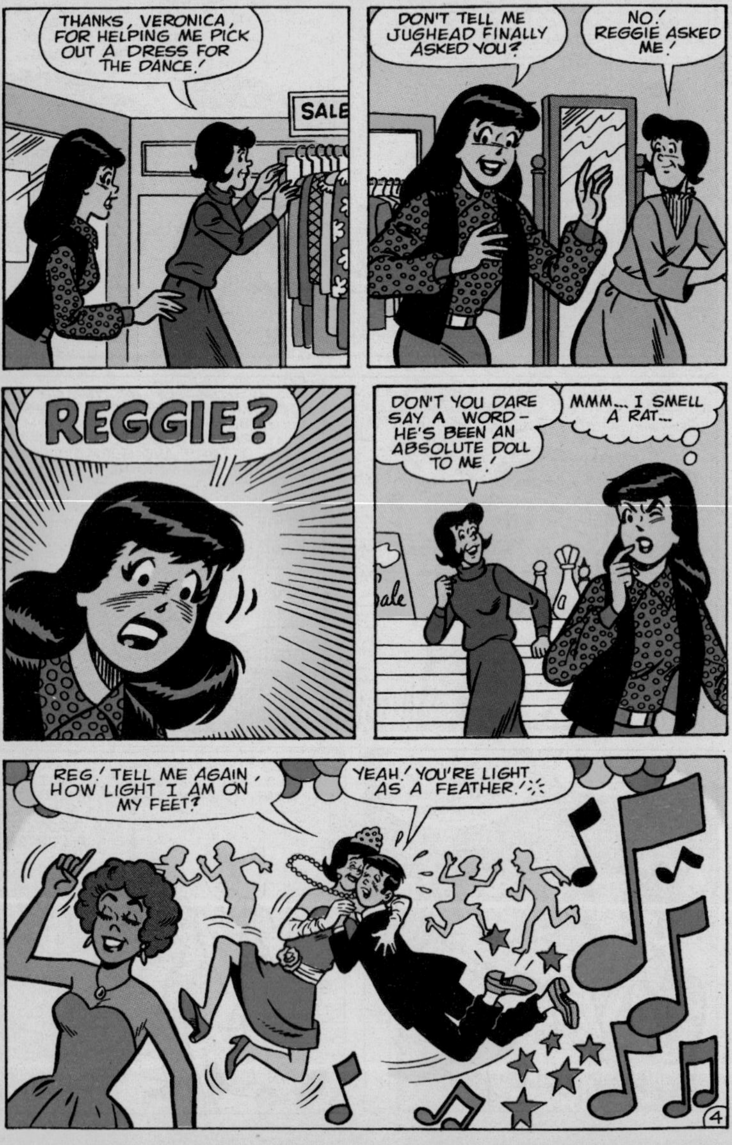
THANKS, VERONICA, FOR HELPING ME PICK OUT A DRESS FOR THE DANCE!
SALE
DON'T TELL ME JUGHEAD FINALLY ASKED YOU?
NO! REGGIE ASKED ME!
REGGIE?
DON'T YOU DARE SAY A WORD— HE'S BEEN AN ABSOLUTE DOLL TO ME!
MMM... I SMELL A RAT...
Sale
REG! TELL ME AGAIN, HOW LIGHT I AM ON MY FEET?
YEAH! YOU'RE LIGHT AS A FEATHER!
4

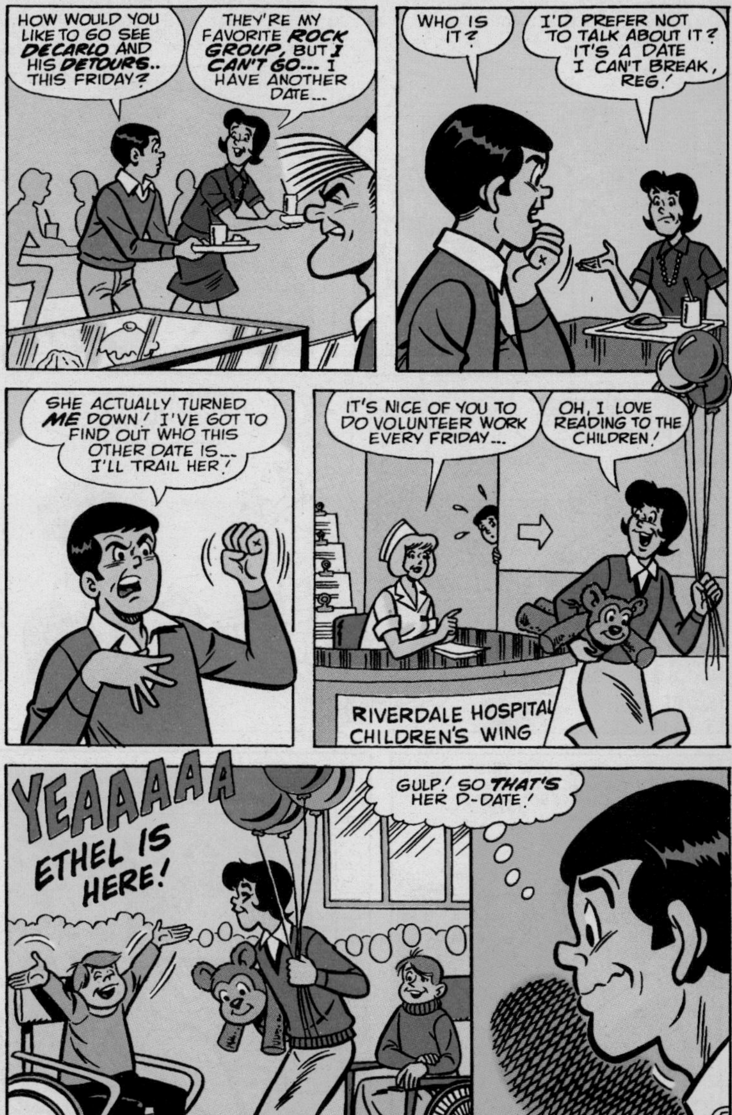
HOW WOULD YOU LIKE TO GO SEE DECARLO AND HIS DETOURS.. THIS FRIDAY?
THEY'RE MY FAVORITE ROCK GROUP, BUT I CAN'T GO... I HAVE ANOTHER DATE...
WHO IS IT?
I'D PREFER NOT TO TALK ABOUT IT? IT'S A DATE I CAN'T BREAK, REG!
SHE ACTUALLY TURNED ME DOWN! I'VE GOT TO FIND OUT WHO THIS OTHER DATE IS... I'LL TRAIL HER!
IT'S NICE OF YOU TO DO VOLUNTEER WORK EVERY FRIDAY...
OH, I LOVE READING TO THE CHILDREN!
RIVERDALE HOSPITAL CHILDREN'S WING
YEAAAAA
ETHEL IS HERE!
GULP! SO THAT'S HER D-DATE!
5

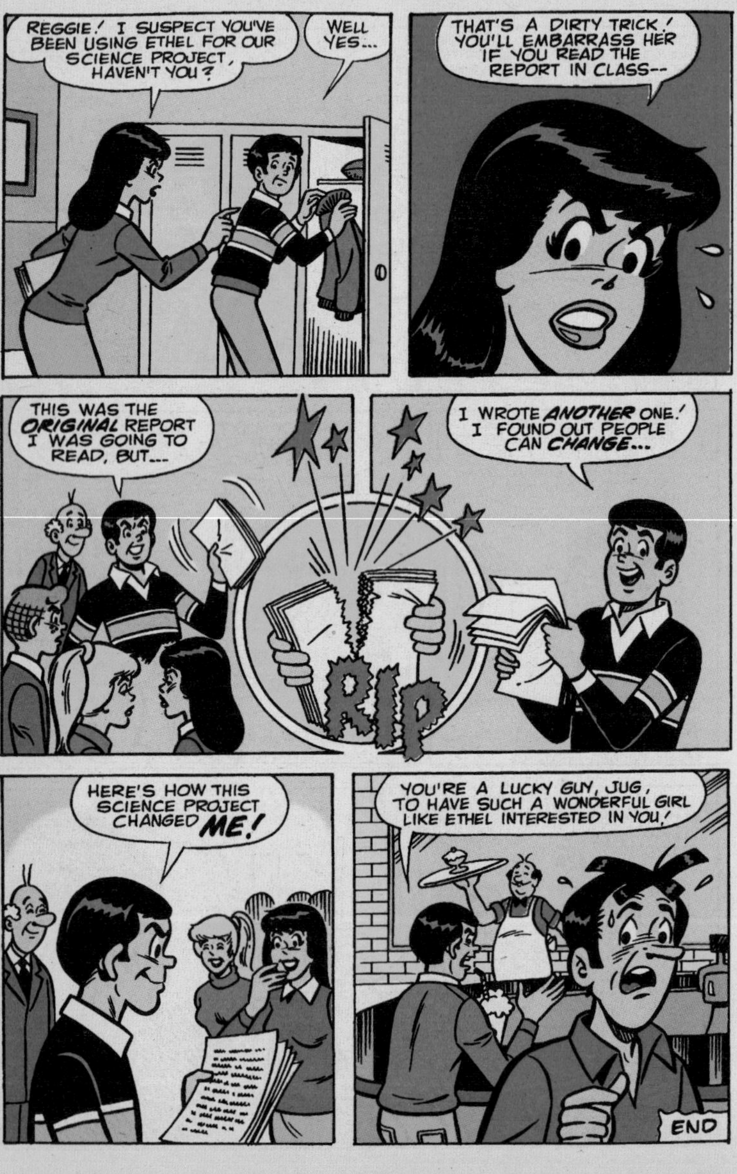
REGGIE! I SUSPECT YOU'VE BEEN USING ETHEL FOR OUR SCIENCE PROJECT, HAVEN'T YOU?
WELL YES...
THAT'S A DIRTY TRICK! YOU'LL EMBARRASS HER IF YOU READ THE REPORT IN CLASS--
THIS WAS THE ORIGINAL REPORT I WAS GOING TO READ, BUT...
RIP
I WROTE ANOTHER ONE! I FOUND OUT PEOPLE CAN CHANGE...
HERE'S HOW THIS SCIENCE PROJECT CHANGED ME!
YOU'RE A LUCKY GUY, JUG, TO HAVE SUCH A WONDERFUL GIRL LIKE ETHEL INTERESTED IN YOU!
END

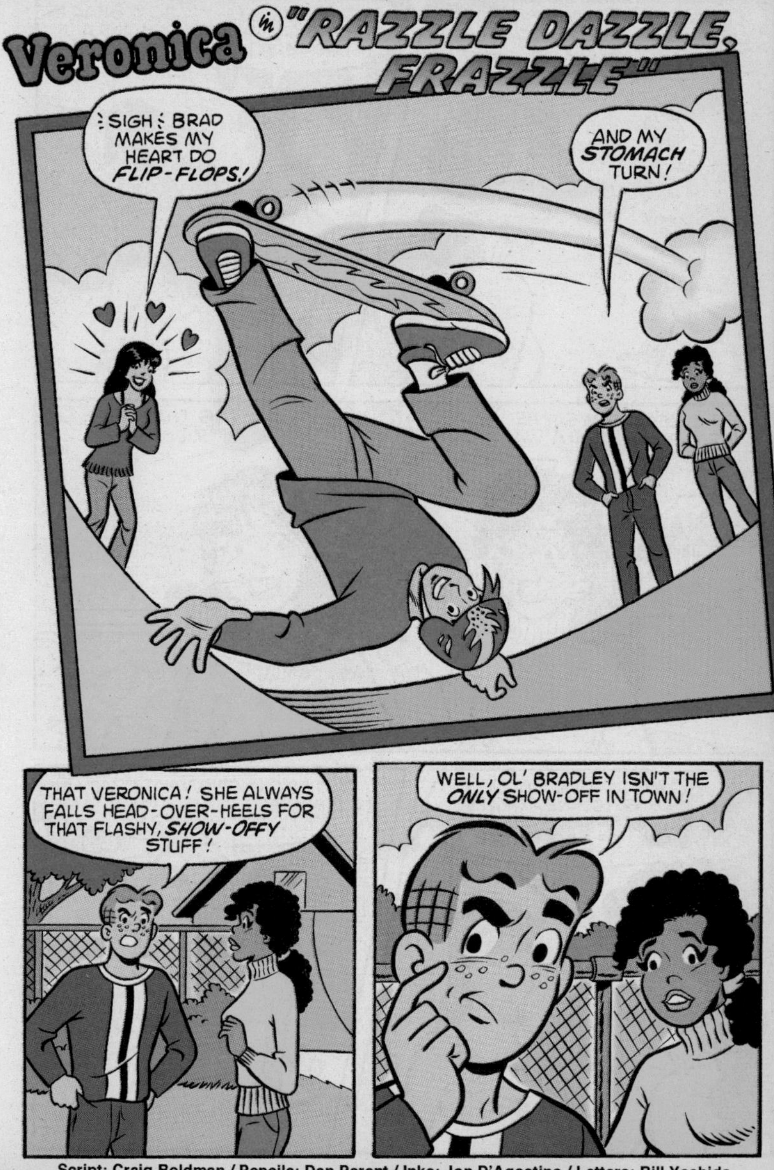
Veronica in "RAZZLE DAZZLE, FRAZZLE"
SIGH BRAD MAKES MY HEART DO FLIP-FLOPS!
AND MY STOMACH TURN!
THAT VERONICA! SHE ALWAYS FALLS HEAD-OVER-HEELS FOR THAT FLASHY, SHOW-OFFY STUFF!
WELL, OL' BRADLEY ISN'T THE ONLY SHOW-OFF IN TOWN!

Script: Craig Boldman / Pencils: Dan Parent / Inks: Jon D'Agostino / Letters: Bill Yoshida

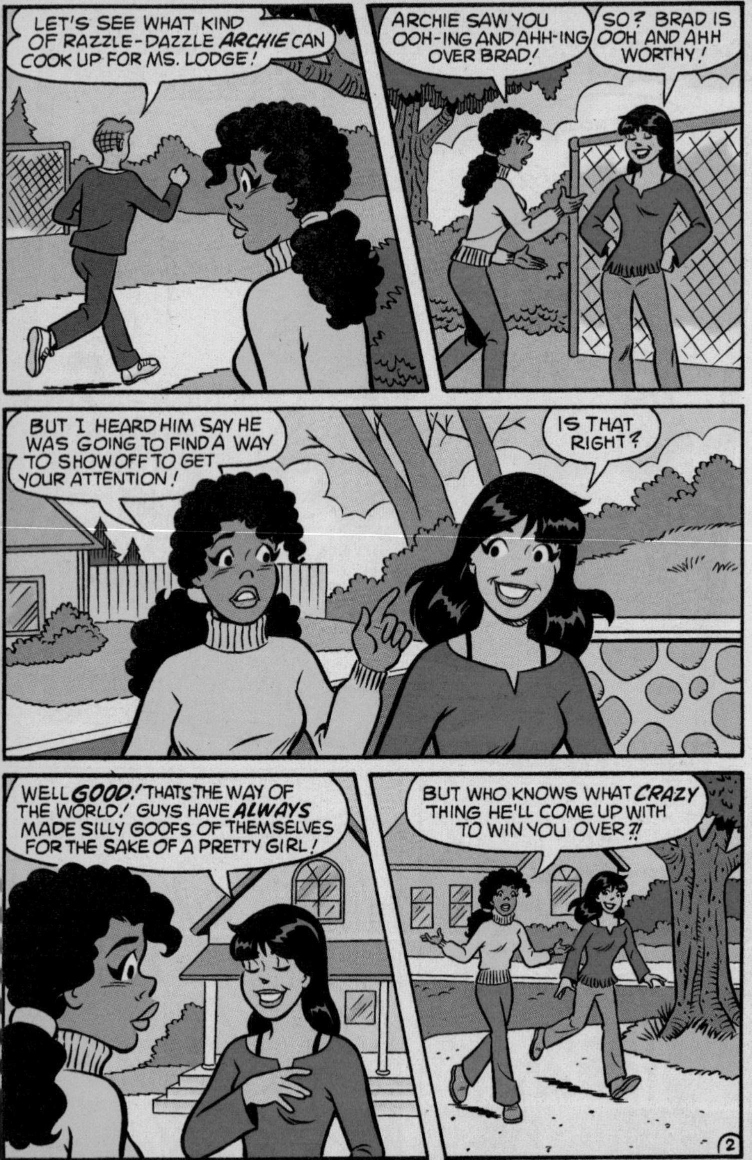
LET'S SEE WHAT KIND OF RAZZLE-DAZZLE ARCHIE CAN COOK UP FOR MS. LODGE!
ARCHIE SAW YOU OOH-ING AND AHH-ING OVER BRAD!
SO? BRAD IS OOH AND AHH WORTHY!
BUT I HEARD HIM SAY HE WAS GOING TO FIND A WAY TO SHOW OFF TO GET YOUR ATTENTION!
IS THAT RIGHT?
WELL GOOD! THAT'S THE WAY OF THE WORLD! GUYS HAVE ALWAYS MADE SILLY GOOFS OF THEMSELVES FOR THE SAKE OF A PRETTY GIRL!
BUT WHO KNOWS WHAT CRAZY THING HE'LL COME UP WITH TO WIN YOU OVER?!
2

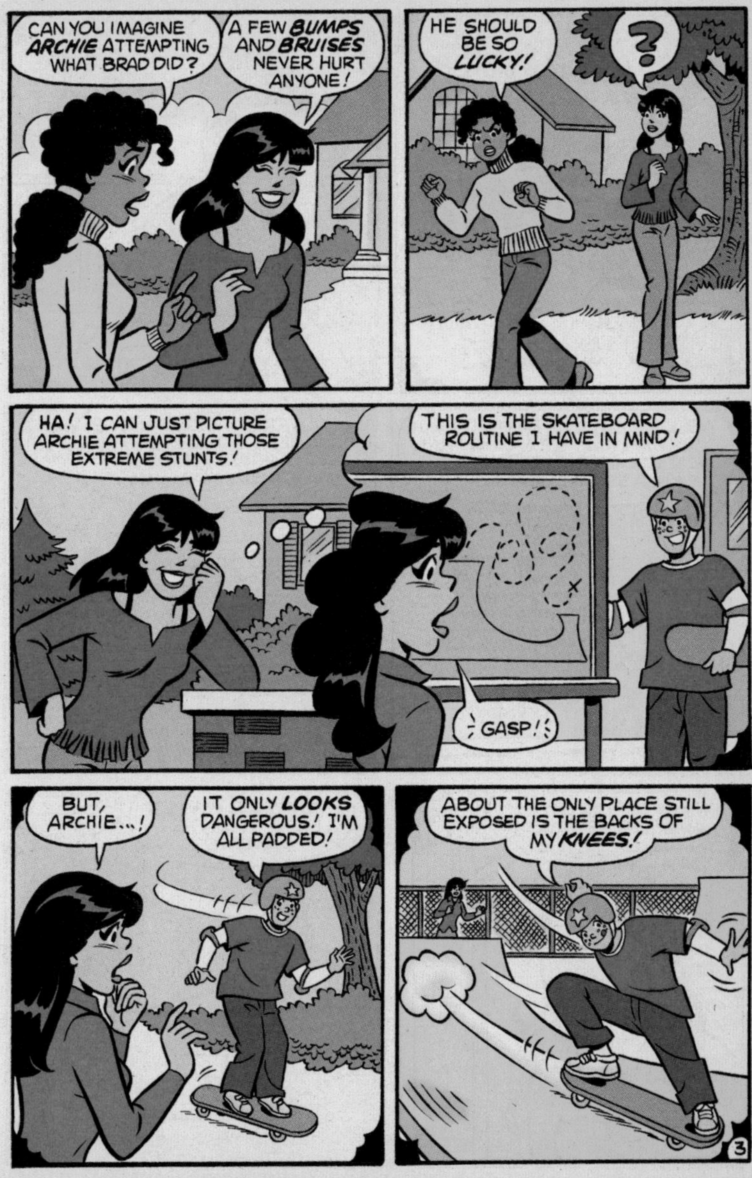

CAN YOU IMAGINE ARCHIE ATTEMPTING WHAT BRAD DID?
A FEW BUMPS AND BRUISES NEVER HURT ANYONE!
HE SHOULD BE SO LUCKY!
?
HA! I CAN JUST PICTURE ARCHIE ATTEMPTING THOSE EXTREME STUNTS!
THIS IS THE SKATEBOARD ROUTINE I HAVE IN MIND!
GASP!
BUT, ARCHIE...!
IT ONLY LOOKS DANGEROUS! I'M ALL PADDED!
ABOUT THE ONLY PLACE STILL EXPOSED IS THE BACKS OF MY KNEES!

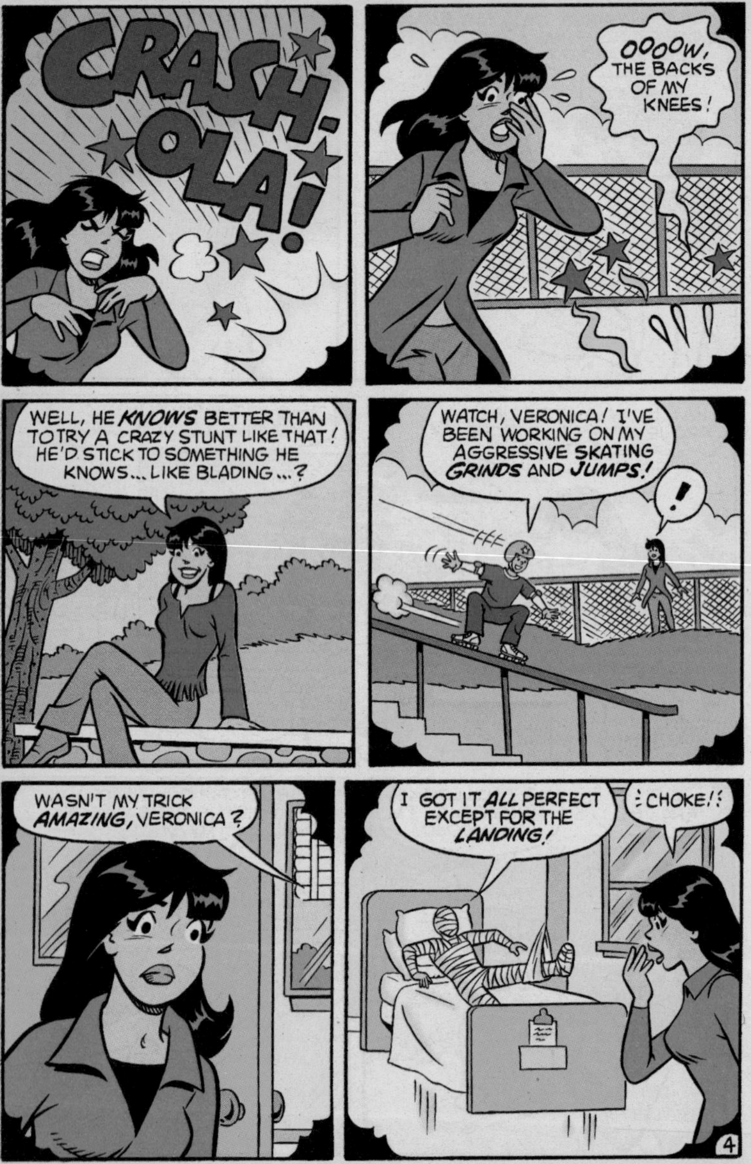
CRASH-OLA!
OOOOW, THE BACKS OF MY KNEES!
WELL, HE KNOWS BETTER THAN TO TRY A CRAZY STUNT LIKE THAT! HE'D STICK TO SOMETHING HE KNOWS... LIKE BLADING...?
WATCH, VERONICA! I'VE BEEN WORKING ON MY AGGRESSIVE SKATING GRINDS AND JUMPS!
!
WASN'T MY TRICK AMAZING, VERONICA?
I GOT IT ALL PERFECT EXCEPT FOR THE LANDING!
CHOKE!
4

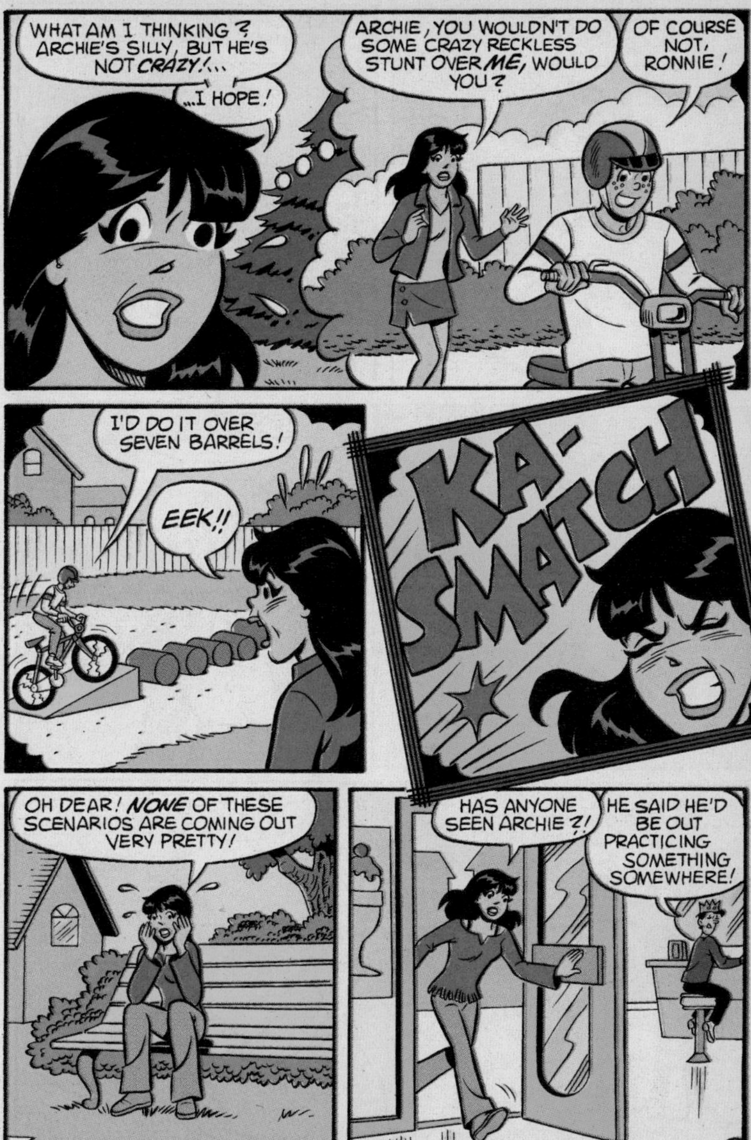

WHAT AM I THINKING ? ARCHIE'S SILLY, BUT HE'S NOT *CRAZY*!...
...I HOPE!
ARCHIE, YOU WOULDN'T DO SOME CRAZY RECKLESS STUNT OVER *ME*, WOULD YOU ?
OF COURSE NOT, RONNIE!
I'D DO IT OVER SEVEN BARRELS!
EEK!!
KA-SMATCH
OH DEAR! *NONE* OF THESE SCENARIOS ARE COMING OUT VERY PRETTY!
HAS ANYONE SEEN ARCHIE ?!
HE SAID HE'D BE OUT PRACTICING SOMETHING SOMEWHERE!
5

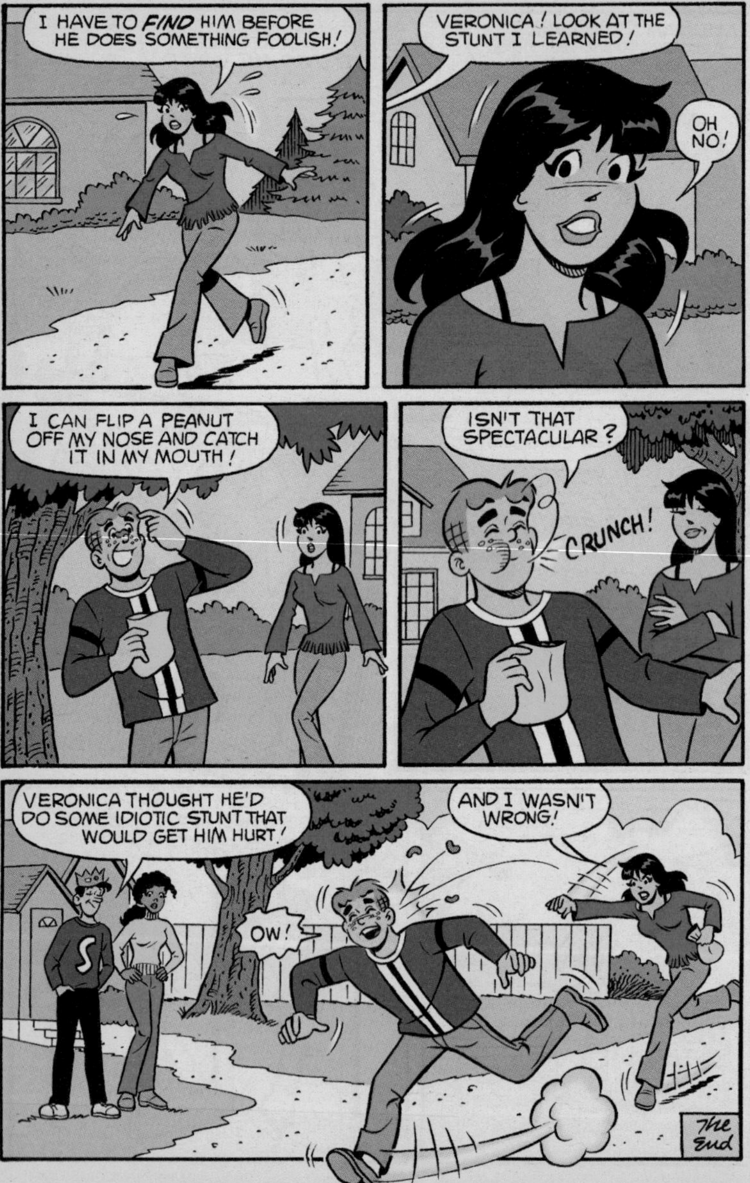
I HAVE TO FIND HIM BEFORE HE DOES SOMETHING FOOLISH!
VERONICA! LOOK AT THE STUNT I LEARNED!
OH NO!
I CAN FLIP A PEANUT OFF MY NOSE AND CATCH IT IN MY MOUTH!
ISN'T THAT SPECTACULAR?
CRUNCH!
VERONICA THOUGHT HE'D DO SOME IDIOTIC STUNT THAT WOULD GET HIM HURT!
AND I WASN'T WRONG!
OW!
The End

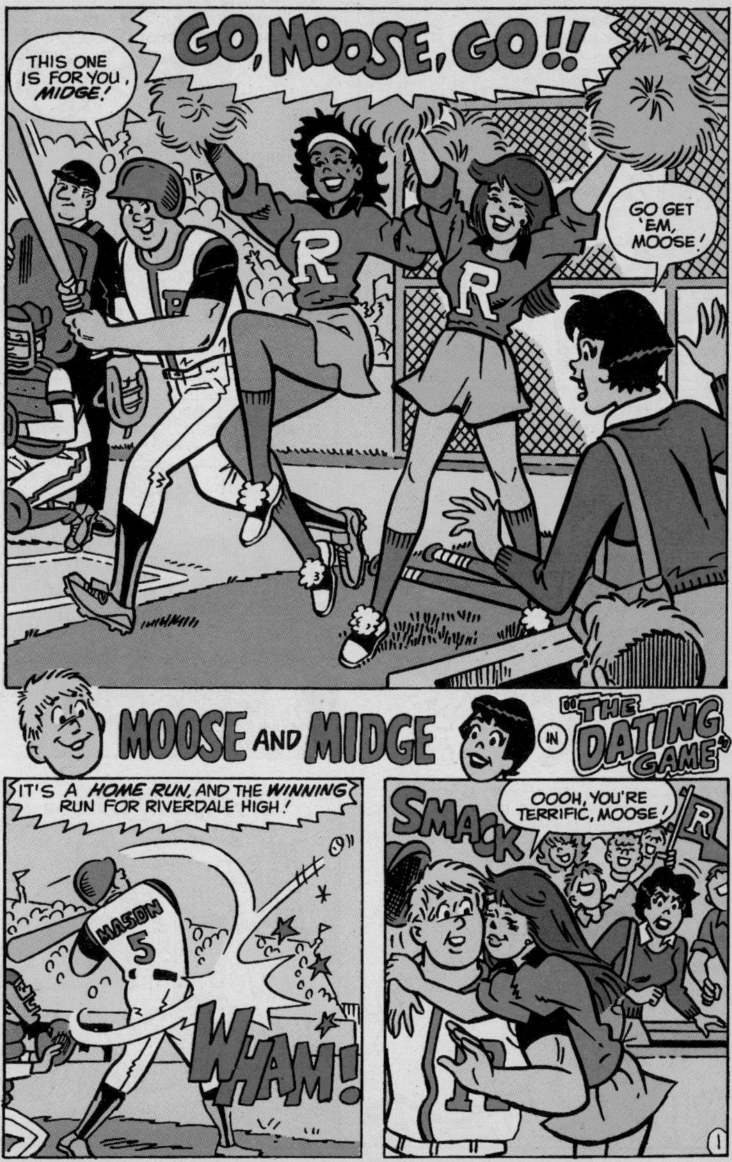
THIS ONE IS FOR YOU, MIDGE!
GO, MOOSE, GO!!
GO GET 'EM, MOOSE!
MOOSE AND MIDGE IN "THE DATING GAME"
IT'S A HOME RUN, AND THE WINNING RUN FOR RIVERDALE HIGH!
MASON
5
WHAM!
SMACK
OOOH, YOU'RE TERRIFIC, MOOSE!
1

Script: Joe Edwards / Pencils: Stan Goldberg / Inks: Rudy Lapick / Letters: Bill Yoshida / Colors: Barry Grossman

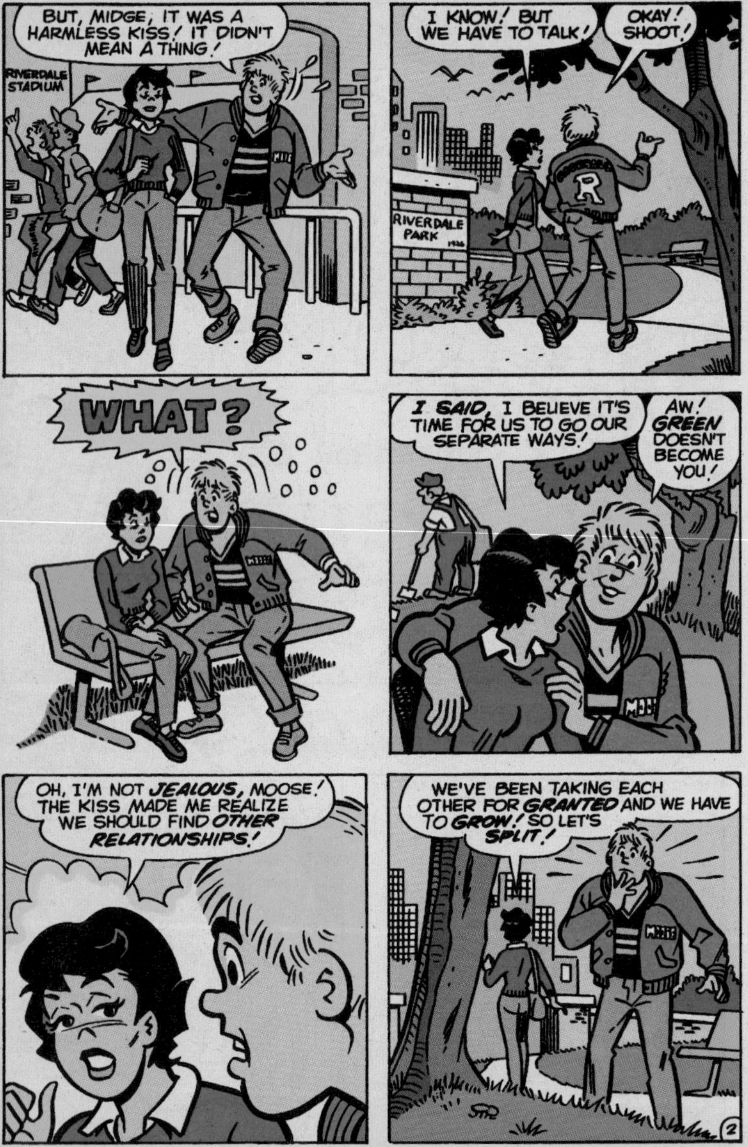
BUT, MIDGE, IT WAS A HARMLESS KISS! IT DIDN'T MEAN A THING!
RIVERDALE STADIUM
I KNOW! BUT WE HAVE TO TALK!
OKAY! SHOOT!
RIVERDALE PARK
WHAT?
I SAID, I BELIEVE IT'S TIME FOR US TO GO OUR SEPARATE WAYS!
AW! GREEN DOESN'T BECOME YOU!
OH, I'M NOT JEALOUS, MOOSE! THE KISS MADE ME REALIZE WE SHOULD FIND OTHER RELATIONSHIPS!
WE'VE BEEN TAKING EACH OTHER FOR GRANTED AND WE HAVE TO GROW! SO LET'S SPLIT!
2

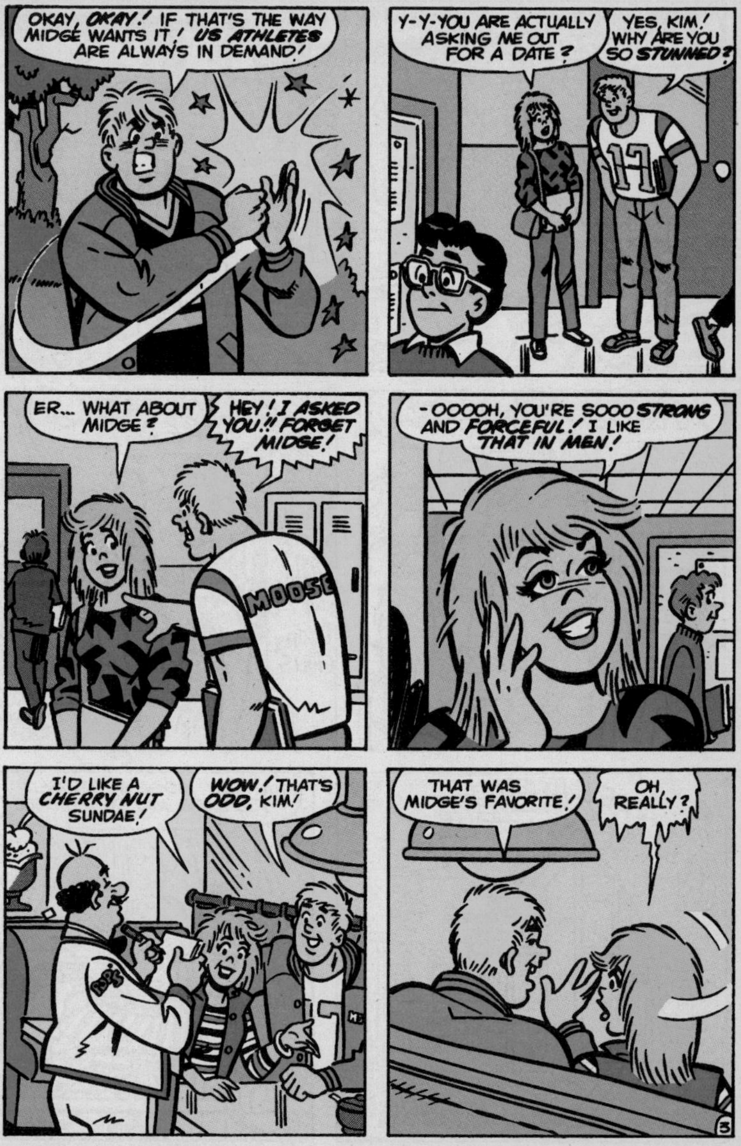

OKAY, OKAY! IF THAT'S THE WAY MIDGE WANTS IT! US ATHLETES ARE ALWAYS IN DEMAND!
Y-Y-YOU ARE ACTUALLY ASKING ME OUT FOR A DATE?
YES, KIM! WHY ARE YOU SO STUNNED?
ER... WHAT ABOUT MIDGE?
HEY! I ASKED YOU!! FORGET MIDGE!
MOOSE
-OOOOH, YOU'RE SOOO STRONG AND FORCEFUL! I LIKE THAT IN MEN!
I'D LIKE A CHERRY NUT SUNDAE!
WOW! THAT'S ODD, KIM!
POP'S
THAT WAS MIDGE'S FAVORITE!
OH, REALLY?
3

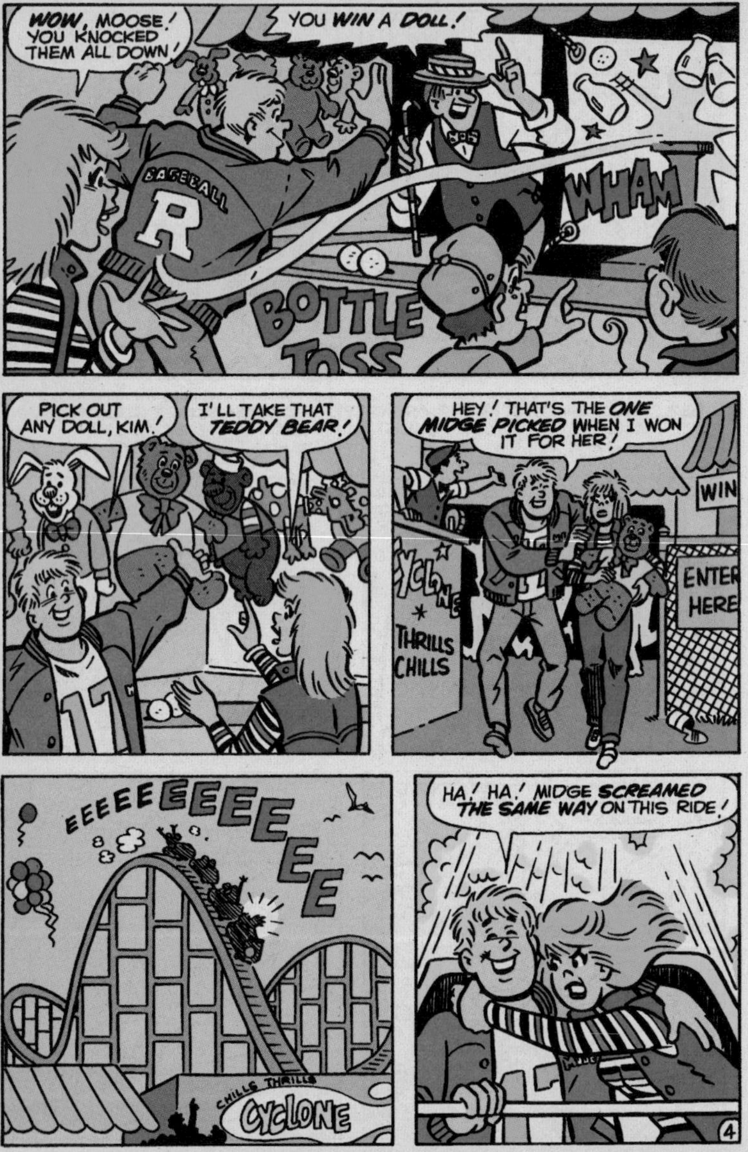
WOW, MOOSE! YOU KNOCKED THEM ALL DOWN!
YOU WIN A DOLL!
WHAM
BASEBALL
BOTTLE TOSS
PICK OUT ANY DOLL, KIM!
I'LL TAKE THAT TEDDY BEAR!
HEY! THAT'S THE ONE MIDGE PICKED WHEN I WON IT FOR HER!
WIN
ENTER HERE
CYCLONE
THRILLS CHILLS
EEEEEEEEEEEE
CHILLS THRILLS
CYCLONE
HA! HA! MIDGE SCREAMED THE SAME WAY ON THIS RIDE!
4

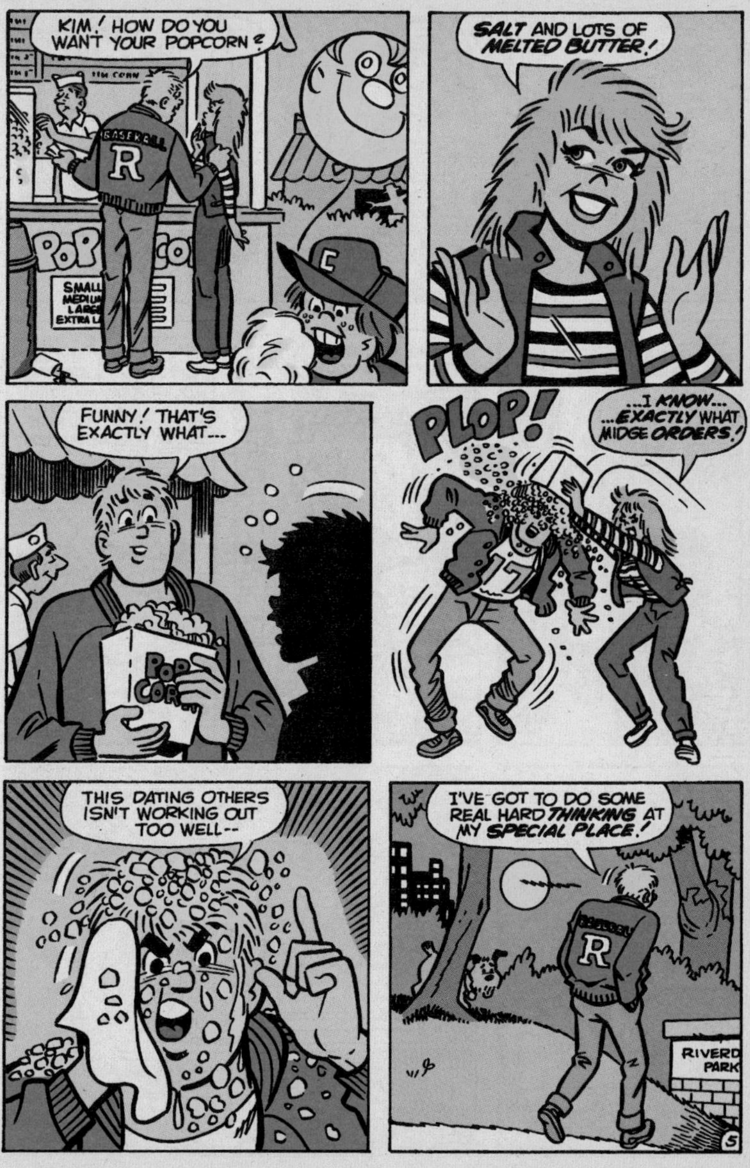
KIM! HOW DO YOU WANT YOUR POPCORN?
BASEBALL
R
POP CORN
SMALL MEDIUM LARGE EXTRA L
C
SALT AND LOTS OF MELTED BUTTER!
FUNNY! THAT'S EXACTLY WHAT...
POP CORN
PLOP!
...I KNOW... ...EXACTLY WHAT MIDGE ORDERS!
17
THIS DATING OTHERS ISN'T WORKING OUT TOO WELL--
I'VE GOT TO DO SOME REAL HARD THINKING AT MY SPECIAL PLACE!
R
RIVERD PARK

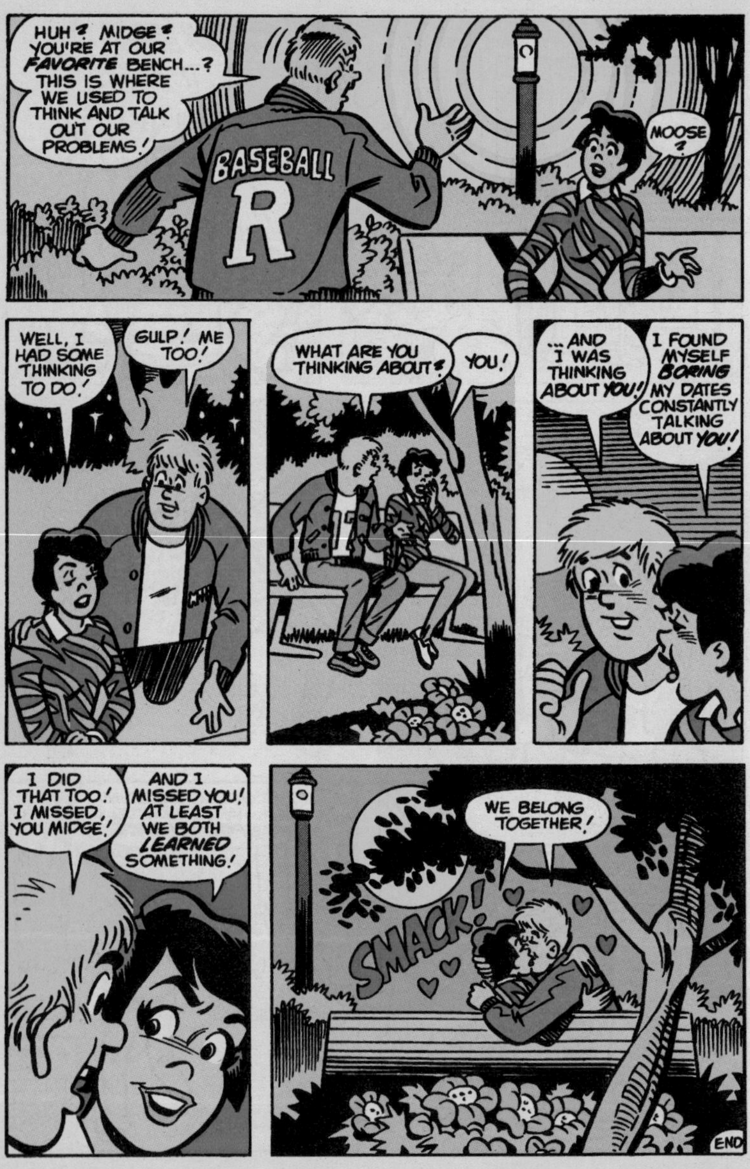
HUH? MIDGE? YOU'RE AT OUR FAVORITE BENCH...? THIS IS WHERE WE USED TO THINK AND TALK OUT OUR PROBLEMS!
MOOSE?
BASEBALL
R
WELL, I HAD SOME THINKING TO DO!
GULP! ME TOO!
WHAT ARE YOU THINKING ABOUT?
YOU!
...AND I WAS THINKING ABOUT YOU!
I FOUND MYSELF BORING MY DATES CONSTANTLY TALKING ABOUT YOU!
I DID THAT TOO! I MISSED YOU MIDGE!
AND I MISSED YOU! AT LEAST WE BOTH LEARNED SOMETHING!
WE BELONG TOGETHER!
SMACK!
END

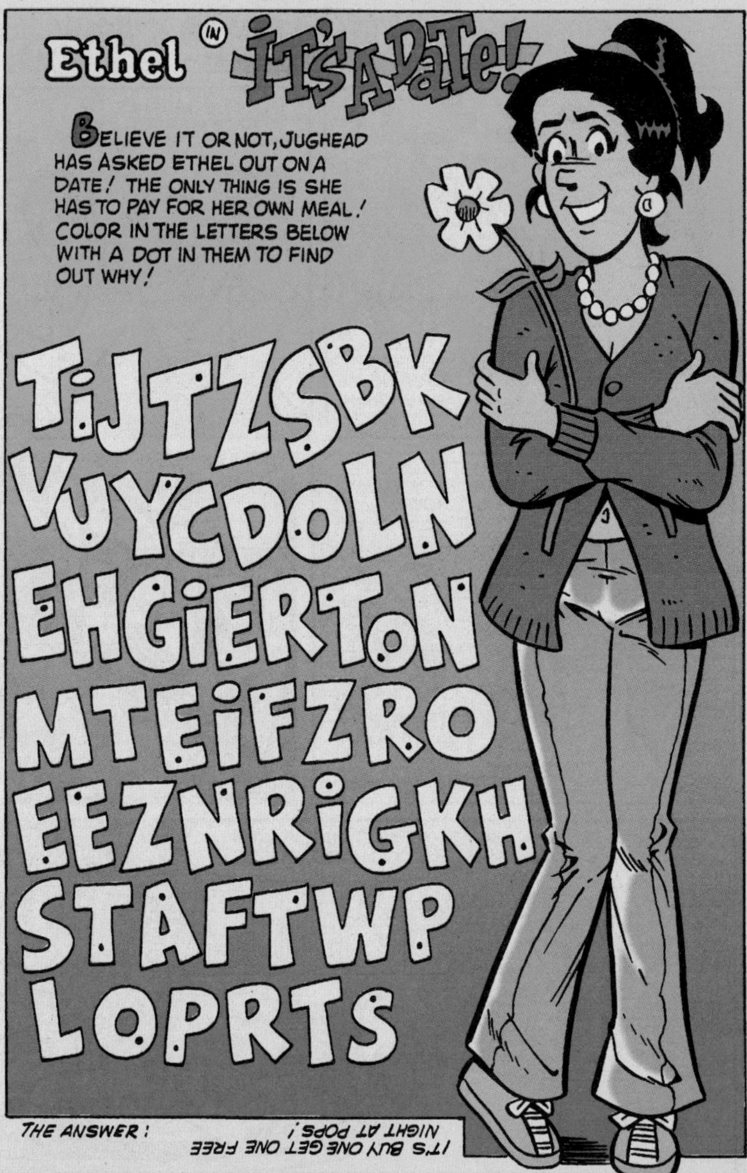
Ethel (IN) IT'S A DATE!
BELIEVE IT OR NOT, JUGHEAD HAS ASKED ETHEL OUT ON A DATE! THE ONLY THING IS SHE HAS TO PAY FOR HER OWN MEAL! COLOR IN THE LETTERS BELOW WITH A DOT IN THEM TO FIND OUT WHY!
TIJTZSBK
VUYCDOLN
EHGIERTON
MTEIFZRO
EEZNRIGKH
STAFTWP
LOPRTS

THE ANSWER: IT'S BUY ONE GET ONE FREE NIGHT AT POPS!

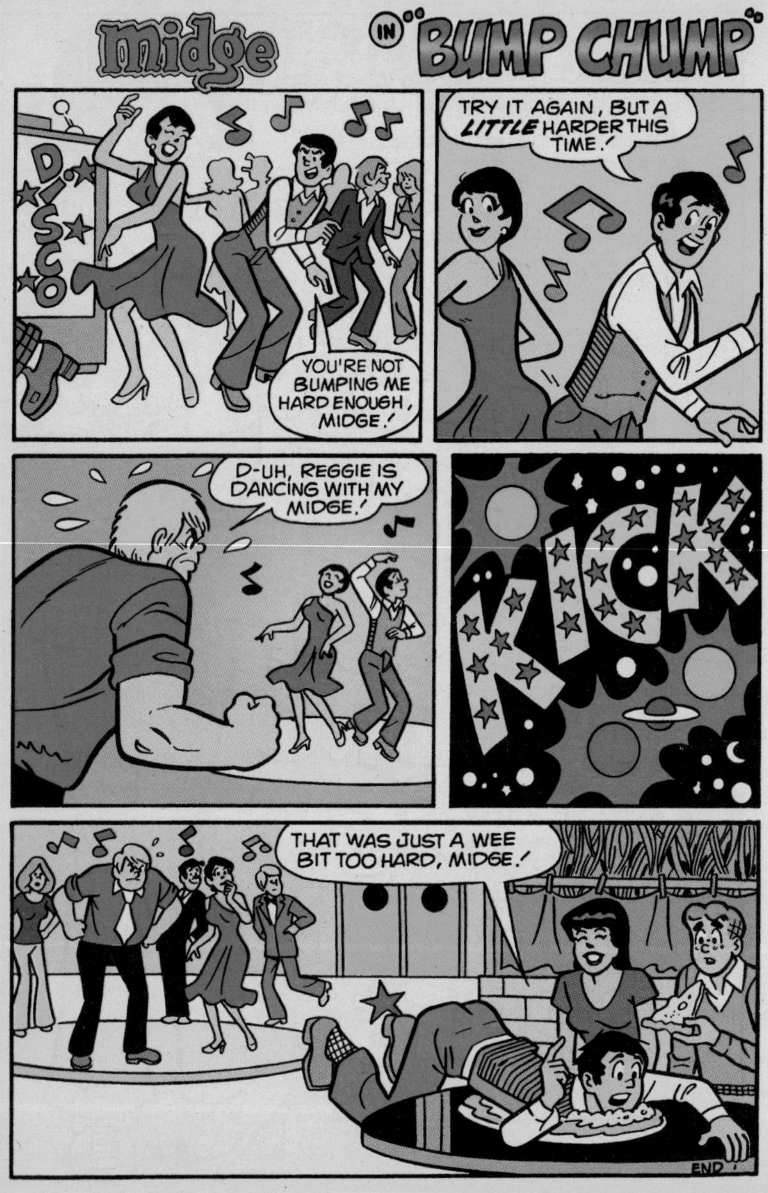
Midge
IN "BUMP CHUMP"
DISCO
YOU'RE NOT BUMPING ME HARD ENOUGH, MIDGE.!
TRY IT AGAIN, BUT A LITTLE HARDER THIS TIME.!
D-UH, REGGIE IS DANCING WITH MY MIDGE.!
KICK
THAT WAS JUST A WEE BIT TOO HARD, MIDGE.!
END

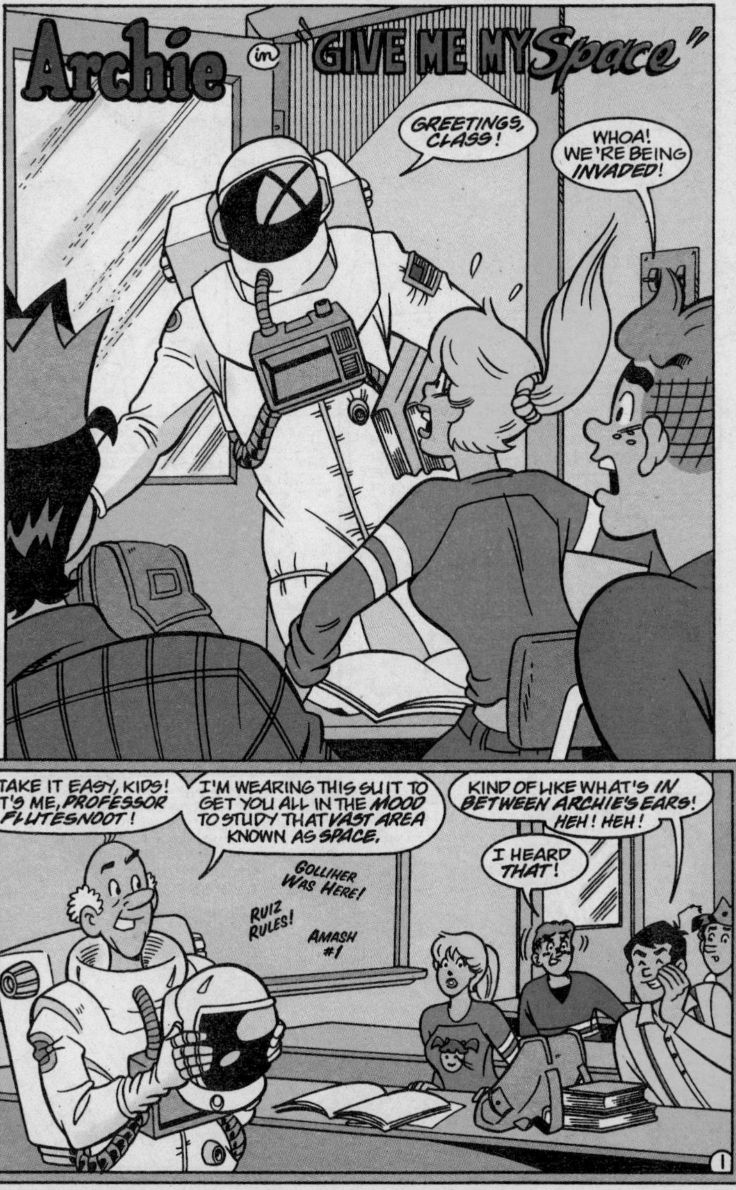

Archie in "GIVE ME MY Space"
GREETINGS, CLASS!
WHOA! WE'RE BEING INVADED!
TAKE IT EASY, KIDS! IT'S ME, PROFESSOR FLUTESNOOT!
I'M WEARING THIS SUIT TO GET YOU ALL IN THE MOOD TO STUDY THAT VAST AREA KNOWN AS SPACE.
KIND OF LIKE WHAT'S IN BETWEEN ARCHIE'S EARS! HEH! HEH!
I HEARD THAT!
GOLLIHER WAS HERE!
RUIZ RULES!
AMASH #1
1

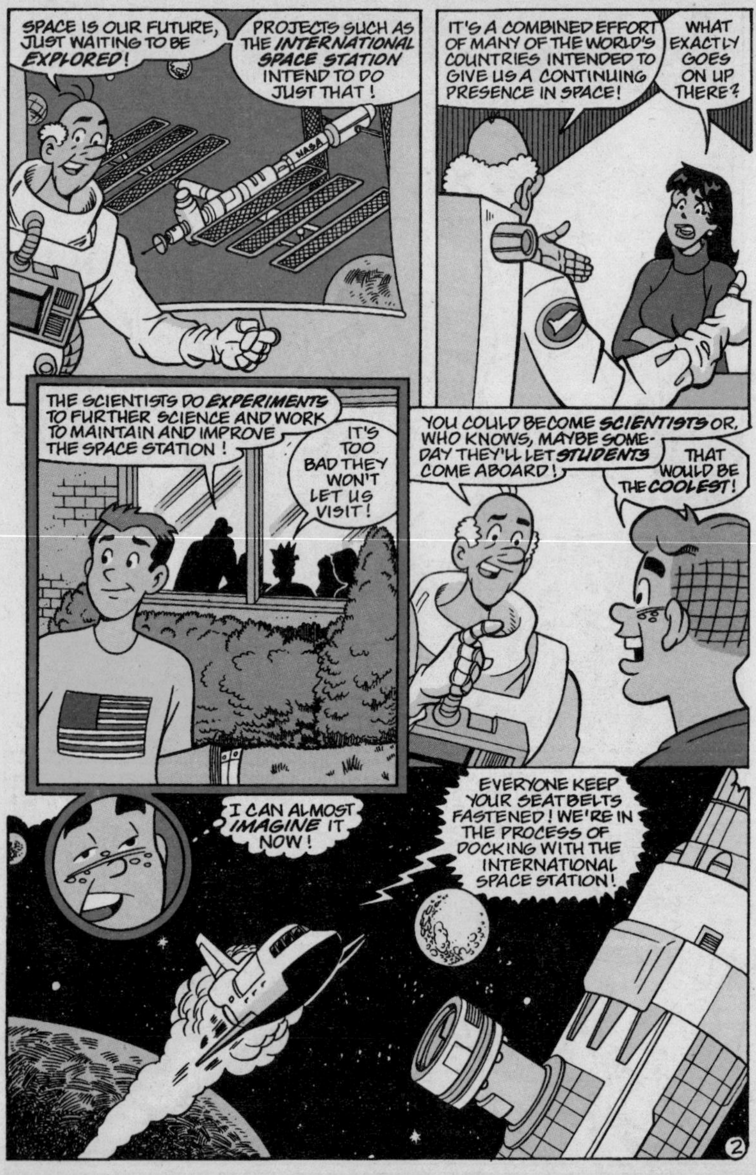

SPACE IS OUR FUTURE, JUST WAITING TO BE *EXPLORED*!
PROJECTS SUCH AS THE *INTERNATIONAL SPACE STATION* INTEND TO DO JUST THAT!
NASA
IT'S A COMBINED EFFORT OF MANY OF THE WORLD'S COUNTRIES INTENDED TO GIVE US A CONTINUING PRESENCE IN SPACE!
WHAT EXACTLY GOES ON UP THERE?
THE SCIENTISTS DO *EXPERIMENTS* TO FURTHER SCIENCE AND WORK TO MAINTAIN AND IMPROVE THE SPACE STATION!
IT'S TOO BAD THEY WON'T LET US VISIT!
YOU COULD BECOME *SCIENTISTS* OR, WHO KNOWS, MAYBE SOME-DAY THEY'LL LET *STUDENTS* COME ABOARD!
THAT WOULD BE THE *COOLEST*!
I CAN ALMOST *IMAGINE* IT NOW!
EVERYONE KEEP YOUR SEATBELTS FASTENED! WE'RE IN THE PROCESS OF DOCKING WITH THE INTERNATIONAL SPACE STATION!

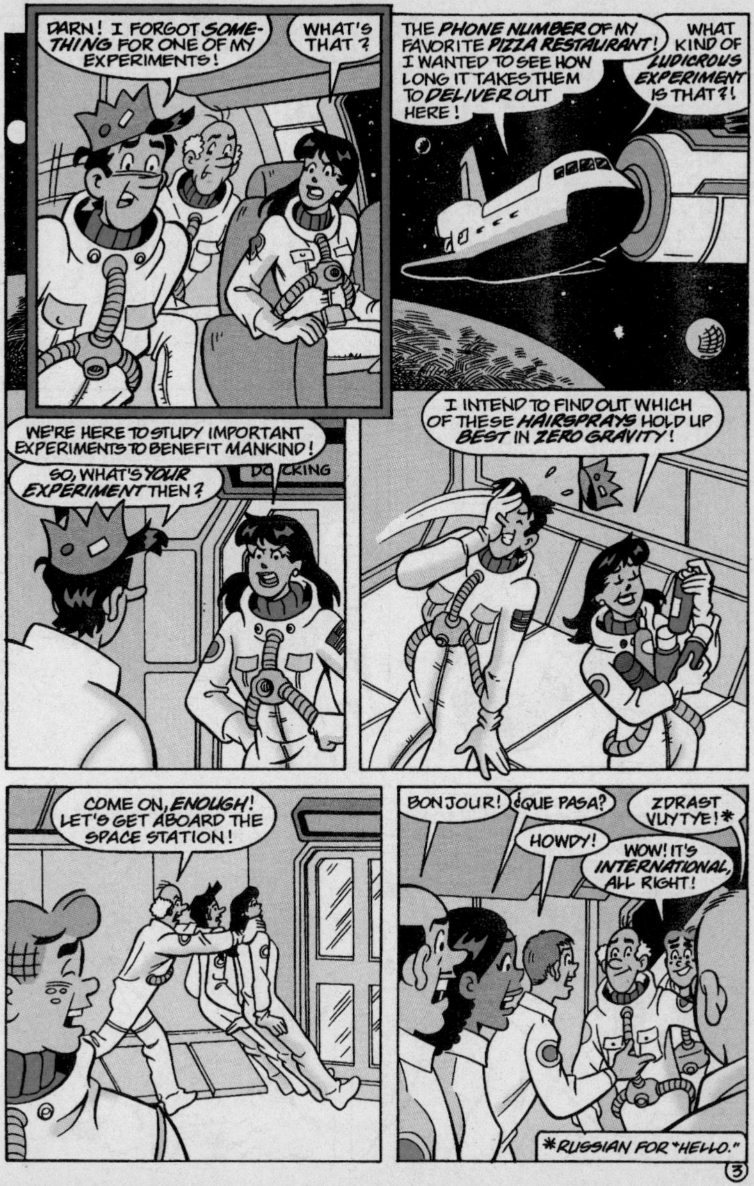
DARN! I FORGOT SOME-THING FOR ONE OF MY EXPERIMENTS!
WHAT'S THAT?
THE PHONE NUMBER OF MY FAVORITE PIZZA RESTAURANT! I WANTED TO SEE HOW LONG IT TAKES THEM TO DELIVER OUT HERE!
WHAT KIND OF LUDICROUS EXPERIMENT IS THAT?!
WE'RE HERE TO STUDY IMPORTANT EXPERIMENTS TO BENEFIT MANKIND!
SO, WHAT'S YOUR EXPERIMENT THEN?
DOCKING
I INTEND TO FIND OUT WHICH OF THESE HAIRSPRAYS HOLD UP BEST IN ZERO GRAVITY!
COME ON, ENOUGH! LET'S GET ABOARD THE SPACE STATION!
BONJOUR!
¿QUE PASA?
HOWDY!
ZDRAST VUYTYE!*
WOW! IT'S INTERNATIONAL, ALL RIGHT!
*RUSSIAN FOR "HELLO."

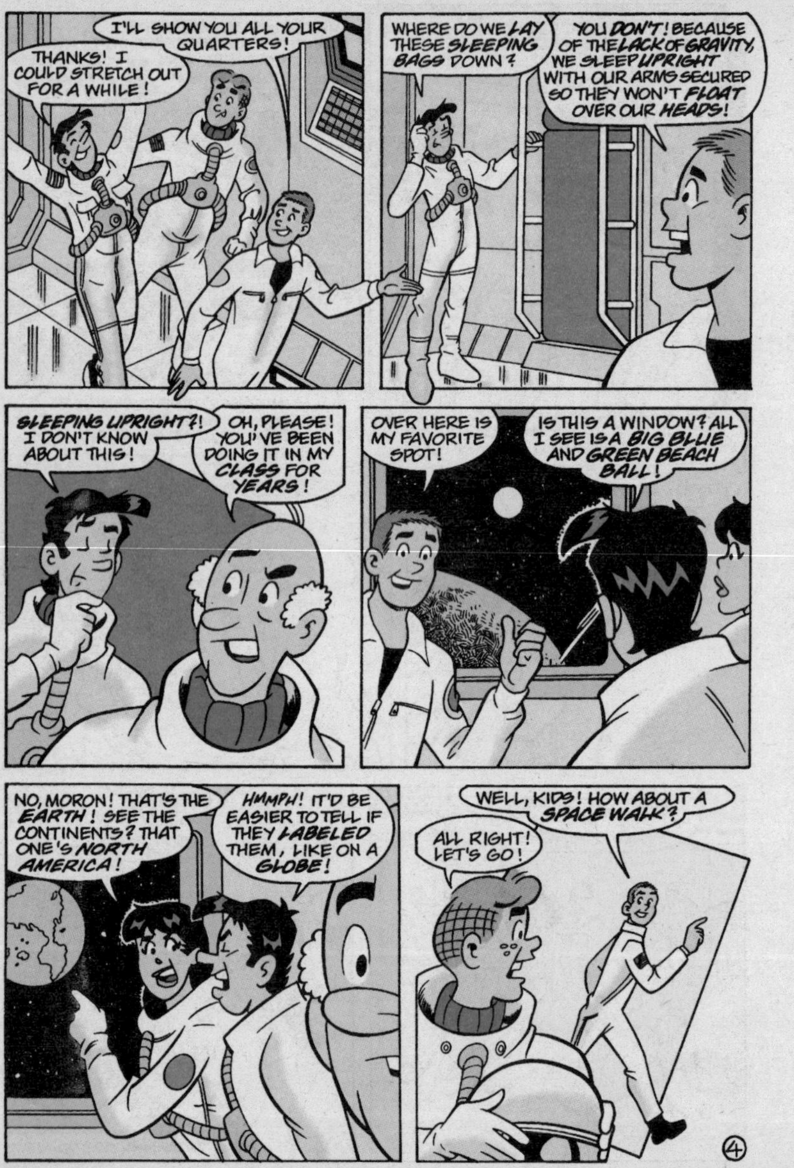
THANKS! I COULD STRETCH OUT FOR A WHILE!
I'LL SHOW YOU ALL YOUR QUARTERS!
WHERE DO WE LAY THESE SLEEPING BAGS DOWN?
YOU DON'T! BECAUSE OF THE LACK OF GRAVITY, WE SLEEP UPRIGHT WITH OUR ARMS SECURED SO THEY WON'T FLOAT OVER OUR HEADS!
SLEEPING UPRIGHT?! I DON'T KNOW ABOUT THIS!
OH, PLEASE! YOU'VE BEEN DOING IT IN MY CLASS FOR YEARS!
OVER HERE IS MY FAVORITE SPOT!
IS THIS A WINDOW? ALL I SEE IS A BIG BLUE AND GREEN BEACH BALL!
NO, MORON! THAT'S THE EARTH! SEE THE CONTINENTS? THAT ONE'S NORTH AMERICA!
HMMPH! IT'D BE EASIER TO TELL IF THEY LABELED THEM, LIKE ON A GLOBE!
WELL, KIDS! HOW ABOUT A SPACE WALK?
ALL RIGHT! LET'S GO!
4

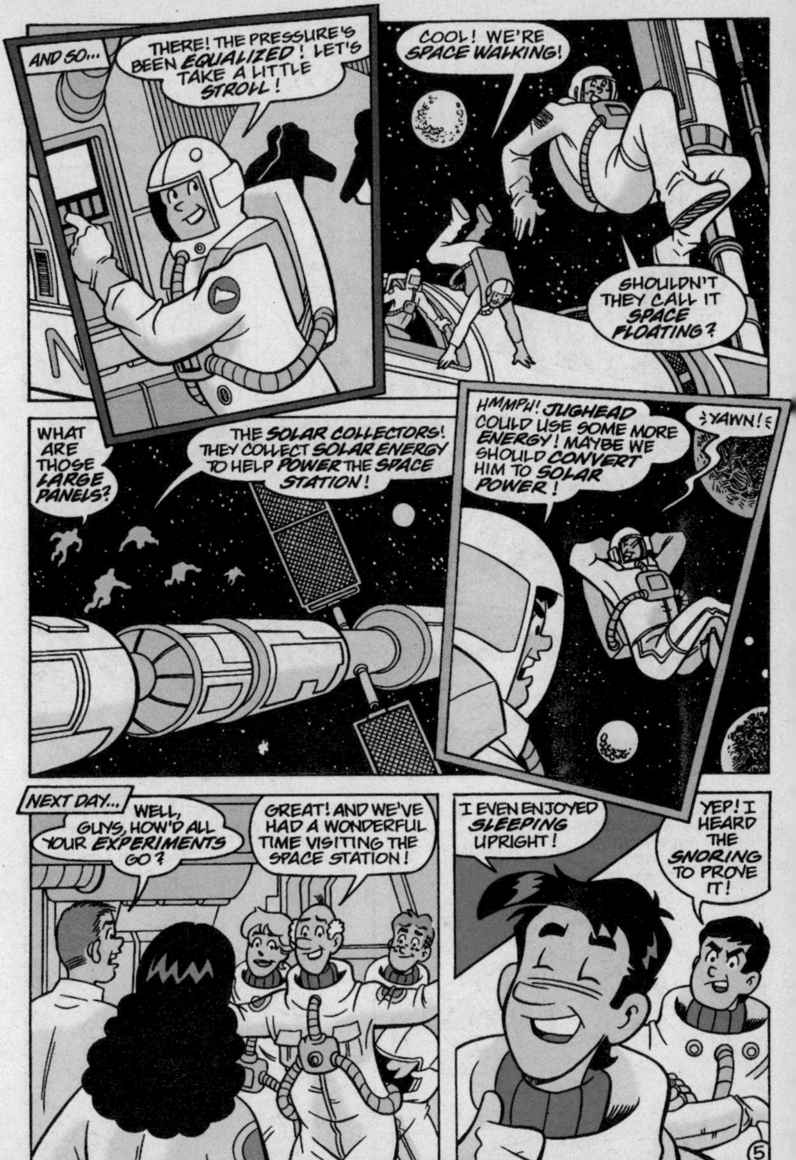
AND SO...
THERE! THE PRESSURE'S BEEN EQUALIZED! LET'S TAKE A LITTLE STROLL!
COOL! WE'RE SPACE WALKING!
SHOULDN'T THEY CALL IT SPACE FLOATING?
WHAT ARE THOSE LARGE PANELS?
THE SOLAR COLLECTORS! THEY COLLECT SOLAR ENERGY TO HELP POWER THE SPACE STATION!
HMMPH! JUGHEAD COULD USE SOME MORE ENERGY! MAYBE WE SHOULD CONVERT HIM TO SOLAR POWER!
YAWN!
NEXT DAY...
WELL, GUYS, HOW'D ALL YOUR EXPERIMENTS GO?
GREAT! AND WE'VE HAD A WONDERFUL TIME VISITING THE SPACE STATION!
I EVEN ENJOYED SLEEPING UPRIGHT!
YEP! I HEARD THE SNORING TO PROVE IT!
5

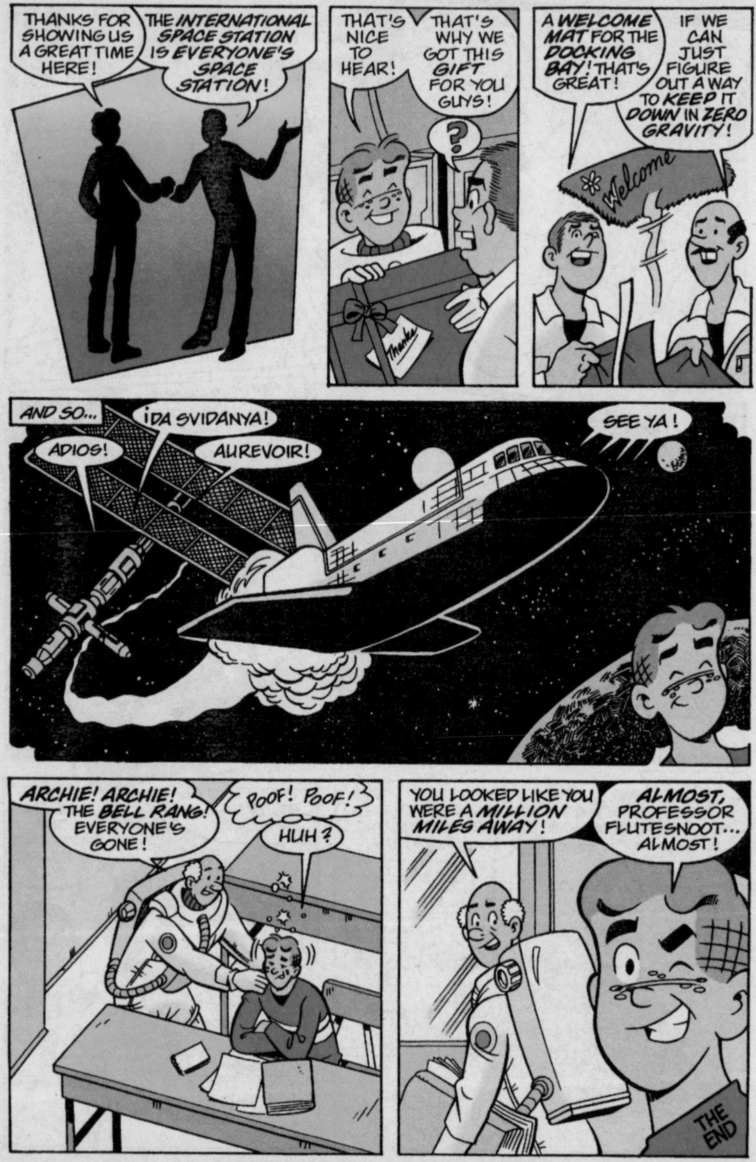
THANKS FOR SHOWING US A GREAT TIME HERE!
THE INTERNATIONAL SPACE STATION IS EVERYONE'S SPACE STATION!
THAT'S NICE TO HEAR!
THAT'S WHY WE GOT THIS GIFT FOR YOU GUYS!
?
Thanks
A WELCOME MAT FOR THE DOCKING BAY! THAT'S GREAT!
IF WE CAN JUST FIGURE OUT A WAY TO KEEP IT DOWN IN ZERO GRAVITY!
Welcome
AND SO...
¡DA SVIDANYA!
ADIOS!
AU REVOIR!
SEE YA!
ARCHIE! ARCHIE! THE BELL RANG! EVERYONE'S GONE!
POOF! POOF!
HUH?
YOU LOOKED LIKE YOU WERE A MILLION MILES AWAY!
ALMOST, PROFESSOR FLUTESNOOT... ALMOST!
THE END

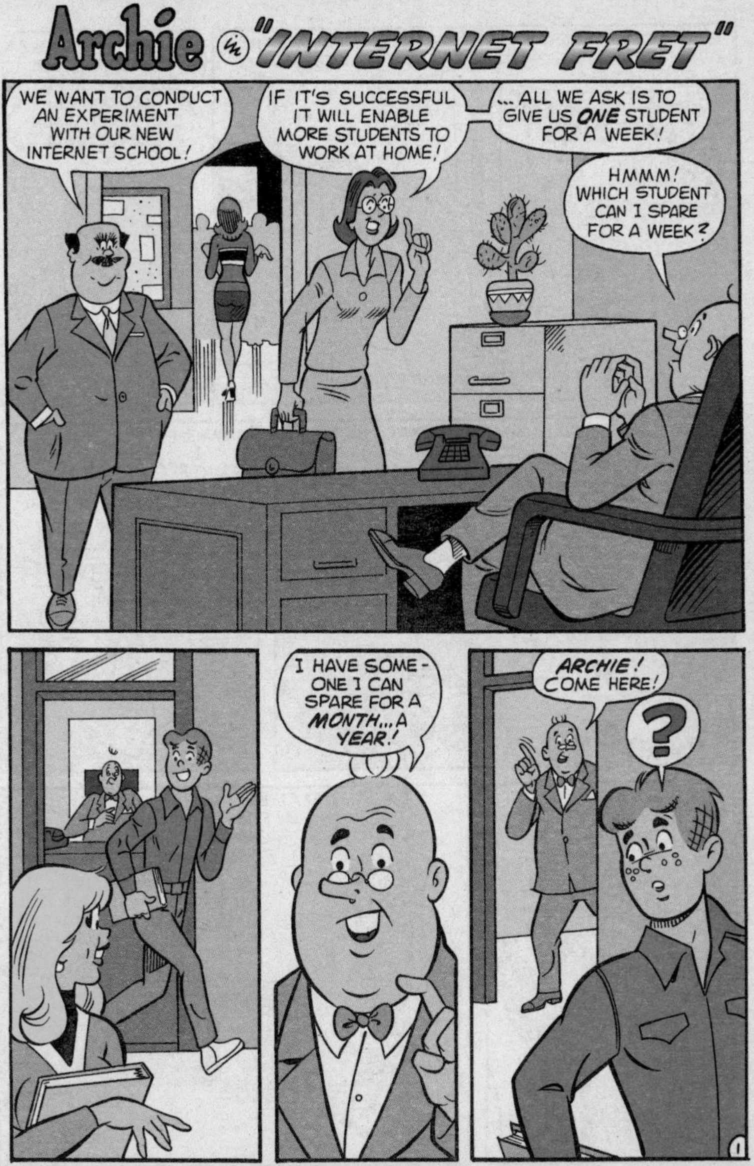
Archie in "INTERNET FRET"
WE WANT TO CONDUCT AN EXPERIMENT WITH OUR NEW INTERNET SCHOOL!
IF IT'S SUCCESSFUL IT WILL ENABLE MORE STUDENTS TO WORK AT HOME!
... ALL WE ASK IS TO GIVE US ONE STUDENT FOR A WEEK!
HMMM! WHICH STUDENT CAN I SPARE FOR A WEEK?
I HAVE SOME-ONE I CAN SPARE FOR A MONTH... A YEAR!
ARCHIE! COME HERE!
?
1

Script: George Gladir / Pencils: Bob Bolling / Inks: Bob Smith / Letters: Bill Yoshida / Colors: Barry Grossman

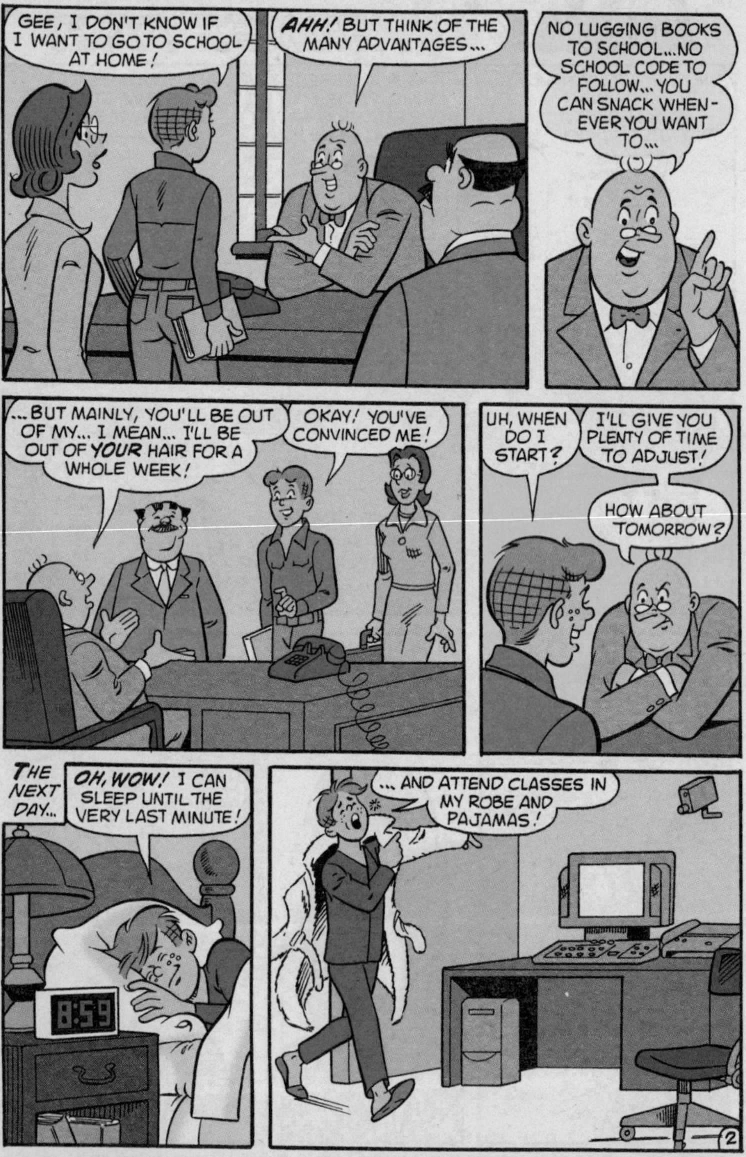
GEE, I DON'T KNOW IF I WANT TO GO TO SCHOOL AT HOME!
AHH! BUT THINK OF THE MANY ADVANTAGES...
NO LUGGING BOOKS TO SCHOOL...NO SCHOOL CODE TO FOLLOW... YOU CAN SNACK WHEN-EVER YOU WANT TO...
...BUT MAINLY, YOU'LL BE OUT OF MY... I MEAN... I'LL BE OUT OF YOUR HAIR FOR A WHOLE WEEK!
OKAY! YOU'VE CONVINCED ME!
UH, WHEN DO I START?
I'LL GIVE YOU PLENTY OF TIME TO ADJUST!
HOW ABOUT TOMORROW?
THE NEXT DAY...
OH, WOW! I CAN SLEEP UNTIL THE VERY LAST MINUTE!
8:59
... AND ATTEND CLASSES IN MY ROBE AND PAJAMAS!
2

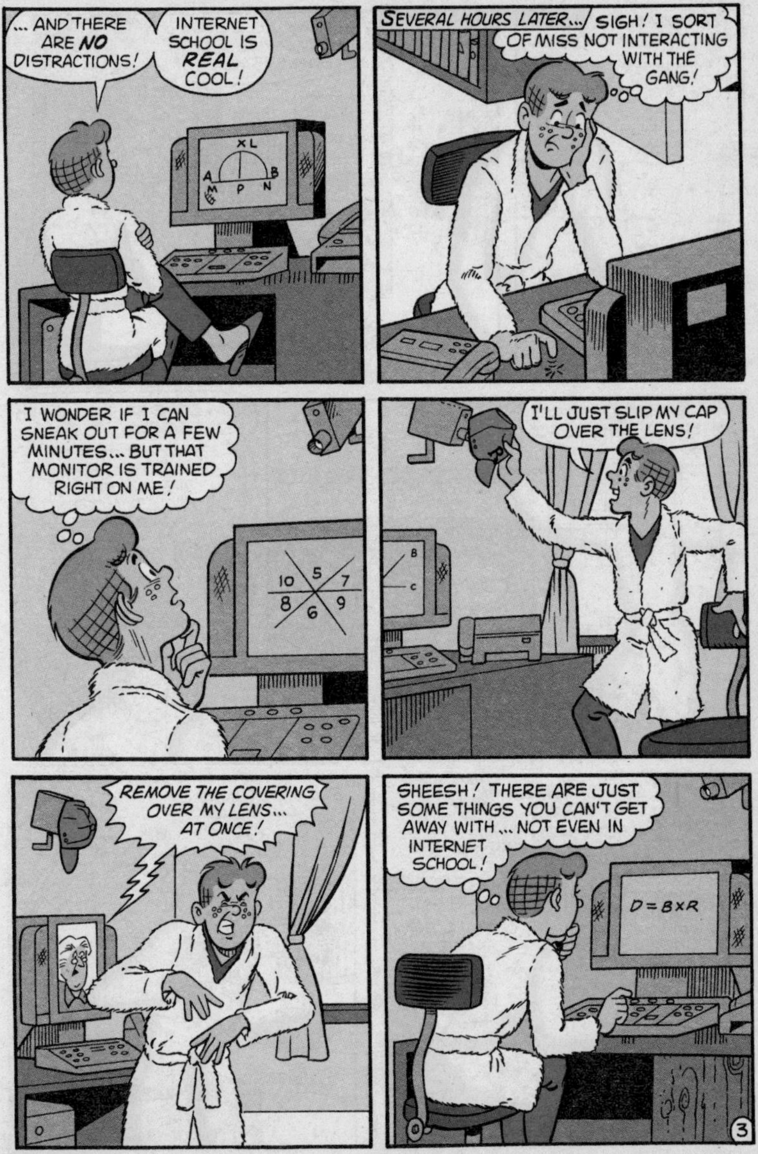

... AND THERE ARE NO DISTRACTIONS!
INTERNET SCHOOL IS REAL COOL!
XL
A
B
M
P
N
SEVERAL HOURS LATER...
SIGH! I SORT OF MISS NOT INTERACTING WITH THE GANG!
I WONDER IF I CAN SNEAK OUT FOR A FEW MINUTES... BUT THAT MONITOR IS TRAINED RIGHT ON ME!
10
5
7
8
6
9
I'LL JUST SLIP MY CAP OVER THE LENS!
B
C
REMOVE THE COVERING OVER MY LENS... AT ONCE!
SHEESH! THERE ARE JUST SOME THINGS YOU CAN'T GET AWAY WITH... NOT EVEN IN INTERNET SCHOOL!
D = B×R
3

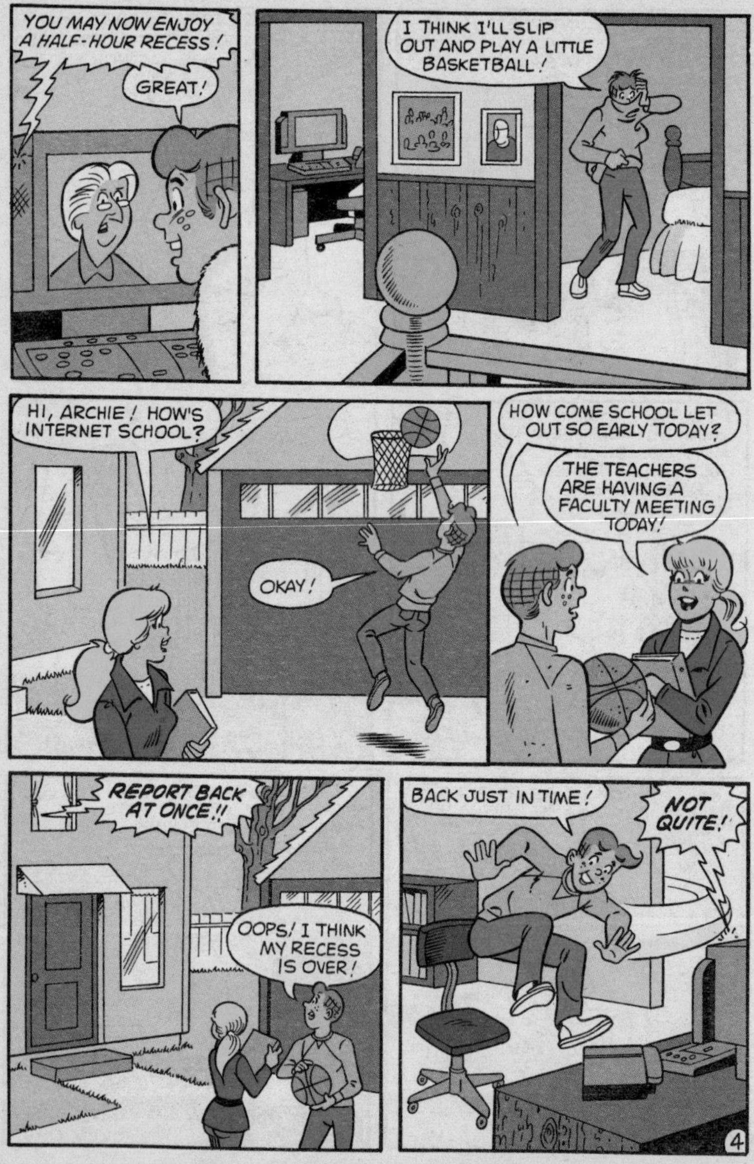
YOU MAY NOW ENJOY A HALF-HOUR RECESS!
GREAT!
I THINK I'LL SLIP OUT AND PLAY A LITTLE BASKETBALL!
HI, ARCHIE! HOW'S INTERNET SCHOOL?
OKAY!
HOW COME SCHOOL LET OUT SO EARLY TODAY?
THE TEACHERS ARE HAVING A FACULTY MEETING TODAY!
REPORT BACK AT ONCE!!
OOPS! I THINK MY RECESS IS OVER!
BACK JUST IN TIME!
NOT QUITE!
4

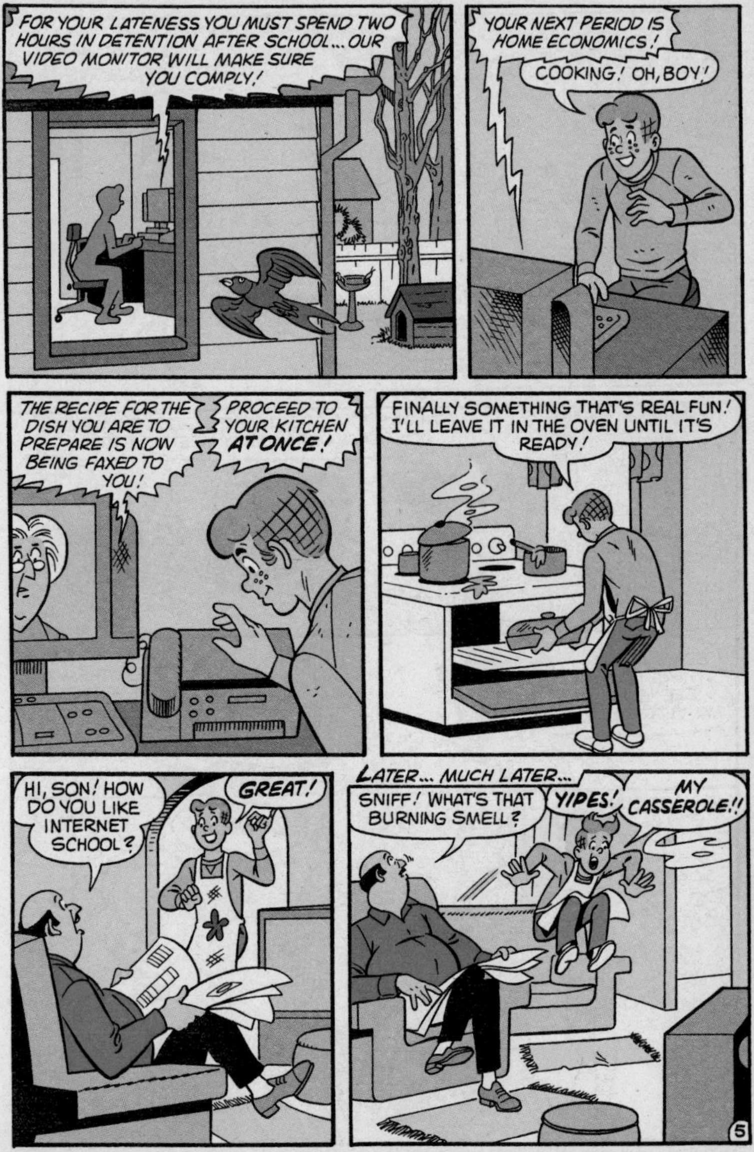
FOR YOUR LATENESS YOU MUST SPEND TWO HOURS IN DETENTION AFTER SCHOOL... OUR VIDEO MONITOR WILL MAKE SURE YOU COMPLY!
YOUR NEXT PERIOD IS HOME ECONOMICS!
COOKING! OH, BOY!
THE RECIPE FOR THE DISH YOU ARE TO PREPARE IS NOW BEING FAXED TO YOU!
PROCEED TO YOUR KITCHEN AT ONCE!
FINALLY SOMETHING THAT'S REAL FUN! I'LL LEAVE IT IN THE OVEN UNTIL IT'S READY!
HI, SON! HOW DO YOU LIKE INTERNET SCHOOL?
GREAT!
LATER... MUCH LATER...
SNIFF! WHAT'S THAT BURNING SMELL?
YIPES!
MY CASSEROLE!!
5

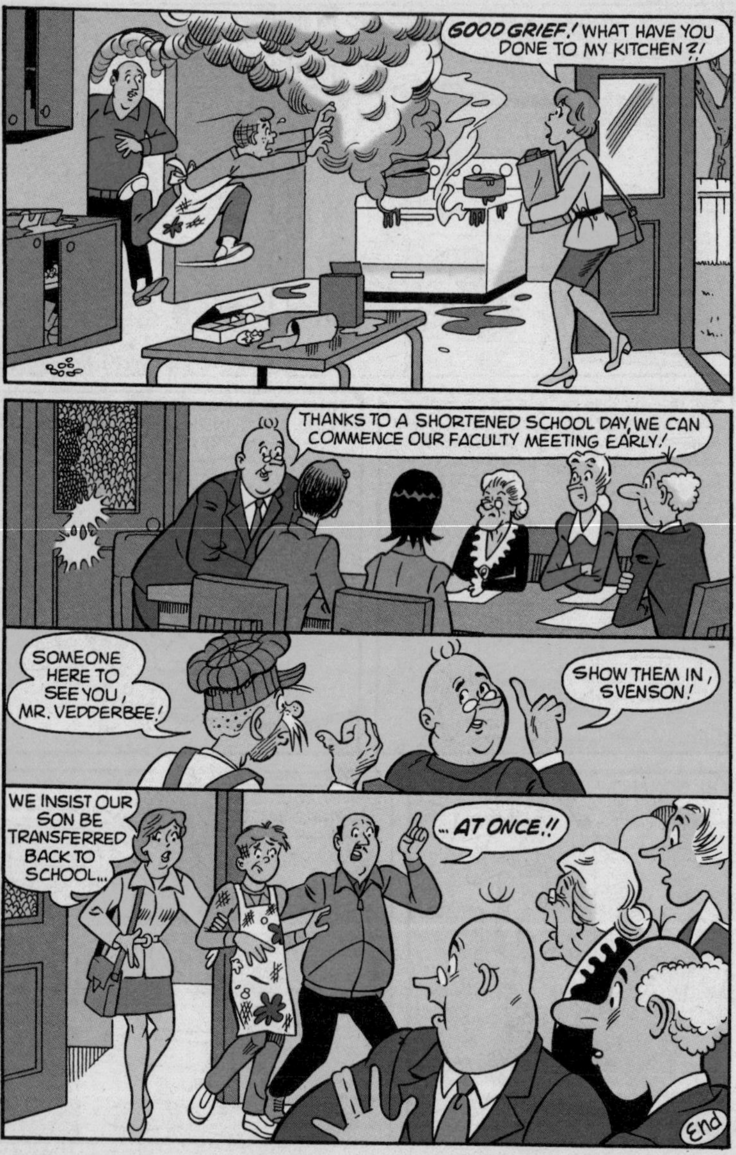
GOOD GRIEF! WHAT HAVE YOU DONE TO MY KITCHEN?!
THANKS TO A SHORTENED SCHOOL DAY, WE CAN COMMENCE OUR FACULTY MEETING EARLY!
SOMEONE HERE TO SEE YOU, MR. VEDDERBEE!
SHOW THEM IN, SVENSON!
WE INSIST OUR SON BE TRANSFERRED BACK TO SCHOOL...
...AT ONCE!!
End

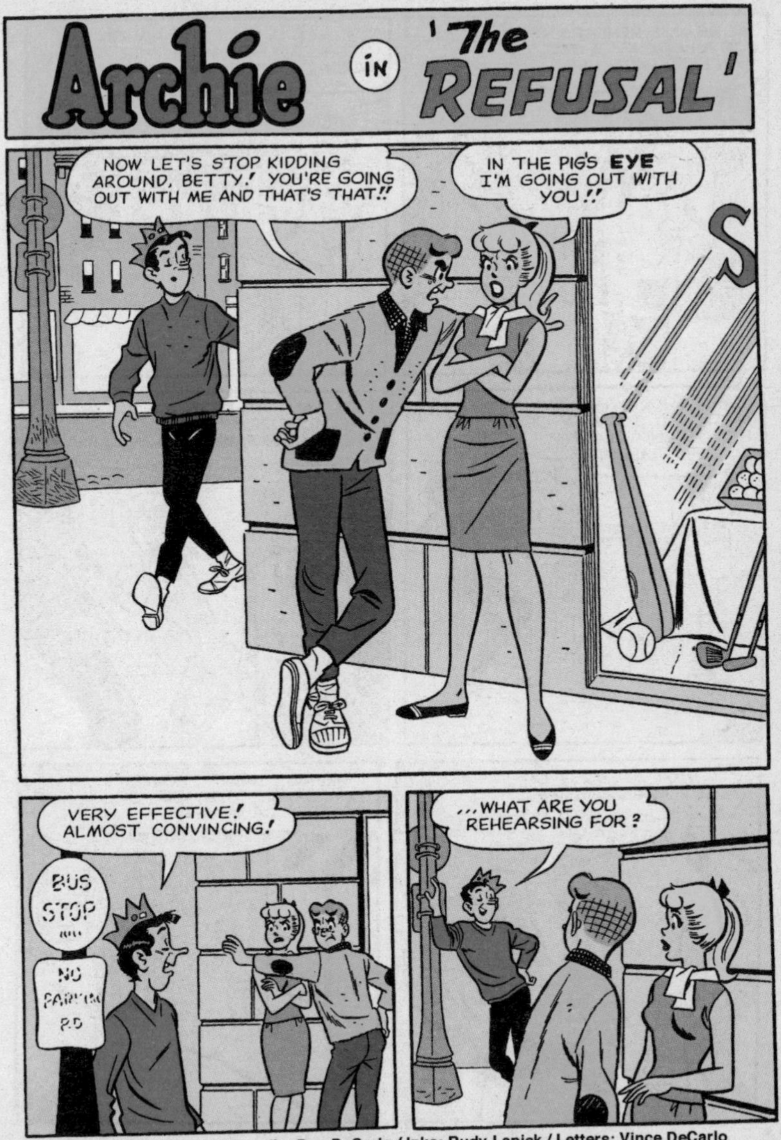
Archie in 'The REFUSAL'
NOW LET'S STOP KIDDING AROUND, BETTY! YOU'RE GOING OUT WITH ME AND THAT'S THAT!!
IN THE PIG'S EYE I'M GOING OUT WITH YOU!!
VERY EFFECTIVE! ALMOST CONVINCING!
BUS STOP
...WHAT ARE YOU REHEARSING FOR?

Script: Frank Doyle / Pencils: Dan DeCarlo / Inks: Rudy Lapick / Letters: Vince DeCarlo

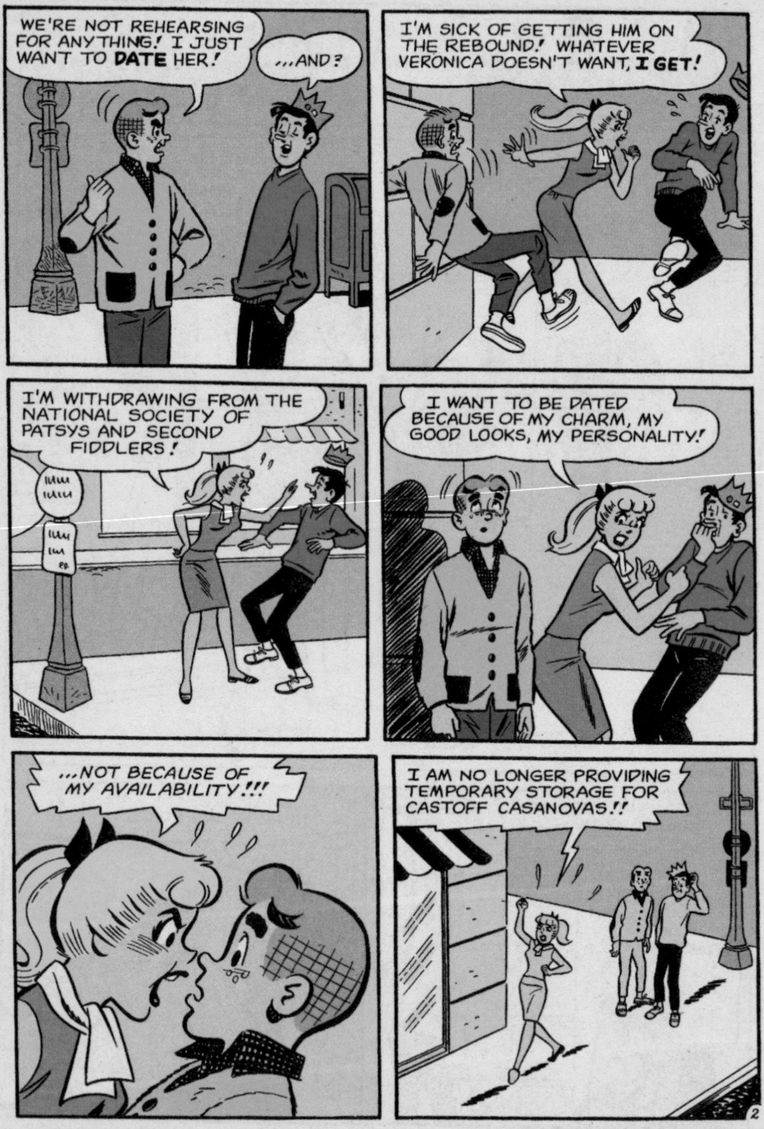

WE'RE NOT REHEARSING FOR ANYTHING! I JUST WANT TO **DATE** HER!
...AND?
I'M SICK OF GETTING HIM ON THE REBOUND! WHATEVER VERONICA DOESN'T WANT, **I GET**!
I'M WITHDRAWING FROM THE NATIONAL SOCIETY OF PATSYS AND SECOND FIDDLERS!
I WANT TO BE DATED BECAUSE OF MY CHARM, MY GOOD LOOKS, MY PERSONALITY!
...NOT BECAUSE OF MY AVAILABILITY!!!
I AM NO LONGER PROVIDING TEMPORARY STORAGE FOR CASTOFF CASANOVAS!!

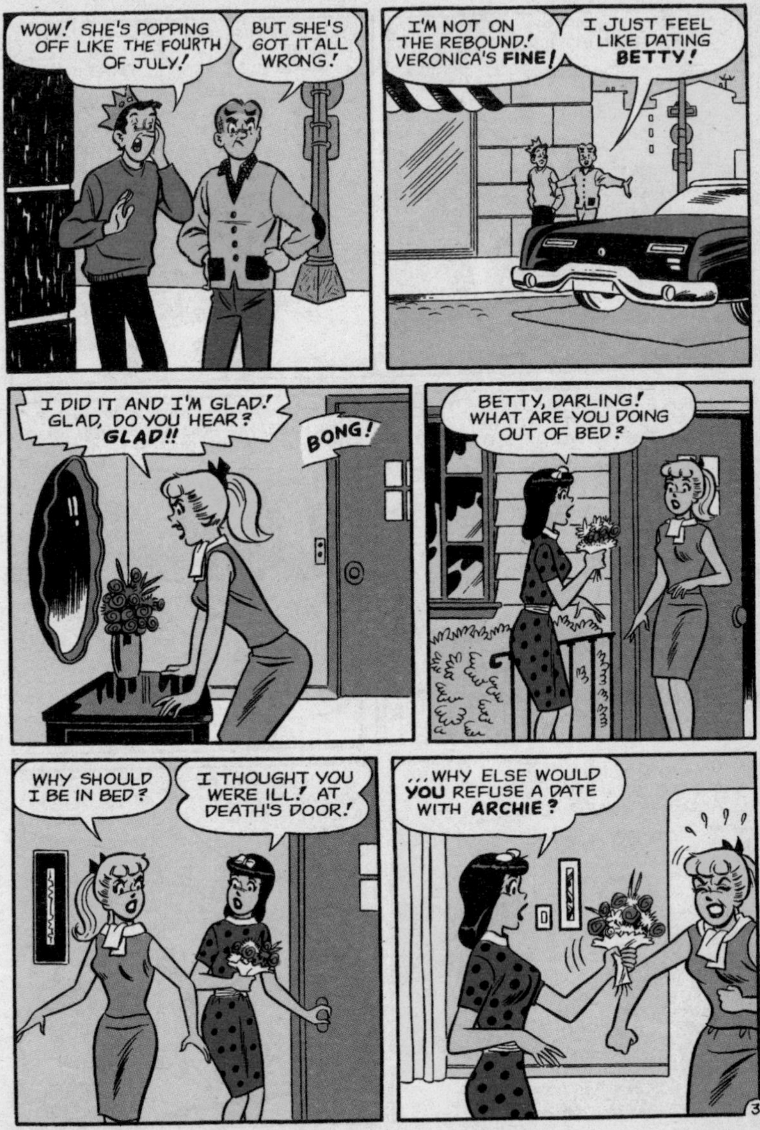

WOW! SHE'S POPPING OFF LIKE THE FOURTH OF JULY!
BUT SHE'S GOT IT ALL WRONG!
I'M NOT ON THE REBOUND! VERONICA'S FINE!
I JUST FEEL LIKE DATING BETTY!
I DID IT AND I'M GLAD! GLAD, DO YOU HEAR? GLAD!!
BONG!
BETTY, DARLING! WHAT ARE YOU DOING OUT OF BED?
WHY SHOULD I BE IN BED?
I THOUGHT YOU WERE ILL! AT DEATH'S DOOR!
...WHY ELSE WOULD YOU REFUSE A DATE WITH ARCHIE?

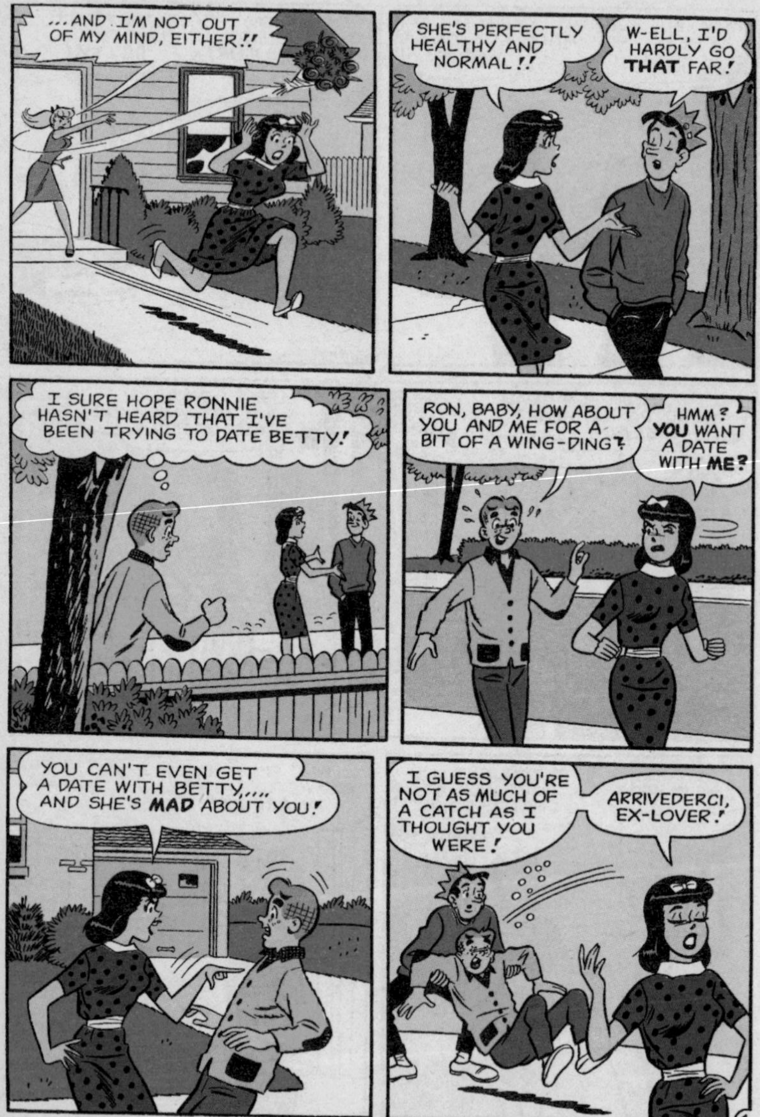
...AND I'M NOT OUT OF MY MIND, EITHER!!
SHE'S PERFECTLY HEALTHY AND NORMAL!!
W-ELL, I'D HARDLY GO **THAT** FAR!
I SURE HOPE RONNIE HASN'T HEARD THAT I'VE BEEN TRYING TO DATE BETTY!
RON, BABY, HOW ABOUT YOU AND ME FOR A BIT OF A WING-DING?
HMM? **YOU** WANT A DATE WITH **ME?**
YOU CAN'T EVEN GET A DATE WITH BETTY,.... AND SHE'S **MAD** ABOUT YOU!
I GUESS YOU'RE NOT AS MUCH OF A CATCH AS I THOUGHT YOU WERE!
ARRIVEDERCI, EX-LOVER!
4

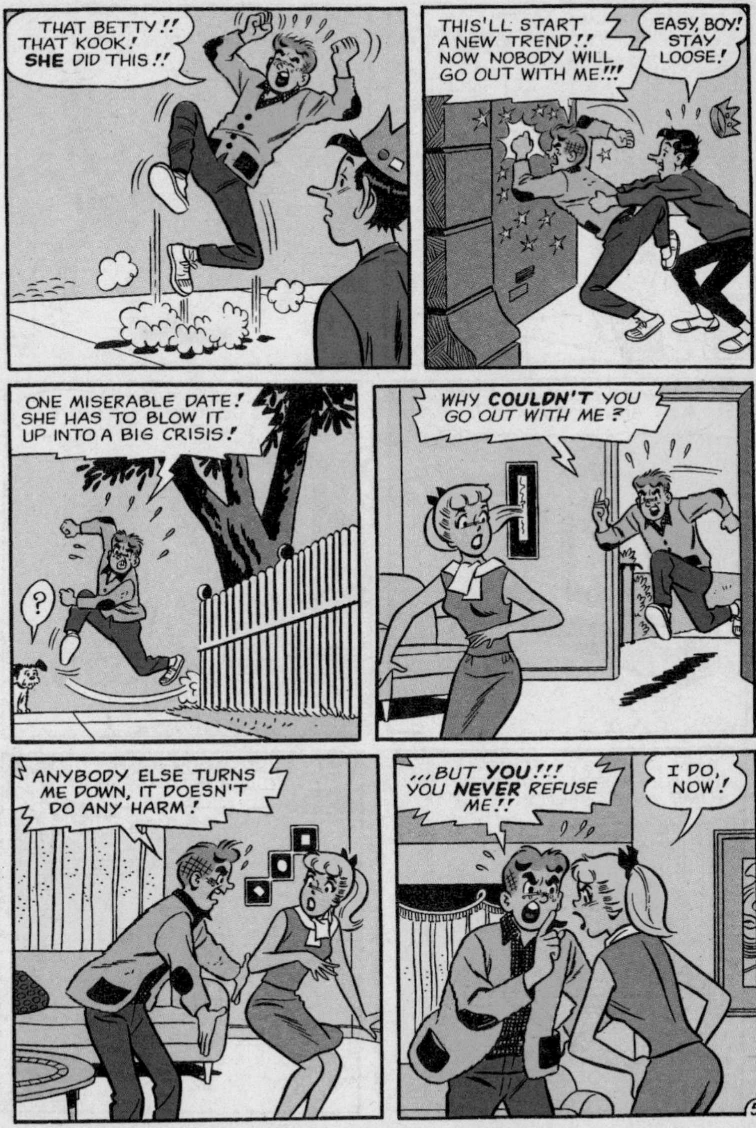
THAT BETTY!! THAT KOOK! SHE DID THIS!!
THIS'LL START A NEW TREND!! NOW NOBODY WILL GO OUT WITH ME!!!
EASY, BOY! STAY LOOSE!
ONE MISERABLE DATE! SHE HAS TO BLOW IT UP INTO A BIG CRISIS!
?
WHY COULDN'T YOU GO OUT WITH ME?
ANYBODY ELSE TURNS ME DOWN, IT DOESN'T DO ANY HARM!
...BUT YOU!!! YOU NEVER REFUSE ME!!
I DO, NOW!

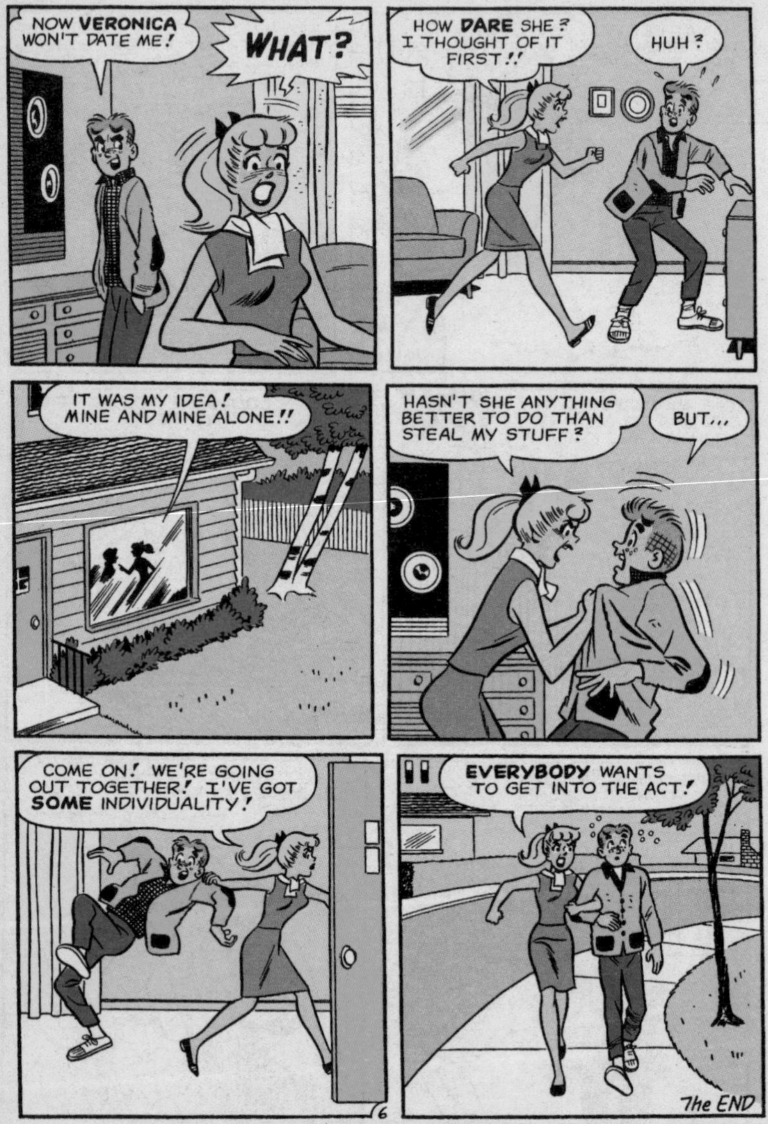
NOW **VERONICA** WON'T DATE ME!
WHAT?
HOW **DARE** SHE? I THOUGHT OF IT FIRST!!
HUH?
IT WAS MY IDEA! MINE AND MINE ALONE!!
HASN'T SHE ANYTHING BETTER TO DO THAN STEAL MY STUFF?
BUT...
COME ON! WE'RE GOING OUT TOGETHER! I'VE GOT **SOME** INDIVIDUALITY!
EVERYBODY WANTS TO GET INTO THE ACT!
The END

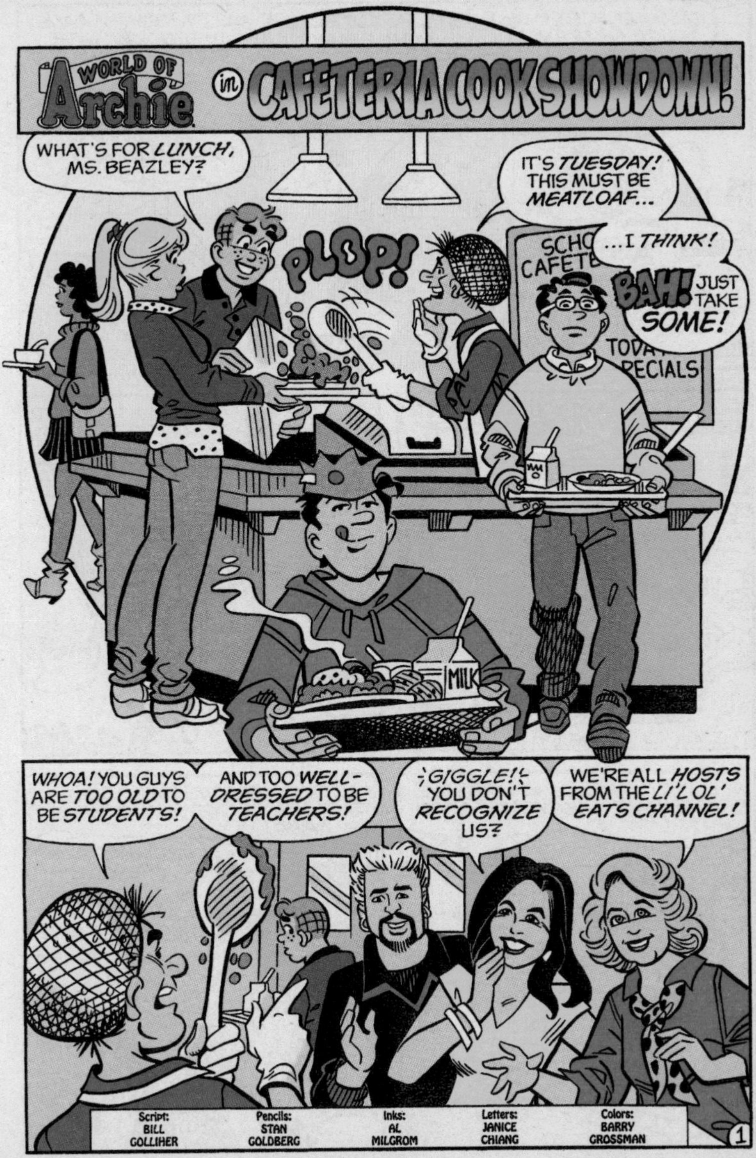
WORLD OF Archie in CAFETERIA COOK SHOWDOWN!
WHAT'S FOR LUNCH, MS. BEAZLEY?
IT'S TUESDAY! THIS MUST BE MEATLOAF...
...I THINK!
PLOP!
BAH! JUST TAKE SOME!
TODAY SPECIALS
MILK
WHOA! YOU GUYS ARE TOO OLD TO BE STUDENTS!
AND TOO WELL-DRESSED TO BE TEACHERS!
GIGGLE! YOU DON'T RECOGNIZE US?
WE'RE ALL HOSTS FROM THE LI'L OL' EATS CHANNEL!
Script: BILL GOLLIHER
Pencils: STAN GOLDBERG
Inks: AL MILGROM
Letters: JANICE CHIANG
Colors: BARRY GROSSMAN
1

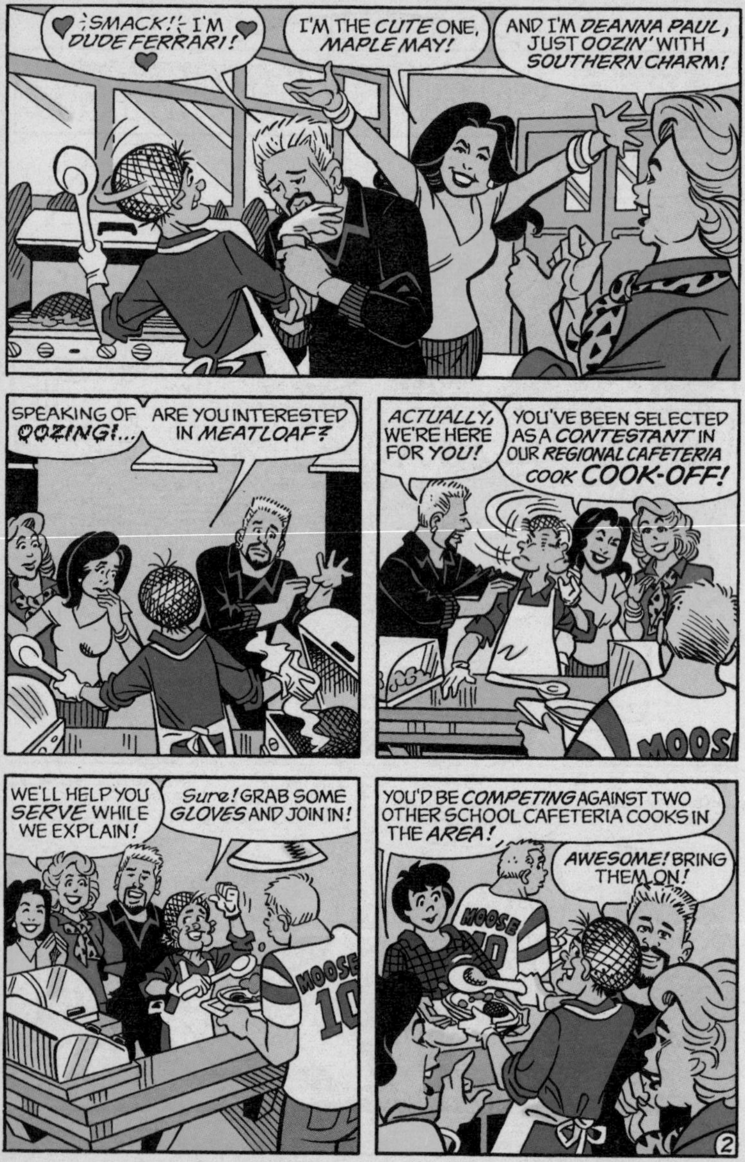

SMACK! I'M DUDE FERRARI!
I'M THE CUTE ONE, MAPLE MAY!
AND I'M DEANNA PAUL, JUST OOZIN' WITH SOUTHERN CHARM!
SPEAKING OF OOZING!...
ARE YOU INTERESTED IN MEATLOAF?
ACTUALLY, WE'RE HERE FOR YOU!
YOU'VE BEEN SELECTED AS A CONTESTANT IN OUR REGIONAL CAFETERIA COOK COOK-OFF!
MOOS
WE'LL HELP YOU SERVE WHILE WE EXPLAIN!
Sure! GRAB SOME GLOVES AND JOIN IN!
MOOSE 10
YOU'D BE COMPETING AGAINST TWO OTHER SCHOOL CAFETERIA COOKS IN THE AREA!
AWESOME! BRING THEM ON!
MOOSE

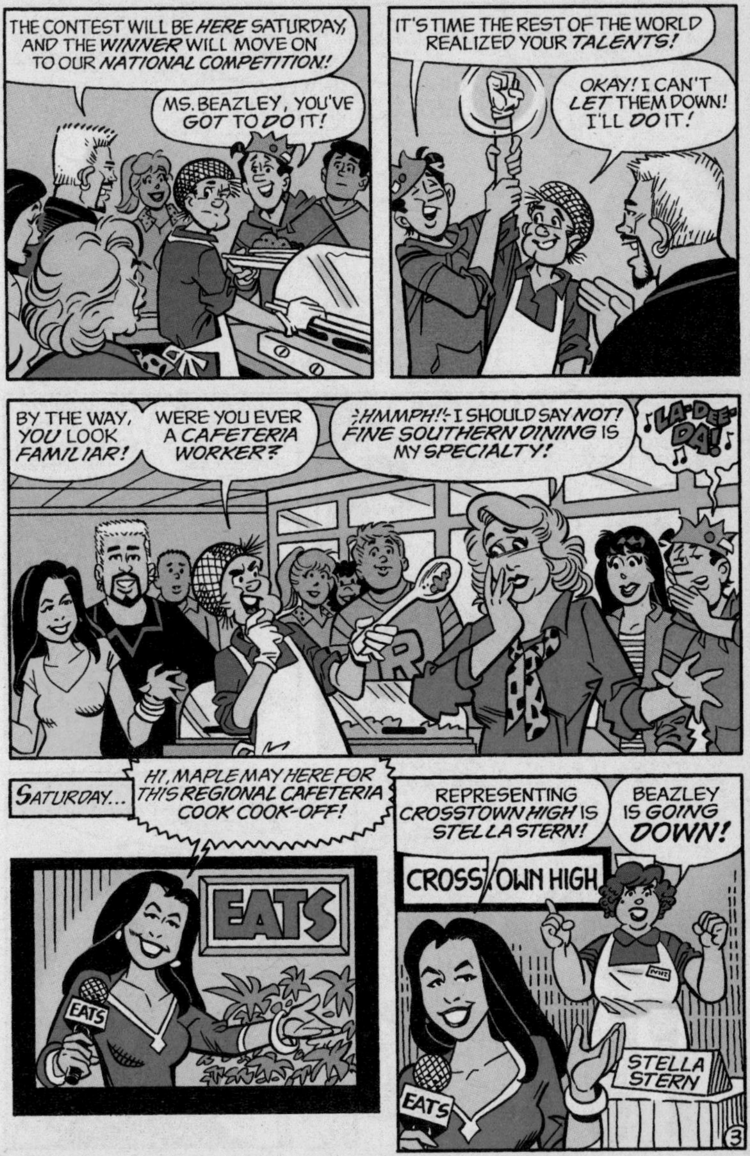

THE CONTEST WILL BE HERE SATURDAY, AND THE WINNER WILL MOVE ON TO OUR NATIONAL COMPETITION!
MS. BEAZLEY, YOU'VE GOT TO DO IT!
IT'S TIME THE REST OF THE WORLD REALIZED YOUR TALENTS!
OKAY! I CAN'T LET THEM DOWN! I'LL DO IT!
BY THE WAY, YOU LOOK FAMILIAR!
WERE YOU EVER A CAFETERIA WORKER?
HMMPH!! I SHOULD SAY NOT! FINE SOUTHERN DINING IS MY SPECIALTY!
LA-DEE-DA!
SATURDAY...
HI, MAPLE MAY HERE FOR THIS REGIONAL CAFETERIA COOK COOK-OFF!
EATS
EATS
REPRESENTING CROSSTOWN HIGH IS STELLA STERN!
BEAZLEY IS GOING DOWN!
CROSSTOWN HIGH
STELLA STERN
EATS

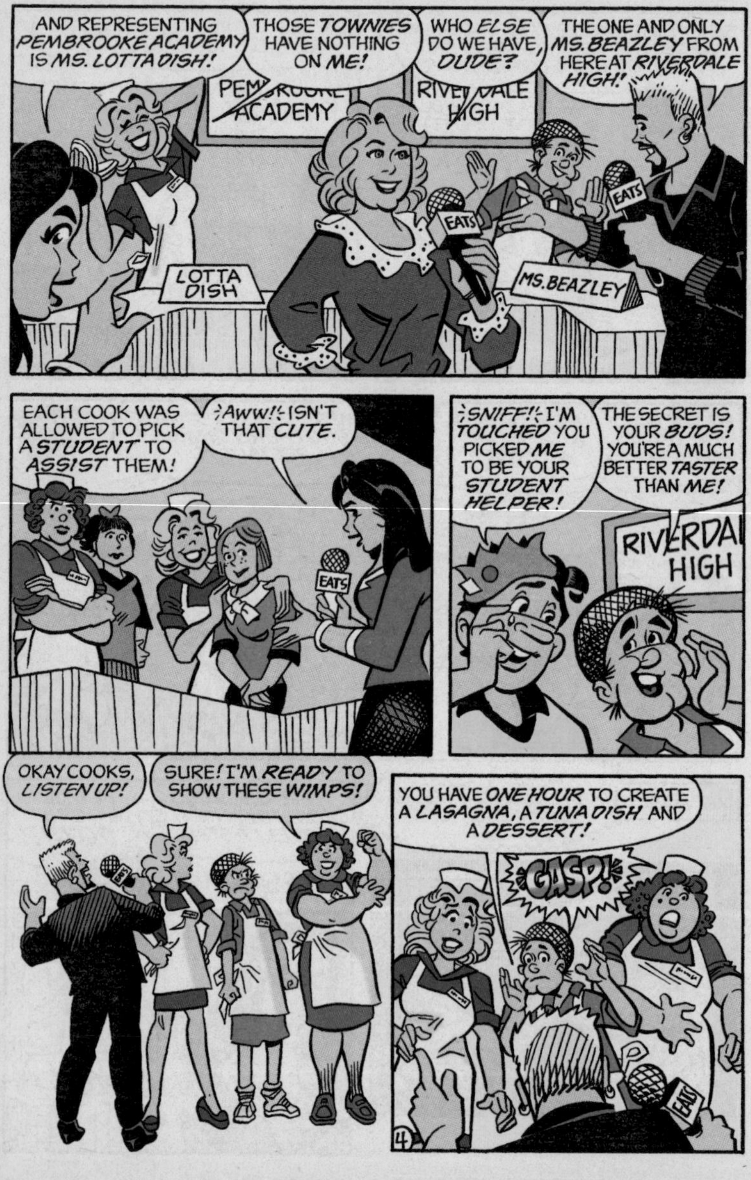

AND REPRESENTING PEMBROOKE ACADEMY IS MS. LOTTA DISH!
THOSE TOWNIES HAVE NOTHING ON ME!
WHO ELSE DO WE HAVE, DUDE?
THE ONE AND ONLY MS. BEAZLEY FROM HERE AT RIVERDALE HIGH!
PEMBROOKE ACADEMY
RIVERDALE HIGH
EATS
LOTTA DISH
MS. BEAZLEY
EACH COOK WAS ALLOWED TO PICK A STUDENT TO ASSIST THEM!
Aww! ISN'T THAT CUTE.
SNIFF! I'M TOUCHED YOU PICKED ME TO BE YOUR STUDENT HELPER!
THE SECRET IS YOUR BUDS! YOU'RE A MUCH BETTER TASTER THAN ME!
RIVERDA HIGH
OKAY COOKS, LISTEN UP!
SURE! I'M READY TO SHOW THESE WIMPS!
YOU HAVE ONE HOUR TO CREATE A LASAGNA, A TUNA DISH AND A DESSERT!
GASP!
4

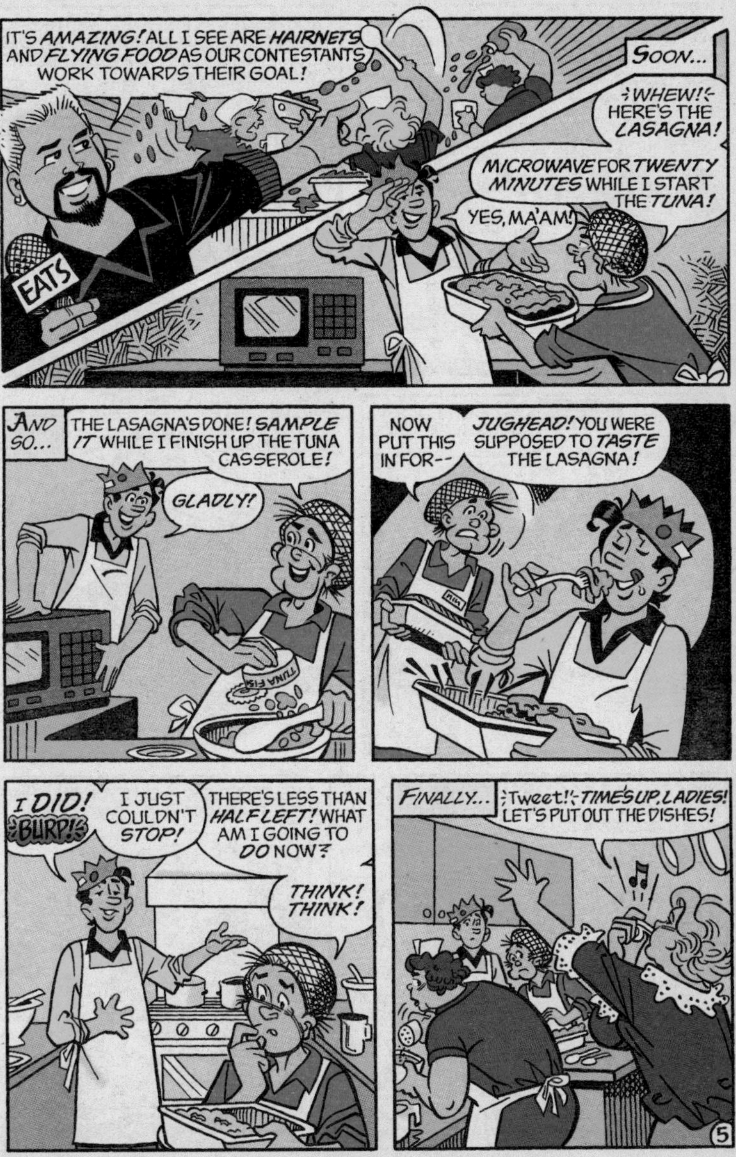
IT'S AMAZING! ALL I SEE ARE HAIRNETS AND FLYING FOOD AS OUR CONTESTANTS WORK TOWARDS THEIR GOAL!
EATS
SOON...
WHEW! HERE'S THE LASAGNA!
MICROWAVE FOR TWENTY MINUTES WHILE I START THE TUNA!
YES, MA'AM!
AND SO...
THE LASAGNA'S DONE! SAMPLE IT WHILE I FINISH UP THE TUNA CASSEROLE!
GLADLY!
TUNA FISH
NOW PUT THIS IN FOR--
JUGHEAD! YOU WERE SUPPOSED TO TASTE THE LASAGNA!
I DID! BURP!
I JUST COULDN'T STOP!
THERE'S LESS THAN HALF LEFT! WHAT AM I GOING TO DO NOW?
THINK! THINK!
FINALLY...
Tweet! TIME'S UP, LADIES! LET'S PUT OUT THE DISHES!
5

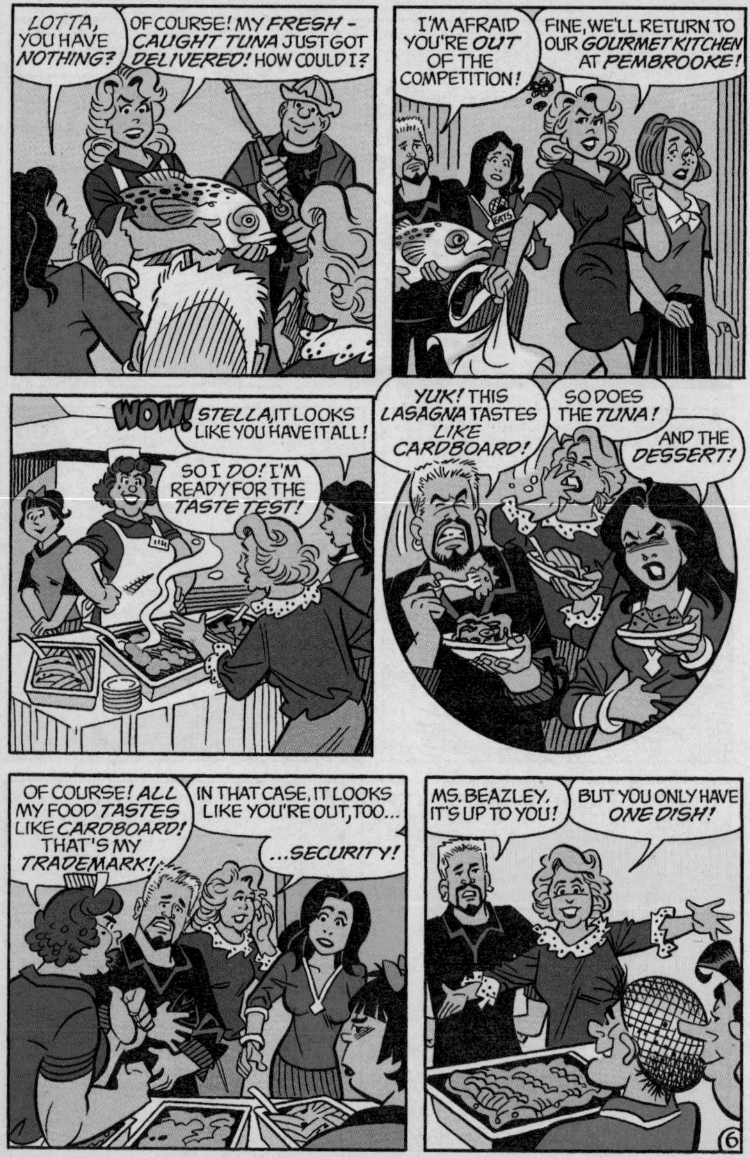

LOTTA, YOU HAVE NOTHING?
OF COURSE! MY FRESH-CAUGHT TUNA JUST GOT DELIVERED! HOW COULD I?
I'M AFRAID YOU'RE OUT OF THE COMPETITION!
FINE, WE'LL RETURN TO OUR GOURMET KITCHEN AT PEMBROOKE!
EATS
WOW! STELLA, IT LOOKS LIKE YOU HAVE IT ALL!
SO I DO! I'M READY FOR THE TASTE TEST!
YUK! THIS LASAGNA TASTES LIKE CARDBOARD!
SO DOES THE TUNA!
AND THE DESSERT!
OF COURSE! ALL MY FOOD TASTES LIKE CARDBOARD! THAT'S MY TRADEMARK!
IN THAT CASE, IT LOOKS LIKE YOU'RE OUT, TOO...
...SECURITY!
MS. BEAZLEY, IT'S UP TO YOU!
BUT YOU ONLY HAVE ONE DISH!
6

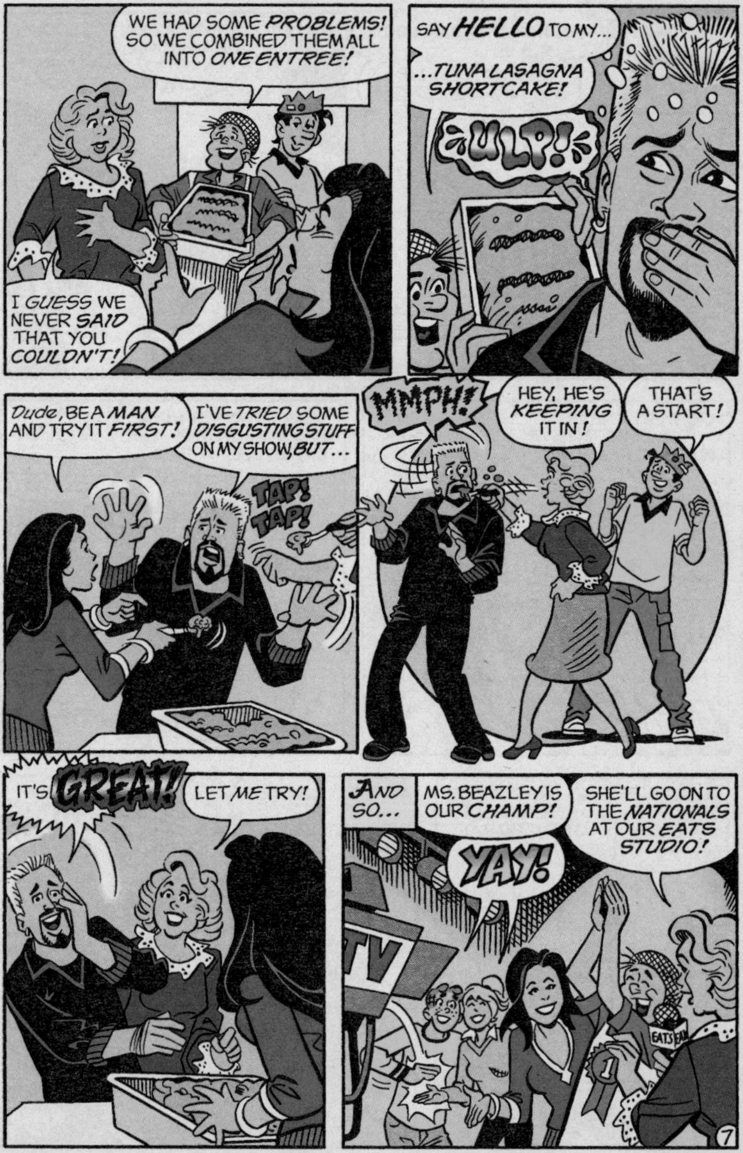
WE HAD SOME PROBLEMS! SO WE COMBINED THEM ALL INTO ONE ENTREE!
I GUESS WE NEVER SAID THAT YOU COULDN'T!
SAY HELLO TO MY...
...TUNA LASAGNA SHORTCAKE!
ULP!
Dude, BE A MAN AND TRY IT FIRST!
I'VE TRIED SOME DISGUSTING STUFF ON MY SHOW, BUT...
TAP! TAP!
MMPH!
HEY, HE'S KEEPING IT IN!
THAT'S A START!
IT'S GREAT!
LET ME TRY!
AND SO...
MS. BEAZLEY IS OUR CHAMP!
SHE'LL GO ON TO THE NATIONALS AT OUR EATS STUDIO!
YAY!
TV
EATS
1
7

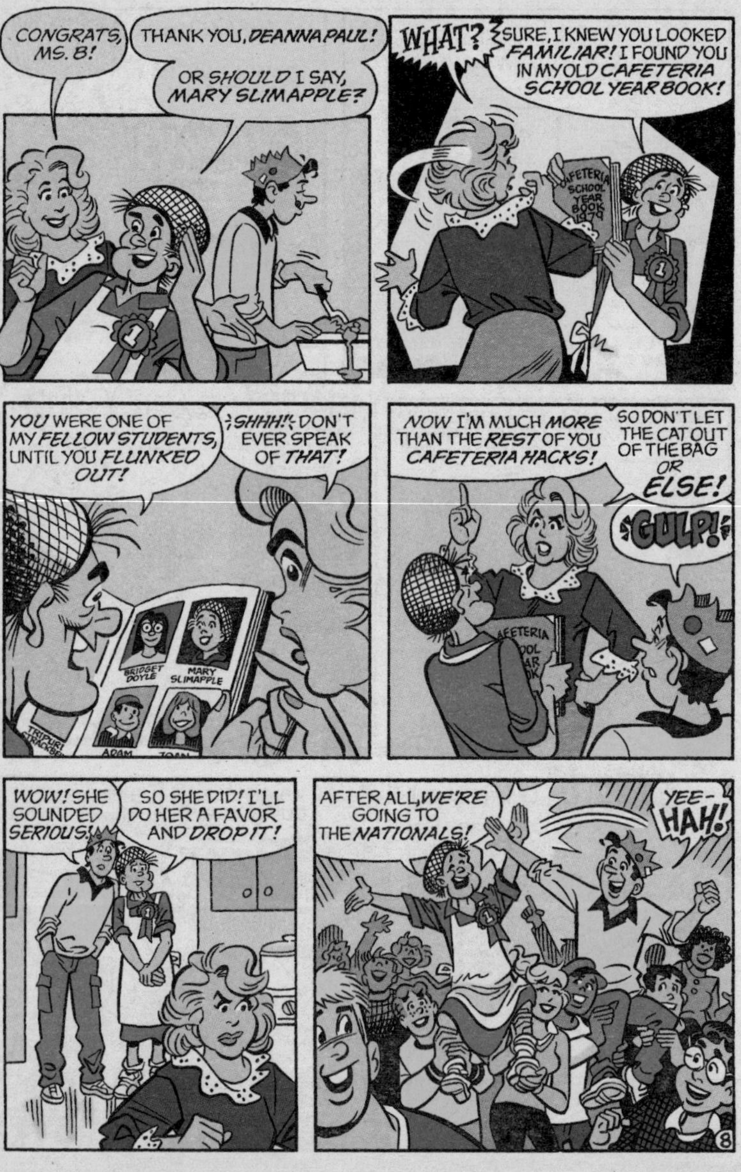

CONGRATS, MS. B!
THANK YOU, DEANNA PAUL!
OR SHOULD I SAY, MARY SLIMAPPLE?
WHAT?
SURE, I KNEW YOU LOOKED FAMILIAR! I FOUND YOU IN MY OLD CAFETERIA SCHOOL YEAR BOOK!
CAFETERIA SCHOOL YEAR BOOK 1979
YOU WERE ONE OF MY FELLOW STUDENTS, UNTIL YOU FLUNKED OUT!
SHHH! DON'T EVER SPEAK OF THAT!
BRIDGET DOYLE
MARY SLIMAPPLE
NOW I'M MUCH MORE THAN THE REST OF YOU CAFETERIA HACKS!
SO DON'T LET THE CAT OUT OF THE BAG OR ELSE!
GULP!
WOW! SHE SOUNDED SERIOUS!
SO SHE DID! I'LL DO HER A FAVOR AND DROP IT!
AFTER ALL, WE'RE GOING TO THE NATIONALS!
YEE-HAH!

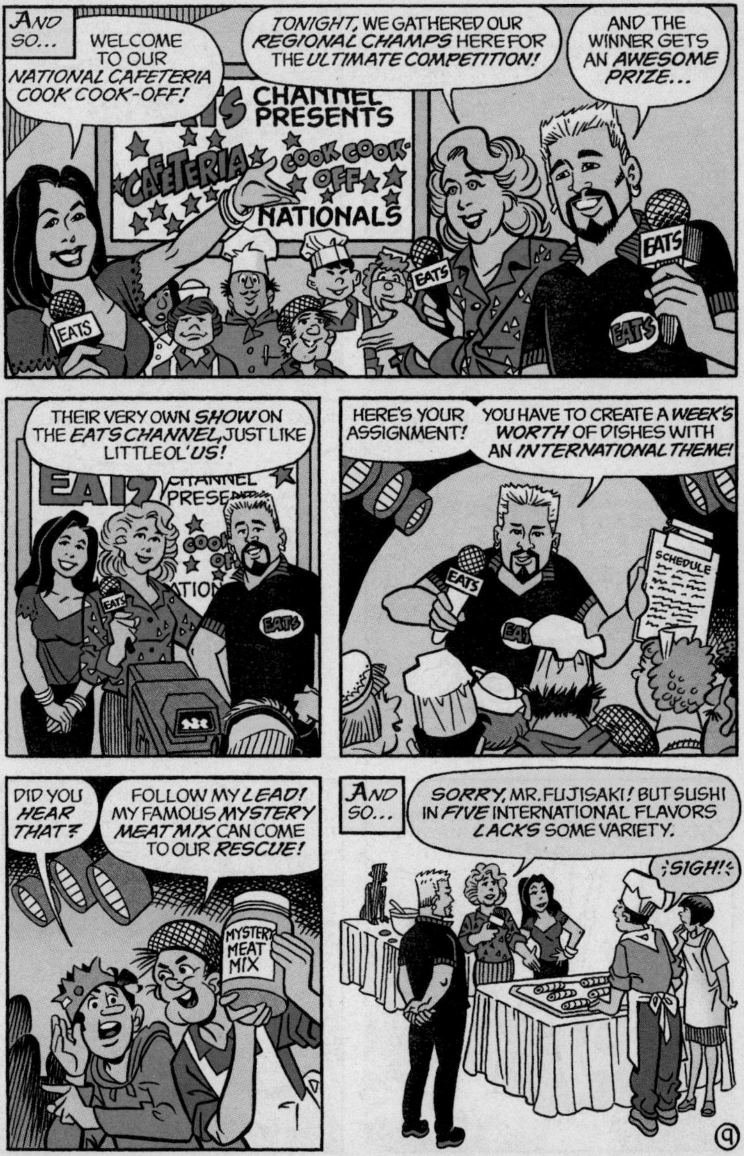

AND SO...
WELCOME TO OUR NATIONAL CAFETERIA COOK COOK-OFF!
TONIGHT, WE GATHERED OUR REGIONAL CHAMPS HERE FOR THE ULTIMATE COMPETITION!
AND THE WINNER GETS AN AWESOME PRIZE...
EATS CHANNEL PRESENTS CAFETERIA COOK COOK-OFF NATIONALS
EATS
THEIR VERY OWN SHOW ON THE EATS CHANNEL, JUST LIKE LITTLE OL' US!
HERE'S YOUR ASSIGNMENT!
YOU HAVE TO CREATE A WEEK'S WORTH OF DISHES WITH AN INTERNATIONAL THEME!
SCHEDULE
DID YOU HEAR THAT?
FOLLOW MY LEAD! MY FAMOUS MYSTERY MEAT MIX CAN COME TO OUR RESCUE!
MYSTERY MEAT MIX
AND SO...
SORRY, MR. FUJISAKI! BUT SUSHI IN FIVE INTERNATIONAL FLAVORS LACKS SOME VARIETY.
SIGH!

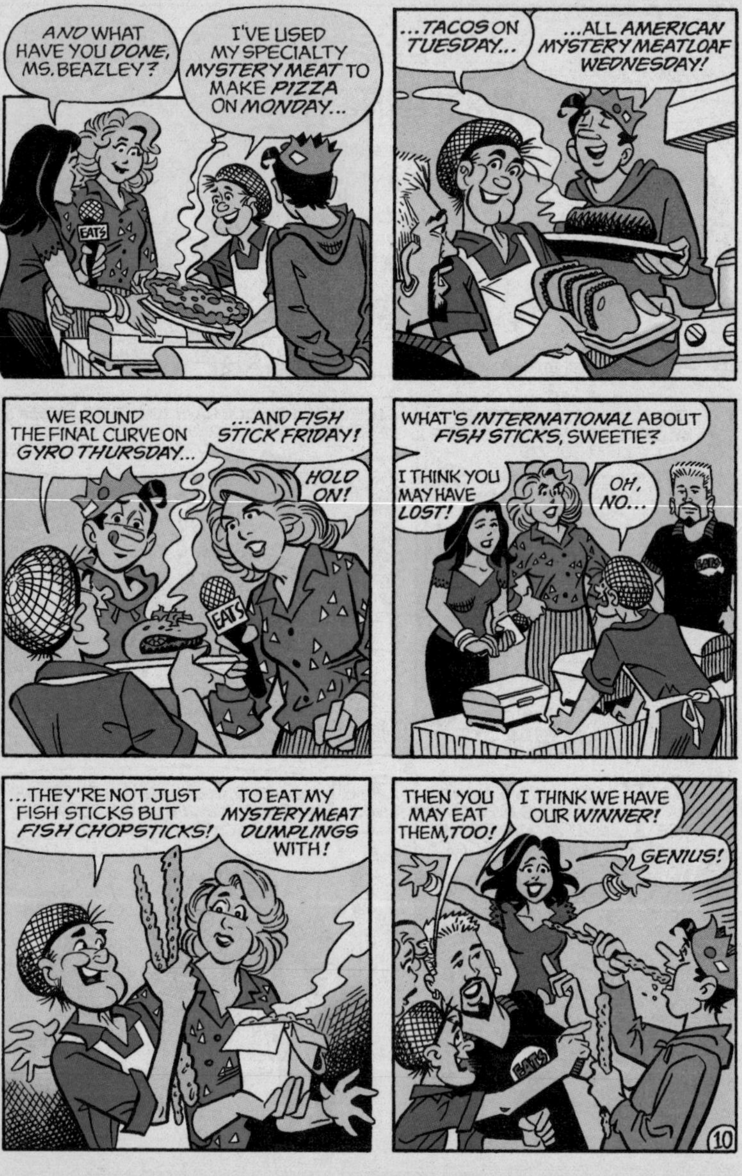
AND WHAT HAVE YOU DONE, MS. BEAZLEY?
I'VE USED MY SPECIALTY MYSTERY MEAT TO MAKE PIZZA ON MONDAY...
EATS
...TACOS ON TUESDAY...
...ALL AMERICAN MYSTERY MEATLOAF WEDNESDAY!
WE ROUND THE FINAL CURVE ON GYRO THURSDAY...
...AND FISH STICK FRIDAY!
HOLD ON!
EATS
WHAT'S INTERNATIONAL ABOUT FISH STICKS, SWEETIE?
I THINK YOU MAY HAVE LOST!
OH, NO...
...THEY'RE NOT JUST FISH STICKS BUT FISH CHOPSTICKS!
TO EAT MY MYSTERY MEAT DUMPLINGS WITH!
THEN YOU MAY EAT THEM, TOO!
I THINK WE HAVE OUR WINNER!
GENIUS!
EATS
10

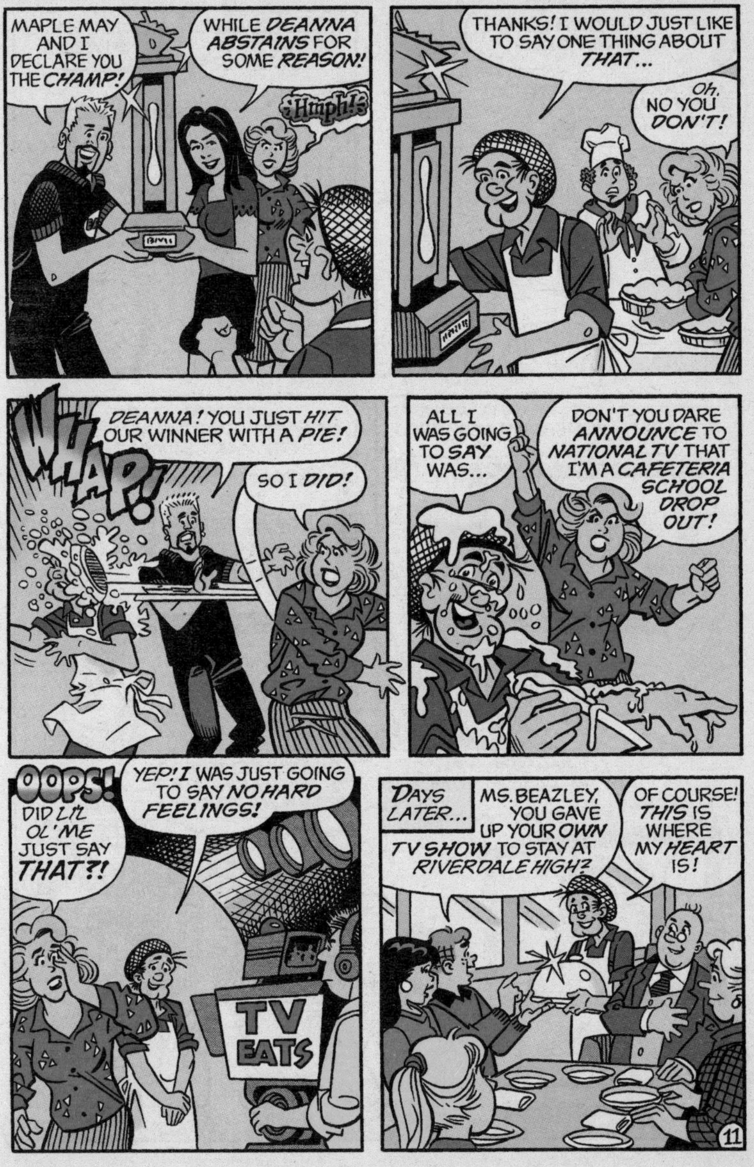
MAPLE MAY AND I DECLARE YOU THE CHAMP!
WHILE DEANNA ABSTAINS FOR SOME REASON!
Hmph!
THANKS! I WOULD JUST LIKE TO SAY ONE THING ABOUT THAT...
Oh, NO YOU DON'T!
WHAP!
DEANNA! YOU JUST HIT OUR WINNER WITH A PIE!
SO I DID!
ALL I WAS GOING TO SAY WAS...
DON'T YOU DARE ANNOUNCE TO NATIONAL TV THAT I'M A CAFETERIA SCHOOL DROP OUT!
OOPS!
DID LI'L OL' ME JUST SAY THAT?!
YEP! I WAS JUST GOING TO SAY NO HARD FEELINGS!
TV EATS
DAYS LATER...
MS. BEAZLEY, YOU GAVE UP YOUR OWN TV SHOW TO STAY AT RIVERDALE HIGH?
OF COURSE! THIS IS WHERE MY HEART IS!

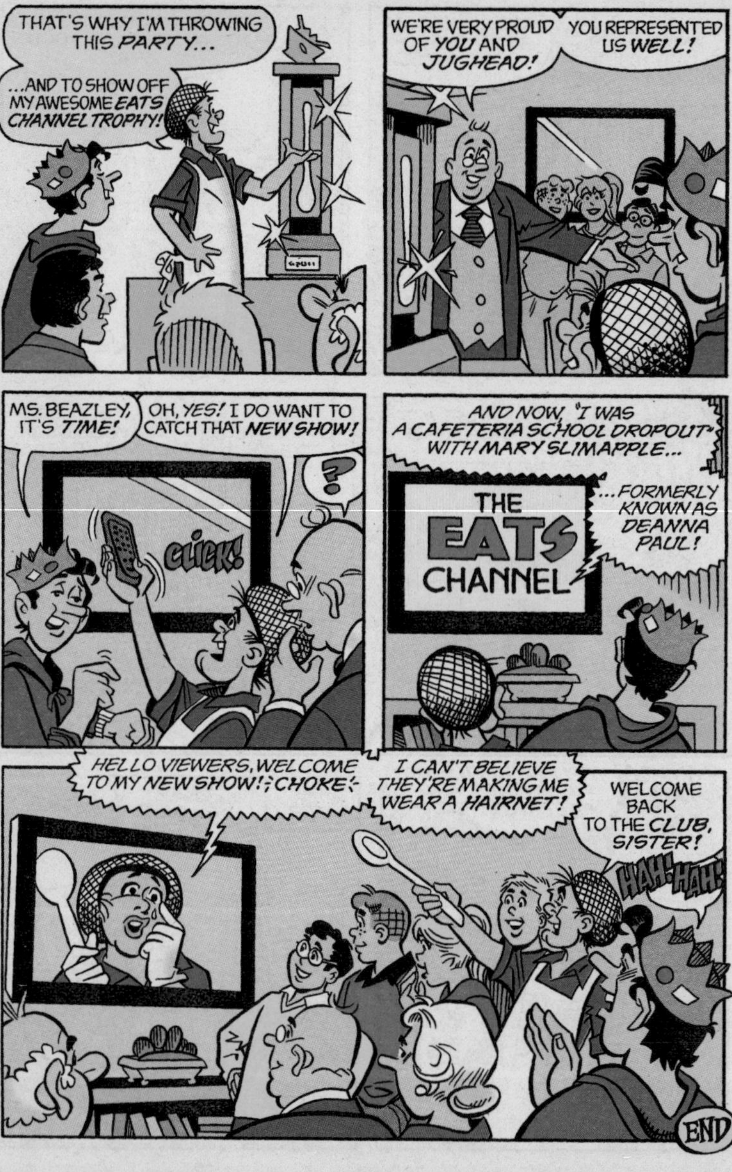
THAT'S WHY I'M THROWING THIS PARTY...
...AND TO SHOW OFF MY AWESOME EATS CHANNEL TROPHY!
WE'RE VERY PROUD OF YOU AND JUGHEAD!
YOU REPRESENTED US WELL!
MS. BEAZLEY, IT'S TIME!
OH, YES! I DO WANT TO CATCH THAT NEW SHOW!
?
CLICK!
AND NOW, "I WAS A CAFETERIA SCHOOL DROPOUT" WITH MARY SLIMAPPLE...
THE EATS CHANNEL
...FORMERLY KNOWN AS DEANNA PAUL!
HELLO VIEWERS, WELCOME TO MY NEW SHOW! -CHOKE-
I CAN'T BELIEVE THEY'RE MAKING ME WEAR A HAIRNET!
WELCOME BACK TO THE CLUB, SISTER!
HAH! HAH!
END

MR. WEATHERBEE HONOR ROLL!!
UNSCRAMBLE THE LETTERS TO FIND OUT WHO MISTER WEATHERBEE HAS TO CHOOSE FROM FOR THE HEAD OF THE CLASS !! ...ANSWERS BELOW !!
1 NOLTID
2 TYBTE
oh me!
3 DIGEM
ANSWERS:
1. DILTON 2. BETTY 3. MIDGE

Archie's GAG BAG

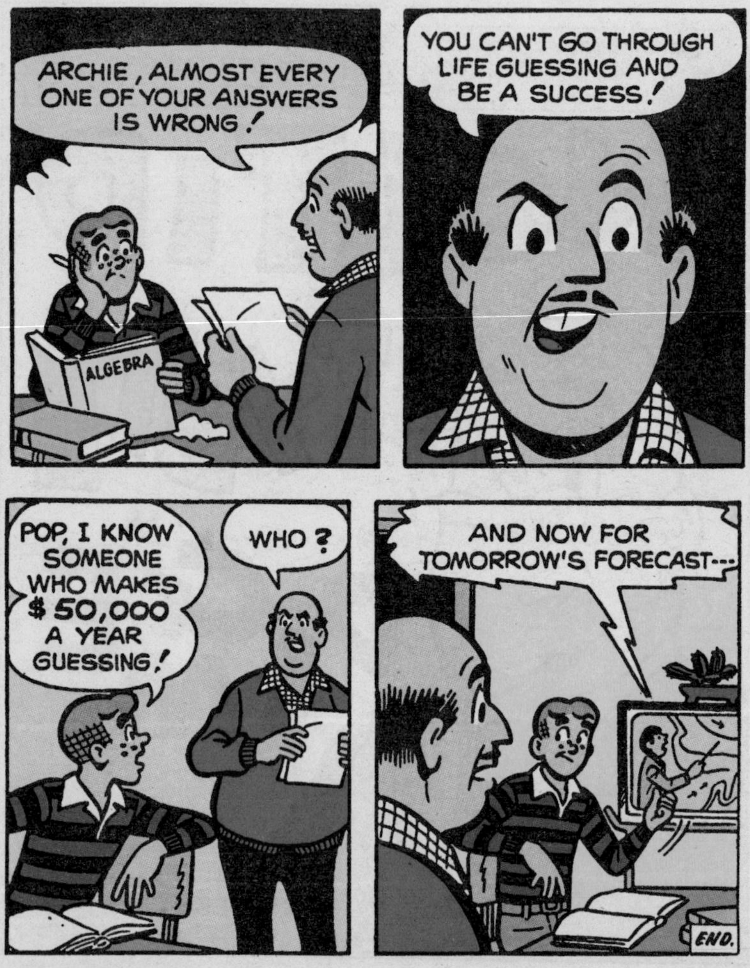
ARCHIE, ALMOST EVERY ONE OF YOUR ANSWERS IS WRONG!
ALGEBRA
YOU CAN'T GO THROUGH LIFE GUESSING AND BE A SUCCESS!
POP, I KNOW SOMEONE WHO MAKES $ 50,000 A YEAR GUESSING!
WHO?
AND NOW FOR TOMORROW'S FORECAST---
END.

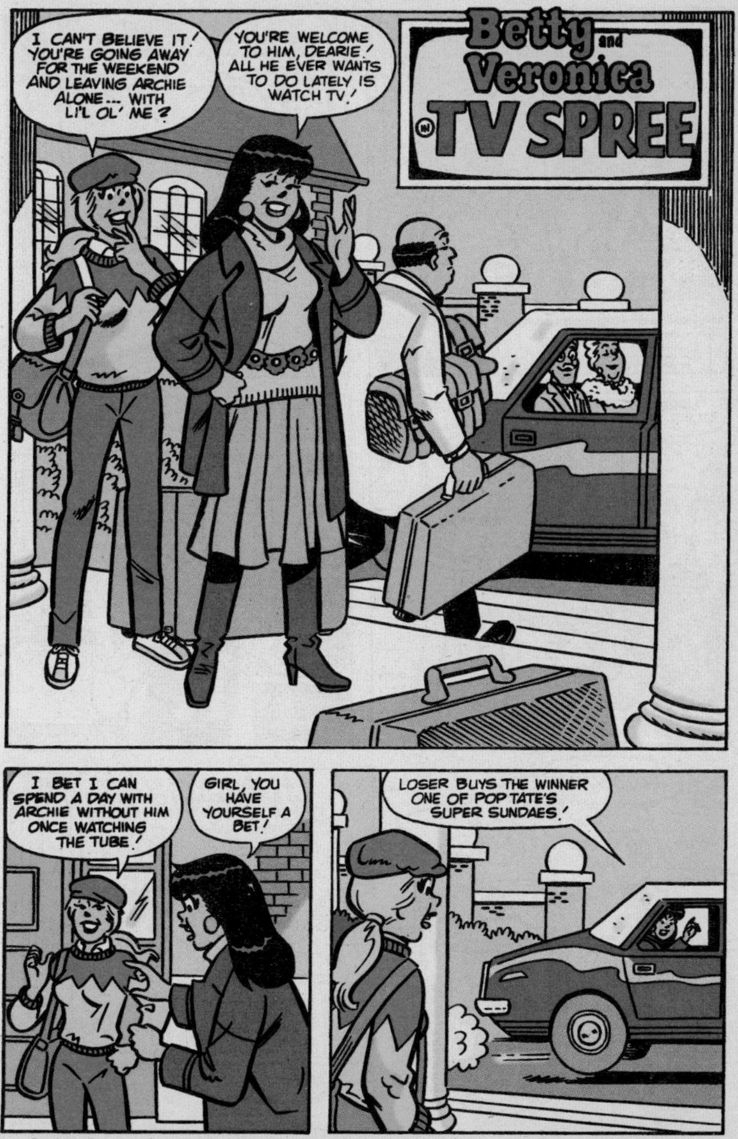
Betty and Veronica
in TV SPREE
I CAN'T BELIEVE IT! YOU'RE GOING AWAY FOR THE WEEKEND AND LEAVING ARCHIE ALONE... WITH LI'L OL' ME?
YOU'RE WELCOME TO HIM, DEARIE! ALL HE EVER WANTS TO DO LATELY IS WATCH TV!
I BET I CAN SPEND A DAY WITH ARCHIE WITHOUT HIM ONCE WATCHING THE TUBE!
GIRL, YOU HAVE YOURSELF A BET!
LOSER BUYS THE WINNER ONE OF POP TATE'S SUPER SUNDAES!

Script: George Gladir / Pencils: Stan Goldberg / Inks: Rudy Lapick / Letters: Bill Yoshida

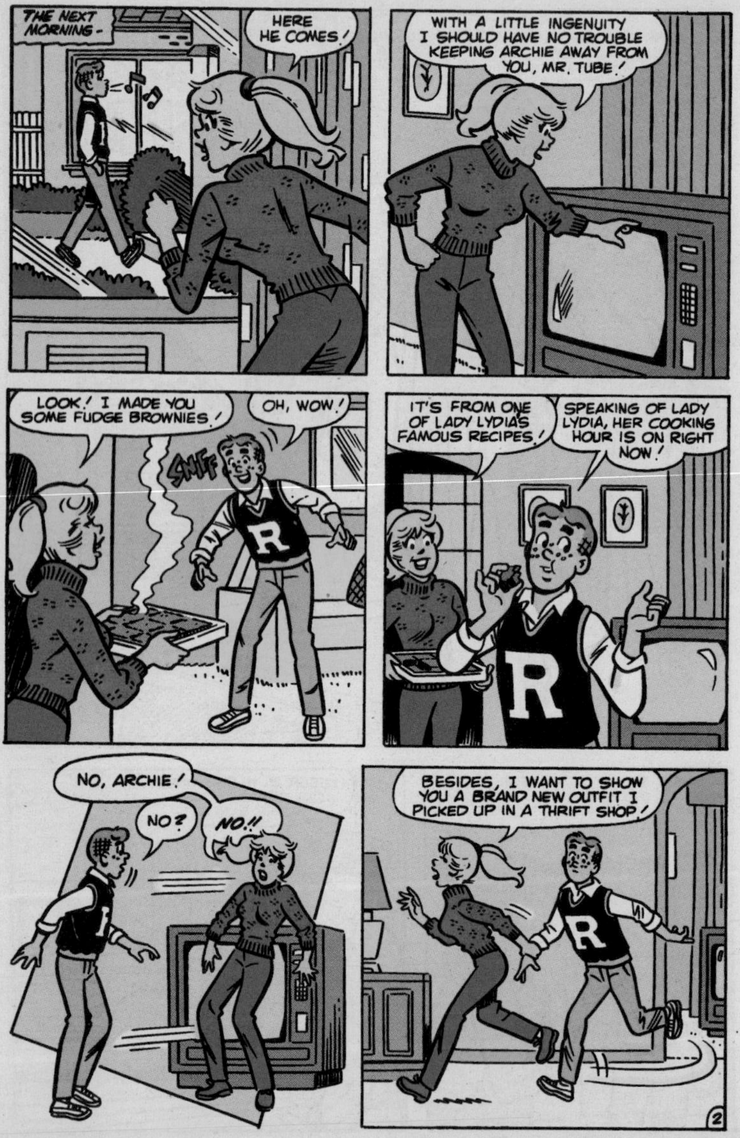
THE NEXT MORNING -
HERE HE COMES!
WITH A LITTLE INGENUITY I SHOULD HAVE NO TROUBLE KEEPING ARCHIE AWAY FROM YOU, MR. TUBE!
LOOK! I MADE YOU SOME FUDGE BROWNIES!
OH, WOW!
SNIFF
IT'S FROM ONE OF LADY LYDIA'S FAMOUS RECIPES!
SPEAKING OF LADY LYDIA, HER COOKING HOUR IS ON RIGHT NOW!
NO, ARCHIE!
NO?
NO!!
BESIDES, I WANT TO SHOW YOU A BRAND NEW OUTFIT I PICKED UP IN A THRIFT SHOP!
2

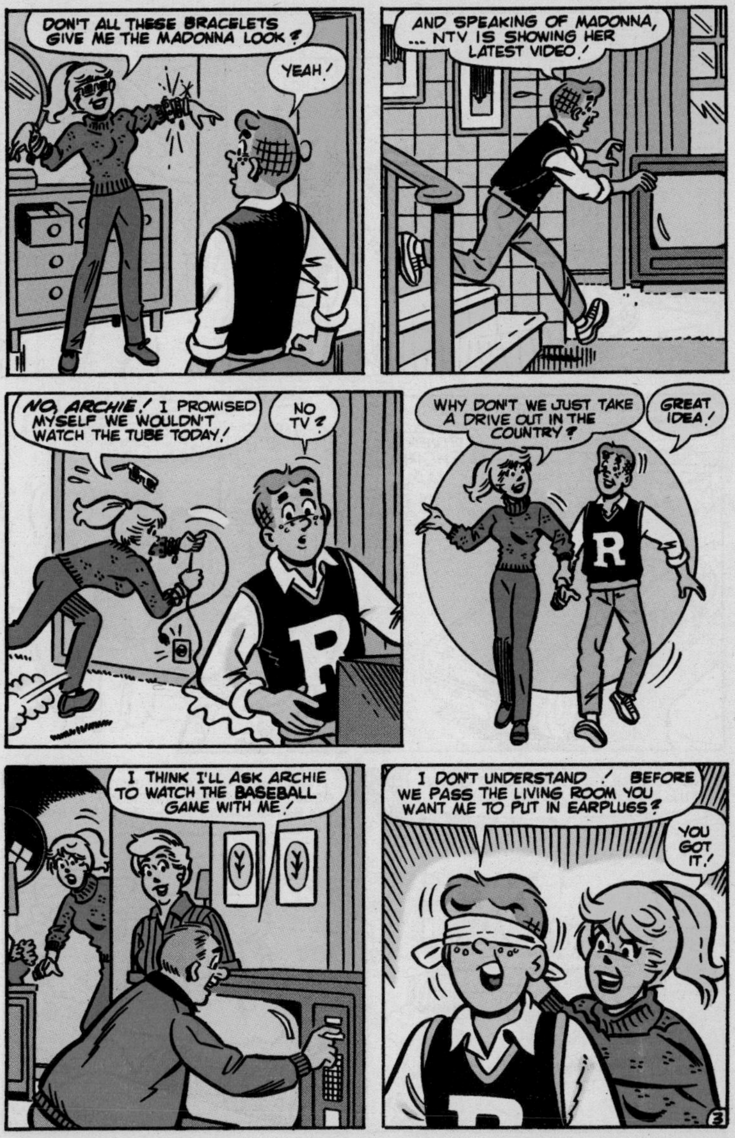

DON'T ALL THESE BRACELETS GIVE ME THE MADONNA LOOK?
YEAH!
AND SPEAKING OF MADONNA, ... NTV IS SHOWING HER LATEST VIDEO!
NO, ARCHIE! I PROMISED MYSELF WE WOULDN'T WATCH THE TUBE TODAY!
NO TV?
WHY DON'T WE JUST TAKE A DRIVE OUT IN THE COUNTRY?
GREAT IDEA!
I THINK I'LL ASK ARCHIE TO WATCH THE BASEBALL GAME WITH ME!
I DON'T UNDERSTAND! BEFORE WE PASS THE LIVING ROOM YOU WANT ME TO PUT IN EARPLUGS?
YOU GOT IT!
3

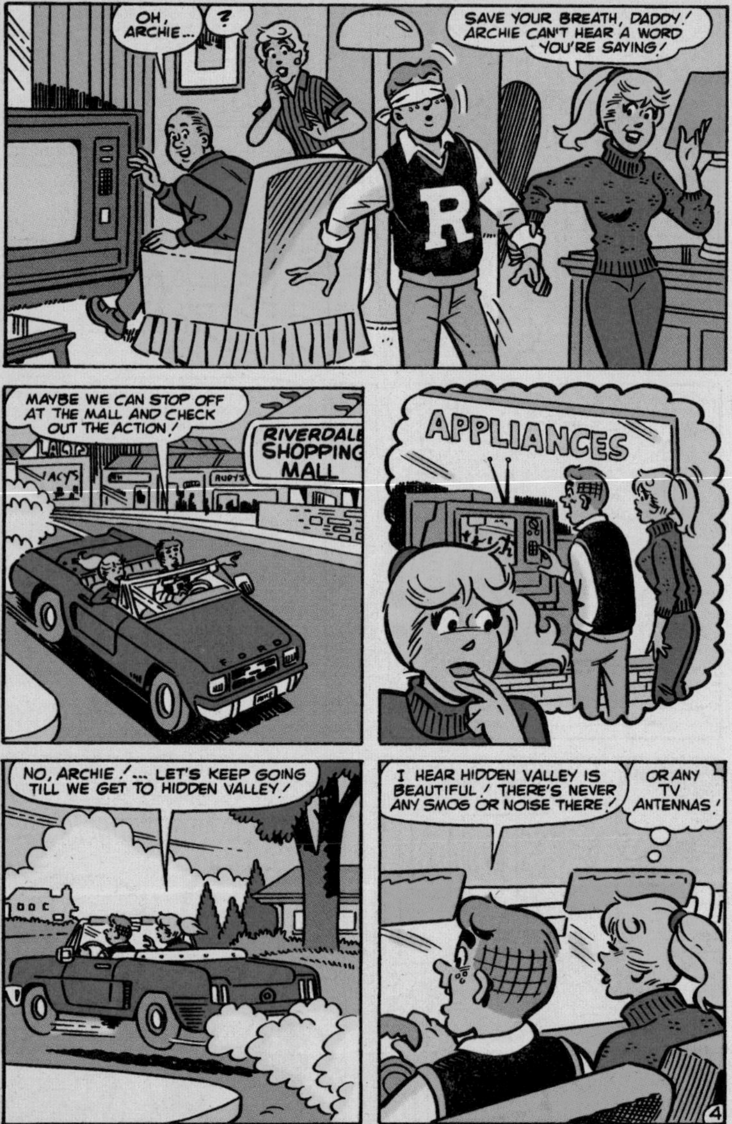
OH, ARCHIE...
?
SAVE YOUR BREATH, DADDY! ARCHIE CAN'T HEAR A WORD YOU'RE SAYING!
MAYBE WE CAN STOP OFF AT THE MALL AND CHECK OUT THE ACTION!
RIVERDALE SHOPPING MALL
APPLIANCES
NO, ARCHIE!... LET'S KEEP GOING TILL WE GET TO HIDDEN VALLEY!
I HEAR HIDDEN VALLEY IS BEAUTIFUL! THERE'S NEVER ANY SMOG OR NOISE THERE!
OR ANY TV ANTENNAS!
4

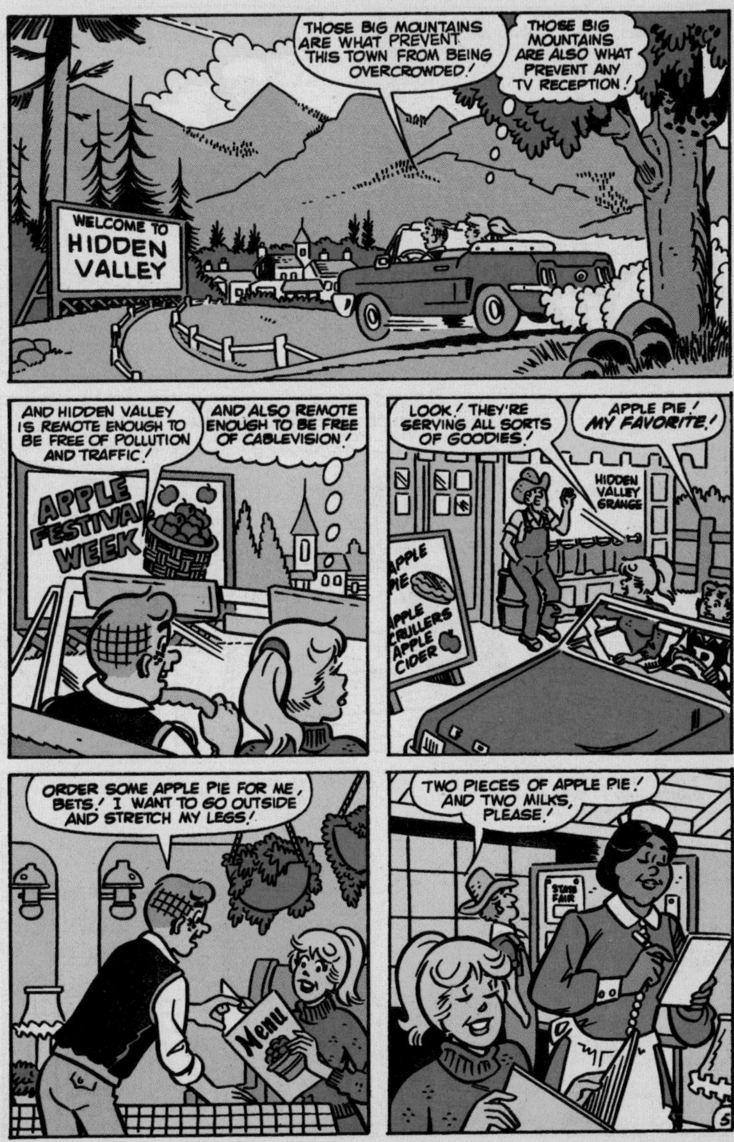
THOSE BIG MOUNTAINS ARE WHAT PREVENT THIS TOWN FROM BEING OVERCROWDED!
THOSE BIG MOUNTAINS ARE ALSO WHAT PREVENT ANY TV RECEPTION!
WELCOME TO HIDDEN VALLEY
AND HIDDEN VALLEY IS REMOTE ENOUGH TO BE FREE OF POLLUTION AND TRAFFIC!
AND ALSO REMOTE ENOUGH TO BE FREE OF CABLEVISION!
APPLE FESTIVAL WEEK
LOOK! THEY'RE SERVING ALL SORTS OF GOODIES!
APPLE PIE! MY FAVORITE!
HIDDEN VALLEY GRANGE
APPLE PIE
APPLE CRULLERS
APPLE CIDER
ORDER SOME APPLE PIE FOR ME, BETS! I WANT TO GO OUTSIDE AND STRETCH MY LEGS!
Menu
TWO PIECES OF APPLE PIE! AND TWO MILKS, PLEASE!
STATE FAIR
5

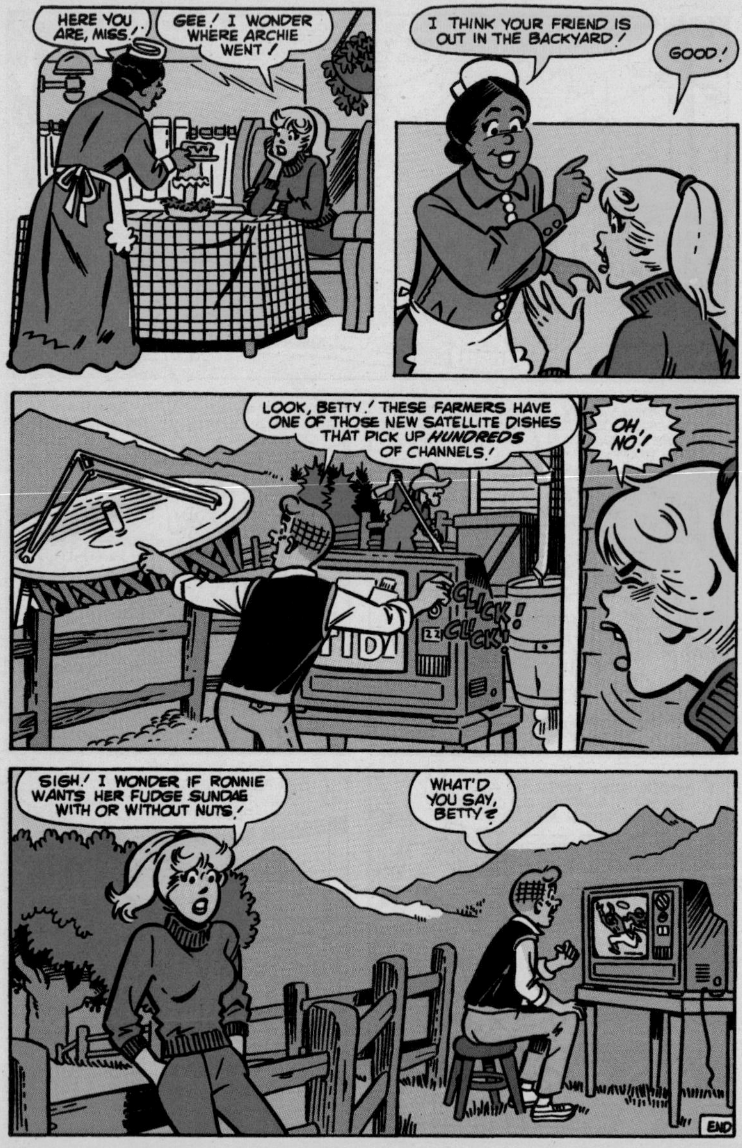
HERE YOU ARE, MISS!
GEE! I WONDER WHERE ARCHIE WENT!
I THINK YOUR FRIEND IS OUT IN THE BACKYARD!
GOOD!
LOOK, BETTY! THESE FARMERS HAVE ONE OF THOSE NEW SATELLITE DISHES THAT PICK UP HUNDREDS OF CHANNELS!
CLICK! CLICK!
OH, NO!
SIGH! I WONDER IF RONNIE WANTS HER FUDGE SUNDAE WITH OR WITHOUT NUTS!
WHAT'D YOU SAY, BETTY?
END

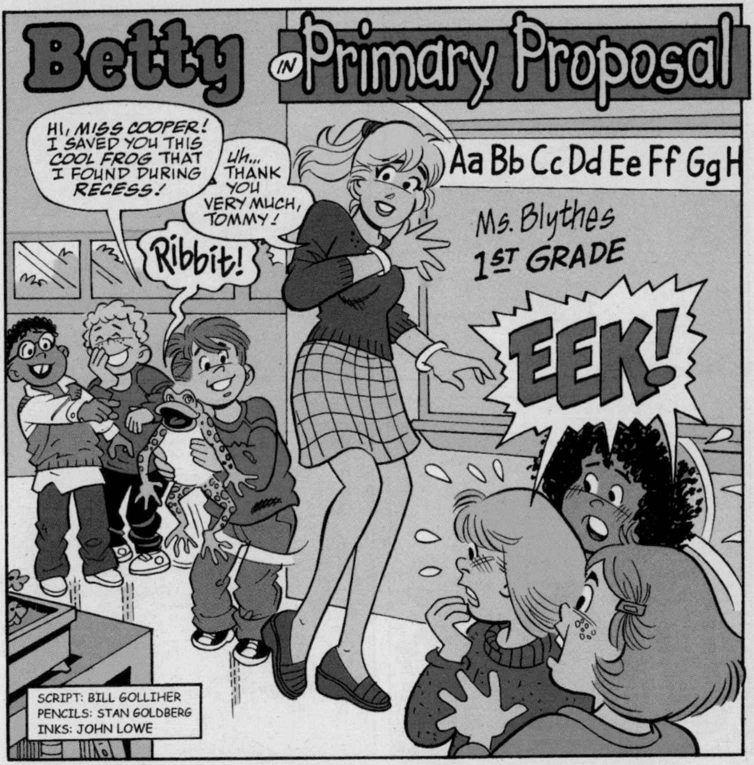
Betty in Primary Proposal
HI, MISS COOPER! I SAVED YOU THIS COOL FROG THAT I FOUND DURING RECESS!
UH... THANK YOU VERY MUCH, TOMMY!
Ribbit!
Aa Bb Cc Dd Ee Ff Gg H
Ms. Blythes 1ST GRADE
EEK!
SCRIPT: BILL GOLLIHER
PENCILS: STAN GOLDBERG
INKS: JOHN LOWE

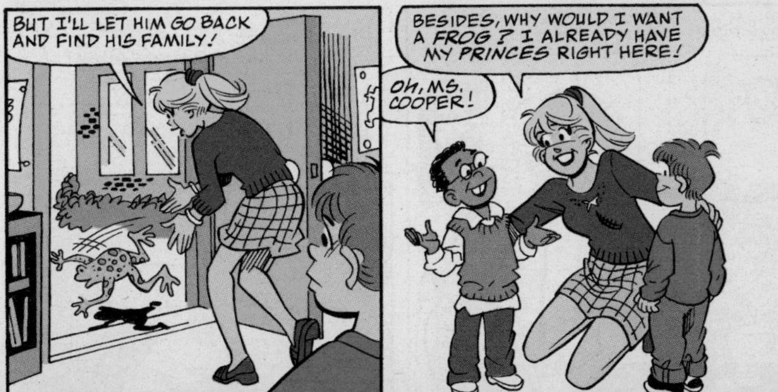
BUT I'LL LET HIM GO BACK AND FIND HIS FAMILY!
BESIDES, WHY WOULD I WANT A FROG? I ALREADY HAVE MY PRINCES RIGHT HERE!
OH, MS. COOPER!

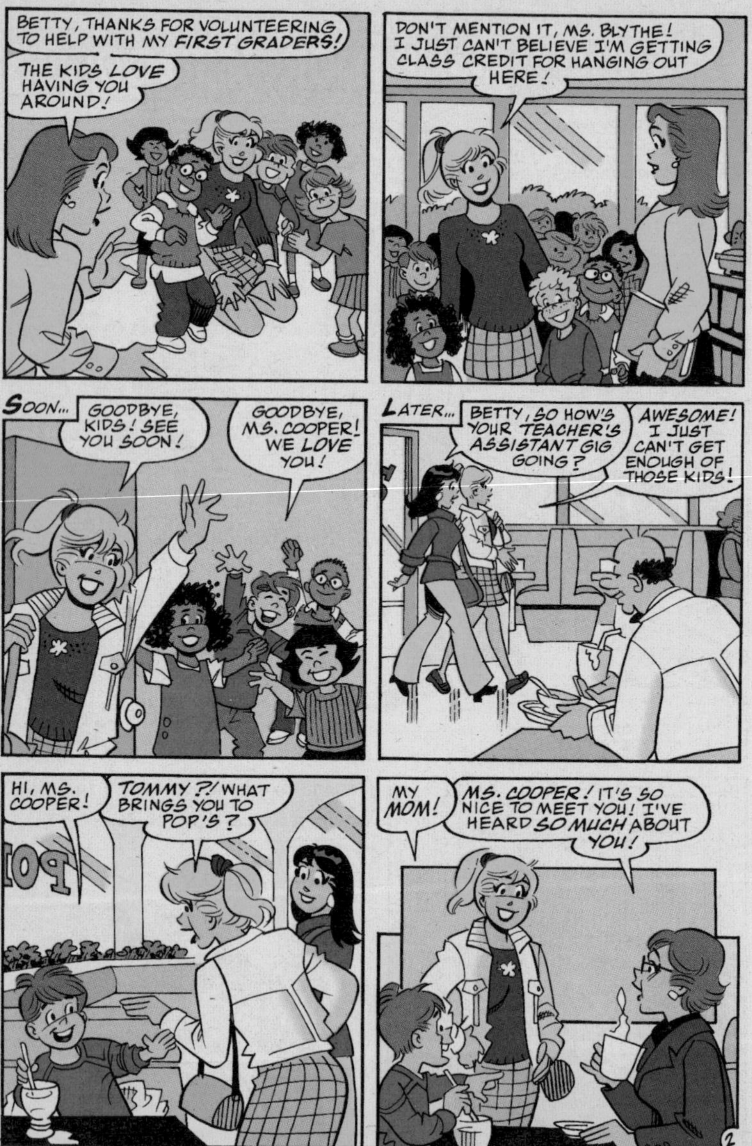
BETTY, THANKS FOR VOLUNTEERING TO HELP WITH MY FIRST GRADERS!
THE KIDS LOVE HAVING YOU AROUND!
DON'T MENTION IT, MS. BLYTHE! I JUST CAN'T BELIEVE I'M GETTING CLASS CREDIT FOR HANGING OUT HERE!
SOON...
GOODBYE, KIDS! SEE YOU SOON!
GOODBYE, MS. COOPER! WE LOVE YOU!
LATER...
BETTY, SO HOW'S YOUR TEACHER'S ASSISTANT GIG GOING?
AWESOME! I JUST CAN'T GET ENOUGH OF THOSE KIDS!
HI, MS. COOPER!
TOMMY?! WHAT BRINGS YOU TO POP'S?
MY MOM!
MS. COOPER! IT'S SO NICE TO MEET YOU! I'VE HEARD SO MUCH ABOUT YOU!
2

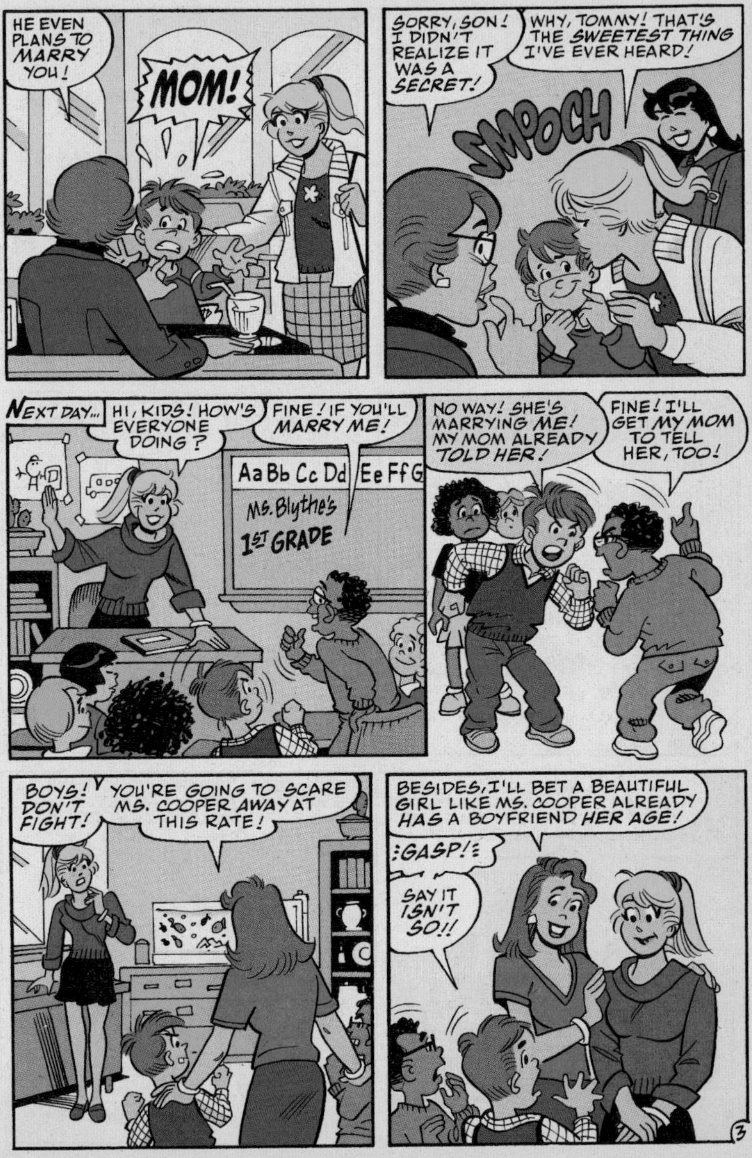

HE EVEN PLANS TO MARRY YOU!
MOM!
SORRY, SON! I DIDN'T REALIZE IT WAS A SECRET!
WHY, TOMMY! THAT'S THE SWEETEST THING I'VE EVER HEARD!
SMOOCH
NEXT DAY...
HI, KIDS! HOW'S EVERYONE DOING?
FINE! IF YOU'LL MARRY ME!
Aa Bb Cc Dd Ee Ff G
Ms. Blythe's 1ST GRADE
NO WAY! SHE'S MARRYING ME! MY MOM ALREADY TOLD HER!
FINE! I'LL GET MY MOM TO TELL HER, TOO!
BOYS! DON'T FIGHT!
YOU'RE GOING TO SCARE MS. COOPER AWAY AT THIS RATE!
BESIDES, I'LL BET A BEAUTIFUL GIRL LIKE MS. COOPER ALREADY HAS A BOYFRIEND HER AGE!
GASP!
SAY IT ISN'T SO!!

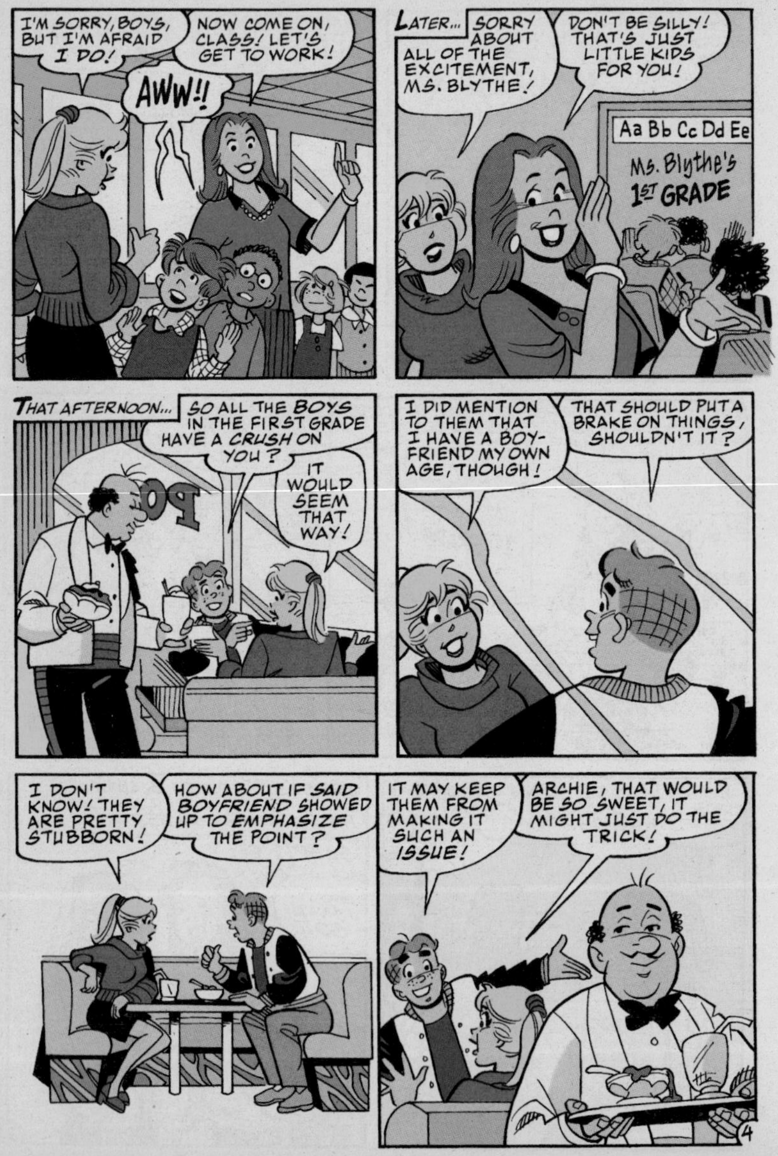
I'M SORRY, BOYS, BUT I'M AFRAID I DO!
NOW COME ON, CLASS! LET'S GET TO WORK!
AWW!!
LATER...
SORRY ABOUT ALL OF THE EXCITEMENT, MS. BLYTHE!
DON'T BE SILLY! THAT'S JUST LITTLE KIDS FOR YOU!
Aa Bb Cc Dd Ee
Ms. Blythe's 1ST GRADE
THAT AFTERNOON...
SO ALL THE BOYS IN THE FIRST GRADE HAVE A CRUSH ON YOU?
IT WOULD SEEM THAT WAY!
I DID MENTION TO THEM THAT I HAVE A BOY-FRIEND MY OWN AGE, THOUGH!
THAT SHOULD PUT A BRAKE ON THINGS, SHOULDN'T IT?
I DON'T KNOW! THEY ARE PRETTY STUBBORN!
HOW ABOUT IF SAID BOYFRIEND SHOWED UP TO EMPHASIZE THE POINT?
IT MAY KEEP THEM FROM MAKING IT SUCH AN ISSUE!
ARCHIE, THAT WOULD BE SO SWEET, IT MIGHT JUST DO THE TRICK!
4

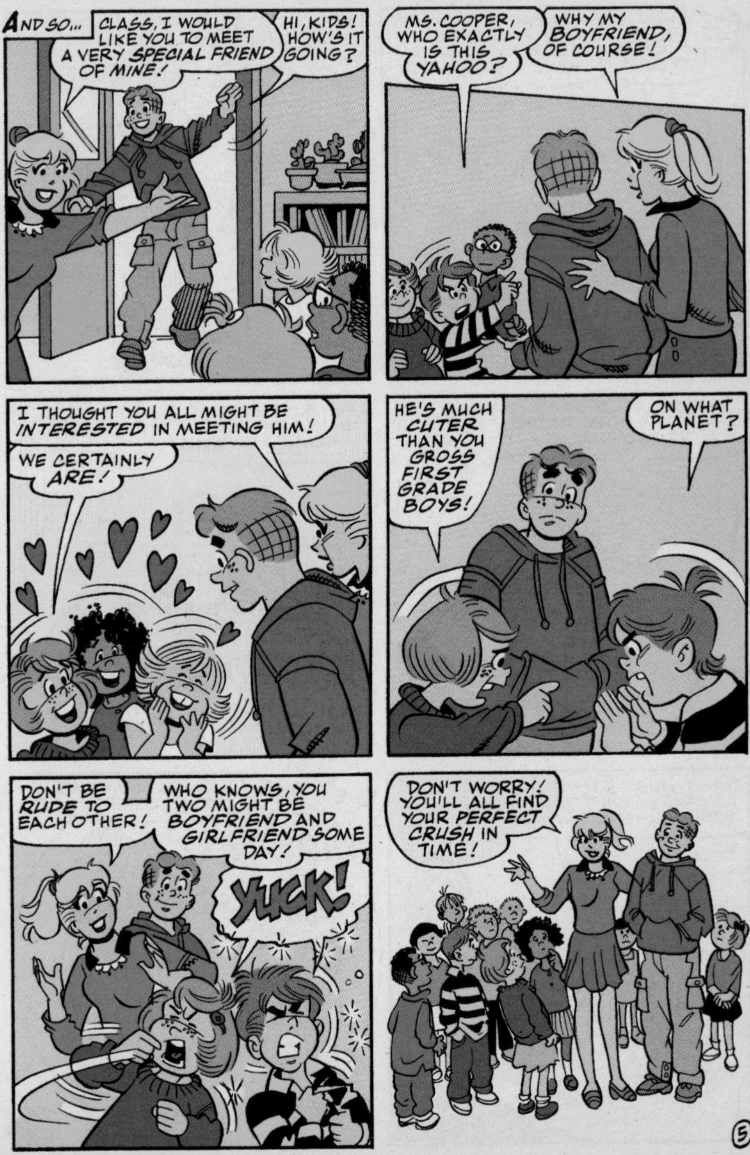

AND SO...
CLASS, I WOULD LIKE YOU TO MEET A VERY SPECIAL FRIEND OF MINE!
HI, KIDS! HOW'S IT GOING?
MS. COOPER, WHO EXACTLY IS THIS YAHOO?
WHY MY BOYFRIEND, OF COURSE!
I THOUGHT YOU ALL MIGHT BE INTERESTED IN MEETING HIM!
WE CERTAINLY ARE!
HE'S MUCH CUTER THAN YOU GROSS FIRST GRADE BOYS!
ON WHAT PLANET?
DON'T BE RUDE TO EACH OTHER!
WHO KNOWS, YOU TWO MIGHT BE BOYFRIEND AND GIRLFRIEND SOME DAY!
YUCK!
DON'T WORRY! YOU'LL ALL FIND YOUR PERFECT CRUSH IN TIME!

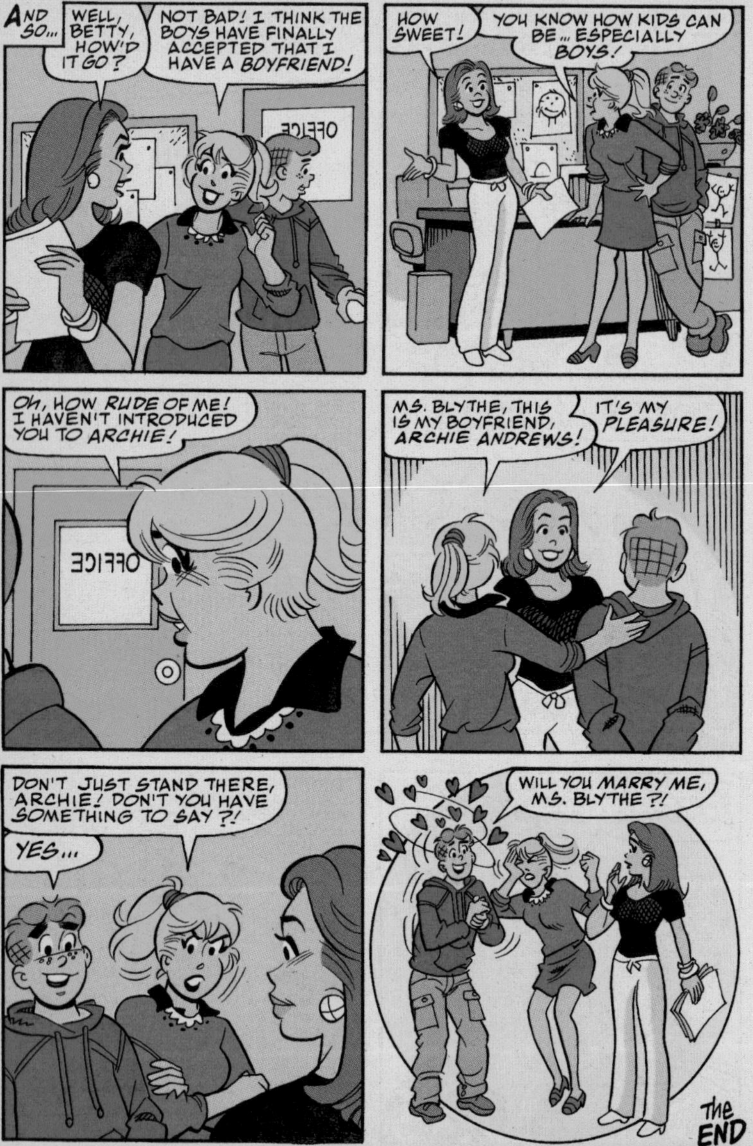
AND SO...
WELL, BETTY, HOW'D IT GO?
NOT BAD! I THINK THE BOYS HAVE FINALLY ACCEPTED THAT I HAVE A BOYFRIEND!
OFFICE
HOW SWEET!
YOU KNOW HOW KIDS CAN BE... ESPECIALLY BOYS!
OH, HOW RUDE OF ME! I HAVEN'T INTRODUCED YOU TO ARCHIE!
OFFICE
MS. BLYTHE, THIS IS MY BOYFRIEND, ARCHIE ANDREWS!
IT'S MY PLEASURE!
DON'T JUST STAND THERE, ARCHIE! DON'T YOU HAVE SOMETHING TO SAY?!
YES...
WILL YOU MARRY ME, MS. BLYTHE?!
THE END

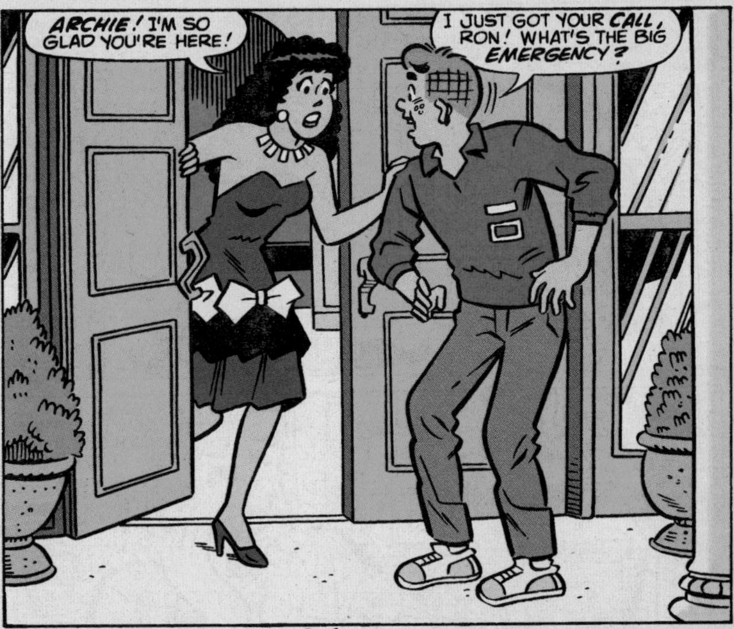
ARCHIE! I'M SO GLAD YOU'RE HERE!
I JUST GOT YOUR CALL, RON! WHAT'S THE BIG EMERGENCY?

Veronica in "SETTING THINGS STRAIGHT"

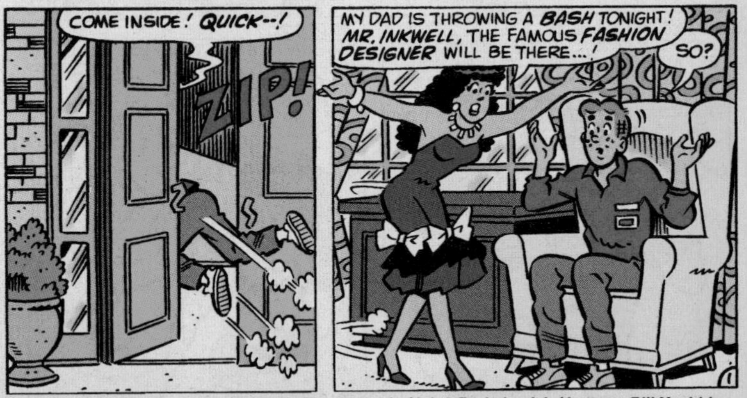
COME INSIDE! QUICK--!
ZIP!
MY DAD IS THROWING A BASH TONIGHT! MR. INKWELL, THE FAMOUS FASHION DESIGNER WILL BE THERE...!
SO?

Script: Rich Margopolous / Pencils: Tim Kennedy / Inks: Rudy Lapick / Letters: Bill Yoshida

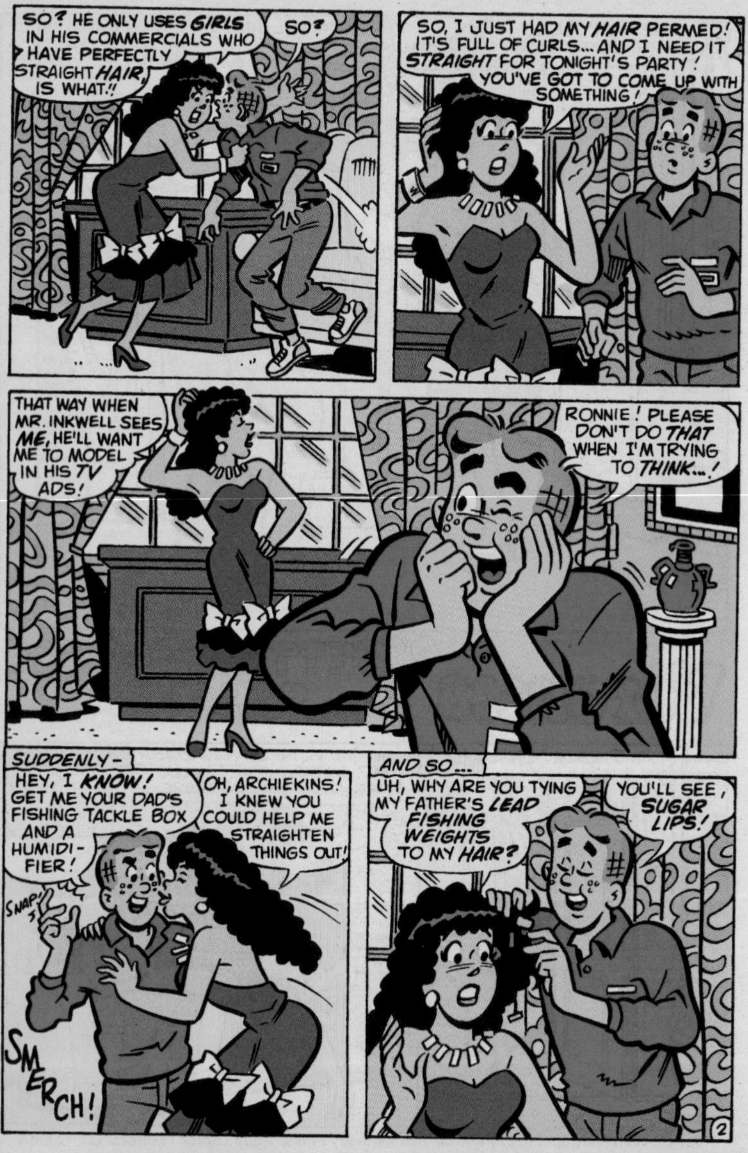

SO? HE ONLY USES GIRLS IN HIS COMMERCIALS WHO HAVE PERFECTLY STRAIGHT HAIR, IS WHAT!!
SO?
SO, I JUST HAD MY HAIR PERMED! IT'S FULL OF CURLS... AND I NEED IT STRAIGHT FOR TONIGHT'S PARTY! YOU'VE GOT TO COME UP WITH SOMETHING!
THAT WAY WHEN MR. INKWELL SEES ME, HE'LL WANT ME TO MODEL IN HIS TV ADS!
RONNIE! PLEASE DON'T DO THAT WHEN I'M TRYING TO THINK...!
SUDDENLY-
HEY, I KNOW! GET ME YOUR DAD'S FISHING TACKLE BOX AND A HUMIDI-FIER!
OH, ARCHIEKINS! I KNEW YOU COULD HELP ME STRAIGHTEN THINGS OUT!
SNAP!
SMERCH!
AND SO...
UH, WHY ARE YOU TYING MY FATHER'S LEAD FISHING WEIGHTS TO MY HAIR?
YOU'LL SEE, SUGAR LIPS!
2

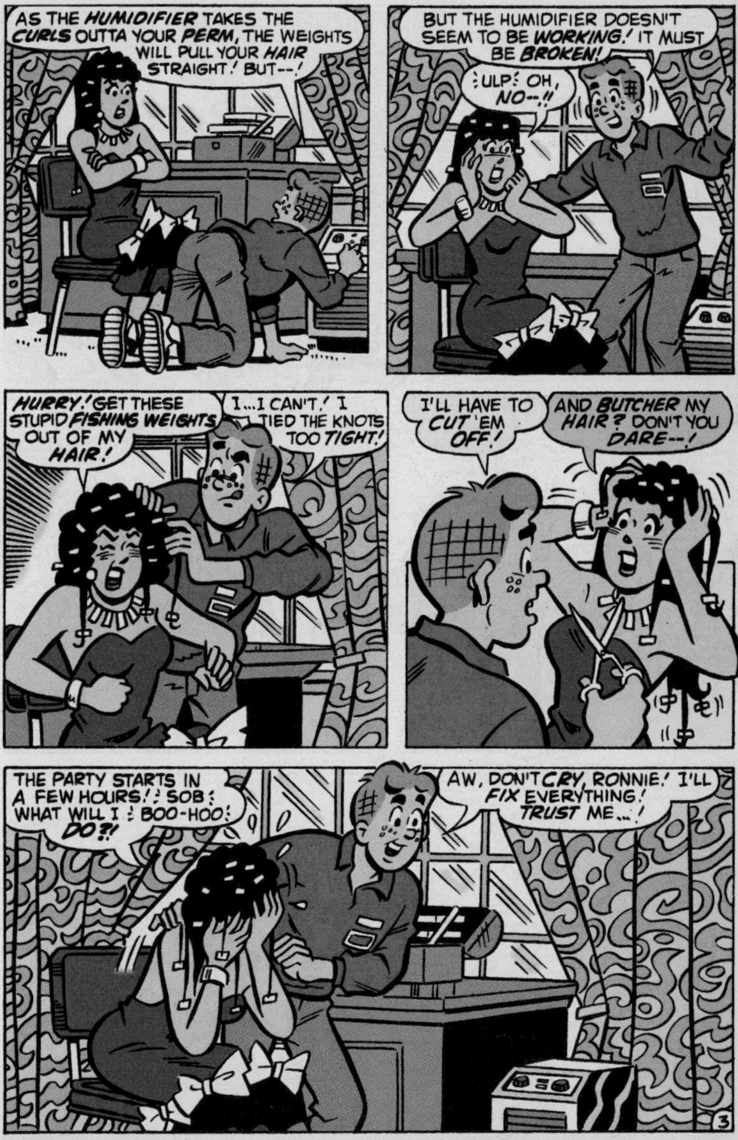
AS THE HUMIDIFIER TAKES THE CURLS OUTTA YOUR PERM, THE WEIGHTS WILL PULL YOUR HAIR STRAIGHT! BUT--!
BUT THE HUMIDIFIER DOESN'T SEEM TO BE WORKING! IT MUST BE BROKEN!
ULP! OH, NO--!!
HURRY! GET THESE STUPID FISHING WEIGHTS OUT OF MY HAIR!
I...I CAN'T! I TIED THE KNOTS TOO TIGHT!
I'LL HAVE TO CUT 'EM OFF!
AND BUTCHER MY HAIR? DON'T YOU DARE--!
THE PARTY STARTS IN A FEW HOURS! SOB! WHAT WILL I BOO-HOO! DO?!
AW, DON'T CRY, RONNIE! I'LL FIX EVERYTHING! TRUST ME...!
3

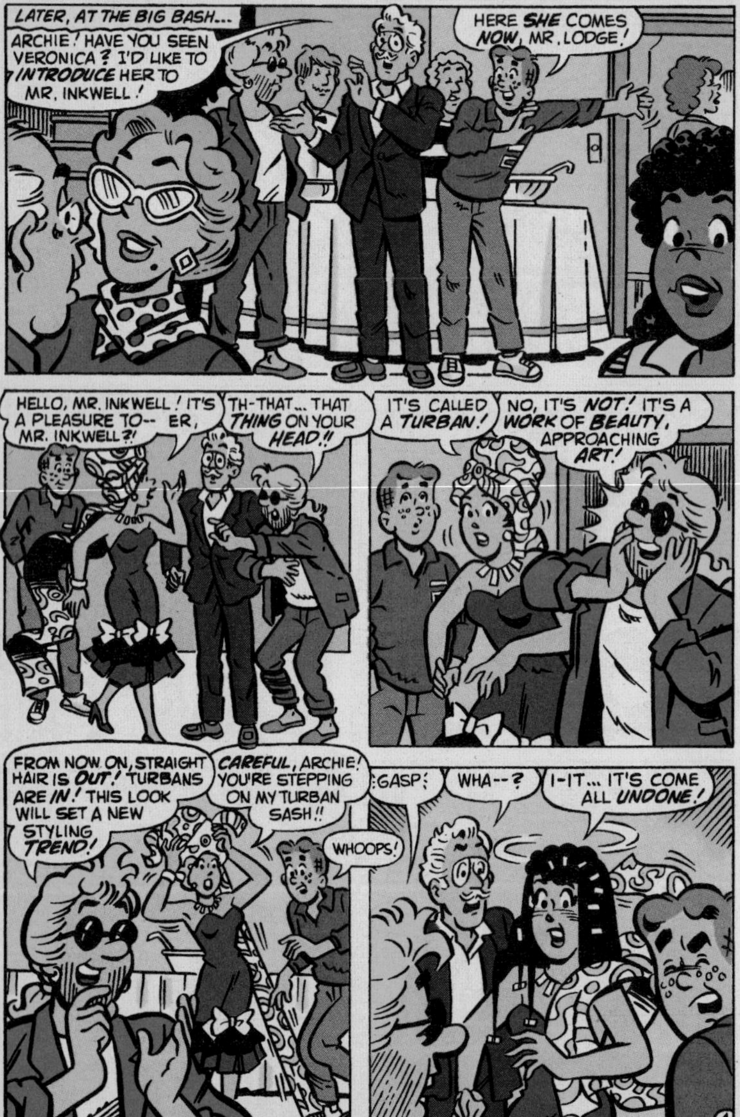

LATER, AT THE BIG BASH...
ARCHIE! HAVE YOU SEEN VERONICA? I'D LIKE TO INTRODUCE HER TO MR. INKWELL!
HERE SHE COMES NOW, MR. LODGE!
HELLO, MR. INKWELL! IT'S A PLEASURE TO-- ER, MR. INKWELL?!
TH-THAT... THAT THING ON YOUR HEAD!!
IT'S CALLED A TURBAN!
NO, IT'S NOT! IT'S A WORK OF BEAUTY, APPROACHING ART!
FROM NOW ON, STRAIGHT HAIR IS OUT! TURBANS ARE IN! THIS LOOK WILL SET A NEW STYLING TREND!
CAREFUL, ARCHIE! YOU'RE STEPPING ON MY TURBAN SASH!!
WHOOPS!
GASP
WHA--?
I-IT... IT'S COME ALL UNDONE!
4

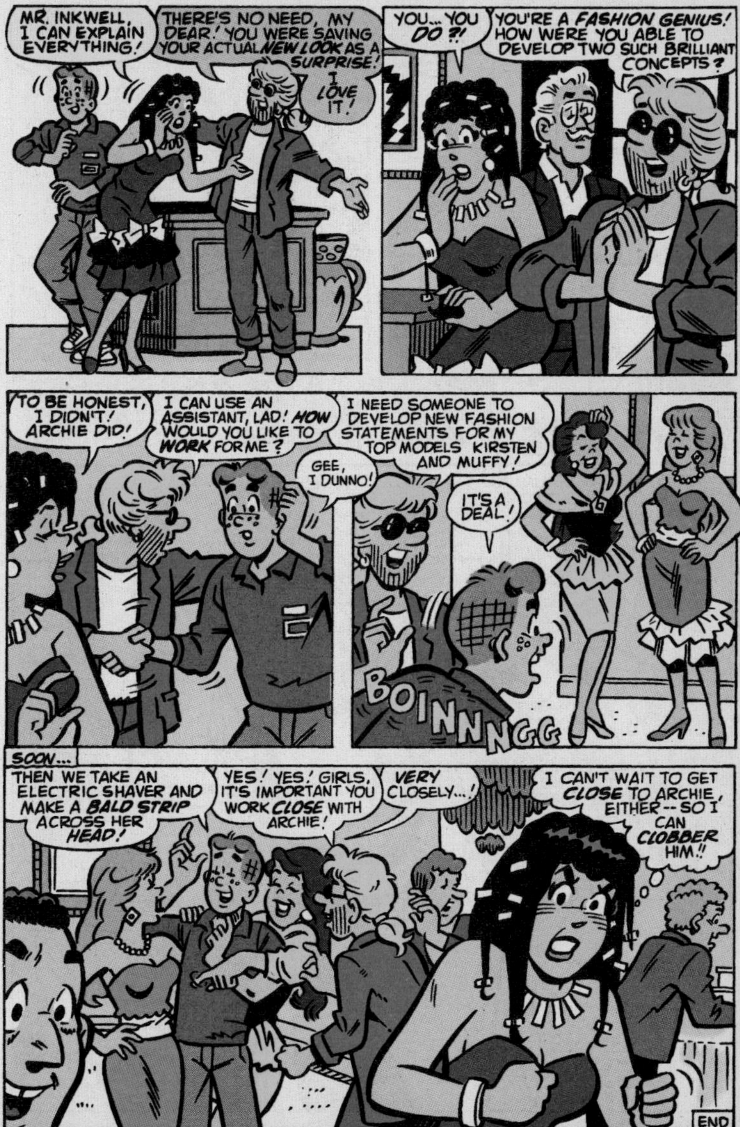

MR. INKWELL, I CAN EXPLAIN EVERYTHING!
THERE'S NO NEED, MY DEAR! YOU WERE SAVING YOUR ACTUAL NEW LOOK AS A SURPRISE!
I LOVE IT!
YOU... YOU DO ?!
YOU'RE A FASHION GENIUS! HOW WERE YOU ABLE TO DEVELOP TWO SUCH BRILLIANT CONCEPTS ?
TO BE HONEST, I DIDN'T! ARCHIE DID!
I CAN USE AN ASSISTANT, LAD! HOW WOULD YOU LIKE TO WORK FOR ME ?
GEE, I DUNNO!
I NEED SOMEONE TO DEVELOP NEW FASHION STATEMENTS FOR MY TOP MODELS KIRSTEN AND MUFFY!
IT'S A DEAL!
BOINNNNGG
SOON...
THEN WE TAKE AN ELECTRIC SHAVER AND MAKE A BALD STRIP ACROSS HER HEAD!
YES! YES! GIRLS, IT'S IMPORTANT YOU WORK CLOSE WITH ARCHIE!
VERY CLOSELY...!
I CAN'T WAIT TO GET CLOSE TO ARCHIE, EITHER -- SO I CAN CLOBBER HIM!!
END

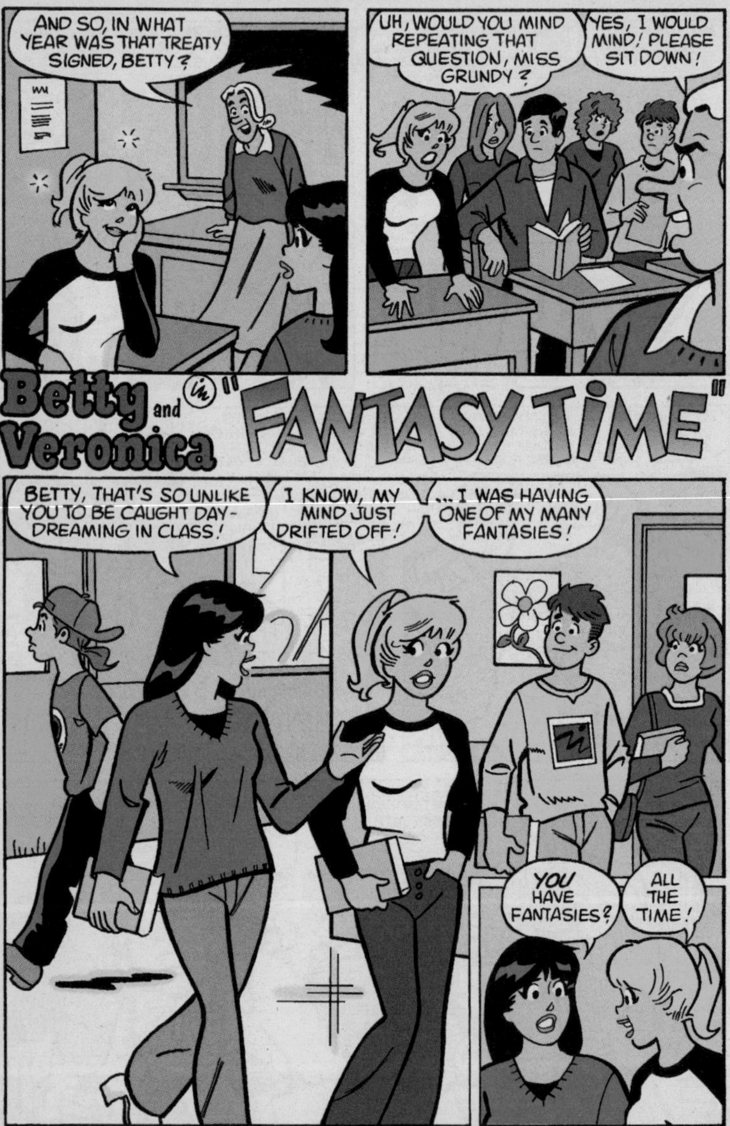
AND SO, IN WHAT YEAR WAS THAT TREATY SIGNED, BETTY?
UH, WOULD YOU MIND REPEATING THAT QUESTION, MISS GRUNDY?
YES, I WOULD MIND! PLEASE SIT DOWN!
Betty and Veronica in "FANTASY TIME"
BETTY, THAT'S SO UNLIKE YOU TO BE CAUGHT DAY-DREAMING IN CLASS!
I KNOW, MY MIND JUST DRIFTED OFF!
...I WAS HAVING ONE OF MY MANY FANTASIES!
YOU HAVE FANTASIES?
ALL THE TIME!

Script: George Gladir / Pencils: Jeff Shultz / Inks: Henry Scarpelli / Letters: Bill Yoshida / Colors: Barry Grossman

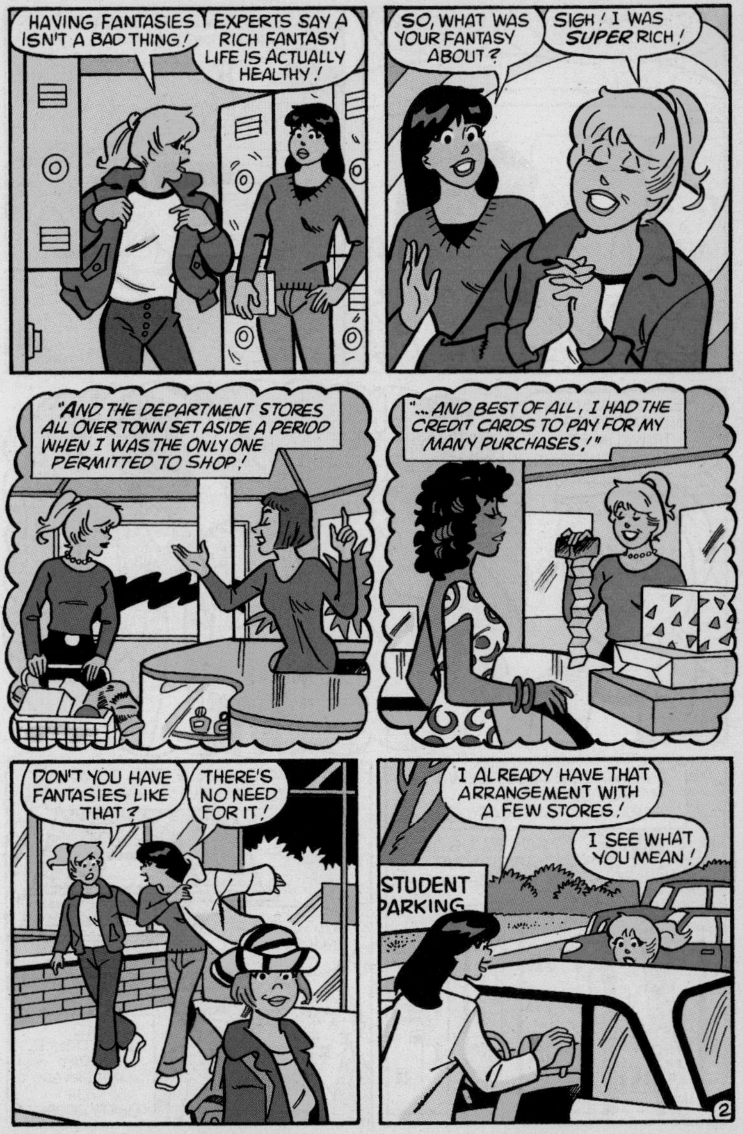

HAVING FANTASIES ISN'T A BAD THING!
EXPERTS SAY A RICH FANTASY LIFE IS ACTUALLY HEALTHY!
SO, WHAT WAS YOUR FANTASY ABOUT?
SIGH! I WAS SUPER RICH!
"AND THE DEPARTMENT STORES ALL OVER TOWN SET ASIDE A PERIOD WHEN I WAS THE ONLY ONE PERMITTED TO SHOP!
"...AND BEST OF ALL, I HAD THE CREDIT CARDS TO PAY FOR MY MANY PURCHASES!"
DON'T YOU HAVE FANTASIES LIKE THAT?
THERE'S NO NEED FOR IT!
I ALREADY HAVE THAT ARRANGEMENT WITH A FEW STORES!
I SEE WHAT YOU MEAN!
STUDENT PARKING
2

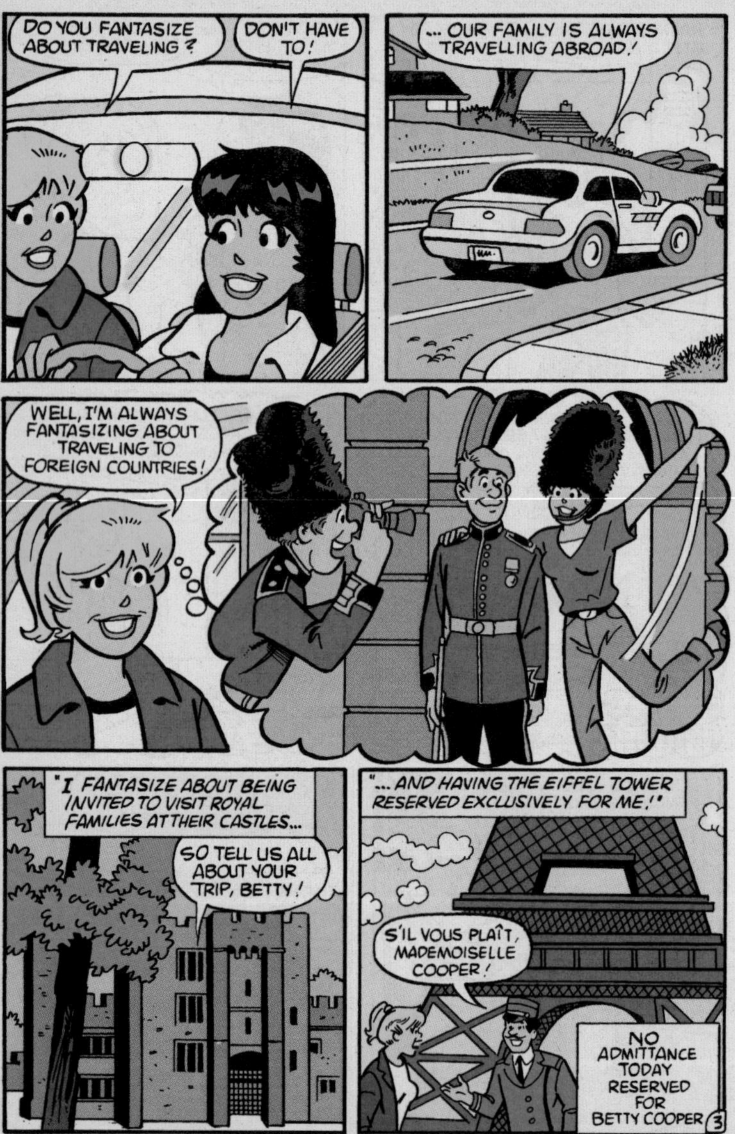
DO YOU FANTASIZE ABOUT TRAVELING?
DON'T HAVE TO!
... OUR FAMILY IS ALWAYS TRAVELLING ABROAD!
WELL, I'M ALWAYS FANTASIZING ABOUT TRAVELING TO FOREIGN COUNTRIES!
"I FANTASIZE ABOUT BEING INVITED TO VISIT ROYAL FAMILIES AT THEIR CASTLES...
SO TELL US ALL ABOUT YOUR TRIP, BETTY!
"... AND HAVING THE EIFFEL TOWER RESERVED EXCLUSIVELY FOR ME!"
S'IL VOUS PLAÎT, MADEMOISELLE COOPER!
NO ADMITTANCE TODAY RESERVED FOR BETTY COOPER
3

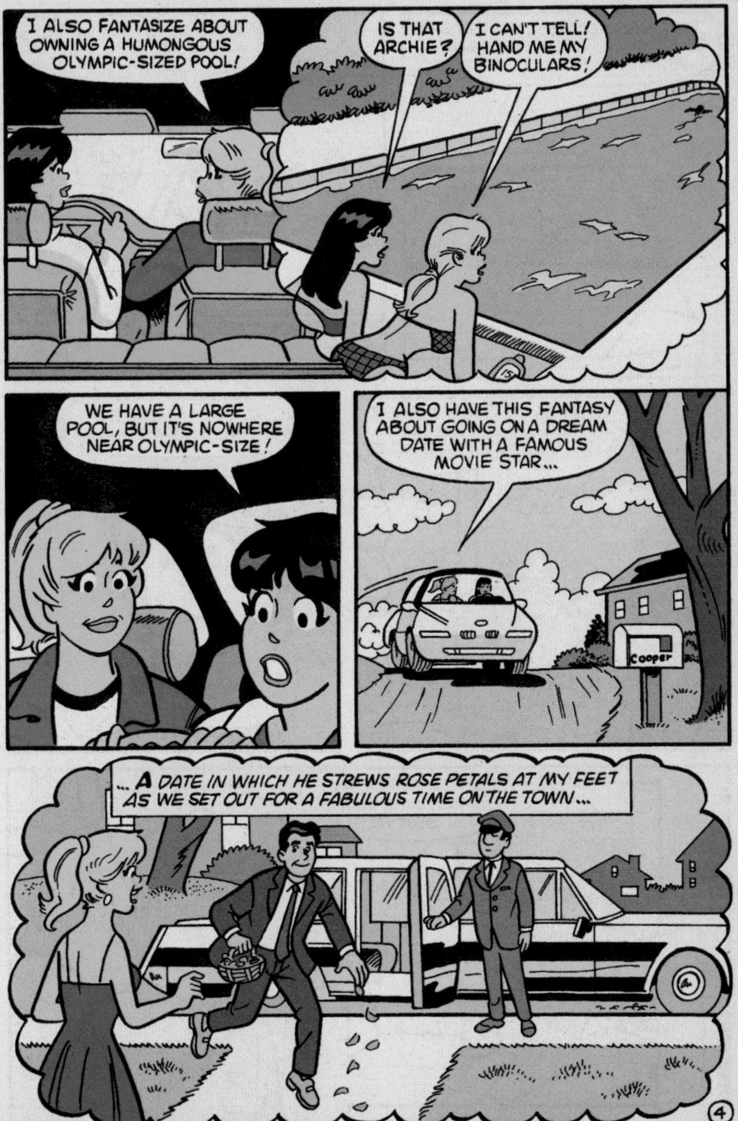
I ALSO FANTASIZE ABOUT OWNING A HUMONGOUS OLYMPIC-SIZED POOL!
IS THAT ARCHIE?
I CAN'T TELL! HAND ME MY BINOCULARS!
WE HAVE A LARGE POOL, BUT IT'S NOWHERE NEAR OLYMPIC-SIZE!
I ALSO HAVE THIS FANTASY ABOUT GOING ON A DREAM DATE WITH A FAMOUS MOVIE STAR...
COOPER
...A DATE IN WHICH HE STREWS ROSE PETALS AT MY FEET AS WE SET OUT FOR A FABULOUS TIME ON THE TOWN...
4

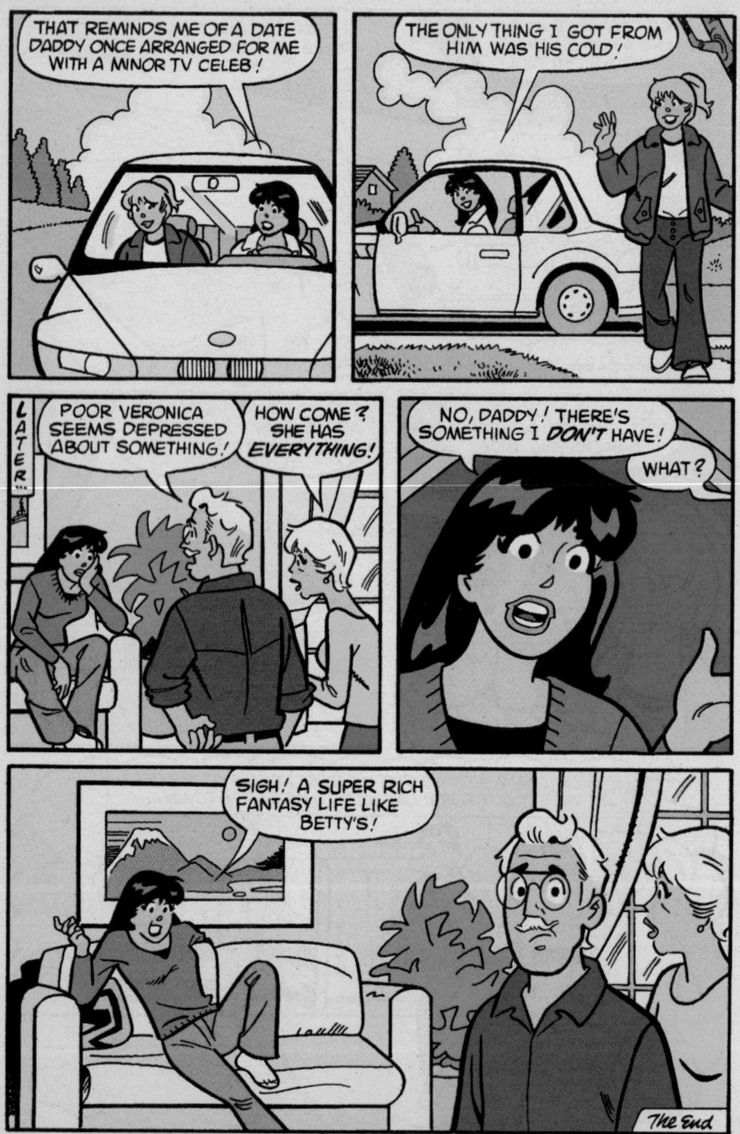
THAT REMINDS ME OF A DATE DADDY ONCE ARRANGED FOR ME WITH A MINOR TV CELEB!
THE ONLY THING I GOT FROM HIM WAS HIS COLD!
LATER
POOR VERONICA SEEMS DEPRESSED ABOUT SOMETHING!
HOW COME? SHE HAS EVERYTHING!
NO, DADDY! THERE'S SOMETHING I DON'T HAVE!
WHAT?
SIGH! A SUPER RICH FANTASY LIFE LIKE BETTY'S!
The End

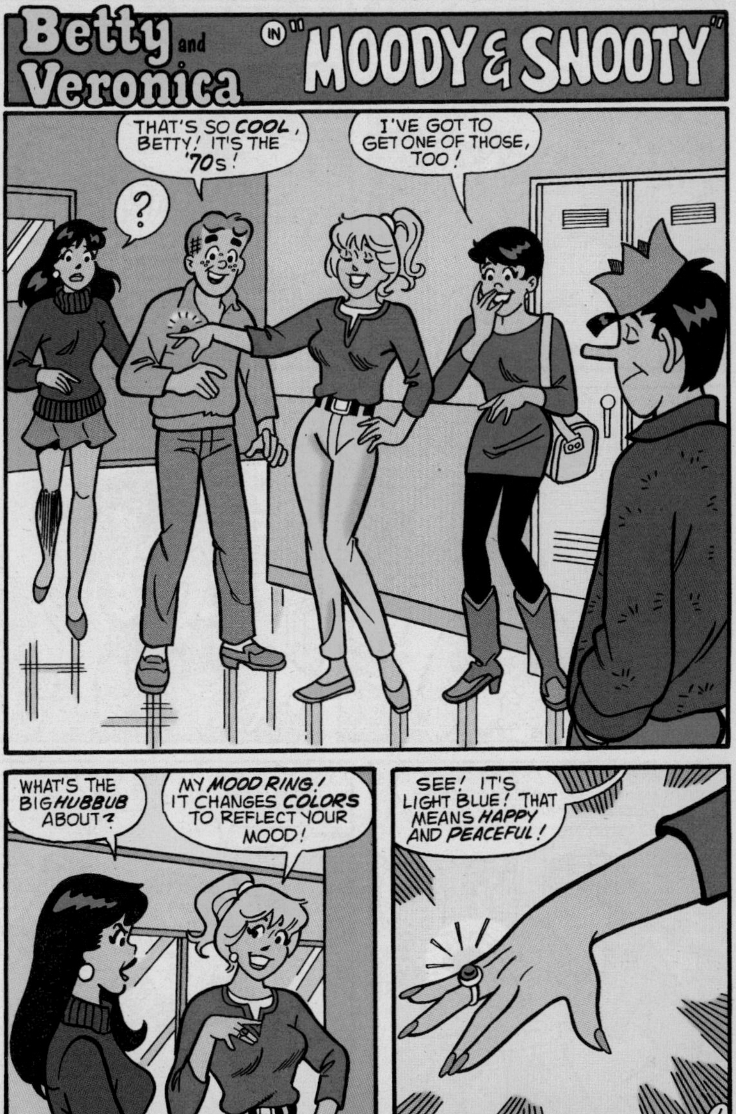
Betty and Veronica
IN "MOODY & SNOOTY"
THAT'S SO COOL, BETTY! IT'S THE '70s!
?
I'VE GOT TO GET ONE OF THOSE, TOO!
WHAT'S THE BIG HUBBUB ABOUT?
MY MOOD RING! IT CHANGES COLORS TO REFLECT YOUR MOOD!
SEE! IT'S LIGHT BLUE! THAT MEANS HAPPY AND PEACEFUL!
1

Script: Dan Parent / Pencils: Dan DeCarlo & Dan Parent / Inks: Henry Scarpelli / Letters: Bill Yoshida

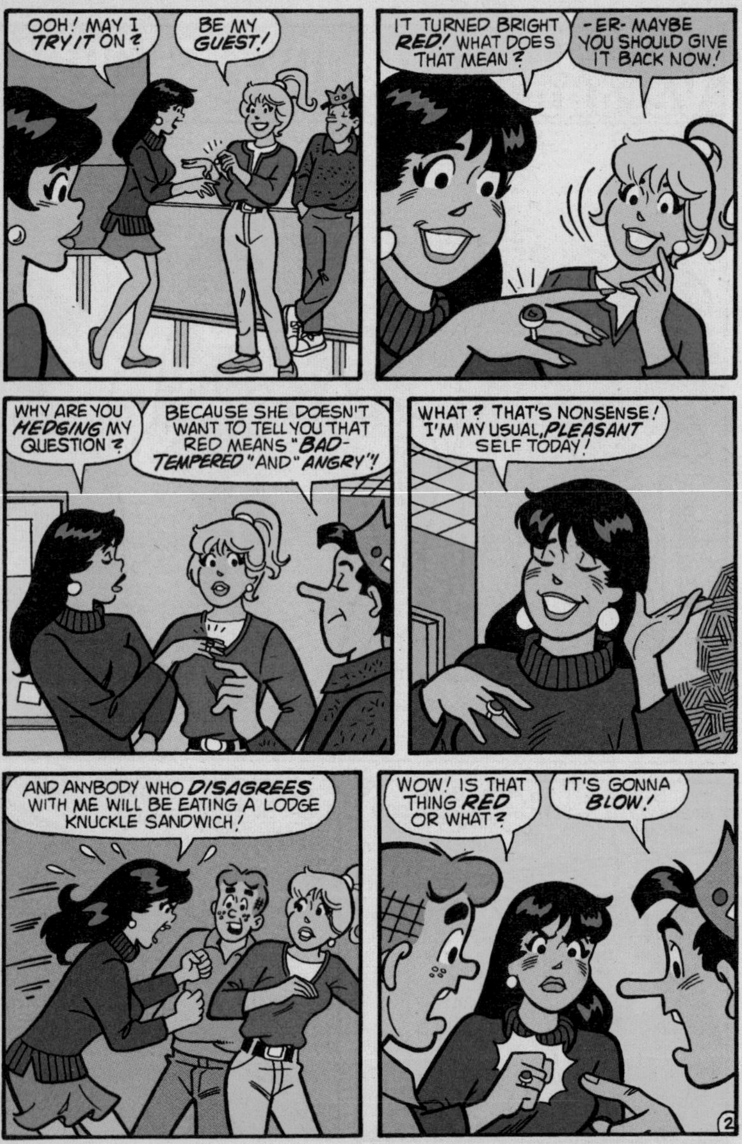
OOH! MAY I TRY IT ON?
BE MY GUEST!
IT TURNED BRIGHT RED! WHAT DOES THAT MEAN?
-ER- MAYBE YOU SHOULD GIVE IT BACK NOW!
WHY ARE YOU HEDGING MY QUESTION?
BECAUSE SHE DOESN'T WANT TO TELL YOU THAT RED MEANS "BAD-TEMPERED" AND "ANGRY"!
WHAT? THAT'S NONSENSE! I'M MY USUAL, PLEASANT SELF TODAY!
AND ANYBODY WHO DISAGREES WITH ME WILL BE EATING A LODGE KNUCKLE SANDWICH!
WOW! IS THAT THING RED OR WHAT?
IT'S GONNA BLOW!
2

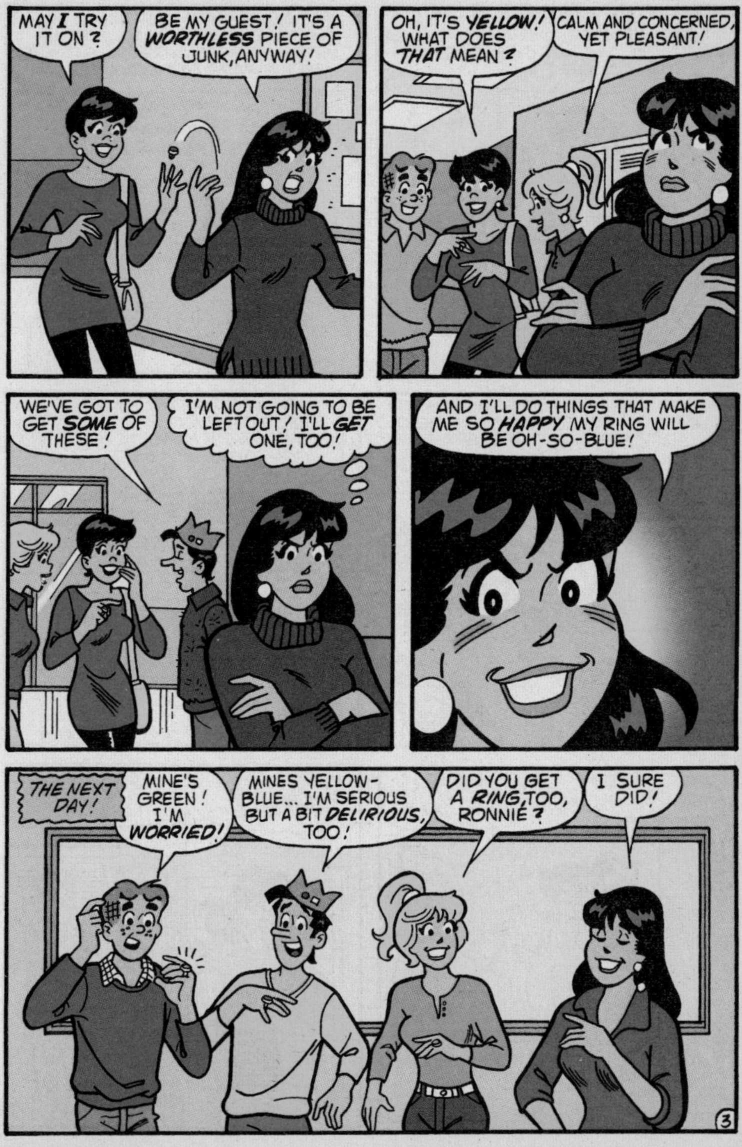
MAY *I* TRY IT ON?
BE MY GUEST! IT'S A *WORTHLESS* PIECE OF JUNK, ANYWAY!
OH, IT'S *YELLOW!* WHAT DOES *THAT* MEAN?
CALM AND CONCERNED, YET PLEASANT!
WE'VE GOT TO GET *SOME* OF THESE!
I'M NOT GOING TO BE LEFT OUT! I'LL *GET* ONE, TOO!
AND I'LL DO THINGS THAT MAKE ME SO *HAPPY* MY RING WILL BE OH-SO-BLUE!
THE NEXT DAY!
MINE'S GREEN! I'M *WORRIED!*
MINES YELLOW-BLUE... I'M SERIOUS BUT A BIT *DELIRIOUS,* TOO!
DID YOU GET A *RING,* TOO, RONNIE?
I SURE DID!
3

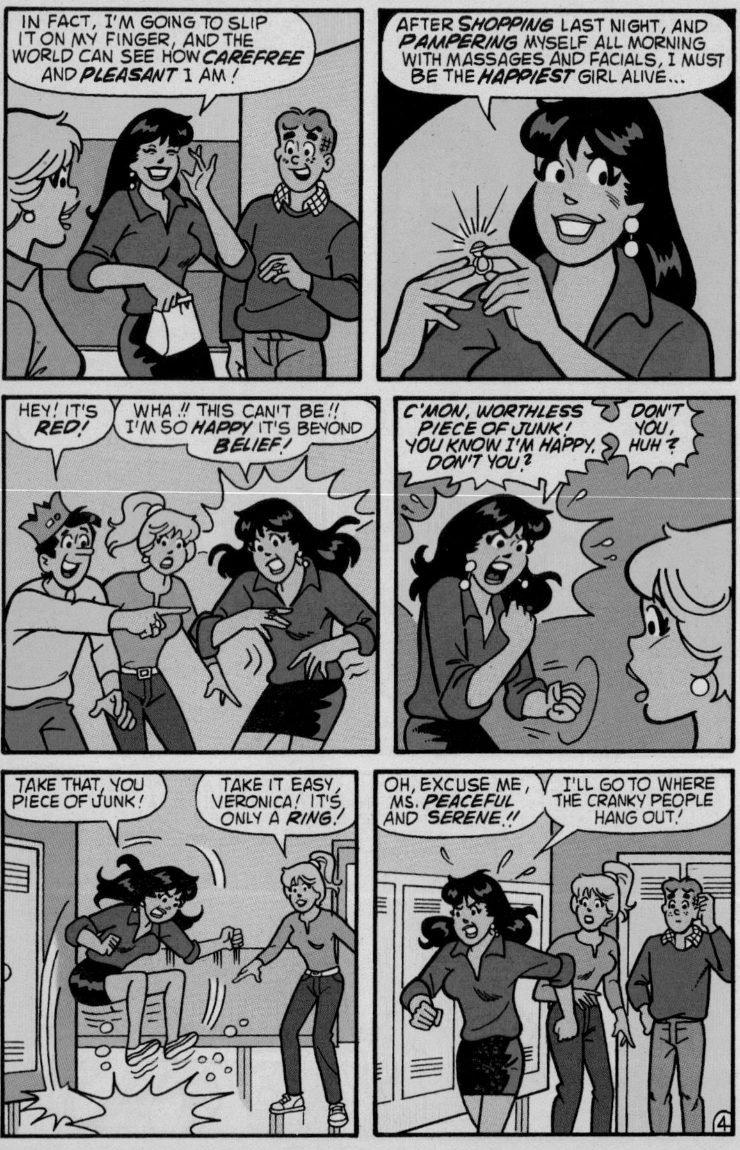
IN FACT, I'M GOING TO SLIP IT ON MY FINGER, AND THE WORLD CAN SEE HOW CAREFREE AND PLEASANT I AM!
AFTER SHOPPING LAST NIGHT, AND PAMPERING MYSELF ALL MORNING WITH MASSAGES AND FACIALS, I MUST BE THE HAPPIEST GIRL ALIVE...
HEY! IT'S RED!
WHA!! THIS CAN'T BE!! I'M SO HAPPY IT'S BEYOND BELIEF!
C'MON, WORTHLESS PIECE OF JUNK! YOU KNOW I'M HAPPY. DON'T YOU?
DON'T YOU, HUH?
TAKE THAT, YOU PIECE OF JUNK!
TAKE IT EASY, VERONICA! IT'S ONLY A RING!
OH, EXCUSE ME, MS. PEACEFUL AND SERENE!!
I'LL GO TO WHERE THE CRANKY PEOPLE HANG OUT!
4

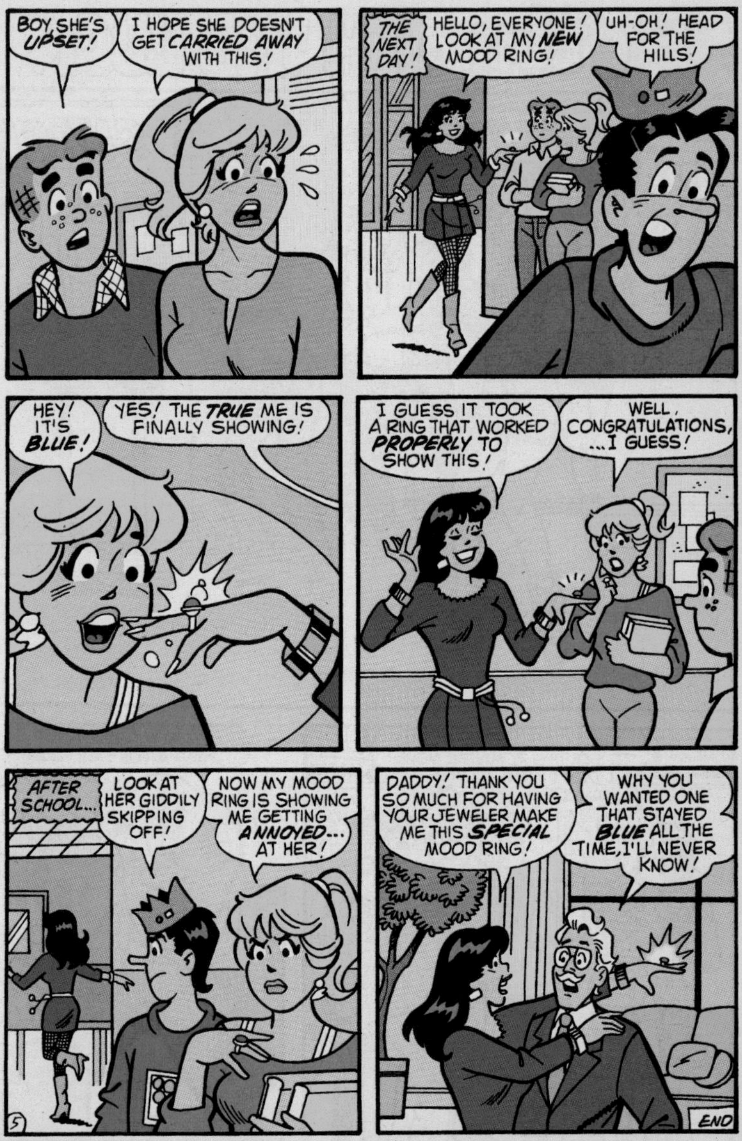

BOY, SHE'S UPSET!
I HOPE SHE DOESN'T GET CARRIED AWAY WITH THIS!
THE NEXT DAY!
HELLO, EVERYONE! LOOK AT MY NEW MOOD RING!
UH-OH! HEAD FOR THE HILLS!
HEY! IT'S BLUE!
YES! THE TRUE ME IS FINALLY SHOWING!
I GUESS IT TOOK A RING THAT WORKED PROPERLY TO SHOW THIS!
WELL, CONGRATULATIONS, ...I GUESS!
AFTER SCHOOL...
LOOK AT HER GIDDILY SKIPPING OFF!
NOW MY MOOD RING IS SHOWING ME GETTING ANNOYED... AT HER!
5
DADDY! THANK YOU SO MUCH FOR HAVING YOUR JEWELER MAKE ME THIS SPECIAL MOOD RING!
WHY YOU WANTED ONE THAT STAYED BLUE ALL THE TIME, I'LL NEVER KNOW!
END

Betty in "THUMB LUCK"

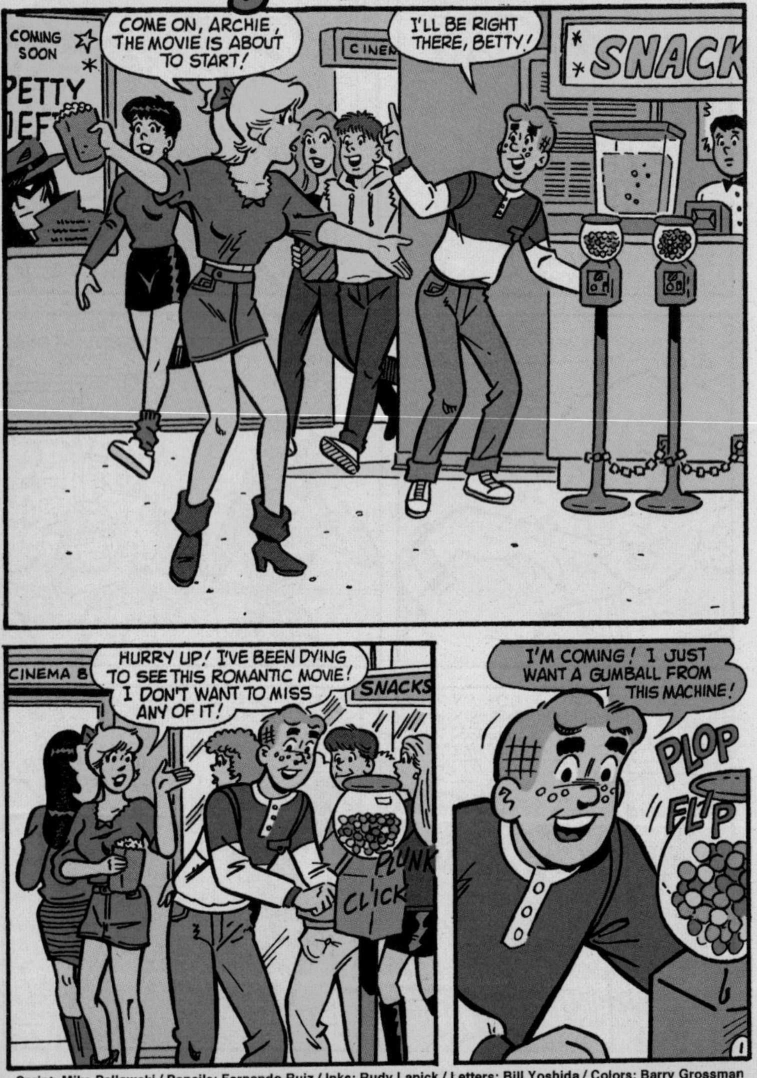
COMING SOON
PETTY DEFT
COME ON, ARCHIE, THE MOVIE IS ABOUT TO START!
I'LL BE RIGHT THERE, BETTY!
SNACK
CINEMA 8
HURRY UP! I'VE BEEN DYING TO SEE THIS ROMANTIC MOVIE! I DON'T WANT TO MISS ANY OF IT!
SNACKS
PLUNK
CLICK
I'M COMING! I JUST WANT A GUMBALL FROM THIS MACHINE!
PLOP
FLIP
1

Script: Mike Pellowski / Pencils: Fernando Ruiz / Inks: Rudy Lapick / Letters: Bill Yoshida / Colors: Barry Grossman

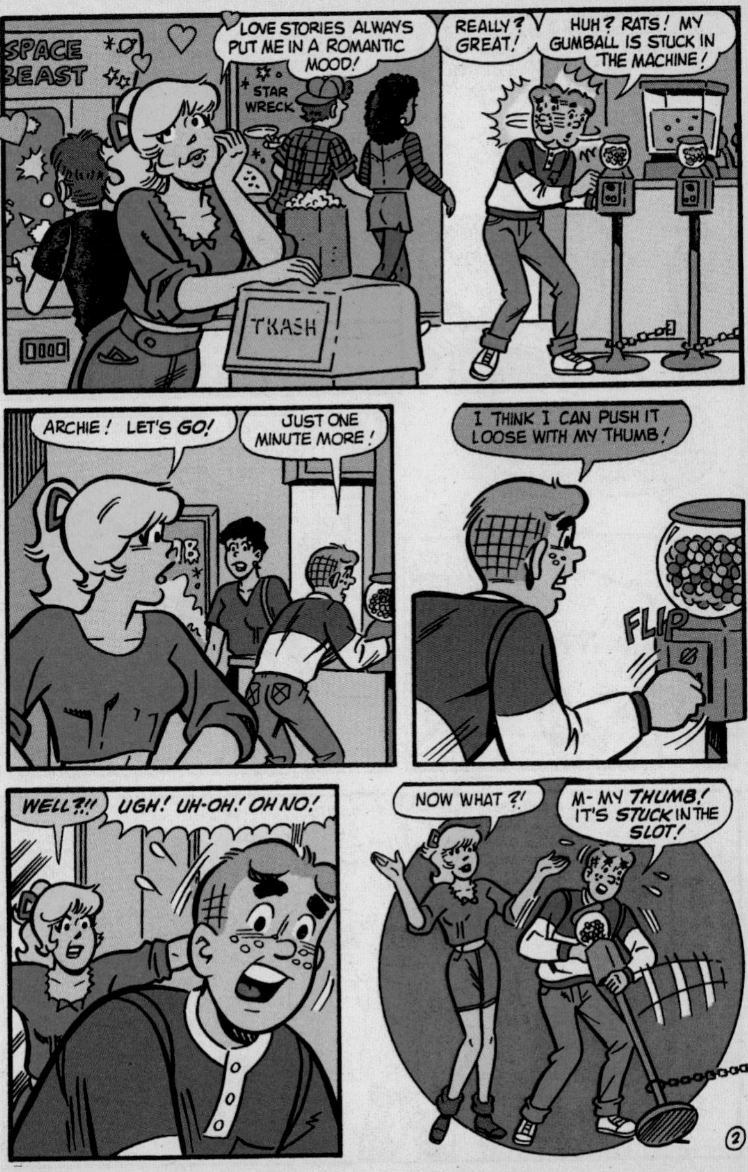
SPACE BEAST
LOVE STORIES ALWAYS PUT ME IN A ROMANTIC MOOD!
STAR WRECK
TRASH
REALLY? GREAT!
HUH? RATS! MY GUMBALL IS STUCK IN THE MACHINE!
ARCHIE! LET'S GO!
JUST ONE MINUTE MORE!
I THINK I CAN PUSH IT LOOSE WITH MY THUMB!
FLIP
WELL?!!
UGH! UH-OH! OH NO!
NOW WHAT?!
M-MY THUMB! IT'S STUCK IN THE SLOT!

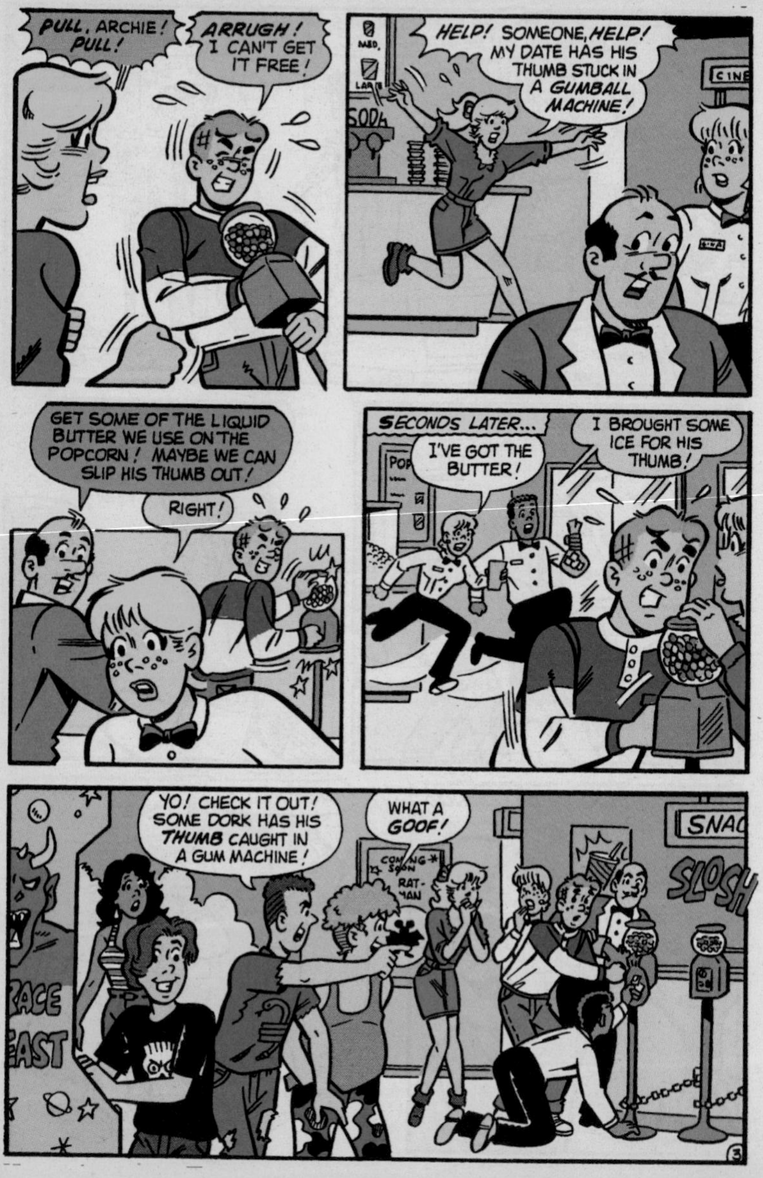
PULL, ARCHIE! PULL!
ARRUGH! I CAN'T GET IT FREE!
HELP! SOMEONE, HELP! MY DATE HAS HIS THUMB STUCK IN A GUMBALL MACHINE!
GET SOME OF THE LIQUID BUTTER WE USE ON THE POPCORN! MAYBE WE CAN SLIP HIS THUMB OUT!
RIGHT!
SECONDS LATER...
I'VE GOT THE BUTTER!
I BROUGHT SOME ICE FOR HIS THUMB!
YO! CHECK IT OUT! SOME DORK HAS HIS THUMB CAUGHT IN A GUM MACHINE!
WHAT A GOOF!
COMING SOON
RAT-MAN
SLOSH
SNAC
3

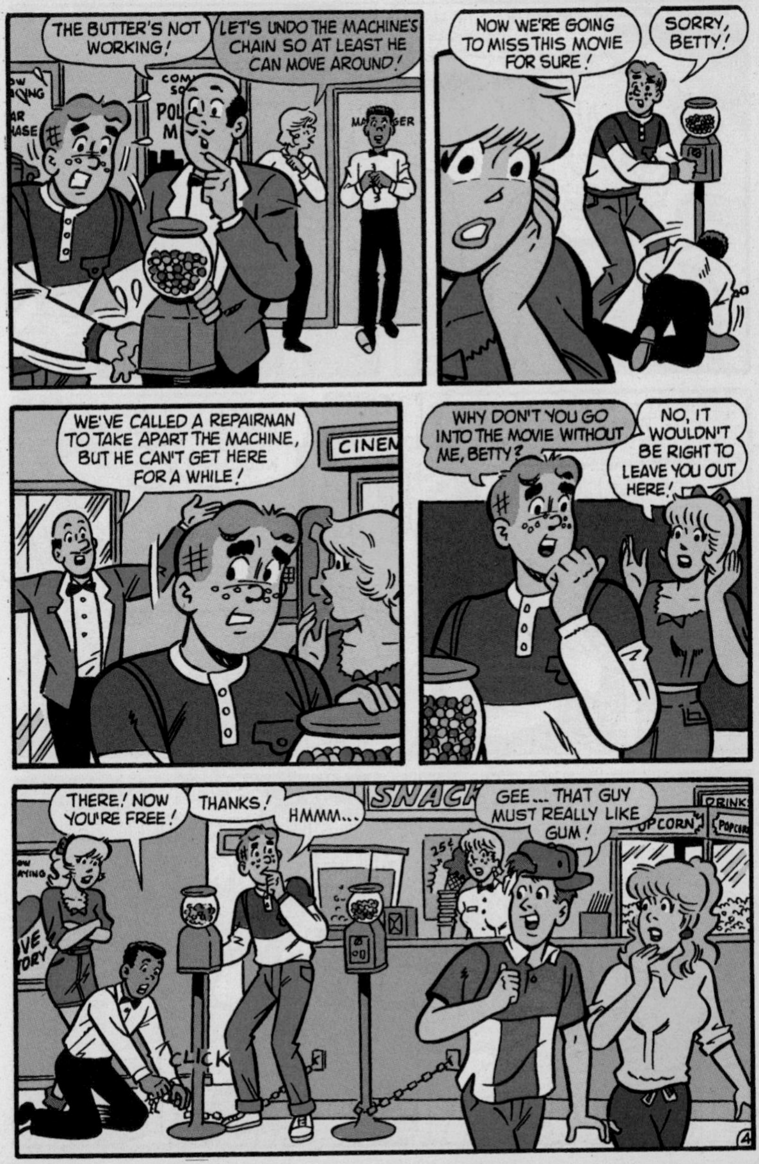

THE BUTTER'S NOT WORKING!
LET'S UNDO THE MACHINE'S CHAIN SO AT LEAST HE CAN MOVE AROUND!
MANAGER
NOW WE'RE GOING TO MISS THIS MOVIE FOR SURE!
SORRY, BETTY!
WE'VE CALLED A REPAIRMAN TO TAKE APART THE MACHINE, BUT HE CAN'T GET HERE FOR A WHILE!
CINEM
WHY DON'T YOU GO INTO THE MOVIE WITHOUT ME, BETTY?
NO, IT WOULDN'T BE RIGHT TO LEAVE YOU OUT HERE!
THERE! NOW YOU'RE FREE!
THANKS!
HMMM...
SNACK
GEE... THAT GUY MUST REALLY LIKE GUM!
POPCORN
DRINKS
CLICK
25¢
4

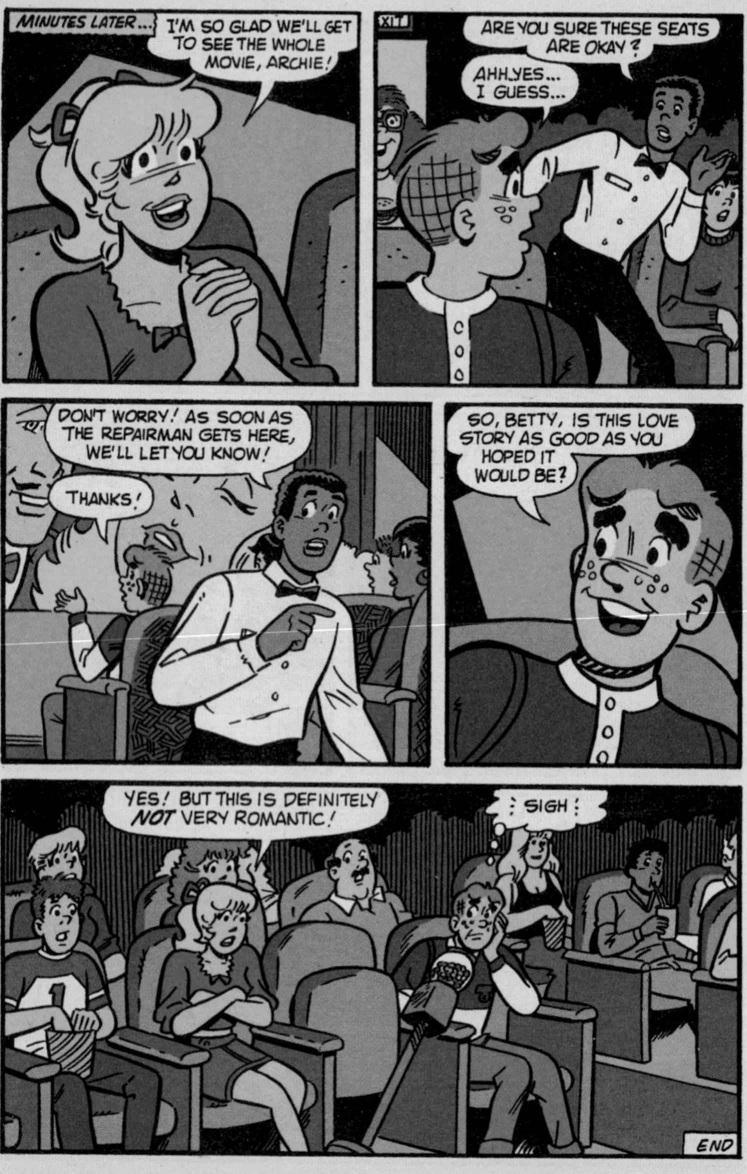
MINUTES LATER...
I'M SO GLAD WE'LL GET TO SEE THE WHOLE MOVIE, ARCHIE!
ARE YOU SURE THESE SEATS ARE OKAY?
AHH..YES... I GUESS...
DON'T WORRY! AS SOON AS THE REPAIRMAN GETS HERE, WE'LL LET YOU KNOW!
THANKS!
SO, BETTY, IS THIS LOVE STORY AS GOOD AS YOU HOPED IT WOULD BE?
YES! BUT THIS IS DEFINITELY NOT VERY ROMANTIC!
SIGH
END